JOHN SAUL

Three Complete Novels

JOHN SAUL

Three Complete Novels

HELLFIRE

THE UNWANTED

SLEEPWALK

WINGS BOOKS
NEW YORK / AVENEL, NEW JERSEY

This edition contains the complete and unabridged texts of the
original editions. They have been completely reset for this volume.

This omnibus was originally published in separate volumes under the titles:
Hellfire, copyright © 1986 by John Saul
The Unwanted, copyright © 1987 by John Saul
Sleepwalk, copyright © 1990 by John Saul

This 1992 edition is published by Wings Books,
distributed by Outlet Book Company, Inc., a Random House Company,
40 Engelhard Avenue, Avenel, New Jersey 07001, by
arrangement with Bantam Books, Inc.

Random House
New York • Toronto • London • Sydney • Auckland

Printed and bound in the United States of America

Library of Congress Cataloging-in-Publication Data

Saul, John.
    [Novels. Selections]
    John Saul : three complete novels.
        p.   cm.
    Contents : Hellfire—The unwanted—Sleepwalk.
    ISBN 0-517-08477-5
    I. Title.   II. Title: Three complete novels.
  PS3569.A787A6   1992
  813'.54—dc20   92-21554
                                                                      CIP

8   7   6   5   4   3   2   1

Contents

HELLFIRE

FOR THE SACK FAMILY—
Burt, Lynn and the boys

Prologue

The boy turned off the path that wound down from the big house on the hill—his house—and wandered along the river-bank. A hundred yards ahead, he could see the wooden trestle that carried the railroad tracks over the rushing stream. He had always imagined that the stream was a boundary, a visible line that separated him from everyone else in the little town. If the river weren't there, he sometimes thought, then he would be part of the town.

But of course it wasn't just the river; there was far more to it than that.

He came to the trestle, and paused. Partly, he was listening for the sound of a train, for he knew that if he could hear the low rumblings of an engine, it wasn't safe to cross the river.

You had to wait until the train had come and gone, or until the sound had faded away into silence.

Sometimes, though, he was tempted to try the crossing even though he could hear a train coming, just to see if he could make it in time.

But of course he'd never tried it. It was too big a risk.

Not that he didn't like risks. He did. There was nothing he liked more than going off by himself, exploring the woods that covered the hillside, poking along the riverbank, skipping from stone to stone, though sooner or later he would miss his footing and slide into the rushing waters.

But the rushing waters wouldn't kill him.

A train, catching him defenseless in the middle of the trestle, would.

For a moment, he visualized himself, crushed under the weight of the streamliner that roared past the town twice a day, his mutilated body dropping into the river below. . . .

He put the thought out of his mind, and instead—as he often did—pictured himself already dead.

He saw himself in a coffin now, with flowers all around him. His parents, their eyes wet with tears, sat in the front pew of the little Episcopalian church in the middle of the town. Behind them, he could see all the other people of the town, staring at his coffin, wishing they'd been nicer to him, wishing they'd been his friends.

Not that he cared, he assured himself. It was more fun to be by yourself anyway. Besides, he had friends most of the time anyway, and when he came home from school in the summer it was nice to be able to play by himself, without anyone else wanting to do something he might not want to do.

Abandoning the fantasy, he listened carefully. When he heard no sound of an approaching train, he started across the trestle, carefully stepping from tie to tie, then continued along the tracks as they swept around the village in a long and gentle curve.

Suddenly he felt eyes watching him, and glanced off to the left. A quarter of a block down the road two boys stood side by side, staring at him.

He smiled, but as he was about to wave to them they turned away. He could hear them snickering as they whispered to each other.

His face burning with sudden anger, he hurried along the railroad tracks until he was certain he could no longer be seen from the road. Between himself and the other boys, separating him from the village, stood the forbidding brick walls of a building that had fascinated him for as long as he could remember.

The boy hesitated, remembering the stories he'd heard from his father, remembering the legends about what had happened in that building so many years ago. Terrible things that could only be spoken of in whispers.

No one knew if the legends were really true.

As he stared at the building, he began to feel as if the other boys—the village boys—were still watching him, challenging him, laughing at him because they knew he didn't have the courage to go inside.

Always before, when he'd stood here contemplating the old building, he'd eventually lost his nerve, and turned away.

But today would be different.

Ignoring the knot of fear that now burned hot in his belly, he left the railroad tracks and scrambled down the slope of the roadbed.

He started along a weed-choked path that paralleled the side of the building. Halfway along the wall, he came to a small door, covered over with weathered boards that had long since shrunken with age. Through the gaps between the boards he could make out the door itself, held closed only by a padlock on a rusted hasp.

Gingerly he tested one of the boards. The corroded nails groaned for a second, then gave way. A moment later, two more boards lay on the ground at the boy's feet.

The boy reached out and grasped the padlock. He paused, knowing that if it gave way, he would then be committed to go inside.

He took a deep breath, tightened his grip, and twisted.

The rusted hasp held for a moment, then broke loose. The lock, free from the door it had guarded so long, lay in the boy's hand. He stared at it for several long seconds, almost wishing he had left it in place.

Then, struggling against a strange fear he could feel growing within him, the boy pushed the door open and squirmed through the gap left by the three planks he had torn away.

For a moment the deep shadows blinded him, but then his eyes adjusted to the dim light of the interior, and he looked around.

Inside, the building seemed even larger than it looked from the outside, and emptier.

Except, the boy realized, it didn't feel empty at all.

Somewhere, he was certain, there was someone—or some*thing*—lurking within these walls, waiting for him.

Almost against his will, his eyes began exploring the old building. Emptiness stretched away in all directions, and far above him, just visible in the shadowed light that barely penetrated the immense space, the tangled iron struts supporting the roof seemed to reach down to him, as if trying to grasp him in their skeletal arms.

In the silence, the boy could hear the pounding of his own heart.

Suddenly a cacophony of sound filled the enormous building, and the boy felt a scream rising in his throat. He choked it back at the last second, then forced himself to look up.

A flock of pigeons, frightened by the boys's intrusion, had burst from their nests and now wheeled beneath the roof. As the boy watched, they began settling once more into their nests.

Seconds later, silence once more cast an eerie spell over the vast emptiness.

The boy gazed into the gloom, and saw, far away at the back of the building, the top of a flight of stairs.

Beneath him, then, was not simply a solid floor. Below this floor, there was a basement.

The stairs seemed to beckon to him, to demand that he come and explore that which lay beneath.

The boy's heart began pounding once more, and a cold sweat broke out on his back.

Suddenly he could stand the silence no longer.

"No! I won't!"

His voice, far louder than he had intended, echoed back to him, and once again the pigeons milled madly among the rafters, fluttering in confusion. Gasping, the boy shrank back against the reassuring solidity of the brick wall.

But when the silence came once more, the compelling fascination of those downward-leading stairs gripped him once again. He forced his fear down. Slowly, he began moving toward the back of the building.

He had moved only a few yards when suddenly the boy felt his skin crawl.

Something, he was certain, was watching him.

He tried to ignore it, keeping his, eyes on the far wall, but the strange sensation wouldn t go away.

The hair on the back of his neck was standing up now, and he could feel goose bumps covering his arms. He could stand it no longer, and whirled around to face whatever was behind him.

Nothing.

His eyes searched the semidarkness, looking for something—anything!

The vast expanse seemed empty.

And then, once again, the hair on the back of his neck stood up, and his spine began to tingle.

He whirled once more. Once more there was nothing.

Yet something seemed to fill the emptiness, seemed to surround him, taunt him.

He should never have come inside. He knew that now, knew it with a certainty that made his blood run cold.

But now it was too late. Now there was no turning back.

Far away, and seeming to recede into the distance, he could barely make out the small rectangle of brightness that marked the door he had come through only a few minutes before.

The door was too far away.

It seemed as if he had been in the mysterious gloom forever, and already, dimly, he began to understand that he was never going to leave.

There was something here—something that wanted him.

Charged with the inexorable force of his own imagination, he moved once more toward the vortex that was the stairwell.

He paused at the top of the stairs, peering fearfully into the blackness below. He wanted to turn now, and run away, run back toward that distant speck of light, and the daylight beyond.

But it was too late. The gloom of the building held him in its rapture, and though there was nothing but darkness below, he knew he had no choice but to continue down the stairs.

He started down the steps, straining to see into a blackness that seemed to go on forever.

There was a mustiness in the air below, and something else— some faint odor he couldn't quite identify, but that seemed oddly familiar.

He came to the bottom of the stairs, and stopped, terrified.

Again, he wanted to turn around, turn away from the evil he felt in the darkness, but he knew he wouldn't.

Knew he couldn't.

Then he heard a sound—barely distinguishable.

He listened, straining his ears.

Was it real, or had he only imagined it?

He heard it again.

Some kind of animal. It had to be. A rat, perhaps, or maybe only a mouse.

Or was it something else, something unreal?

A voice, whispering to him so quietly he couldn't make out the words, calling to him, luring him on into the darkness and the unknown. . . .

The strange odor grew stronger, its acridity burning in his nostrils.

He stepped off the last stair, and began groping his way through the darkness.

He thought he could feel unseen hands guiding him, feel a strange force drawing him on.

And then, though he could still see nothing, he sensed a presence.

It was close to him—too close.

"Who—" he began, but his question was cut off as something struck him from behind. Staggering, he pitched forward, his balance gone, then tried to break his fall by throwing his arms in front of him.

But it was too late, and even as he fell, he knew it.

He opened his mouth to scream, but his throat felt choked, as though strangling hands held him in a deadly grip. No sound emerged from his throat.

In an instant that seemed to go on forever, he felt a coldness slide through his clothing, piercing his skin, an icy pain that slipped between his ribs deep into his chest.

The object—the thing; the unidentifiable evil—plunged into his heart, and he felt himself begin to die.

And as he died, he slowly recognized the familiar odor that had filled his nostrils.

Smoke.

For some reason, in that long-abandoned basement, he smelled smoke. . . .

Then, as the last vestiges of life drained from his body, he saw flames flickering out from beneath the stairway, and in the faint remnants of his consciousness, he heard laughter.

Laughter, mixed with screams of terror.

The laughter and the screams closed in on him, growing louder and louder, mingling with the ice-cold pain until there was nothing but blackness. And for the boy, the terror was over. . . .

One

Rain at a funeral is a cliché, Carolyn Sturgess reflected as she gazed abstractedly out the window of the limousine that moved slowly through the streets of Westover. Though it was June, the day was chilly, with a dampness that seemed to seep into the bones. Ahead, through the divider window and the streaked windshield beyond, she could see the car carrying her husband, her mother-in-law, and her stepdaughter, and ahead of that—barely visible—the hearse bearing the body of her father-in-law. Carolyn shuddered, feeling chilled.

Barely visible.

The words, she realized, described Conrad Sturgess perfectly, at least in his last years. For more than a decade, he had seldom left the mansion on the hill above the town, seldom been seen in the streets of the village that his family had dominated for more than a century. But despite his reclusiveness, the old man had still been a presence in Westover, and Carolyn found herself wondering how the village would change, now that Conrad Sturgess was dead.

As the long black car turned left on Church Street, Carolyn glanced back at the small crowd that still lingered in front of the white-clapboard Episcopal church that stood facing the square, its

sober New England facade seeming to glare with faint disapproval at
the small business district that squatted defensively on the other side
of the worn patch of lawn beyond the bronze statue of a long-
forgotten Revolutionary hero that gazed out from the middle of the
square.

"Will any of them come up to Hilltop for the other service?"

Her daughter's voice interrupted her reverie, and Carolyn reached
over to give Beth's hand an affectionate squeeze. "The interment,"
she automatically corrected.

"The interment," Beth Rogers repeated, her brows furrowing as
she concentrated on getting the word exactly right. She pictured the
look of scorn she would get from Tracy Sturgess, her stepsister, if
she mispronounced it later. Not, she told herself, that she cared
what Tracy Sturgess thought, but she still hated it when Tracy and
her friends laughed at her. Just because Tracy was almost thirteen,
and went to private school, didn't make her any better than Beth.
After all, she was almost twelve herself. "How come they call it that?
An . . . interment?"

"Because that's what it is," Carolyn explained. "Anyway, that's
what Abigail calls it, so that's what we must call it, too. After all,
we're Sturgesses now, aren't we?"

"I'm not," Beth said, her brown eyes darkening in exactly the
same way her father's did when he got angry. "I'm still Beth Rogers,
and I always will be. I don't want to be a Sturgess!"

"Oh, Lord, Carolyn thought. Here we go again. When would she
learn to stop trying to convince her daughter to accept Phillip Sturgess as her father? And why, really, *should* Beth transfer her affec-
tion to her stepfather, when her real father still lived right here in
Westover, and she saw him every day? She wished, though she'd
never say it, that Alan Rogers would simply disappear from the face
of the earth. Or at least, from Westover, Massachusetts. "Of course
you are," she said aloud. "Anyway, it doesn't really matter what you
call it, because an interment and a burial are the same thing. Okay?"

"Well, *are* the other people from the church coming?"

Carolyn shook her head. "The service at Hilltop is only for family
and our closest friends."

"But we know everybody who was there," Beth replied, her
voice reflecting her puzzlement. "Why can't they all come?"

"Because—" Carolyn floundered for a moment, knowing that
whatever she said, Beth would immediately see through her words
and grasp the truth of the matter. "Because they aren't all friends of
the Sturgesses," she ventured.

"You mean they aren't all rich," Beth replied.

Bingo! Carolyn thought. And there was no point in trying to deny it, at least not to Beth.

The car turned again, and Carolyn glanced out the window to see the bleak form of the old shoe factory—the building everyone in Westover referred to as "the mill"—looming above Prospect Street, its soot-covered red bricks giving it an even more forbidding appearance than its bleak nineteenth-century architecture had intended.

Carolyn, as always, felt a slight shudder pass through her body at the sight of the mill, and quickly looked away. Then it was gone, and the village was left behind as the cortege moved out River Road to begin winding its way up the long narrow lane that led to Hilltop.

"Mom?" Beth suddenly asked, interrupting the silence that had fallen over the big car. "What's going to happen, now that—" She hesitated for a moment, then used the term her mother had asked her to use. Until today she had refused to utter it. "—now that Uncle Conrad's dead?"

"I don't know," Carolyn replied. "I suppose everything will go on just as it always has."

But of course she knew it wasn't true. She knew that without Conrad Sturgess silently controlling his family's interests from the privacy of his den, everything in Westover was going to change.

And she knew that she, at least, wasn't going to like the changes. As the limousine pulled through the gates of Hilltop, she remembered the old adage about sleeping dogs.

Her husband, she knew, had no intention of letting them lie.

The six pallbearers carried the casket containing Conrad Sturgess's body slowly up a narrow path through the forest. Behind the casket, Abigail Sturgess walked alone, head held high, unmindful of the rain that still fell in a dense drizzle. Though she leaned heavily on a cane, her back was as stiffly erect as ever. Behind her walked her son, Phillip, with Carolyn on his arm. Following the couple were their two children, Beth Rogers and Tracy Sturgess. Then, bringing up the rear of the short procession, came the mourners: the Kilpatricks and the Baileys, the Babcocks and the Adamses—the old families whose ties to the Sturgesses went back through the generations.

The cortege rounded a bend in the trail, and came to a sudden stop as Abigail Sturgess paused for a moment to gaze at the wrought-iron grillwork that arched over the path.

Two words were worked into the pattern:

ETERNAL VIGILANCE

*   *   *

She seemed to consider the words for a few moments, then walked on. A few minutes later, Conrad Sturgess, followed by his family and friends, arrived at the spot he had always known would be his final resting place.

Worked carefully into the earth, and covered with moss, there was a short flight of stone steps. At the top of the steps, looming out of the forest like some sort of strange temple, stood the Sturgess-family mausoleum.

The structure was circular, and made entirely of pale pink marble. There were seven columns, each of them nearly twenty feet high, topped by a marble ring that was almost fifty feet across. All around, the forest seemed to be crowding in on the strange edifice, and only a few rays of sunlight ever glinted on the polished marble. Today the lowering skies seemed to hover only a few feet above the strange monument, and the stone, slick with rain, seemed to have had its color washed away.

Six of the columns were in perfect condition.

The seventh pillar was broken; all that remained of it was its base, and the top two feet, hanging oddly from the surmounting marble drum.

In the center of the circle of columns, on a marble floor, stood a large round marble table, with space around it for seven marble chairs.

Six of the chairs were there.

The seventh place at the table, the place with the broken pillar behind it, was empty.

Beth, her eyes glued to her mother's back, climbed the steps uncertainly. She'd been here before, but always before the mausoleum had seemed to her to be nothing more than some strange ruin from the past. But today it was different, and she felt a chill pass through her as she stepped between two of the columns and found herself inside the stone ring.

She glanced nervously around, but everyone else seemed to know exactly what to do. The mourners, all of them clad in black, the women's faces veiled, had spread themselves in a semicircle around the chairs. The pallbearers placed the coffin carefully on a bier that stood at the empty seventh place. Abigail Sturgess, her face impassive, stood behind the coffin, gazing at the massive stone chair that stood opposite.

Beth's eyes shifted to the back of the marble chair upon which the old woman s eyes were fixed.

On the back of the chair, chiseled deep into the marble, was an inscription:

SAMUEL PRUETT STURGESS
May 3, 1822—August 12, 1890

Beth's hand reached out and took her mother's. She tugged gently, and when Carolyn leaned down, the little girl whispered in her ear.

"What's she doing?" she asked.

"She's presenting Conrad to his grandfather," Carolyn whispered back.

"Why?"

"It's a tradition, sweetheart," Carolyn replied, glancing nervously around. But it was all right—no one seemed to notice them at all.

Beth frowned slightly. Why were they "presenting" Uncle Conrad to old Mr. Sturgess? It didn't make any sense to her. She tugged at her mother's hand once more, but this time her mother only looked down at her, holding a finger to her lips and shaking her head.

Silently, wishing she were somewhere else—anywhere else—Beth watched the rest of the service. The minister's voice droned on, repeating everything he'd said about Conrad Sturgess in the church only half an hour ago, and Beth wondered if this time he was telling Samuel Pruett Sturgess about Uncle Conrad. Then she began looking around at all the unfamiliar faces of the people around her.

None of them were the people she'd known all her life, the people she'd known when her mother and father were married. They were all strangers, and she knew that they were somehow different from her.

It wasn't that they were rich, even though she knew they were. They all lived in big houses, like Hilltop, though none was quite so grand as Hilltop itself.

It was the way they acted.

Like this morning, before the funeral, when she'd been sitting by herself in the breakfast room, and one of them—she thought it was Mrs. Kilpatrick—had come in, and smiled at her. It had been a nice smile, and for a minute Beth had hoped she and the woman might be friends.

"And a good morning to you, young lady," the woman had said. "I don't believe we've met, have we?"

Beth had shaken her head shyly, and offered the woman her hand. "I'm Beth Rogers."

"Rogers?" the woman had repeated. "I don't believe I know any Rogerses. Where are you from? Do I know your mother?"

Beth had nodded. "I live here. My mother's—"

And then she'd seen the woman's smile disappear, and her eyes, the eyes that had been so warm and sparkling a minute before, had suddenly turned cold. "Oh," she'd said. "You're Carolyn's little girl, aren't you? How nice." Before Beth could say anything else, the woman had turned and silently left the room.

Now, Beth realized she must have been staring at the woman, for the woman—she was almost sure it was Mrs. Kilpatrick—was glaring at her. She felt her mother tugging at her arm, and realized that the service was over.

The pallbearers were carrying the casket down another flight of steps, and as Beth, walking beside her mother, followed Tracy and Phillip Sturgess—at old Abigail's side now—she saw that there was a tiny cemetery in the forest behind the mausoleum. An open grave awaited, and Conrad Sturgess's coffin was slowly lowered into it. Abigail Sturgess stepped forward, reached stiffly down to pick up a clod of sodden earth, and dropped it into the grave. Then she turned away, and began making her way back through the mausoleum, and down the path that led to the house.

Beth noticed that Abigail Sturgess, once she had turned away from her husband's grave, never looked back. It was very much like Mrs. Kilpatrick this morning. Beth wasn't sure why, but for some reason it bothered her.

Carolyn Sturgess stood uncomfortably in the walnut-paneled library doing her best to chat with Elaine Kilpatrick. She was finding it difficult. It wasn't anything that Elaine said, really; the woman was perfectly polite. It was just that there seemed to be a chasm between them, and Carolyn had no idea of how to bridge that chasm. It wasn't that she had no interest in the things Elaine talked about; indeed, one of the things that had attracted her to Phillip Sturgess when she'd first met him a year before had been his own interest in all the things Elaine Kilpatrick seemed to know everything about.

And that, of course, was the trouble. Elaine seemed to know everything about everything, and Carolyn was feeling once again, like an uneducated, provincial fool.

Carolyn Rogers Sturgess was no fool. She'd graduated from Boston University with a degree in art, and even though it wasn't Smith, and the degree wasn't *cum laude*, Carolyn was proud of it.

And she and Alan had done their share of traveling, too. Of course it hadn't been Paris and London, nor had she seen the museums in Florence, but she had certainly done her share of galleries in New York.

"But of course we don't really appreciate art in this country, do we?" she heard Elaine asking earnestly, and silently chided herself for wondering if she detected a note of condescension in the other woman's tone. Certainly if it was there, it wasn't reflected in Elaine's luminous brown eyes, which seemed to concentrate on her with undivided attention.

And yet, as she nearly always did when she was with Phillip's friends, she had a feeling she was being talked down to.

"No," she said lamely, "I don't suppose we do." Then she offered Elaine what she hoped was a radiant smile. "Do excuse me, won't you?" she asked. "I see Frances Babcock over there, and there's something I have to talk to her about."

"Of course," Elaine said smoothly, immediately turning to Chip Bailey and plunging into another conversation.

As Carolyn started toward Frances Babcock, whom she secretly loathed, she wondered how Elaine did it. And worse, she wondered if she would ever learn the trick of it, or whether these women had simply been born with all the social graces bred into them over the generations. But whatever it was they had, she knew she lacked it. She lacked it, and her daughter lacked it.

She realized then that she hadn't seen Beth for more than an hour, not since the receiving line had broken up and the family had come into the library to join their guests. Beth, in fact, had not come into the library at all. Veering away from Frances Babcock, Carolyn slipped out of the library, and glanced down the broad corridor that ran through this wing of the house. It was empty.

But coming out of the living room, she saw her stepdaughter. "Tracy?"

The girl, her blond hair twisted up in a French knot that Carolyn thought was too old for her, paused at the bottom of the broad staircase that swept from the entry hall up to the second floor. She glanced around furtively, then glared at Carolyn when she saw that they were alone. "What do you want?"

Carolyn felt a twinge of anger. If Phillip had been there, Tracy's reply would have been guardedly polite. But when they were alone, no matter what Tracy said to her, it always contained a note of challenge, as if she were daring Carolyn to try to exercise any form of control over her.

"I was looking for Beth," Carolyn replied evenly, refusing to let Tracy see her anger. "I thought she was coming into the library with the rest of us."

"Well, if she's not there, then obviously she didn't, did she?" Tracy countered.

"Have you seen her?"

"No."

"Well, if you do see her, will you tell her I'm looking for her?"

Tracy's eyes narrowed, and her lips curled in what should have been a smile, but wasn't. "Maybe I will, and maybe I won't," she said. Then she started up the stairs, disappearing from Carolyn's sight.

Ignore it, Carolyn told herself. She's not used to you yet, and she's not used to Beth, and you have to give her time. Then, guiltily, she found herself wishing that it were not June, and that Tracy were not home for the summer. It had been bad enough at Christmas, when she and Phillip had gotten married, and Tracy had refused to speak to her at all, and worse during the spring break, when Tracy had furiously demanded that she and Beth leave, telling them they had no place in this house. Tracy had been careful to deliver her ultimatum when her father wasn't around, and Carolyn had finally decided not to tell Phillip about the incident at all. But now the girl was home for the summer, and though there had been no major scenes yet, Carolyn could feel one building. The only question, she was sure, was when Tracy's anger at her father's second marriage would boil over once more. She hoped that when it did, she would bear the brunt of it, not Beth. Beth, she knew, was having a hard enough time of it already. Sighing, she started up the stairs. Perhaps, as she often did, Beth had retreated to her room.

As she reached the second floor, the imperious voice of her mother-in-law stopped her.

"Carolyn? Where are you going?"

Carolyn turned, and fleetingly wondered how Abigail Sturgess had managed to materialize so suddenly. But there she stood, her ebony cane gripped firmly in her right hand, her head tipped back as she surveyed Carolyn with her blue eyes—the same eyes she had passed on to her son and her granddaughter.

Except that Phillip's eyes were as warm as a tropical sea.

Abigail's and Tracy's were chipped from ice.

And now, as they were so often, those eyes were fixed disapprovingly on Carolyn.

"I was just looking for Beth, Abigail," Carolyn replied.

Abigail offered her a wintry smile. "I'm sure Beth is perfectly capable of taking care of herself. And a good hostess doesn't leave her guests by themselves, does she? Come. There are some people with whom I wish you to speak."

Carolyn hesitated, then, with a quick glance up the stairs, followed Abigail back to the library.

No one but Abigail seemed to have noticed that she had left.

No one but Phillip, who, spotting her from his position next to the fireplace, offered her a smile.

Suddenly she felt better, felt that perhaps, after all, she did belong here. At least Phillip seemed to think she did.

Alan Rogers leaned back in his desk chair and unconsciously ran his hand through the unruly mop of black hair that never, no matter how hard he tried, seemed to stay under control. He glanced out the window; the rain seemed finally to have stopped, at least for a while. He couldn't help smiling to himself as he pictured the scene that must have been going on up at the Sturgesses' an hour ago.

All of them dressed in black, standing in the rain, but regally ignoring it while they finally put the old bastard to rest.

If Conrad Sturgess would ever rest in peace. Alan Rogers sincerely hoped he wouldn't.

Perhaps, he thought, he should have gone to the burial. No one, after all, would have told him to leave. That wasn't their way. They would simply have looked down their patrician noses at him, and done their best to let him know, subtly, of course, that he wasn't wanted there.

And if it hadn't been for Beth, he might have done just that, and the hell with Carolyn.

She would have been furious with him, naturally, but that wouldn't really have bothered him at all. After all these years, he was used to Carolyn's fury. Indeed, sometimes he wasn't sure he could remember a time when she had not been furious with him.

There must have been a time, though, when they had loved each other. Maybe the first couple of years of their marriage, before Carolyn's ambitions for him had taken over their lives. Alan had been a carpenter and a good one, who took pride in practicing his craft, but that had not been enough. Carolyn had decided he should become a contractor, a businessman. He'd always refused, telling her he just didn't want the responsibility.

The arguments grew more bitter and, finally, had broken up the marriage.

The irony was that two years after the divorce, he'd wound up getting his contractor's license anyway. It had finally become an economic necessity. If he was going to support himself, along with Carolyn and Beth, he simply had to have more money coming in. And so he'd done what Carolyn had always wanted him to do in the first place.

And what had happened?

She'd upped and married Phillip Sturgess, and he was off the hook for everything except child support. For that matter, he didn't suppose it would matter a whit to Carolyn anymore whether he sent the monthly support check or not. Phillip, he knew, would make up the balance, and do it cheerfully.

But it was a matter of principle. Beth was his daughter, and he wanted to support her, whether she needed his support or not.

The money, he suspected, was probably going into a trust fund for her. That would be very much like Phillip—children should have trust funds from their fathers, and he would see to it that Beth had one, whether Alan knew anything about it or not.

Grinning to himself, he wondered if Carolyn knew how well he and Phillip really got along together. In fact, if Carolyn hadn't married Phillip, they would probably have become good friends, despite the difference in their backgrounds.

For Phillip, alone among the Sturgesses, had somehow managed to overcome the sense of superiority that had been bred into him from the day he was born.

He'd gone to the right schools, played with the right children, met the right women—even married one of them, the first time around—but no matter how hard his parents had tried, Phillip had never been able to put on the aristocratic airs the Sturgesses were renowned for. Now that Phillip had married Carolyn, the two men should have kept a wary distance, but, in fact, Alan could not help liking Phillip Sturgess. Now that Carolyn had what she wanted— position, money, all the comforts of life he had not been able to provide—he hoped the marriage would thrive. For one thing was certain, Phillip loved her—as much as Alan himself once had.

He wanted his ex-wife to be happy, if only for his daughter's sake, knowing that if Phillip and Carolyn found it rough going, somehow Beth would get caught in the middle.

Whatever happened, Alan would never allow his daughter to be caught in it. It wasn't Beth's fault that things hadn't worked out for him and Carolyn. In fact, if he really thought about it, it was probably the Sturgesses' own fault.

For as long as he'd known Carolyn—and they'd grown up together—she had been fascinated by the Sturgess family.

Fascinated by them, and repulsed by them.

And yet she'd married Phillip.

So maybe the revulsion of them that she'd always professed had not been quite what she'd said.

Maybe it had been envy, and a wish that she'd been born one of them.

At any rate, when Phillip Sturgess had suddenly reappeared in Westover a year ago after living abroad for nearly a decade, Carolyn had wasted no time in snaring him. Which, Alan realized, wasn't really a fair thing to say. The two of them had met and fallen in love, and Carolyn had resigned her job in the local law office when she'd married Phillip, claiming that continuing as assistant to an attorney when she was marrying his major client involved a conflict of interest.

Perhaps it did; perhaps it didn't. None of it mattered, not anymore. The fact was that Carolyn had married Phillip, and Alan hoped she would be happy. When Abigail followed Conrad to the grave, he thought, maybe she would have a chance at that. Until then, Alan was certain his former wife had an uphill battle ahead of her.

The door opened, and his secretary walked in. She dropped a stack of mail on his desk, then surveyed him critically. "Thoughtful," she said. "Always a bad sign."

"Just thinking about the Sturgesses, and hoping they didn't all drown in Conrad's grave."

Judy Parkins snickered. "That would be something, wouldn't it? And after Carolyn worked so hard to get Phillip, too."

The smile faded from Alan's face, and Judy immediately wished she hadn't spoken. "I'm sorry. I didn't really mean that."

Alan shrugged wryly. "Well, let's just hope they're happy, and wish them well, all right?"

Judy regarded her employer with a raised brow. "How come you always manage to be so damned *good?* And if you are, how come Carolyn wanted to trade you in for Phillip Sturgess in the first place?"

"First, I'm not so damned good, and second, she didn't trade me in. She chucked me. And it's over and done, with. All right?"

"Check." Judy turned, but as she was about to leave the office, Beth burst in, her face blotched and streaked with tears. She threw herself into her father's arms, sobbing. Judy Parkins, after offering Alan a sympathetic look, slipped out of the office, quietly closing the door behind her.

"Honey," Alan crooned as he tried to calm his daughter. "What is it? What happened?"

"Th-they hate me," Beth wailed. "I don't belong there, and they all hate me!"

Alan hugged the unhappy child closer. "Oh, darling, that isn't true. Your mother loves you very much, and so does Uncle Phillip—"

"He's *not* my uncle," Beth protested. "He's Tracy's father, and he hates me."

"Now who told you that?"

"T-Tracy," Beth stammered. She stared up into her father's face, her eyes beseeching him. "She . . . she said her father hates me, and that by the end of the summer, I'll have to go live somewhere else. Sh-she said he's going to make me!"

"I see," Alan replied. It was exactly the sort of thing that had happened in the spring, when Tracy had last been home from school. "And when did she tell you this?"

"A little while ago. Everyone was in . . . in the library, and I was by myself in the living room, and she came in, and she told me. She said that now that her grandfather's dead, her father owns the house, and . . . and he's going to make me go away!"

"And was anybody else there?"

Beth hesitated, then shook her head. "N-no . . ."

"Well, I'll bet if Uncle Phillip had heard Tracy say that, he'd have turned her over his knee and given her a spanking. Maybe I'd better just give him a call, and tell him."

Beth drew back, horrified. "No! If you call him, then Tracy will know I told, and it'll just be worse than it already is!"

Alan nodded solemnly. "Then what do you think we ought to do?"

"Can't I come and live with you, Daddy? Please?"

Alan sighed silently. This, too, was something they'd been through before, and he'd tried to explain over and over why it was best for Beth to live with her mother. But no matter how often he explained it to her, her reply never changed.

"But I don't belong there," she always said. "They're different from me, and I just don't belong. If you make me stay there, I'm going to die."

And sometimes, when he looked into her huge brown eyes, and smoothed back her soft dark hair—the hair she'd inherited from Carolyn—he almost believed she was right.

He stood up, and took his daughter by the hand. "Come on, honey," he said. "I'll drive you home, and we'll talk about it on the way."

"Home?" Beth asked, her eyes suddenly hopeful. "To your house?"

"No," Alan replied. "I'll drive you back to Hilltop. That's where you live now, isn't it?"

Though Beth said nothing, the eager light faded from her eyes.

Two

Alan Rogers turned off River Road, shifted his Fiat into low gear, and started up the drive.

"Almost there." When there was no response from Beth, he glanced at her out of the corner of his eye. She sat huddled against the door, her eyes clouded with unhappiness.

"Act as if," Alan said. Beth turned to face him.

"Act as if? What does that mean?"

"It means if you act as if things are all right, then maybe they will be. Don't think about what's wrong—think about what's right. It helps."

"How can it help? Pretending doesn't change anything."

"But it can change how you think about things. Like that apartment I lived in for a while. The one above the drugstore?"

A hint of a smile played around Beth's mouth. "You hated that place."

"Indeed I did. And why shouldn't I have? I wasn't living with you anymore, and I missed you terribly. And the apartment was small and dark and empty. It was awful. And then one day Judy came over."

"Judy Parkins?"

"The very same. Anyway, I was griping about how bad the place was, and she asked me what I'd do with it if I liked it."

"But you didn't like it," Beth protested. "You hated it!"

"That's what I said. And Judy said, 'So pretend you like it. What would you do with it?' So I thought about it, then told her that I'd start by getting rid of the venetian blinds, and put shutters in, and I'd paint it, and cover the floor with grass mats. And the next weekend she came over, and we did it. And guess what? It turned out the place wasn't so bad after all."

The Fiat passed through the gates of Hilltop House, and Alan drove slowly along the wide circular driveway that skirted a broad expanse of lawn in front of the Sturgess mansion. He brought the car to a halt between a Cadillac and a Mercedes, then sat for a moment staring at the immense house. As always, he was struck less by its size than its strange appearance. Whoever had designed it had apparently been less interested in creating a thing of beauty than in making a declaration of power.

"All right, all right," he said, turning a deadpan face to his daughter as though she had spoken. "I'll admit that grass mats and paint won't help this place."

Built primarily of carved stone, the house spread in two flat-roofed wings from a central core, the main feature of which was an immense stained-glass window—which Alan thought more appropriate to a cathedral than a home—over the massive double front doors. The facade was nearly devoid of decoration, and the only breaks in the roof line were provided by a few chimneys, scattered haphazardly wherever the floor plan had required them.

There was something vaguely forbidding about the structure, as if the house were trying to defend itself against a hostile world.

"It's not like a house at all," Beth said. "It's like a museum. I always feel like I'm going to break something."

"You've only lived here a few months, sweetheart. Give yourself a chance to get used to it." But even as he spoke the words, Alan wondered if it would be possible for his daughter to be at home in a house such as this. Certainly, he knew, he never could have. "Come on," he sighed. "Let's get you back inside."

Beth reluctantly got out of the Fiat as Alan held the door open for her, then slipped her hand into her father's. "Couldn't I stay with you tonight?" she pleaded. "Please?"

Alan pulled his daughter close, and dropped his arm over her shoulder. "Don't make me feel like I'm feeding you to the lions," he replied, but his attempt at humor sounded hollow even to himself. He reached out and pressed the bell. A moment later the door was opened by the old woman who had been the Sturgesses' housekeeper for as long as anyone could remember.

"Beth! Why, where have you been? Your mother's been, looking everywhere for you!"

"She came down to say hello to me, Hannah. I guess she didn't tell anyone where she was going."

Hannah's eyes narrowed in mock severity. "Well, you might have told me, mightn't you, young lady?"

"I . . . I'm sorry, Hannah. But I just . . . I—"

"I know," Hannah broke in. She glanced over her shoulder nervously, then lowered her voice. "All the swells standing around acting like they care about old Mr. Conrad, and each other too, for that matter. Don't see how they can stand themselves." She reached out and gently drew Beth away from her father and into the house.

"Come on into the kitchen and have a cup of cocoa. You too, Alan—"

"I don't think so, Hannah. I'd better—"

"Hannah?" Carolyn's voice called from inside. "Hannah, who is it?" A second later Carolyn, her face drawn, appeared at the door. Seeing Alan, she fell silent for a few seconds, then nodded with sudden understanding. "She came to you again?"

Alan's head bobbed in agreement, and Carolyn hesitated for a moment, then slipped her arms around her daughter. "Darling, what happened? Why didn't you tell me where you were going?"

"Y-you were busy."

"I'm never too busy for you. You know that—"

"It was just too much for her," Alan interjected. "She didn't know anyone, and—"

Carolyn glanced at him, then turned to Hannah. "Take her up to her room, will you, Hannah?"

"I was going to give her some cocoa, ma'am."

"Fine. I'll be there in a minute." She waited until Hannah and Beth were gone, then faced her ex-husband. "Alan, did something happen? Something Beth won't want to tell me about?"

Alan shook his head helplessly. "Carolyn, what can I say? If there's anything she wants to tell you, she'll tell you."

"But you won't," Carolyn said, her voice cool.

"No, I won't. We agreed long ago that—"

"We agreed that we wouldn't use Beth against each other. But if something happened that I need to know about, you have to tell me."

Alan considered his wife's words carefully, then shook his head. "If you want to know what's happening with Beth, talk to her. After all, she lives with you, not with me."

Carolyn stood at the door until Alan was gone and she could no longer hear his car. Then she closed the immense carved-oak front door and started toward the kitchen. But before she had crossed the foyer, her mother-in-law's icy voice stopped her.

"Carolyn, we still have guests."

Carolyn hesitated, torn. Then, as if drawn like a puppet on a string, she turned to follow Abigail Sturgess back to the library.

It was nearly midnight when Carolyn finally went through the house for the last time, making her nightly check to be sure the windows were closed and the doors locked. It was unnecessary— she knew that. Hannah went through the house too, as she had done each night for the last four decades, but Carolyn did it anyway. When Phillip had asked her why one night, she hadn't really been able to tell him. She'd said that checking the house helped make her feel that it was really hers, and that it was a habit left over from all the years before she'd married Phillip. But it was more than that.

Part of it was a simple need to reassure herself, for every night before she went to sleep, she listened to the old house creaking and groaning in the darkness until she could stand it no longer, and giving in to what she knew were irrational fears, got up to search through the rooms to make sure everything was as it should be. After the second month—last February—she had decided it was easier simply to make her rounds before she went to bed.

But it was more than that. There was something about Hilltop House at night—after Abigail had gone to bed—that drew her with a fascination she rarely felt in the daylight. During the day, Hilltop always seemed to her to be trying to shut her out. But at night, it all changed, and the cold stone took on a different feeling, less forbidding and chilly, cradling her, assuring her that no matter what else happened, the house would always be there.

She wandered slowly through the rooms, pausing in the dining room to gaze, as she often did, at the portraits of all the Sturgesses who had once lived in this house, and were now in the mausoleum or the small graveyard behind it. They gazed down on her, and she sometimes imagined that they—like Abigail—were disapproving of her. But of course that was ridiculous. Their expressions of vague contempt had nothing to do with her.

Nothing to do with her personally, at any rate.

Tonight she sank into the chair at the end of the immense dining table, and stared up at the portrait of Samuel Pruett Sturgess. The soft light from the crystal chandelier glowed over the old picture. Carolyn examined it carefully. For some reason she had almost expected the old man's demeanor to have softened tonight, as if meeting his grandson that afternoon had pleased him.

But if it had, the portrait gave no hint. Samuel Pruett Sturgess glowered down from the wall as he always had, and Carolyn caught herself wondering once again if the founding Sturgess had been as cruel as he seemed in the artist's depiction of him, a mean-faced, stern-looking patriarch.

Had the artist heard the rumors about Samuel Pruett, too, or had the rumors about him only begun after his death? There had been so many stories whispered about the old man, his rages, his ruthlessness, that some of them must have been true. And in Carolyn's own family . . .

She shuddered involuntarily, and was once more glad that both her parents had died long before she married Phillip Sturgess. In her family, hatred for the Sturgesses had run deep, and all the rumors had been accepted as fact. For the last child of the Deavers to have married a Sturgess would have been, for both her father and mother, the ultimate shame.

The Deavers had lived in Westover as long as the Sturgesses, perhaps longer. And in Carolyn's family, the legend had always been that Charles Cobb Deaver—Carolyn's great-great-grandfather—had been in partnership with Samuel Pruett Sturgess. Charles Deaver had been a cobbler, and the legend had it that Samuel Pruett Sturgess had used him to get the shoe mill started, then squeezed him out. As the mill had grown, and the Sturgess fortunes risen, the Deaver fortunes had declined. Charles had ended up as nothing more than a shift foreman, and found himself in the position of overseeing the labor of his own children. In the end, he had killed himself, but it was an article of faith to Carolyn's parents that Samuel Pruett Sturgess had murdered him, as surely as if he'd held the gun himself.

Looking at the portrait of Samuel Pruett Sturgess, Carolyn found it hard to doubt the legend. Certainly there was nothing in the man's face that hinted at any sort of kindness. It was a pinched face, an avaricious face, and often Carolyn wished it didn't hang in the dining room, where she had to see it every day. But at the same time, she found the portrait held a strange fascination for her, as if somewhere, buried in the portrait, was the truth behind all the legends.

She stood up, switched off the light, and made her way back through the vast expanse of the living room to the entry hall. She checked the front door once more, then started up the stairs. On the second-floor landing, she glanced down the north wing, and saw a sliver of light beneath the door to Abigail's suite. For a moment, she was tempted to go and tap on the door and say good night to the old woman. But in the end, she turned away, knowing that it would do no good. She would only be rebuffed once more. She turned the other way, and hurried down the wide hall to the suite she and Phillip occupied at the opposite end of the house.

"Are we safe for another night?" Phillip asked as she came into the bedroom. He was propped up against the headboard of the king-size bed, clad in pajamas, paging through a magazine. "No thieves or rapists prowling the corridors?"

Carolyn stuck her tongue out at him, then went to perch on the edge of the bed, presenting her back to him. "The only rapist around here is you, and I happen to like it. Unzip me?"

She felt the warmth of Phillip's fingers on her skin, and shivered with pleasure, but as he started to slip his arms around her, she wriggled away and stood up. Stepping out of the black dress, she started toward her dressing room.

"People should die around here more often," she heard Phillip say. Startled, she turned around to find him grinning at her. "I like you in black."

"I look terrible in black," Carolyn, protested. "And anyway, that's a horrible thing to say."

"I like to say horrible things. And you don't look terrible in black. Anyway not in black undies."

"Well, it's still a horrible thing to say on the day we buried your father."

"Who was beginning to show signs of never dying at all," Phillip remarked dryly.

"Phillip!"

"Well, it's true, isn't it? And don't go all pious on me. As for dear old Dad," he went on, "I'm not going to pretend I'm sorry to see him go. At least not to you."

"Your father was—" Carolyn began, but her husband cut her off.

"My father was a half-senile old man who had outlived his time. My God, Carolyn, you should be the first to admit that. He never faced up to the fact that the nineteenth century ended, even though he never lived in it."

"All right, he was difficult," Carolyn admitted. "But he was still your father, and you owe him some respect."

The mischievous glint in Phillip's eyes died, and his expression turned serious. "I don't have to respect him at all," he said. "We both know how he was, and we both know how he treated you. He acted as though you were one of the servants."

"And I survived it, didn't I?" Carolyn asked. "After all, we could have moved out, if we'd really wanted to."

"Agreed," Phillip sighed. "And we didn't, which probably doesn't speak very well for either one of us. Anyway, it's over now."

"Is it?" Carolyn asked. "What about your mother? And Tracy? They haven't been a bed of roses either." Then, at the look of pain that came into Phillip's eyes, she wished she could take back the words. "I'm sorry. I shouldn't have said that, should I?"

"You shouldn't have had to say it," Phillip replied quietly. Then his eyes met hers. "Carolyn, do you want to move? We can take the girls, and go anywhere we want. Away from Westover. Without Mother's influence, Tracy will come around."

It was something Carolyn had thought about often, and always, in the end, rejected. Leaving Westover, she knew, was not the solution. "We can't, Phillip. You know we can't. We can't leave Abigail alone here—it would kill her. It's going to be hard enough for her without your father. Without you and Tracy, she'd have nothing left. Besides," she added, "this is your home."

"And your home, too."

Carolyn shook her head ruefully. "Not yet. Maybe someday, but not yet. This is your home—and your mother's. And I'm afraid I still feel . . . like a guest here," she offered hesitantly. She had almost said, "an unwelcome guest."

"You don't have to, you know."

"I know," Carolyn replied. "Lord knows you've told me to spend what I want redoing the place, but I can't. I'd be afraid of bankrupting us, and besides, I wouldn't know where to start. And I'm not about to open another front for Abigail."

"She's just set in her ways. If you just began—"

"She's not just set in her ways, and you know it. She's Abigail Sturgess, and she's frozen in time." Suddenly her voice broke. "And she thinks I'm a toy you found on the wrong side of the tracks, and brought home to play with for a while!"

Immediately, Phillip was on his feet, and his arms were around her. "Darling, don't think that. Don't think that for even a minute."

Carolyn fought back the tears that were burning her eyes and shook her head. "I don't. You know I don't. I'm just having a weak moment. Let me finish undressing, and then let's talk about something else, all right?"

Reluctantly Phillip released her, and went back to the bed. Carolyn moved through the dressing room into the bathroom, and quickly ran cold water in the sink, then washed her face, and began running a brush through her hair.

Maybe it had been a mistake to marry Phillip—maybe, no matter how badly she wanted it to work, it was an impossible situation.

But she had to make it work.

After Alan—

She tried to force the thought out of her mind, but couldn't. The problem, she knew, was that Phillip and Alan were too much alike.

Good, kind, decent men.

And she'd lost Alan, simply because she hadn't been able to accept him as he was. She'd always wanted more.

She wouldn't make the same mistake with Phillip. Westover was his home; this house was his home. He belonged here. And no matter what happened, she wouldn't ask him to leave. She would figure out a way to deal with his mother, and she would win his daughter over. And she would never ask him to leave.

She'd married him for what he was. A large part of that identity was defined by the fact that Phillip was a Sturgess. And Sturgesses lived at Hilltop.

Suddenly fragments of the old stories flitted through her mind—stories she'd grown up with, stories about the Sturgesses. But as quickly as they came, she rejected them. They were only the unkind

whisperings of people who had less than the Sturgesses and therefore envied them. Legends. And they had nothing to do with Phillip.

She put the hairbrush away, and returned to the bedroom, then
slid into the bed next to her husband. Switching off the lamp on her
bed table, she snuggled close, feeling the tension drain out of her
body. And then—a thought occurred to her.

"Phillip."

"Hm?"

"Phillip, that plan you've been working on—the one to refurbish
the mill?"

"Mm-hmm. What about it?"

"You're not . . . you're not thinking of going ahead with it, are
you?"

Phillip drew away slightly, and looked down at her. "Don't tell me
you've been talking to Mother?"

"Abigail? What made you think that?"

"Because we were talking about the mill today. On the way up
here, after the church service. She asked me if the plan was ready."

Carolyn felt her heart beat faster. "What did you tell her?"

"That it was all set. Everything's on paper."

"And what did Abigail say?" Carolyn realized that she was holding
her breath.

Phillip chuckled. "For once, Mother agreed with me. She said that
now that Father's gone, it's time I went ahead with that project."

Carolyn lay silent for a long time, then spoke again. "Phillip,
maybe you shouldn't go ahead. Maybe . . . maybe your father was
right."

Now Phillip sat full upright, and turned on the light. When she
looked at him, she saw his eyes flashing angrily.

"Right? All Father would ever say about the mill was that it was
evil, and should never be touched. Not restored, not converted to
some other use, not even torn down. Just left to rot, for God's sake!
How can that be right?"

Carolyn shook her head unhappily. "I don't know. But there have
been so many stories. And you don't know how everyone in town
feels about the mill."

"They feel the same way I feel about it," Phillip declared. "That
it's a hideous old eyesore, and that something ought to be done with
it."

"But that's not it," Carolyn replied. "It's something else. It's a
reminder of how things used to be here—" She stopped herself, not
wanting to hurt her husband, but it was already too late: she could
see the pain in Phillip's eyes.

"You mean a reminder of the bad old days, when my family used to work children to death in the shoe factory?"

Mutely, Carolyn nodded.

Phillip stared at her for a moment, then flopped back down on his pillow, averting his eyes.

"I think that's another reason to renovate it," he said tiredly. "Perhaps the best reason. Maybe all those old stories will finally be forgotten if I do something with the mill and some people in Westover make some honest money from it."

"But maybe . . . maybe the stories shouldn't be forgotten, Phillip. Maybe we always need to remember what happened there."

"My God," Phillip groaned. "You sound just like Father. Except that he'd never say exactly what he was talking about. It was always vague references, and dark hints. But nothing I could ever put my finger on." He propped himself up on one elbow, and his tone lightened. "And you know why I could never put my finger on any of it?" he asked.

Carolyn shook her head.

"Because maybe there was nothing to put my finger on! Just a bunch of stories and legends about terrible abuses in the shoe mill. But that sort of thing went on all over New England. Christ, child labor was our answer to slavery. But it's all over now, Carolyn. Why should we keep torturing ourselves with it?"

"I don't know," Carolyn admitted. "But I just can't help feeling that somehow your father was right about the mill."

Phillip reached over and turned off his light again, then drew her close. "Well, he wasn't," he said. "He was as wrong about the mill as he was about everything else. He was my father, darling, but I have to confess I didn't like him very much."

Carolyn made no reply, and lay still in her husband's arms. Here, in bed with Phillip, she felt secure and safe, and she would do nothing to threaten that security. But as Phillip drifted into sleep, and she lay awake, she couldn't help feeling that Phillip was wrong about the mill, and that old Conrad Sturgess, whom they had buried that day, was right.

The mill should be left alone; left to crumble away until there was nothing left of it but dust.

Three

Tracy Sturgess lay in her bed listening to the faint echoes of the old grandfather clock that had stood in the entry hall for as long as she could remember. She counted the chimes, then checked her tally against the little clock on her night table.

Eleven.

She threw the covers back, put on her robe, then went into the bathroom that adjoined her bedroom. Switching on the light, she inspected herself in the mirror.

She didn't look quite right.

Carefully she mussed her hair until she was satisfied that it looked as though she'd been tossing in her bed for the last hour. Then she turned the bathroom light off and moved quickly through the darkness to her bedroom door. Opening it a crack, she peered out into the dimness of the corridor, lit only by a small nightlight that sat on the marble-topped commode midway between the stairs and her grandmother's rooms.

The hall was empty, and silence hung over the house. But at the far end of the hall, as she had known it would, light glowed from beneath her grandmother's door.

Smiling, she hurried down the hall.

She paused outside her grandmother's door, and listened. From within, she could hear the faint sounds of her grandmother moving restlessly around her sitting room, then a silence. Tracy smiled. Composing her face into a mask of worried unhappiness, she rapped softly at the door. For a moment there was no response from within, then she heard her grandmother's voice.

"Come in."

Tracy twisted the brass knob, and gently pushed the door open just far enough to slip through. "G-Grandmother?" she asked, letting her voice tremble just the slightest bit. "I couldn't sleep. I miss Grandfather so much . . ." She reached up and brushed at her eyes.

Her grandmother's response, as always, was immediate.

"Tracy, darling, come in. Please." From her chair, Abigail held her arms wide, and Tracy, after hesitating only a second, ran across the room, dropped to her knees, and buried her face in the old woman's lap. Abigail, her own eyes flooding, gently stroked Tracy's hair.

"What is it, child? What's wrong?"

Tracy sniffled slightly, then looked up. "I . . . I just don't know what's going to happen to us, now that Grandfather's . . ." She let her voice trail off, and held still as Abigail brushed the beginnings of a tear away from her eye.

"It's going to be all right, my darling," Abigail assured her. "We have to learn to accept these things. We all die sooner or later, and it was time for your grandfather to go."

"But I didn't *want* him to die!" Tracy wailed. "I loved him so much!"

"Of course you did. We all did. But we have to understand that he's gone now, and that our lives go on."

"But without him, everything's going to be different!"

"Different?" Abigail asked. "How are things going to be different?"

Tracy hesitated for a long time, waiting for her grandmother to urge her to speak.

"Go on, Tracy. Whatever it is, you know you can tell me."

Tracy took a deep breath. "It . . . it's Carolyn. What's going to happen to me, now that Grandfather isn't here to help me? She hates me."

Abigail slipped her arms around her granddaughter, and drew her close. "How could she hate you? You're a lovely child."

Tracy allowed herself a small pout. "But she does hate me. She always tells Daddy that I'm spoiled, and that you've raised me wrong." She felt her grandmother's body stiffen.

"I've raised you precisely as your mother would have raised you," Abigail replied. "And your father knows that."

"But he married *her!* And now she's going to try to change everything!"

"Everything? How?"

Tracy's eyes clouded, and she drew a little away from her grandmother. "I . . . I guess I shouldn't talk about it tonight," she said. She stood up as if to leave, but Abigail stopped her.

"Nonsense. Whatever is upsetting you, we should deal with it. Now, what is it?"

Tracy turned to face her grandmother again. "M-my birthday party," she stammered. "Are we still going to have it next week, like we planned?"

Abigail blinked, then remembered. Tracy's party, planned for weeks, had slipped her mind when Conrad died. "Why—I don't know." Then, seeing the disappointment in Tracy's eyes, she immediately made up her mind. "But I don't see why we shouldn't have it. In fact, I'm certain your grandfather would have wanted it that way."

Suddenly Tracy brightened. "And I can invite anybody I want?"

"Absolutely," Abigail assured her. "After all, it's your party, isn't it?"

"But what about—" Tracy fell silent, as if once again she was hesitant to tell her grandmother what was on her mind.

"What about what?" Abigail pressed.

"Beth," Tracy whispered. She hesitated as her grandmother's jaw tightened slightly, and wondered if she'd made a mistake. But when Abigail spoke a moment later, Tracy knew it was going to be all right.

"I don't think the little Rogers girl would enjoy your party."

"But what are we going to do?" Tracy asked. "Carolyn will make me invite her."

"Perhaps," the old woman said softly, but her eyes were glinting now. "Perhaps she will. But perhaps she won't, either. At any rate, we'll deal with it tomorrow. All right?"

Tracy came back, and leaned down to give her grandmother a hug. "I love you, Grandmother," she whispered.

"And I love you, too," Abigail replied. "And you mustn't worry about anything. Just because your grandfather's gone doesn't mean you're all alone. You've still got me."

A few minutes later, Tracy left her grandmother's room, and started back down the long corridor. But the smell of the room—a mixture of mustiness and toosweet cologne as well as something else—was still with her. She took several deep breaths, trying to rid herself of that cloying scent she had always hated: it was the smell of old people.

She wondered how her grandmother could stand it. And the room, too. Though she was always careful to tell her grandmother how much she liked the old-fashioned sitting room, with its Victorian furniture and worn Oriental rugs, the truth was that she hated the look of her grandmother's suite as much as its smell. When her grandmother finally died, and Tracy talked her father into letting her move into the big suite, she'd change it all.

Everything.

But until then, she had to go on pretending to her grandmother. Grandparents, after all, had been known to cut people out of their wills. Tracy, even though she wasn't quite thirteen yet, wasn't about to let something like that happen.

Suddenly she stopped, listening. From behind a closed door she could barely make out the sounds of one of her favorite rock bands. She frowned, and listened harder.

The music was coming from Beth's room.

She listened for a moment, her body unconsciously swaying to the familiar rhythms. Then, her eyes narrowing, she strode to Beth's door, and pushed it open without knocking.

Startled at Tracy's sudden entry, Beth sat up in bed and stared at the other girl.

"What do you think you're doing?" she heard Tracy hiss.

"Tracy? What . . . what's wrong?"

"That music, stupid! Don't you know we're mourning my grandfather?"

Beth stared at Tracy for a second, trying to understand what she'd done. "But—I was playing it soft."

"You shouldn't be playing it at all," Tracy said. "How can anybody sleep, with you blaring your radio?"

"But you can hardly hear it—" Beth protested.

"*I* could hear it," Tracy insisted. "And my grandmother could, too! Shut it off!"

Beth's eyes widened, and she reached over to turn the knob on the clock-radio. "I'll turn it down—"

"Turn it off!" Tracy insisted. She marched over to the night table, and punched at the button on top. The radio went silent. Beth, her eyes frightened, stared at her stepsister.

"I don't see why I can't listen to it if it's so soft no one else can hear—"

"You can't listen to it, because I said you can't. It's my house— not yours—and if you don't like it here, you can just go live somewhere else!"

"But Mom said—"

"Who cares what your mother says?" Tracy demanded. "Just because your stupid mother married my father doesn't give you the right to—"

Suddenly Beth's anger overcame her confusion. "You take that back, Tracy Sturgess!"

Tracy, startled by the unexpected outburst, stepped back: "Don't you talk to me like that!"

"Don't you call my mother stupid!"

Tracy's eyes hardened, and her mouth set petulantly. "I'll call your mother anything I want, and you can't stop me!"

Beth stared at Tracy, fighting back her anger. "Just go away," she finally managed to say. "Just go away and leave me alone."

The, two girls stared at each other for several long seconds, Tracy's eyes glittering with rage while Beth struggled against the tears that threatened to overwhelm her. Then, at last, Tracy turned and stamped out of the room.

As soon as Tracy was gone, Beth ran to the door and locked it, then returned to her bed. Sobbing, she buried her head in the pillow.

It wasn't going to get any better, despite what her father had told her. It was only going to get worse, and it wouldn't matter what she did, or how much she pretended.

Tracy would still hate her.

Her sobs slowly subsided, and she lay in bed wondering what tomorrow would be like.

But she already knew.

It would start at breakfast.

She would sit miserably at the table in the breakfast room, trying to figure out which spoon to use for what.

Old Mrs. Sturgess would ignore her, just like she always did.

But Tracy would watch her, waiting for her to make a mistake, so that she could laugh when Beth made one.

And she would say or do something wrong. She always did.

But what if she didn't go down for breakfast? What if she got up early, and sneaked down to have breakfast with Hannah? Then she could go down to the stable and see the horses, and after that—

—What?

Tracy would come, and tell her she didn't know anything about horses, and that she should leave them alone.

And the trouble was, Tracy was right.

Beth didn't know anything about horses. She didn't know anything about anything in this house, and she'd never learn.

She snuggled deeper under the covers, and closed her eyes. Maybe, if she pretended hard enough, she could convince herself that she was back in the house on Cherry Street, where she'd lived before. And she could pretend that her parents were still married, and—

—and she couldn't do it.

Her parents *weren't* still married. Her mother was married to Uncle Phillip, and she had to get used to it.

She had to, and she would. Her mother wanted her to, and so did her father.

She turned over, telling herself that it wasn't really so bad. It was a nice house, even if it was too big, and Uncle Phillip was always kind to her.

If she could only figure out some way to make Tracy like her.

Slowly, sleep reached out to her.

And in the night, she dreamed of Tracy.

Tracy was trying to kill her.

*   *   *

Despite the June warmth in the glassed-in breakfast room, Carolyn could feel the chill emanating from her mother-in-law, and the cold hatred from her stepdaughter. Phillip, engrossed in the financial pages of *The Wall Street Journal,* appeared oblivious of the strain in the room, though she was certain that he was listening to every word spoken. And when he at last felt compelled to put an end to the argument that had been going on for the last twenty minutes, she knew that he would come down firmly on her side.

It had begun when Carolyn had first come in that morning, and seen that her daughter's place was not occupied.

"Isn't Beth down yet?" she'd asked.

Abigail had peered at her over the tops of her reading glasses.

"I believe she took her breakfast with Hannah this morning," she'd said, managing to convey that though she didn't approve of members of her family eating with the servants, she was willing to overlook the breach in Beth's case.

Beth, after all, wasn't a Sturgess, and couldn't be expected to meet the Sturgess standards of behavior.

Then she'd offered Carolyn a bright smile, and suggested that, since Beth was not present, perhaps they should discuss Tracy's birthday party.

Carolyn's guard had immediately gone up, particularly when she saw the slight smile on Tracy's lips.

Now, almost half an hour later, Tracy was glaring at her, her blue eyes glittering with barely controlled fury beneath her creased brows.

"But Beth won't even *enjoy* my party," Tracy began, taking a new tack. "She won't know how to dress, or what to say. She doesn't know any of my friends, and they don't know her!"

"Then perhaps it would be good for them to get to know her," Carolyn said placidly, unwilling to reveal her own anger. "And perhaps we ought to invite some of Beth's friends, too. It certainly seems to me that it would be good for you to get to know them. After all, you're going to be going to school with them next year."

"That has hardly been decided yet," Abigail put in, laying her napkin aside in a gesture Carolyn had long since learned to recognize as a danger signal. "After Phillip and I have discussed the quality of the Westover schools, we'll make the final decision."

"We've already talked about it, Mother," Phillip said, putting his newspaper aside. "The decision has been made. Next year Tracy goes to public school."

"I've told you, I'm quite willing to pay her tuition out of my own funds—" Abigail began, but Phillip cut her off.

"Funds are not the point. The point is that neither I nor Carolyn is pleased with Tracy's school."

"And just what would Carolyn know about Tracy's school?" Abigail asked, her voice taking on an acid quality she no longer tried to hide. "I hardly think," she went on, casting a haughty half-smile in her daughter-in-law's direction, "that your Carolyn is in any position to judge the quality of private schools."

"That is not what we are talking about right now," Carolyn replied, ignoring Abigail's frosty gaze. Then, noting the beginnings of a grin playing around Phillip's mouth, she stretched her foot under the table and kicked him. The grin threatened to grow for a split second, then he managed to suppress it. Carolyn continued, "What we're talking about is Tracy's party, and it seems to me that we're making a mountain out of a molehill. Aside from the fact that my daughter is a perfectly nice girl, whose feelings I have no intention of letting either of you trample on, I think that you, Abigail, might keep in mind that her father happens to be an Alderman, and while that doesn't make him a Sturgess—or a Babcock, a Kilpatrick, or a Bailey, either—it does give him a certain amount of power." She let her eyes bore directly into Abigail's. "Back when you were Tracy's age, the Board of Aldermen consisted of your father, Phillip's grandfather, Jeremiah Bailey, and Fred Kilpatrick. Aside from the fact that they were the Aldermen, they were also very rich."

"The people voted for them," Abigail snapped.

"Of course they did. The people worked for them, too, which might have had something to do with the way they cast their votes. But all that's over, and it's time you understood it. There are no Baileys, Kilpatricks, Babcocks, or Sturgesses on the board anymore. But the board still runs Westover, and the board still has to pass on all the permits that Phillip is going to need for future projects." She paused, noting that Abigail flinched slightly, and surreptitiously glanced at her son.

Phillip, she was almost certain, was suppressing another grin.

"Given what you want to do with the mill, Abigail, you should understand the value of being on good terms with the board. There are a lot of people—and I am among them—who feel the mill should be left as it is, or torn down. I, of course, won't fight Phillip. But others will. And snubbing Beth on Tracy's birthday isn't going to help your cause. It will hurt me, and I don't even want to think about what it will do to Beth. But it will infuriate Alan."

"I can't imagine that Alderman Rogers is even aware of Tracy's party," Abigail observed archly.

"I wouldn't count on that," Carolyn replied. "Beth talks to her father about everything. In all of the talk about Tracy's party, it was never suggested that Beth not be invited."

"*I* didn't invite her," Tracy said sullenly. "And it's my party. If I don't want her to be here that day, she doesn't have to be here! Does she, Grandmother?"

"Of course not, dear," Abigail assured her. She turned her gaze back to Carolyn. "I'm sure you understand that our family has never mixed with children like Beth, and I see no reason why Tracy should be forced to do something that is unnatural to her. As for Beth, I'm sure she won't feel the least bit snubbed. Those kinds of people rarely do—particularly the children."

Steeling herself, Carolyn managed to keep her voice level. "Since I can't imagine that you've ever been snubbed, Abigail, I'm sure you wouldn't know how it feels. I, on the other hand, know very well, since it happens to me quite regularly. I can tolerate it. But there's no reason why Beth should have to." She paused, then decided it was time to let both Abigail and Tracy see how angry she truly was. "My God," she went on. "Beth lives here! This is supposed to be her home, and the two of you do your best to make her feel as if she doesn't belong here. And perhaps she doesn't. Perhaps neither of us does. But here we are, and here we shall stay. And Beth will be at Tracy's party, and you will both be polite to her. Is that clear?" She took a breath, and hoped Abigail couldn't see that her hands were trembling. "Now, I think we might as well talk about something else, since this discussion is over," she finished, somehow managing to force a smile. "More toast, Abigail?"

Abigail ignored her. "Phillip, I will not be treated this way. I don't understand how you can—"

"She's right, Mother," Phillip interrupted, and Carolyn breathed a silent sigh of relief. "Aside from the moral issues, which we Sturgesses have never been too strong on, I think you'd better consider long and hard before you offend Alan Rogers. Not, mind you, that I think Alan would be petty enough to hold up any permits over a birthday party." He smiled ironically. "Somehow that sort of thing strikes me as being much more our style than his. But there are a lot of projects coming up, and we're going to need cooperation from the town. It's not only Tracy who should start getting acquainted with everyone else who lives in Westover, all of us should." He turned finally to his daughter. "I'm sorry, honey, but your stepmother's right. Beth will be included in your party, or there won't be a party."

Tracy, her face twisting into a grimace of frustration and fury, burst into tears and stormed from the table. Immediately, Abigail rose to follow her, but Phillip spoke once more. "Leave her alone, Mother."

"I will *not* leave her alone," Abigail replied. "Ever since you married Carolyn, you've become insensitive to your own family. But you're making a mistake, Phillip, and you will live to regret it." She started out of the breakfast room, then turned back. "And as for the mill, Carolyn, whatever is done with it is no concern of yours. It is Sturgess property, and always has been. We shall do as we please with it, and what we please to do is to restore it as a monument to the foresight of Phillip's great-grandfather. If the people of Westover cannot appreciate that, then the people be damned." Her back ramrod straight, she swept out of the room.

There was a long silence, finally broken by Carolyn's tired sigh. "I'm sorry," she said. "I know how unpleasant that was for you. And maybe she's right. Maybe Tracy shouldn't be forced to include Beth in her party."

Phillip shook his head. "Not a chance. It's time all of us got dragged into the modern world. You've done it for me, and maybe Beth can do it for Tracy. We'll just keep on plugging, and eventually things will all work out." He glanced at his watch, then drained the last of his coffee. "And as for me, I've got to meet one of the wrong sort of people at the mill, and if I don't hurry, I'll be late."

"Wrong sort of people?" Carolyn asked archly. "Who?"

"The worst," Phillip replied, dropping his voice to a conspiratorial level. "Your ex-husband!" Then, before she could reply, he was gone.

Alone, Carolyn sat for a few minutes staring down on the village below. Always, when she'd lived down there and gazed up at Hilltop, the house had seemed to her to be the most peaceful place on earth.

Now she was here, and there was no peace.

Four

Beth pushed open the screened kitchen door, and stepped out onto the little flagstone patio that led to the back gardens. The door slammed shut behind her, and she jumped slightly at the crash, calling a quick apology over her shoulder.

"It's all right," Hannah replied mildly from the shadows of the kitchen. "No harm done."

Beth stood in the small enclosure, feeling the early-morning sunshine, and looked around. Here, away from the vastness of the rest of the house, she almost felt at home. The patio, in fact, was almost like the one her father had built behind the house on Cherry Street.

At Hilltop, though, there was another terrace, a wide veranda that extended across most of the length of the house, filled with tables and chairs and chaise lounges. It overlooked the tennis court and the rose garden, and Beth didn't really like it: like everything else here, it was too big and too ornate.

She skipped down the steps, then started along a path that led under an arbor, then skirted the edge of the rose garden. Beyond that, hidden from the house by a high hedge, was the stable.

The stable was Beth's favorite part of Hilltop. In the barn, where it was warm in winter, but cool now that summer was here, and everything smelled like horses and hay, she always felt better. In fact, she'd even made friends with one of the horses, a large black-and-white one named Patches, who always whinnied when she came into the barn, and nuzzled at her pockets looking for carrots.

She turned a corner, and almost tripped over the gardener, who was on his knees carefully digging up a border of tulip bulbs and replacing them with tiny marigolds.

"Hi, Mr. Smithers."

The old gardener looked up, then rocked back on his heels, dangling his trowel in his right hand. "Morning, Miss Beth. You're out bright and early today."

"I had breakfast with Hannah this morning."

Smithers's brows rose slightly, but he said nothing.

"Well, what's wrong with that?" Beth asked. "If I want to eat breakfast with Hannah, why shouldn't I?"

"No reason—no reason at all," the old man assured her. Then a little grin cracked his weathered face. "But I bet Mrs. Sturgess didn't like that."

Beth frowned uncertainly. "Why wouldn't she like that?"

Now Smithers's brows arched in a caricature of disapproval. "A member of the family eating with the servants? Tut-tut, child! It simply isn't done!"

"But I'm not a member of the family! I'm just who I always was. Remember?" Then her voice dropped. "And I wish you wouldn't call me Miss Beth, either. You never used to do that."

"And your mother never used to be married to Mr. Phillip, either," Smithers replied, his voice gentle. "Things are different now, and you have to learn what's expected of you. And part of that is that

I call you Miss Beth, and you call me Ben. I'm the gardener here, and you shouldn't call me 'mister.' "

"But when we lived next door to you, I always called you Mr. Smithers."

"That was before," the gardener explained once more. "And I used to call your mother by her first name, too. But everything's changed now." Ben Smithers shrugged, shaking his head. "It's just the way of the world, Miss Beth. Everything changes, and there's not much you can do about it," Then he brightened. "Except my garden," he added. "Every year, I try to make it look just the way it always has. 'Course, even that doesn't work out, when you get right down to it. It's always a little different, and every year the soil gets a little more worn out." He smiled ruefully. "Sort of like me, I guess. Every year, a little more worn out. Now, you run along, and let me get my work done, all right?"

"I could help you," Beth offered, but even as she uttered the words, she knew what the old man's answer would be.

"Not for you to help me," he said. "It's for you and the rest of the Sturgesses to pick 'em. It's for me to grow 'em. Which is just as well, since growin' 'em is what I like to do."

His grip on the trowel tightened, and he rocked forward. A moment later a clump of tulip bulbs appeared, and Ben Smithers carefully brushed the dirt away from it before slipping it into a labeled bag. A moment later, a young marigold had replaced the tulip.

Beth watched for a few minutes, then silently continued on her way down to the stable.

Beth let herself into the stable and heard Patches whinny softly. Fishing in her pocket, she found a stump of carrot, then scratched the horse affectionately between the ears as the animal munched the treat. There was a movement at the back of the barn, and Beth quickly withdrew her hand from the horse, afraid that Tracy Sturgess was about to appear, but when she looked up, all she saw was Peter Russell, the stableboy, grinning at her.

"Hi, twerp. Come down to help me muck out the stalls?"

"Can I?" Beth asked eagerly.

Peter looked puzzled. "Why not?"

"I just—" Beth hesitated, then plunged on. "Peter, am I any different since I moved up here?"

"Jeez," Peter replied. "How would I know? Why don't you ask Peggy? She's your best friend, isn't she?" He handed a shovel to Beth, and pointed to a large pile in one of the empty stalls. Making a face, Beth let herself into the stall, and gingerly slid the shovel under the pile of manure.

"But Peggy never comes up here," Beth replied. Peggy Russell was Peter's younger sister and Beth and Peggy had been best friends since second grade. Balancing the shovel carefully, Beth moved outside and added the manure to the pile that grew steadily behind the stable each week until a truck came on Monday afternoons to take it all away. When she went back into the stall, she found Peter staring at her with the contempt he usually reserved for his kid sister.

"You know, you can be almost as dumb as Peggy sometimes. The reason she doesn't come up here is because I work here. Mom says if she came up here it would look like she was tagging along on my job, and then Mr. Sturgess might fire me."

Beth stared at Peter. "He wouldn't do that!"

"Tell that to my mom."

"I will! Peggy's my friend. Uncle Phillip wouldn't fire you just because your sister came to see me!"

"Uncle Phillip?" Peter echoed, his voice suddenly tinged with scorn. "Since when is he your uncle?"

Beth felt herself redden, and turned away. "It . . . it's what I'm supposed to call him," she mumbled.

"Why don't you just call him Dad?" Peter asked.

Beth spun around to face him again, the sting of his words bringing tears to her eyes. "He s not my father! And why are you being so mean? I thought you were my friend!"

Peter stared at his sister's friend, wondering what she was so angry about. Didn't she have everything now? She lived in a mansion, and had servants, and a tennis court, and horses. She was living a life all the other kids in Westover only dreamed about.

"We're not friends," he said finally. "You're the kid who lives in the mansion now, remember? Since when have any of the kids like you ever been friends of the rest of us? Now, if you want to help, help. If you don't, just go away. Okay? I've got work to do."

Beth dropped the shovel and ran from the stall, certain her tears were going to overcome her. She started toward the door, but before she could get out of the stable, the big black-and-white horse in the first stall whinnied again, and stretched its neck out to snuffle at her.

Beth paused, and automatically reached up to pet the horse. Suddenly she knew what she should do. If Peter was going to treat her like she was Tracy Sturgess, she would act like Tracy.

"Peter," she called; then, when there was no answer, she called again, louder. "Peter!"

The stableboy stuck his head out of one of the far stalls. "What do you want now?"

"Saddle Patches," Beth told him. "I want to go for a ride."

Peter stared at her. "Are you nuts? You don't know how to ride."

"Do it!" Beth demanded, hoping she didn't sound as frightened as she suddenly felt. "Let Patches out in the paddock, and put the saddle on!"

Peter only grinned at her, and shook his head.

"Then I'll do it myself," Beth cried. Opening the gate, she let herself into the stall. The horse backed away, then reared up, snorting.

Beth darted across the stall and threw open the door on the other side, and the horse immediately bolted through into the paddock beyond. A moment later, Beth followed.

Outside, she paused, then reached up and took the lead rope off the nail it was coiled over. As she started toward the horse, she tried to remember what it was that Tracy did when she was going to saddle a mount.

Patches eyed her as she approached, pawing at the ground and whinnying softly. When she was only a few feet away, the horse reared up, pawed at the air, then cantered off to the other end of the paddock.

From the stable, Beth heard Peter laughing. She spun around, glaring at him.

"Don't just stand there! Help me!"

"You let Patches out—it's your problem!"

Beth looked from Peter back to the horse, and suddenly felt herself begin to panic. The animal, so friendly in the stall, suddenly looked much bigger, and somehow threatening. But she had to get the horse onto the lead. She had to!

She started forward once more, moving slowly and carefully, feeling her heart pound. Patches, apparently no longer interested in her, had reached down and torn a clump of grass up. But when Beth moved in close, the horse suddenly shied away, snorted a warning, then once more trotted away.

Suddenly Beth felt the lead rope being torn from her hand, and heard Tracy's voice.

"What are you doing, stupid? Give me that!" Then, while Beth stood watching, Tracy trotted over to the horse, grasped its halter just as it began to rear, and snapped the lead in place. She jerked sharply on the lead, and Patches came back to earth, neighing softly.

"You idiot," Tracy shouted to Beth as she led the horse back to its stall. "What were you doing?"

"I . . . I just wanted to go for a ride. And Peter wouldn't saddle him for me, so I tried to do it myself."

"Well, you can't," Tracy snapped. "You don't know anything about horses."

"I do, too—"

"You just called Patches 'him,' didn't you? Well, it just so happens Patches is a mare. If you can't even tell that, you should stay out of the stable. And besides, Patches is *my* horse!"

"Aw, come on, Tracy," Peter Russell began, but Tracy, whirled around, glaring at him.

"You stay out of this, or I'll make Father fire you. And don't ever let her back in the stable again."

Peter's lips tightened, but be said nothing. When Tracy had led the horse back into the stable and closed the door, Beth ran over to the boy.

"Peter, I'm sorry. I didn't mean to—"

"Didn't you hear her?" Peter demanded, his anger at Tracy now refocused on Beth. "Just stay away, all right?" Then he turned, and also disappeared into the stable.

Beth hesitated, then felt the tears she'd been fighting overflow. Scrambling through the paddock fence, she ran along the path back toward the rose garden, then veered off to the right, going around the end of the house, crossing the front lawn. On the far side two immense stone lions flanked the foot of the trail that led up to the mausoleum. Beth passed between them unseeingly, almost blinded by the stinging tears.

Phillip Sturgess and Alan Rogers stood on Prospect Street, gazing across at the sullen brick facade of the long-abandoned mill. Its windows, long since bereft of glass, were boarded over, and the once-red bricks bore a thick accumulation of grime that had turned them nearly black. At the top, some of the crenellations that had once been the building's sole claim to architectural interest had crumbled away, giving the abandoned factory a ruined look.

The two men stood silent for a long time. Alan finally sighed, and shook his head.

"I don't know. On paper, it all looks great, but when you look at what we really have to work with—well, I just don't know. It might be easier to tear it down and start over."

Phillip nodded. "It would be cheaper, too. But we'd lose something if we did that. There's history in that building, Alan. Almost the whole history of Westover is tied up in the mill."

"Don't you mean the history of the Sturgesses?" Alan replied.

"I'm not sure there's a difference." Then he saw the grin on Alan's face, and chuckled. "All right, so I sounded like my parents. But the whole attraction of the place will be the fact of the restoration, so we don't really have any choice, do we? And the structure's sound, believe it, or not. I had an engineer survey it a few months ago."

Alan regarded the other man skeptically. "Did your father know that?"

"You know how Father felt about the mill."

"And he had a right to, after what happened to your brother."

There was a silence; then Phillip spoke again, his voice softer. "What happened to Conrad Junior was an accident, despite what Father believed." Then, when Alan said nothing, Phillip turned to face him. "Alan, you don't believe all those stories, do you?"

"The ghost stories? Of course not. But apparently your father did."

Phillip's expression tightened. "He's dead now."

"Yes." Alan paused, then chose his words carefully. "What about Carolyn? What does she think of all this?"

Phillip eyed Alan shrewdly. "The fact that you asked the question suggests to me that you know the answer."

"I just wondered," Alan replied, shrugging noncommittally. "She just always hated this place, that's all." Then, meeting Phillip's eyes, he went on. "A lot of people in Westover hate this mill, Phillip. They see it as a symbol, and the memories it evokes aren't pleasant ones. A lot of the children of Westover died in that building—"

"That was a long time ago, Alan," Phillip interrupted. "And while I'm not pretending it was right, child labor went on all over New England back then. It wasn't just here, and it wasn't just the Sturgesses."

"I'm not saying it was," Alan agreed. "All I'm saying is that a lot of people here still look at that mill, and think about what went on in it."

"Something none of them really remembers," Phillip pointed out. "Let's not forget that the mill's been closed for a century, and stories get exaggerated. If Father had been smart, he'd have done something with the property years ago." Suddenly Phillip cocked his head, and gazed at Alan suspiciously. "Alan, is there something you're not telling me? Is the board likely to hold up the permits just because of the history of the building?"

Alan shook his head. "Nope. The permits will go through without a murmur. As far as the board's concerned, history is history. If turning this old wreck into a mall full of cute little shops will make people in Westover some money, the aldermen are all for it."

"But you doubt that it will," Phillip stated.

"I do," Alan agreed, but then smiled ruefully. "Of course, as your wife will tell you, I'm not the most imaginative son-of-a-bitch around, and never think anything will work. So why don't we go inside and have a look around, and I can tell you just why the dump will collapse when we start working on it."

"And I," Phillip laughed, "will expect you to buy me a drink when nothing collapses at all."

They crossed Prospect Street, walked to the corner of the vast building, then turned left onto a weedchoked path that paralleled the building's long northern wall. Halfway down, they came to a metal door, its paint badly weathered. But when Phillip slipped a key into the padlock that hung from an oversized hasp, it opened easily.

"Father had the lock checked every month, from the day Conrad Junior died. Sometimes he did it himself. When I was a kid, I used to beg him to bring me along and show me the inside of the mill, but he never would. I guess—well, I guess he never got over my brother's death at all."

"He really never even let you look around?" Alan asked.

Phillip shook his head. "It used to drive me nuts. Sometimes I'd lie awake nights, looking down at it from my window, plotting how I could sneak in. But then I'd think about what Father would do to me if I got caught, and I never tried it." His face twisted into an abashed grin. "Do you know, even when I came down here with the engineer, I almost couldn't bring myself to go inside? I kept thinking Father was watching me from Hilltop, and when I got home, he'd skin me. Forty-three years old, and still afraid of my father. Some tycoon, huh?"

Alan chuckled, and thumped his friend's back. "Afraid you just don't pull off the tycoon act very well at all, Phillip, and that's the truth. You sure you're a real Sturgess?"

"I'm going to accept that little bit of snideness as a compliment, thank you very much," Phillip replied. Then pulled the door open, and stood back. "After you."

Alan stepped through the door, and looked around curiously. It was almost pitch black in the interior, for only a little light filtered through the boarded windows. High overhead, a latticework of iron strutting supported the ceiling.

"In its day, that roof was considered quite an accomplishment. There weren't many buildings this size with no pillars for the roof. It's almost the size of a football field."

"And almost as empty, too," Alan observed. He kicked at the floor, and was surprised when there was no give.

"It's oak. Solid oak and three inches thick. Downstairs, there are beams and pillars everywhere. The engineer said he'd never seen anything quite like it."

They prowled through the building, but Alan quickly realized there was little to see. It was simply an immense shell, with a few remnants of partitions still in place at the back, where the mill offices had been. Though it had suffered badly from neglect, the structure did, indeed, seem basically sound. After exploring the main floor, they headed toward a stairway leading to the basement.

Phillip switched on a flashlight, and they started down. At the bottom of the stairs, Phillip suddenly stopped.

"This is where they found Conrad Junior," he said softly. "Apparently he tripped, and fell on some kind of tool."

Alan frowned, then took the flashlight from the other man and cast its beam around the expanse of the basement. Shadows from the closely spaced columns were everywhere, and the beam of light finally seemed to lose itself in the distance. But except for the forest of supporting pillars, the basement, like the floor above, seemed empty.

"What was a tool doing here? It looks like the place was cleared out a hundred years ago."

"Search me," Phillip replied. "When it happened, I hadn't even been born yet. In fact," he added, his voice taking on a note of melancholy that Alan had never heard before, "I guess I was the replacement child. I don't think Mother intended having more than one, but when Conrad Junior died, they decided to have me."

"They didn't do so badly," Alan said, deliberately making his voice light. "I don't know what your brother was like, but—"

"—But he was the son my father loved," Phillip said, his voice suddenly bitter. "Father never failed to let me know that I was no substitute for my brother," he added. Then, embarrassed by what he had confided, he cleared his throat, and grasped Alan's arm. "Come on. Let's get out of here."

Though he would have liked to examine the massive wooden beams that supported the main floor, and take a closer look at the building's foundations, Alan followed Phillip up the stairs and across the barren building.

Their footsteps echoed loudly in the silence, and neither man spoke again until they had once more emerged into the bright sunlight of the summer morning.

"Well," Phillip asked, "what do you think?"

Alan once more regarded the building thoughtfully before he spoke. Then, at last, he nodded.

"It can be done. And it won't take long either. If we get started right away, we should be able to have it open by Labor Day."

The two men stared at each other, both of them recognizing the irony at the same time.

"Labor Day," Phillip repeated softly. "Given the history of the building, that seems somehow fitting, doesn't it?"

"I suppose so," Alan agreed. "And a tad macabre, too, when you think about it."

Phillip relocked the metal door, and they started back up the path toward Prospect Street. Then, when they were once more in front of the old factory, Phillip spoke once more.

"Alan, when we were down in the basement, did you smell something?"

Alan frowned thoughtfully, then shook his head.

"It was probably nothing," Phillip went on. "But for a minute there, while we were talking, I thought I smelled smoke."

Five

"**H**annah?"

The old housekeeper looked up from the bowl of peas she was shelling, then started to pull her weight up from the battered easy chair she'd long ago moved from her room into the enormous kitchen.

"Don't get up," Carolyn told her. "I was just wondering if you'd seen Beth."

"She was right here till after breakfast," Hannah replied, sinking gratefully back into the depths of the chair. "Helped me with the dishes." She glanced up at Carolyn over the rims of her half-glasses. "She's a mighty nice girl, that daughter of yours."

Carolyn nodded absently, and Hannah's gaze sharpened slightly. "Something wrong, Miss Carolyn? Have I done something to displease you?"

"Of course not," Carolyn replied immediately. "You're wonderful, and I don't know what I'd do without you." She hesitated, knowing she should probably leave Hannah alone in her domain, then lowered herself onto one of the straight-backed wooden chairs that sat at the kitchen table. Her fingers began nervously twisting at a button on her blouse. "I . . . I'm not really sure," she went on. "It's just that . . ." She let her voice trail off, afraid that whatever she might say would sound somehow disloyal to her husband.

But Hannah, her face imperturbable nodded wisely, and finished the sentence for her. ". . . it's just that things up here aren't like you thought they'd be, and it's not as easy as it looked?"

How did she know? Carolyn wondered. Is it all that obvious? Instinctively, without thinking about it at all, she reached out for a handful of the peas, and began shelling them.

"You don't have to do that, Miss Carolyn," Hannah said quietly, but there was something in her tone that made Carolyn look at the housekeeper. As she'd suspected, Hannah's eyes were fixed on her, as if challenging her to speak her mind clearly.

But she won't ever ask me anything, Carolyn suddenly realized. If I need to talk, I can, but she'll never initiate a conversation.

"Yes, I do," Carolyn replied, making up her mind. "I have to do something. I'm just not used to sitting around all day with no work to do. And I'm afraid I'm not good at lunches, either," she added, remembering the few times she'd accepted invitations from the wives of men her husband had grown up with, only to spend a few miserable hours listening to them chat about people she didn't know and places she'd never been.

"I'm good at fixing lunches," Hannah said mildly. "But I'm afraid I'd have to agree with you about them fancy luncheon parties. Some of us just can't abide that sort of twaddle."

"Beth couldn't abide facing breakfast with the family this morning, could she?" Carolyn asked pointedly.

Hannah's lips pursed, and Carolyn was afraid she'd asked the old servant to step beyond some invisible limit.

"She'll get used to things here," Hannah said at last. "She likes it out here because it's familiar." She glanced up again, and there was a slight twinkle in her eyes. "She tells me when she lived on Cherry Street, the family practically lived in the kitchen."

"What family doesn't?" Carolyn replied, then rolled her eyes as she realized the ridiculousness of the question. "Never mind. That was a stupid thing to say."

"Not so stupid. Mr. Phillip used to spend a lot of time here when he was a boy. In fact," she added, "sometimes I feel like I raised him myself. Anyway, he certainly turned out the way I'd want a son to turn out, if I'd had one. And I have to say, it's nice to have a child in my kitchen again. Particularly one who already knows how to wash dishes and take out the trash."

She fell silent, and Carolyn found herself wondering exactly what the old woman was trying to tell her.

"What about Tracy?" she asked. "Doesn't she ever come out here?"

"Only when she wants something," Hannah replied, and though

there was nothing condemnatory in her voice, Carolyn noticed that the old woman's eyes stayed on the bowl of peas as she spoke. "Tracy's a different kind of child. Takes after her grandmother, if you know what I mean."

"I'm afraid I do," Carolyn replied. "She—well, she seems determined to make Beth feel as if she doesn't belong here."

Hannah opened her mouth, then seemed to change her mind. But an opaqueness came into her eyes, and Carolyn knew that now she had gone too far.

"I wouldn't know about that," Hannah finally said. "But as for that little girl of yours, I have an idea of where she might be." Her eyes drifted toward the window.

Following Hannah's lead, Carolyn gazed out the window. Barely visible through the treetops, she could make out the marble ring that surmounted the mausoleum.

"The mausoleum? Why would she have gone up there?"

Hannah shrugged. "She might not have. But there was a bit of a ruckus down at the stable a while ago, and I've noticed that when people want to be alone around here, they often go up to the mausoleum." Her eyes met Carolyn's once more. "If she wants to tell you what happened, she will. But don't push her, Miss Carolyn. She's doing her best to fit in. Just let her do it her way."

Then, as Carolyn hurried out the kitchen door, Hannah went back to shelling her peas. But as she worked, she wondered if either Beth or Carolyn would ever be allowed to fit into this house. If it were up to Tracy, she knew, they wouldn't.

Tracy would die first.

Beth sat alone in the coolness that pervaded the mausoleum despite the growing heat of the morning. Her tears had long since dried, and she'd spent a few minutes reading the inscriptions on the backs of each of the chairs that surrounded the marble table. Now she was perched on the edge of Samuel Pruett Sturgess's marble chair, staring out at the village she'd grown up in.

From here, Westover almost looked like a miniature village—like one of the tiny model-train layouts her father had taken her to see at a show in Boston last year. She could see the tracks coming around the hillside, crossing the river, then disappearing behind the mill and reemerging to curve in a wide arc around the village until they disappeared into the distant hills.

But it was the mill that interested her most. From where she sat, the old brick building was framed exactly between two of the marble pillars. The town itself was mostly to the left of the mill, but from this vantage point the mill was precisely centered below her.

In fact, if the seventh pillar—the pillar that had once stood op-posite Samuel Pruett Sturgess's chair—hadn't been broken, the mill would be completely invisible.

For a while, she'd sat trying to decide whether the mausoleum had been built the way it was on purpose, or if, after the whole thing was finished, someone had noticed that if one of the pillars was broken out, then old Mr. Sturgess would be able to look down at his factory from his chair.

For that's the way it had struck Beth.

It was almost as if the table was for all the dead Sturgesses to meet around, as though they were still alive, and had business to discuss, and the oldest of them—Samuel Pruett Sturgess—was sitting where he could watch over the whole town, and especially his mill.

Then, while she had been pretending to be Mr. Sturgess, she had seen it.

It was a flash, like some kind of explosion. Suddenly, it had seemed as if the mill was on fire.

At first she'd thought it was the sun, reflecting off the windows of the building.

But then she remembered that all the windows were boarded up, and there wasn't any glass in them.

Now she was staring at the old building, waiting to see if it would happen again. So far, it hadn't.

"Beth?"

She jumped, startled, and turned to see her mother coming up the steps from the path to the house. Quickly, she slid off the marble chair.

"Honey? Are you okay?"

Beth felt a sudden stab of embarrassment. Did her mother know what had happened down at the stable? Had Tracy told on her? But she hadn't really done anything—not really. Just let Patches out into the paddock.

"I . . . I'm fine," she said.

Carolyn surveyed the little girl carefully. She could see from the puffiness around her eyes that Beth had been crying, but she seemed to be over it now. Panting slightly, Carolyn eased herself into the chair next to the one Beth had been occupying, then sighed as the cool of a faint breeze touched her forehead.

"Go on," she said. "Sit down again." Then she lowered her voice slightly, and glanced around as if she was looking to see if they were being watched. "Actually, I've been dying to sit in these chairs ever since Phillip told me no one's allowed to sit in them."

Beth's eyes widened. "They aren't? I didn't know that. I didn't mean to—"

"Of course you didn't mean to do anything wrong. And you didn't, either, so don't worry about it. I, on the other hand, know perfectly well that I shouldn't be sitting in this chair, and I'm rather enjoying breaking the rules. Whose chair is it, anyway?"

Beth hesitated, then giggled slightly. "His wife's," she pronounced solemnly.

Carolyn frowned. "Whose?"

"You mean you haven't read it?" Beth said, laughing out loud now. "Go on, read it. You're going to hate it." As Carolyn rose, and moved around behind the chair, Beth stopped her. "You have to read his first, though."

Thoroughly puzzled, Carolyn studied the back of the chair that contained the ashes of Samuel Pruett Sturgess. Aside from his dates of birth and death, also etched in the stone were the facts of his life, at least those he had apparently considered important. The marble proclaimed that he had been a member of Sigma Alpha Gamma, a thirty-second-degree Mason, an Episcopalian, a Republican, and the father of four children.

After she had read through all the information, Carolyn's eyes shifted to the chair in which she had been sitting.

The inscription on the back was simple:

HIS WIFE

"Do you believe it?" Beth giggled. "Not even her name!"

Though she tried to contain herself, Carolyn couldn't help laughing. "So much for women's lib, hunh? I wonder what the poor woman's life must have been like?"

"I bet he made her walk three steps behind him," Beth replied. "Can you imagine Daddy putting something like that on your tombstone?" Then, suddenly remembering the divorce, she reddened.

"It's all right," Carolyn assured her. "And you're right. Your father wouldn't dare put something like that on my tombstone. And neither would Phillip, for that matter."

The mischievous light that had been in Beth's eyes a moment before faded, and Carolyn wished for an instant that she hadn't mentioned Phillip's name. But now it was too late.

"Phillip loves you very much, you know," she said.

Beth nodded. "I know. It's just—" She fell suddenly silent, then shook her head. "Oh, never mind. It doesn't matter. Can we just talk about something else?"

But Carolyn could see that whatever had happened, it did matter. Beth's eyes were damp, and she could see that the little girl was struggling once more against her unhappiness. But then Hannah's words of a few minutes before came back to Carolyn. Reluctantly, she nodded. "All right. What shall we talk about?"

Beth thought for a minute, then grinned crookedly. "Let's not talk about anything. Let's go for a hike!"

"A hike?" Carolyn echoed. "Where?"

"Down the hill. Look. There's a little trail over there. See?" Beth pointed past the broken seventh pillar.

Carolyn's eyes followed her daughter's gesture, and she saw what had apparently once been a path leading down the hill, though what now remained of the trail was overgrown with weeds and brush.

"Good Lord," she groaned. "Can we even get through? Where does it go?"

"I bet it goes down to the river! Can we go down, Mom? Please? It'll be just like it used to be!"

Carolyn eyed the trail carefully. To her it looked both steep and difficult. Then she turned back to Beth, and the eager light in the little girl's eyes made her mind up for her.

"Hit it, Tarzan. I'm right behind you."

As Beth, dressed in jeans and a white shirt that Carolyn recognized as having once belonged to Alan, plunged into the brush, Carolyn had a sudden fleeting memory. There had been days like this before—days when the three of them, she and Alan and Beth, had hiked around the countryside, just following the paths and trails. Even then the strain between herself and Alan had been all too evident, festering just below the surface. Now here she was, hiking again, and once again there was something festering just below the surface.

But this time, the infection had invaded Beth.

From now on, she determined, she would spend more time with her daughter. Her daughter, right now, needed her very badly.

Abigail rapped once on Tracy's closed bedroom door, then let herself in. Tracy sat propped on her bed, her arms folded against her chest. The sophistication that sometimes lent her the look of an older girl was nowhere to be seen. Right now she looked exactly like the angry almost-thirteen-year-old she was.

"I hate her," she said. Then, again: "I hate her, hate her, hate her. I hate Beth, and I hate Carolyn, too!"

Abigail seated herself on the edge of the bed, and took one of Tracy's hands in her own. "Hate is a very unattractive emotion that we should do our best to keep out of our hearts."

"I don't care." Tracy sulked. "They hate me, too!"

"No, I don't think they do," Abigail went on, her voice soothing. "At least not Carolyn. She simply doesn't understand you, that's all.

You have to remember where she came from, Tracy. She never had any of our advantages, and we should pity her, not hate her. But of course," she added, "pitying her doesn't mean we should give in to her, either."

Tracy looked up, a glimmer of hope in her eyes. "But Daddy said—"

"I know exactly what your father said. I may be eighty-three years old, but I'm neither deaf nor blind. I heard your father, and I see every day how that woman treats him."

"I just wish she'd go away."

"One day she will," Abigail promised. "Mark my words, one day your father will realize the mistake he's made, and understand that he needs a woman of his own background. But until then, all we can do is try to ignore her, and the child, too."

"She was chasing Patches," Tracy stormed. "She chased her out of the stall, and Patches was terrified."

Abigail, who had watched the incident at the stable from her sitting-room window, said nothing.

"And what about my party?" Tracy went on. "Having Beth there will wreck it! My friends will think I actually *like* her."

"Not if she isn't here," said Abigail. "Now it seems to me that all you have to do is change the day of your party. Beth always spends Saturdays with her father, so we'll simply move your party from Sunday to Saturday. You tell Hannah," she finished, "and I'll tell Carolyn." Her patrician lips curled into a smile. "I'm an old lady, and I suppose there's a chance I might just forget to speak to her, of course."

Tracy reached out to hug her grandmother. "Will you do that?" she asked. "Will you really do that for me?"

"Of course I will. What are grandmothers for?" Disentangling herself from Tracy's embrace, she stood up. "Now, I want you to go down and talk to Hannah. And don't look too pleased with yourself. While I don't question Hannah's loyalty, I sometimes think she has a tendency to talk too much to your father's wife."

Giggling, Tracy rolled off her bed and left the room. Abigail followed her slowly, then watched her as the girl hurried down the hall toward the stairs. From the back, even at her age, she looked so much like her mother that tears came to Abigail's eyes. Lorraine Kilpatrick Sturgess had been exactly the right girl for Phillip and Abigail had never quite adjusted to the fact of her death. And yet, Tracy seemed sometimes almost to be a reincarnation of the woman who had died giving birth to her. Except for the eyes. Tracy's eyes had come from her father, who had inherited that clear blue from Abigail herself. But the rest of Tracy was pure Lorraine.

And dear Lorraine would never have had anything to do with a woman like Carolyn, nor allowed Tracy to associate with a child like Beth. Abigail would see to it that Tracy never felt any differently.

When Tracy had disappeared down the stairs, Abigail retreated to her suite. Here, in the rooms that hadn't changed since she'd come here as a bride, life seemed to her to be as it should have been. Here, nothing ever changed. Whatever happened in the outside world had no meaning for her here, for in these rooms were all the portraits of her family, and of Conrad, and the mementos of times past, when the Sturgesses had run Westover.

When the mill was reopened, the Sturgesses would once again resume their rightful place. Perhaps the people wouldn't be working directly for her family, but at least they would be paying rent.

Abigail, almost against her will, glanced up at the portrait of her husband, and heard once again the words he had uttered so often in the years before he had died.

"It is an evil place, but it must never be torn down. It must stand as it is, a constant reminder to us all. It is evil, Abigail, but it is our conscience. We must never lose it, and never change it."

Abigail had listened to him, and pitied him, but in the end had realized that her husband had simply lost his mind.

And she knew exactly when it had started.

It had started on the day that Conrad Junior had died, and his father had refused to accept it as the accident it had been.

Instead, he had blamed the mill, insisting that the mill itself had somehow claimed their son's life.

Then, in the last few years of his life, when his mind had begun to fail as rapidly as his body, he had become fixated on a box of old records from the last days of the mill's operations.

He had kept them in a metal box in the closet, and as he drew closer and closer to death, he had spent more and more time poring over them, and mumbling about the evil in the mill.

She took the metal box off the closet shelf now, and went to sit in her favorite chair by the window. Opening the box, she carefully removed the old journals with which it was filled. The pages were yellowed with age and threatened to crumble in her fingers. Slowly, she began reading.

Strange records of odd things happening at the mill.

Horrible things that seemed, on a bright sunny morning like to-day, far too terrible to believe.

And Abigail didn't believe, despite her husband's fanatic ravings. She turned the pages one by one, shaking her head sadly as she thought of the manner in which Conrad had wasted his life because of a few lines in an ancient journal.

Even on the day he died, he had demanded that she bring him the box, then, propped up in his bed, he had pored over the journals for the last time, his hands trembling as he fingered the pages, muttering to himself as he deciphered the words once more. Abigail had watched him, knowing that his mind was no longer in the present, that he had taken himself to another era. Finally, late in the afternoon, his breathing had suddenly changed, and the hollow rattles of death had gripped him as his worn-out heart began its last spasmodic flutterings.

Abigail had pried his fingers loose from the journals, but even as she put them back in the box and carried the box itself back to the closet, Conrad had reached out for them, as if by grasping the past one last time he could stave off death and prolong the final moment.

When she had returned to his bed, he had struggled to speak, his words barely audible as they bubbled through the fluids gathering in his lungs.

"She's there," he'd gasped at last. "She's still there, and she hates us all. . . . Keep her there, Abigail. Keep her there for me. . . ."

And then, clutching at her hand, he'd died.

Abigail had pondered his last words since then, but only now, as she sat fingering the crumbling documents, did she decide that whatever he had been trying to say, the words had been nothing more than the fragmented ramblings of a dying man.

Now Abigail put the journals back in the box, closed and locked it, and returned it to its place on her husband's closet shelf. Then she went to the window, and gazed out across Westover, as she had so many times before. At the other side of the town, silent and forbidding, lay the ancient hulk of the long-abandoned mill.

When she and Phillip had finished with it, though, it would once again be the proudest building in Westover.

Nothing and no one would stop them.

Neither Conrad's insane superstitions, nor Carolyn's inane prattling, would ever convince her that the mill was anything but an ordinary building.

And it was there—had always been there—to make money for the Sturgesses.

Certainly there was nothing either shameful or evil in that.

Hannah eyed Tracy suspiciously.

"Isn't it a little late to be switching a party?"

Tracy sighed dramatically, and did her best to look as upset by the whole thing as Hannah seemed to be.

"Well, of course it is," she said. "But I *can't* have my party without Alison Babcock, and she won't be able to come on Sunday! So we'll just have to have it on Saturday, instead.''

"What about the other kids? What if they can't come on Saturday?''

"They can," Tracy lied smoothly. "I've already talked to them, and they can all come on Saturday. I don't see why you want to make such a big deal about it.''

Hannah's brows arched skeptically. "And just when did you talk to Miss Alison? The phone hasn't rung here all morning.''

Tracy's eyes narrowed, and glinted dangerously. Who did Hannah think she was, anyway? Didn't she know she was just a servant? "I called her. We were talking about something else, and she remembered. So I've been calling all the other kids ever since. Okay?''

Hannah's eyes went to the telephone extension on the counter, with its two buttons, one of which glowed when either of the telephone lines was in use. Then she saw Tracy silently daring her to challenge her words.

"I'll speak to Miss Carolyn about it," she said, deciding there was no point in calling the lie. The girl already knew she'd been caught, and didn't care.

"That won't be necessary," Tracy said, her voice petulant, though her eyes glowed with her apparent victory. "Grandmother's going to talk to Carolyn. And if Grandmother says it's all right to change the party to Saturday, then it is. So just do it.''

"Now see here," Hannah began, but her words were suddenly cut off by a scream coming from outside.

Turning away from Tracy, Hannah squinted out the window into the brightness of the morning.

Beth was charging across the lawn, her face pale, and her hair streaming out behind her.

"Hannah!" the little girl shouted. "Hannah! Mr. Smithers! Come quick! It's Mom! Something's happened to Mom!''

Six

Carolyn opened her eyes, and for a moment thought she was in her room in the little house on Cherry Street. But that was impossible. She'd been on a trail below Hilltop, hiking with Beth. And then—

Then what? She searched in her mind for details, and as she probed the recesses of her memory, her eyes fixed on the ceiling of the little room.

A hospital room, painted the same pale green that her room on Cherry Street had always been.

Hospital green, Beth had always called it, and now Carolyn had to admit she was right.

Something in her mind clicked.

She'd fainted.

They had been on the path leading down from the mausoleum, and then they'd turned off to the left, along a steep side trail. After a few yards, they'd come to a little clearing, and while Beth explored, Carolyn had sat down to rest.

She'd been looking out over the village, enjoying the view, and then, gradually, she'd begun to notice something at the far side of town. It seemed to her that it had crept slowly into her consciousness, but then, as she'd become aware of it, she'd found herself staring at the mill.

It was burning.

Clouds of smoke were billowing from it, and flames licked out from the windows.

And even though the entire village separated her from the mill, she could hear screams, as if people were trapped inside.

The memory seemed to wobble in her mind, and Carolyn found herself struggling to keep it in focus.

Struggling.

That was it.

She had struggled to her feet, and called out to Beth, and then the whole sky had seemed to turn black, as if smoke were covering it.

And she had felt dizzy.

After that, there were only fragments.

59

Beth, calling to her, begging her to wake up.

Then Hannah's face, a mask of worry, looming above her.

How had Hannah gotten there?

Then hands, lifting her, carrying her.

And now she was in the hospital.

For the first time since waking, she tried to move, and immediately felt, a warm pressure on her hand.

"Don't, honey."

At the unexpected sound of a voice, the memories faded out of her mind.

Phillip's voice. Why hadn't she been aware that he was here? Had he been holding her hand all along? She turned her head slightly, and saw him, sitting by the bed, his blue eyes clouded with worry.

"Phillip? How . . . how did I get here? What happened?"

"You fainted. Hannah and Ben managed to get you back to the house, then had you brought down here."

"Hannah and Ben?" Carolyn repeated. "How did they—?"

"You helped. You were half-conscious, and you kept talking about a fire. They said you seemed to think there was a brush fire or something."

Carolyn frowned. "No . . . no, it was something else." Her hand tightened on Phillip's. "It was the mill. I saw the mill burning."

"The mill? What on earth are you talking about?"

Carolyn hesitated. Now that she thought about it, it seemed much more like a memory from a dream than something that had actually happened. "I . . . I don't know. It was all so strange . . ." Her voice trailed off, and she glanced around the room. "Where's Beth?"

"Right outside," Phillip replied. "I'll get her."

A moment later her daughter appeared at the bedside, her eyes wide with worry. "Mom? Are you okay? I . . . I was afraid you'd—"

"Died?" Carolyn chuckled, managing to lend her voice a strength she didn't feel. "Not quite yet. Your old mother has a few more years in her." She smiled, and hitched herself a little higher in the hospital bed. "But let me tell you, if that's your idea of a fun little hike, you can get somebody else to go next time."

Phillip's brows arched, and he winked at, Beth. "Obviously she's feeling better. All of a sudden its your fault."

Carolyn twisted her face into a grimace of comic indignation. "Well, you don't expect me to take the blame, do you? I'm the one who wound up in the hospital. The least the two of you can do is make sympathetic noises and tell me it wasn't my fault. Right?" she added, turning to her daughter.

"Oh, absolutely," Beth replied, nodding solemnly. "You were just standing there yelling at me, and pointing, so I thought, wouldn't it be fun to make Mother faint? And you fell right over."

"See?" Carolyn asked Phillip. "That's the kind of child every mother dreams of having." Then her expression turned serious. "Beth, did you see anything? Just before I fainted, did you see anything happening down in the village?"

Beth frowned uncertainly. "Like what?"

"Well, it was strange," Carolyn said. "I could have sworn that I saw the mill burning. You didn't see anything like that?"

Beth shook her head, then suddenly remembered what had happened up at the mausoleum before her mother had arrived. For a minute, while she'd been sitting in the marble chair, she *had* seen something like that. But before she could tell them about it, the door opened, and a doctor entered the room.

Phillip immediately rose to his feet, but the doctor waved him back into his chair, turning to Carolyn with a little smile playing around the corners of his mouth.

"Mrs. Sturgess," he asked, "you and your daughter wouldn't by any chance have been rabbit hunting this morning, would you?"

Carolyn blinked. Rabbit hunting? What on earth was he talking about?

"Because if you were, the hunt was a success. You've killed a rabbit. Or, if you haven't yet, I'm prepared to guarantee that you will."

Carolyn stared at the doctor, and slowly the light began, to dawn. "You mean—I'm pregnant?"

"Congratulations. And to you too, Mr. Sturgess."

Phillip's eyes fixed on the doctor, then slowly shifted to his wife. "A baby?" he asked. "You and I are going to have a baby?"

Carolyn nodded, suddenly feeling almost stupidly happy. "That's what the man says," she said, grinning foolishly. "You know—little tiny critters, with ten little fingers, and ten little toes? Keep you up late at night? That's what he's talking about." Phillip looked dazed, and Carolyn's surge of happiness was suddenly tinged with fear. What if he—

But then his arms were around her, and he was hugging her close. "Who ever thought—I mean I just didn't think—we never even talked about it!" Suddenly he drew away, and his forehead creased with worry. "Honey, is it all right with you?"

Carolyn squeezed him hard. "Of course it's all right with me. I can't think of anything I'd rather do."

As Carolyn and Phillip gazed happily at each other, neither of them saw Beth slip quietly out of the room.

* * *

A baby.

The idea of her mother and Uncle Phillip having a baby had never occurred to her before, and as Beth left the little Westover hospital, walking slowly along Prospect Street, her eyes fixed on the sidewalk in front of her, she wasn't at all sure how she felt about it.

It was bad enough living at Hilltop already. What would happen when there was a baby there, too?

Her mother would spend all her time with the baby, and not have any time for her.

Which wasn't fair, and Beth knew it.

In fact, now that she thought about it, she knew that she'd always wanted to have a baby brother. Or a sister—it hadn't really mattered. But after her parents had gotten the divorce, she'd just sort of given up the idea.

And then, when Carolyn had married Phillip Sturgess, it had just never entered her head that her mother might have another baby.

Which was kind of a dumb thing to have thought, really. After all, lots of the kids in Westover had half-brothers and half-sisters. Why shouldn't she?

The more she thought about it, the more she liked the whole idea of it.

Suddenly she felt better, and looked up to see that she'd walked almost four blocks. In the next block, the mill stood, looking dark and threatening even in the noontime sun.

Beth stared at it for a few minutes, wondering what it was about the big old building that had always made her friends, especially the boys, talk about what might be inside it, and wonder what had really happened to the boy—Uncle Phillip's brother—who had died in there long before they had even been born.

To her, it was just an ugly building.

Or anyway it had been, up until this morning.

She started walking again, coming closer to the building, trying to figure out what the sun might have been reflecting off. But there didn't seem to be anything. The windows were boarded over, and so were the massive doors, set back into the front of the building at the top of a short flight of stairs.

But she *had* seen something that morning, and so had her mother. Her mother had said it looked as if the building were on fire.

She stepped back, tipping her head up to gaze toward the roof line. As she reached the edge of the sidewalk, she bumped into a car.

Her father's car.

But her father's office was several blocks away. Why was his car here? She scanned the street, but saw nothing.

Puzzled, she stared once more at the mill.

Could her father be inside?

She trotted up the steps, and carefully inspected the boards over the front door. All of them were nailed tight, and there didn't seem to her to be any way to get in.

And yet, even as she stood there, she could almost feel that the mill wasn't empty.

Her father *had* to be inside.

She went back down the steps, and turned toward River Road. On that side of the building, she knew, there was another door—a big metal door—and she knew there was a padlock on it. Since she'd been six years old, every week at least one of the kids she knew had come down to check, always hoping that maybe this time, someone had left the lock open.

She came to the corner of the building, and looked down the long brick wall.

Halfway down to the railroad tracks, the door stood open.

She broke into a run, and a moment later stood in the doorway, gazing into the gloomy interior of the abandoned factory.

The silence of the building seemed to gather around her, and slowly Beth felt the beginnings of fear.

And then she began to feel something else.

Once again, she felt that strange certainty that the mill was not empty.

"D-Daddy?" she called softly, stepping through the door. "Are you here?"

She felt a slight trickle of sweat begin to slide down her spine, and fought a sudden trembling in her knees.

Then, as she listened to the silence, she heard something.

A rustling sound, from up above.

Beth froze, her heart pounding.

And then she heard it again.

She looked up.

With a sudden burst of flapping wings, a pigeon took off from one of the rafters, circled, then soared out through a gap between the boards over one of the windows.

Beth stood still, waiting for her heartbeat to calm. As she looked around, her eyes fixed on the top of a stairwell at the far end of the building.

He was downstairs. That's why he hadn't heard her. He was down in the basement.

Resolutely, she started across the vast emptiness of the building. As she reached the middle of the floor, she felt suddenly exposed, and had an urge to run.

But there was nothing to be afraid of. There was nothing in the mill except herself, and some birds.

And downstairs, her father.

After what seemed like an eternity, she reached the top of the stairs, and peered uncertainly into the darkness below.

Her own shadow preceded her down the steep flight of steps, and only a little light spilled over the staircase to illuminate the nearer parts of the vast basement.

"Daddy?" Beth whispered. But the sound was so quiet, even she could barely hear it.

And then there was something else, coming on the heels of her own voice.

Another sound, fainter than the one her own voice had made, coming from below.

Something was moving in the darkness.

Once again Beth's heart began to pound, but she remained where she was, forcing back the panic that threatened to overcome her.

Finally, when she heard nothing more, she moved slowly down the steps, until she could place a foot on the basement floor.

She listened, and after a moment, as the darkness began closing in on her, the sound repeated itself.

Panic surged through her. All her instincts told her to run, to flee back up the stairs and out into the daylight. But when she tried to move, her legs refused to obey her, and she remained where she was, paralyzed.

Once again the sound came. This time, though it was almost inaudible, Beth thought she recognized a word.

"Beeetth . . ."

Her name. It was as if someone had called her name.

"D-Daddy?" she whispered again. "Daddy, is that you?"

There was another silence, and Beth strained once more to see into the darkness surrounding her.

In the distance, barely visible, she thought she could see a flickering of light.

And then she froze, her voice strangling as the sound came again, like a winter wind sighing in the trees.

"Aaaammmyyy."

Beth gazed fearfully into the blackness for several long seconds. Then, when the sound was not repeated, her panic began to subside. At last she was able to speak again, though her voice still trembled. "Is someone there?"

In the far distance, the light flickered again, and she heard something else.

Footsteps, approaching out of the darkness.

The seconds crept by, and the light bobbed nearer.

And once more, the whispering voice, barely audible, danced around her.

"Aaaammmyyy."

"D-Daddy?" Beth called once more, her fear surging back. "Daddy, is that you?"

The light stopped moving, and for a moment Beth felt a flash of fear. What if it wasn't her father? What if it was someone else?

And then, at last, she heard it.

"Beth? Honey? What are you doing here?"

Beth ran toward the light, and threw herself into her father's arms.

"Daddy! I—for a second, I was afraid it wasn't you!"

"Sweetheart! What are you doing here?" Alan asked again. He loosened himself from his daughter's grip, then began leading her back toward the stairs.

"I was walking home from the hospital, and I saw your car," Beth began, her voice still quavering. But Alan interrupted her.

"The hospital? What were you doing at the hospital?"

Beth's eyes widened in the darkness, and for a moment she wondered what she should say. But before she could make up her mind, she had blurted out the truth.

"It was Mom. We were hiking, and all of a sudden she fainted. She . . . she's going to have a baby!"

There was a momentary silence, and then Alan said quietly, "Well, how about that. You finally get your wish."

They were at the bottom of the stairs now, and he switched off the flashlight. In the dim light that filtered down the stairwell, he looked into his daughter's face. But instead of the happiness he had been expecting to see, there was something else. "Hey! You always wanted a baby brother or sister. Aren't you happy about your mom being pregnant?"

Beth hesitated, then seemed to come out of a reverie. But when she spoke, she wasn't looking at him. Instead, her eyes were fixed on a spot somewhere in the darkness beneath the stairs. "I . . . I guess I'm glad," she said, but Alan was sure she wasn't thinking about what she was saying.

"Beth?" he asked now. "Honey, what is it? Is something wrong?"

Beth shook her head uncertainly. "I don't know. I just—I thought I heard something—"

"Down here?" Alan started up the stairs, and Beth, almost reluctantly, followed.

"Unh-hunh. It was like a . . . a voice. Only not really, you know?"

"No," Alan chuckled. "I don't know. It was probably just a mouse or something."

Beth stopped, shaking her head, and turned back to peer once again down into the darkness of the basement.

And then, barely audible, she could hear it again.

A chill passed through her, and she concentrated, straining her ears.

"Don't you hear it, Daddy?" she asked. "Don't you hear it at all?"

Alan paused, and turned back.

For the last hour, he'd heard all kinds of noises in the basement of the mill.

Rats had scrambled out of his way as he'd poked around the foundations of the building, and at least once a snake had slithered over his hand. That time, he'd clearly heard his own muffled yelp of sudden fright.

Now he listened again, but there was nothing. "Sorry, hon. I don't hear a thing."

But still Beth hesitated, frowning deeply.

It had been there. She knew it had.

It was a voice, and it was calling out to her.

Why couldn't her father hear it?

And then, slowly, she realized what the answer was.

He couldn't hear it, because he wasn't supposed to.

The voice was calling out only to her.

A chill passed through her, and her skin suddenly felt as if something were crawling over it.

She knew she was right.

In the darkness of the basement, something had reached out and touched her.

Something in the blackness wanted her.

She had no idea what was in the basement, and part of her hoped never to find out. But another part of her felt a faint twinge of curiosity. That part of her, indeed, wanted to go back, wanted to plunge back into the darkness, and discover what was there.

She hesitated, struggling with that part of her that wanted to go back into the blackness. But the moment was gone. Her father had already turned away, going on up the stairs.

She followed him, her feet carrying her slowly, for the memory of what had happened filled her mind.

There was something there, something that wanted her.

Something that chilled her to the depths of her soul.

She hurried up the stairs after her father, catching up with him halfway across the great empty building.

"Take a good look at it," she heard him say just before they stepped out into the sunlight. "It won't look like this much longer."

Beth looked up at her father. "It won't? How come?"

Alan grinned happily. "You mean your mom didn't tell you?"

Beth frowned. "Tell me what?"

"We're going to reopen this place. Starting tomorrow, I'm going to begin partitioning it off, and putting in skylights, and sandblasting it, and by the end of the summer, it's going to be open and functioning again. We're turning it into a shopping mall."

Beth turned and stared back into the gloomy depths of the building.

She tried to picture the dark, cavernous mill as her father had just described it, but she couldn't.

Instead, her mind filled with the voice she had heard in the basement, and from deep in some part of her being she could not identify, a terrible knowledge surfaced. It was then Beth knew that what her father was saying was wrong.

They mustn't change the mill. Not ever.

For some reason she didn't yet understand, the mill should stay just as it was.

Abandoned, and empty.

But it wasn't empty, not really.

In the basement, somewhere under the stairs, something lived.

Seven

"I'm fine," Carolyn Sturgess insisted, gazing at her husband fondly, but with just a touch of annoyance. "This is all a bit ridiculous."

Phillip merely leaned down to adjust one of the pillows, and brushed her forehead with his lips. "It's not ridiculous. You heard what Dr. Blanchard said."

"Of course I heard what he said," Carolyn groused. "He said I should take it easy, which I fully intend to do. And I'm perfectly willing to admit that I probably shouldn't have gone blundering through the underbrush, given my condition. But I didn't know about my condition, did I?"

"No, you didn't," Phillip agreed. "But now you do, and I intend to see to it that you don't go against doctor's orders."

Carolyn glanced around the big bedroom, and fleetingly wondered if Phillip really intended her simply to lie here for the next seven months, forcing Hannah to carry her meals up the stairs three times a day. But of course, she realized, he wouldn't intend that at all.

He'd bring the meals himself.

And an ambulance to bring her home from the hospital. That, too, was just like Phillip.

She'd felt perfectly capable of walking out of the hospital, getting into the car, and driving herself home, but Phillip had insisted on a wheelchair and an ambulance, and it had been easier to give in than to argue with him.

Once they'd arrived at Hilltop, though, she'd wished she *had* argued, for there was Alan, just leaving the house after driving Beth home. The look of concern on his face when he'd first seen her had quickly given way to amusement, and she'd waited for him to make some allusion to *Camille* or *Wuthering Heights.* The fact that he'd confined himself to an arched eyebrow hadn't made her feel any less foolish.

Now, she looked up at Phillip and shook her head. "I won't do it, you know. You can't stand guard over me through an entire pregnancy, and as soon as your back is turned, I'll be up and about my business. All that happened was that I fainted. Even Dr. Blanchard didn't think I was in any danger of losing the baby."

"We're not going to take any chances—" Phillip protested, but Carolyn didn't let him finish.

"I don't intend to take any chances," she insisted. "If I'd known I was pregnant, I wouldn't have gone with Beth." Then she narrowed her eyes mischievously. "Or are you trying to say that I'm too old to be having a baby?"

Phillip reddened. "I didn't mean—"

"Of course you didn't," Carolyn broke in, suddenly unable to contain her laughter any longer. "It's all just too silly, darling. I'm starting to feel like I'm stuck in a movie or something. I keep expecting you to start using phrases like 'in a family way' or refer to my 'delicate condition.' It's just all so Victorian, that's all."

"I suppose we should expect you to feel that way," another voice said, and Carolyn looked up to see Abigail Sturgess standing in the doorway. "But after what happened to our dear Lorraine, you can't really blame Phillip for being concerned, can you?"

Carolyn's mouth tightened in anger as she saw the misery that came over Phillip's face, and she reached out to take his hand in her own. "I know you're concerned for me, Abigail," she said smoothly. "But I have no intention of losing the baby, or of dying in delivery."

"Of course not," Abigail agreed, her thin lips curving in a cool smile. "And you needn't worry about anything. I shall see to it that everything in the house runs exactly as it should."

For a moment the two women's eyes met, and then Carolyn sighed, and allowed herself to sink into the pillows. "I'm sure you will, Abigail," she said softly. "I'm sure you'll run everything exactly as Lorraine would have wanted it." Through eyes that were nearly closed, she saw the old woman watching her, and felt for a moment like a mouse being examined by a coiled cobra. But then, her appetite apparently satisfied for the moment, Abigail turned, and stiffly left the room. Only when Carolyn was sure that Abigail was out of earshot did she speak again.

"I'm sorry, Phillip. I shouldn't have mentioned Lorraine."

Her husband's forehead wrinkled into a sympathetic frown. "She's the one who brought Lorraine up, not you. Now, just get some rest, and don't worry about anything. Promise?"

"I promise. And you have to promise not to start mother-henning me. Hannah's perfectly capable of doing that."

As if to prove the point, the old housekeeper elbowed the door open, then came into the room, a pot of tea balanced on a bed tray. "See?" Carolyn asked, then hitched herself back into a sitting position as Hannah set the tray over her legs. "Thank you, Hannah. But please don't start treating me as if I'm sick."

"Who says you're sick?" Hannah retorted. "Being pregnant and being sick are two different things—despite what some people think. But a nice pot of tea never hurt anybody." She poured two cups, and handed one to Phillip. "And as for Miss Tracy's party, I don't want you to worry about anything. I can take care of it all. Although I must say," she added, making no attempt to keep the grumpiness out of her voice, "changing it from Sunday to Saturday isn't going to make my life any easier."

"Changing it?" Carolyn asked. "Hannah, what on earth are you talking about?"

Hannah peered at Carolyn for a moment; then her eyes narrowed slightly. "You mean Mrs. Sturgess didn't talk to you about it?"

"She hasn't talked to me about anything," Carolyn replied.

"But Miss Tracy said—" Hannah began, then abruptly fell silent, her lips closing tightly.

"Said what, Hannah?" Phillip urged. "It's all right. What did Tracy say?"

"I don't like to talk out of turn," Hannah mumbled. She busied herself refolding the already perfectly folded bedspread.

Phillip opened his mouth to speak again, but Carolyn held up a restraining hand. "Hannah, telling us about a change in Tracy's birthday plans is hardly speaking out of turn. Now, what is this about changing the party from Sunday to Saturday?"

Hannah hesitated, then repeated what Tracy had said in the kitchen that morning. "She told me that Mrs. Sturgess was going to talk to you," she finished. "It just must have been forgotten in all the excitement. Now, if there's nothing else, I'd better get back to my kitchen."

She bustled out of the room. Neither Carolyn nor Phillip said a word for a moment. Finally Phillip spoke.

"Did Mother talk to you about switching the party?"

"No," Carolyn replied. "She didn't."

"Well, I'm sure there was a reason for the change—" Phillip began, but fell silent as Carolyn pushed the tray to the foot of the bed and threw back the covers.

"There was a reason," she agreed, swinging her feet off the bed and getting shakily to her feet. "And I intend to put a stop to it right now."

Phillip set his teacup on the bed table, and rose to steady his wife. "Hey, take it easy. Whatever it is can wait. Let me deal with it."

"But it can't wait," Carolyn insisted. "And I have to deal with it myself." She began struggling into her robe, then met her husband's eyes. "Don't you see? There's a very simple reason why they changed the party, and why Abigail didn't tell me. Oh, I'm sure she would have on Saturday morning, right after Beth left to spend the day with Alan!" Her eyes blazed with anger, and her mouth twisted into a parody of Abigail's supercilious smile. "I can hear her now: 'Oh, Carolyn dear, didn't I tell you? Tracy's party is going to be today. Such a pity Beth will miss it.' Only it's not going to happen that way!"

"You don't think—"

"Of course that's what I think, Phillip. And if you think about it, you'll know I'm right. Tracy doesn't want Beth at her party, and Abigail's figured out a way to give Tracy what she wants."

Now it was Phillip's eyes that glittered with anger. "I'll deal with Mother myself. In fact, I'll deal with both of them. This has all gone far enough." He turned and started out of the room, but Carolyn stopped him.

"No, Phillip. I've got to do it myself. What's happening in this house is between Abigail and me, and I can't hide behind you. Abigail will only see that as weakness, and hate me more than she already does."

"And what about Tracy? Isn't she part of it?"

"Tracy takes her lead from your mother. I'm not going to say a word to her about it. I'm going to let Abigail do that."

Phillip smiled. "It'll be the first time in years that Mother's had to go back on a promise to Tracy. Maybe it'll be good for both of them. But you're sure you don't want me to take care of it?" he added, his voice anxious. "You should be in bed."

"I'll be fine," Carolyn promised him. Tying the belt of her robe firmly around her waist, she left Phillip alone in the bedroom.

Carolyn found Abigail in the library, sitting placidly in a chair by the window, a book open on her lap. The old woman glanced up, then, surprised, put the book aside.

"Why, Carolyn," she said. "Shouldn't you be in bed?"

"Perhaps I should," Carolyn replied. "But right now, I'm afraid you and I need to have a little talk, Abigail." For the first time in her memory, Carolyn saw uncertainty flicker in the old lady's eyes.

"I'm sure whatever it is can wait," Abigail began.

"No, it can't," Carolyn said softly. She closed the door behind her, then moved across the room to lower herself into the chair opposite her mother-in-law. "We'll talk now, Abigail."

"Very well," Abigail said. Her voice was chilly, but her eyes darted nervously toward the closed door. "And just what is it you'd like to discuss? The weather? It seems to be a nice afternoon—"

"Nice enough for a birthday party," Carolyn interrupted, matching the old lady's smile. "I do hope the weather holds until Sunday, don't you?"

Abigail's eyes widened for a split second, but then she recovered herself. "I meant to talk to you about that," she said. "But of course after what happened, I didn't want to worry you with something so petty."

" 'Petty' does seem to be the right word, I suppose," Carolyn mused, letting her eyes drift around the room. For once, she knew, Abigail was on the defensive.

"I'm sure I don't know what you're talking about," Abigail replied, but her nervousness betrayed her.

"And I'm sure you do." Carolyn's eyes moved back to the old woman. Abigail sat stiffly in the armchair, her posture rigidly erect. "Abigail, all this has to stop. I know what you think of me, and I know what you think of Beth. But I am married to Phillip, and that's not going to change. I am also Tracy's stepmother, and I would like that to be a pleasant relationship for both her and myself. I'd appreciate it if you'd stop interfering."

Abigail expertly feigned puzzlement. "Carolyn, I don't know what all this is about, and I do wish you'd explain it to me. Whatever has happened, I'm sure we can straighten it out. Now, why don't you just start at the beginning-''

"No, Abigail. I've already taken care of it. I was just in the kitchen, where I told Hannah that Tracy's party will be on Sunday afternoon, as planned. I do hope it won't inconvenience Tracy, having to call all her friends again." Now Carolyn saw the cold fury in the old woman's eyes, which Abigail made no attempt to hide.

"Except that Tracy will not be calling them again," Abigail rasped. "The fact that I failed to mention the change to you is my fault. There's no reason why Tracy should suffer. All the plans have been made, and Hannah has everything under control. I really fail to see the problem."

"The problem is that Beth will be with her father on Saturday afternoon, as she always is. A fact both you and Tracy are perfectly aware of."

"Are we?" Abigail replied, allowing her voice to turn venomous. "I think you lend your child's activities an importance they don't deserve, my dear."

Carolyn smiled benignly, betraying none of her inner fury. "The same might be said of your attitude about Tracy, Abigail. At any rate, that's not the issue. The fact of the matter is simply this: Tracy's party will take place on Sunday afternoon, or it will not take place at all."

Abigail's eyes flashed with pure hatred now. "If that's what you and Phillip have decided, I'm sure there's nothing I can do about it," she said. "Perhaps you'd better tell Tracy about the change in plans. I believe she's outside playing tennis."

"I'll tell her," Carolyn replied. "And I'll be sure to be as careful about telling her as you were about telling me."

"I had intended to tell you!" Abigail fumed.

"All right," Carolyn sighed. "Have it your own way, if it's so important to you. But you're wasting your time, and making life harder for all of us."

"Am I?" Abigail asked, her voice icy. She rose to her feet and, grasping her cane, started toward the French doors. "Perhaps I am. But perhaps I'm not. I don't know why Phillip married you, Carolyn, but I do know that he is still my son, and still a Sturgess. In time, he will come to his senses. As to the party, I shall explain things to Tracy myself, and we shall deal with the situation. And hereafter, I shall do my best to protect Tracy, and bring her up in a manner of which Lorraine would approve." Leaving Carolyn still sitting in her chair, Abigail swept regally out of the room.

But she's dead, Carolyn wanted to scream. *Don't you understand that Lorraine is dead?* But, of course, it wasn't Lorraine at all. It was

Abigail herself, desperately trying to hang on to a way of life that had all but disappeared. Carolyn sighed once more, feeling suddenly worn out. She allowed herself to sink deeper into the chair.

Like so much of the furniture in the old house, the overstuffed wing chair needed reupholstering. Nothing had been repaired or refurbished here for years, for Abigail refused to see how threadbare it had all become. The old woman saw only the splendor of her youth, when the house had been staffed by a butler, five maids, a cook, and a gardening staff.

Now all that was left were Hannah and Ben Smithers, who did their best to cope with all the work that had to be done, aided occasionally by a few people who came in part-time when things could be put off no longer.

But Abigail wouldn't see it. Sometimes, as now, when she was feeling dispirited by the constant battle, Carolyn thought that nothing would change until the day Abigail finally died.

And sometimes Carolyn was certain that Abigail would live forever.

Abigail flung open the French doors, stepped out onto the terrace, and looked down toward the tennis court, where Tracy, dressed in spotless whites, was playing with Alison Babcock. Abigail watched the game for a few minutes, remembering the days before concrete courts, when the young ladies and gentlemen of her own generation had played genteel lawn tennis here—days long ago that Abigail still missed sorely. How much more civilized life had been then. Life went on, some things never changed. That was what Carolyn would never understand. She would never understand that being a Sturgess was something special, with rights and privileges that had to be protected. To Carolyn, the Sturgesses were just like anyone else.

Abigail knew better, and always had.

And Tracy knew it, too.

The game ended, and Tracy, grinning joyfully, was running toward her.

"Three sets, Grandmother," she crowed. "I won three straight sets!"

"Good for you," Abigail told her. "Why don't I have Hannah bring us some lemonade, and we can sit for a while?"

Tracy's face immediately crumpled. "But Alison and I wanted to go to the club. Her mom's picking us up."

"Well, I'm sure a few minutes won't matter, and I want to talk to you about something."

"What?" Tracy asked. "Why can't we talk about it later?"

"Because I think we'd better talk about it now," Abigail replied in a tone that warned Tracy not to push her luck too far. Reluctantly, the girl accompanied her grandmother to a small wrought-iron table surrounded by four chairs, and sat down.

"I'm afraid our little plan didn't work out quite the way we intended," Abigail began. "Carolyn has changed your party back to Sunday."

Tracy's eyes flared dangerously. "But she can't do that! I've already told everyone it's Saturday!"

"I know, and I'm sorry," Abigail replied. "But there doesn't seem to be anything we can do. Beth is going to be here. And," she added, smiling tightly, "I shall expect you and your friends to treat her exactly as I would myself."

Tracy's eyes clouded threateningly, but then, as she began to understand, a smile spread over her face. "We will, Grandmother," she replied. A horn sounded from the front of the house, and Tracy leaped to her feet. "Is it okay if I go now, Grandmother?"

"Of course," Abigail replied. Tracy bent over, and the old woman gave her a quick peck on the check. "You have a good time, and don't worry about the party. I'm sure you know exactly what to do."

When Tracy was gone, Abigail suddenly had a sense of being watched, and turned.

Standing at the French doors, looking at her thoughtfully, was Carolyn.

It doesn't matter, Abigail told herself. Even if she heard, she won't know what I was telling the child. The woman doesn't even speak our language.

Beth retreated to her room right after dinner that evening. The meal itself had been horrible—her mother hadn't come down at all, and she'd had to sit at the table, picking at her food, while Tracy glared at her and old Mrs. Sturgess ignored her. Uncle Phillip had been nice to her, but every time he started to talk to her, Tracy had interrupted him. Finally, pretending that she didn't feel well, she'd asked to be excused.

Now she lay sprawled on her bed, trying to read a book, the radio playing softly in the background. Suddenly there was a knock at the door, and Beth rolled over and guiltily switched the radio off. A second later the door opened. With relief, Beth saw that it was not Tracy this time.

Phillip stuck his head inside. "Okay if I come in?"

Beth nodded. "I'm sorry the radio was too loud. I didn't think anyone could hear it."

Phillip's brow knit into a frown. "It isn't even on, is it?"

"I turned it off. I was afraid Tracy—" Then she fell silent, suddenly embarrassed.

"Tracy's downstairs, listening to the stereo in the music room," Phillip replied. "If you want the radio on, turn it on."

"I don't want to bother anyone."

Phillip hesitated, then crossed the room and sat on the edge of the bed. "How come it's not all right for you to bother anyone, but it's all right for everyone else to bother you?"

Beth regarded her stepfather shyly. "But it's Tracy's house."

"It's your house too, Beth," Phillip told her. "And it seems to me you ought to be sticking up for yourself a little more. Your mother can't fight all your battles for you."

Beth looked away, then felt Phillip's hand on her shoulder. She started to pull away, but couldn't. Finally she turned to face him again. "I . . . I just don't know what to do," she said. "I want to do the right thing, but all that ever happens is that I mess it up. Like this morning, down at the stable."

"All that happened down there was that you didn't know what you were doing. And whatever Tracy might have said, there wasn't any harm done. In fact, I'll bet Patches was happy to get out of the stall, even if it was only for a couple of minutes. Most of the time, all she does is just stand there." He smiled reassuringly. "Would you like to learn how to ride her?"

Beth's eyes widened eagerly. "Could I?"

"I don't see why not. In fact, if you want to, we could go out tomorrow morning. We can both get up early and have breakfast with Hannah and be back before anyone else even knows we're gone. What do you say?"

"That would be neat!"

"Then it's a date," Phillip said. He stood up, and started toward the door. "And for God's sake, turn the radio back on. This place is too big, and too quiet." Then he was gone, and Beth was alone again.

She switched the radio back on, then flopped over onto her back, staring up at the ceiling. Suddenly, for the first time since Tracy had come home, she felt a little better. Maybe if Uncle Phillip really would teach her to ride . . .

With the radio playing softly, she drifted into sleep.

When she woke up, the dream was still clear in her mind.

She lay still, thinking about it, reliving it, then rolled over to switch off the radio that was still humming softly on the nightstand.

She had been back in the mill, but it hadn't been at all the way she remembered it from this afternoon.

Instead, it had been filled with people working at all kinds of machinery she'd never seen before. But they hadn't seemed to be able to see her, and she'd wandered around for a long time, watching them work.

And then, faintly, she'd heard someone calling to her. The voice had been muffled at first, and she'd barely been able to hear it. But as she'd wandered toward the back of the building, the voice had grown stronger. She'd suddenly realized that it was coming from downstairs.

She'd gone to the top of the stairs, and listened, hearing faintly but distinctly, the voice, calling to her again.

But then, as she'd started down the stairs, a hand had fallen on her shoulder.

"You can't go down there," a man's voice said.

She had stared up into the face of the man, and realized that he looked strangely familiar. His hair was iron gray and there was a hardness in his eyes that frightened her.

"But I have to," she'd protested weakly. "Someone's calling me."

"You can't go down there," the man had said again.

Then the voice had called to Beth again, and she'd struggled with the man, trying to twist away from his grip. But it hadn't done any good. The man's hands had only tightened on her, and begun dragging her away from the stairs.

And then, with the voice from the basement still ringing in her ears, she'd awakened.

Now, in the silence of the room, with the darkness of the night gathered around her, she could almost hear the voice again, still calling to her, even though she was awake.

She got up from the bed, and went to the window, peering out into the night.

A full moon hung in the sky, and the village, its lights twinkling, lay spread out below. In the distance, almost lost in the darkness, was the dark silhouette of the mill.

Beth waited, half-expecting to see the same strange light glowing from it that she'd seen from the mausoleum this morning, but tonight there was nothing.

She watched for several long minutes, then finally turned away and began undressing. But when she finally slipped under the covers and closed her eyes, the memory of the dream came back to her once more. Once more she heard the strange voice calling out to her, a strangled, needy cry.

"Beeettthhh. Beeettthhh."

And in the depths of her memory, the same voice echoed back, calling out the other word, the word she had seemed to hear in the mill that afternoon.

"Aaaaammmyyy . . .''

Amy.

Amy was calling to her. Amy needed her.

But who was Amy?

As Beth tossed in her bed, trying to fall back into sleep, she knew that somehow she would have to go back to the mill. She had to find out.

T racy Sturgess woke up early on Sunday morning, her eyes going immediately to the open window.

Outside, the day was bright and sunny, without a cloud in the sky. That meant they'd be able to play tennis and croquet that afternoon, two games Tracy was an expert at and that Beth Rogers could barely play at all.

Tracy smiled to herself as she thought about it. She could picture Beth now, clumsily running around the tennis court—barely able to return a serve—while the rest of them watched, clucking sympathetically while they tried to keep from giggling out loud. Maybe they'd even play doubles, and Tracy would get Alison Babcock to be Beth's partner. Alison was almost as good at tennis as Tracy herself, and the two of them had already planned it out. Alison would act as if she was going for the ball, then step aside at the last minute, telling Beth that she was only giving her more room. And Beth, not knowing what was going on, would keep on trying harder, and it would get funnier and funnier. And the best part of it was that even if Carolyn was watching, she wouldn't be able to do anything about it, because it would look like they were all doing their best to help Beth have a good time.

Tracy stretched, then lazily got out of bed and wandered over to the window to look out onto the grounds. On the lawn, Ben was setting up the croquet court, laboriously studying a book, then measuring the distances with a tape measure. Tracy had insisted on an English court, with a single stake in the center and six wickets arranged around it. She and Alison had planned this, too, then practiced the unfamiliar layout with Jeff Bailey and Kip Braithwaite. Tracy could hardly wait until she saw the look on Beth's face, particularly when Beth had to ask how the game was played.

"Oh," she'd say, pretending to be surprised. "I thought you said you knew—" And then she'd pretend she'd suddenly remembered, and offer Beth her best sympathetic expression. "You meant *American* game, didn't you? None of us plays that." Then, while Beth squirmed in embarrassment, and her friends looked politely bored, she'd carefully explain to Beth the sequence of the wickets, graciously allowing her to go first.

And then, of course, all the rest of them would use Beth's ball to get around the court fast.

As Ben placed the last wicket into the lawn, Tracy's eyes wandered down toward the stable, and suddenly her happy mood vanished. Her father and Beth were in the paddock, saddling Patches. Next to Patches, already saddled, was her father's favorite horse, an enormous black Arabian gelding named Sheik.

Tracy's chin trembled with fury. She turned from the window and began struggling into a pair of jeans and one of her father's old shirts. Ignoring the tangled mess of her hair, she slammed out of her room, and started toward the stairs.

"Tracy?" she heard her grandmother call from the far end of the corridor. "Tracy, darling, what on earth is wrong? Where are you going?"

Tracy spun around, her eyes glittering with anger. "He's doing it again! He's down in the paddock with her, and he's going to let her ride my horse again!"

Abigail, framed in the door of her room, frowned in puzzlement. "Peter?" she asked. "But I thought you'd told him not to let Beth anywhere near the stable."

"I did. But it's not Peter—it's Father! He's down there with her, and he's going to take her riding. Just like day before yesterday!"

Abigail's brows arched, and she started toward Tracy, but Tracy had already turned away. And then, when Abigail was halfway to the landing, she heard a muffled thump and a scream. Hurrying forward, she reached the landing, and peered down over the railing.

Near the bottom of the stairs, Carolyn sat nearly doubled over, clutching herself in pain, while Tracy glared at her furiously.

"What were you doing there?" she heard Tracy demand. "You could see me coming down! Why didn't you get out of my way?"

"And you could see me, too, couldn't you?" Carolyn replied. "If you hadn't been running, it wouldn't have happened at all."

"I can run if I want to," Tracy said, fixing a malevolent stare on

Carolyn now. "And you can't stop me! You'd better just watch where you're going."

Carolyn pulled herself painfully to her feet, then reached out and grasped Tracy's wrist just as the girl began to turn away. When she spoke again, her voice was level, but carried an edge that made Tracy turn back and face her.

"That will be quite enough, young lady. You may be thirteen years old today, but you're not so old that I can't turn you over my knee and give you a good spanking. I've put up with just about as much from you as I intend to tolerate, and I suggest you think long and hard before you speak to me again that way. Me, or anyone else. And as for running up and down the stairs, I don't really care if you do it or not, so long as you don't run into people. You could have hurt me very badly, you know. You might even have made me lose my baby."

Tracy's mouth quivered, and she suddenly twisted loose from Carolyn's grip. "I wish I *had* hurt you," she hissed. "I wish I'd killed you and your baby, too!" Then she spun around. She charged through the French doors at the rear of the foyer, and dashed across the lawn to push her way through the hedge to the paddock. But when she got there, it was too late.

The paddock was empty.

Carolyn, shocked at the hatred in Tracy's voice, sank back down onto the stairs, burying her face in her hands.

Abigail remained where she was, watching her daughter-in-law silently. After nearly a minute had passed, she spoke.

"Carolyn? Carolyn, are you all right?"

Carolyn stiffened, then looked up to see Abigail gazing down at her from the landing above. She managed a weak smile, and got once more to her feet. "I'm all right, Abigail. I just had a bad moment, that's all."

The old woman's lips curved into a tight line of disapproval. "I thought I heard a scream. You didn't fall, did you?"

Carolyn hesitated, then shook her head. "No. No, I'm really perfectly all right."

"Perhaps you're trying to do too much," Abigail suggested, her voice taking on the slight purring quality that Carolyn had long since learned to recognize as a danger signal. "Why don't you spend the rest of the day in your room? After all, you'd never forgive yourself if something happened to the baby, would you? And I hate to think how Phillip would feel."

She heard! Carolyn suddenly knew. *She heard every word we said!* And she doesn't care. She knows what happened, and what could have happened, and she won't say a word to Tracy, or a word to Phillip. She feels the same way as Tracy. *She hopes I lose my baby.*

Her heart was thumping now, and when she spoke she had to make an effort to keep her voice from trembling. "But nothing's going to happen to my baby, Abigail. It's going to be perfectly all right."

The two women gazed at each other for a moment; then, at last, Abigail turned away, and started slowly back down the corridor toward her rooms.

Only when she was gone did Carolyn gingerly touch her abdomen once more, hoping to feel a movement that would tell her the baby was all right.

But it was too early to expect any movement from the life within her, and finally she moved painfully across the wide entry hall to the telephone and called the hospital. Despite the fact of Tracy's party that afternoon, she made an appointment to see Dr. Blanchard at two o'clock.

Phillip and Beth dismounted, and Beth carefully tied Patches's reins to a low branch before flopping down onto the soft grass of the little meadow. Then she sat up, and looked around, remembering the last time she'd been here.

"This is where Mom fainted, Uncle Phillip. Right over there by that big rock."

Phillip's eyes followed Beth's pointing arm, then he stood up and wandered over to the rock on which Carolyn had been sitting that morning a few days earlier. A moment later Beth was beside him. "Remember what Mom said that morning? About it looking like the mill was on fire?"

Phillip glanced down at Beth, nodding. "And she asked you if you'd seen the same thing."

"And I did," Beth said, her voice suddenly shy. "At least, I think I did." Slowly, trying to reconstruct the memory, she told Phillip what she'd seen that day from up at the mausoleum. "I thought it was an optical illusion at first," she said when she was finished. "But Mom saw the same thing."

"Maybe you both saw an illusion," Phillip replied. "From up here, the sun can play funny tricks on you. It reflects off the roof of one building and lights up another. And sometimes when it catches the windows just right, it looks as though the whole village is on fire."

"But it wasn't the whole village," Beth protested. "It was just the mill. And it couldn't have been reflections, because all the windows at the mill are boarded up."

Phillip nodded thoughtfully, and looked once more at the old building at the far side of the town. Already it had changed. The boards were torn away from the windows now, and scaffolding had been constructed around it. Already the sandblasting had begun, and here and there areas of bright red brick were beginning to show through the thick layers of grime that had built up over the decades. In his mind's eye, Phillip began to picture the mill as it would be in a few more months, with shutters softening the stark rows of evenly spaced windows, a porte cochere extending from the front entrance out over the sidewalk, and wrought-iron tracery decorating the roof line.

"How come it was closed?" he suddenly heard Beth ask. He glanced down once more, and saw her looking back at him with earnest curiosity.

"Economics," he replied, "The place just wasn't making money anymore."

"But what about all the stories?" Beth pressed.

"What stories are those?" Phillip countered, though he was fairly certain he knew.

"About the children that used to work there. I thought something happened, and they made your family close it up."

"Well, those stories certainly aren't anything new, are they? I've heard them all my life. And I suppose there's some truth to them, too."

"You mean children really did work in the mill?"

"Absolutely. And it wasn't just this mill, either. There were mills and factories all over the Northeast where children worked. And it wasn't much fun, either. Most of the children your age had to work as much as twelve hours a day, six days a week."

"Th-that's what Mom told me," Beth stammered. "And she said that a lot of the children died."

Phillip's eyes clouded slightly. "Yes, I suppose that's true, too. But it's all over now, isn't it? All that happened a hundred years ago."

But Beth didn't seem to be hearing him. Instead, she was once more looking out over the town. Even without following her gaze, Phillip knew that her eyes were fixed on the mill.

"Uncle Phillip? Did . . . did the mill ever catch on fire?"

"On fire?" Phillip echoed. "What on earth makes you think that?"

"It just—I don't know," Beth floundered. "I was just thinking about what Mom and I saw the other day, that's all."

"I thought we'd agreed that was just an optical illusion," Phillip said carefully.

"But what if it wasn't?" Beth asked. Her eyes brightened, and the beginnings of an eager smile came over her face. "What if we were sort of looking into the past? What if it did burn, and sometimes you can still see it?''

"Now, that,'' Phillip chuckled, "is a story I haven't heard before. How on earth did you come up with that one?''

"But what if it's true?'' Beth pressed, ignoring her stepfather's question. "Could something like that happen?''

Phillip shrugged. "It depends on whom you ask, I suppose. If you ask me, I'd say no. But there are plenty of people who claim that whatever happens in a building never goes away. That's the whole idea of ghost stories, isn't it? That people die, but instead of going to heaven they stay around the place they died, scaring people?''

Beth fell silent, thinking about what Phillip had said. Was that what had happened to her the other day? Was that what she had heard? A ghost?

Beth didn't believe in ghosts.

Still, she'd heard something in the mill, and she had seen something from the mausoleum that same day.

And there was the dream, too. . . .

She turned away from the view of the town, and wandered back into the meadow. From the tree where she was tied, Patches whinnied softly, and pawed at the ground. Beth started across the meadow toward the horse, then stopped as something caught the corner of her eye.

She looked around, and frowned slightly.

A few yards away, a small depression, almost barren of the lush grass that filled the rest of the meadow, dipped slightly below the clearing's floor. In the morning light, it almost looked as if the grass on that spot had been burned away.

And from where she stood, the spot looked exactly like a grave.

Suddenly she became conscious of her stepfather standing next to her.

"Beth? What is it?''

"Over there,'' Beth said, pointing. "What's that?''

Phillip's eyes scanned the meadow, but he saw nothing unusual. It looked exactly as it had always looked. "What?'' he asked.

Beth hesitated, then shook her head. "Nothing,'' she replied as she untied Patches and remounted the big mare. "I just thought I saw something, that's all.'' Then she grinned. "It must have been another optical illusion.''

"Either that,'' Phillip laughed, "or you're seeing things. Come on. We don't want to be too long, or you'll be late for Tracy's party.'' He swung easily up onto the Arabian, and cantered out of the meadow onto the trail that led around the hillside to the paddock. But before Beth followed him, she looked once more around the little meadow.

The strangely sunken area was still there, and the more she looked at it, the more certain she became that it was, indeed, a grave.

And in her own mind, she decided whose grave it was.

It was Amy's grave.

By the time lunch began, Beth wished the floor would open up, and she could just fall through.

It had begun after she'd spent almost an hour trying to decide what to wear for the party, and finally settled on a green dress that she'd found in the thrift shop almost a year ago. Now, of course, she never shopped at the thrift shop, but she missed it. The thrift shop was an adventure. You never knew what you were going to find there, and she and her mother used to spend hours rummaging around, looking for things they wouldn't have been able to afford new. The green dress had been one of their best discoveries. It had been almost new, and her mother had had it cleaned and pressed, and then they'd put it away for a special occasion. And today, Beth had decided, was the special occasion.

But when she'd gone downstairs after all Tracy's friends had arrived, she'd realized her mistake.

All the other kids, Tracy included, were dressed in jeans and Lacoste shirts.

Beth had burned with humiliation as Tracy had eyed the dress scornfully, then said, "I guess I should have told you it was informal, shouldn't I? I mean, how could you have known?" Beth had flinched at the slight stress on the word "you," but said nothing.

Then Tracy began making introductions, and Beth squirmed miserably as Tracy's friends asked her questions that weren't really quite questions.

"You go to school right here in Westover? How can you *stand* it?"

"Where do you go during the summer? My family's always in Maine, but it gets *sooo* boring up there, don't you think?"

"You mean you've never *been* to Maine? I thought *every*body went to Maine."

"How come you never go to the country club? Everything else here is so tacky!"

It was a boy named Jeff Bailey who delivered the final blow. He looked at Beth with large blue eyes, and a smile on his face. "I like your dress," he said. Then his smile turned into a malicious grin. "I even liked it when my sister bought it three years ago."

That was when Beth had suddenly fled back upstairs and quickly changed her clothes, shoving the offending green dress back into a corner of the closet where she'd never have to see it again. Finally, after washing her face and recombing her hair, she'd gone back downstairs.

Tracy and her friends were playing croquet, and when they offered to start over again so she could play, she should have known what was going to happen.

Instead, she'd thought they were being nice to her.

Half an hour later, she had still not made it through the first wicket, and all the rest of them were finished.

"In croquet, you never want to go first," Tracy had told her after it was all over, then dropped her voice and glanced around to see if Carolyn was within earshot. "But you wouldn't know *that* either, would you?"

When they had asked her to play tennis, Beth had only shaken her head.

Now all she had to do was get through lunch and the movie Tracy had talked her father into getting for them, and it would all be over.

Tracy opened the curtains over the library windows, then turned and grinned maliciously at Beth. "You were scared, weren't you?" she asked.

"N-no," Beth replied, not quite truthfully. Even though she had kept telling herself it was only a movie, she *had* been scared. Horror movies always frightened her, no matter how much she told herself they weren't true.

"Well, I think you were," Tracy insisted. "If a silly old movie scares you so much, I don't see how you can stand to live in this house."

Beth frowned uncertainly. "What are you talking about? There isn't anything so scary about this house." That wasn't really true, but Beth wasn't about to admit that when she'd first moved into Hilltop, she'd spent several nights lying awake listening to the strange sounds that had seemed to fill the old house.

"Isn't there?" Tracy asked. "What about the ghost?"

Beth's frown smoothed out as she realized that Tracy just wanted her to look stupid again. "What ghost?" she asked, trying to make her voice as scornful as Tracy's.

"We're not sure." Tracy's voice took on a tone of smug self-importance, and she glanced at Alison Babcock. "But we think she's friendly. She's an old lady, dressed in black, and she prowls around the house late at night, looking for something."

"That's your grandmother," Beth ventured, but nobody laughed, and Tracy only shook her head.

"No, it's not," she replied. She turned to Jeff Bailey. "It isn't Grandmother, is it?"

"It didn't look like her to me," Jeff said, picking up the game. "She's real old, and her eyes are all sunken in, like she's blind or something. And she carries a candle," he added, in his most sepulchral tone.

"When did you see her?" Beth demanded.

"Last year," Jeff replied. "There were a bunch of us here for the weekend, and we all saw her. Isn't that right?"

Brett Kilpatrick nodded. "I saw her the same time Jeff did. She was in the upstairs hall, right by the top of the stairs. And when we spoke to her, she disappeared."

Beth looked around at the rest of Tracy's guests. All of them were nodding agreement and looking a little bit frightened. Maybe, after all, it was true. Then, slowly, an idea began to form in her mind. "Maybe . . . maybe she was looking for Amy," she said.

Tracy Sturgess's eyes clouded uncertainly. "Amy?" she repeated. "Who's Amy?"

"The ghost who lives in the mill," Beth replied, her confidence beginning to grow. "Don't you know about her?"

Tracy shook her head slowly, glancing at her friends out of the corner of her eyes. "Tell us about her."

Beth shrugged. "She's a little girl," she improvised. "And she's lived in the mill practically forever."

"Oh, sure," Jeff scoffed. "But have you ever seen her?"

Beth felt herself flush. "No," she admitted. "But . . . but I've heard her."

"Really?" Tracy asked. She was smirking now. "What did she say?"

"She said—" But before Beth could think of anything a ghost might have said, Jeff and Brett looked at each other and broke into loud laughter.

"She believes it!" Brett crowed. "She really believes there's a ghost in the mill."

As the boys' raucous whoops filled the room, Beth felt her face flush with humiliation once again. "Well, if there's a ghost here, why couldn't there be one in the mill?" she demanded, her face scarlet and her voice desperate as the laughter grew among Tracy's friends.

"Because there *isn't* any ghost here," Tracy said triumphantly. "I just made all that up! And you believed it, just like I thought you would. You really *are* stupid, aren't you?"

Beth stood up, her chin quivering. "Not as stupid as you and your dumb friends, Tracy! There is a ghost in the mill, and I know who it is! And I'm leaving!"

"So leave," Tracy taunted, dropping the last vestige of politeness from her voice. "Who wants you here anyway?"

Beth fled from the room, intent on finding her mother.

And then she remembered.

Her mother had made an emergency appointment to go see Dr. Blanchard. Neither she nor even Uncle Phillip was home.

Her father.

She would go and see her father.

Tears welling from her eyes, she hurried out the front door, and started toward the driveway.

And then, as she came to the lawn, she remembered the trail leading down the hill.

It was a shortcut, and would get her to the village much faster. She ran across the lawn, and plunged through the brush until she came to the trail from the paddock, then hurried along to the path that led down the hill.

It was when she was halfway down the hill that the idea came to her.

She wouldn't go see her father after all. Instead, she would go to the mill, and find a way to get inside.

And once she was in the mill, she would find out if Amy was truly there or not.

But even as she started on her way again, she knew what she would find in the mill.

Amy would be there—because Beth wanted her to be there.

Nine

Jeff Bailey and Brett Kilpatrick presented an odd contrast as they walked along River Road. Though they were distant cousins, Jeff was blond and gangling, while Brett's thatch of dark curly hair gave the same clear evidence of Celtic descent as did his compact body. They were approaching the point at which River Road crossed the railroad tracks, where they would turn right, cross the trestle over the river, and head north toward their homes near the country club. It was the long way around from Hilltop, but neither of them had felt like taking the shortcut directly down the hillside to the river.

"How come she was even there?" Jeff asked, casually kicking a battered beer can that lay by the road. It arced into the air, then dropped back into the drainage ditch. "Tracy hates her."

"She lives there," Brett replied. "Tracy tried to switch the party, but her stepmother found out. She's sure a creep, isn't she?"

"She's a local—they're all like that." Jeff watched idly while Brett took careful aim on the beer can, then snickered when it rolled only a few feet ahead. "And you think you're going to make the soccer team next year?" At St. Francis Academy, where both of them spent nine months of each year, the soccer team was *the* team to be on.

Brett ignored the gibe. "Can you believe the dress she was wearing?" he asked, bringing the subject back to Beth Rogers. "It looked even uglier on her than it did on your sister. And when Tracy started telling that story about the ghost, and she *believed* her, I thought I was gonna piss my pants."

Jeff skidded down the shoulder into the ditch, and kicked the can neatly back up onto the road. Then, as they came to the railroad tracks, he glanced across the street, his eyes falling on the scaffold-covered walls of the mill.

"What about the ghost she claimed lives in there?" he asked.

"Give me a break," Brett groaned. "She was just trying to look smart. Or she's so dumb she really believes there's something in there."

Jeff eyed his friend, a mischievous grin playing around the corners of his mouth. "Want to go in and take a look?" he challenged.

Brett hesitated. All his life he'd heard stories about the mill, and he knew as well as everyone else in Westover that Mr. Sturgess's older brother had gotten killed in the building years earlier.

And according to Brett's father, no one had ever found out exactly what had happened to Con Sturgess. It was supposed to have been an accident, but everyone knew that old man Sturgess had always claimed it wasn't.

Then he saw Jeff watching him, a smirk on his face. Ignoring the knot of fear in his gut, he nodded. "Why not?" he asked, aiming one last kick at the battered can and missing completely. He followed Jeff down the tracks toward the back of the mill. "How do we get in?"

Jeff surveyed the building, then shrugged. "It's got to be a cinch. I bet they aren't even keeping it locked up."

Brett's eyes followed Jeff's, but he didn't feel nearly as confident as Jeff sounded. "What if someone catches us?"

"So what? All we're going to do is look around. What's the big deal? Besides, they're working on it, right?"

Brett nodded.

"So everybody pokes around buildings that are being restored. If anybody catches us, we'll just tell them we wanted to see what was going on. Come on.''

They followed a spur from the main line that led to the long-abandoned loading dock at the rear of the mill, skirted around a pile of trash that had accumulated against the dock itself, then scrambled up to try the freight door. It was securely locked, as was the door to what had once been the dispatcher's office. After trying two more doors, they jumped off the dock, rounded the corner of the building, and started walking along a newly cleared path that paralleled the side of the building. Halfway to Prospect Street they came to the metal door that had always before been carefully locked.

Today the lock was open, hanging loosely from the hasp.

"See?" Jeff asked. "What'd I tell you? It's not even locked up. We can just walk in." He reached out and grasped the knob, then twisted it.

It turned easily.

"H-how *come* it's not locked?" Brett asked, his voice dropping to a whisper. "S'pose someone's inside?"

Jeff's eyes raked him scornfully. "It's not locked because the workmen were too stupid to lock it," he said. He pushed the door open, and stepped through, but Brett still hung back. "You coming, or not?"

"Maybe we shouldn't," Brett suggested. He glanced to the west, where the sun was sinking toward the horizon. "Isn't it pretty dark in there?"

"You can see fine." Jeff sneered. "Either come in, or stay out, but I'm gonna look around."

Struggling against his fear, Brett stepped through the door and closed it behind him. For a moment the deep shadows blinded him, but then his eyes adjusted to the dim light of the interior, and he looked around.

Somehow, he had expected it to be empty.

But it wasn't.

Already, the floor had been subdivided by the skeletal shapes of newly constructed framework, and in the roof, several holes had been cut for skylights. Now, in the late afternoon, little light came through the holes, and it seemed to Brett that all they did was make the place even spookier than it already was.

And the framework, he realized, was almost like a maze. Almost anywhere, there could be someone hiding.

In the silence, Brett could hear the pounding of his own heart.

"Hey!"

The sudden sound jabbed Brett like a needle, and he felt his whole body twitch with a sudden release of tension. Then he realized the sound had come from Jeff. "Jeez!" he whispered loudly. "What did you do that for?"

Jeff gazed at his friend with disgust. "Because," he explained, "if anybody had answered, we could have said we were looking for someone, and then left. No one ever thinks you're sneaking in some-where if you make a lot of noise." He called out once more: "Any-body here?" A pair of pigeons, frightened by the sudden disturbance, burst from their nests in a flapping of wings.

When silence had fallen once more, Jeff raised his hand, pointing toward the rear wall. "If there's anything in here, I bet it's back there," he said.

Brett gazed into the gathering gloom, and saw the top of the stairs that led down into the basement below. It was in the basement, his father had told him, that Con Sturgess's body had been found. Brett's heart pounded harder, and he felt a cold sweat breaking out on his back. "I bet there's nothing there at all," he said, though his voice quavered slightly in spite of his efforts to keep it steady. Jeff, catch-ing the slip, grinned.

"Scared?"

"Hell, no," Brett lied. "What's to be scared of?"

"Ghoooosts," Jeff intoned, then snickered. "Come on."

They started toward the back of the building, with Brett following reluctantly. They had gone only a few yards when Brett felt his skin crawl.

He had the eerie feeling of unseen eyes watching him.

He tried to ignore it, keeping his eyes on Jeff's back, but the feeling wouldn't go away.

Instead, it got worse.

There was something else in the mill—he was sure of it. But he couldn't be sure where it was. It seemed to be all around him, following him. Suddenly he could stand it no longer, and whirled around to face whatever was stalking him.

Nothing.

His eyes scanned the tangle of structural supports, searching for a movement, but there was nothing there. Nothing, at least, that he could see.

And then, once again, the hair on the back of his neck stood up, and his spine began to tingle.

There was a sudden feeling of movement behind him. His stom-ach lurched. Something touched his shoulder.

Screaming, he jerked free, and whirled once more.

Jeff was staring at him, laughing. "Gotcha!"

"Jesus Christ! You scared the shit out of me!"

Jeff regarded him with knowing eyes. "You were already scared, weren't you?"

"I . . . I thought I heard something," Brett lied again.

"Well, you didn't, 'cause there's nothing here," Jeff replied. "Let's go see what's downstairs."

Without waiting for Brett to reply, Jeff headed once more for the staircase. Brett, unwilling to stay where he was, or admit by leaving that he was frightened, followed close behind. But when Jeff started down the stairs, Brett stopped, peering fearfully, into the blackness below. "I'm not going down there."

"Chicken," Jeff taunted.

This time, Brett ignored the taunt. "It's dark down there, and you can't see anything."

"I can see all the way to the bottom of the stairs, and I'm going down whether you come or not."

Brett said nothing, only shrugged. He was staying where he was.

Jeff started down the stairs, but with each step he took, a little more of his confidence slipped away.

He began to wonder what might actually be waiting in the darkness below.

According to Beth Rogers, there was a ghost here.

But that was ridiculous. He didn't believe in ghosts.

He tried to remember how funny the ghost story had been a couple of hours ago, when they'd all been lying around on the floor of Tracy's library.

But it didn't seem so funny now, not with the dank gloom of the old building gathering around him.

In fact, now that he thought about it, the darkness itself was almost like something alive, reaching out for him.

He stopped near the bottom of the stairs, and tried to shake the feeling off.

He wasn't scared of the dark. He'd never been scared of the dark, at least not since he was a baby.

But now, here, he found that the dank blackness below was something very much to be afraid of.

Here, he didn't know what the darkness concealed. It wasn't at all like being in the dark at home, where you knew everything that was in the room around you, and could identify every sound you heard.

Here, the darkness seemed to go on forever, and the sounds—the little rustling sounds he was beginning to hear now—could be anything at all.

Mice. They could be mice, or even rats.

Or something else.

Something you couldn't touch, but that could touch you.

He wanted to go back now, but it was too late. Brett was waiting above, and he'd laughed at Brett. If he came back up now, and admitted he'd been afraid to go any farther, Brett would never let him forget it.

Holding his breath, he took another step.

He listened to the noises, and began to imagine that they were voices.

Voices, whispering so quietly he could barely hear them.

He took another step, which brought him to the basement floor. Bracing himself, he edged into the horrible blackness around him.

And then, out of the darkness, he sensed something coming for him.

He opened his mouth, but fear choked his throat and no sound came out. From behind him, he felt himself being pushed. He staggered in the darkness, and reached out to find something to brace himself with.

There was nothing.

Now, as he realized what was happening to him, his fear released him, and a scream erupted from his throat—cut off a moment later as he pitched forward and fell.

In a flash, he remembered the story he'd heard about how Tracy's uncle had died, long before he had even been born. It's happening again, he thought. Just like it happened before.

In an instant that seemed to go on forever, something hard and sharp pressed against his chest, so cold it seemed to burn as it punctured his shirt, then his skin.

His own weight as he fell thrust the object into his heart, and he heard himself gasp, felt the final racking stab of pain, then heard his own blood bubbling into his lungs.

As he died, a draft of cool air blew around him, and then he smelled a familiar odor.

Smoke.

To Jeff Bailey, death smelled like smoke. . . .

Brett heard the soft thump of something falling, then silence closed around him once more. "Jeff?"

There was no answer. He called out again, louder, sure that his friend was trying to scare him as he had before. "Come on, Jeff. Quit fooling around."

Still there was no answer, and Brett took a tentative step down the stairs.

And then, a chill passing through him, he was suddenly certain that Jeff was not fooling around. Turning, he dashed toward the door they had come through twenty minutes earlier, hurled it open, and charged out into the gathering dusk.

"Help!" he yelled. "Somebody help me!" In panic, he began running toward the street in front of the mill.

"All right, son," Sergeant Peter Cosgrove said a few minutes later. "Just try to calm down, and tell me where your friend is."

"D-down there," Brett quavered. He pointed down the stairs, now brightly lit by the worklights that were strung throughout the building. "Something happened to him. I . . . I don't know what."

Cosgrove's partner, Barney Jeffers, trotted down the stairs, a flashlight in his hand. A moment later, as he flashed his light around the darkness of the basement, they heard him swear. At the same moment, brakes squealed outside, then an ambulance crew with a stretcher hurried through the door.

"Over here," Cosgrove called. He turned his attention back to Brett. "You stay right here, son. I'm gonna find a light for the basement. Okay?"

Brett nodded mutely, his eyes fixed on the staircase. What seemed like an eternity later, the lights in the basement suddenly flashed on, and he could see Jeff lying on the basement floor. Blood, mixed with dirt, soaked his shirt, and the stillness of death lay over him like a shroud. Brett's stomach heaved, and he turned away.

"What do you think?" Cosgrove asked Jeffers half an hour later. The ambulance was gone, and they were standing at the top of the stairs while a crew worked below, photographing the site and searching for evidence. Cosgrove was ninety-percent certain they wouldn't find anything.

"Same as you," Jeffers replied. "I think the Kilpatrick kid was telling the truth. Looks to me like the boy went down to look around, couldn't see anything, and tripped. If he'd been anywhere else, he might have skinned his knee. As it was, he landed on that pick."

"What the hell was it doing lying there?" Cosgrove muttered angrily.

"You want to charge someone with criminal negligence?" Jeffers inquired.

"I'd love to," Cosgrove replied, his voice tight. "But who do you charge? Might just as well charge the Bailey boy. If he hadn't been trespassing—"

"It was an accident," Jeffers interrupted. "Sometimes things happen, Pete. There's nothing we can do about it."

Cosgrove sighed, letting the tension drain from his body. "I know," he agreed. "But it's weird, too, you know?"

"Weird?" Jeffers echoed.

Cosgrove looked around, his eyes surveying the interior of the mill. "Yeah," he said. "Weird. All my life, I've heard stories about this place, and how dangerous it is. Stupid stories. So now they're fixing it up, and what happens? They aren't even done, and we already got someone dead. That's what I call weird."

Jeffers looked at his partner curiously. "You're not saying what I think you're saying, are you?"

Cosgrove shrugged. "I don't know," he said softly. "You didn't grow up here, like I did. Something like this happened once before. Must have been forty-odd years ago. That time it was Phillip Sturgess's brother. Conrad Junior."

Barney Jeffers frowned. "You mean he died? Here in the mill?"

"Not just in the mill, Barney," Cosgrove said darkly. "Right here. At the bottom of the stairs."

Jeffers uttered a low whistle. "Jesus. What happened?"

"That's the thing," Cosgrove went on. "No one ever found out. No one ever knew if it was an accident, or murder, or what. But it was just like this one." He fell silent for a few seconds, then shook his head. "Weird," he muttered. "It's just—well, it's weird, that's all."

Then, his face grim, he started toward the patrol car, bracing himself for what was ahead. He was about to call Jeff Bailey's parents to tell them their son had died in the mill, a pickax through his heart.

Ten

Hannah was in the midst of serving dessert when the telephone rang. Carolyn slid her chair back and started to stand up, but Abigail's voice, quiet yet firm, made her sink back into her chair. "Hannah will get it." Silently, Hannah placed the pie she had been serving on a sideboard, and left the room. A moment later she came back.

"It's for Mr. Phillip. It's the police, and they say it's an emergency. I explained you were in the middle of dinner, but they insisted—"

"It's all right, Hannah," Phillip said. "I'm sure it's important." He turned to his mother. "If you'll excuse me?"

Abigail glared at her son. "Really, Phillip, it's most impolite of them to call you now. I simply don't understand—"

"Maybe you will, after I talk to them," Phillip interrupted. "Go ahead with dessert."

When he was gone, Abigail turned her attention to Carolyn. "You simply must learn a few rudimentary things, Carolyn. First, it's very impolite to call people during the dinner hour. There is, however, little we can do to stop *that*. It seems that *no one* has manners anymore. But if the phone does ring while we are dining, Hannah will answer it."

From the corner of her eye, Carolyn saw Tracy's smirk, but ignored it. Beth, intently studying her plate, appeared suddenly to have found something fascinating in her pie. Smiling tightly, Carolyn patted Abigail's hand. "I'll try to remember that, Abigail," she promised as the old woman jerked away as if she'd been burned. "But suppose Hannah weren't here? Suppose it were her day off?"

"One of the other servants—" Abigail began, then abruptly fell silent as she remembered that there were no other servants. "In that case," she finally admitted, her voice stiff, "I suppose one of us would have to answer it."

Score one for our side, thought Carolyn as Tracy's smirk faded and a tiny smile played around the corners of Beth's mouth. In silence, the four of them began eating their pie. After four or five minutes that seemed to Carolyn like an eternity, Phillip returned, his expression grim.

"I have to go downtown," he informed them.

"Now?" Abigail immediately asked. "Surely whatever it is can wait until we've finished dinner?"

"What's happened?" The look on Phillip's face told Carolyn that something was terribly wrong.

"An accident," he replied. "A couple of kids got into the mill after the party this afternoon."

Beth's eyes widened, and her fork stopped in midair. Then, as her hand began to tremble, she carefully put the fork back on her plate.

"And what happened?" Abigail Sturgess asked. Her voice, normally strong and commanding, suddenly sounded hollow. When Carolyn looked at her, the old woman was pale, and there was an anxiety in her eyes that Carolyn had never seen before. "Tell me, Phillip," she insisted. "What has happened?"

Phillip hesitated a fraction of a second. "Jeff Bailey," he said at last. "He's—well, I'm afraid he's dead."

There was a sudden shocked silence as the name sank in. It

wasn't a stranger—not even someone they had known only casually. It was a boy they all knew, who had been in their home only that afternoon.

"Jeff?" Tracy echoed. "Jeff's dead?"

"But—how?" Carolyn asked. "What happened?"

Phillip shook his head. "I'm not sure exactly. I have to go down there immediately."

Abigail rose to her feet. All the blood had drained from her face now, and she was swaying, as if she might faint at any moment. "My God," she whispered. "It's like your brother. He was the same age as Jeff when he—when he—" She fell suddenly silent, unable to continue.

Phillip stared at his mother. "Like Conrad?" he echoed. "Mother, what on earth are you talking about? We don't even know what happened yet—"

But Abigail was shaking her head, and her eyes had taken on a strangely empty look, as if she were seeing something far removed from the dining room. "Your father," she whispered. "He always said something like this would happen. He was always afraid—"

"Mother, please," Phillip said, taking her arm and guiding her back into her chair. "We don't even know what happened," he repeated.

"What did they say?" Abigail demanded. "Phillip, tell me what they said about Jeffrey."

Phillip swallowed, and glanced at Tracy and Beth, reluctant to repeat what he had been told in front of the girls. But both girls were staring at him, Tracy's eyes glinting strangely, Beth's wide and frightened. "Apparently he tripped," he said quietly. "There was a pick lying on the floor. He fell on it."

"Oh, God," Carolyn moaned.

Abigail gasped, and sank limply into her chair. "Like Conrad," she whispered. "It's just like Conrad." Her eyes seemed to focus again, and fixed on her son. "Phillip, maybe your father was right about the mill. Maybe we've made a mistake. Perhaps we should simply board it up again."

But Phillip shook his head, his face setting grimly. "For heaven's sake, Mother," he began. "It was an accident. It wasn't anybody's fault. Jeff shouldn't have been in there in the first place. He was—" And then he broke off his own words, the look in Abigail's eyes telling him she wasn't listening. Once again she seemed to have disappeared into another world. "I'll be back as soon as I can," he told Carolyn. He kissed her quickly on the cheek, then was gone.

"I must call Maggie Bailey," Abigail said suddenly. "I must try to apologize to her for what we've done." She started from the dining room, but before she reached the door, Carolyn blocked her path.

"No," Carolyn said. "If you call Maggie Bailey, it will only be to tell her how sorry you are about Jeff. But you will not begin filling her head with any superstitions about the mill."

Slowly, Abigail turned to face her. "Superstitions?" she echoed. Then she smiled bitterly. "Well, I suppose that's easy for you to say. But you don't remember the last time something like this happened, do you? Of course not—you weren't even born then. But it was an evening very much like this. And the telephone rang, and the police told us that Conrad Junior had been found in the mill. He'd tripped, they said. Tripped, and fallen on an old tool." Her voice dropped to a whisper. "It was the same thing, Carolyn. My husband always said that what happened to our son was not an accident, but I never believed him. But now? What do you expect me to think? It's happened again, just as my dear husband was afraid it would."

Almost in spite of herself, Carolyn felt a flicker of sympathy for the old lady. "Abigail, what you're saying just doesn't make any sense. The mill is dangerous—we all know that. And it was locked up precisely in order to prevent any more accidents like the ones that happened to your son and Jeff Bailey."

"But what if it wasn't an accident?" Tracy suddenly asked. "What if there was someone else in there?"

Carolyn glanced at Tracy, then felt her stomach tighten as she saw that although Tracy had directed the question to her, the girl's eyes were fixed on Beth. "Just what are you suggesting, Tracy?" she asked, her voice cool.

"Nothing," Tracy replied with exaggerated innocence. "I was just asking a question."

Before Carolyn could reply, Abigail spoke again. "Conrad's last words," she said so quietly that Carolyn wasn't sure if she was speaking to them or to herself. "He said, 'She's still there. She's there, and she hates us. . . .'"

Tracy's eyes brightened. "Who, Grandmother? Who hates us?"

But Abigail shook her head. "I don't know," she whispered. "It was the last thing he said. I . . . I didn't think it meant anything. But now—"

"And you were right," Carolyn declared. "It didn't mean anything. As it happens, I agreed with your husband about the mill—I don't think it should be reopened. It was an evil place, a place where people were exploited, worked till they dropped, and I think it should be torn down and forgotten. But let's not start inventing ghost stories. All right?"

Abigail hesitated, then shook her head. "And what if you're wrong?" she asked. "What if my husband was right? What if there *is* something about the mill, and the only way we can keep it safe is by keeping people out of it?"

"For heaven's sake, Abigail, don't start filling the children's heads with a lot of nonsense."

"But I *want* to hear," Tracy protested.

"And I *don't* want to hear," Carolyn said firmly. "And neither does Beth. The mill is nothing but an old building that's been an eyesore in this town for nearly a hundred years. Frankly, I can't understand why it wasn't torn down years ago." Her eyes fixed on Abigail. "In fact, Abigail, I'd like to know why your husband didn't tear it down years ago when your son died there."

Abigail's strength seemed to flow back into her, and she gazed imperiously at Carolyn. "He didn't tear it down because he always said that it *mustn't* be torn down. He always said that it must stand as a reminder to us."

"A reminder?" Carolyn replied. Suddenly she had had enough, and did nothing to conceal the fury that welled in her as she stared at the old woman. "A reminder of how big a fortune your family once made in that building? A reminder of all the children who spent their lives in that building, working twelve hours a day for next to no money at all so that your family could build this monstrosity of a house and staff it with the few people in town who weren't working in your mill? Was that it, Abigail? Did he want the mill to stand there forever to remind us all of the good old days? Well, for my family, those days weren't so good, though I'm sure you're not aware of that!"

Abigail remained silent for several long seconds, then finally said, "I don't know what Conrad thought at the end, Carolyn," she began quietly. "But I do know that he was terrified of the mill. Until tonight, I paid no attention to it. But now I think perhaps we all ought to rethink the matter." She walked from the dining room, her back straight, her proud old head held high.

A moment later Tracy followed her grandmother, leaving Carolyn and Beth alone in the dining room. There was a long silence, and finally, for the first time, Beth spoke.

"Mom? What . . . what if she's right? What if there is something in the mill? What would it mean?"

Carolyn sighed, and shook her head. "It wouldn't mean anything, sweetheart," she said. "It wouldn't mean anything, because it's not possible. It doesn't matter what old Mr. Sturgess thought, or what Abigail thinks now. There's nothing in the mill." But even as she said the words, a memory flashed through Carolyn's mind—a memory of that morning the day after the funeral, when she'd been out hiking with Beth.

For a moment, just before she'd fainted, the mill had looked as if it were burning.

But that was silly. The mill hadn't been on fire, and she hadn't actually seen anything. It had simply been a delusion, caused by the fainting spell.

She put the memory out of her mind, and began helping Beth and a silent Hannah clear the table. Surely there was a reasonable explanation for what had happened in the mill that day. When Phillip came home, they would know what it was.

Phillip Sturgess sat in Norm Adcock's office, facing the chief of the Westover Police Department over a desk that looked even more worn than Phillip felt. In the chair next to him, Alan Rogers sat, his eyes grim as he waited for Phillip to finish reading the report Cosgrove and Jeffers had filed. They'd already listened to Brett Kilpatrick's story.

For Phillip, there was a dreamlike quality to the whole thing, as if something out of the past were being replayed. And, of course, it was—the events of that afternoon were an eerie replay of what he'd heard about the day his brother had died.

The police, he was beginning to understand, were much more interested in the minutiae of what had happened than in the death of Jeff Bailey. Of course, he knew why that was. Jeff Bailey, like Phillip himself, was one of "them" to Norm Adcock. One of the rich ones—the ones who lived in Westover but were seldom seen in the town. Not, to Adcock, really a part of the town at all. Had it been this way when his brother had died?

Undoubtedly it had.

He finished reading the report, and put it back on the police chief's desk. "But the door *had* to be locked," he said now, in response to the question he'd heard Adcock asking Alan Rogers. "I can't believe no one checked it before the workmen left Friday."

His eyes went to Alan, who shook his head. "I'm sorry, Phillip. I'm almost sure I checked the lock myself, but I suppose it's possible I didn't. At any rate, it doesn't matter now. The lock was open, and doesn't show any signs of being forced. So part of the responsibility for what happened is mine."

Adcock shrugged. "Or maybe one of the kids had a key that fit. It's unlikely, but it's a possibility."

"What about charges?" Phillip asked. "Will there be any?"

Adcock shrugged noncommittally. "That's not really up to me, Mr. Sturgess. That'll be up to the prosecutor. I s'pose he could make a case that the mill is an *attractive nuisance*, and probably a few other things, too." He leaned back in his chair, his fingers fiddling with a ballpoint pen. "And I think you can probably count on being sued by the boy's folks."

"Which is between their attorneys and mine," Phillip said tightly. Then, hearing how cold his own words sounded, he tried to recover: "I couldn't feel worse about this if Jeff had been my own son."

Adcock nodded, though the expression of contempt in his eyes didn't change. He laid the pen back on the desk. "Then you won't object to fencing the place off, will you?" he asked, making no attempt to disguise the fact that his words had not been a question but an order.

"You don't even have to mention it," Phillip replied. "Alan, you can start the work tomorrow, can't you?"

"Of course."

"I'll post a guard on the place until the fence is finished," Phillip added.

"I already put a man out there for tonight," Adcock said. "I know it seems like closing the barn door after the horse is gone, but things like this have a way of gettin' out of hand. Unless I miss my guess, there's already kids in town planning to try to sneak in there tonight."

Phillip nodded. "Bill us for your man's time, Chief. The mill's my responsibility, not yours."

"I wasn't planning to do anything else," Adcock observed coolly. He stood up. "Well, I guess there isn't much else we can do tonight. I better get back home before Millie comes looking for me." He shook his head as he fished in his pocket for his car keys. "Hell of a thing," he said. Then, again: "Hell of a thing."

The three men walked together through the small police station, Adcock greeting each of his men by his first name.

All of them replied to the chief, all of them spoke to Alan Rogers.

For Phillip Sturgess, there were no greetings, not even a nod of the head.

Then they were outside, and the chief had gone. Alan and Phillip stood for a moment next to Alan's car. Silence hung over them until finally Alan reached out and put his hand on the other man's shoulder.

"I really don't know what to say, Phillip."

"There's not much *to* say, is there?"

"If you want to fire me, I'll understand. In fact, I've already written a letter withdrawing from the contract."

Phillip said nothing for a moment, then shook his head. "No. I can't see how that will solve anything. It won't bring Jeff Bailey back, and the job still has to be finished."

Alan nodded, then got into his car. "Can I buy you a drink? I know I could use one."

Again Phillip shook his head. "Thanks, but not tonight. I think I'd better go home and start taking care of things."

"Okay." He turned the key in the ignition. The engine of the old Fiat coughed twice, then caught. "Phillip, try not to let this get to you. What happened today was just an accident, nothing more. But people are going to talk—it's all too much like what happened to your brother. All I can tell you is, don't listen to them. Don't listen to any of them." Then, before the other man could answer, Alan put his car in gear and drove off into the night, leaving Phillip Sturgess alone on the sidewalk.

Phillip parked his car on Prospect Street, and sat for a few minutes, staring at the mill, wondering what his father had meant all those years when he'd insisted over and over that it was an evil place. Though Phillip had pressed him to explain, Conrad Sturgess had gone on pronouncing his dire words as though the statement itself were sufficient, adding only that someday he would understand.

But it was all nonsense. There was no such thing as a building that was evil, not even a building as ugly as the mill, with its stark facade and unadorned utilitarian lines.

He switched off the ignition, then reached into the glove compartment for the flashlight he always kept there. Locking the car, he crossed Prospect Street, and started toward the side of the building and the metal door.

"Hold on there, mister," a voice said from behind him. "Just where do you think you're going?"

Phillip turned, and was immediately blinded by the bright beam of a halogen light. Two seconds later the light went out. "Sorry, Mr. Sturgess," the voice went on. "I didn't recognize you." A man stepped forward. Phillip recognized his police uniform, but not his face.

"It's all right. I was just going home, and thought I'd stop to have a look around."

The officer hesitated, then reluctantly nodded. "Well, I suppose you can go in if you want to. It's your building." Another hesitation, and then, with even more reluctance: "Want me to go with you?"

"No, thanks," Phillip immediately assured him. "I'll only be a few minutes." Then, with the officer still watching him, he used his key to open the door, and stepped into the black emptiness of the mill. He stood still, listening, then reached out and groped for the light switch. The darkness was washed away by the big worklights suspended from the roof.

Phillip glanced around, then headed toward the back of the building, and the stairs leading downward.

He paused at the top of the stairs, looking into the blackness below, and wondered if perhaps he shouldn't leave now, and simply go home.

But he couldn't.

A boy had died here today, and it had happened down below, in the black reaches of the basement.

For some reason—he wasn't really certain why—he had to see the place where Jeff Bailey had died.

Turning on the flashlight, he started down the stairs.

At the bottom, he paused again, and shone the light around the basement.

Nothing.

As far as the weak beam of the flashlight could penetrate, there was nothing. Only a worn wooden floor, covered with dirt, and a scattering of tools.

He turned the light onto the area beneath the stairs.

There, the dust had been disturbed by many feet. In the midst of the footprints, Phillip saw a brownish smear.

The stain left by Jeff Bailey's blood.

Swallowing hard in an attempt to quash the wave of nausea that threatened him, Phillip turned away, switched off the flashlight, and started up the stairs.

Halfway up, he stopped.

From the darkness below, he was certain he had heard something.

He listened, waiting for it to come again.

All he could hear was the pounding of his own heartbeat.

Once more, he started up the stairs.

And he heard it again.

It was faint, almost inaudible, but he was nearly certain that it was there.

It was a crackling noise, almost as if something were burning.

He froze again, straining his ears, struggling to hear the sound once more, hear it clearly.

It didn't come.

The minutes passed, and his heart finally slowed to a normal pace. In the mill, there was only silence. At last, Phillip went on up the stairs, and walked slowly toward the door. He paused one final time, his hand poised over the light switch, and looked around.

Everything was as it should be.

He switched out the lights, plunging the building back into darkness, then carefully locked the door. From a few feet away, the policeman spoke. "Everything all right, Mr. Sturgess?"

Phillip nodded, about to start back toward his car. Then: "You didn't hear anything, did you?" he asked. "While I was in the mill?"

The cop frowned in the darkness. "Hear anything, Mr. Sturgess? No, I don't think so."

Phillip thought for a moment, then nodded once again. "All right," he said. "Thanks."

He walked quickly to his car, unlocked it, and got in. Then he put the flashlight back in the glove compartment, started the engine, and shifted the gears into drive.

He looked at the mill once more.

He decided he hadn't heard anything. It had only been his imagination, and the stress of the day.

Phillip Sturgess drove away into the night.

Beth woke up just after midnight, screaming.

The dream was still vivid in her memory, and her pajamas were soaked with perspiration. Her heart pounded as her scream faded away.

The door to her bedroom flew open, and the light went on.

"Beth?" she heard her mother's voice asking. "Beth, what is it? Are you all right?"

Beth shook her head, as if the gesture would shake the hideous images from her mind. "I saw it," she breathed. "I saw it all!"

"What?" Carolyn asked, crossing the large room to sit on the bed and gather Beth into her arms. "What did you see, honey?"

"Jeff," Beth sobbed. "I saw what happened to him, Mom."

"It was a nightmare, sweetheart," Carolyn crooned, gently stroking her daughter's forehead. "It was only a dream."

"But I *saw* it," Beth insisted. "I . . . I was in the mill, downstairs, and there was someone else there. And then there was a sound, and I could hear Jeff's voice."

She broke off, sobbing, and Carolyn cradled her. "No," she whispered. "It was a dream. Only a dream."

It was as if Beth didn't hear her. "And then the wall slid away, and all of a sudden I could see Jeff. And then—and then someone pushed him!"

"Pushed him?" Carolyn asked. "What do you mean, honey?"

"I . . . I don't know," Beth stammered. "But someone pushed him, and he fell onto the pick. He didn't trip, Mom! She pushed him. She killed him!"

"No, sweetheart," Carolyn insisted. "All that happened was that you had a bad dream. And what happened to Jeff Bailey today was an accident."

Beth looked up at her mother with worried eyes. Carolyn brushed the hair back from the child's forehead with gentle fingers. "A dream?" Beth asked. "But . . . but it was so real—"

"I know," Carolyn assured her. "That's what makes nightmares so scary, honey. They seem so real that even when you wake up, sometimes they seem as if they're still happening. Is that what happened to you?"

Beth nodded. "I woke up, and it was dark, and it seemed like I was still in the mill. And I could still see it, and . . . and—"

"And now it's all over with," Carolyn finished for her. "Now you're all wide-awake, and you know it was just a dream, and you can forget all about it." She eased Beth back onto the pillow, and carefully tucked her in.

"Do you want me to leave the light on for a few minutes?"

Beth hesitated, then nodded.

"Okay. Now, you just try to go back to sleep, and I'll come back in later, and turn the light off. How's that?"

"C-can't we leave it on all night?" Beth asked.

Carolyn hesitated, thinking about the nightmares that had plagued Beth in the months after she and Alan had separated, and how the only thing that had finally solved them was leaving the light on through the night. It had been less than a year since Beth had finally been able to start sleeping in darkness once again. Was it all about to start over? "All right," she said. "For tonight, we'll leave the light on. But just tonight. All right?"

Beth nodded, and Carolyn leaned down and kissed her on the cheek. "Now, go back to sleep, honey, and if you have another bad dream, you call me."

Beth said nothing, but turned over and drew the covers tightly around her. Carolyn straightened up, and looked at her daughter for a moment, wishing she could simply take Beth in with her and Phillip. But of course that could never happen. No matter how bad the nightmares had been, Beth had always refused to leave her own bed for the safety of her mother's. That would have been giving in to her fears, and Beth would never do that.

Giving the little girl a reassuring smile, Carolyn kissed her again, then quietly left the room, pulling the door closed behind her.

Alone, Beth rolled over again, and lay staring at the ceiling in the soft glow of the bedlamp.

She knew what had happened now; knew what had taken place during the time that had disappeared from her day.

She'd been on her way to visit her father, running away from the party—the horrible party where everything had gone so wrong—and she'd stopped at the mill.

Stopped just for a moment, hoping to find out if Amy was really there or not.

And then she'd gone on her way, but something had been different. The light had changed, and the sun had dropped over the horizon.

It was suddenly much later than she'd thought.

So instead of going to see her father, she'd come back home, climbing back up the trail on the hillside. No one had even missed her; no one had even known she was gone.

But now, after the dream, she knew exactly what she'd done.

She had found Amy, and told her what had happened at the party, told her how mean Jeff Bailey had been to her.

And Amy had gotten revenge.

It hadn't been she who had killed Jeff; she was sure of it.

If Beth had killed him, she would have remembered it.

So it had to have been Amy who killed him.

Beth reached up and switched out the light.

The darkness no longer frightened her, for now she had a friend. A friend named Amy, who liked the dark.

From now on, Beth wouldn't be alone anymore. There would be someone to talk to, someone to confide in.

Someone who understood her.

Eleven

The morning was bright and cool, and as Beth came slowly awake, she had a strange feeling of peace. Her nightmare of a few hours earlier was almost forgotten, and she lay comfortably in bed, her eyes closed, planning the day. Maybe she and Peggy Russell—

And then, as always happened on mornings when she woke up feeling happy and relaxed, the feeling of contentment fled.

She remembered where she was.

She wasn't back home in her bedroom on Cherry Street. She was still at Hilltop.

She was still at Hilltop, and she'd had a bad dream last night, in which she'd seen Jeff Bailey die.

Suddenly a shadow fell across her, and Beth's eyes snapped open. A few feet away, between her and the window, stood Tracy Sturgess.

"I know what you did," Tracy said, her voice so low that for a moment Beth wasn't quite sure she'd spoken at all.

She sat up in bed, and instinctively pulled the covers up around her chest.

Tracy was glaring at her angrily, but there was something in the half-smile on her lips that Beth found even more frightening than the words she had spoken.

"D-did what?" she stammered. The clock on her nightstand told her that it was only seven A.M. "What are you doing here?"

"I know what you did," Tracy repeated, louder this time. Now the smile widened into a malicious grin. "You killed Jeff, didn't you? You sneaked into the mill yesterday, and when he came down the stairs, you killed him."

Beth's eyes widened. "No—I—"

"I heard you," Tracy pressed. "Last night, when you were talking to your mother, I was out in the hall. And I heard everything you said!" There was a taunting lilt to her voice now that made Beth cower back against the headboard, clutching the covers even tighter.

"But I didn't do anything," she protested. "It was only a dream."

Tracy's eyes narrowed. "It wasn't either a dream. You just made that up to tell your mother. And she's dumb enough to believe you. But I'm not. And wait'll I tell my father!"

"Tell him what?" Beth asked.

"That you're crazy, and you killed Jeff Bailey just because he was teasing you at my party."

"But I didn't kill him," Beth said, her heart suddenly beating harder. "It . . . it was Amy who killed him."

Tracy's lips twisted into a scornful sneer. "Amy? You mean the ghost in the mill you were talking about?"

Beth nodded mutely.

"There's no such thing as ghosts," Tracy told her. "All you did was make up a story. But no one's going to believe you!"

"But it's true," Beth suddenly flared. "Amy's real, and she's my friend, and all she did was just try to help me. And if you don't watch out, maybe she'll kill you, too!"

The grin faded from Tracy's face. "Don't you say things like that," she hissed. "Don't you ever say things like that to me."

"I can say what I want," Beth replied, her fear washed away by her anger. "And you get out of my room."

"It's not your room," Tracy replied. "This is my house, and if I wanted to, I could take this room away from you. You shouldn't even be on this floor anyway—you should be upstairs where the servants used to live, because that's all you're good for."

"You take that back!" Beth shouted. She was out of the bed now, standing in her pajamas, her fists clenched.

"I won't take it back!" Tracy shouted. "I hate you, and I hate your mother, and I wish both of you were dead!" Suddenly she threw herself at Beth, her fingers reaching out to grab Beth's hair.

Beth ducked and tried to twist away, but it was too late. Tracy's body hurtled into her own, and she fell to the floor with Tracy on top of her. Then she felt Tracy's hands grabbing at her hair, pulling and jerking at it. With a violent lurch, she managed to roll over, and covered her face with her arms.

"I'll kill you!" she heard Tracy screaming.

And then, just as she was expecting Tracy to start clawing at her, she heard another voice.

"Beth? Beth, are you all—My God, what's happening in here?" A second later she felt Tracy's weight being lifted off her and opened her eyes to see her mother staring down at her.

And beyond her mother, she saw her stepfather, his hand clamped tightly on Tracy's forearm. Wiping at her face with one hand, she pulled herself together, then got to her feet.

"What on earth were you doing?" she heard her mother demand. "What's going on?"

Beth glanced at Tracy out of the corner of her eye, then shook her head. "Nothing," she said. "She . . . she wanted me to shut off my radio, and I wouldn't do it."

Carolyn turned to Tracy. "Well? Is that true?"

Tracy's chin jutted out, and she glared at Carolyn. "I don't have to answer you! You're not my mother!" Then she winced as her father's hand tightened on her arm.

"You do have to answer Carolyn," Phillip said, his voice calm but firm. "It's true that she's not your mother, but she's my wife, and you will respect that. Now, is what Beth said the truth?"

Tracy remained silent for another few seconds, her eyes flashing venomously at Beth. "No!" she said at last. "She didn't even have her dumb radio on! She was threatening to kill me, just like she already killed Jeff Bailey!"

As Beth's eyes widened, and her skin turned ashen, a silence fell over the room. Both Phillip and Carolyn stared at Tracy in shocked horror.

It was Phillip who finally spoke. "The only threat I heard was yours. Now, go to your room, and stay there until either Carolyn or

I tell you to come out. And in the future, stay out of Beth's room unless she invites you in."

"It's not her room—" Tracy protested, but her father let her go no further.

"That's enough, Tracy!"

Tracy's eyes glittered angrily, but she said nothing more. She stamped out of the room, slamming the door behind her. When she was gone, Carolyn sat down on the edge of the bed, and motioned Beth to join her.

"Did you threaten to kill Tracy?" she asked.

Beth hesitated, then nodded silently.

"But why?"

Beth's chin trembled, but she managed to keep herself under control. "B-because she said I killed Jeff Bailey," she whispered. "She came in, and said she knew what I did, and that she was going to tell Uncle Phillip."

"But you didn't do anything," Phillip interjected. "What did she think she knew?"

"She was listening last night when I was talking to Mom," Beth explained. "She heard me telling Mom about my dream, and said I was just making it all up."

Phillip's eyes darkened. "I see," he said. Then: "Excuse me, Carolyn. I think it's time my daughter and I had a private talk."

Before Carolyn could protest, he was gone. Beth, her eyes damp, looked up at her mother. "I'm sorry, Mom."

"So am I, darling," Carolyn replied. "I wish you and Tracy didn't fight and I'm sorry she's so mean to you. I guess you'll just have to do the same thing with Tracy that I do with Abigail. No matter what she says, and how much it hurts, you have to ignore it. After a while, if you don't react, it won't be any fun for Tracy anymore, and she'll stop."

"But why does she hate me?" Beth asked. "I never did anything to her."

Carolyn put her arms around her daughter, and drew her close. "It's not you, honey. That's what you have to understand. Right now, she'd be just as mean to anybody else who was living here. She's afraid we're going to take her father away from her, that's all."

"But I don't want to do that," Beth replied. "I already have a father. Doesn't she know that?"

"Of course she does." Carolyn rose from the bed and started toward the door. "But you have to understand that what Tracy knows doesn't really matter right now. It's what she feels. And she's still very angry that her father married me. So she's taking it out on you."

"But . . . but that's not fair," Beth said, unconsciously echoing the words Tracy had used only a few moments before.

"I know it," Carolyn agreed. "But that's the way life is. It isn't always fair, and it doesn't always make sense. But we still have to do the best we can." She smiled fondly at the little girl. "So why don't we forget all this and get dressed and go down to breakfast. Okay?"

Beth nodded. She said nothing, but when her mother had gone, instead of going to her closet to begin dressing, she went to the window, and gazed down over the village to the mill.

In the depths of her mind, Tracy's words still reverberated.

I know what you did.

Was it possible? Was it possible that just as she had seen Amy in the dream last night, seen Amy pushing Jeff, making him fall on the pick . . .

She shuddered slightly, and turned away from the window.

But still the thought lurked in her mind. .

What if Tracy was right? What if there were no Amy?

But there had to be. If Amy wasn't real, if she hadn't heard her, if she hadn't seen her in the dream, then that meant—

She shut the thought out of her mind, for if there were no Amy, then maybe Tracy was right.

Maybe she, Beth, really had killed Jeff.

But she wouldn't have . . . she *couldn't* have. . . .

Alan Rogers glanced at his watch, then signaled to the foreman to call the lunch hour. As the workmen moved from the heat of the day into the relative coolness of the mill itself, Alan began his normal twice-daily inspection of the job. He had found out long ago that it was impossible to hire workers with standards as high as his own, but he'd also understood that he couldn't demand as much of his crews as he demanded of himself. They, after all, were working for an hourly wage, and didn't share his fanaticism for getting things done right. To them, a job was a job, and what counted was the hours put in. For Alan, the work itself was more important than the money he earned. His satisfaction in getting the job done right usually outstripped his interest in squeezing out the last dollar of profit.

Today the work was going well. Already all the fence posts were in place, and by this afternoon, with any luck at all, the fence should be complete. It wouldn't be pretty—nothing more than sheets of plywood hastily nailed to the posts and stringers, but it would be effective. Tomorrow they could get back to the real work—the reconstruction.

He had come to the last post, and was about to join the rest of the crew in the shadowy interior, when he heard Beth calling to him. He looked up to see his daughter pedaling her bicycle furiously along River Road, leaning into the turn at Prospect Street with a lot more courage than Alan himself would have had, then jumping it up the curb as she barreled onto the grounds of the mill itself. As he watched, the rear wheel of the bike lost its traction and began to skid out of control, but Beth merely put a foot down, pivoted the bicycle in a neat Brodie, and came to a stop in front of him, grinning.

"Pretty good, hunh?"

Alan nodded appreciatively. "Very neat. But if you break your neck, don't coming whining to me. You're nuts."

"Didn't you ever Brodie your bike when you were a kid?"

"Of course I did," Alan agreed. "And I was nuts, too. So what brings you down here?"

"I came down to have lunch with you," Beth replied, holding up a brown bag that she'd fished out of the pouch slung under the racing seat on the bike. "Hannah made me some sandwiches. Peanut butter and jelly. Want one?"

"I might swap you for a tuna fish."

Beth made a face. "I hate tuna fish. Is that all you have?"

Alan chuckled. "Don't get picky. It may be tuna fish, but I made it myself."

"Big deal," Beth replied, rolling her eyes. "You probably icked it all up with mayonnaise, didn't you?"

Alan regarded his daughter with mock exasperation. "If you only came down here to pick on me, you can go right back home. I don't need any grief from any eleven-year-old smart-asses, thank you very much!"

Beth stuck out her tongue, but when Alan started back toward the mill, she followed along behind him. Grabbing a hard hat from the portable site shack, Alan dropped it over her head, then stepped aside to let her precede him through the door into the vast building. Beth promptly took the hat off, adjusted the headband so it wouldn't sink down over her eyes, then put it back on.

As soon as she stepped inside, her eyes went to the stairs at the far end of the mill.

"No," Alan said, as if reading her mind. "You can't go down there."

Beth's brow furrowed. "Why not? I just want to look."

"Because it's morbid," Alan told her. He opened his lunchbox and pulled out a sandwich, offering Beth half. She shook her head.

"But all I want to do is see where it happened," she pressed. "What's wrong with that?"

Alan sighed, knowing there was really no way to explain it to her. If he'd been her age, he'd have been dying to see the spot where the accident had happened, too. This morning, as he'd expected, there had been a steady stream of kids coming by the mill, some of them stopping to stare, others trying to look as though the last thing in the world they had come to see was the place where someone had died the day before. "There isn't any reason for you to see it," he said. "There's nothing there, anyway."

"Not even any blood?" Beth asked with innocent curiosity.

Alan swallowed, then concentrated on the sandwich, though he was suddenly losing his appetite for it. "Why don't we talk about something else? How's everybody up at your house?" Beth's eyes clouded, and Alan immediately knew that something had gone wrong that morning. "Want to talk about it?"

His daughter glanced at him, then shrugged. "It wasn't any big deal," she said. "I just had a fight with Tracy, that's all."

"Is that why you came down here? 'Cause things got too rough up there?"

"I don't know. Anyway, there isn't anyone home. They went over to the Baileys'."

"All of them?"

"Mom and Uncle Phillip. Tracy's got some friends over. And they're all talking about what happened to Jeff."

So much for changing the subject, Alan thought. And then, suddenly, he thought he understood. "Might be kind of neat if you could go back and tell 'em all what the spot looks like, hunh?"

Beth's eyes widened slightly. "Could I? Could I go down there just for a minute?"

Helplessly, Alan gave in. "All right. After lunch, I'll take you down. But just for a minute. Promise?"

Beth nodded solemnly. "I promise."

With the darkness washed away by the blazing worklights, the basement looked nothing like it had before. It was simply a vast expanse of space, very much like the main floor, except that down here the space was broken by the many columns that supported the floor above. As she looked out into the basement, Beth could hardly remember how terrifying it had been when it was dark. Now there was nothing frightening about it at all.

Except for the spot on the floor.

It was a slightly reddish brown, and spread from a spot a few yards from the bottom of the stairs. It looked to Beth as though someone had tried to clean it up, but there was still a lot left, soaked into the wooden floor.

Still, if her father hadn't told her what it was, she wasn't sure she would have known. Somehow, she had sort of expected it to be bright red, and glistening.

She stared at the spot for several long seconds, searching her mind for a memory.

But all that was there was the memory of the dream.

Surely, if she had killed Jeff herself, seeing the place where she had done it would have brought it all back.

And then, as she was about to turn away, her eyes scanned the rear wall, under the stairs. She frowned, then tugged at her father's arm. "What's that?" she asked.

Alan's eyes followed his daughter's pointing finger. For a moment he saw nothing—just a blank wall. Then, as he looked again, he realized that under the stairs the wall wasn't made out of concrete.

It looked to him like it was made out of metal.

He stepped into the shadows below the stairs, and took a closer look.

"Well, I'll be damned," he said softly.

"What is it, Daddy?" Beth asked. Suddenly her heart skipped a beat and she felt a slight thrill of anticipation.

"It looks like some kind of fire door," Alan replied. He reached up and felt in the darkness, and his fingers found a rail bolted to the concrete behind the metal. Moving his hands along the rail, he came to a metal roller.

He pounded on the metal, and heard a low echoing sound.

"Is it hollow?" Beth asked.

Alan nodded. "It sure seems like it's some kind of fire door. Give me a hand, and we'll see if we can open it."

Gingerly, Alan felt for the end of the door nearest the staircase, and curled his fingers around its edge. Then he leaned his weight into it, and tugged.

The door didn't budge.

Frowning, he stepped back, surveyed the door, then moved to the other end.

Near the ceiling, he found what he was looking for. A metal pin, protruding from the concrete. When he tried to remove it, it too held fast.

"What is it, Daddy?" Beth asked.

"Don't know," Alan muttered. "And it's going to take a couple of wrenches to find out."

"Is there another room back there?"

"That's what's weird," her father replied. "According to the plans I have, all that's back there is the loading dock, and it's supposed to be solid concrete."

"Then why would they need a fire door?"

"Good question. Unless it's not a fire door. It might be something else entirely. I'll be back in a minute."

As her father trotted up the stairs, Beth stared at the strange, barely visible door in fascination.

There was a room behind the door—she was sure of it.

And she knew what the room was.

It was Amy's room.

It was the room where Amy lived, and that's why, when she'd heard the strange voice the other day, it had sounded so faint.

It had been muffled by the door.

She moved closer to the door, letting her imagination run free.

There could be anything behind the door. She imagined an old forgotten room, still filled with the kind of furniture they sold in antique stores. It was probably an office of some kind, so there would be desks, and maybe a big black leather chair. There might even be one of those old-fashioned braided rugs still on the floor.

It would all be covered with dust, but there would still be papers on the desks, and stuff in the wastebasket, for in Beth's mind she was sure the room had simply been closed up one day, and forgotten. And then, when the mill had been closed, no one had even remembered that this room was there.

Suddenly she heard footsteps on the stairs, and her father reappeared, carrying a large monkey wrench.

"This should do it," he said, giving her a conspiratorial wink. "All set?"

Beth nodded, and stood back while Alan adjusted the wrench to the pin, then applied pressure to it.

The pin held for a moment, then squealed, and slowly began to turn. With some further effort, it fell away, and once more Alan gripped the end of the metal door and leaned his weight into it.

This time the door groaned and moved slightly. After two more pulls its rusty rollers screeched in protest, and it slid reluctantly to one side.

Instantly, a rush of ice-cold air flowed out of the gap.

Beth froze, the chill seeming to cut through her, and she could feel goose bumps rippling her skin as the hair on her neck stood on end. It was as if something physical had emerged from whatever lay behind the door. Beth's first instinct was to turn and run.

And then the blast of icy air stopped, almost as if it had never happened. She looked up at her father.

"What was that?" she asked, her voice trembling slightly.

"What?" Alan replied.

"The cold," Beth explained. "Didn't you feel the cold coming through the crack?"

Alan frowned slightly, then shook his head. "I didn't feel anything at all." He pulled on the door again, opening it far enough for them both to peer inside.

Alan shone his flashlight into the darkness beyond the metal door.

It was a room, perhaps twenty feet long and fifteen feet deep.

Its walls were blackened, and the floor was covered with a thick layer of dust.

It was completely empty.

Then, as Beth gazed around the long-forgotten room, she noticed a familiar odor in the stale air.

The little room smelled strongly of smoke.

Twelve

There was nothing comfortable about the silence that reigned in the Mercedes-Benz as Phillip maneuvered it up the long drive and brought it to a stop in front of Hilltop. It was as if, by mutual consent, all of them were waiting until they were once more inside the mansion before they faced the argument that all of them now knew was inevitable.

For Carolyn, it was particularly difficult, for she was in the unique position of finding herself in agreement with her mother-in-law, albeit for reasons that Abigail would never understand. Still, the fact remained that for the first time Carolyn was about to side with the woman who hated her, against the husband who loved her.

She waited for Phillip to come around and open the door for her, and offered him an uncertain smile that was part gratitude and part apology. Getting out of the car, she started up the front steps. Hannah opened the door for her, and she nodded a greeting to the old woman before crossing the foyer to turn right down the wide corridor that led to the library. Beyond the French doors and the terrace outside, she could see Tracy and three of her friends playing tennis.

Beth was nowhere to be seen.

She dropped her purse on a table, and glanced at the fireplace, where—as always—a fire was laid, ready to be lit. For a moment she was tempted to put a match to it, despite the warmth of the day. But warming the room even further would do nothing to alleviate the chill that was emanating from Abigail.

"It won't help," Abigail said as she entered the room, apparently reading Carolyn's mind. Then, stripping off her gloves and expertly removing the pin from her veiled hat, she turned to her son. "I don't think there can be any question now of continuing with your project. We shall order Mr. Rogers to begin closing the mill tomorrow."

Phillip's brows rose a fraction of an inch, and his arms folded over his chest. He leaned back against the desk that had once been his father's. "Indeed?" he asked, "And when did it become my project, Mother? Until yesterday, it was our project, unless I'm suddenly getting senile."

Abigail's sharp eyes raked over her son, and her lips curved into a tightly cynical smile. "If that remark was intended to suggest that I'm losing my grip, I don't appreciate it. I've simply changed my mind, and in light of what happened to Jeff Bailey—"

"What happened to Jeff Bailey was an accident, Mother. We've seen the reports, and there's nothing to suggest there was anything more to it than the simple facts. He tripped, and fell on a pick. That's that."

"He tripped and fell on a tool on the precise spot where your brother tripped and fell on a tool. Don't you consider that a bit more than a coincidence?"

"No, Mother, I don't," Phillip replied, his voice and manner clearly indicating that his mind was made up on the subject.

But Abigail was not about to give in so easily. "I'm sorry you can't see that which is perfectly clear," she went on. "But it doesn't really matter, does it? I shall speak to Mr. Rogers myself."

"Will you?" Phillip asked. There was a hardness in his tone that neither Carolyn nor Abigail had ever before heard. Carolyn gazed curiously at her husband, while Abigail's eyes suddenly flickered with uncertainty. "You may certainly speak to Alan if you wish, but I hope you understand that he won't act on your orders. He's working for me, not for you."

The uncertainty vanished from Abigail's eyes. She regarded her son with undisguised fury. "You?" she asked, making no effort to conceal her contempt. "Working for you? How dare you suggest that my wishes will not be obeyed. Particularly when all I am doing is seeing to it that your father's own wishes are honored."

"Enough, Mother," Phillip said, his voice suddenly sounding tired. "You might be able to buffalo everyone else that way, but it won't work with me. I've read Father's will. He left me in charge of all Sturgess business enterprises, and it is my decision to go ahead with the mill project. If you want to give in to Father's superstitions, that's up to you. But don't expect me to go along with them."

"Your brother's memory should mean something to you," Abigail flared.

But Phillip only shook his head. "My brother's memory?" he repeated. "Mother, I wasn't even born until a year after Conrad Junior died. And I wouldn't have been born at all if he hadn't died."

Abigail, looking as if she'd been struck, sank into one of the wing chairs. "Phillip, that isn't true!"

"Isn't it?" Phillip demanded. "I'm not a fool, Mother. Don't you think I know that I was nothing more than a replacement for Conrad? God knows, you and Father certainly never let me forget it. I grew up being compared to a brother I never even met! And now you want me to close down the restoration of the mill, simply because there have been two accidents there in the space of forty years? Well, you can forget it, Mother. What you choose to do is your own decision, but I won't be bound by Father's superstitions."

Abigail sat coiled in her chair like a serpent ready to strike. "I'll stop you," she hissed. "I'll use everything in my power to stop you from finishing that mill."

"Fine!" Phillip said in a mild tone. "Start calling your lawyers, and mobilizing your forces. But you won't get anywhere. The power resides in me. Or have you forgotten that particular Sturgess tradition?"

Carolyn, who had said nothing throughout the exchange, preferring to remain as invisible as Abigail sometimes made her feel, suddenly spoke for the first time. "Tradition?" she asked. "Phillip, what are you talking about?"

Phillip turned to face her, a glint of triumph playing in his eyes. "Something I'm sure Mother's never mentioned to you. In my family, while the women have always been strong—we Sturgesses seem to attract strong women—there has always been a carefully drawn line. And that line, as Mother knows perfectly well, is the line where personal affairs stop, and business affairs begin. There has never been a female Sturgess who has had anything to say about our business affairs. That is always left up to the men. So when Father died, sole control over the family's assets passed to me. In short," he finished, smiling grimly, "Mother can make my life as miserable as she wants, and scream to her lawyers as much as she wants. But in the end, there isn't a thing she can do. When it comes to the mill, or anything else outside of this house, she is totally without power. Indeed, Mother," he added, his voice taking on the same chill Carolyn had felt so often from the old woman, "if I chose to, I could throw you out of this house."

Abigail was on her feet again, her eyes blazing. "How dare you?" she demanded of her son. "How dare you speak to me that way? And in front of her, of all people?" She wheeled around, and the full force of her anger was focused on Carolyn. "This is all your fault," she went on. "Before Phillip met you, he never would have talked to me this way. He would have asked for my advice, and heeded my words. But not anymore. You've hypnotized him! You've come into our lives—you and your common little daughter—and done your best to take Phillip away from us. But you won't succeed! Do you understand me? Somehow, I shall find a way to stop you!" She started toward the door, her anger making her stagger slightly, even though she leaned heavily on her cane. Carolyn took a step toward her, wanting to reach out to her, to steady her. But Phillip shook his bead, and made a gesture that kept Carolyn where she was.

A moment later they were alone, with Abigail's fury hanging between them like a cloud.

"I'm sorry," Phillip said. "She shouldn't have attacked you and Beth. But she knows there's nothing she can do to stop me from finishing the mill project, so she had to turn elsewhere. And you were convenient." He moved toward her, his arms spread wide, but instead of stepping forward to meet him, Carolyn turned away, and sank into the chair Abigail had vacated only seconds earlier.

"Maybe she's right," Carolyn replied. Conflicting emotions were battering at her now. All the control she'd developed so carefully in the months since she'd moved to Hilltop seemed to be deserting her at the moment she needed it most. "Maybe our marrying *was* a mistake, Phillip. Maybe you should never have met me. Maybe you should have stayed away from Westover for the rest of your life."

"You don't believe that," Phillip said, his face ashen, his eyes pleading. "Darling, you can't mean that!"

"Can't I? I don't know what I mean. But I can't go on much longer living with a woman who hates me. And it isn't just me. It's Beth, too. Phillip, Beth knows how Abigail and Tracy feel about her. Even though she tries to pretend it isn't happening, she feels every slight they inflict on her! I'd hoped we could be a family—all of us. But it's not like that! As long as we've been married, it's been like a war, with Beth and me on one side, and Abigail and Tracy on the other. And you're caught in the middle."

"Well, at least the sides are balanced," Phillip said in a wry but futile attempt to defuse the situation. "At least you're not ganging up on me!"

Suddenly Carolyn laughed, but it was a high-pitched, brittle parody of her normal laughter, and Phillip realized how close she was to slipping into hysteria. "Aren't we?" she asked. "Abigail made a mistake just now, but I don't think she knows it. On the subject of the mill, I would have sided with her. Isn't that funny? Isn't that just about the funniest thing you ever heard?" And then she crumpled in her chair, sobbing.

Phillip came to her then, kneeling by the chair and gathering her into his arms. Carolyn neither resisted him nor moved closer to him, and even as he held her, he could sense the loneliness she was feeling.

"It's all right, darling," he whispered, stroking her hair gently. "We'll get through this. Somehow, we'll put all of this behind us. But you mustn't even think of leaving me without you, I'd have nothing."

"Nothing?" Carolyn echoed. "You'd have your mother, and your daughter, and Hilltop, and all the rest of everything the Sturgesses have always had. You'd hardly miss me at all."

Phillip groaned silently, and held her closer. "It's not true, darling. The only thing that matters to me is you. You and our baby."

Carolyn stiffened in his arms. For that moment—that moment of overwhelming anguish she'd forgotten about the baby. She drew back slightly, and tipped her face up to look at Phillip. In his eyes, she could see his love for her, and she felt a glimmer of hope.

"You do love me, don't you?" she asked, the need for his reassurance gripping her once more.

"More than anything," Phillip replied.

"And the baby? You really do want the baby? You haven't just been saying that for my sake?"

Phillip smiled fondly at her. "How could I not want the baby?" he asked. "It's going to be our baby. *Ours!* It won't be anything anyone can use to try to drive us apart. In fact, it might even help. It will be Mother's grandson, and she'll fall in love with him the moment he's born."

Deep in Carolyn's mind, a warning sounded. "Son?" she asked. "What makes you so sure it will be a boy?"

"What else can it be?" Phillip asked. He was grinning broadly now, the crisis behind him. "I've already got a daughter, and so have you. And I need a son. After all, if it's not a boy, who will there be to carry on the Sturgess line?"

The Sturgess line.

The phrase echoed in Carolyn's mind. She tried to tell herself that he hadn't meant anything by it, that he'd meant it as a joke. But deep inside, the warning sounded stronger.

He wants an heir. He wants a boy, to name after himself, and to raise in his own image. Abigail's right. He's a Sturgess, and I mustn't ever forget it.

"And what if it's a girl?" she asked, careful to keep her tone as lightly bantering as his had been.

"Then I'll spoil her," Phillip assured her. "I'll give her everything she wants, and treat her like the princess she'll be, and she'll be the happiest little girl who ever lived."

But she'll be a girl, Carolyn said to herself. And to the Sturgesses, girls just aren't quite as good. Nice to have around, but just not quite as good.

She kissed Phillip on the cheek, and stood up. "Well," she said as blithely as possible, "I shall certainly do my best to produce a boy for you. But if I fail," she added, "it will be your own fault. As I understand it, the gene that determines sex comes directly from the father. If the Sturgesses want boys, their chromosomes better be able to handle it."

Phillip nodded affably, and his eyes once again took on the gentleness that Carolyn had fallen in love with. There wasn't a trace left of the cold anger with which he had told his mother that she was little more than a guest in her own home. "And what about the mill?" he asked. "Are you really planning to form some kind of unholy alliance with my mother?"

Carolyn hesitated, then shook her head. "I suppose not," she said. "For one thing, in their own way, my reasons for keeping it closed are just as superstitious as hers. And I have a feeling that she'd change her position before accepting support from me anyway. So I'll just stay out of it, bite my tongue, and hope for the best."

But as she slowly climbed the stairs and started toward the master suite at the end of the hall, Carolyn wondered, once more, what the best would be. Perhaps, indeed, she had been right in her hysterical outburst, and the marriage—no matter how much she and Phillip loved each other—was doomed to failure already.

Or perhaps (and much more likely, she told herself) she was simply suffering from her pregnancy, which, despite her insistence that she was feeling fine, was beginning to bother her. Though she wouldn't admit it to Phillip, she was secretly glad that Dr. Blanchard bad insisted that she get at least two hours' rest every day.

If nothing else, at least it provided her with an escape from the tensions of the house.

She slipped into the bedroom, and closed the door behind her. Lying down on the bed, she stretched luxuriously, and then let her eyes wander out the window to the enormous maple that stood a few yards away, its leaves completely blocking out the sunlight.

Concentrating on the cool peacefulness of the greenery, she drifted into sleep.

*   *   *

At the other end of the house, in her rooms that were almost an exact mirror image of those her daughter-in-law occupied, Abigail Sturgess was wakeful and wary. She was staring out the window, her eyes focused angrily on the forbidding building that had represented so much tragedy for her family.

More and more, she was becoming convinced that her husband had been right.

There was something evil about the mill, and though she wasn't yet sure what it was, she had made up her mind to find out.

Beth pedaled away from the mill, but instead of heading out River Road to start the long climb back up to Hilltop, she turned the other way, riding slowly along Prospect Street, then turning up Church toward the little square in the middle of the village. Once there, she slowed her bike, looking around to see if any of her old friends might be playing softball on the worn grass. But the square was empty, and Beth rode on.

Almost without thinking about it, she turned right on Main Street, then left on Cherry. A minute later she had come to a halt in front of the little house in which she'd lived until she had moved to Hilltop.

The house, which had always seemed big to her, looked small now, and the paint was peeling off its siding. In the front yard, weeds were sprouting in the lawn, and the bushes that her mother had planted along the front of the house didn't have the neatly trimmed look of the gardens at Hilltop.

But still, it was home to Beth, and she had a sudden deep longing to go up to the front door, and ask whoever lived there now if she could go into her own room, just for a few minutes.

But of course she couldn't—it wasn't her room anymore, and besides, it wouldn't look the same as it had when she had lived there. The new people would have changed it, and it just wouldn't feel right.

She got back on the bike, and continued down the block, looking at all the familiar houses. At the corner, she turned right again, then left on Elm Street.

In front of the Russells' house, Peggy was playing hopscotch with Rachel Masin, and Beth braked her bike to a stop.

"Hi," she said. "What are you guys doing?"

Peggy, whose lager was in one corner of the number-four square, was concentrating hard on keeping her balance in the number-five, while she leaned down to pick up the key chain she had won from Beth herself last summer. Finally, snagging the chain with one finger and taking a deep breath, she hopped quickly down the last three squares and out of the pattern.

"Playing hopscotch," she announced. "And I'm winning. Rachel can't even get past number three."

"But I'm using a rock for a lager, like you're supposed to," Rachel protested. "Anybody can do it with a key chain. They always stay right where you throw them."

"Can I play?" Beth asked. She leaned the bike against a tree, and fished in her pocket for something to use as a lager. All she came up with was the key chain—identical to the one she had lost to Peggy—that held her house key. "I'll start at one."

Peggy looked at her with open hostility. "How come you're not out riding your horse? Peter says you go out every day now."

Beth's heart sank. Why couldn't Peter have kept his mouth shut? Now Peggy thought she was just like Tracy. "I don't have a horse," she said. "It's Uncle Phillip's horse, and all he's doing is teaching me to ride it. And we don't go out every day. In fact, we've only been out a couple of times."

"That's not what my brother says," Peggy challenged as if daring Beth to contradict her big brother.

"Well, I don't care what Peter says," Beth began, and then stopped, realizing she sounded just like Tracy Sturgess. "I . . . I mean we don't really go out every day. Just sometimes." Then she had an idea. "You could go with us sometime if you want to." Peggy said nothing, but her face blushed pink, and Beth belatedly remembered what Peter had told her. "Uncle Phillip wouldn't fire Peter," she blurted out. "Really he wouldn't."

The red in Peggy's face deepened, and her eyes brimmed with tears. "Why don't you just go away?" she demanded. "We were having fun until you showed up!"

"But we're supposed to be friends," Beth protested. "You're supposed to be my best friend!"

"That was when you lived on Cherry Street. You were just like us then. But now you live up on the hill. Why don't you be friends with Tracy Sturgess?"

"I hate Tracy!" Beth shot back, on the verge of tears herself now. "I hate her, and she hates me! And I'm not any different than I ever was! It's not fair, Peggy! It's just not fair!"

Rachel Masin, looking from Peggy to Beth, then back to Peggy, suddenly stooped down and picked up her lager. "I gotta go home, Peggy," she said hurriedly. "My—" She searched around for an excuse, and seized on the first one that came to mind. "My mom says I have to baby-sit my little brother." Without waiting for either of the other girls to reply, she ran off down the street and around the corner.

"Now look what you did," Peggy said, glowering at Beth. "We were having a good time till you came along."

"But I didn't do anything. How come you don't like me anymore?"

Peggy hesitated for a moment, then planted her fists on her hips, and stared at Beth.

Beth stared right back.

The two girls stood perfectly still, their eyes fixed on each other, each of them determined not to be the first to blink. But after thirty seconds that seemed like ten minutes, Beth felt her eyes beginning to sting.

"You're gonna blink," Peggy said, seeing the strain in Beth's face.

"No I'm not!"

"You are too. And if you do, you owe me a Coke. That's the rules."

Beth renewed her concentration, but the harder she tried not to blink, the more impossible it became. Finally giving up, she closed her eyes and rubbed at them with her fists.

"You owe me a Coke," Peggy crowed. "Come on—you can ride me down to the drugstore."

The spat forgotten, Peggy climbed onto the rack that was mounted over the back fender of the bike, and wobbling dangerously, Beth pedaled them away. Ten minutes later they were in their favorite booth in the rear corner of the drugstore, sipping on cherry Cokes.

"What's it really like up there?" Peggy asked. "I mean, what's it like living in that house? Isn't it scary?"

Beth hesitated, then shook her head. "It's not really scary. But you have to get used to it. The worst part is Tracy Sturgess."

Peggy nodded wisely. "I know. Peter says she's the meanest person he ever met."

"She is," Beth agreed. "And she really hates me."

"How come?"

Beth shrugged. "I don't know. I guess she thinks Mom and I are just hicks. She's always acting like she's better than everybody." Then she grinned. "But wait till next year—she's going to be going to school right here!"

Peggy's eyes widened in astonishment. "You mean she isn't going back to private school?"

"That's what I heard."

"Wow," Peggy breathed. "Wait'll the other kids hear about that!"

Then she snickered maliciously. "And wait till the first day of school. I bet everybody cuts her dead."

"I hope they do," Beth said, her voice edged with bitterness. "I hope they're all just as mean to her as she is to me."

Peggy nodded, then sighed despondently. "But they prob'ly won't be. They'll prob'ly start kissing up to her just because she's a Sturgess." She sucked the last of the Coke through the straw, then tipped the glass up so that the crushed ice slid into her mouth. She munched on it for a minute, then looked across the table at Beth again. "Do you know what really happened to Jeff Bailey?"

Beth felt a slight chill go through her. "I—he just tripped and fell, didn't he?"

"Search me," Peggy replied. "But I heard my parents talking about it last night, and they kept talking about the other boy that got killed in the mill—"

"Uncle Phillip's brother," Beth put in.

Peggy nodded. "Anyway, my mom said that she didn't think it was a coincidence at all. She said there's always been stories about the mill, and she thinks maybe there's something in there."

Beth hesitated, then nodded. "There is," she said.

Peggy stared at her. "How do you know?" she asked.

Beth hesitated, then made up her mind. "Come up to Hilltop tomorrow, and I'll show you something. And I'll tell you what's in the mill. But you have to promise not to tell anyone else, all right? It's a secret."

Peggy nodded eagerly. "I promise."

"Cross your heart?"

"Cross my heart," Peggy repeated. "Cross my heart, and hope to die."

Thirteen

Eileen Russell looked at her daughter doubtfully, then shook her head as she slid two perfectly fried eggs out of the skillet onto the child's plate. "I don't know. I just don't like the idea of Peter getting into trouble over it."

"But Peter *won't* get in trouble," Peggy insisted. "Beth promised.

She even said I could go riding with them sometime, if I wanted to. With her and Mr. Sturgess!''

Eileen's gaze shifted to her son. "Well?" she asked. "Does that sound like Mr. Sturgess to you?''

Peter shrugged noncommittally, but at the pleading look in his sister's eyes, he nodded his head. "He's pretty nice, and he takes Beth riding sometimes. I don't think he'd care if Peg went along.'' Then he grinned. "But Tracy'd piss her pants. She hates it bad enough when her dad goes riding with Beth. If Peg was along— she'd shit.''

"Watch your language, young man,'' Eileen said, more out of habit than any particular prudery. She turned the matter over in her mind once more. She knew how much Peggy had missed Beth over the last few months, but her main concern was still that nothing threaten Peter's job. Jobs, particularly in the summer, were scarce, and they needed the money. Her job hostessing at the Red Hen barely covered the bills, and if something should happen to Peter's job—

Finally she decided to compromise, and call Carolyn Sturgess. Except that even something as simple as that suddenly presented a problem. It was stupid, and Eileen knew it. After all, when they'd been growing up together, Carolyn Deaver had been one of her best friends, and after Dan Russell walked out on her about the same time Carolyn had divorced Alan Rogers, they'd become even closer.

But then Carolyn had married Phillip Sturgess, and moved up to the mansion on top of the hill, and everything had changed.

Still, Eileen had to admit that part of the problem was her own fault. She'd gone up to Hilltop a couple of times, but the very size of the house had made her uncomfortable, and old Mrs. Sturgess had been blatantly rude to her. Finally she'd stopped going, telling herself that from now on, she'd invite Carolyn to her own house.

Except she'd never really done it. She'd tried to tell herself that she just kept putting it off because she was busy, but she knew that the real reason was that in comparison to Hilltop, her house was little more than a slum. And after getting used to the splendor of the mansion, Carolyn would be sure to notice the shortcomings of Eileen's place. So the invitation had never been issued, and as the months went by, Eileen thought about it less and less.

Still, there was no reason why Peggy and Beth's friendship should end simply because their mothers' had withered. She picked up the receiver and dialed the number that was still written in pencil on the wall next to the phone. To her relief, Carolyn herself answered the phone on the second ring, sounding sleepy. With a sinking heart,

Eileen realized that there was no longer any reason for Carolyn to be up by seven A.M.

"It's Eileen," she said. "Eileen Russell. Did I wake you?"

Instantly, the sleepiness was gone from Carolyn's voice. "Eileen! It's been months!"

"I know," Eileen replied. "And I'm sorry. But—well, you know how it goes."

There was an instant's hesitation before she heard Carolyn's reply, and some of the enthusiasm seemed to have gone out of her voice. "Yes," she said. "of course. I . . . I understand, Eileen."

"The reason I'm calling," Eileen plunged on, "is that Beth ran into Peggy yesterday, and invited her to come up to Hilltop this morning. I just wanted to be sure it wouldn't be any problem."

"Problem?" Carolyn echoed. "Eileen, it would be wonderful. Beth's missed Peggy so much, and so have I. You know she's welcome here anytime."

Suddenly Eileen felt ashamed of herself. Carolyn hadn't changed— hadn't changed at all. Why had she been so sure she had? Or was she herself busy being a snob, attributing to Carolyn airs that she herself would have taken on in the same situation? She had to admit that the possibility existed.

"Okay," she said. "She'll be up sometime in the middle of the morning." She hesitated, then went on. "And maybe this afternoon I could come up myself. We haven't had a talk for a long time."

"Could you?" Carolyn asked. "Oh, Eileen, that would be wonderful. What time?"

Eileen thought quickly. "How about three-ish? I have to do lunch at the Hen, but it's a split shift. I don't have to be back until seven."

"Great!" Carolyn agreed.

When she hung up a moment later, Eileen grinned happily at Peggy. "Looks like the drought's over," she said. "You can go up anytime you want."

Peggy, winded from the hike up the hill, paused when she came through the gates of Hilltop, and stared at the mansion while she caught her breath. It still seemed to her impossible that anybody could really live in it. But Beth? That was really weird. Beth should still be living on Cherry Street, where they could run back and forth between each other's houses four or five times a day. Up here, just the driveway was longer than the whole distance between their houses used to be.

She started toward the front door, then changed her mind, and skirted around to the far end of the house. Somewhere, she knew, there had to be a back door, and all her life she'd been used to using her friends' back doors. You only went to the front door on special occasions.

Finally she found the little terrace behind the kitchen, and knocked loudly on the screen door. A moment later, Beth herself appeared on the other side of the door. "I knew you'd come around here," she said, holding the door open so Peggy could come into the kitchen. "Want a doughnut or something?"

Peggy nodded mutely, and Beth helped herself from the plate on the kitchen table, handing one to the other girl. "Come on," she said. "Let's get out of here. I want to show you something." They pushed the screen door open, and let it slam behind them, Beth calling out an apology even before Hannah could admonish her. Then, with Peggy following behind, Beth led her back around the corner of the house, and across the lawn toward the trail to the mausoleum.

Patches snorted, pawed at the stable floor, then stretched her neck out over the half-door, whinnying eagerly.

"Not yet," Tracy Sturgess told the big mare. "Not till I'm done grooming you." She gave the horse's lead a quick jerk, but instead of obediently backing away from the door, the horse only snorted again, and tossed her head jerking the lead from Tracy's hand.

"Stop it!" Tracy snapped, grabbing for the lead, but hissing. "Peter! Come make Patches hold still."

"In a minute," Peter called from the other end of the stable.

"Now!" Tracy demanded. She moved carefully around Patches, then grasped the horse's halter, and tried to pull her back into the stall. Again, the horse snorted, reared slightly, and tried to pull away.

"What's wrong with you?" Tracy asked. Then, her hand still clutching the halter, she looked out into the paddock to see what had attracted the mare's attention. The paddock, though, was empty.

Tracy raised her eyes, and then, past the rose garden, saw the movement that had distracted the horse.

It was Beth, walking across the lawn with someone else, a girl Tracy didn't recognize. Tracy frowned, then jerked the horse's lead again. Patches whinnied a loud protest, but a moment later Peter came into the stall, took the lead from Tracy, and gently pulled the animal away from the door. Tracy remained where she was, staring out at the retreating figures of the two girls.

"Who's that?" she asked, her back still to Peter.

"Who?"

"That girl with Beth."

Peter shrugged. "My sister. Her name's Peggy."

Now Tracy turned around to glare angrily at the stableboy. "Who cares what her name is? What's she doing up here?"

Peter reddened slightly. He'd known this would happen. Now he'd be in trouble for sure. "Beth invited her up."

"Who said she could do that?" Tracy demanded. "This isn't her house. She doesn't have the right to invite people up here."

"Her mom said it was okay. She said Peggy could come up anytime she wanted to."

"Well, she can't!" Tracy exclaimed. "And I'm going to tell her so!" She stamped out of the stall, leaving Peter to finish the job she'd begun, then ran through the rose garden and around the corner of the house just in time to see Beth and Peggy starting up the trail toward the mausoleum.

She was about to call out to them, and tell Peggy Russell to go home, when she changed her mind. Maybe it would be more fun to follow them, and find out what they were doing.

Peggy stood staring in awe at the strange marble structure that was the tomb of the Sturgesses. "Wow," she breathed. "What is it?"

Beth explained the mausoleum as best she could, then pulled Peggy away. "But this isn't what I wanted to show you," she said. "It's down here. Come on."

They started down the overgrown path on the other side of the mausoleum, walking carefully, their feet crunching on the thick bed of fallen leaves and twigs that covered the old trail. Here and there the path seemed to Peggy to disappear completely, and several times they had to scramble over fallen trees. And then, just as Peggy was sure the trail was coming to an end, it suddenly branched off to the left. Peggy looked around. At the place where the two paths converged, she spotted a sign, old and rusty, its paint peeling away, hanging crookedly on a tree.

PRIVATE PROPERTY
NO TRESPASSING

"Maybe we'd better come back," Peggy said, her voice dropping to a whisper as she glanced around guiltily.

"It doesn't mean us," Beth replied. "It's just marking the place where Uncle Phillip's property starts. It's for people coming up the hill, not going down. Come on."

With Peggy following somewhat reluctantly now, Beth started along the track that would lead to the little meadow.

"Where are you going?" Peggy asked.

"You'll see," Beth replied. "Don't worry."

"But what if we get lost?" Peggy argued. "How do you know

which trail to follow?'' More and more, she was wishing they hadn't come down here at all. It seemed to her that the woods were closing in around her. She wished she were back up on the top of the hill where at least everything was open.

"I've been down here before,'' Beth replied. "Mom and I came down here one day, and Uncle Phillip and I came out here on the horses. Stop being chicken.''

Peggy hesitated, wondering what to do. Maybe she should turn around, and try to find her own way back. But if she did that, she'd have to go by herself.

Making up her mind, she followed Beth. They had gone only about a hundred yards when Beth stopped. "Look,'' she said softly. "Here it is.''

Peggy stared around the little meadow. Saplings stood here and there in the clearing, and the underbrush came nearly to her waist. But there didn't seem to her to be any difference between this meadow and any of the others that dotted the woods around Westover.

"What's so special about this?'' Peggy complained. "It's just a clearing, isn't it?''

Beth shook her head, and led Peggy across the meadow to the place where she'd found the small depression last time she had been there.

She pointed to it silently, and Peggy frowned in puzzlement. "What is it?''

"It's a grave,'' Beth said.

Peggy's eyes widened. She glanced around nervously, wishing she were somewhere else. "H-how do you know?'' she breathed.

"I just know,'' Beth replied. "I found it the other day.''

"Whose is it?'' Peggy whispered, her wide eyes fixed on the odd depression. "Who's buried here? Is it one of the Sturgesses?''

Beth shook her head. "They're all buried up in the mausoleum. I think—'' She hesitated, then took a deep breath. "I think this is where Amy's buried.''

"Amy?'' Peggy repeated blankly. "Who's Amy? What's her last name?''

"I . . . I don't know,'' Beth admitted.

The two girls stood silently for a moment, their eyes -fixed on the odd sunken spot.

"Maybe it isn't a grave at all,'' Peggy suggested. "If it was a grave, wouldn't there be a headstone or something?''

Beth's eyes flicked up the hill, toward the spot where the mausoleum lay hidden in the woods. "There isn't any headstone because they didn't want anyone to know,'' she said in a whisper. "They didn't want anyone to know who she was, or that she's even here.''

"But who is she?" Peggy pressed.

Beth turned to look at Peggy, and there was something in her eyes that made Peggy feel suddenly nervous.

"She's my friend," Beth said.

"Y-your friend?" Peggy repeated. "But . . . but I thought she was dead.''

"She is," Beth agreed. "But she's still alive, too. She lives in the mill.''

"The mill?" Peggy echoed. Suddenly she felt a small knot of fear forming in her stomach.

Beth nodded, her mind racing now. "I think she must have worked there," she said, her voice quiet. "I think something terrible happened to her, and they buried her up here. But she's not up here. Not really. She's still in the mill.''

Peggy watched Beth warily. Something seemed to have come over her now. Though Beth was looking at her, Peggy wasn't sure her friend was seeing her. And what she was saying didn't make any sense at all.

In fact, it sounded crazy.

"B—but what's she doing in the mill?" Peggy finally stammered. "What does she want?"

Beth's eyes darkened. "She wants to kill them," she said at last. "Just like she killed Jeff Bailey.''

As the words sank into Peggy's mind, the knot of fear grew, reaching out into her arms and legs, making her knees tremble.

"Why?" she whispered. "Why would she kill Jeff?"

Beth heard the words, and as her eyes remained fixed on what she was now certain was Amy's grave, she began to understand. She remembered the party, and the way Tracy and her friends had treated her.

She remembered the humiliation, and the pain.

"Because he was mean to me," she said softly. "He was mean to me, so she killed him.'' The words became the truth in her own mind even as she spoke them. For her, Amy was real now. "She's my friend, Peggy. Don't you understand? She's my best friend.''

Peggy felt her heart beating faster. "But she's dead, Beth," she protested. "She's not even alive, and you don't even know who she is. How can she be your best friend?''

But Beth wasn't listening to her. In fact, Peggy wasn't even sure Beth could hear her anymore. Slowly, one step at a time, Peggy began backing away. If Beth noticed, she gave no sign, for her eyes were still fixed on the depression in the ground that she had decided was a grave.

But it wasn't anything, Peggy told herself. It was just a little dip in the ground where the grass seemed dried up, not bright green like the rest of the meadow, and there wasn't anything there. Nothing at all.

She backed up another three steps, then turned and fled from the meadow back into the woods, hurtling back along the path toward the "No Trespassing" sign. But when she got there, she didn't turn right, up the hill toward the mausoleum.

Instead, she turned left, and began thrashing her way down the hillside toward the river below.

Beth stood rooted to the spot, staring at the grave. Unaware that Peggy was gone now, she began telling Peggy about the dream she'd had—the dream that was like a memory.

"I saw it," she said. "I was in the mill, under the stairs. And I heard something, and waited. And then Jeff came down the stairs, and he . . . he died. But it wasn't me that killed him. It was Amy. There's a little room under the stairs, and that's where Amy lives. But she came out of the room, and she killed Jeff. And I wasn't scared," she finished. "I watched Amy kill Jeff, and I wasn't scared at all."

And then, as she tore her eyes away from the grave and looked around for Peggy, the silence of the forest was shattered by the sound of laughter.

Tracy Sturgess stepped into the little clearing, her mocking eyes fixed on Beth.

Beth, her own eyes suddenly clearing, felt herself flushing red with humiliation. Had Tracy just gotten there, or had she been following them all along, listening to them and watching them? "How long have you been there?" she asked, her voice quavering now.

Tracy laughed cruelly. "Just long enough to find out you're crazy!" she said.

"I'm not crazy," Beth flared. "There's a grave here, and Peggy saw it too! Didn't you, Peggy?" She turned around, and discovered that Peggy was no longer there.

Tracy snickered. "She left. And you better get out of here, too. If you don't, the ghost might get you!"

Beth looked frantically around, searching for Peggy, but there was no sign of her. "Where is she?" she demanded. "Where's my friend?"

"She isn't your friend." Tracy sneered. "When she found out how crazy you are, she ran like a scared rabbit." Then, her mocking laughter echoing strangely in the bright morning sunlight, she disappeared back into the woods.

Beth stood still, her eyes flooding with tears of anger and humiliation. Then she sank down into the coolness of the grass, drawing her knees up to her chest.

They didn't believe her. Peggy didn't believe her, and Tracy thought she was crazy.

But it was true.

She *knew* it was true!

Her sobs slowly subsided, and finally she sat up. Her eyes fixed on the small depression in the earth, and she tried to figure out how she could prove that she was right.

But there wasn't any way. Even if she dug up the grave and found Amy's bones, they still wouldn't believe her.

Almost unconsciously, her fingers began probing at the soft earth, as if looking for something. And then, a moment later, her right hand touched something hard and flat, buried only an inch below the surface.

She began scraping the dirt away, exposing a weathered slab of stone. It was deeply pitted, its cracks and crevices packed with the rich brown soil, and Beth at had no idea what it might be. But then, as she scraped more of the earth away, the slab began to take shape.

One edge was rough and jagged, but from that edge, the stone had been worked into a smooth, clean semicircular curve, its edges trimmed in a simple bevel. After a few minutes, Beth had cleared the last of the dirt off its surface, and managed to force her fingers under the stone's edge. When she tried to lift it, though, it held fast, and all she succeeded in doing was to break a fingernail, and bare the knuckles of her left hand. Wincing with pain, she wiped her injured hand as clean as she could, then held the smarting knuckles to her mouth. While she waited for the pain to ease, she searched the clearing for a stick, and finally found one that looked thick enough lying a few feet from the mouth of the trail.

She picked it up, and returned to the stone slab. Forcing one end of the stick under its edge, she pressed down on the other end. For a moment, nothing happened. Then the stone came loose. Dropping the stick, Beth crouched down and turned the slab over.

The other face had been polished smooth, and Beth knew immediately that her first feeling about it had been right—it was the top of what had once been a headstone.

With growing excitement, she rubbed the dirt away from the shallow engraving just below the upper curve. The letters were fuzzy, almost worn away by the ravages of time. But even so, she was able to read them:

AMELIA

The was nothing else, nor could she find the rest of the broken gravestone.

But it was enough.

Amy was real.

Beth thought about Tracy, and her mocking laughter.

And Peggy, who hadn't believed her, and had run away from her.

But she had found the proof. Now, no matter what they said, they wouldn't be able to take Amy away from her.

If they tried, she knew what would happen to them. Amy would do to them what she had done to Jeff Bailey.

For Beth and Amy were friends now—best friends—and nothing would ever be allowed to come between them again.

Fourteen

Tracy let herself in through the French doors leading to the foyer, and started up the stairs to the second floor. All the way back from the clearing in the woods, she'd been trying to figure out the best way to use what she'd overheard Beth saying, but she still hadn't made up her mind.

Of course, she'd tell all her friends, starting with Alison Babcock.

But who else? What if she told her father? If he believed her, maybe he'd send Beth away somewhere.

But what if he didn't believe her? What if he thought she was just making up a story? Then he'd get mad at her.

Her grandmother.

That's who she'd tell. Her grandmother always believed her, no matter what she said. And if she had to, she'd make her grandmother walk all the way out there, and show her where Beth had been, standing over that stupid sinkhole, talking about a ghost like it was something real.

She hurried on to the top of the stairs, and started down the hall toward the far end. Just as she got to her grandmother's closed door, she heard Carolyn's voice calling her name. But instead of turning around, or even acknowledging that she'd heard, she simply ignored her stepmother, turned the knob of her grandmother's door, and let herself in.

Abigail sat in a chair by the window. Her eyes were closed, and one hand rested in her lap. The other one hung limply at her side, and a few inches below her hand, a book lay open, facedown, on the floor.

Tracy stared at her grandmother. Was it possible she'd died, just sitting there in her chair?

Tracy's heart skipped a beat.

She edged slowly across the room. How could you tell if someone was dead?

You had to feel for a pulse.

Tracy didn't want to do that. It had been horrible enough having to look at her grandfather when he was dead. But to actually have to touch a dead body . . . she shuddered at the thought.

She paused. Maybe she should go and get her father, or even Carolyn.

But then, as she was about to back away, her grandmother's eyes flickered slightly, and her hand moved.

"Grandmother?" Tracy asked.

Abigail's eyes opened, and Tracy felt a surge of relief.

Relief, and a twinge of disappointment. Telling Alison Babcock about finding her grandmother's body would have been even better than telling her about how crazy Beth Rogers was.

"Tracy?" Abigail said, coming fully awake, and straightening up in her chair. "Come give me a kiss, darling. I must have dozed off for a moment."

Tracy obediently stepped forward and gave her grandmother a reluctant peck on the cheek.

"What are you doing here, child?" Abigail asked. "Why aren't you outside? It's a beautiful morning."

"I was," Tracy said. She searched her mind, trying to figure out how to tell her grandmother what she'd heard without admitting that she'd followed Beth. "I . . . I went for a walk in the woods," she went on, deliberately making her voice shake a little. As she'd hoped, her grandmother looked at her sharply.

"Did something happen?" she asked. "You look as though something frightened you."

Tracy did her best to appear reluctant, and, once again, the ruse worked.

"Tell me what happened, child," Abigail urged her.

"It . . . it was Beth," Tracy began, then fell silent once more as if she didn't really want to tell on her stepsister.

Abigail's eyes darkened. "I see. And what did Beth do to you?"

"N-nothing, really," Tracy said.

Abigail's sharp eyes scanned her granddaughter carefully. "Well, she must have done something," Abigail pressed. "If she didn't, why do you look so worried?"

Still Tracy made a show of hesitating, then decided it would be better to let her grandmother pull the whole story out of her. "Grandmother," she said, "do you think maybe Beth could be crazy?"

"Crazy?" Abigail repeated, her brows arching slightly. "Tracy, what on earth happened? What would make, you say such a thing?"

"Well, I was out in the woods, just hiking around, and all of a sudden I heard something," Tracy explained. "It sounded like Beth—like she was talking to someone, so I went to find her. But when I got there—" She paused, wondering if she should mention Peggy Russell at all. She decided not to. "Well, she was talking to herself. She was out there in the woods, and she was talking to herself!"

Abigail's forehead wrinkled into a frown. "And what was she saying?" she asked.

Slowly, as if struggling to remember every fragment of what she'd heard, Tracy repeated the words she'd heard Beth speak. "It was weird, Grandmother," she finished. "I mean, she was talking like there was really a ghost. She had a name for her, and everything. She called her Amy, and she said the ghost killed Jeff! She said it killed Jeff, and she watched it happen! Doesn't that sound like she's crazy?"

Abigail sat silently for several long minutes, feeling the erratic pounding of her heart.

Amy.

"Amy" was a corruption of "Amelia."

And Amelia was a name she'd heard before.

Her husband had used it sometimes, when he was muttering to himself about the mill, and about Conrad Junior.

"Where?" Abigail finally asked, her blue eyes fixing intently on Tracy. "Where did all this happen, child?"

"In a little clearing," Tracy replied. "Down the hill from the mausoleum. There's a trail to it." She hesitated, then went on. "Do you want to go down there, Grandmother? I can show it to you. I can even show you the thing Beth thinks is a grave. Only it's not a grave. It's just a little sunken spot. " She fell silent for a moment, but when her grandmother didn't say anything, she spoke again. "Well? What do you think? Is she crazy?"

Abigail glanced up at her, and Tracy suddenly realized that her grandmother was no longer listening to her.

"What?" Abigail asked.

Tracy's expression tightened into an angry pout. "Nothing," she said. "Nothing at all." Then she turned and stamped out of her grandmother's little parlor, slamming the door behind her.

Abigail, sitting thoughtfully in her chair, ignored the slam of the door. Indeed, she didn't even hear it.

Her mind was occupied with other things.

Eileen Russell parked her five-year-old Chevy in front of Hilltop, and wished once more that she hadn't agreed to come up here. She'd considered calling Carolyn and asking her to come down to the village instead, pleading a heavy workload and suggesting they just get together for a quick drink in the bar. She'd quickly rejected that idea; what she had to talk to Carolyn about couldn't be discussed in a public place.

Perhaps it couldn't be discussed at all, given the fact that they hadn't seen each other for several months, and Carolyn's life had changed so radically in the interim.

Still, for old times sake, she had to try.

She got out of her car, slammed the door shut, and strode up the broad steps to the front door. She pressed the bell, and, when she heard nothing, pressed it again. Then, assuming it must be broken, she raised the huge brass knocker, and let it fall to its anvil with a resounding thump.

After what seemed an eternity, the door opened, and Hannah peered out. She blinked in the sunlight, then nodded a greeting. "Peter's out in the stable," she said. "You can just go around the back if you want to."

"I'm not here for Peter, Hannah," Eileen replied. "I came to see Carolyn."

Hannah looked momentarily taken aback, then recovered herself. "I'm sorry," she said. "She didn't tell me to be expecting anyone. Come on in, and I'll go find her." She held the door wide, and Eileen stepped into the huge entry hall. "Just make yourself at home," Hannah went on, closing the door and starting the long climb to the second floor.

After what seemed an eternity to Eileen, Carolyn appeared at the curve of the stairs. "Eileen! Come on up. If I'd been thinking, I'd have had Hannah send you right up, but I forgot to tell her." As Eileen climbed the stairs, Carolyn smiled ruefully. "I'm afraid I can't get used to the idea of having someone to answer the door for me. It seems so decadent. I'd have answered myself, but I never heard the bell. I was resting and I must have fallen asleep."

Eileen frowned, studying her old friend. "If you're not feeling well, I can—"

"I'm fine," Carolyn broke in. "But unfortunately, I can't convince either Phillip or Dr. Blanchard that there's no problem having a baby at my age."

They were halfway down the corridor now, and Eileen came to an abrupt stop, staring at Carolyn. "A baby?" she repeated.

Carolyn nodded happily.

"Well, for heaven's sake." Then a thought occurred to her, and she blurted it out before she had considered it. "Does Alan know?"

Carolyn stared at her for a moment, then burst out laughing. "Of course he knows! Beth told him right off the bat." Her smile faded slightly. "I'm afraid Beth was a little upset at first, but she's used to the idea now. In fact, I think she's looking forward to having a baby brother. Anyway, I hope she is."

She opened the door to the master bedroom, then stepped back to let the other woman go in ahead of her. Eileen surveyed the room quickly, taking in the rich antique furnishings, the sheer size of the room, then whistled appreciatively. "If this were my bedroom, I'd never leave it. My God, Carolyn, it's bigger than my living room."

"I know," Carolyn sighed. "And if you want to know the truth, sometimes I hate it." She saw the skepticism in Eileen's eyes, and shrugged helplessly. "I think you have to be born to this kind of thing. Sometimes I feel so out of place, all I want is to be back on Cherry Street."

Eileen said nothing, but crossed to the window and looked out. The view took in the entire estate, the village, and the countryside beyond. Indeed, if she looked carefully, she could pick out the roof of her own little house, looking from here like nothing more than a speck in the landscape. "What about Beth?" she asked without turning around. "How's she handling living up here?"

Carolyn started to make a casual reply, but there was something in Eileen's voice that stopped her. "What do you mean?" she asked instead. "Eileen, did something happen this morning? With Peggy?"

Now Eileen turned to face Carolyn, her expression serious. "I almost didn't come up here," she confessed. "Peggy showed up at the Red Hen about eleven. First she told me nothing was wrong, but I didn't believe her. You know Peggy—she can't hide her feelings at all. And she was pretty upset."

Carolyn sank into one of the twin love seats that faced each other in front of the window. "What happened?"

"Beth didn't say anything?" Eileen countered.

Carolyn shook her head. "But I haven't seen her. In fact, I thought Peggy was still with her, and they were out on the grounds somewhere."

"They went for a hike," Eileen explained. "Apparently yesterday

Beth told Peggy there was something she wanted to show her, and today she showed it to her."

"What was it?" Carolyn asked.

"That's the thing," Eileen went on, perching nervously on the couch opposite Carolyn. "From what Peggy said, it didn't sound like anything. Just a sort of a depression in a little clearing somewhere down the hill. But Peggy says that Beth insisted that it was a grave, and that it belonged to some little girl who used to work at the mill."

Carolyn studied Eileen for a moment, trying to decide if her old friend was pulling her leg. But Eileen's eyes were serious, and her brow was furrowed with worry. "I . . . I'm not sure I understand," Carolyn said at last.

"I'm not sure I do, either," Eileen replied. "At first, it sounded as though Beth was playing a joke on Peggy—telling her a ghost story. You know Peggy—she believes everything anybody tells her. But when she told me what happened up there, she said it wasn't as if Beth was even talking to her. She said it sounded crazy, that Beth really seemed to believe there was some kind of ghost living in the mill."

"But that's ridiculous," Carolyn said. "Beth knows there's no such thing as ghosts—"

"We all know that," Eileen agreed. "And ordinarily I wouldn't have thought anything about it. But Peggy was so frightened by the whole thing that I thought I'd better come up here and tell you about it. And I guess I wanted to find out if it really happened."

"I don't know," Carolyn replied. "But—well, I'm sure there's a reasonable explanation for whatever happened." Then, when Eileen said nothing, Carolyn had a sudden feeling that there was something the other woman wasn't saying. "Eileen? What is it? What's wrong?"

Eileen looked away, and when she spoke, her eyes were fixed on something outside the window. "Peggy said that the way Beth was talking, it sounded as though Beth was at the mill the night Jeff Bailey died. Peggy got the feeling that maybe Beth had killed him herself."

"Oh, my God," Carolyn groaned, suddenly understanding. Quickly she told Eileen about the dream Beth had had that night, and how real it had seemed to her. "That's all she was doing," she finished. "She was just telling Peggy about the dream."

Eileen hesitated, then rose to her feet. "Well," she said, "I hope you're right—I hope that's all it was. But I'm not sure there'll be any convincing Peggy of that. I'm afraid—" She hesitated, then decided to go ahead. "Well, I'm afraid Peggy doesn't want to see Beth anymore."

"Not see her anymore!" Carolyn exclaimed. "But, Eileen, that's crazy. They're best friends. They always have been."

Eileen stood silently for a moment, then shook her head. "They were best friends," she said quietly. "But not anymore. Everything's changed now, Carolyn. Things aren't the way they used to be. I'm sorry." As she started toward the door, Carolyn rose to her feet, but Eileen waved her back onto the couch. "I'll let myself out," she said.

Then she was gone, and Carolyn knew that she would never be back.

But it had nothing to do with Beth. Of that, she was absolutely positive.

It had to do with the fact that she herself had married Phillip Sturgess, and Eileen, like all her other old friends, didn't believe she hadn't changed, didn't believe she was the same Carolyn they'd known for years. They were sure that since she had married a Sturgess, she had taken on the airs of a Sturgess, and her daughter had, too.

Peggy's story was just that—a story.

The real reason Peggy Russell didn't want to play with Beth anymore, Carolyn insisted to herself, was nothing more than simple resentment of the way Beth lived now.

And there was nothing Carolyn could do about that. It was just a matter of time. In time, Beth would adjust to her new life, and make new friends.

Soon, too, there would be a new baby in the house. That would help. The baby would be a halfbrother to both Beth and Tracy, and maybe, at last, the two of them could be friends.

As for the story of the ghost that Peggy was so certain Beth believed in, Carolyn dismissed it from her mind.

Her daughter, she knew, was far too sensible ever to believe in something like a ghost.

Abigail Sturgess stood in the mausoleum, gazing down through the fading afternoon sun at the foreboding silhouette of the mill. Earlier, when she'd first come up to the mausoleum, the newly sandblasted bricks had glowed red in the sunlight, and for a moment it had looked to Abigail as if the building were on fire. But it was, she knew, only an illusion.

Abigail Sturgess didn't believe in illusions.

Still, somewhere inside the mill there was something that her husband had believed in, and that now she, too, was beginning to believe in.

Coming to a reluctant decision, she turned and began making her laborious way down the steps to the forest path. Abigail moved steadily along until she emerged onto the lawn in front of the house, but instead of going into the house, she crossed to the garage, and entered it through a side door. Turning on the lights, she reached into her purse and found the keys to the old Rolls-Royce that her husband had steadfastly refused to sell, though he hadn't driven it in years. Instead, he had kept it in the garage, insisting that it be taken out on a monthly basis, to be driven a few miles, gone over by a mechanic, then returned to the garage, where it would be available on the day when he finally decided to take it out himself. That day had never come. When he died, he hadn't been behind the wheel of the car for nearly a decade. But it was in perfect condition, ready for Abigail now.

She got stiffly behind the wheel, found the slot for the key, and twisted the starter.

Immediately, the engine purred into nearly silent life. Abigail reached up and pressed the button attached to the sun visor, and the garage door opened behind her. Putting the car in gear, she backed carefully out into the driveway, changed gears, and rolled sedately around the lawn and out the gates.

A few seconds later, she had left the estate, and was starting down the hill into Westover.

She parked the car on Prospect Street, across from the mill, and sat for a long time, wondering whether or not she was doing the right thing.

On the day nearly forty-five years before, when they had buried Conrad Junior, Abigail had accompanied her husband to the mill. There, she had watched as he placed the padlock on the door, then turned to her and made her swear never to set foot inside the building again. To humor him she had agreed. And though she had helped Phillip plan the reconstruction, she had not toured the building with him. Now, as she steeled herself to her task, the oath came back to her and she felt herself shiver slightly.

But it was ridiculous. She was going into the mill this time not to violate Conrad's wishes, but to implement them.

She left the car, and crossed Prospect Street, unaware that the men who were finishing up their day's work on the scaffolding covering the mill's facade were staring at her.

She made her way down the path along the northern wall of the mill, ignoring the stream of workmen coming the other way, making them step off the path to make way for her. Finally she stepped through the open door that broke the wall halfway to the end.

She paused. The worklights glittered with a surprising intensity that cut away the gloom she had expected. Almost immediately, she heard a voice behind her. She turned to see Alan Rogers emerging from the construction shack. "Mrs. Sturgess," he was saying. "Can I do something for you?"

Abigail's lips tightened slightly, and she regarded him with open contempt. "I have decided that we shall stop work," she said without preamble. "You may dismiss your crew, Mr. Rogers. I have changed my mind."

Alan stopped abruptly, and stared at the old woman. What the hell was she talking about? "I beg your pardon, Mrs. Sturgess," he said aloud. "Did you say you'd changed your mind?"

"I did," Abigail replied.

"About what?" Alan asked, deciding to buy some time while he decided how to handle her.

"Don't pretend to be more of a fool than you are, Mr. Rogers," Abigail said coldly. "I have decided not to go ahead with the reconstruction. I want the mill sealed up again."

Alan licked his lips uncertainly. The last thing he wanted to do right now was get into a fight with Abigail Sturgess. "Well, I'm afraid it isn't quite that simple, Mrs. Sturgess," he began, but Abigail cut him off.

"Of course it's that simple," she snapped. "It's my mill. You will be paid, of course. But the work is to stop immediately."

Alan said nothing, but shook his head.

Abigail's eyes flashed dangerously. "Did you hear me, Mr. Rogers?"

Alan sighed, then nodded. "I did, Mrs. Sturgess. But I'm afraid I can't stop the work on your authority. It was Phillip who signed the contract. If he's changed his mind, he'll have to tell me himself. He was here this morning," he added with elaborate casualness, "and he didn't say a word about stopping the project. In fact, just the opposite. We were figuring out ways to speed the job up."

Abigail was silent for a moment, then nodded curtly. "I see." She turned away, and started back into the cavernous interior of the building. Before she had taken two steps, though, she felt Alan's hand on her arm.

"I'm sorry, but you can't go in there."

She brushed his hand away as if it were an annoying insect. "Of course I can go in," she snapped. "If I wish to inspect my property, I have the right to do so." Her eyes met his, as if challenging him to stop her. "The men are gone, Mr. Rogers," she went on. "I'll hardly be in the way."

Alan nodded a reluctant agreement. "All right. But I'll go with you."

"That's not necessary," Abigail replied.

"I'm afraid it is," Alan told her. "You may own the mill, Mrs.

Sturgess, but right now I'm responsible for it. I don't leave in the afternoon until I know that it's empty, and locked. And I'm not about to allow you to wander around by yourself."

Abigail's nod of assent was almost imperceptible. "Very well."

Twenty minutes later they stood at the top of the stairs to the basement. Without looking at Alan, Abigail spoke. "Give me your flashlight, Mr. Rogers. I wish to go downstairs."

"Mrs. Sturgess—" Alan began, but Abigail cut him off.

"Mr. Rogers, one of my sons died down there many years ago, and my dearest friend's grandson died in the same place two days ago. I wish to visit the spot where the tragedies occurred, and I wish to visit it alone. You will give me your flashlight, and then you will wait for me at the door."

Alan hesitated. "Let me at least turn on the lights down there." He started toward the electrical panel, but Abigail stopped him.

"No," she said. "I wish to see it the way my son and Jeff Bailey saw it." When Alan still hesitated, she allowed the faintest note of pleading to enter her voice. "I have my reasons, Mr. Rogers. Please."

Reluctantly, Alan turned his flashlight over to the old woman, then, as she started slowly down the stairs, headed back to the site shack. He would give her twenty minutes, no more.

Only when she reached the basement, and the darkness of it had closed around her, did Abigail turn on the flashlight and let its beam wander through the dusty expanse of the cellar.

There seemed to be nothing there.

Only piles of crates and stacks of plasterboard.

She stepped onto the floor of the basement, and turned right. She took five more steps, then turned right again, so that she was facing the area below the stairs.

Holding the flashlight firmly, she played its beam into the darkness there.

Abigail's thoughts were fueled by the memory of her husband's strange fixations about this place, and her eyes began to play tricks on her.

A face loomed out of the darkness, pale skin stretched over sharp cheekbones, the mouth drawn back in a grimace of terror.

Eyes glared at her, sparkling with hatred.

Another face, twisted in agony.

A mouth, hanging in the blackness—open—screaming silently.

Abigail's heart began to pound as the faces surrounded her, all of them hanging in the darkness, all of them staring at her, accusing her, judging her.

Laughter began to ring in Abigail's ears. Then the laughter turned to screams of agony and anguish. A stabbing pain shot through Abigail's left arm, up into her shoulder, and through her chest.

The flashlight dropped to the floor, its lens and bulb shattering on the hard concrete.

Her knees buckled beneath her, and she began to sink to the floor.

But still the faces—faces of children—loomed in the darkness, coming closer, closing in on her. Their screams echoed through the old building, and rang in her ears, louder and louder, until the screaming seemed to be inside her head. Then, as she felt herself losing consciousness, she thought she saw a flash of light, a glow, thought she saw flames licking from the edges of the fire door.

It's true, she thought, as the flames receded and blackness engulfed her, *Conrad was right. It's all true....*

Fifteen

Abigail Sturgess sat propped up in bed, three pillows behind her back, her frail shoulders covered with the cashmere afghan that was the first thing she had demanded after awakening to find herself in the hospital. Her skin, almost translucent, seemed to sag around her features, but her eyes were as bright as ever as she regarded her family with something that Carolyn felt was very close to disdain.

"It's nothing more than a minor inconvenience," the old woman insisted. "If anyone sends flowers, I shall have them thrown away—flowers are for funerals, and a slight heart attack hardly qualifies me for the grave."

"There was nothing slight about it, Mother," Phillip replied. "You're probably going to be here for a while."

"I'd rather be dead, and I shall tell that to the first doctor who suggests that I can't rest just as well in my own home as I can here." But despite her words, Abigail knew she would stay in the hospital until her strength returned, however long it took. And right now she felt much worse than she was prepared to admit.

"But what happened, Grandmother?" Tracy demanded. "What were you doing down there?"

Abigail turned to smile at her granddaughter. "Why, I wasn't doing much of anything, darling. I simply went down to see just what it was that your father is doing to the old place, that's all."

Tracy's eyes narrowed suspiciously. "After everybody had gone home, Grandmother?"

"Mr. Rogers had not gone home," Abigail sniffed. "Although had I wished to go in alone, who was to stop me?"

"The liability laws, and the fine print in the contract might have given you a certain amount of pause," Phillip observed dryly, "had you bothered to read them. But Tracy's right—whatever possessed you to go down there today? And why didn't you ask me to take you? I would have been more than glad to show you around."

"And bore me with a lot of technical claptrap I care nothing about," Abigail said with more peevishness than she truly felt. "I was up in the mausoleum and suddenly I had an urge to go down to the mill and have a look around." She glanced at Tracy, who was watching her with more shrewdness than she would have expected from a girl of thirteen. "At any rate, it doesn't really matter, does it? All that happened was that I went down to the basement, and I had a heart attack. I'll grant you it was inconvenient, and it would have been a lot easier for us all if I'd done this at home, but I didn't, and that's that."

Phillip gazed at his mother speculatively. "The mausoleum," he repeated. "Why did you go up there?"

Abigail's eyes hardened slightly. "Your father is buried there, Phillip. Do you need more of an explanation as to why I might go there?"

"Under the circumstances, Mother, I think I do," Phillip replied. "You've never been in the habit of walking up that trail by yourself, and you certainly haven't driven a car in years. Yet today you not only hiked up to the mausoleum, but you then took the car and drove yourself down to the mill, where you proceeded to have a heart attack."

"Perhaps," Abigail grated, "the walk and the drive were simply too much for me."

"And perhaps," Phillip shot back, "there's something else going on. Something you're not telling us about."

Abigail glared at her son. "I do not intend to be cross-examined by you, Phillip." Then, appearing to relent, she eased herself back against the pillows. "I was thinking about Conrad, that's all. So I went up to the mausoleum to be nearer to him. I find it peaceful up there." She smiled bitterly. "One day, I suppose, I shall find my peace there on a more permanent basis, shan't I?"

No one said anything.

"As for the mill, today I simply decided to go down there and see if I could discover what it was about it that so upset your father."

The door opened, and a smiling nurse bustled in. "I'm afraid our time's up," she announced with exaggerated cheer. "Doctor made us promise to keep our visit short this evening, and now we need our nap."

Carolyn rose from her chair, and picked up her purse, while Tracy leaned over to kiss her grandmother. Abigail accepted the kiss, but her eyes remained fixed on the nurse. "I made no such promises," she announced. "Furthermore, I have no intention of taking a nap. I intend to talk to my son for a few more minutes."

"Mrs. Sturgess—" the nurse began.

"It won't work, Nurse," Phillip said, sighing and lowering himself into the chair his wife had just vacated. "Better to give her a few more minutes than waste your time arguing with her, and end up giving in to her anyway."

"But Doctor said—"

"Doctor was a stupid child, and I can't imagine that he's grown into a much brighter adult," Abigail announced. "Now please leave me alone with my son."

The nurse hesitated, then gave up. Besides, she privately agreed with Abigail Sturgess's assessment of the doctor, and from what she'd seen of Mrs. Sturgess in the two hours since she'd arrived in the hospital, she suspected the old woman was a lot stronger than the doctor thought. "All right," she said. "But please, Mrs. Sturgess, not all night, okay?"

Abigail nodded slightly, and offered her hand to Carolyn when the younger woman made as if to kiss her on the cheek. "I expect to be home in a few days," she said. "I shall have to trust you to supervise Hannah until then. Please tell her—"

"I'm sure Hannah knows exactly what to do, Abigail," Carolyn interjected. "Just try to relax, and get well, all right?"

Abigail's lips tightened, but she didn't speak again until Carolyn and Tracy had followed the nurse out of the room and the door was shut. "As if she really wants me to get well," she began, but this time Phillip cut her off.

"Of course she wants you to get well, Mother," he said. "But sometimes I can't imagine why, considering the way you treat her. Now, what is it you want to tell me that you wouldn't say in front of Carolyn?"

"And Tracy," Abigail pointed out.

"Indeed?" Phillip asked. "Somehow I thought it was mostly Carolyn you wanted to be rid of."

Abigail shook her head. "Not this time. What I have to say, I shall say only to you." Her head turned, and her eyes fixed on her son with an intensity Phillip had rarely seen. "Phillip, you must close the mill."

Phillip groaned. "For God's sake, Mother. This is absolutely ridiculous. I thought when Father died, we could be done with all that nonsense. Please don't you start in on it now. Besides, it's far too late to change our minds. The investment is too big, and the contracts have been signed. I couldn't cancel them, even if I wanted to, which I don't. There's no way—"

"If you don't close the mill, more people will die there," Abigail interrupted. "It isn't going to stop, Phillip—don't you see? It happened to Conrad Junior, and now it's happened to Jeff Bailey—"

"Jeff Bailey's death was an accident—nothing more. It's been investigated, and there's no evidence of anything other than the fact that he tripped, and fell on a pick."

"Which is almost exactly what happened to your brother," Abigail replied.

"And that was more than forty years ago, Mother. We've been through all this before."

Abigail reached out and clutched Phillip's hand. "And what about me?"

Phillip eyed her impatiently. "You? Mother, you yourself said that what happened to you could as easily have happened at home or anywhere else."

"I lied," Abigail said softly.

Phillip leaned forward. "You *lied*?"

"I didn't want to frighten Tracy, or talk about it in front of your wife, but something happened today." She looked at Phillip again, and he thought he saw something in her eyes that he'd never seen there before.

Fear.

"I saw something down there, Phillip. I can't tell you exactly what it was, because I can't truly remember it. But I know that this afternoon, when I was in the basement of the mill, I was in the presence of death. I could see it, and I could hear it, and I could feel it. It's there, Phillip. Death lives in the mill, and if you don't close it, it will kill us all."

Phillip sat still, wondering what to say to his mother. Was it possible that her age was finally catching up with her, and she was beginning to suffer from delusions? But her voice was so strong, and she seemed so sure of what she was saying. "Mother, I'm sure you believe you felt something today, and there's no reason why you shouldn't. My God! You had a heart attack! It must have been terrifying." He smiled sympathetically. "In a way, you *were* in the presence of death, as you put it—"

"Don't patronize me, Phillip," Abigail rasped. "I know what I felt, and I know when I felt it. It had nothing to do with the heart attack, except to cause it. Oh, I was frightened all right. What do you think brought the attack on? It was fear, Phillip. Pure, unadulterated fear. I've never been a coward, but I saw something in that basement that frightened me more than anything has ever frightened me in my life. Whatever it is, it killed Jeff Bailey, and it tried to kill me. And there's no way to get rid of it. Your father was right. The only thing you can do is close the mill."

Phillip rose to his feet, knowing that arguing with his mother was useless. "I'll think about it, Mother," he said softly as he leaned over to kiss her. "I can't promise you anything right now, except to think about it."

Abigail turned away from Phillip's kiss, her head sinking tiredly into the pillows. "Not good enough," she whispered so quietly that Phillip could barely make out her words. "It's just not good enough." She closed her eyes, and for a moment Phillip thought she had fallen asleep. But then her eyes blinked open, and her body stiffened. "Beth," she said.

Phillip stared at her. "Beth?" he repeated.

Abigail's eyes narrowed slightly, and she nodded. "Where is she?"

The question threw Phillip into confusion. What on earth was she thinking of now? "She's with her father," he replied. "Alan was still here when we arrived, and we asked him if he'd take Beth for the evening."

"I want to see her," Abigail announced. "Get her, and bring her to me."

Phillip's eyes widened. "Now? Tonight?"

"Of course, tonight!" the old woman snapped. "If I'm as sick as you'd like to think, I could be dead by tomorrow!"

Phillip felt a sudden uneasiness. "Mother, what is all this about? I know how you feel about Beth—"

"You know nothing," Abigail whispered in a voice as venomous as Phillip had ever heard her use. "Apparently you're as much of a fool as your father always said you were."

Anger surged through Phillip, and he felt a vein in his forehead begin to throb. "I hardly think you'll get my cooperation this way, Mother," he replied, biting the words off one by one. "And if you think I'll expose Beth to you while you're in a mood like this, you're quite wrong."

Abigail glared at him for a moment, her entire body trembling as if it were palsied. Then, slowly, she eased herself back down, and when she spoke, her voice was calm.

"I'm sorry," she said, though there was no hint of regret in her voice. "I suppose I shouldn't have spoken to you that way. But I wish to see Beth, and I wish to see her tonight." When Phillip said nothing, she went on. "If she doesn't wish to see me, I shall understand, Phillip. And you may tell her that she may feel free to walk out of this room at any time."

"But why, Mother?" Phillip pressed. "Why do you want to see Beth?"

Abigail hesitated, then shook her head. "I can't tell you," she said quietly. "It wouldn't make any sense to you." Then she turned her head away, and closed her eyes once more. Phillip watched her for a moment, then slipped out of the room to join Carolyn and Tracy in the reception area.

"What did she say, Daddy?" Tracy immediately demanded while Carolyn asked the same question with her eyes.

"Nothing much," Phillip replied, his voice pensive. "She told me she wanted the mill closed, and she . . ." His voice trailed off, and there was a long moment of silence.

"What, Phillip?" Carolyn finally asked. "What else did she say?"

Phillip glanced at his daughter, then his eyes fell on his wife. "She says she wants to see Beth. Tonight."

Carolyn's eyes widened in surprise. "But—Phillip, she always acts as if Beth doesn't even exist!"

"I know," Phillip agreed. "Don't ask me why she wants to see her—she wouldn't say. All she said is that she wants to talk to Beth, but that if Beth doesn't want to come, she doesn't have to."

As confused as her husband, Carolyn slipped her hand into his, and let him guide her out of the reception room onto the street.

In their preoccupation with Abigail's strange request, neither of them noticed the look of pure hatred that came into Tracy's eyes as soon as her stepsister's name was spoken.

Sixteen

"What do you say we have supper at the Red Hen?" Alan asked dolefully as he stared into the nearly empty refrigerator. He hadn't expected to have Beth with him that evening, so hadn't stocked up on the food he knew she liked. Nor had he bothered to stop at the store on the way back to his apartment from the hospital. He was too tired, and he'd known from Beth's silence that something was wrong. Now, when she didn't answer his question, he decided to face the issue directly.

"You might as well tell me what's up," he said, closing the refrigerator door and moving into the tiny living room of the apartment. He dropped down onto the sofa next to Beth, and slipped his arm around her. "If you can't tell your old dad, who can you tell?"

Beth looked up at him, her eyes filled with worry.

"I . . . I think I know what happened to Mrs. Sturgess," she said after a silence that had threatened to stretch into minutes. "I think Amy must have done something to her, just like she did to Jeff Bailey."

Alan frowned thoughtfully, and wished—not for the first time—that he knew more about psychology. Then he reminded himself that parents had dealt with children for centuries before psychologists had ever invented themselves, and decided that his own instincts were all he needed. Right now, his instincts told him not to challenge the existence of Beth's imaginary friend. "Why would Amy want to do something to Mrs. Sturgess?" he asked.

"I'm not sure," Beth replied. "I think she hates the Sturgesses, though. And I think she hates all their friends, too."

"But why?" Alan pressed. "That doesn't really make sense, does it?" But of course he knew that it did. Amy, as Beth's "friend," would be angry at all the people who had hurt Beth, but whom Beth would not let herself hate. But how could he explain that to his daughter now, after what had happened that morning? She was already feeling friendless, and taking Amy away from her—trying to explain to her that the child didn't exist outside her own imagination—seemed to him as if it would be too much.

He'd heard about what had happened up on the hill that morning.

At least he'd heard what Peggy Russell had had to say when she'd come bursting into the Red Hen while Alan was having lunch that afternoon.

But he hadn't, he now realized ruefully, connected Peggy's wild tale with Abigail Sturgess's unexpected visit to the mill. He should have, especially when the old woman insisted on going into the basement, but he hadn't.

Beth, obviously, had, and now it was up to him to try to find a way to convince his daughter that what had happened to Abigail was nothing more than a heart attack brought on only by her age. But it was certainly not connected to the presence in the mill of any sort of being, either real or imaginary. He was trying to figure out how to explain this to Beth when the doorbell rang. To his surprise, he found Phillip and Carolyn, with Tracy between them, standing in the hall.

Instinctively, he stepped out of the apartment and closed the door behind him, rather than invite them all inside. As Phillip began to explain the reason they were there, Alan's feeling of apprehension grew. There could only be one possible reason why Abigail wanted to talk to Beth, and the last thing he wanted to do was discuss that subject in front of Tracy. Why, he wondered, couldn't they have left her at home?

"Beth and I were just going out for supper," he said at last, not really intending the statement as anything more than an attempt to buy some time to think. But Phillip immediately suggested that they all go together, and Alan, taken off guard, was unable to invent a polite way to refuse.

It was a mistake.

Alan realized it was a mistake even as he pulled into the parking lot at the Red Hen, to be greeted warmly a few moments later by Eileen Russell. When the Sturgesses appeared behind him, Eileen's welcoming smile all but disappeared, and Alan felt a distinct chill between Carolyn and Eileen as Eileen led them to a large round table near the fireplace, that, even on this warm early-summer evening, was ablaze with the false warmth of poorly designed gas logs.

"This is totally tacky," Tracy announced as they spread themselves around the table. "No wonder Grandmother never comes here."

"How is Mrs. Sturgess?" Alan asked immediately. Out of the corner of his eye, he'd seen Phillip opening his mouth to admonish his daughter, and all his instincts told him that if he let that happen, Tracy would do her best to make the meal as difficult as possible for all of them. And for Beth, it would become sheer misery. As if to confirm his feeling, he saw Carolyn shoot him a grateful look.

"Much better," Phillip replied, his attention diverted from Tracy. "In fact, she's doing her best to make life miserable for everyone at the hospital, which, for Mother, is a good sign."

"Did she say what happened?" Alan asked warily, still certain the woman's experience in the mill had to be the reason she now wanted to talk to Beth.

Phillip hesitated, but shook his head. "Not really. She said something in the basement frightened her, but she couldn't say exactly what."

A nervous silence fell over the table, which Alan finally broke with an attempt at a lightness he didn't feel. But he still wasn't ready to discuss Abigail's request with Beth, so he tried to put it off with black humor. "Aside from the darkness, the smell, and the rats that live down there, what's to be scared of?"

It didn't work. Beth, who had said nothing until then, turned serious eyes to him. "Smell? What kind of smell?"

Alan winked at his daughter. "The smell of dirt, damp, and age. That place was closed up so long, I'm not sure I'll ever be able to get it aired out."

"Of course you will," Phillip replied. "It's just a matter of getting a decent furnace in, and letting it dry out."

"It might not be that simple," Carolyn said quietly. "With the mill, it seems that nothing is as simple as it appears, doesn't it?"

Alan eyed his ex-wife carefully. "Do I hear a note of skepticism?" he asked. "Don't tell me you've joined forces with your mother-in-law and decided the mill shouldn't be reopened."

Carolyn shot him a look of annoyance, but then decided that under his bantering tone, he'd meant the question seriously. "It has to do with a lot of things," she replied. "Aside from the history of the place, it just seems to me that Westover isn't big enough to support the kind of shops that always go into places like Ye Olde Mill." In an attempt to take the sting out of her words, she purposely pronounced the final E in "olde," and was relieved when Phillip joined in Alan's chuckle.

But then Phillip's laughter died away, and when he spoke, his voice was serious. "I'm afraid that despite what everyone else thinks—including my wife—I'm still convinced it'll be a success. If it turns out the way Alan and I have planned it, I'm hoping it will draw people from the whole area. And that could give the entire town a boost."

"Well, God knows Westover could use that," Alan sighed. He

picked up his menu, and glanced at the list of appetizers. "How does escargots sound?"

"*Here?*" Tracy asked. "You've got to be kidding." Her father shot her a warning glance, but Tracy ignored it. "Why couldn't we have gone to a nice restaurant?"

"There's nothing wrong with this place, Tracy," Phillip said quietly.

Tracy's eyes narrowed, and her mouth set into a sullen pout. "If Grandmother weren't in the hospital, we wouldn't have had to come here at all."

"We're here because we want to be," Phillip replied, and though his voice remained quiet, it had taken on a certain edge.

Carolyn seemed to be doing her best to ignore the exchange, and Alan, certain that anything else he said—no matter how innocuous—would only exacerbate the situation, concentrated on his menu even though he was quickly losing his appetite. And this, he thought as he began eliminating entrees to narrow his choices, is what Carolyn and Beth have to put up with every day. He felt a flicker of sympathy for Carolyn, and wondered if this marriage, like their own, was also going to be a failure for her. If Tracy had anything to do with it, he was certain it would be.

And more and more, it was becoming clear to him why Beth had found it necessary to invent a friend.

Surreptitiously, he stole a glance at his daughter. She seemed to be trying to disappear behind the menu. But she couldn't disappear all the time. How did she cope with Tracy's constant hostility and snobbery?

And why should she have to? Maybe, after all, he should try to find a way to make it possible for her to come and live with him. "Anything look good to you, honey?" he finally asked when the silence at the table began to become uncomfortable.

"I like the shrimp," Beth replied, but when she tried to tell Tracy how they were cooked, Tracy merely glared at her, and turned away. Beth once more fell silent, and as the meal wore on, the conversation became increasingly strained.

Then, over coffee, Phillip Sturgess suddenly came to the point of their unannounced visit to Alan's apartment. Without a word to Alan, he turned to Beth.

"Beth, Tracy's grandmother would like to see you."

Carolyn stiffened slightly, as Beth's eyes widened in surprise. Alan, who had been sipping his coffee, set his cup down as he felt his daughter staring at him accusingly from across the table.

"Is that why they came to the apartment?" she asked.

"Well, we didn't come because we wanted to see you," Tracy hissed, then fell silent when her father glared at her.

"I'm afraid so, honey," Alan confessed. He turned to Phillip. "But I really don't understand why she wants to see Beth," he went on. "I thought—" Then he stopped himself, embarrassed to utter the words that had been on the tip of his tongue.

"That Mother isn't particularly fond of Beth?" Phillip finished. Then, when everyone except Tracy—whose mouth was now twisted into a smug smile—seemed as embarrassed as Alan had been, he went on. "I don't think there's any reason for any of us to pretend the truth doesn't exist. But today she specifically asked to see Beth. I don't know why—she wouldn't tell me. But she did say that Beth doesn't have to come if she doesn't want to." He turned to Beth, who was now looking at him with a mixture of fear and curiosity. "And she also told me that if you do decide to come and see her, you can leave anytime you want to."

Alan frowned. "What in the world did she mean by that?"

Now it was Phillip who looked uncomfortable. "I'm not sure about that either," he replied. "But I have to assume that Mother is well aware of how she's treated Beth, and this is her way of apologizing for it."

Alan felt a sudden surge of anger for his daughter. "It seems to me," he said tightly, "that your mother is still busy acting like the queen of the world. If she's been mean to Beth—and I think we all know damned well that she has—then I see no reason for Beth to go see her, now. Frankly, I'm surprised you'd even ask, Phillip."

Tracy's eyes flashed angrily. "Don't you talk about my grandmother that way—" she began, but Alan had finally had enough.

"Shut up, Tracy," he said, not even glancing at the girl, but instead keeping his eyes on Phillip, as if challenging him to try to defend his daughter's rudeness. Out of the corner of his eye, he saw the shock on Tracy's face. Apparently her own father had never spoken that way to her.

"Of course you're right," Phillip said quietly, his shoulders slumping. "Mother's treated Beth shamefully—and Carolyn too, for that matter. And perhaps I should have simply told her it was out of the question." He turned to Beth. "I'm sorry," he said. "I shouldn't have even brought it up."

"I don't see why Grandmother even wants to talk to Beth at all," Tracy said as her father fell silent.

Beth, who had been sitting silently as the others talked, turned to face her stepsister. "Why not?" she asked. "Why wouldn't she want to talk to me?"

Tracy glared malevolently at Beth. "Because you're nothing but trash," she said, her voice quivering with anger. "You should be living with your stupid father in that crummy apartment, and you never should have come to Hilltop in the first place."

"Tracy!" Phillip interrupted. He put his napkin aside, and for a split second, Alan thought he might actually be about to strike the girl. But suddenly Carolyn, her voice low, stopped him.

"Leave her alone, Phillip," she said. "We might as well let her speak her piece." She turned to Tracy. "Go on," she said.

The reasonableness of Carolyn's voice only seemed to fuel Tracy's fury, and her eyes flashed dangerously. "Don't you talk to my father like that," she said, her voice rising to fill the room so that people at other tables turned to stare. "All you ever do is try to tell us what to do. Well, why don't you do something about Beth, instead of picking on me all the time? She's the one who's crazy, and everybody knows it!"

A deathly silence fell over the entire restaurant. After a moment Alan laid his napkin aside and stood up. "Come on, sweetheart," he said to his daughter. "I think we've heard all we need to hear."

But Beth didn't move. Instead she stared silently at Tracy for a moment, then shook her head. "It's all right," she said quietly. "I'll go see Mrs. Sturgess. And I don't care what you think, Tracy. I don't care what you think, and I don't care what you say. I'm not crazy, and your grandmother knows it." She said the words with as much bravado as she could summon up, but it wasn't enough to still the pain Tracy's words had caused her.

The only way she could shut out that pain was to concentrate on something else, on something that wouldn't hurt her.

And right now, the only thing that wouldn't hurt her was Amy.

From now on, she would concentrate on Amy, and then she would be safe from whatever Tracy might say or do.

Beth glanced nervously down the corridor to the waiting room where her mother, Phillip, and Tracy were waiting. Phillip nodded to her, and her mother gave her an encouraging smile, and she reached out and shyly knocked at the closed door. From inside, Abigail Sturgess's voice weakly called out for her to come in. She opened the door, and slipped inside.

The room was much bigger than she'd thought it would be, and there were flowers everywhere. It seemed as if there should have been a second bed in the room, but it wasn't there. She wondered if they'd really taken it out just for Mrs. Sturgess. Finally, after taking in the room, she made her eyes go to the bed. There, propped up against two pillows, and looking much smaller than Beth remembered her, was the old woman.

For her own part, Abigail surveyed the child with more interest than she ever had before. Until today, Beth had been nothing more to her than an unwelcome intrusion in her life, one best ignored until such time as Phillip finally came to his senses and left Carolyn.

Now, as she studied the girl, she slowly came to realize what a pretty child she truly was. Not that she wasn't perfectly familiar with Beth's features; she was. But today, for the first time, she really looked at Beth. There was a softness to her face, she realized, that was totally lacking in Tracy's face. Indeed, there was an innocence in Beth's eyes that she couldn't remember having seen in a child for years. Until now, she'd simply attributed the sophistication of Tracy and her friends to the hardening effect of growing up in the modern world. But in Beth, there was no trace of a knowing glint in her eyes. Rather, they appeared to be totally guileless.

"Come here, Beth," she said softly, patting the edge of the bed. "I—" She hesitated, almost unable to speak the words. "I want to thank you for coming to see a sick old lady," she finally managed.

Slowly, like a nervous animal, Beth approached the bed, but stopped short before she was within range of Abigail's hands. "I'm sorry you're sick," she offered shyly, then stood as if waiting to have her sympathy rebuffed.

"Well, perhaps I'm not that sick," Abigail replied. Then she twisted her lips into a grimace that was intended to be a warm smile. "Don't you want to know why I asked that you be brought here?"

Beth hesitated, then nodded silently.

"I want to talk to you about your friend," Abigail went on. She searched Beth's face for a reaction, but saw none. "Amy," she added.

For a moment, she thought Beth was going to turn around and flee from the room. But instead, Beth's eyes only showed the hurt of betrayal. "Tracy shouldn't have told you," she said. "She wasn't even supposed to know about Amy."

"I agree with you," Abigail said evenly, then watched carefully to see what Beth's reaction would be. As she'd hoped, Beth's eyes brightened slightly. "But since she did tell me about Amy, I thought we might talk about her." When Beth's forehead creased into a worried frown, Abigail hastened to reassure her. "It will be our secret. I promise not to tell anyone else about Amy, unless you say it's all right."

Beth chewed thoughtfully on her lip, then looked warily at the old woman in the bed. "Wh-what do you want to know about her?" she stammered.

Abigail let herself relax. It was going to be all right. "Well, to start with, how old is she?"

Beth hesitated. She wasn't quite sure. "My age," she said at last. "I think she's eleven, going on twelve."

"Eleven," Abigail repeated. "And do you know what she looks like?"

Beth shook her head.

"But I thought she was your friend," Abigail pressed. "Haven't you ever seen her?"

"Y-yes—"

"Then you must know what she looks like, mustn't you?"

"It . . . it was dark."

"Dark. Like it is in the mill?"

Beth nodded.

"And is that where you saw her? In the mill?"

Once more, Beth nodded.

"What does she do there?"

"She . . . she lives there," Beth replied, then stepped back almost as if she expected to be punished for what she'd said.

"But I thought—I thought she was dead," Abigail said.

Beth's eyes widened once more, and again Abigail was afraid she was going to run from the room. But instead, she swallowed hard, and stood her ground.

"She *is* dead," she said. "She used to work in the mill a long time ago, and something terrible happened to her. And she's still there."

"I see," Abigail breathed. "Do you know what happened to her?"

Beth thought, and then remembered the smell she'd noticed when she'd been in the basement of the mill with her father. "I think there was a fire," she whispered. "I think there was a fire, and she couldn't get out."

Abigail gasped, suddenly sitting up in the bed. Her hand shot out, clutching Beth's arm. "How do you know that?" she demanded. "How do you know there was a fire?"

Beth, suddenly terrified, wrenched herself loose from Abigail's grip, and ran to the door. Then she turned back to face the old woman once again.

"I know!" she said, her voice reflecting her sudden desperation. She wished she hadn't come here after all, wished she hadn't agreed to come and see this old woman who hated her for reasons she couldn't understand at all. "I just know, that's all!" she repeated.

She reached for the door handle, but just as she was about to pull on it and run from the room, Abigail spoke again.

"I can tell you about Amy," the old woman said. "I can tell you everything about her that you want to know."

Beth froze, and then, very slowly, turned away from the door.

Abigail's eyes seemed to reach out to her, gripping her, drawing her inexorably back toward the bed. . . .

Tracy sat in the waiting room, her fury growing inside her.

It should have been *her* her grandmother wanted to see, not that stupid Beth. What could they possibly be talking about? Her grandmother didn't even like Beth—in fact, she hated her almost as much as Tracy herself did.

Then she remembered the conversation she'd had that afternoon when she'd told her grandmother how crazy Beth was. And her grandmother hadn't really said anything.

But she'd gone down to the mill later on.

Was it possible that her grandmother didn't believe Beth was crazy? Could she actually believe what Beth had been saying?

It wasn't fair.

None of it was fair!

Everyone was paying attention to Beth, and no one was paying attention to her!

In fact, her own father hadn't even done anything when that horrible Alan Rogers at dinner had told her to shut up. Instead of defending her, he'd actually apologized to Beth, like he was Beth's father, instead of her own.

And now her grandmother was acting like Beth was her grandchild, instead of herself.

All of a sudden, Tracy knew what was happening. Beth was stealing her family. She was stealing her father, and she was stealing her grandmother.

Tracy clutched at the magazine she was pretending to read, and saw her knuckles turn white as her anger turned her hands into tight fists.

Well, she wouldn't put up with it, and if any of them thought she would, they were wrong!

She'd get even. She'd get even with them all!

Beth sat silently in the back seat of the Mercedes, staring out the window, watching the darkness outside as the big car made its ponderous way along Prospect Street toward River Road. As it came abreast of the mill, though, she stirred slightly, and leaned forward, as if by the slight movement her eyes would be able to pierce the brick walls of the ancient building, and see into its depths.

It was impossible, though. All she saw was the blank facade of bricks. But still, as Phillip turned left onto River Road, her eyes remained on the great mass of the building, then fixed on the loading dock that extended out from behind the mill.

There.

It was in there, in the dark cold room beneath the loading dock, that Amy had died.

Unless old Mrs. Sturgess had been lying to her.

Ever since she'd left the hospital room, she'd been trying to decide if the old woman had been telling her the truth or not, and she still hadn't made up her mind. But eventually she'd know.

Amy would find a way to tell her.

The mill disappeared into the darkness as the car moved on, and finally Beth let herself sink deep into the seat. Then, feeling eyes on her, she glanced over to where Tracy, her lips tight with anger, sat glaring at her.

"I want to know what my grandmother told you," she whispered so quietly that Beth was certain no one in the car but herself could hear it. But from the front seat Phillip Sturgess spoke.

"That's enough, Tracy. If she wants to tell us, she will. But she certainly doesn't have to."

"Why not?" Tracy demanded. "And why did Grandmother want to talk to her instead of to me?" Her eyes, which had never left Beth, grew angrier. "I'll find out," she said. "I'll get my grandmother to tell me."

Beth said nothing, only turning away to face the window once more. But this time her eyes were closed. She didn't open them again until she heard the familiar crunching noises of the car's tires on the gravel of the circular driveway. Wordlessly, she got out of the car the moment Phillip stopped, hurried up the steps, and was the first one through the front door.

Hannah—waiting in the foyer—spoke to her, but Beth went past the old servant as if she hadn't seen her, and ran up the stairs. A moment later Hannah turned puzzled eyes to Carolyn as the rest of the family came into the house.

"Is Miss Beth all right?" she asked, her voice anxious.

"She's fine," Tracy replied before either her father or her step-mother could say anything. "Aren't you going to ask about my grand-mother?"

Hannah reddened slightly, but nodded. "I was just going to, Miss Tracy. How is she? Is she better?"

"She's doing very well," Phillip said before Tracy could go on. "In fact, she'll probably be home in a few weeks."

Hannah's brows rose. "Shall I get one of the downstairs rooms ready?"

"Don't bother. Mother won't budge from her rooms until the day she dies, and that doesn't look like it's going to be for quite a while yet." Then, understanding what Hannah was really saying, he reached out and patted her shoulder. "Don't worry, Hannah—if Mother needs extra help, we'll bring in a nurse. I'm not going to ask you to spend all day running up and down the stairs."

"Thank you, Mr. Phillip. I'm not as young as I used to be, I'm afraid. Would you like a nice pot of tea?"

Phillip and Carolyn glanced at each other, then shook their heads at the same time.

"I'll have a Coke, Hannah," Tracy said. "You can bring it to my room." She started toward the stairs, but Carolyn stopped her.

"If you want a Coke, Tracy, you can get it for yourself."

Tracy turned, her chin trembling. "I don't have to. It's Hannah's job."

"It is not Hannah's job," Phillip said quietly, but with a firmness in his voice that silenced Tracy. "Things are going to be difficult enough around here when your grandmother comes home, and it will be appreciated if you will do your part without making life even more difficult for us. All of us," he added, nodding pointedly toward Carolyn.

Tracy said nothing for a moment, and Carolyn could almost see her calculating the effects of various responses. In the end, she produced an apologetic expression, and looked shyly at the floor. "I'm sorry, Daddy," she said. Then, the Coke she had wanted ap-parently now forgotten, she dashed up the stairs two at a time. A moment later her door slammed loudly.

Carolyn sighed. "I'm sorry," she said. "I suppose I should have overlooked that, shouldn't I?"

"Why?" Phillip asked. He led her into the library, and poured each of them a stiff drink. "If you ask me, she was just testing, to see how far she could go. And I have to confess I'm getting just as tired of it as you are." Handing her the drink, he smiled ruefully. "I'm afraid I wasn't much of a father to her, which isn't an excuse—only an apology."

"Nothing to apologize for," Carolyn replied. She held the drink up in a silent toast, but as Phillip drank from his glass, she put her own back on the bar. "Pregnant ladies shouldn't drink." Then, feeling the built-up strain of the evening, she lowered herself tiredly into one of the wing chairs. "Do you want to tell me what's going on?" she asked.

Phillip looked at her quizzically, but said nothing.

"Come on," Carolyn pressed. "Your mother said something to you that you didn't want Tracy to hear. What was it?"

Phillip said nothing, but wandered over to the fireplace, where he stood leaning against the mantel, staring into his glass. Finally, instead of answering her question, he asked one of his own. "You don't think I should go ahead with the mill project, either. Is it just because of the way it used to operate, or is it something else?"

Carolyn frowned, wondering what, exactly, he was getting at. And then, slowly, the pieces began falling together in her mind. But what it added up to made no sense. It was as if Conrad Sturgess had suddenly risen from his chair in the mausoleum, and come back into the house with all his superstitions, and ramblings of evil in the mill. "It's the history," she said at last. "My great-great-grandfather was driven to suicide because of the mill. That my family blamed old Samuel Pruett is something you know, Phillip. It's been a sore spot in my family for generations."

"And yet you married me," Phillip pointed out.

"I love you," Carolyn replied.

Phillip nodded perfunctorily, and Carolyn had the distinct feeling that he hadn't really heard her, that his mind was on something else. "Was your family afraid of the mill?" she finally heard him ask.

Carolyn hesitated. Again, more pieces fell into place. "There were stories," she said, almost reluctantly.

"What kind of stories?"

"There was a story that several children disappeared from the mill. And right after that, your family closed it."

"Disappeared?" Phillip asked, his eyes reflecting a genuine puzzlement that told Carolyn he'd never before heard the story.

"That's what I was told. One day some of the children went to work, and didn't come home again. The story the mill put out was that they'd run away. And I suppose it was plausible, given the working conditions. But a lot of people in Westover didn't believe it. My great-grandparents certainly didn't.''

Phillip's forehead furrowed into a deep frown, and he refilled his glass. "What did they think happened?"

"They thought the children had died in the mill, and that the Sturgesses covered it up.'' She hesitated, then went on. "One of the missing children was a member of my family."

Phillip was silent for a moment. "Why didn't you ever tell me that story before?"

"There didn't seem any point,'' Carolyn replied. "It all happened so long ago, and I've never been quite sure whether to believe it or not.'' She smiled ruefully. "Well, to be perfectly honest, I was more than ready to believe it until I met you. Then I decided no one as nice as you could have sprung from a family that would have done something as awful as that, so I decided that the tales my grandmother told me must have been exaggerated. Which they probably were,'' she added, attempting a lightness she wasn't quite feeling. "You know how old family stories go."

"Don't I just," Phillip agreed, smiling thinly. "So now you don't believe the story?"

Carolyn shrugged. "I don't know that I ever believed it, truly. And I don't know that I disbelieve it now. It's just there, that's all. And whether I believe it or not, I'll never be comfortable about that mill. It gives me the willies, and it doesn't matter what you do to it, it always will."

Phillip sighed heavily. "Well, if what Mother said is true, it gave her considerably more than the willies this afternoon." Then, as Carolyn listened in silence, he repeated what Abigail had told him at the hospital. When he was finished, she picked up her glass from the bar, took a large sip, then firmly replaced it. "She really said it was the fear that brought on the heart attack, not the other way around?"

Phillip nodded. "She was very positive about it. And you know how positive Mother can be,'' he added archly. "Anyway, right after that, she asked me to bring Beth to her."

Carolyn's heart sank as she remembered the conversation she'd had with Eileen Russell that very afternoon. Had Eileen spent the rest of the day spreading Peggy's story all over town? She must have, since apparently Abigail had already heard.

"So that's why your mother went to the mill today,'' she said out loud, then repeated her conversation with Eileen to Phillip. "It must have gotten back to your mother,'' she finished, suddenly angry. "So she tied it all together with your father's nonsense and Jeff Bailey's accident, and went down there looking for something. But there's nothing there—only Beth's imagination, and your father's craziness!"

"And your family's stories," Phillip added. "If you mix it all together, it gets pretty potent, doesn't it?"

"But it's just stories," Carolyn insisted, her eyes imploring her husband. "And besides, Beth never heard them. My family all died before she was even born, and I never told them to her."

"But Beth's grown up in Westover," Phillip observed. "Everyone in town must know those stories, and she's probably heard them in one version or another all her life." He left the fireplace, and sank onto a sofa.

"Maybe Mother's right," he said. "Maybe you're both right. If everybody in Westover's heard all those stories, probably no one will come anywhere near the mill. Wouldn't that be something?" he added wryly. "All that money, and I'll wind up boarding the place up again."

"No!" Carolyn suddenly exclaimed. "Phillip, we're being ridiculous. And I've been ridiculous right along. But it's going to stop right now. I don't believe in ghosts, and neither do you. There's nothing in the mill. And as soon as it's opened, all the old stories will be forgotten!"

Before Phillip could make a reply, they both heard the screams coming from upstairs.

Tracy had appeared at Beth's door five minutes earlier, letting herself in without knocking. Beth, lying on the bed staring at the ceiling, had not moved, and for a minute Tracy had thought she was asleep. But then she'd seen that Beth's eyes were open.

"Look at me!" she'd demanded.

Beth, startled, had jumped up, then, when she saw who it was, sat back down on her bed. "What do you want?"

"I want to know what my grandmother said," Tracy told her. She advanced across the room a few steps, then stopped, still ten feet from the bed.

Beth hesitated. She could see the anger in Tracy's eyes, and was sure that if she tried to make something up, Tracy would know she was lying.

Maybe she should call her mother. But what good would that do? Tracy would just wait until they were alone, then start in on her again.

"She . . . she wanted to talk about Amy," she finally blurted.

Tracy looked at her scornfully. "You're crazy," she said. "There's no such person as Amy."

"There is, too," Beth shot back. "She's my friend, and your grand-mother knows all about her."

"She only knows what I told her." Tracy sneered. "And I told her everything you were saying to that stupid Peggy Russell."

"Peggy's not stupid!"

"Maybe she's not," Tracy conceded. "At least she's not stupid enough to believe all that junk you were telling her. And neither am I, and neither is my grandmother!"

"You don't know anything," Beth replied. Tears were welling up in her eyes now, and she was struggling to keep them from over-flowing. "You think you're so smart, but you don't know anything, Tracy Sturgess!"

"You shut up!"

"I don't have to!" Beth cried. "I live here too, and I can say what I want to say! And I don't care if you don't believe me! I don't care if anybody believes me. Now, go away and leave me alone!"

Tracy's eyes glowed with fury. "Make me! Just try to make me, you stupid little bitch!"

"You take that back!"

"I don't have to, 'cause it's true! You're stupid, and you're crazy, and when I tell my father, he'll make you go away. And I'll be glad when he does!"

Beth's tears overflowed now, but they were tears of anger, not of pain "Who wants to live in your stupid house anyway! I never wanted to come here!"

"And nobody ever wanted you to come here!" Tracy screamed. "Don't you know we all hate you? I hate you, and my grandmother hates you, and my father hates you! I bet your mother even hates you!"

The blood drained from Beth's face, and she lunged off the bed, hurling herself at Tracy. But Tracy, seeing her coming, spun around, yanked the door open, and dashed down the hall. Beth caught up to her just as she was opening the door to her room. Grabbing Tracy's hair, she tried to pull her back out into the hall.

"Let go of me!" Tracy screamed. Her arms flailing, she tumbled into her room, with Beth on top of her. "Daddy! Daddy, help me! She's trying to kill me!"

She was lying on her stomach, Beth astride her, pummeling at her shoulders. With a violent wrench, Tracy twisted herself over onto her back, and, still screaming, began clawing at Beth's face.

And then, just as she was sure she was going to be able to throw Beth off her and give her the thrashing she deserved, her father suddenly appeared, his hands sliding under Beth's shoulders, lifting her up.

"Get her away from me," Tracy wailed, her hands immediately falling away from Beth to cover her face. "Get her off me, Daddy! She's hurting me!"

With a quick tug Phillip pulled Beth to her feet, then let her go. Sobbing, she ran to her mother, who was now standing just inside the door, and threw her arms around her. Carolyn knelt down, pulling her daughter close.

"Beth! Honey, what happened?"

But before she could reply, Tracy's voice filled the room. "She's crazy!" Tracy yelled. "I was just lying on my bed, and all of a sudden she came in and jumped on me! I didn't do anything, Daddy!"

Carolyn, bewildered, looked from Tracy to Beth. "Beth? Is that true?"

Beth, tears streaming from her eyes, shook her head. "She came into my room," she replied. "She came in and started telling me I was crazy, and that everyone hates me. And . . . and—" She broke off, choking back her sobs.

"That's not true—" Tracy said hotly. "I didn't go anywhere near her room!"

"That's enough!" Phillip declared. "It doesn't matter who started it. You're both quite grown up enough not to be fighting like this. Now I want you both to apologize to each other."

"I won't!" Tracy shouted. "I didn't do anything, and I don't have to apologize to anyone! Why don't you make Beth apologize? She started it!"

Phillip took a deep breath, and silently counted to ten. When he spoke, his voice was quiet, but there was an edge to it that cut through his daughter's fury. "I don't care who started it, Tracy. All I'm interested in is ending it. Now, apologize to Beth."

Tracy's eyes narrowed. "I'm sorry," she whispered in a voice that was barely audible.

Phillip turned to the other girl. "Beth?"

Beth hesitated, then sniffled. "I'm sorry," she said at last. "I shouldn't have jumped on you."

"See?" Tracy crowed. "She admitted it!"

"She apologized, Tracy," her father replied. "That's all. Now get into bed, and I'll be back in a little while to say good night."

Tracy glanced at the clock, then decided not to press her luck by protesting that it wasn't even ten yet. Instead, she looked up at her father appealingly. "Is it all right if I watch television?"

"For an hour," Phillip agreed. "Say good night to Carolyn and Beth."

Tracy hesitated, then spoke the words while she looked at the floor.

"Good night, Tracy," Carolyn said quietly, then led Beth out of the room and back to her own. Neither mother nor daughter said anything while Beth undressed, put on her pajamas, then slipped under the covers. Finally Carolyn leaned over, and kissed her daughter's forehead.

"I'm sorry, honey," she said.

Beth looked up at her mother. "Do you believe me, Mommy?" she said so quietly that Carolyn could barely hear the words.

"Of course I do," Carolyn assured her. "Why would I ever think that you'd pick a fight with Tracy?" She forced herself to grin. "After all, she's bigger than you."

"But why does she hate me?" Beth asked.

"I don't know," Carolyn replied, the smile fading from her lips. "And I don't know what we can do about it, either. But we'll think of something. I promise." She kissed Beth once more, then went to the door. Then, as she let herself out, she heard Beth speak once more, almost as if she were talking to herself—

"Sometimes I wish Amy would just kill her."

Chilled, Carolyn said nothing, but pulled Beth's door closed behind her.

Phillip glanced up as Carolyn came into their bedroom. "You look white as a sheet," he said. Taking her hand, he led her to the bed, but she pulled away from him and went to sit at her vanity instead.

In the mirror, she could see that he was right. Her skin looked ashen, and there seemed to be dark circles under her eyes. Helplessly, she shook her head.

"I just don't know how much more of it I can stand," she said, her voice trembling with the tears that were suddenly threatening to overwhelm her. "It's not getting any better, Phillip. And I don't think it's going to!"

Phillip came to stand beside her, his strong hands resting gently on her shoulders. "But what can we do?" he asked. "They're our children." Then he smiled tightly. "Maybe I was wrong," he suggested. "Maybe I shouldn't have stopped the fight. In the end, they may just have to fight it out."

"That's boys," Carolyn said. She reached for a Kleenex, and blew her nose, then threw the tissue into the white wicker basket at her feet. "Girls don't do that sort of thing."

"Ours do," Phillip said quietly.

Carolyn shook her head hopelessly. "And what's it going to be like when the baby comes? Phillip, I just don't think I can cope with it all."

"Of course you can," Phillip began, but Carolyn shook her head again.

The last words Beth had spoken before Carolyn had left her room echoed in her mind. Should she repeat them to Phillip? But she couldn't. It would be almost like betraying Beth. Besides, the words hadn't meant anything—they'd been nothing more than the venting of childish anger.

"I . . . I've been thinking maybe I ought to let Beth go live with Alan for a while," she finally said. "At least until the baby is born." In the mirror she could see her husband's worried frown. "And she'd like to go—I know she would."

"What about Alan?" Phillip asked. "Don't you think you ought to ask him about it?"

"I don't have to," Carolyn sighed. "You know as well as I do that he'd take her in a minute. He'd rearrange his whole life for her."

There was a melancholy note in her voice that made Phillip wonder if Carolyn was having more second thoughts about their marriage. "And I wouldn't?" he asked quietly, hoping he didn't sound defensive.

Carolyn patted one of his hands gently. "You'd do anything for anybody, if you could," she told him. "In that way, you and Alan are very much alike. And I know how much you've tried to do for Beth. But you have Tracy and Abigail to worry about, too."

"And you," Phillip added.

"And me, and in a few months, a new baby as well. And I just keep thinking maybe I'm being unfair to Beth. She's so unhappy here, and it doesn't seem to matter what you or I do. Sometimes I feel as though we're both caught in the middle."

"I know," Phillip agreed. Giving her shoulders one more squeeze, he wandered over to the window, and looked out into the night. From here, at the front of the house, he could barely make out the upper ring of the mausoleum, glowing softly in the moonlight. Up there, at least, it looked peaceful. If only they could make the house peaceful, too.

"Let's not make any decisions now," he said. "Let's give it a little more time, and see what happens. I hate giving up. Another few days, all right? And then we'll talk to Alan."

Carolyn nodded, and looked at herself in the mirror once more.

She not only looked tired now, she thought. She looked defeated as well.

In the corridor outside, Tracy padded silently away from the door to her father's bedroom.

She hadn't heard every word—the wood was too thick for that—but she'd heard enough.

They were thinking about sending Beth away. That was exactly what Tracy wanted. But it wouldn't be forever.

When the baby came, they'd bring her back, and then it would be worse than ever.

She had to figure out how to convince them that Beth was crazy so they'd send her away and never let her come back again.

She went back to her room, and got into bed. The television was on, and though she was looking at it, she wasn't really seeing it. She was thinking.

By the time her father came in to say good night twenty minutes later, she had figured it out. When he leaned over to kiss her, she slipped her hands around his neck, and hugged him tightly. "I love you, Daddy," she said quietly. "I love you, and I really am sorry about what happened with Beth tonight. From now on, I'll do my best to be nice to her. All right?"

She felt her father's body stiffen for a moment, then relax as he returned her hug. "Thanks, Princess," he said into her ear. "That would really help out."

"Then I'll do it," Tracy whispered, giving him one more kiss, then rolling over in bed. "Good night, Daddy."

When he was gone, she rolled back over and lay staring at the ceiling. When the house was silent and she was sure everyone had gone to sleep, she got out of bed, and quickly dressed.

A minute later, she was down the stairs and out of the house, moving across the terrace, then disappearing into the night.

Eighteen

The warmth of the morning woke Beth early, and she stretched luxuriously, then kicked the covers off and got out of bed. But a moment later, as she came fully awake and remembered last night's fight with Tracy, her good feeling vanished.

It would be another day just like all the rest—a day of trying not to make any mistakes, of trying to stay out of Tracy's way, of not knowing what to do next.

Maybe she should go down to the village and find Peggy.

Or maybe, instead of looking for Peggy, she should go to the mill.

Maybe, if she promised to stay out of everyone's way, her father would let her spend the day at the mill. Then, while everyone was busy, she could go down into the basement, and sneak into the little room under the stairs. And Amy would be there, waiting for her.

They could sit in the dark together, and Beth could talk to her. It would be nice, Beth thought, to be alone in someplace cool and dark and quiet, with no one around except a friend who wouldn't laugh at you, or tease you, no matter what you said. That's the kind of friend, she was sure, that Amy would be to her. Someone for her to talk to when she got so lonely she felt like no one in the world wanted her, or understood her, or cared about her.

She began dressing, then looked at the clock. It was only seven-thirty. Hannah would be in the kitchen, starting breakfast, but neither Peter nor Mr. Smithers would have come to work yet.

Maybe she should go down to the stable and visit Patches before Peter got there. Because Peggy, she was sure, would have told Peter what happened yesterday. Peggy always told everybody everything, and by now Peter probably would have decided she was crazy, too.

What if he told her she couldn't come to the stable anymore? That, she decided, would be awful. Going down to see the horses in the morning was the best part of every day. Still, it hadn't happened yet, and even if it did, she could just start getting up earlier every day.

She tied her tennis shoes, then quickly made her bed and put away the clothes she'd been wearing last night. Then she left her room, and glanced down the hall in both directions, listening. She heard nothing. Both Tracy's door and her mother's door were still closed. Everybody but her was still asleep. She scurried down the stairs, and through the long living room, then slowed down as she crossed the dining room. She could almost feel the portraits of all the dead Sturgesses glaring disapprovingly down on her, even though she always did her best not to look at them. When she came to the butler's pantry, she let out an almost audible sigh of relief. Here, in Hannah's territory, she always felt more comfortable. Finally she pushed open the kitchen door.

"Must be a quarter to eight," Hannah said without turning from the stove where she was scrambling some eggs. "You're getting to be as regular as clockwork. Orange juice is in the refrigerator, and the eggs'll be done in a minute."

"I could have made my own eggs," Beth said as she reached into the refrigerator and brought out the pitcher of freshly squeezed orange juice. Even though she hated the pulp in it, she wouldn't hurt Hannah's feelings by telling her so, so she poured a big glass, then took a deep breath, squeezed her eyes shut tight, and tried to drink it all in one gulp. When she was finished, she opened her eyes to see the housekeeper shaking her head sympathetically.

"Don't see how you can do that," Hannah said, her face serious but her eyes twinkling. "The pulp in that stuff makes me gag. I always have to strain it, myself."

Beth's eyes widened in surprise; then she giggled, and sat down at the table to dig into the plate of eggs that was now waiting for her. When she was finished, she scraped the leavings into the sink, rinsed the plate, then picked up the waiting bag of garbage and headed out the back door. She dumped the trash in the barrel as she crossed the little terrace, then waved to Ben Smithers, who was busy in the rose garden.

She ran all the way to the door of the stable. As soon as she stepped inside, she knew that Peter, as she'd hoped, was not there yet. There was a stillness in the little barn—a quiet that was broken only by the soft snufflings of the horses as they became aware that someone had come into the stable.

Beth let herself relax as she closed the stable door behind her, and started down the aisle toward Patches's stall. The big mare was stretching her neck out as far as she could, and whinnying softly.

"Hi, Patches," Beth whispered, reaching up to scratch the horse's ears. "Have you had breakfast yet?"

The horse snuffled, pawing at the floor of her stall, then tried to poke her nose into the pocket of Beth's jeans. Across the stall, the feed trough was empty.

"I don't see why Peter can't leave you something to eat during the night," Beth told the big mare, scratching her affectionately between the ears. "What if you get hungry?"

The horse snorted softly, and her head bobbed as if she had understood every word Beth said, and agreed with her. That, Beth decided, was the neatest thing about Patches—she could say anything to her, and never have to worry about whether the horse believed her or not.

It wasn't at all like it was with people. With people, if you said something that sounded just a little bit strange, they started calling you crazy.

Either that, or they didn't believe you were telling them the truth.

Beth sighed, hugged Patches's neck, then started down the aisle toward the feed bins to find something for the horse to eat. The hay wasn't down yet, but there was a big sack of oats beneath the hayloft.

As she found a pail and began filling it with oats, Beth wondered if anyone would ever believe that Amy was real.

So far, it didn't seem like anyone would.

Except for old Mrs. Sturgess.

But had the old lady really believed her, or was she just pretending to for some reason that Beth couldn't understand? Yet if she was only pretending, why would she have said that when she came home from the hospital she'd show Beth something that proved there really was a girl named Amy? And why would she have asked Beth what Amy wanted?

Beth didn't think Amy wanted anything. All she wanted was for them to be friends.

She took the pailful of oats back to Patches's stall, opened the door, and let herself inside.

"Look what I've got for you," she said, holding the pail up close to the big mare's nose.

The horse sniffed at the pail, then backed away, tossing her head.

"It's only oats," Beth said, moving slowly forward until she could reach out and take hold of Patches's halter. "You like oats, remember?"

She offered the pail once more, but the horse, sniffing at it again, tried to pull her head away. But Beth, prepared for it, tightened her grip on the halter, and held Patches in place.

"Maybe she doesn't want any," she heard a voice say from behind her. "Maybe she's not hungry."

Beth felt herself redden, and whirled around to see Tracy standing at the stall door, smiling in that superior way of hers that never failed to make Beth feel stupid. "She likes oats," she said. "She just wants me to feed her, that's all."

"She doesn't want you to feed her." Tracy sneered. "She doesn't even like you. She just wants you to go away!"

"That's not true!" Beth flared, stung. "Watch!"

Still holding on to the horse's halter with one hand, she set the pail on the floor, then took a handful of the grain and held it up for Patches's inspection.

The big horse eyed the grain, then tentatively opened her mouth and licked. Beth raised her hand, and the horse's lips curled out, closed, and pulled in the oats. As she munched slowly, then swallowed, Beth reached down for another handful.

"That's the way," she crooned softly as the horse ate the second handful. "See how good they are?"

"Big deal," Tracy replied, her voice scornful. "A horse will eat anything, if you shove it into its mouth." Snickering, she turned away, and left the stable as silently as she'd come.

Beth felt a sudden stinging in her eyes, and glared after Tracy. "But you do like me," Beth said to Patches when she was once again alone with the horse. "You like me better than anyone, don't you?"

She picked up the pail, and held it while Patches, snuffling with apparent contentment, finished off the oats. Then, patting the horse on the neck, Beth let go of her halter and left the stall to take the bucket to the sink, wash it, and return it to its place by the tackroom door.

She was just about to turn Patches out into the paddock when she heard her mother's voice calling her to come in. She hesitated, then patted the horse once more. "I'll be back later," she promised. "And maybe we can go for a ride. Okay?" The horse whinnied softly, and her tail flicked up. Then her tongue came out to give Beth's hand a final lick. "Who cares what Tracy thinks? Who cares what anyone thinks?"

But as she left the stable, Peter Russell was coming in, and Beth could tell by the way he looked at her that Peggy had, indeed, told him all about yesterday morning. And though he said nothing, Beth felt herself redden.

She did, after all, care what people thought.

Beth was just coming back into the stable an hour later when she heard Patches's first high-pitched whinny, followed by the crash of hooves against the wooden walls of the stall.

She raced down the broad aisle between the two rows of stalls and got to the big mare just in time to see the horse rear up, her forelegs lashing at the air, then drop back down. She stamped her feet, then once more reared, her teeth bared and her mouth open as if she were trying to bite some unseen enemy.

Terrified, Beth backed away from the stall. "Peter!" she yelled. "Come quick!"

But Peter was already there, coming out of the stall that belonged to the big Arabian stallion named Thunder. He stared at Patches in amazement for a moment, then dashed down the aisle between the two rows of stalls, climbed the fence into the paddock, and hurried back toward Patches's stall. As the mare, her eyes glazed now, bolted out of the stable, Peter made a grab for her halter, but missed. Bucking and snorting, Patches moved out into the center of the paddock, then stopped for a moment, glancing around wildly, as if searching for the unseen attacker. Then she dropped to the ground, and began rolling over, her legs thrashing violently. A moment later Beth, her face ashen, appeared at the open stall door.

"Peter, what's wrong with her?"

Peter hesitated, his eyes fixed on the agonized horse. "I don't know," he said. "Get me the lead, then go up to the house and have someone call the vet."

Beth darted back into the stable, grabbed a lead, then ran back outside and gave it to Peter. She stared at Patches for a moment, then dashed to the paddock fence, climbed over it, and charged up the slope toward the house.

A moment later she burst through the back door, calling out for Hannah.

"What is it, child?" Hannah asked, bustling out of her room.

"It's Patches," Beth gasped. "Hannah, we have to call the vet right away. Something's wrong with Patches! I . . . I think she's dying!"

As Beth and her mother, together with Phillip and Tracy Sturgess, looked on, Paul Garvey shook his head, and slid a large needle into a vein in Patches's right foreleg. He pressed the plunger on the hypodermic home, and a moment later Patches shuddered, seemed to sigh, then lay still.

"It's better this way," the veterinarian said softly, rising to his feet. "There wasn't any way to bring her out of that."

"But it was colic, wasn't it?" Phillip asked, his eyes leaving the dead horse to fix anxiously on Garvey.

"I never saw a case that violent before," Garvey replied. "If I had to bet, I'd put my money on poison."

"Poison?" Carolyn echoed, her eyes widening. "But who—"

"I'd like to check her feed," Garvey interrupted, his attention shifting to Peter Russell. "Any of the other horses showing any symptoms like this?"

Peter shook his head. "They hadn't even been fed yet. At least not Patches. I'd just filled Thunder's trough, and Patches would have been next."

The vet frowned. "The horse hadn't eaten anything?" he asked, his voice conveying his doubt.

It was Tracy who answered him. "It was Beth," she said, her voice quivering with apparent fury. "Beth was feeding her oats this morning."

Garvey's frown deepened. "Oats?" he echoed. "How much?"

"A whole bucketful," Tracy said. "They're in that bag over there." She pointed to the big feedsack that still sat against the wall beneath the hayloft, and Garvey walked quickly over, reached deep into the sack, and pulled out a handful. Holding the feed close to his nose, he sniffed deeply. Garvey frowned, then sniffed again.

"Well?" Phillip asked.

"Doesn't smell right," Garvey said. "I'll take some of this back to my lab. In the meantime, don't let any of the other horses anywhere near this stuff."

There was a moment of silence as the import of his words sank in, and then suddenly Tracy's voice, shrill and angry, sliced through the stable once more. "She poisoned her! She poisoned my horse!"

Beth gasped, and turned to look at Tracy, who was pointing at her accusingly. "I didn't do anything—" she began, but Tracy cut her off.

"You killed her!" she screamed. "Just because you hate me, you killed my horse! She didn't even want those oats! I saw you, and you were making her eat them. You were shoving them right into her mouth!" She lunged toward Beth, but her father grabbed her, holding her back.

"Tracy, nobody would try to kill Patches—"

"She did!" Tracy wailed. "She poisoned the oats, and then made her eat them."

Beth stared at Tracy for a moment, and suddenly remembered the way Patches had snorted, and tried to pull away from the pail. It wasn't until she'd taken the food in her own hand, and almost shoved it into the horse's mouth, that the animal had finally eaten it. Bursting into tears, she wheeled around and fled from the barn.

As Phillip held his crying daughter close, he and Carolyn exchanged a long look. Finally, after what seemed an eternity of silent decision-making, he spoke.

"I'll call Alan," he said quietly. "I guess maybe it's time we did something."

As he spoke the words, he thought for a moment that he felt Tracy relax against his body, and her sobbing seemed to ease.

Tracy Sturgess emerged from the swimming pool at the Westover Country Club, grabbed a towel, and flopped down on the lawn, shaking the water out of her hair. She'd been at the club for an hour, and even though no one had told her, she was almost sure she knew why her father had suddenly suggested—even insisted—that she come here this afternoon.

They were going to move Beth out of the house while she was gone.

And almost as good as that was the fact that her father had promised her a new horse, and even given in when she'd demanded an Arabian just like Thunder. She'd had to cry, of course, and act as though losing Patches was the worst thing that had ever happened to her, but that was easy. She'd always been good at things like that.

Now she propped her head up on one arm, and grinned at Alison Babcock, who was her best friend this summer. "What's everybody talking about?" she asked.

"Your grandmother," Alison replied. She rolled her eyes toward

Kip Braithwaite, who was sprawled on a towel next to her. "Kip thinks someone tried to kill her."

Tracy's eyes widened, and she turned to stare at Kip. "Why would anyone want to kill Grandmother?"

"Well, someone wanted to kill Jeff Bailey, and they did it, didn't they?"

"Aw, jeez," Brett Kilpatrick groaned. "Nobody killed Jeff. He tripped and fell on a pick."

"That's what you think," Kip replied.

"Well, I ought to know," Brett shot back. "I was there, wasn't I?"

"But what did *you* see?" Kip taunted. "You were too chicken even to go downstairs."

"But what about Grandmother?" Tracy demanded. "How come you think someone tried to kill her?"

Kip shrugged. "Well, she had her heart attack right on the same spot where they killed Jeff, didn't she?"

"So what?" Alison Babcock asked. "That doesn't prove anything."

"And it doesn't disprove anything, either," Kip taunted.

"Well, if you're so smart, who did it?" Brett asked. Kip glared at his friend. "What about Beth Rogers?"

Brett began laughing. "Her? You gotta be kidding."

"Didn't you see her at Tracy's party? She almost wet her pants just watching that movie!"

"But she was talking about a ghost in the mill," Kip pointed out. "Maybe she went looking for one."

"Are you kidding?" Alison giggled. "Beth Rogers? Give me a break."

"Well, I think she killed Jeff," Kip insisted. "And I think she tried to kill Tracy's grandma, too."

"Big deal." Alison sneered. "So that's what you *think*. But how do you *know*?"

"Well, I know she killed Tracy's horse," Kip shot back. "Tracy says that's why they're kicking her out. She's crazy."

"Oh, come on," Alison started, but Tracy interrupted her.

"But she is crazy, Alison," she insisted. "I was hiking up near the mausoleum yesterday, and she was up there. I heard her talking about someone named Amy that she thinks killed Jeff."

Alison stared at her. "Amy?" she repeated. "Who's she supposed to be?"

Tracy rolled her eyes. "She's the ghost! And I heard her talking about how this Amy killed Jeff because he was teasing her at my party."

The other three fell silent, eyeing each other uneasily, and Tracy could see that she hadn't yet convinced them. "Well, she *is* crazy," she insisted. "And I bet Kip's right. I bet she's so crazy that she killed Jeff, and doesn't even know it. I bet she really believes a ghost did it."

Alison's eyes narrowed, and she stared suspiciously at Tracy. "What about your grandmother?" she asked. "Do you think Beth tried to kill her too?"

Tracy hesitated, then nodded.

"Why?" Alison demanded. "What did your grandmother ever do to her?"

"Nothing," Tracy replied. "Except she can't stand Beth either, and Beth knows it. But crazy people don't need a reason to do things—they just do them." Then she had an idea. "And my grandmother was acting real weird last night, too. First she talked to Daddy, and then she made us go get Beth and bring her to the hospital. And afterward, Beth wouldn't tell any of us what she and Grandmother talked about."

"Think maybe she saw Beth down there yesterday?" Kip asked.

"If she'd seen her, why would she want to talk to her?" Alison asked. "I mean, if somebody tried to kill me, the last thing I'd want to do is *talk* to them!"

"Maybe she wasn't sure it was Beth," Kip suggested. "Maybe she wanted to talk to her to see if she could trap her, like they do on TV all the time."

Alison rolled her eyes impatiently. "Oh, who cares what they talked about? There's no way we can find out, anyway."

There was a momentary silence, and then Tracy grinned conspiratorially. "I bet I can find out."

"How?" someone asked.

"I'll go visit Grandmother," Tracy went on. "And I'll bet I can pry whatever she told Beth out of her. I can always get Grandmother to do whatever I want, because she hates Carolyn so much."

"I bet she doesn't hate her as much as you do," Alison said, rolling over onto her back, and closing her eyes.

"I bet she doesn't, either," Tracy agreed. She, too, flopped back and closed her eyes. "In fact, I wish I could figure out a way to get Daddy to throw her out, too. Or maybe I could even get Beth to kill her. Wouldn't that be neat? Getting her to kill her own mother?" She giggled maliciously, and after a moment, the others joined in.

Tracy left the club at four o'clock, deciding it was better to walk the two miles into town than to ask her father to take her to the hospital when he came to pick her up. He'd want to know why she suddenly wanted to visit her grandmother, and she wasn't about to tell him. She started along River Road, wondering how she would get the information she wanted out of her grandmother. She couldn't just ask her—she already knew that. If she'd made Beth promise not to talk, she wouldn't just start talking herself. And then, as she approached the railroad tracks, she knew the answer.

Get her talking about the past. If there was anything her grandmother liked to do, it was to talk about the "good old days" before Tracy was born. And then, when she had her grandmother's guard down, she'd figure out how to lead her into talking about what had happened last night.

She was crossing the railroad tracks on River Road when she suddenly felt as if she was being watched. Turning, she saw Beth Rogers standing a few yards away, staring at her.

She froze, wondering what was going to happen. What if Beth had already figured out what she'd done to the oats? Would she have the nerve to say anything? But it wouldn't happen—Beth, she was sure, was too dumb to figure out what had really happened to Patches, just as Patches had been too dumb to refuse the poisoned oats. Raising her chin defiantly, and studiously ignoring Beth, she continued on to Prospect Street, then turned right past the mill toward the hospital that lay a few blocks further on.

Ignoring the sign announcing that visiting hours were from six until eight P.M., Tracy made her way to her grandmother's room, and let herself inside. Lying in the bed, her eyes closed and her breathing regular, Abigail Sturgess slept peacefully.

Tracy gazed at the frail form in the bed for a few moments, then reached out and shook her grandmother.

"Grandmother? Wake up."

Abigail stirred slightly, and tried to roll over.

Tracy shook her again. "Grandmother! It's Tracy. Wake up!"

Abigail started slightly, coughed, and opened her eyes. Squinting against the light, she peered up into her granddaughter's face. "Tracy?" she asked weakly. "What are you doing here?"

Tracy wreathed her face in a smile. "I came to visit you, Grandmother. I thought you must be lonely."

Abigail struggled to sit up. "Well, aren't you sweet," she said, as Tracy stuffed an extra pillow behind her. She blinked, then reached unsteadily for a glass of water on the table next to the bed. "Did your father come with you?"

Tracy shook her head. "I walked. I was afraid if I told anyone I was coming, Carolyn would have stopped me."

"She probably would have," Abigail agreed. "She's a hard one, that woman." Then she smiled. "Not like your mother at all."

Sensing an opening, Tracy smiled again. "Tell me about her," she said. "Tell me all about Mommy!"

Abigail sighed contentedly, and her eyes took on a faraway look as she let her mind drift back into the past. "She was a wonderful woman, your mother. Pretty as a picture, and just like you." She reached out to Tracy, squeezing her hand affectionately. "And she knew her place in the world. You wouldn't find her working in the kitchen, except once a week to give Cook the menus. But I suppose those days are gone forever." Her voice trailed off, and she fell silent.

Tracy gazed at the shriveled form of her grandmother, wondering if she'd gone back to sleep again. "Well, if the mill starts making money again—" she began, and Abigail's eyes snapped open.

"It won't!" she said, her voice suddenly strong. "We don't need the money, and I told your father to close it. I intend to see that he does!"

Tracy grinned to herself "But why?" she asked. "Why should he close it?"

Abigail's head swung slowly around, and her eyes fixed on Tracy's, but Tracy had the eerie feeling that her grandmother wasn't really seeing her.

"Because she's evil," the old woman whispered, almost to herself. "She killed my son, and she killed Jeff Bailey, and she tried to kill me!"

Tracy's heart beat faster. It was exactly what she'd wanted to hear, even though her grandmother was confused. Beth couldn't possibly have killed Uncle Conrad—she hadn't even been born yet. But it didn't matter. So what if her grandmother had part of it wrong? She did her best not to show her excitement. "She tried to *kill* you?" she whispered. "Who?" Then, when her grandmother made no reply, she decided to gamble. "You saw her, didn't you?" she asked. "You saw her down there, and she did something to you, didn't she?"

Abigail's eyes widened, and she felt her heart constrict as her mind suddenly opened and the memories of the previous night flooded back to her. Again her hand reached out to Tracy, but now that hand was a claw, and when she grasped the girl's wrist, Tracy felt a stab of pain.

"The children," Abigail gasped. "Yes . . . I saw the children."

"Beth," Tracy whispered excitedly. "You saw Beth Rogers, didn't you?"

Abigail was nodding now, and her jaw began working as she struggled to speak again. "Children," she repeated. "I saw them. I saw them just as if they were really there. . . ."

Tracy's heart was thumping now. "You did, Grandmother," she said. "You saw her, and she tried to kill you."

"Dead," Abigail whispered. "She's dead, and she wants to kill us." Her grip on Tracy's arm tightened, and the girl winced with pain. "She wants to kill us all, Tracy. She hates us, because of what we did to her. She hates us, and she'll kill us if we let her."

Tracy tried to pull away, but Abigail seemed to find new strength as her words rambled on. "Stay away, Tracy. Stay away from there. Promise me, Tracy. Promise me you'll stay away."

Suddenly frightened by her grandmother's surge of power, Tracy twisted her arm loose from the old woman's grip. As if she'd been disconnected from her source of strength, Abigail went limp, her arm falling by her side as she sank back into the pillows.

"Promise me," she muttered softly as her eyes, clouded now with her years and infirmities, sought out Tracy's.

Tracy began edging toward the door. "I . . . I promise," she mumbled. Then she was gone, pulling the door closed behind her, wanting to shut out the image of the ancient woman in the bed.

As she left the hospital, she turned her grandmother's words over in her mind, and decided that, after all, she had been right.

Her grandmother *had* seen someone in the basement of the mill last night, and whoever she had seen had tried to kill her.

And Tracy knew who the old woman had seen.

Beth Rogers.

She walked back along River Road until she came to Prospect Street, where she stopped to stare curiously at the old building that was suddenly coming back to life. What, she wondered, had really happened there so many years ago?

Nothing, she decided.

Her grandmother was old, and sick, and didn't know what she was talking about.

And promises made to her, Tracy also decided, didn't really count. In fact, Tracy had long ago figured out that promises didn't mean anything. If you wanted something, you made promises in order to get it. Then you went ahead and did what you wanted, and nobody ever said anything. At least her father and her grandmother didn't, and that was all that mattered.

If she felt like going into the mill and looking around, she would, and no one was going to stop her.

Nineteen

The somnolence of summer had settled into Westover, and by August the town had taken on a wilted look. People moved slowly in the damp warmth of July, and slower still as August's heat closed oppressively down on them.

For Beth, life had taken on a strange routine, each day much like the day before.

At first it had all been terribly confusing. The memory of Patches dying while she watched was still fresh in her mind—etched indelibly there, still waking her up in the middle of the night sometimes.

But the rest of that day had taken on a dreamlike quality. The sudden arrival of her father; the explanation that it had been decided that for a while, at least, she should live with him; the hasty packing of her bags; her departure from Hilltop with her father, barely aware of what was happening while she tried to figure out *why* it had happened.

Her father had tried to explain it to her, tried to tell her that while no one was blaming her for what had happened to Patches, it had just seemed better to all of them for her to live with him for a while. Mrs. Sturgess would be coming home, and her mother was pregnant, and Tracy . . .

His voice had trailed off after he'd mentioned Tracy's name, but Beth had known what he meant. Hilltop was Tracy's house, not hers, and they both couldn't live there anymore. So she had to move out.

It wasn't fair, but it was the way things were, and even at her age, Beth already knew that life was not always fair.

But living with her father had not turned out to be quite what she'd thought it would be, either. Before she'd moved in with him, they'd always gone out to dinner on the evenings she'd spent with him, and he'd always seemed to have lots of time to spend with her.

But now, when she was there all the time, it was different. She understood why—he had to go to work every day, and he couldn't afford to take them both to restaurants every night. So they stayed home most evenings, and he cooked dinner for them, and the food wasn't as good as the food Hannah had fixed at Hilltop. And her room was a lot smaller, and didn't look out over the whole village. Instead, it looked out over a parking lot, and only a little corner of the mill was visible through a gap between two buildings across Fourth Street.

But at least Tracy wasn't there, and that was good.

What wasn't good was what had happened when she'd gone to see Peggy Russell. Peggy had only opened the door a few inches, and she hadn't invited Beth to come in. Instead she'd said that she couldn't play with Beth anymore, and that Beth better stay away from her house.

Beth, her eyes blurred with tear's, had gone back home, but the emptiness of her father's little apartment had made her feel even more lonesome than Peggy's rejection. So she'd gone down to the mill, and spent the rest of the day there.

As the days had turned into weeks she'd tried to make friends again with the kids she'd known before she moved up to the top of the hill, but it hadn't worked. All of them had heard about what had happened to Patches, and all of them had heard Peggy's story about the grave up on the hillside, and about the fact that Beth thought the person who was buried there still lived in the mill. At first, they'd simply ignored her when she tried to make friends with them, but when she'd persisted, they'd started calling her names, and invented a nickname for her.

Crazy Bethy.

They called it out at her when she walked down the street, and if their parents were with them, and they couldn't yell it out loud, they'd whisper to each other, and point at her.

Her father told her not to worry about it—that in a few weeks something else would come along, and the kids would forget all about it.

But Beth wasn't at all sure that would ever happen.

She started spending more time at the mill, and finally it got so that the workmen expected her to be there, and stopped worrying about her every minute. They were always friendly to her, and she wandered around anywhere she wanted, watching them work, bringing them tools, sometimes even helping them.

It wasn't so bad, really, except on the days that Phillip Sturgess came to inspect the progress of the work, and brought Tracy with him.

Phillip was always friendly to Beth, interested in how she was, and what she was doing.

But Tracy never spoke to her. Instead she just stared at her, a little smile on her mouth that told Beth she was laughing at her. Beth tried to pretend she didn't care, but of course she did.

Sometimes, during the afternoons, she'd see Tracy outside, just standing there watching the mill, and Beth knew what she wanted.

She wanted to come inside, and go down into the basement.

But she couldn't. All day there were people there, and at night, when everyone had gone home, the building was carefully closed up, and the padlock on the one gate in the fence was always checked twice.

But for Beth, going down to the basement, and the little room under the loading dock, was simple. No one ever missed her, and part of every day she spent sitting alone in the darkness of that room, feeling the presence of Amy, who was now her only real friend.

At first it had been a little bit scary being down there by herself. For a long time she'd always left the door open and kept her flashlight on, using its beam to search out every corner. But soon she'd decided there was nothing to fear in the darkness of the room, and began closing the door behind her, turning off the light, and imagining that Amy—a real Amy—was there with her.

After a while even the strange smoky odor of the room didn't bother her anymore, and in late July, she'd brought an old blanket to the mill. Now she kept it in the little room, where sometimes she'd spread it out, then lie on it while she daydreamed about Amy.

She knew a lot about Amy now. She'd gone to the library, and found books about what the towns like Westover had been like a hundred years ago when Amy had been alive.

She'd read about children like Amy, who'd spent most of their lives in buildings like this, working all day long, then going home to little houses that had no heat, and no electricity, and no plumbing.

One day, she'd wandered around Westover, trying to decide which house Amy might have lived in.

Finally, in her own mind, she'd decided that Amy's house was the one on Elm Street, right by the railroad tracks. Of course she knew that part of the reason she'd decided on that house was that her mother had showed it to her a long time ago, and told her that the house, abandoned now, its roof sagging and its windows broken, with weeds growing wild around its weathered walls, had once been her own family's home, long ago, even before she herself had been born.

As Beth had stood on the cracked sidewalk that day, staring at it, imagining that this was where Amy had lived, she'd thought she could hear Amy's voice whispering to her, telling her that she was right, that this was the place which had been her home.

Then she'd begun dreaming about Amy. The dreams came to her only when she was in the little room behind the stairs, and she wasn't even sure they were really dreams, for she couldn't remember being asleep when they came to her, nor could she remember waking up when they were over. Indeed, she decided that they weren't dreams at all.

They were visions.

They were visits from Amy, who came to show her things, and tell her things.

She never talked to anyone about Amy's visits She'd learned by now not to talk about Amy to anyone. The one time she had, no one had believed her. And now everyone thought she was crazy.

Everyone, that is, except old Mrs. Sturgess, and Beth hadn't seen her since the day after she'd gone to the hospital. Once Beth had gone back to visit her again, but the nurse had told her that there was a list of people who were allowed into the old woman's room, and her name wasn't on the list.

So Amy had become her secret, and it didn't really matter to Beth anymore if old Mrs. Sturgess could prove that there had really been someone named Amy or not.

To Beth, Amy was as real as anyone else.

Amy was a part of her.

And then one day late in August, in the little room in the basement of the mill, she actually became Amy for a little while, saw what Amy saw, felt what she felt.

It was a particularly hot afternoon, but down there, in the darkness, it felt different. It felt cool, almost as if it were a perfect morning in spring. Beth spread the blanket out on the floor, then lowered herself down onto it, switched off the flashlight, and let the visit happen. . . .

It was the kind of spring morning Amy had long since learned to dread: the sun was shining brightly, and the air was warm even at a little before six. By ten, she knew, it would be getting hot, but there would be just enough breeze to make lying in the square and staring—daydreaming—up into the spreading maples the most alluring experience she could think of. And in the afternoon, when the heat reached its peak, and the air was getting so muggy that breathing was hard, there would be the stream, just a few yards away, its cool waters beckoning to her.

Yes, today was the kind of day she had come to dread, because for some reason, this kind of day never seemed to come on a Sunday, when she might have had at least a few minutes to enjoy it. On Sundays, even though she didn't have to go to work, there was too much to do at home, taking care of her sisters and brothers, keeping out of her father's way, helping her mother with all the things she never had time to do during the week.

Almost unconsciously, she slowed her pace, as if by taking a few more minutes now, she could put off the inevitable. But she knew it was impossible. As she turned off the railroad tracks to make her way up the path toward Prospect Street, and the shadow of the shoe mill blotted out the sunlight, she began steeling herself for the hours ahead. Long ago her mother had taught her the trick of survival in the mill. All you had to do was shut everything out, until the little room you worked in was your whole world, and nothing beyond that little room could enter your head at all. Then all you thought about was the work: cutting the little pieces of leather out of the tanned hides, making sure they were all exactly the same size, stacking them carefully but quickly in neat piles so that when they went to the assembley room upstairs the assemblers would have the right piece at the right time. And you had to work fast, because you got paid by the piece.

You had to ignore the smells, too, or you'd quickly get sick and not be able to work at all. Sometimes Amy wondered which smells were the worst—the acrid odor of the lye used for tanning the hides, or the sour smell of the dyes used to color the leather after it was tanned. Or maybe, she sometimes thought, the worst smell was the smell of the people themselves, all of them sweating in the heat, their eyes fastened on their work for fear that if they looked toward the filthy windows the light and air outside would overpower them, and they'd drop their work and run away from the mill forever.

But they couldn't do that—Amy least of all. This was 1886, and there weren't many jobs, and at home her mother, who had no job at all, always told her how lucky she was to have a job in the middle of the depression. And even though Amy wasn't quite sure what a depression was, she knew that she couldn't give in to her impulse to run away from the mill, because if she did, there wouldn't be any money at all, and her mother and sisters and brothers would have nothing to eat.

The door of the mill loomed a few steps ahead of her now, and she paused. According to the clock on the church steeple above the square, she still had four minutes before the morning whistle blew and everyone had to be at the tables, ready to work. Her eyes darted around, as if gathering images to put away for examination later, but then fixed on a group of three children—children her own age—who were walking along the other side of the street. She knew their names, but had never spoken to them, as they had never spoken to her.

Fleetingly, she wondered if they knew her name.

Probably not, since they didn't work at the mill.

They didn't work at all.

They were the lucky ones, whose fathers ran the mill, and who lived in nice houses, and went to school in the winter and played outside all summer. And they had pretty clothes, clothes that never looked as though someone else had worn them before; never looked as though they needed mending two or three times a week. Involuntarily, Amy's hands dropped down and ran over her own dress, as if by some unseen force she could make the stains on it disappear, or smooth over the rough stitches that held its tattered pieces together.

For a moment, she wondered where they were going today, then decided it didn't matter. The only thing that mattered, really, was that now she had only one minute to get to her table, and if she was late, the shift supervisor would yell at her; might even fire her. And if that happened—

She put the thought out of her mind, and hurried through the door into the dimness of the mill, doing her best to put the rest of the world out of her mind.

A few people spoke to her as she started toward the stairs at the far end of the building, and she nodded a brief response. But most of the people were already hard at work, their fingers moving quickly in unchanging routines that had long since become automatic as they assembled shoes from the piles of leather around them. The people seemed to have a sameness about them: their eyes were vacant, and their skin seemed to have the look of worn leather. Their clothes, shabby and ill-fitting, all looked alike, and marked them for what they were—millworkers. For a fleeting instant, she wondered if they, like herself, dreamed of getting out of the mill, but then she decided they didn't. For most of them, the mill was their life, and they would be here until they died.

As the whistle sounded, its piercing scream slashing through her like a knife, Amy hurried down the stairs and into the little room under the loading dock where she worked with the other children her age, cutting the freshly dyed hides into the many pieces that went into the shoes.

It was here she had started working three years ago, when she was eight, tending to the vats in which the hides were soaked, then moving on to the dyeing itself. Finally, she had begun training as a cutter, and now she worked her twelve-hour shifts, six days a week, cutting soles from the rough leather, training herself to work as the others worked, without thinking.

Even as she put on her apron and took up her position at the cutting table, she began the process of closing down her mind.

She started with her eyes.

She had to keep her eyes on her work, even though it had been months since she really needed to watch every move she made. But if her eyes stayed on the leather, and the hypnotically moving knife in her right hand, they wouldn't stray to the children around her, and she wouldn't see things she didn't want to see. She wouldn't see her cousin, who worked only a few feet away, and whose face was always streaked with tears. She knew why her cousin cried while he worked, but he had sworn her to secrecy, knowing that if anyone found out he was allergic to the dyes he worked with he would lose his job. So he worked on, and even though the dyes hurt him to the point where he cried all day, he never said anything, and turned away whenever the foreman was in the area.

Amy closed her ears as well, for if she didn't, she would hear the other children talking and if she let herself listen, she would soon begin talking, too. And if she talked, she would think, and if she thought, she didn't know what might happen.

The only way to get through it was to close herself down, let herself be hypnotized by the dull routine of the work, and get through the hours one at a time.

She picked up the knife, and began cutting. Within thirty seconds, she was into the rhythm of movement that would carry her through the day. Hold the hide down with her left hand, cut straight through with her right, cutting out a strip exactly three inches wide. Pick up the three-inch-wide strip in her left hand, and give a quick cut, twisting the knife slightly to turn the curve of the heel. Flip the heel over, repeat the cut. Put the heel piece in the box, and start the next one. Slowly, as happened every day, her senses began closing down until all she was aware of was her tiny area of the workbench, the knife in her hand, and the leather in front of her. Soon time would have no meaning for her, and she would continue to work, oblivious not only of what was going on around her but also of the pain in her arms and shoulders, the pain that would creep up on her every day. She would not allow herself to feel it until the evening whistle had sounded, and she was on her way home. Then, as her senses came back to her, the pain would come too, and by the time she got home she would be unable to move her arms. But her mother would have a tub of hot water waiting for her, water she'd been heating on the wood-burning stove, and she would sink into it, waiting for the pain to turn to numbness, and then the numbness to turn into the tingling sensation that meant soon she would be able to move her arms again.

But during the day, the only thing she could do was shut the pain out, as she had learned to shut everything else out. Shutting things out was the only way to get through it.

And then, when things were shut out, and she was no longer

aware of the mill, she would live in her own world for a while, a world where there was no mill. In her world, she would live outside, in the warmth of the sun, with the breezes blowing through her long hair, caressing her skin. The air would be filled with the scent of flowers, and she would lie by the stream for hours, letting the water play over her fingers. And someday, she knew, she would go to live in that world. Someday, she would find a way to leave the mill, and then she would never have to shut things out again. And when that day came, she would take her cousin with her, and all the other children who, like her, were slowly dying in the mill. . . .

She had no idea what time it was when something encroached on her closed senses. Indeed, for the first few minutes, she wasn't even sure what it was that was playing around the edges of her mind. All she knew was that something wasn't quite the way it should be. Something, somewhere, was disturbing her protective trance.

Slowly, almost imperceptibly, she began opening her mind to the world around her.

It was the smell.

The room, always airless, always choked with fumes and the sour odor of sweat, contained something new. Hesitating at her work, the knife poised in mid-stroke, she sniffed at the air.

There was an acrid smell, somehow familiar, but out of place.

And her eyes were stinging.

Her senses coming fully alert now, she felt tears welling in her eyes, running down her cheeks. She dropped the knife, and painfully raised her right hand to wipe away the tears.

The smell was stronger now, and she turned, forcing herself to look around the room.

And then she saw it.

In the corner near the door a pile of rags, stained dark with oily dyes, had burst into flames.

Amy stared at the flames for a moment, uncertain they were really there. And then she looked around.

The other children, the children she thought spent their days talking among themselves while they worked, were standing at their stations, their expressions glazed over as their hands moved in the same metronomically regular rhythm she herself experienced every day.

A few yards away, his eyes streaming, her cousin stood at one of the dye vats.

And even though he was crying, she knew immediately that he, too, had retreated into a private world where the mill could not penetrate. He, like herself—like all the children—had escaped into another world, oblivious of the world in which his body toiled.

The fire was spreading now, sending tongues of flame out across the floor as billows of smoke rose from the rags and filled the room with a choking fog.

And then, from beyond the little room, she heard the sounds of people calling out: "Fire! Fire in the cutting room !" And then the voices were cut off by the scream of the whistle, this time not signaling the end of the morning shift, but blaring out in short, urgent bursts, alerting the workers to the danger. In a moment, the fire squad would appear, and begin dousing the flames.

All around her, she could feel the other children coming alive, hear them begin coughing, hear the first sounds of their terror.

Out.

She had to get them out.

She crossed to her cousin, and took his hand. The boy, a year younger than herself, stared at her for a moment, then tried to pull away.

"Come on," Amy begged. "Willie, we have to get out of here." But Willie, staring beyond her, only shook his head, and tried to pull away. Turning, Amy saw what her cousin had already seen: the door, barely visible now, was blocked by the rising flames.

"Through!" she yelled. "We have to go through the fire! Come on!" Grasping Willie's hand, she began dragging him toward the door, the heat of the growing fire searing her face, singeing her hair.

But there was no other way out. She pressed on, two of the other children following her. And then, just as she was about to charge through the flames, she heard a voice on the other side.

"Close that door, dammit! Do you want the whole place to go up?"

She froze, recognizing the voice, and knowing its command would be obeyed. Then, helplessly, she watched as the heavy metal fire door slid quickly into place. Just as it slammed shut, she saw the face of the man who had issued the order. He was looking at her, but in his eyes she saw nothing. No love, no pity, no sorrow for what he had done.

Then the face disappeared and she was trapped.

Barely comprehending, she stepped backward, then let Willie pull her away from the angry flames.

Finally, she turned away, and stared into the terrifed eyes of the other children. All of them seemed to be looking at her, waiting for her to do something. But there was nothing she could do.

Finally, one of the children came to life, and, screaming, ran into the flames to pound on the closed fire door, begging someone to open it, to let them out, to save them.

Amy knew that even if someone heard the screaming child, the door would not be opened.

The child's screams began to fade, and as the girl watched, he sank slowly to his knees, his clothes on fire, his hair burned away. Then he slid lower, and the last thing the girl saw before she turned away was his hand, outstretched, still reaching toward the safety that wasn't there.

Willie was clinging to her now, and with the other children close around her, she stumbled to the far side of the room. But even as she moved away from the fire, she knew it was useless.

Except for the window.

Above her, high up, was a small window.

If she could get to the window, break it . . .

Closing her mind against her rising panic, as she had learned to close it against her life in the mill, she looked around for something to stand on.

A stool. In the corner, there was a stool.

She let go of Willie's hand, and dragged the stool over until it stood beneath the window. Climbing up, she could barely reach the sill.

The window was locked.

And then one of the other children gave her a mallet, and, ignoring the pain in her arms and shoulders, she swung it at the glass.

As the glass shattered, she realized her mistake.

Fresh air rushed into the vacuum created by the fire, and, with new oxygen to feed on, the fire exploded with new life.

Instantly, the room filled with smoke and flames, and the screams of children who knew they were about to die.

For a moment, time seemed to stand still, and the girl watched as the fire came to consume her. Then, as her dress caught fire, and she began falling toward the floor, she heard Willie calling out her name.

"Amy!" he screamed. And then once more. "Aaaammyyyy!"

It was the last word Willie spoke, the last word Amy heard. And his was the last face she ever saw.

But the last memory that flashed through her mind, the memory she died with, was the memory of another voice, and another face.

A voice ordering the fire door to be closed.

A voice ordering her death.

A voice commanding that she never leave the mill. And the face she saw, the face that went with that terrible voice that had ordered her death, was the face of the man she knew was her father.

As Amy died, she knew that she never would leave the mill. But as it had killed her, so would she kill others.

She would have her revenge.

Twenty

For Alan Rogers, that late-August afternoon had been the day on which, for the first time, he'd finally begun to see the results of the summer's labors. The outside of the mill was finished. Its surfaces, stripped clean of their layers of grime, were now the warm dark red of old brick, set off with white trim around the windows. The windows themselves, formerly no more than symmetrically placed holes in the otherwise blank facade of the building, had been widened with shutters, and now gave the building a vaguely colonial look.

The fence, no longer serving any useful purpose, had been torn down a week ago.

The main entrance on Prospect Street was done, a broad flight of steps leading to a rank of glass doors that opened directly onto the main concourse of the first floor. Halfway down, the concourse widened into a huge skylit atrium, above which a rainbow-hued dome of stained glass had been installed. Beyond the atrium, the concourse continued to the end of the building, where a waterfall would eventually cascade down to a small pool. The old offices had long since been torn out, but the staircase to the basement still remained one of the last vestiges of the original structure still to be replaced.

Above him, the construction of the open mezzanine was two weeks ahead of schedule, and already the dividing walls of the second-level shops were in place. Their facades, like those on the main level, would not be completed until the tenants had signed their leases and submitted designs for completion of their storefronts. All of them would be different, but there were strict guidelines within which the tenants could exercise their imaginations. In the end, Alan was now certain, the mill would look exactly as Phillip had hoped it would—an ornate nineteenth-century arcade of the sort one would be likely to run across in London, but that one could scarcely hope to discover in a fading industrial town fifty miles outside of Boston.

Until today, Alan had not been certain that the September 1 deadline would be met. Even now he wasn't positive that every detail would have been completed. But it would be close enough for the Labor Day dedication ceremony to take place, and for the Old Mill to be opened to the public. Some of the stores would be occupied, and the rest of them would have intriguingly painted wooden fronts, announcing the names of their future tenants, and hinting at what the contents of the shops might eventually be.

The construction crew was gone, and silence hung over the building. But in his mind, Alan could almost hear the murmur of a crowd of shoppers, and the faint gurgling of the waterfall. He walked slowly around the main floor, inspecting the work that had been done that day, and reinspecting what had been accomplished over the previous weeks.

He did this every day, correcting as many of the mistakes as he could himself, and making copious notes with exact instructions on what was to be done the following morning so that no time would be wasted while he had to accompany the men from place to place, giving them verbal instructions. But for the most part, the work was perfect—the men had long since discovered that Alan Rogers would allow nothing to slip by, and that he would not appreciate having to pay their wage while they corrected their own mistakes. It hadn't hurt that Alan had let it be known that the bonus for early completion would be divided equally among the workers, rather than going directly into his own pocket.

His inspection of the first floor completed, he mounted the stairs to the mezzanine.

Up here, although ahead of schedule, the work had not progressed as quickly as it had downstairs, but that was only to be expected. No one expected the mezzanine to be open by Labor Day.

Still, it was coming along faster than he'd dared hope, and the subdivisions were all but completed. Now the lowered ceiling that would cap the shops was being installed. Though to the casual observer that ceiling would appear to be supported by the walls it surmounted, it was actually being suspended from the spiderlike struts that held up the roof of the building itself. Almost ten feet would separate the false ceilings of the shops from the intricate ironwork above them, and from the main concourse on the first floor, all the old strutwork would be clearly visible, framing the new skylight in the center.

Alan gazed up at the skylight, admiring it once more. Though it was massive, it appeared to be light as a feather, the effect of lightness achieved through the artist's use of pale greens and blues and almost pastel reds and oranges.

Then, as his eyes scanned the intricate glasswork, he suddenly frowned.

One of the panes, near the base of the dome, appeared to be cracked.

He hesitated, started to make a note of it, then wondered if perhaps he was mistaken. It might not be a crack at all—it could be nothing more than an imperfection in the glass, magnified by the angle of the slowly setting sun.

He moved closer, but even then he couldn't make the crack out clearly. Glancing around, he saw a ladder propped up against the strutwork, left there by one of the workmen for use again in the morning.

Alan moved quickly to the ladder, and a moment later was up in the ironwork, moving carefully out above the concourse toward the dome.

He'd never been afraid of heights—indeed he'd always rather enjoyed them—and before he moved all the way out to the center of the roof, he looked down. As always, the distance between floor and ceiling was amplified by the angle of viewing it from above, but for Alan there wasn't even the slightest feeling of dizziness or tightening in his groin. He glanced around the empty building, enjoying the new perspective on his work, then moved confidently onward toward the dome.

When he was directly beneath the spot where he thought he'd seen the cracked glass, he looked up, but the angle was far too acute. The pane in question was almost invisible, extending almost straight up from where he was.

He leaned out, his full weight suspended above the floor below by the strength of his fingers alone.

Still, he couldn't quite see the pane. But if he stretched upward, reaching with his left hand, perhaps he could feel it.

He clutched one of the crosspieces tight in his right hand, and groped upward with his left.

His fingers touched the cool surface of the glass, and carefully explored it.

Nothing.

He reached further, his left foot leaving the iron beam on which he stood.

And then, with only one foot on anything solid, and only his right hand checking his balance, it happened.

Time seemed to stop as the small piece of wrought iron in his right hand suddenly cracked in his grip, then gave way.

Instinctively, he looked down.

The distance seemed to telescope away from him, the floor, forty feet below, receding quickly into the distance. Now, for the first time in his experience, the dizziness of heights came upon him, he felt an almost sexual tightening in his groin, and a sudden wave of fear washed over him. His entire body broke out in an icy sweat.

What was happening to him wasn't possible.

The ironwork had all been examined, the badly rusted pieces replaced weeks ago.

And yet, somehow, this piece had been missed. This very piece on which he had depended today.

His fingers, acting independently from his brain, clutched desperately at the broken piece for a moment, then, too late, dropped the fragment and reached for the solid bar that was suddenly just out of his reach.

He felt himself teeter, and slowly arc away from the I-beam.

Then he was plunging downward, his eyes wide open, his arms stretched out as if to break his fall.

He opened his mouth, and screamed.

It was the scream that jerked Beth back into the present. For just the smallest instant she was sure it was Amy's scream, that last, horrible sound as she'd died, but then Beth knew it was more. For a second she could still hear it, even now that the vision was gone, and she was once more alone in the cool darkness of the room behind the stairs.

And then the scream was cut short by a loud thumping noise, followed by the kind of empty silence that Beth had never experienced before.

The silence of death happening suddenly, unexpectedly.

She sat frozen, and slowly the silence was intruded upon, by her own heartbeat.

"Daddy?" she whispered softly. Even as she spoke the word, she knew instinctively there would be no answer.

She rose slowly to her feet. The pleasant cool of the room had shifted to a bone-chilling cold, and she reached down without thinking, picked up the blanket, and wrapped it around herself.

She moved slowly toward the door, but then hesitated, something in her not wanting to leave the safety and isolation of the little room, wanting rather to stay there in the darkness and isolation, as if that alone could protect her from whatever waited for her outside.

But she had to go out, had to go and see for herself what had happened.

She slid the door open just far enough to slip through, then slid it closed again behind her. Then, using the flashlight to guide her even though she knew the steps by rote, she crept out from under the stairs and started upward.

She could see him as soon as her head came above floor level.

He lay in the center of the mill, beneath the stained-glass dome. Sunlight, streaming in from one of the high side windows, illuminated his body, and motes of dust danced in the air above him.

He was very still, lying facedown, his arms outstretched as if he was reaching for something.

Beth froze.

It couldn't be real.

She was imagining it. Or she was seeing something else, something out of the past like the things Amy had shown her.

It wasn't her father on the floor. It was someone else—someone she didn't know—someone she didn't care about.

As she forced herself to move slowly forward, she kept repeating it to herself.

It isn't Daddy.

It isn't Daddy, and it isn't even real.

It's only a dream.

It's only a dream, and I'll wake up.

But then she was there, standing beneath the dome, her father's body at her feet. Beneath his head, a pool of blood had formed.

She knew it was real, and that she wasn't going to wake up.

She felt her body go numb as her mind tried to reject it all. But that was impossible. He lay there, not moving, not breathing, with the stillness that only death could produce.

And slowly, almost against her will, the connections in her mind began to form.

It was Amy.

Amy had killed her father.

It had happened at the same time, to the very instant.

She'd been in that room with Amy, been there when the fire broke out, been there when Amy died.

She had felt Amy die, felt as though she was dying with her. She'd felt the heat of the flames, felt the despair when she knew there would be no escape.

And she'd felt the fury—Amy's fury—in that final moment when she'd heard again the words of her father, and seen his face.

Not my father. Amy's father.

But the wish—the dying wish for vengeance—had been hers as well as Amy's.

And now her own father was dead.

She pulled the blanket, filthy with soot, closer around her body as if its warmth could shut out the chill she was feeling, and sank slowly to her knees. She reached out with one arm, the tips of her fingers touching the flesh of her father's face.

It was still warm, but despite that warmth, she could feel that there was no life there.

He was gone.

She wasn't even aware of the sound that began emanating from her throat, the high, thin wail of anguish, that built slowly until it was the scream of a wild animal caught in the vicious jaws of a trap.

A scream that was part agonizing pain, part stark terror.

The scream built, filling the enormous building, echoing off the walls and roof, building on itself until it almost seemed the walls themselves must give way under its force.

"NNNNOOOOOOOOOO—"

She was prone now, stretched out over her father's body, her fingers clutching at him, poking him, prodding him, pulling at him, as if at any moment he might respond, might move beneath her, then turn over, put his arms around her, and tell her that everything was all right, that he was alive, that he loved her and would still be there to take care of her.

And still, the scream built. . . .

Phillip was driving the Mercedes at no more than fifteen miles an hour, and doing his best to avoid the worst of the potholes in Prospect Street. Beside him, Carolyn was staring straight ahead through the windshield, but he could see a slight smile playing around the corners of her mouth as she listened to Abigail's diatribe pour forth from the back seat.

"There's hardly a need to proceed at the pace of a snail, Phillip. I'm not going to break, and I shall be much more comfortable back in my own room than I am trapped in the back seat of this car."

"I asked you to use an ambulance, Mother," Phillip reminded her, but was silenced by an indignant sniff.

"Ambulances are for sick people. If I'm still sick after six weeks in that terrible place, then I should be dead. And, if I may say so, Phillip, it is a miracle that I'm not. One would think that considering the amount of money we have given that wretched little clinic, the least they could have done was serve me decent food. And as for the doctors, I can't imagine how any of them even qualified for medical school, let alone graduated. In my day—"

"I know, Mother," Phillip interrupted. "These days they're letting just anybody be doctors, aren't they?"

Abigail's lips tightened as she heard Tracy snicker from the seat next to her. She glared at her son in the rearview mirror. "Are you mocking me, Phillip?" she asked, her voice cold.

Phillip did not answer her. He slowed the car to a complete halt in front of the mill, and pressed the button that would lower his window. "Well, there it is," he said proudly. "I thought you might want to see it."

"I do not," Abigail declared, turning her head away. "All I want is to be taken home—" And then she fell silent. A strange sound was filling the air, and it seemed to be coming from the mill.

The sound grew louder, and within seconds all four of them knew what it was.

Inside the mill, someone was screaming.

Carolyn froze in her seat; her heart had begun pounding. From the back, she heard Abigail's voice, uncertainly asking what the scream could be. Then she heard her husband's voice.

"I'll go see."

"I'll go with you," Carolyn said immediately. Phillip's voice had the effect of releasing her from her paralysis, and she opened the car door, then hurried around to the sidewalk.

The scream was getting louder, sending a chill through Carolyn's very soul.

"You'd better not," Phillip told her. "Take Tracy and Mother home. I'll find out what's happened, and call you as soon as I can." When Carolyn seemed to hesitate, he gripped her arms tightly. "Do it!" he said. Then he released her arms and started toward the steps that now rose to the newly installed front doors.

Carolyn remained where she was for a moment, then, reluctantly, got into the driver's seat of the Mercedes, and closed the door.

Phillip, even as he mounted the steps, realized it would be pointless. The doors would be locked, and he had no key.

He should abandon the steps, and head for the side door. But he couldn't. He had to look now.

With the unearthly scream still ringing in his ears, he came to the top of the steps, shielded his eyes, and peered through the glass doors.

One hundred and fifty feet away, barely visible in the dim light within, he saw a shape huddled on the floor. Then, as he watched, the shape moved and a face appeared.

Caught in the strange light of the sun, he saw Beth, her features twisted into a mask of anguished grief. Blood smeared her face, and her hands seemed to be clawing spasmodically at the air.

Phillip felt his stomach tighten for a moment, and fought against the nausea that was threatening to overwhelm him.

Then he felt a movement at his side, and heard another voice.

"What is it?" Tracy asked. "What's happening in there?"

Almost against his will, Phillip looked down. Tracy, her eyes glinting with malicious curiosity, looked back at him. "She killed someone, didn't she?" he heard his daughter saying. But there was no fear in Tracy's voice, nor so much as a hint of compassion or pity.

Only eagerness, and a strange note of satisfaction.

Clamping his hand on Tracy's wrist, Phillip jerked the child away from the door.

"Stop it!" Tracy screeched as Phillip dragged her down the steps. "You're hurting me!"

Phillip shoved Tracy into the back seat, slammed the door, then spoke through her open window. "Don't say anything, Tracy," he commanded. "If you say one word, I swear that the next time I see you I will give you a thrashing you will never forget!"

Then, at the look of anguish in Carolyn's eyes, he shook his head. "It looks bad," he said quietly. "Just get them home. I'll be there as soon as I can." Then, as Carolyn put the car in gear and drove away, he dashed around the corner of the building and started toward the side door.

Phillip recognized Alan's car parked next to the construction shack, and had an instinctive feeling of relief. Whatever had happened, Alan would already be taking care of it.

Then he was at the door, and even before his eyes had fully taken in what he was seeing, he recognized the body that lay broken on the floor.

He rushed into the area beneath the dome, and dropped to his knees, his arms instinctively going around Beth, trying to draw her away.

She fought him for a moment, clutching at her father's body, but then let go, burying her face against Phillip's chest, her arms encircling his neck, her hysterical screams dissolving into a series of racking sobs that shook her entire body.

Phillip reached out and laid his fingers on Alan's neck, feeling for a pulse.

As he had expected, there was none.

His breath caught, and he rose to his feet, staggering back a step. Beth still clung to him, and he made no attempt to set her down, or try to get her to stand on her own legs. Instead, he hoisted her higher, his right arm supporting her while he caressed her gently with his left hand.

"It's all right," he whispered as he turned away and started back toward the door. "I'm here, and it's going to be all right."

In the shack, he picked up the phone and quickly dialed the number of the police station.

"There's been an accident," he said as soon as the phone was answered at the other end. "This is Phillip Sturgess. I'm at the mill, and we've had a terrible accident. Get some men and an ambulance down here right away." Without waiting for an answer, he hung up the phone, then stepped out of the shack and sank to a sitting position on its steps.

In his arms, Beth continued sobbing, and for a moment that was all he could hear in the quiet of the afternoon.

Then, in the distance, he heard a siren begin wailing, then another, and another.

In less than a minute the sirens had reached a crescendo, then cut off abruptly as brakes squealed and dust rose up around him.

As if from nowhere, two police cars and an ambulance had appeared, and people seemed to be everywhere.

Two men in uniform, followed by a pair of white-clad paramedics, dashed past him, disappearing immediately into the cavernous interior of the mill.

Then there was someone beside him, and he looked up to see Norm Adcock's craggy face gazing down at him.

"It's Alan," he said quietly. "I don't know what happened to him. I—" He fell silent, unsure what else to say.

In his arms, Beth stirred, her sobbing having finally subsided a little. Then he felt her arms tighten around him once more, and heard her speak, her voice distorted, barely audible as it passed through a throat worn raw from her screams of a few moments ago. But still, the words themselves were clear.

"I killed him," she whispered. "I didn't mean to—really I didn't."

Then, as Phillip Sturgess and Norm Adcock exchanged a long look, her sobs overtook her once more.

Twenty-one

"Well?" Phillip Sturgess asked. "What do you think?"

It was past ten o'clock, but to look at the little Westover police station, anyone would have thought it was the middle of the day. Most of the force was there, and people filled the small lobby, asking questions of anyone whose attention they could get. But everyone on the force had been told to reply to all questions in the same way. Over and over again the answer was repeated: "We don't know yet exactly what happened. As soon as we have some information, there will be an announcement."

The rumors, of course, had been running rampant, feeding off one another, passed from person to person.

All of them, naturally, centered on Beth Rogers, and all of them were variations on the same theme.

"Mr. Sturgess found her right over the corpse. It wasn't even cold yet, and she was covered with blood." Then there would be a falsely sympathetic clucking of the tongue, and a heavy sigh. "She's always been an odd child, though, and these last few weeks—well, I don't like to repeat the stories I've heard."

But of course the stories *were* repeated, and embellished, and exaggerated, until by nightfall there were few people in Westover who hadn't heard that Beth had already killed Jeff Bailey, but had been protected by the power of the Sturgesses, who hadn't wanted a scandal.

And, of course, there was the horse—Phillip Sturgess's prize mare—that Beth had slaughtered in its stall. Would a sane person kill an innocent animal? Of course not.

And they'd all seen Beth, hadn't they? Seen her wandering around town by herself? And talking to herself? Certainly they had.

The kids had known, of course, and their parents had been foolish not to have listened to them. Children always know when something's wrong with someone—they have a sixth sense about those things. In a way, the more sanctimonious citizens declared, Alan's death was the responsibility of them all, for they'd all seen the signs of Beth's illness, but no one had done anything about it.

They came and went from the police station, gathering in the square to enjoy the warmth of the summer evening, and speculate on what would happen next. Some of them dropped in at the Red Hen to have a drink, and listened with serious faces as Eileen Russell repeated over and over again what had happened to Peggy the last time she had gone to visit Beth. All of them agreed that Peggy Russell had been lucky to escape with her life.

Bobby Golding, who was an orderly at the clinic, got off shift at eight, and went directly to the Red Hen, where he reported that Beth was currently being held in a locked room, where she was held into a bed with restraints, and would be transferred to the state mental hospital in the morning. And, he added, she would never stand trial for what she'd done, because schizophrenics never did.

And that, of course, wasn't fair, someone argued. There wasn't really anything crazy about Beth at all. She was just damned clever. All she really wanted to do was get back up to Hilltop, and she couldn't do that as long as her father was still alive. So she'd pretended to be crazy, and killed him, knowing perfectly well that they'd just put her in a hospital for a couple of months, then let her go. And when she came back to Westover, then nobody would be safe.

And so it went, until by ten o'clock Beth had been charged, tried, and convicted.

Except by Norm Adcock, who now leaned back in his chair and rubbed his tired eyes, then tried to stretch the knots out of his aching shoulders. "Only way I can figure it is an accident," he said in reply to Phillip's question. He gestured to the reports that sat in a neat stack on his desk. "We found the broken brace three feet away, and there were traces of both paint and rust on Alan's hands and shoes that match what we got off the girders. I suppose the rust could have come from anywhere, but the paint was only used on the struts supporting the roof. Couldn't have come from anywhere else. Besides, we even found his fingerprints on the glass over the spot where that brace broke. He must have been up there checking the dome for something, and his own weight broke the brace."

Phillip nodded. "And what about Beth? Is there any way she could have been up there, too?"

"I don't see how. You know as well as I do that Alan wouldn't have let her start climbing around up there. He wouldn't have let anybody do that, let alone his own daughter."

"But he'd do it himself," Phillip commented, not really expecting a reply.

"That was Alan. He wouldn't let anyone else take a risk like that, but he'd never think about it himself."

There was a silence, while Phillip turned it over in his mind. "What if he was already up there, and she climbed up without his permission?"

"Already thought of that," Adcock replied. "If traces of the paint showed up on Alan's shoes, then they would have shown up on hers, too. And they didn't. There's no way she was up there, and no way she had anything to do with what happened to Alan."

Phillip felt the tension he'd been unconsciously building up in his body suddenly ease. He hadn't yet told Carolyn about the strange words Beth had uttered when she'd finally been able to speak that afternoon, and now he wouldn't have to. But he still didn't understand them.

"What do you think about what she said?" he asked.

"Not my department," Adcock replied, shrugging. "You'll have to ask the docs about that one. But offhand, I'd say it was nothing more than shock. She was the only one there, Mr. Sturgess, and she's a little girl." He stood up, stretched, and once more rubbed at his shoulders. "I'd better get out there and talk to the folks. Hope I can convince them that I'm telling them the truth. And you," he added, "might want to think about going out the back way."

Phillip frowned, wondering what the police chief was getting at. "Why?"

"Because if you're with me, someone's bound to suggest that you've pressured me to gloss over what happened." He smiled bitterly. "People are like that. They don't want a simple answer. They'd rather have a scandal, and they're about to be disappointed." He hesitated a moment, then went on, but his tone of voice had changed slightly, become less official. "Alan was a friend of yours, wasn't he?"

"He was," Phillip replied. "In other circumstances, I suspect he might have been my best friend. We—well, we understood each other, Alan and I."

Adcock's lips pursed thoughtfully. "He was my friend, too. So I guess, in a strange sort of way, you and I should be friends, Mr. Sturgess."

Phillip hesitated, uncertain what the chief was getting at. "Friends usually call each other by their first names," he observed quietly. "And mine's Phillip."

The chief's head bobbed. "And mine's Norm. And if you want my opinion, I'd say you're going to be in for some very rough times."

"I'm not sure I follow you—"

"Beth. What do you plan to do about her?"

"Do about her?" Phillip repeated. "I'm going to take her home, and do whatever I can to help her get through all this."

"Six weeks ago you kicked her out of your house."

Phillip's eyes narrowed, and he felt sudden anger make a vein in his forehead throb. But before he could speak, he realized that there had been nothing condemnatory in the chief's voice. Adcock had spoken as if he were simply delivering information. "Is that what people have been saying?" he asked.

"That's what they've been saying. And all evening I've been getting reports from my boys." Briefly, he told Phillip about the gossip that was already sweeping through the town. "I can't tell you what to do, but if Beth were my daughter, I'm not sure I'd want her to stay here. It's not going to matter what I say, Mr. —Phillip. People are going to talk, and the stories are going to get worse and worse."

"But Beth hasn't done anything—"

"What about the horse?" Adcock asked bluntly. "Are you going to tell me the poison got into those oats all by itself?"

Suddenly, unbidden, a memory flashed into Phillip's mind. A memory of his daughter, looking up at him earlier that afternoon, and asking him if Beth had killed someone.

She hadn't cared.

He'd seen it in her eyes.

She hadn't cared that someone had died. All she'd cared about was that once more Beth Rogers might be in trouble.

"Beth didn't poison the oats," he said now, the pain of the truth wrenching at him. "But I know who did." He turned, and started out of the office, but Adcock's voice stopped him.

"Mind telling me?" the chief asked.

Phillip didn't turn around. "Yes," he said quietly. "I mind very much." He pulled the door open and stepped out into the squad room. Glancing around, he spotted the back door that led out to the alley behind the building, and started toward it. He could feel the eyes of everyone in the room following him, but no one spoke.

Phillip slipped quietly into the room at the clinic. Carolyn, her face pale, looked up at him from her chair next to the bed in which Beth lay sleeping, but made no attempt to rise. He could see by the redness of her eyes that she had been crying. A damp handkerchief was still clutched in her left hand. With her right, she held her daughter's hand. He moved around the bed, and leaned over to kiss his wife's forehead.

"How is she?" he asked.

"Asleep," Carolyn sighed. "Finally. They had to give her a shot. She didn't want one, but she finally gave in."

Phillip's sympathetic smile slowly faded into a look of grim determination. "And maybe that's the problem," he muttered to himself. "Maybe she's always given in too easily."

Carolyn looked up at him dazedly. "Given in? Phillip, what are you talking about?"

Phillip shook his head as if trying to clear it of unwanted thoughts. "I'm not sure," he said. "I've just been thinking, that's all. And I'm not liking what I'm thinking." He hesitated, then decided there was no point in putting it off. "We were wrong to send her to Alan," he said.

Carolyn swallowed, and for a moment Phillip was afraid she was going to start crying again, but then she recovered herself. "Phillip, will you please tell me what you're talking about? I just don't understand. Alan's dead, and Beth keeps saying she killed him, and now you say—" And then a thought struck her, and her face paled. "Phillip," she whispered, "you don't believe she had anything to do—"

"Of course not," Phillip assured her immediately. "I didn't from the first minute she said it, and I'd hoped you hadn't even heard it. Norm Adcock is positive it was an accident. He says there's no way Beth could have caused Alan's fall. But that's not exactly what I'm talking about."

Carolyn relaxed just a little. "Then what *are* you talking about?"

Phillip replied, "The more I think about it, the more I keep thinking that this whole mess might not have happened if Beth weren't so damned determined to try to please everyone. Which," he added bitterly, "is a trait she inherited from her father, God rest his soul."

Now Carolyn's tears did overflow. "Will you please tell me what you're talking about?" she begged.

Suddenly Beth stirred in the bed, and Phillip reached down to stroke her forehead. Still asleep, she reached up and clutched his hand in her own for a moment, then let it go and rolled over. After a few more seconds had passed, she was sleeping peacefully once again.

"Come on," Phillip said quietly, drawing Carolyn to her feet. "Let's find someplace where we can talk."

He led her out of the room, then spoke to the duty nurse, who let them into a vacant office. Phillip guided Carolyn to a chair, then paced the little room for a moment, wondering where to start.

"I keep wondering why they were there at all, at that time of the afternoon," Phillip finally said. "The men had gone home an hour earlier, but they were still there. Anybody else would have knocked off, but not Alan. I'd asked him to rush the schedule, and instead of telling me he couldn't, he just went ahead and did it. He's been working late every day, and working on weekends, too. And on top of that, we dumped Beth on him."

Carolyn gasped, her eyes widening. "We didn't dump her," she protested. "You know what the situation was like at home. And it was just getting worse."

"I know," Phillip agreed. "But did either of us stop to think about the situation at Alan's? Carolyn, we know what's been going on, and all we've done is tell ourselves it would blow over. But what can the last six weeks have been like for Beth? No friends—every kid in town down on her—spending all her time in the mill because she had no place else to go! My God, she must have been out of her mind with loneliness. And she wouldn't complain, either. Not her. All she ever wanted was for people to love her, but none of us ever managed to have time for her."

"That's not true!" Carolyn objected. "I always had time for her, and you used to get up and take her riding."

"Three times, maybe," Phillip replied. "But you know as well as I do that we were both walking on eggs, trying to be fair to everyone. You were trying to fit in just as hard as Beth was. And then when Patches died, we were both willing to believe that she'd poisoned the oats."

"We didn't," Carolyn breathed, but Phillip held up a hand in a silencing gesture.

"Maybe we didn't. But we let it be the last straw, and we didn't try too hard to find out what really happened. It was easier just to avoid the situation by letting Beth move in with Alan."

"We thought it was best," Carolyn insisted. "We talked it over, and we agreed that it would be best for all of us. It wasn't just ourselves we were thinking about! It was Beth and Tracy, too!"

"Tracy," Phillip breathed. He'd been standing at the window, looking out into the darkness, but now he turned and faced Carolyn. "It was Tracy who poisoned Patches," he said.

Carolyn stared at him. "No . . . even Tracy wouldn't—"

"Wouldn't she? Try this—what if Tracy heard us talking the night before?" He knew he was guessing, but even as he spoke the words, he knew they were the truth. "What if she knew that if anything else happened—anything at all—we'd decided to let Beth go live with Alan? You know as well as I do that she's always resented Beth."

"But she loved that horse—"

Phillip shook his head tiredly, feeling the exhaustion of the conflicting emotions that had been boiling within him over the last hour. "It wasn't the horse she loved," he said. "It was having the horse. I . . . I'm not sure Tracy is really capable of loving anything or anyone. This afternoon—" He fell silent for a moment, then made himself tell Carolyn what had happened in front of the mill that day. "She didn't care about Alan being dead," he finished, his own eyes flooding with tears now. "All she cared about was that it might be blamed on Beth. And she hoped it would be. I could see it in her eyes."

Carolyn groaned softly, her eyes fixed on the floor as her hand unconsciously kneaded the limp handkerchief. Then, finally, she looked up.

"But what do we do?" she asked. "What can we possibly do?"

"I don't know," Phillip confessed. "But we can take Beth home, and try to make it up to her some way. Somehow, we have to make her understand that she's not alone. We have to make her know that we love her very much."

Carolyn nodded mutely. And then, after a long moment she spoke the other question, the question that was in both their minds.

"What about Tracy? What do we do about her?"

Phillip had no answer.

Twenty-two

Phillip left the hospital a few minutes later. Carolyn, unwilling to leave her daughter alone that night, had asked for a cot to be brought into Beth's room, and phoned Hannah to pack an overnight case for her.

Phillip walked slowly along Prospect Street, feeling the aura of tension in the village around him. There was still a crowd of people gathered in front of the mill, talking quietly among themselves, but they fell silent as he approached. There was something condemnatory in their glances, though none of them seemed willing to look directly at him. But he was all too aware of the eyes that raked over him, then quickly looked away. He wondered if he should stop and talk with them, then decided there was nothing he could say.

As he made his way quickly through the small crowd, and came to the north side of the old brick structure, his instincts told him to walk on, leaving the mill and all thoughts of it until tomorrow. But he couldn't do that. There were decisions that had to be made, and he couldn't allow himself to put them off. At the corner of the building, he turned left, starting once more toward the side entrance.

He used his key to open the construction shack, then rummaged around in Alan's battered desk until he found a spare set of keys to the building. In the darkness of the evening, he opened the door and slipped inside the mill itself. He stood still for several seconds, rejecting once more the strange urge to turn his back on the old building and simply walk away.

He told himself that the anxiety he was suddenly feeling meant nothing. It wasn't the building itself he was reacting to, but rather the tragedy that had occurred there only a few hours ago. The mill was only a building, and there were practical decisions to be made.

And yet his anxiousness began to congeal into something like fear, gathering around him, challenging him. He answered the challenge by reaching for the switch by the door that would turn on the naked bulbs of the worklights, certain that by banishing the darkness he would alleviate the irrational panic that was threatening to overwhelm him now.

At first it worked. Harsh white light flooded the building, and the familiar forms of the new construction reassured him. There was, after all, nothing to fear.

As his eyes scanned the progress Alan had made, Phillip realized immediately that there could be no reasonable argument for abandoning the project now. It was all but complete, needing little more than a few days' work on the mezzanine level.

And yet he still had an uneasy feeling that there was something here that he had yet to fully comprehend. Even with the worklights on, it was as if some dark shadow lingered in the vast spaces beneath the roof.

He moved forward to the spot where Alan Rogers had died only a few hours before. Though the floor had already been washed clean, and there was no evidence of the tragedy that had occurred there, still he could see Alan's broken body all too clearly in his mind's eye, and see Beth, her face ashen, crouching brokenly over the corpse, keening her grief into the echoing spaces above.

He paused for a moment, then, almost against his will, turned to face the front of the mill. On the steps, separated from him by the glass of the front doors, were the curious people of Westover, watching him with what he imagined to be suspicion. Suddenly he felt like an actor on a stage, caught unexpectedly in the spotlight without having rehearsed his role.

And then, as he stood alone in the mill, he realized that he had not come here tonight simply to make a decision about the future of the mill.

It was something else.

There was something he was looking for.

He turned away, and started toward the back of the mill, pausing at the enormous lighting panel that had been completed only a week ago. A moment later every light in the mill blazed into life, washing the shadows cast by the worklights away, suffusing the entire building with the even illumination of hundreds of fluorescent tubes.

When he looked down the stairs into the basement, the darkness there was gone too, driven away by the surge of electricity.

He started down the stairs, moving slowly, for still the light had not completely freed him from the near-panic that had threatened him when he'd first entered the building.

At the bottom of the stairs he gazed out into the far reaches of the basement, but there was nothing there that seemed the least bit unusual. It was as it had always been, nothing more than a vast expanse of space interrupted at regular intervals by the huge wooden columns that supported the floor above. There was nothing that Phillip could see that would induce the unease that was again growing within him.

He looked down at his feet, at the spot where his brother had died, and Jeff Bailey had died, and his mother had nearly died.

This, he realized, was the true reason he'd come here tonight. To stand alone at this spot, waiting to see if the fear his mother had described to him six weeks ago would come to him now, threaten him as it had threatened her.

Was it the same fear that had killed his brother?

He had to know.

And yet, as the seconds stretched into minutes, there was nothing.

He turned finally, and for the first time saw the little room tucked away behind the stairs. Its door stood slightly agape, but beyond the door there was only darkness.

It was from that darkness that tentacles of true fear finally began to reach out to him.

He told himself that what he was feeling was irrational, that there was nothing beyond that door but an empty room. And yet, as he approached the door he found himself stepping to one side so that the door itself separated him from whatever might lie beyond. His pulse rate suddenly rising, he reached out, grasped the door, and began sliding it to the left until it was fully open. Now the space was nearly six feet wide, and the light from the basement spilled into the room, only to be swallowed up by the blackness of the walls beyond.

There seemed to Phillip to be nothing unusual about the room. A simple rectangle, with a single small window high up on the far wall, and barren of furniture. The only sign that anyone had been in here in years was the area on the floor where the accumulated dust of a century had been recently disturbed.

All that set the room apart from the rest of the basement was its smell.

Emanating from the room was a strong odor of smoke, as if there had recently been a fire here.

As the smoky odor filled his lungs, Phillip began to feel a strange roiling of emotions that seemed to come not from within himself but from the room.

The fear was stronger now, but mixed with it there was a sense of pent-up rage. It was almost as if the room were coiling in upon itself preparing to strike him.

And yet there was a strange feeling of longing, too. A deep melancholy, tinged strongly with sadness. As he stood staring into the room, resisting a compelling urge to step inside and meet whatever was truly there, Phillip found his eyes flooding. A moment later the tears overflowed, and ran unheeded down his cheeks.

He took a tentative step forward, his arms reaching out as if to touch whatever was in the room, but then he suddenly veered away, and instead of entering the room, grasped the edge of the door and quickly rolled it shut.

As it slammed home, he imagined that he heard a short cry from within, a childish voice calling out to him.

"Father!"

He hurried up the stairs, turned off the lights, and started toward the side door.

And then, at the far end of the mill, he saw the faces.

They were still there—the people of Westover, their faces pressed to the glass, their features distorted into strange grimaces. Their hands seemed to be reaching out to him, and at first he had the feeling that they were beseeching him. Then, as he moved into the rotunda beneath the soaring glass dome of the building, he perceived something else.

The faces, though vaguely familiar, were unrecognizable. The men, clad in shabby clothing, all wore caps low on their foreheads, and their faces were unshaven.

The women, all of them gaunt with what seemed to be hunger, were also dressed shabbily, in long thin dresses that covered them from their wrists to their ankles and were buttoned high on their necks. They all wore their hair alike, twisted back into buns at the napes of their necks.

And they were not beseeching him.

They were reaching out to him not because they wanted anything of him.

They wanted *him.*

Their eyes showed it clearly. The eyes, all of them fixed on him now, glittered with hatred. He could almost feel it radiating out from them, surging through the glass of the doors—rolling toward him in an angry wave down the broad corridor of the mill.

He froze for a moment, his panic building within him, then turned and ran to the side door, reaching out to the switch and plunging the mill back into the darkness that had filled it a few moments earlier. He stepped through the door, closed it, and locked it.

He glanced toward the front of the mill, half-expecting to see an angry crowd moving toward him. Instead, there was nothing. Only a single man, silhouetted against a streetlight, waving to him.

"Mr. Sturgess?" he heard a voice calling. "Are you all right?"

Phillip hesitated. "I'm okay," he called back softly. "I just wanted to take a look around." Then he raised his hand, and returned the man's wave. But instead of going back to Prospect Street, he turned the other way, walking down the path until he came to the railroad tracks.

As he hurried through the night, he tried to convince himself that what he'd seen had existed only in his imagination.

When he got home twenty minutes later, Phillip found Tracy waiting for him. She was sitting on the stairs, halfway up, and when the door opened, she stood up and looked eagerly down at him. He glanced up at her, then dropped his keys in the drawer of the commode that sat near the front door. Neither of them said anything until he started toward the library, intent on fixing himself a drink. As he was sure she would, his daughter followed him into the big walnut-paneled room.

"Well?" she demanded as Phillip poured a generous slug of Scotch into a Waterford tumbler, then added a couple of ice cubes and some water. Only when he finished making the drink did he turn to face her.

"Well what?" he asked evenly.

Tracy hesitated. There was something in her father's eyes she'd never seen before. Though he was looking at her, she had the funny feeling that he wasn't seeing her. "Well, did she kill him?" she asked at last.

Phillip frowned, swirling his drink in his glass, then went over to the French doors to stare out into the night. "Why would she do that?" he asked, his back to Tracy.

"Well, isn't that obvious?" he heard his daughter say. "She wants to come back here. So she killed her father, because if he's dead, there's no place else for her to live."

Phillip felt his eyes flood once more, and suppressed the groan that rose in his throat. "Is this place really that wonderful?" he asked so softly that Tracy had to strain to hear him. "Is it really worth killing someone—your own father—just to live here?" Then, when he'd waited long enough for his words to sink in, he swung around and faced Tracy, who was standing in the center of the room, her eyes wide as she stared at him. "Well?" he asked. "Is it really worth all that?"

"It is to her—" Tracy began, but Phillip didn't let her finish.

"How could it be?" he asked. "What would have been so wonderful for her here? Ever since you came home from school you've done your best to make her miserable. You didn't even try to be friends with her. You treated her like a servant, ignored her, snubbed her—"

"So what?" Tracy demanded. Her face had flushed with anger,

and her blue eyes glinted in the light of the chandelier. "She's nothing but trash, just like her mother. She doesn't belong here, and she doesn't fit in here, and if she comes back here, I won't live here anymore!"

"I see," Phillip said calmly. "And just where do you propose to live?"

Tracy's eyes widened, and the color suddenly drained from her face. What was he saying? He couldn't mean what she thought he meant, could he? "I . . . I'll go live with Alison Babcock."

Phillip nodded thoughtfully, and sipped once more at his drink. "Tracy," he said quietly, "I think you'd better sit down. It's a good time for the two of us to have a talk, since Carolyn won't be home."

"I hope Carolyn never comes back here again," Tracy declared, dropping into one of the wing chairs and draping her left leg casually over its arm.

"I'm sure that's what you hope," Phillip replied, sitting down opposite her. "But I'm telling you right now that it's a hope I want never to hear expressed in this house again. You may think anything you like, but you will keep your thoughts to yourself from this moment on."

His words hit Tracy like a physical blow. For a moment she was too stunned to say anything at all. Then she swallowed, and widened her eyes. "Daddy—"

"Put your feet on the floor, and sit up like the lady you think you are," Phillip said.

Tracy's leg came off the arm of the chair, and dropped to the floor. She stared at her father, trying to figure out what had happened. "You're going to let her come back here, aren't you?" she finally asked, her voice heavy with accusation. "Even after what she did to my horse."

"Ah," Phillip said, draining his glass and rising to his feet to fix himself another drink. "The horse." As he passed Tracy he glanced down, and could see by her eyes that his suspicion was correct. "The Babcocks have some pretty good stock in their stable," he commented. He said nothing more until he was once more facing her. "I wonder how safe they'd feel with you living in their house."

Tracy's heart was pounding now, and she had to grip the arms of the chair to keep her hands from shaking. "I didn't do it—" she began, but when her father shook his head, she fell silent.

"I don't believe you, Tracy," she heard him say. "I don't believe you, and I don't know what to do." His eyes flooded with tears once more, and this time he made no effort to hide them. "I guess I haven't been much of a father, have I? I've always tried to give you everything you wanted, but it wasn't enough."

"But I love you, Daddy," Tracy ventured.

"Do you?" Phillip asked. "I suppose you do, in your own way. But it's the wrong way, Tracy. I can't live my life for you. I can't decide whom to fall in love with simply on the basis of what you want. And I can't let you dictate who will live in my house and who won't."

In her own mind, Tracy mistook the sadness in Phillip's words for weakness. "But they don't belong here, Daddy," she protested once more. "I don't see why you can't see that. Carolyn and Beth don't even like it here. All they want is our money!"

The tenseness in her father's jaw told Tracy she had made a mistake, and she instinctively shrank back in her chair. Her father's eyes were coldly furious now.

"I'm not going to hit you," he told her. "Perhaps I should, but I won't. I don't believe in that sort of thing. But I will tell you this now, Tracy, and you had better listen and you had better understand, because I won't tell you again. From this moment on, you will treat Carolyn with all the respect you would give your own mother, or any other adult woman. I don't care anymore how you feel about her. The only thing I care about is how you treat her. From now on, you will be friendly and helpful and polite, whether I am in the house or not. As for Beth, yes, she will be coming back here to live. And it won't be because she has no other place to go. It will be because both her mother and I love her very much. And you will treat her the same way you will treat Carolyn. You will go even further. You will make friends with Beth, unless she's not interested in being friends with you. In that case, you will simply be polite to her, and stay out of her way. When she comes home tomorrow, you will tell her you are sorry about what happened to her father and you will apologize for having poisoned her horse—"

"It was *my* horse," Tracy exploded. Suddenly she was on her feet, glaring at her father with naked fury. "It was my horse, and I had the right to do anything I wanted to it! And it's my house, and I can act any way I want to here, and you can't stop me. I hate you!"

Phillip rose to his feet. "Very well," he said softly. "If that's the way you feel, there's only one thing I can do. In the morning, I'll make some calls and find a school for you."

"Good!" Tracy shot back, her feet planted wide apart on the carpet, her face a mask of angry belligerence. "And I hope it's as far away from here as you can get!"

"Oh, it will be," Phillip replied. "But of course since you'll be there year-round from now on, we'll have to find one that has no vacations. Also, of course, one that has no horses." He looked down, his eyes fixing on his daughter. "No privileges of any sort, I should think," he said softly. "It appears that you've already had far too many of those."

Tracy searched her father's face, trying to see if he really meant what he was saying. "I . . . I'll run away!"

Phillip shrugged. "If you do, then you do. But if I were you, I'd think about it pretty hard. I understand life can be pretty rough out there for a girl of your age." Then he turned and left the library, closing the door quietly behind him. Tracy, frozen with rage and disbelief, stood perfectly still for a moment, then went to the bar and began throwing the glasses at the door, one by one.

Phillip and Hannah met at the bottom of the stairs as the first crash of breaking crystal emanated from the library. The old woman's eyes widened, and she almost dropped the small overnight case she carried in her right hand. She said nothing, but her eyes questioned Phillip.

"It's Tracy," he said mildly. "She's a little upset right now, but I imagine she'll calm down when she runs out of glasses. If she asks you to clean up the mess for her, please do me the favor of playing deaf." He thought he heard her gasp as her head bobbed dutifully. "Oh . . . and, Hannah," he added as he started up the stairs. "From now on, there will be no need for you to do anything about Tracy's room. She'll be cleaning it up herself, starting tomorrow."

Hannah's brows arched, and she eyed Phillip shrewdly. "Is that what this is all about?" she asked, tilting her head toward the library.

"I'm afraid not," Phillip replied. "She doesn't even know about having to clean her own room yet."

"In that case, sir, I'll lock up the rest of the crystal and the china as soon as I get back from the hospital."

"Thank you," Phillip said, and found himself grinning as he went up the stairs and turned toward his mother's suite. He found Abigail sitting in her favorite chair, a book facedown in her lap. The moment he came into the room, her sharp old eyes fell on him suspiciously.

"What in the name of God is that racket, Phillip?" she demanded.

"It's Tracy, Mother," he replied. "I have finally put my foot down with her." As briefly as possible, he explained to his mother what he had told his daughter, and why. When he was done, the old lady gazed at him from beneath hooded eyes.

"You're making a terrible mistake, Phillip."

Phillip shrugged, and dropped into the chair opposite her. "It seems to me I've been making a series of terrible mistakes with Tracy all her life." His mother, though, didn't seem to have heard him. She was staring at him now with the disapproval a mother reserves for a wayward child. What, he wondered, was she angry about now? And then he realized that the chair he had unconsciously sunk into had never been occupied by anyone but his father. "He's dead, Mother," he said quietly. "Is the chair in the mausoleum not enough? Is this supposed to be a shrine as well?"

He immediately regretted the words, but there was no recovering them.

"Sit where you wish," Abigail replied, her voice cold. "Since you seem intent on taking over his place in this house, you might as well take his chair as well. But as for Tracy, you can't simply change the rules on a child like her. She's far too sensitive."

"I'm afraid I can't agree with your assessment of her sensitivity," Phillip observed dryly. "And as to the rules, I haven't changed them. I've simply established some."

"And you expect me to allow it?" Abigail asked, her expression hardening.

"Its not a question of your allowing anything," Phillip replied. "I'm simply setting some limits and rules on my daughter, that's all."

Abigail's lips twisted with scorn. "Your daughter? I suppose you have a biological right to say that, but I'd hardly say you've fulfilled the functions of a father with her."

Phillip refused to rise to the bait. "And of course you'd be right in saying it," he agreed. "But that's not the point. The point is that it's time she learned that being a Sturgess does not make her anything special, and I intend to teach her that."

"By punishing her for being naturally resentful of the wrong sort of people intruding into her life?"

"That's enough, Mother," Phillip said, rising to his feet. "I simply wanted to find out how you were. I didn't come in here to debate with you."

Abigail's voice took on the coldness that Phillip had long since learned to recognize as the ultimate sign of his mother's rage. "And you presumed that I would simply acquiesce?"

"I don't presume anything, Mother," he replied, struggling to retain control of his own anger. "But it does occur to me that you might be just the slightest bit interested in how Beth is doing. Her father died this afternoon. Is protecting Tracy's selfishness really more important than Beth's welfare?"

"There's nothing I can do for Beth Rogers," was Abigail's acerbic reply. "But there is a great deal I can do for my own granddaughter. Not the least of which is preventing you from moving young Beth back into this house."

"Because she's 'the wrong sort of person,' Mother?" Phillip asked wearily.

"Not at all," Abigail shot back. "I do not want her here because I regard her as a danger to us all."

"Oh, for heaven's sake, Mother. You're sounding as paranoid as Father was just before he died."

"I am not the least bit convinced that your father did not have all his faculties intact," Abigail stiffly replied.

Phillip sighed. "All right, Mother. There's obviously no point in discussing it anymore. If you need anything, I'll be in my rooms."

"If I need anything, I shall ring for Hannah, just as I've done for the last forty years."

"Hannah's not here. She's gone to the hospital to take some things to Carolyn."

Tracy stared angrily at the empty bar, looking for something else to throw. But there was nothing. The last of the three dozen crystal tumblers that had sat on those shelves for as long as she could remember now lay smashed at the bottom of the library door. The door itself was marked with a series of crescent-shaped scars where the glasses had struck it, and Tracy, even in her rage at her father, was sure that those marks would never be removed. For the rest of her life they would be there in the door, a constant reminder of this day when her father had turned against her.

But there was still her grandmother.

Her grandmother would take her side, and convince her father that he was wrong, that instead of letting Beth come back to Hilltop, they should make Carolyn leave. They could go back to their crummy little house on Cherry Street. Her father could buy it back for them.

She pulled the library door open, ignoring the broken glass that ground into the polished surface of the floor, leaving deep scratches. Hannah could clean up the mess tomorrow, and call someone to fix the floor.

She hurried up the stairs, glancing down the corridor to see if her father's door was closed. Then she turned and started toward her grandmother's rooms.

She didn't bother to knock; she simply pushed the door open and stepped inside. At first she thought the room was empty. Her grandmother was no longer in her chair, and Tracy started toward the bedroom.

Then, from the window, she heard Abigail's voice.

"Tracy? Are you all right, child?"

Tracy turned and saw the old woman, leaning heavily on her cane, a robe wrapped tightly around her. She looked much smaller than Tracy ever remembered, and she looked sick. Her skin seemed to hang in folds from her face, and her hands were trembling. "Daddy wants to send me away," she said.

Abigail hesitated, then slowly nodded her head. "I know," she sighed. "He told me."

"You have to make him change his mind."

"I've already tried," the old woman replied. "But I don't think I can. He's decided I spoiled you, I'm afraid. If your mother were alive—"

"But she's not!" Tracy suddenly shouted. "She's dead! She went away and left me, just like you did!" She started across the room, her face contorting as her fury, which she'd been holding carefully in check, rushed back to the surface. "You went to the hospital and left me here with them! They hate me! Everybody hates me, and nobody cares!"

Abigail felt her heart begin to pound in the face of the girl's anger, and instinctively turned away. She tried to close her ears to Tracy's fury, and made herself concentrate on the night beyond the window.

She shouldn't even be standing here. The doctor had insisted that she stay off her feet, but after her conversation with Phillip, she'd had to get out of her chair, had to pace the room while she tried to decide how to handle the situation. And finally she'd gone to the window, where she'd looked out toward the mill that was always, inevitably, the source of all her family's troubles.

She concentrated once more on the mill, still trying to shut out the shrill sounds of Tracy's angry voice.

And then, as she stared out into the black night, the dark form of the mill seemed suddenly so close she could almost touch it.

She could see the front doors, and the windows, neatly framed with their shutters, as clearly as if she were only across the street.

It was her imagination; it had to be. It was far too dark, and the mill much too far away, for her to see what she was seeing.

Her heart pounded harder, and once more she felt the bands begin to constrict around her chest.

And then, as the mill seemed to grow ever larger and closer, she saw the strange glowing light of a fire. At first it was only that, a strange glow emanating from the stairs to the basement.

But as she watched, and felt her ancient heart begin to burst within her, the glow turned bright. Flames rose up out of the stairwell, licking at the walls, then reaching out beyond the blackening brick as if they were searching for something.

Searching for her.

"No!" she whimpered. With an effort of pure will, for the pain in her chest was consuming her now, she turned from the window and groped for a chair. "Tracy!" she said, hearing the gasp in her own voice. "Tracy, help me!"

"Why?" Tracy said in a low voice, indifferent to her grandmother's pain. "Why should I help you? What do you ever do for me?"

"My heart—" Abigail whispered. She reached out, but as the pain clamped down on her breast, then began shooting down her arms toward her fingers, she dropped the cane and pitched forward, crumpling to her knees. She stretched out her left arm, and just managed to touch Tracy's leg.

Tracy's breath caught, and she pulled away from the strange apparition on the floor. She scrambled from the room, screaming for her father.

"It's Grandmother!" she yelled. "Daddy, come quick! Grandmother's dying!"

Phillip found his mother on the floor of her parlor. She lay on her side, her hands clutching at her breast as if trying to free herself of the demon that possessed her. He dropped to his knees, and reached down to take her hands.

Her eyes, death already taking possession of them, fixed on him, and she reached up to touch his face.

"Fire," she whispered. "It's burning again. You have to stop her, Phillip . . . you have to . . ."

For a moment Phillip thought his own heart would stop. "Who? Who has to be stopped, Mother?"

The old woman gasped for breath, then made one final effort. "Amy," she croaked. "Amy . . ."

And then she was gone.

Twenty-three

Almost everyone in Westover went to the funeral for Alan Rogers or to the funeral for Abigail Sturgess.

Only a handful went to both.

For a few fleeting moments, Carolyn and Phillip had considered the possibility of combining the two services, but quickly rejected it. There had been no relationship between the two people who had died, nor did their circles of mourners overlap. So, in the end, they had decided that services for Alan would be held in the morning, three days after he died, and for Abigail the following afternoon.

What Carolyn had noticed most as the two long days wore on were the differences between the two services.

For Alan, the little church had been packed full with all the people she had been close to during her childhood and the years she had been married to Alan. The minister, who had grown up with Alan, had talked for forty minutes about the friend he had lost, and carried them all back into the past. It was, for Carolyn, a time of memories shared with people she hardly knew anymore, and she found herself missing all the old friends she had unwittingly cut herself off from when she married Phillip. Alan, for those forty minutes, had come back to life for everyone in the church, and Carolyn had found herself half-expecting to get up at the end of the service, turn, and see Alan himself leaning against the back wall of the church, grinning sardonically at the fuss being made over him. But when the service was over, and she stood at the door of the church with her daughter, her feeling of momentary nostalgia faded quickly away.

No one, she realized almost immediately, knew quite what to say. Should they offer condolences to the woman who had divorced the man they were honoring?

Nor did they know quite what to say to Beth, for the gossip had not yet died down, despite the statement Norm Adcock had issued the day after Alan died. So as Alan's friends filed slowly out of the church, they paused for only the briefest of moments to speak to Carolyn, and eye Beth with ill-concealed curiosity. Then they hurried on. As soon as was decently possible, Phillip shepherded her to the waiting car. Carolyn, as they drove toward Hilltop, had found herself relieved that in his will Alan had specified cremation for his remains. A service at the cemetery, she was sure, would have been too uncomfortable for anyone to have borne. She found herself wondering if Alan had arranged for there to be no graveside service just for that very reason. It would, she decided, have been very much like him.

The next afternoon they had gone back to the church for Abigail's funeral. Once again the church had been full, but for the most part it was a different group. For Abigail, people had come from as far away as Boston, and the streets around the church were lined with Cadillacs and Lincolns. The same minister conducted the service and the eulogy, but this time he spoke about someone he had barely known. The eulogy, rather than evoking memories of Abigail, was little more than a recounting of the accomplishments of the Sturgess family. As Carolyn listened, she quickly became acutely aware that the woman the minister described bore no relationship to the woman Carolyn herself had known.

This time, as she stood at the door next to her husband and her stepdaughter, everyone lingered, offering her condolences on the loss of the mother-in-law they all knew perfectly well had hated her. Carolyn forced herself to play the expected role, her eyes cast down as she murmured the proper words.

In the late afternoon there had been the burial at the mausoleum. Abigail's place, next to her husband, was outside the ring of columns, and she was not, as her husband had been, presented to Samuel Pruett Sturgess. That, Carolyn privately reflected, was apparently an honor reserved only for blood relatives.

After the interment they had all returned to the house, and repeated the reception that had been held for Conrad only a few months earlier. And as with Conrad, the only mentions of the deceased were a few automatic phrases whispered in hushed tones of mourning, after which the men clustered together to catch up on business, and the women finalized plans for various committee meetings and social gatherings, none of which included Carolyn.

And then, at last, it was all over, and Carolyn and Phillip were alone in the library.

Both girls had gone quietly to their rooms as soon as they'd returned from the burial service. Upstairs, there was only silence. For that, Carolyn was grateful. She sat wearily in one of the big wing chairs and sipped the drink Phillip had poured for her, reflecting, with a shudder she could barely conceal, on the way everyone had stared at Beth at the funeral services, as if they were all wondering, still, what had really happened to Alan, though no one had dared speak the question aloud.

At Hilltop, too, the air had been heavy with silence and the weight of unspoken questions for the last three days. Even Tracy had been nothing but demure and polite, the perfect child, appropriately sad at the passing of her beloved grandmother.

Carolyn had observed her cautiously but had so far said nothing. Since the moment she'd brought Beth back from the hospital the morning after Alan died, Tracy seemed to have changed. When she and Beth had come in, Tracy had been waiting for them. She'd told Beth how sorry she was that her father had died, then gone out to the car to bring in Carolyn's overnight case and Beth's suitcase. And when they'd gone upstairs, she'd even offered to help Beth unpack.

And so it had gone. Tracy, as far as Carolyn had been able to see, was finally doing her best to accept both of them.

Except that Carolyn had noticed almost immediately the fact that all the crystal in the library was gone, and that both the door and the floor were severely scarred. Though Phillip had said nothing about it, and she had so far refrained from asking him, she was certain that Tracy had been responsible for the damage. Now, she decided to face the issue.

"I have noticed," she said carefully, "how well Tracy has been behaving. And I've also noticed that something obviously happened in here. Do you want to tell me about it?"

Phillip hesitated, but knew he couldn't conceal the truth from his wife. As briefly as possible, he told Carolyn exactly what had happened the night Abigail had died. When he was finally done, Carolyn sat silent for a long time. Then she stood up and went to the window, gazing out into the fading light of the summer evening. And despite the warmth of the air outside the open French doors, she found herself shivering.

"You think I did the wrong thing, don't you?" Phillip asked when Carolyn's silence had gone on longer than he could bear.

"I hope not," Carolyn replied so softly he could hardly hear her. "But I'm afraid she must hate us now more than she ever did before." Then she turned to face her husband. "I'm afraid, Phillip. I'm so very afraid."

Tracy had the door of her room closed and locked, and now she sat at her desk going through the contents of her grandmother's jewelry box. The best things, she knew, were kept in the vault at the bank, and her grandmother had brought them home only once a year, for Christmas and New Year's. Those were the things Tracy really wanted—the diamond necklace with the big emerald drop, which had a bracelet and earrings to go with it. And there was a sapphire tiara. The stones had been specially chosen to match the color of her grandmother's eyes. Tracy knew they would match her own eyes as well.

But still, there were some nice things in the jewelry box, and she was having a hard time trying to decide which ones to take. She had to leave a lot of it so no one would notice that some of it was gone, and she had to leave some of the best stuff, too.

Except that maybe she didn't.

A lot of the stuff in the box that she really liked, she couldn't remember her grandmother ever even wearing, so there was a good chance that her father wouldn't remember it either.

And some of the things in the box had been her mother's. She'd leave those—surely her father would give her mother's jewelry to Carolyn.

She picked up a large jade pendant, carved so that it had a

different pattern on each side, and held it up to her neck. The chain was a little too long, but that didn't matter. The jade itself, she decided, was a perfect color for her—a very pale pink, and, when she held it up to the light, so transparent that the two patterns on either face combined to form yet a third. She opened her own jewelry box, lifted out the tray, and slipped the pendant into the tiny hidden compartment under what looked like the bottom of the case.

Suddenly there was a soft tapping at her door—two knocks, followed by a short silence, and then a third. It was the code she'd given Beth, telling her it would be a secret between them. And Beth, as Tracy had hoped, was too stupid to realize that all it did was give Tracy a chance to hide things before she let Beth into her room.

The whole thing her father had demanded had, in fact, been a lot easier than Tracy had thought it would be. It was almost like a game, and the object was to find out just how stupid Beth and Carolyn really were.

And with Beth, to find out how crazy she really was, so her father would finally have to send her away.

So far, it looked like they were even dumber than Tracy had thought, though she still hadn't figured out how to get Beth talking about Amy again.

Beth, she'd decided, was really pathetic. When she'd opened the suitcase Beth had brought with her, it had been all she could do to keep from giggling out loud at the junk that was inside. It was nothing but faded jeans, and a bunch of blouses and dresses that had to have come from Penney's. But she'd oohed and aahed and begged Beth to loan her some of the junk sometime, and Beth had fallen for it.

And then, this morning, Tracy had dug around in her closet until she'd found a dress she hadn't worn for two years but hadn't bothered to throw away yet, and offered it to Beth to wear to the funerals. The dress had looked awful on her, as Tracy had known it would, but Beth hadn't noticed, and neither had her mother.

Instead, they'd both thanked her, as though she'd done something nice.

Now, as the knock at the door was repeated, Tracy shut her grandmother's jewelry box, and hurriedly shoved it up on the closet shelf before unlocking the door and opening it. Beth stood in the corridor, her eyes wide. Her face was the color of putty. The dress Tracy had loaned her was on a hanger that Beth held high enough so the hem wouldn't touch the floor.

"I . . . I got a spot on it," Beth whispered, looking to Tracy like a frightened rabbit. "I'm sorry—I don't know what happened."

Tracy composed her features into an expression of what she

hoped was generous forgiveness. "It's all right," she said. "I'm sure it won't cost much to have it cleaned." She saw no point in telling Beth she was going to throw the dress away anyhow. "Come on in."

She opened the door wider, and Beth came into the room, and carefully laid the dress on the bed. Tracy could hardly wait to call Alison Babcock and tell her how Beth treated the old rag like it was a Halston gown.

"I . . . I'm really sorry about your grandmother," Beth said as she started backing toward the door.

"It's okay," Tracy replied. "She was so old it's a miracle she didn't die years ago. I mean, it's not like she was young, like your father." Tracy forced herself not to snicker when Beth's eyes flooded with tears. "I'm sorry," she said quickly. "I guess you don't want to talk about your father, do you?"

Beth quickly wiped the tears away, and managed a smile. "I just can't think about him very much yet. But Mom says I'll get over it." Then she frowned uncertainly. "But I don't know. It just hurts so much. Did you feel like that when your mom died?"

Tracy shrugged. "She died when I was born. I don't even remember her. My grandmother raised me."

Beth's frown deepened. "Then how come you don't miss your grandmother like I miss my father?"

"I told you. She was an old lady." She glanced at Beth out of the corner of her eye, then did her best to work up some tears. "Besides, she didn't love me anymore. She loved you more than she loved me."

Beth gasped. "That's not true—"

Now Tracy managed a little sob. "It is, too! She didn't ask to see me when she was in the hospital. At least not the first night. She only wanted to see you."

"But that was about—" And then Beth stopped short, afraid to speak the name that Tracy had used against her for so long.

"About Amy?" Tracy asked, her voice showing no hint of the mockery of the past.

Hesitantly, Beth nodded.

Tracy's heart beat a little faster. She had to be careful now, or she might scare Beth off. "Grandmother talked about her," she said, thinking as fast as she could. "She told me she wished you could come and live here again, because she wanted to know all about Amy."

"She . . . she did?" Beth stammered, wondering if it could possibly be true, and if maybe Tracy didn't think she was crazy anymore.

Tracy nodded solemnly, remembering her grandmother's last words. Maybe she could use them to get Beth talking. "And she said there was a fire." At the look in Beth's eyes, she knew she'd struck a bull's-eye.

"In the mill?" Beth breathed. "Did she really talk about the fire in the mill?"

Now Tracy hesitated. What if Beth was lying too, trying to trap her just as she herself was trying to trap Beth? But that was silly—Beth wasn't smart enough to do that. "I think so," she said. "When she was in the hospital, what did she tell you?"

"Nothing," Beth replied, and Tracy's heart sank. But then Beth spoke again. "Except that when she got home, she'd show me something that proved Amy's real."

A surge of excitement seized Tracy. *It's in the box,* she thought. *It's in the box Grandfather was always going through.*

But she said nothing.

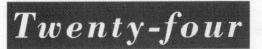

Twenty-four

It was a little past midnight. The house was silent, but from outside her open windows Tracy could hear the soft chirpings of crickets and the murmurs of tree frogs calling to their mates. Her feet bare, and only a light robe over her pajamas, she opened her closet and fished her grandmother's jewelry box off the top shelf. Then she turned off the lights in her room, and carefully opened the door.

The corridor outside was dark, but Tracy didn't even consider turning on the night-light on the commode. Her grandmother's door was only thirty feet away, and she could have walked it blindfolded if she'd had to.

She was halfway down the hall, moving carefully to avoid bumping into the commode that stood at the midpoint, when she realized that the corridor was not completely dark after all. At the far end, there seemed to be a faint glowing, as if a dim light were spilling from beneath a door.

Her grandmother's door.

She froze in the darkness, clutching the jewelry box tighter, her eyes fixed on the light. It seemed now to be flickering slightly. Why would there be light coming from her grandmother's room? It was empty, wasn't it?

Unless it wasn't empty.

But who could be in there? She'd been awake all night, listening.

Her father and stepmother had come in to say good night to her, and then she'd heard them going down the hall to the other end of the house. She'd even opened her door so she could listen, and been able to hear their voices until the closing of their door had cut off their words.

Twice, she'd crept down the hall to listen at Beth's door, and opened it just enough to hear the even rhythm of her stepsister's breathing as she slept.

The only other person in the house was Hannah.

So it had to be Hannah.

Hannah was in her grandmother's room, going through her belongings, looking for things to steal.

Her grandmother had told her about servants, and how they always stole things. "You have to expect it," her grandmother had explained to her. "Servants resent you for what you have, and they think they deserve it. So they simply take things, because they have no sense of right and wrong. You can't stop it—it's simply the price we pay for what we have."

And now, with her grandmother barely dead, Hannah was in her room, using a flashlight to go through her things, looking for things to steal.

Tracy smiled in the darkness, congratulating herself for having already removed the jewelry box from its place in her grandmother's vanity. She turned, and started back toward her own room.

But then she remembered how Hannah had always fawned over Beth, and how, for the last three days, she had refused to do even the simplest thing for Tracy herself. Slowly another idea came to her, and she knew exactly what she would do. She would catch Hannah in her grandmother's room, and then make her father fire her. Hannah could even be blamed for the pieces missing from the jewelry box. Maybe she could even fix it so the old housekeeper would go to jail.

She moved quickly on down the hall, stopping outside the closed door to her grandmother's room. Pressing her ear close, she listened, then stooped down to peer through the keyhole.

The room was dark now, and she could hear nothing.

Maybe Hannah had heard her.

Gingerly, Tracy turned the knob, and pushed the door slightly open. Then she reached in, and flipped the switch just inside the door. The chandelier that hung from the center of the ceiling went on, and the room was flooded with bright light.

Tracy pushed the door open, and looked around.

The room was empty.

But there had been light under the door, she was certain of it. Her eyes scanned the room again, and fell on the door that led to her grandmother's dressing room, and the bathroom beyond.

The dressing room, too, was empty, as was the bathroom. She paused on her way back to the bedroom, and put the jewelry box back in its accustomed place in the top drawer on the right side.

Finally, she returned to the bedroom, and looked around once more. She couldn't have been wrong—she *couldn't.*

And yet, nowhere was there any sign that anyone else had been in these rooms. All was exactly as it had been earlier when she had stolen in to take the jewelry box in the first place. All the clutter—the things her grandmother prized so much, and that Tracy regarded as just so much junk—was exactly as it had always been. The lights, all of them except the chandelier, were off, so that wouldn't account for the strange light coming from beneath the door either.

She went to the window, and looked out into the darkness. In the village there were still a few lights on, and in the distance she could barely make out the shape of the mill. And then, as she watched, she saw the strange flickering light again.

This time, though, it was at the mill. It seemed to light up for just a moment, then disappear once more into the blackness of the night.

And then Tracy was sure she knew what it was. A car, winding along the road, its headlights flashing briefly on the mill as it rounded a bend.

The same thing must have happened when she'd been in the hall—it had been no more than a car coming up the hill, its lights flashing into the room for a few seconds.

Tracy turned away from the window, and started toward the closet that had been her grandfather's.

Had she stayed at the window a few more seconds, she would have seen the strange light at the mill again. She would also have seen that there were no cars moving along River Road.

She found the box where it had sat for as long as she could remember, on the highest shelf of her grandfather's closet. She had seen it often there, but whenever she'd asked her grandfather what was in it, he'd told her only that when the time came, she would know.

Now she stared at it for several moments. There didn't seem to be anything special about it—it was simply a rectangular metal box, with a metal handle. She could tell just by looking at it that it was very old. She reached up and gently eased it off the shelf, then carried it gingerly back to the parlor, where she sat down in her grandmother's chair. When she pressed the button on its front panel, the latch stuck for a second, then popped open.

Inside, there was nothing but some sort of old book. She fingered it for a moment, wondering if she should read it here, then put the box back in her grandfather's closet. But then, as the beginnings of an idea began to form in her mind, she picked up the box and left the suite of rooms, pulling the door shut behind her.

Back in her own room, Tracy put the box on her desk, then took the strange-looking book out of it. Taking the book with her, she went to her bed, got under the covers, then opened the book to the first page.

It was a journal of some sort, written by hand in black ink, that was barely legible. The spiky handwriting looked very old-fashioned, and for a moment Tracy wasn't sure she would be able to read it at all. But then, remembering the book had something to do with Amy, she began studying the words more carefully. Slowly, deciphering the words one by one, she read through the old book.

By the time morning came, and she woke up from what had been a fitful sleep, she knew exactly what she was going to do.

She smiled, and hugged herself, luxuriating in the warmth of the summer morning, and the knowledge that by this time tomorrow, she would finally be rid of Beth Rogers.

I'm being ridiculous, Carolyn told herself as she sat at the breakfast table that morning. Everything is fine. Tracy is behaving like a perfectly ordinary child, and I have no reason to be suspicious.

And there was nothing going on at the table that should have made her suspicious, either. Beth and Tracy were talking together, and Tracy was suggesting that after breakfast, maybe she should give Beth a tennis lesson.

"But I've never even played," Beth said. "I'll just mess up."

"Everybody messes up," Tracy countered. "And besides, you can't go to the club unless you play tennis."

Carolyn felt herself stiffen, ready for the scornful comment that was sure to come. But instead, Tracy simply went on talking, nothing in her voice betraying the contempt for Beth she had always expressed before.

"Look. Everybody at the club plays tennis, right?"

Beth nodded.

"So if you don't play tennis, what are you going to do? Just sit there?"

"Maybe I won't go to the club at all," Beth suggested.

Now Tracy rolled her eyes, and again Carolyn felt a pang of apprehension.

"So what are you going to do? Sit up here all by yourself? What fun will that be? And you know you, don't have any friends down in the village anymore—"

"Tracy—" Phillip interrupted, shooting his daughter a warning look. Instantly, Tracy looked apologetic.

"I'm sorry," she said to Beth. "I shouldn't have said that."

Beth shrugged, and stared at her half-eaten grapefruit. "Why not? It's true. They all think I'm crazy."

"Who cares what they think?" Tracy asked.

Beth eyed Tracy suspiciously. "You think I'm crazy too. You said so."

"That was before," Tracy replied. "I can change my mind, can't I?"

"But what about all your friends?"

"Stop worrying so much. Just let me teach you how to play tennis, and then next week I'll take you to the club. And I'll even let you wear some of my clothes. Or we'll make Daddy take us to Boston, and buy you some of your own."

"But what if I'm no good?" Beth asked, though her eyes were starting to betray her eagerness. "What if I'm terrible at it?"

"You can't be any worse than Alison Babcock," Tracy answered. "She can barely even hit the ball over the net. And when she serves, it's like getting free points."

"You won't laugh at me?"

"I won't laugh at you," Tracy promised, suddenly grinning. "Anyway, I won't laugh very much. Besides, who's going to see you?"

Ten minutes later the girls dutifully cleared the table of everything except their parents' coffee cups, and then were gone. A few minutes later, Carolyn saw them walking across the lawn toward the tennis court, Tracy already showing Beth how to hold a racket.

"Well?" Phillip asked, as if he'd been reading her thoughts for the last half-hour. "You don't believe it, do you?"

Carolyn sighed. "I wish I could, but nobody changes as quickly as Tracy has. So, no, I don't believe it at all. I'm absolutely convinced that she's putting on some kind of performance, but I can't figure out what it's all about."

"Don't forget," Phillip replied. "I gave her a choice—she either behaves herself, or she goes away."

But Carolyn shook her head. "What she's doing goes beyond that,

Phillip, and you know it as well as I do. I keep getting the feeling that she's up to something, and that she needs to get Beth's confidence." Then, at the hurt she saw in Phillip's eyes, she tried to apologize. "I'm sorry. I suppose I'm not being fair to her. But I just can't see her changing overnight."

"She probably hasn't," Phillip conceded. "But even if it's just an act, it's better than the way things were. And we have to give her a chance, don't we? You know as well as I do that if she gets to know Beth, she'll like her."

I don't know that at all, Carolyn thought to herself. *All I know is that I don't believe any of this. I feel like I'm living in a play, and I don't know what it's about.* But despite her private feelings, she made herself smile at her husband. "A couple of months ago that was certainly true enough. But after all that's happened—"

"It's all over now," Phillip declared.

Carolyn wished she thought he was right. "Is it?" she asked. "What about Beth's friend Amy?"

Phillip's eyes clouded, and Carolyn had the feeling he was keeping something from her. But he shook his head. "She'll forget about her. Beth was going through a rough period when she dreamed Amy up, but as things get better, she won't need Amy anymore." He looked at his wife pleadingly. "Honey, haven't we had enough problems this summer? Do we have to start looking for more? And besides," he added, "Beth hasn't mentioned Amy even once since she's been home, has she?"

"Can you blame her?" Carolyn replied more sharply than she'd intended. "Talking about Amy cost her every friend she had. If I'd been her, I'd have stopped talking about Amy long ago. But that wouldn't mean I'd stopped thinking about her."

Phillip frowned. "What are you getting at?"

"I don't know!" Carolyn rose from the table, and moved to the French doors. Beyond the terrace and across the lawn, she could see Beth and Tracy on the tennis court. Had it been any two girls but these, the scene would have looked perfectly natural. But knowing all that had happened that summer, and remembering what Tracy had said in the restaurant the night Abigail had had her first heart attack, there was something frightening about watching Tracy show Beth how to hold the tennis racket. The scene looked so innocent, but Carolyn couldn't rid herself of the feeling that what she was watching was more than a simple tennis lesson. Tracy, she was increasingly certain, was up to something. But what? And then, as her gaze wandered past the tennis court and fell on the massive shape of the mill, it came to her.

Whatever Tracy was up to, it had to do with the mill. She turned back to face her husband. "What about the mill?" she asked. "Have you decided what you're going to do with it?"

Phillip felt dazed by her words. "What does that have to do with Beth and Tracy?" he asked.

"I'm not sure what it has to do with Tracy," Carolyn replied. "But it seems to me that it's obvious what it has to do with Beth. I want you to tear it down."

"Tear it down?" Phillip echoed. "Carolyn, what are you talking about? There's no way I can do that—"

Carolyn's heart beat faster, for even as she had spoken the words, she had known she was right.

"But you have to! Don't you see? It's not just Beth! It's everyone! Sooner or later, that mill destroys everyone in this family. Your brother—your father. Even Abigail and Alan. And I know who will be next! Phillip, if you don't do something, the mill will destroy Beth and Tracy, too!"

Phillip stared at her. It was like hearing his father again, rambling on about the evils and dangers that the old brick building harbored. But there was nothing to it—no more than superstition. "No! Carolyn, I won't have you talking like that. There's nothing in that mill—nothing at all!"

Carolyn heard his words, and desperately wanted to believe them. And yet, deep in her heart, she knew that he was wrong. There *was* something evil in the mill, and it was spreading out now, reaching out toward them. If they didn't do something, it would destroy them all.

But what could they do, short of destroying the mill?

Nothing.

She had to find a way to convince him she was right. And she had to find it soon.

"Did I really do all right?" Beth asked an hour later when Tracy finally called a halt to the tennis lesson.

"You did great," Tracy lied, wondering why she'd even bothered to suggest tennis lessons, when anything else would have done just as well. It had been so boring, standing there in the hot sun, throwing balls gently over the net for Beth to try to hit. And she'd hardly been able to keep from laughing as Beth kept chopping away at them, most of the time not even coming close to hitting one of them. Of course it *had* been kind of fun the last fifteen minutes, when she'd started throwing them all over the place, making Beth run back and forth as fast as she could.

"When are you going to teach me how to serve?"

"Tomorrow," Tracy promised. She jumped easily over the net

and started gathering up the balls that were scattered all over the court. When they were finished, they started toward the house, but Tracy suddenly stopped, as if something had just caught her eye. When Beth turned, Tracy was looking up the hill toward the mausoleum. When she could see Beth watching her out of the corner of her eye, she spoke. "I bet Amy's supposed to be buried up there," she said.

Beth's eyes widened. "A-Amy?" she stammered. "I thought you didn't believe there was any such person."

"I changed my mind," Tracy said. "I told you that this morning, didn't I? That I didn't think you were crazy anymore?"

Beth nodded hesitantly.

"So if I don't think you're crazy, and you think Amy's real, then I have to think she is too, don't I?"

"I . . . I guess so."

"Besides," Tracy went on, her voice dropping, "I snuck into my grandmother's room last night, and found something."

A thrill of anticipation ran through Beth, and her eyes widened. "About Amy?"

Tracy nodded.

"What?" Beth asked. "What did you find?"

"Promise you won't tell anyone?"

"I promise."

Tracy eyed the other girl narrowly. "Swear on your father's grave?"

"Th—that's not fair," Beth protested, struggling against the lump that had suddenly formed in her throat.

"If you don't swear, I won't tell you," Tracy said.

Beth hesitated, then nodded. "I . . . I swear."

"Okay, I found a book, and it tells all about Amy."

"What does it say?"

Tracy smiled mysteriously. "Want to read it?"

"You mean you still have it?"

"I hid it in my room. Come on."

They hurried into the house, and went upstairs. When they reached the landing, Tracy whispered into Beth's ear, "Go into your room and lock the door, and don't let anyone in until I give the secret code. And as soon as I come in, lock the door behind me. All right?"

Beth nodded, and scurried into her room, locking the door behind her. Giggling, Tracy went into her own room, closed the door, then flopped down on the bed and turned on her television. Half an hour later, when she decided that if she waited any longer Beth would decide she'd been joking, she pulled the metal box out from under her bed, checked the upstairs hall, then ran down and knocked twice on Beth's door, waited a second, then knocked again. Instantly the door opened, and Beth let her in.

"What happened?" Beth whispered. "I thought you weren't ever coming."

"I almost got caught," Tracy told her. "Every time I tried to sneak out of my room, Hannah was snooping around. And if she catches us with this, she'll tell my father and he'll whip us both."

Beth gasped. "Whip us? Really?"

Tracy nodded solemnly. "That's why we can't let him know we have it." Then she took the box to Beth's desk, and lifted the lid. Ceremoniously, she took the book out, laid it on the desk, and carefully opened its cover. "Read it," she said.

When Beth had finished deciphering the strange handwriting that covered the pages of the little book, she looked up at Tracy.

"What does it mean?" she asked. "What'll we do?"

"It means they buried her in the wrong place," Tracy replied. "Don't you see? She's supposed to be up in the mausoleum, but she's not. That's what she wants."

Beth's eyes widened. "You mean we have to dig her up?"

Tracy hesitated, then shook her head. "That wouldn't be enough," she said. "What we have to do is get her spirit out of the mill."

Beth swallowed. Her heart was suddenly pounding. "How?" she whispered. "The mill's all locked up, isn't it? How can we get in?"

"I know where Daddy hid the keys," Tracy replied. "So we'll do it tonight. All right? We'll go down there together, and we'll let Amy out, and bring her up to the mausoleum. Then she'll be where she belongs, and she won't be angry anymore, and you can visit her anytime you want to. See?"

Beth nodded, but said nothing.

"Keep the book in here, okay? Hannah's always coming in to clean my room, and if she finds it, we're dead."

"But what if she finds it in here?"

"She won't. But even if she does, it won't be so bad, because you can say you didn't know you shouldn't have taken it out of Grandmother's room. Just stick the book in your desk, and hide the box in your closet."

"But what—?" she began again, but this time Tracy didn't let her finish her question.

"Just hide it, then come down to the stable. There's some stuff we've got to get ready for tonight." Then, before Beth could say anything else, Tracy slipped out of her room, closing the door behind her.

After Tracy was gone, Beth stared at the book for several long seconds, then slowly read it through once more.

Everything she read fit together with what she already knew about Amy.

So Amy was real after all, and even Tracy finally believed her.

Tracy, she decided as she hid the box in her closet and slipped the book into the top drawer of her desk, wasn't so bad. In fact, it was starting to look like they were going to be almost real sisters after all.

Tracy could hardly believe it.

She skipped down the path toward the stable, doing her best to keep from laughing out loud.

Beth had actually fallen for it. Just because of a name written in an old book, she'd actually been stupid enough to think it was proof that her dumb ghost was real.

She sauntered into the stable. Peter Russell was mucking out the stalls. He looked up at her and frowned.

"I thought you weren't supposed to come down here anymore," he said.

"There's some stuff I have to get," Tracy replied, her eyes narrowing angrily.

"What kind of stuff?" Peter challenged. "Your dad told me the stable was off limits."

"None of your business," Tracy replied, but when she tried to brush past Peter, he stepped out into the aisle and blocked her way.

"It is too my business. And until your father says different, you stay out of here."

Tracy hesitated, wondering if she should try to talk him out of it. And then she had an even better idea.

She'd just wait for Beth, and tell her what to get out of the tackroom. And Beth would do it, too. Now that she'd shown Beth that old book, she was sure Beth would do anything she asked her to do.

Anything at all.

Twenty-five

A kind of somnolence hung over the house all that day, and more than once Carolyn had to resist an urge to go to her room, close the curtains, then lie down in the cool half-light and let sleep overtake her. But she hadn't done it, for all day long she found herself obsessed with the idea that hidden somewhere in the house was the key to whatever evil lay within the mill.

For a while, after breakfast, she tried to fight the growing obsession, telling herself that Phillip was right, and that there could not possibly be anything inherently evil about the old building. She reminded herself that Phillip's father, in his last years, had been senile, and that Abigail, in those last weeks of her life when she had changed her mind about the mill, had already been weakened by a heart attack.

And yet every argument she presented herself with fell to pieces in the face of her growing certainty that there was something in the mill that neither Conrad nor Abigail had quite understood, but had nevertheless finally been forced to accept.

Finally, after lunch, she started searching the house.

She began in Abigail's rooms, opening every drawer, searching through the stacks of correspondence the old woman had kept filed away, looking for anything that might refer, even indirectly, to the mill.

There was nothing.

She went to the basement, then, and spent two hours searching through the jumble of furniture that had been stored there. When she finally emerged, covered with the dust and grime that had collected through the years, it was only to climb the long flights of stairs to the attic, where she began the search once more.

Again she found nothing.

But it was strange, for she did find that the Sturgesses, apparently for generations long past, had been inveterate collectors. Aside from enough discarded furniture to fill the house half-again, she had found box after box of old albums, piles of scrapbooks, cartons of personal correspondence, and even yellowed school reports done by Sturgess children who had long since grown up, grown old, and passed away.

And yet, among the collected detritus of the family's life, there had been not one scrap of information about the mill upon which their fortune had been built.

In the end she decided there was a reason for it. The records, she was certain, would have too clearly reflected the realities of the mill—the theft of her own family's share in it, and the appalling conditions under which it had been run. The Sturgesses, she was sure, would not have wanted those records around as a constant reminder of the sins of the past.

Eventually giving up the search, she wandered into the dining room to sit among the portraits of the departed Sturgesses.

She dwelt for a long time on the picture of Samuel Pruett Sturgess, who today seemed to be mocking her, as if he knew it was a descendant of Charles Cobb Deaver who was gazing at him, and was laughing at her efforts to discover the secrets he had long since destroyed.

At last, as the afternoon faded into the kind of hot and sticky evening that promised no relief from the humidity of the day, Phillip came home. He found his wife still in the dining room.

"Enjoying the pleasure of their company?" he asked. When Carolyn turned to face him, he regretted his bantering tone. Her hair, usually flowing in soft waves, hung limply around her shoulders, and her white blouse was smudged with dirt. Her face looked haggard, and her eyes almost frightened. Phillip's smile faded away. "Carolyn, what is it?"

"Nothing," Carolyn sighed. Then she managed a weak smile. "I guess I'm behaving like an hysteric. I've been turning the house upside down all day, trying to find the old records from the mill."

"They're probably in the attic," Phillip observed. "That's where practically everything is."

"They're not," Carolyn replied. She pulled herself to her feet, and started out of the room. "And if you ask me, old Samuel Pruett destroyed them all himself."

For a moment, Phillip thought she must be joking, but there was nothing good-humored in her tone. He followed her into the library, where he fixed himself a drink, then poured her a Coke. "What about the girls?" he asked. "Any problems?"

Carolyn sank into a chair, shaking her head. "None at all. They've been together all day, and I kept waiting for the explosion. But it hasn't come."

Phillip's brows arched hopefully. "Maybe," he suggested, "you were wrong this morning."

"I wish I could think so," Carolyn replied. "But I don't. I just have a feeling something's going to happen. And I wasn't wrong about the mill this morning, either," she added. "I really do want you to close it up again." She met his eyes. "I know it sounds crazy, and I can't explain it, but I've just gotten to the point where 1 believe your parents were right. There's something evil about the place, and I think your whole family knew it. I think that's why I can't find any records. And I mean none at all!"

Phillip hesitated, then, to Carolyn's surprise, nodded. "You might be right," he said at last. "Anyway, I can't really say I think you're wrong anymore." His gaze shifted away from her for a moment, then came back. "I went down there again today, and something happened to me. And it's not the first time."

As clearly as he could, he told Carolyn about the strange experiences he'd had—the odor of smoke he'd noticed in the mill when he'd been there with Alan back when the restoration was just beginning, and the sense of panic he'd had the day Alan had died.

He even told her about the hallucination he'd had, as if he'd slipped back a century in time, and felt as if an angry mob had been reaching out to him, trying to lay their hands on him.

"I felt as though they were going to lynch me," he finished. "And I went back this morning."

"And?" Carolyn prompted him.

Phillip shook his head. "I don't know. I didn't like being in the place alone, but I kept telling myself it was nothing—that the place has so many bad associations for me that I couldn't feel any other way. But the longer I stayed, the worse it got. And I couldn't go into the basement at all. I tried, but I just couldn't do it. Every time I looked down those stairs, I had the feeling that if I went down them, I'd die." He fell silent, then drained his glass and set it aside.

"What did you do?" Carolyn finally pressed when it seemed as if Phillip wasn't going to go on.

"Went to see my accountant." He chuckled hollowly. "When I told him I was thinking about giving the project up, he told me what I told you—we can't. Only he had the numbers to back himself up with."

Carolyn frowned now. "The numbers? What numbers?"

"All the figures on the amount of money we've committed to the project. The loans, the contracts, the cash layouts—the whole ball of wax. And the bottom line is that we literally cannot afford to abandon it. There's just too much money invested." He smiled bitterly. "The best thing that could happen," he added, "would be if the place burned to the ground."

For the rest of the evening, Phillip's last words echoed in Carolyn's mind, and when she at last went to bed, she found it difficult to sleep.

The mill, for her, had become a trap, and she felt its jaws inexorably closing on all of them.

Tracy Sturgess awoke at midnight, just before the alarm on her night table went off. It wasn't a slow wakening, the slight stirring that grows into a stretch and is then followed by reluctantly opening eyes. It was the other kind, when sleep is suddenly snatched away, and the mind is fully alert. At the first sound of the alarm, she reached out and silenced it.

Tracy lay still in the bed, listening to the faint sounds of the night. She had not intended to fall asleep at all—indeed, she had not even bothered to undress that night, and when her father had come in to say good night to her, she had merely clutched the covers tight around her neck. But when he was gone, she'd set her alarm, just in case.

She slid out of her bed and went to the window. The moon, nearly full, hung high in the night sky, bathing the village below in its silvery light. Even from here, each of the houses of Westover was clearly visible, and when Tracy looked at the mill, the moonlight seemed to shimmer on its windows, making it look as if it were lit from within.

Tracy turned away from the window, put on her sneakers, then crossed to the door. Opening it a crack, she listened for several long seconds. From below, the slow regular ticking of the grandfather clock in the foyer seemed amplified by the silence of the house, and Tracy instinctively knew that everyone else was asleep.

She opened the door wider, and stepped out into the corridor, then moved silently toward Beth's room. When she came to the closed door, she paused, listening again before she tried the knob. It turned easily, and when she pushed the door open, there was no betraying squeak from its hinges. Then she was inside, and a moment later she stood by Beth's bed, gently shaking her stepsister.

"Wake up," she whispered as loudly as she dared.

Beth stirred, then woke up, blinking in the dim moonlight. She looked up at Tracy. "Is it time?"

Tracy nodded, then pulled the covers away from Beth. To her disgust, Beth was wearing pajamas. "I told you not to undress," she hissed. "Hurry up, will you?" Beth reached out to the light on her nightstand, but Tracy brushed her hand away. "Don't turn on the lights. What if someone sees? Will you just get dressed?"

Beth scrambled out of the bed, and scurried into her closet. In less than a minute she was back, wearing jeans and a gray sweatshirt. On her sockless feet she had a pair of sneakers almost identical to Tracy's. She sat down at her desk, and quickly tied the laces, then followed Tracy out into the hall. But at the top of the stairs, Tracy suddenly stopped.

"What's wrong?" Beth whispered.

"The bed. We forgot to fix it so it looks like you're still in it."

"But everyone's asleep," Beth protested.

"What if they wake up? Wait for me downstairs by the front door." Then, before Beth could protest, Tracy scurried back to Beth's room and disappeared inside.

But instead of arranging the pillows under the covers of Beth's bed, she went to the desk, opened the top drawer, and took the old book out. Opening the book, she laid it facedown on the desk, then hurried out of the room.

She left the door standing wide open.

Downstairs, she found Beth waiting nervously by the front door. She pulled the drawer of the commode out, fished around until she found the right set of keys, then closed the drawer. A moment later they were outside.

They darted across the lawn, and between the twin stone lions that guarded the path to the mausoleum, then paused to pick up the lantern that Beth had sneaked out of the tackroom that afternoon.

"But why can't we just turn on the lights?" Beth had protested when Tracy had told her what she wanted.

"Are you crazy?" Tracy had replied. "If we turn on the lights, everyone in town will know someone's inside. But who's going to see a lantern?"

Now Tracy checked it once more. Its tank was full, and the wick, which she had carefully trimmed, was still undamaged. The knife she had used to trim the wick—an old rusty jackknife that had also come from the tackroom—was safe in her pocket, along with three books of matches.

Carrying the lantern, Tracy started up the trail to the mausoleum, Beth behind her.

The great marble structure seemed even larger at night, and the moonlight shot black shadows from the pillars across the floor. One of the shadows fell across the chair in which the ashes of Samuel Pruett Sturgess were interred, giving the girls the fleeting illusion that the chair had disappeared entirely. Standing by the broken pillar, they gazed out toward the mill.

"Look," Bed breathed. "It's burning."

Tracy felt a derisive laugh rise in her throat, but choked it off. "It's Amy," she whispered. "She knows we're coming." Out of the corner of her eye she saw Beth hesitate, then nod. "Shall we stop at her grave?" she asked.

This time, Beth shook her head. "She's not there," she whispered. "She's still in the mill. Come on."

Now, with Beth leading, they started down the tangled path that would eventually stop at the river.

"Are you scared?" Tracy asked. They had come to the end of the trestle over the river. On the other side, across River Road, the mill gleamed in the moonlight.

"No," Beth replied with a bravery she didn't quite feel. The wooden bridge stretched out before them, seeming longer and higher at night than it did in the daytime. "Are you?"

Tracy shook her head, and started out onto the narrow span, placing her feet carefully on the ties, keeping to the exact center of the space between the twin rails. Behind her, Beth followed her movements precisely, concentrating on staring at the ties, for when she let her vision shift, focusing on the river below, a wave of dizziness passed over her.

Then they were on the other side of the river, and solid ground once more spread away on either side of the tracks.

They paused at River Road, then darted across.

They came to the back of the mill, and Beth pointed to the loading dock. "That's where she lives," she whispered. "There's a little room under there."

Tracy ignored her, starting up the path along the side of the building. They were exposed now, the full light of the moon shining down on them, and they could easily be seen from any car that might pass by.

The third key Tracy tried fit the padlock on the side door, and when she twisted it the lock popped open. Then, as she pulled the door itself open, she felt Beth freeze beside her. She turned to look, and saw that Beth's eyes were wide, staring in through the open door. Her whole body was trembling slightly, and in the pale moonlight her skin was the color of death.

"What is it?" Tracy whispered. For a second she didn't think Beth had heard her, but then the other girl slowly turned, her fearful eyes meeting Tracy's.

"Daddy," she said softly. "Look. The moon's shining right down on the place where Daddy . . ." Her voice trailed off, and once more her eyes shifted to the interior of the mill.

Tracy followed Beth's gaze.

Inside the building, the moonlight was streaming through the skylight. The colors of the dome itself were faintly visible, but the moonlight had robbed them of their vitality. Instead of sparkling brightly, they cast a nightmare pall over the interior.

Across the floor lay the huge spider's web formed by the shadows of the leaded glass above.

Near the center of the rotunda, a single beam of clear moonlight shone down, illuminating the spot where Alan Rogers had died.

Grasping Beth's hand, Tracy pulled her inside the building, closing the door behind them.

The faint chirping sounds of the summer night disappeared, and silence closed around the two girls. It was as if they'd stepped into another world, a strange dead world that reached out to enclose them, drawing them to its cold bosom.

They started slowly across the floor, unconsciously avoiding the spiderweb shadow cast by the skylight, as if by touching it they could become entangled, to be held prisoner for whatever strange creature might lurk in the shadowy reaches, waiting for its prey.

In the distance, seemingly unreachable, lay the stairs to the basement, and Tracy wanted to run to them, wanted to be away from the strange light and terrifying shadows.

As in a nightmare, her feet seemed mired in mud, each step a terrible effort.

But finally they were there, staring down into the pitch blackness below.

Tracy knelt, set the lantern carefully on the floor, then lifted its chimney off. She struck a match, cupped it in her hands for a moment, then held it to the wick.

The wick sputtered, then caught, the flame spreading quickly along its length. When it was burning brightly, Tracy replaced the chimney, then adjusted the wick. The flame's intensity increased, but still the light was all but lost in the vastness of the building around them.

"Come on," Tracy whispered, getting to her feet once more and picking up the lantern.

But Beth hung back, staring fearfully into the darkness below. In her mind, she began to remember the hellish vision she'd seen last time she had been in the little room behind the stairs. "M-maybe we shouldn't—" she breathed.

But Tracy reached out with her free hand and grasped her wrist once more. "She's your friend, remember?" Tracy hissed, letting her anger begin to show for the first time since Beth had come back to live at Hilltop. "You can't chicken out now. I won't let you!"

She started down the stairs, holding the lantern high. Beth resisted for only a moment, but as Tracy's grip tightened on her wrist, she gave in. Her heart beginning to pound, she reluctantly followed Tracy into the basement.

The yawning blackness seemed to open before them, welcoming them.

Twenty-six

Carolyn rolled over in her sleep, then slowly began to wake up. At first she resisted it, rolling over once more, and keeping her eyes resolutely closed.

It did no good. In a moment she was fully awake, and she sat up, listening, trying to decide what had disturbed her sleep. But there was nothing. The sounds of the crickets and frogs were drifting through the window as they always did, and the faint creaking of the old mansion still complained softly in the background. She glanced at the clock.

One A.M.

She flopped back down on the bed, and felt Phillip stir beside her at the unexpected motion. Once more she tried to go back to sleep. Once more she failed.

Slowly, almost imperceptibly at first, a strange feeling began to grow in her. An uneasy feeling that something was wrong.

The house felt incomplete.

Abigail, she told herself. It's just that Abigail isn't here anymore.

But it was more than that, and she knew it.

She got out of bed, slipped into a robe, then stepped out into the corridor and turned on the lights. Halfway down the long hall, Beth's door stood open. Beth's door, she knew, was never open at night.

Frowning, she hurried down the hall, and switched the light on in Beth's room.

She saw the covers piled at the foot of the empty bed.

Even though all her instincts told her it, too, would be empty, Carolyn crossed the bedroom and checked the bathroom. There was no sign of Beth.

She felt the first flickerings of panic beginning to build inside her, and firmly put them down. Beth might only have gone down to the kitchen to raid the refrigerator. She left the room, and started toward the stairs, but instead of going down them, she went past them, stopping at Tracy's closed door. She hesitated, then turned the knob and pushed the door open just far enough to see inside.

Tracy's bed, too, was empty.

Now Carolyn hurried down the stairs, and searched the house, finally coming to Hannah's bedroom off the kitchen. She rapped softly on the door, then harder. At last there was a stirring from inside the room, the door opened a crack, and Hannah peered out at her, her eyes still red with sleepiness.

"Hannah, I need your help. Something's happened to the girls."

"Our girls?" the old servant asked, opening the door wider, and wrapping her robe tightly around herself. "What do you mean, something's happened to them?"

"They're not here," Carolyn replied. "They're not in their rooms, and they're not down here, either."

Hannah's head shook, and she made a soft clucking sound. "Well, I'm sure they're here somewhere," she said.

"They're not," Carolyn insisted. "I'd better get Phillip. Will you look downstairs?"

Hannah nodded, saying nothing as she started shuffling toward the basement stairs.

Less than a minute later, Carolyn was back in her bedroom, shaking Phillip awake.

Tracy stopped at the bottom of the stairs, and looked around. The lantern's faint glow was quickly swallowed up by the maze of pillars supporting the main floor, and her mind began to play tricks on her as she gazed into the darkness beyond the lantern's reach. There could be all manner of things lurking there in the darkness.

She could almost feel eyes on her, watching her.

Tendrils of fear reached out to her, brushing against her so that her skin began to crawl. When she heard Beth's voice, she turned quickly away from the threatening darkness.

"It's back here," Beth was whispering. "Behind the stairs."

Tracy held the lantern up once more, and its orangish glow spread out in front of her. She saw a large metal door, hung from a rail, standing partly open. And beyond that was the room where Beth was so certain that a ghost dwelt.

To Tracy, the room looked perfectly ordinary. It was empty, and its walls were blackened as if there had been a fire here sometime long ago. In fact, she thought as she stepped inside, she could still almost smell it. There was something in the air, a faint smokiness, that made her wrinkle her nose.

"Where is she?" she asked, still whispering despite the fact that they were alone.

"She's here," Beth said. "I always just came down here and waited. And after a while, she sort of—well, she just sort of came to me."

Tracy set the lantern on the floor, then looked up at Beth.

In the light of the lantern, Beth could see Tracy smiling at her. The way the light struck her face, the smile looked mocking, and Tracy's eyes seemed to have the cruel glint in them that Beth hadn't seen for months.

But that was silly.

Tracy was her friend now.

And then Tracy spoke.

"You really *are* crazy, aren't you?" she asked, reaching into her pocket and fumbling with something.

Beth's breath caught in her throat. "Crazy?" she asked, her voice barely a whisper. "I thought—I thought—"

"You thought I believed you, didn't you? You thought I was dumb enough to think there was really a ghost down here."

Beth froze, her heart pounding. As she watched, Tracy pulled the rusty jackknife out of her pocket, and unfolded its blade. "Wh-what are you doing?" Beth whimpered. She started to back away, but then realized that Tracy was between her and the door.

"You killed him, didn't you?" Tracy asked, her eyes sparkling with hatred now. She moved slowly toward Beth, the knife clutched in her right hand, its blade flashing dully in the light of the lantern. "You killed him just so you could come back and take my father. But I'm not going to let you."

"No," Beth whispered. "I didn't do anything. Amy—it was Amy—"

"There isn't any Amy!" Suddenly moving with the speed of a cat, Tracy leaped at Beth, the knife flashing out.

A stinging pain shot through Beth's left arm, and she looked down to see blood oozing out of a long deep cut. She stared at it for a moment, almost unable to believe what she was seeing. And then she felt a movement close by, and looked up. The knife was arcing toward her, and behind it was Tracy's face, contorted with fury.

"I hate you!" Tracy was screaming. "You're crazy, and I hate you, and I'm going to kill you!"

Beth ducked, and the knife glanced off her shoulder, then ripped down through her right arm. She tried to twist away, but Tracy's left hand was tangled in her hair now.

"*No!*" she screamed, the word almost strangling in her throat. "Please, Tracy! *Nooooo!*"

But it was too late.

Tracy's right arm rose, and then the knife came down once more, plunging into Beth's chest. Tracy twisted at it, then yanked it free, only to plunge it in again.

"Noo . . ." Beth moaned. "Oh, please, no . . ."

Tracy suddenly let go of her hair, throwing her to the floor. Bleeding from both arms and her chest, Beth tried to scramble away, but Tracy's foot shot out, kicking her in the stomach.

As she doubled up, the knife came down again, ripping through her back. Tracy jerked it out, then dropped to her knees, grabbing Beth's hair once again.

Pulling Beth's head back, she tightened her grip on the knife, then pulled it with all the strength she had across Beth's exposed throat.

The knife cut deep, and suddenly there was nothing left of Beth's screams but a sickening gurgling sound as the blood, pumped from a severed artery, mixed with the air being exhaled from her lungs.

For a moment Tracy froze where she was, staring down into Beth's open eyes, etching in her mind every detail of the fear and pain that had twisted Beth's face in the last seconds of her life. Then she dropped the corpse, letting it roll away from her as she rocked back on her heels.

The bloody knife dropped from her hand.

And then, in the flickering light of the kerosene lantern, her clothes stained with her victim's blood, Tracy Sturgess began to laugh. . . .

Phillip came awake slowly, then stared up at his wife's worried face, shading his eyes against the brightness of the chandelier. "What is it?" he asked. "What time is it?"

"Early. It's a little after one-thirty. Phillip, the girls are gone."

Phillip came instantly wide-awake, and sat up. "Gone? What do you mean?"

"They're gone." Quickly she explained what had happened. "Hannah's looking in the basement, but I'm sure they're not there. When I woke up, I had a funny feeling that something was wrong, that something was missing. It's the girls. I haven't searched the whole house, but I'm almost certain they aren't here at all."

Phillip, already out of bed, was pulling on a pair of khaki pants and a golf shirt. With Carolyn at his heels, he strode down the hall, first to Tracy's room, then back to Beth's, where Carolyn was waiting for him.

"They've *got* to be here," he said.

"But they aren't!" Carolyn insisted.

"Did you look upstairs?"

Carolyn shook her head. "No, of course not. It's all closed up. There's nothing up there."

"Well, they have to be somewhere. They wouldn't just take off. Not in the middle of the night." He started down the hall toward the back stairs that led to the long-empty third floor of the old house. Carolyn was about to follow him, when something caught her eye.

On Beth's desk, there was an old leather-hound book.

She stared at it. She'd never seen it before, and she was positive it didn't belong to Beth.

What was it, and why was it here?

She had no ready answer for either question, but suddenly, with the certain knowledge born of instinct, she knew that whatever the little book was, it was directly connected with the girls' absence.

She picked it up and began reading, desperately deciphering the crabbed handwriting that filled the pages. After reading only a few lines she was certain she knew where Beth and Tracy were.

She went to the door, calling out her husband's name. Then, as she was about to call him again, she saw him appear from the back stairs.

"They're not up—"

"Phillip, I know where they are! They went to the mill!"

Phillip stared at her. "The mill?" he echoed. "What on earth are you talking about? Why would they go down there?"

"Here," Carolyn said, holding the old journal out to him. "I found this on Beth's desk. I don't know where they got it, but they must have read it."

Phillip reached out and took the book from her. "What is it?"

"A journal. It tells about the mill, Phillip, and I know that's where the girls have gone. I know it!"

Phillip stared at his wife for a moment, then made up his mind. "I'm calling Norm Adcock," he said at last. "And then I'm going down there."

"I'll go with you," Carolyn said.

"No. Stay here. I . . . I don't know what I'll find. I don't even know what to think right now—"

For a moment Carolyn was tempted to argue with him, but then she changed her mind. For already, in the back of her mind, she knew that something terrible had happened in the mill. Something out of the past had finally come forward, reaching out for an awful vengeance.

Tracy's laughter slowly subsided until it was little more than a manic giggle.

She glanced around the room once more, furtively now, like an animal that was being hunted.

Then, in the soft glow of the lantern light, she dragged Beth's body over near the far wall. High up, beyond her reach, there was a small window. Tracy placed Beth's body beneath the window, one arm leaning against the wall, stretched upward as if it were reaching for the window above.

She returned to the place where Beth's corpse had first fallen, and knelt down to dip her hand into the still-warm blood. When her hand was covered, she went back to the wall, and began smearing her bloodied hand over its blackened surface, leaving crudely formed marks wherever her fingers touched. Over and over she gathered more blood, until at last the message was complete.

Still giggling softly to herself, she went back to the lantern, and bent to pick it up.

And then, suddenly, the lantern light seemed to fade, and the darkness closed in around her.

She was no longer alone in the room. All around her, their faces looming out of the darkness, she saw the faces of children.

Thin faces, with cheeks sunken from hunger, the eyes wide and hollow as they stared at her.

Tracy gasped. These were the children her grandmother had seen. And now she was seeing them, and she knew they could see her too, and knew who she was, and what she had done. They were circling her, closing in on her, reaching out to her.

She backed away from them, and her foot touched something.

She gasped, knowing immediately what it was. She bent down once more, but it was too late. The lantern had tipped over, its chimney shattering.

The cap of the fuel tank had been knocked loose, and the kerosene had spilled out, running quickly in all directions. And then it ignited, and suddenly Tracy was surrounded by flames. She stared at the sudden blaze in horror, and then, dimly, heard the sounds of childish laughter. All around her the faces of the children—the children who couldn't possibly be there—were grinning now, their eyes sparkling with malicious pleasure. She turned to the door, and started toward it. And then, as she came close to it, she saw another child.

A girl, no more than twelve years old.

She was thin, and her clothes were charred and blackened, as if they'd once been burned. Her eyes glowed like coals as she stared at Tracy, and then, as the flames danced close about her feet, she backed away, through the door.

The flames, fed by the spreading kerosene, followed her.

As Tracy watched, the door slowly began to close.

"No," Tracy gasped. She took a step forward, but it was too late. The door slammed shut.

She hurled herself against it, trying to push it aside, but it was immovable. Then she began pounding on it, screaming out for someone to help her, someone to open the door.

But all she heard from beyond the door was the mocking sound of the girl's laughter.

Behind her, she could feel the spirits of the other children gathering around, waiting to welcome her.

The flaming kerosene spread rapidly across the floor of the basement, oozing under a pile of lumber, creeping around the pilings that had for so long supported the weight of the floor above.

The lumber caught first, and now the fire spread quickly, tongues of flame reaching out to find new fuel. Then the pilings began to catch. Tinder-dry after more than a century, they burned with a fury that filled the basement with a terrifying roar. Then the floor itself began to ignite, the fire spreading through its hardwood mass, turning into a living thing as it ranged ever wider.

The temperature rose, and cans of paint thinner began to explode, bursting into new fires that quickly joined the main blaze.

The heat reached the level of a blast furnace, penetrating even the metal door that sealed off the room beneath the stairs.

Tracy was surrounded by blackness now, the kerosene having burned itself out.

But she could feel the fire, and hear it raging beyond the metal door.

And then, as she watched, the door itself began to glow a dull red.

She backed away from it, whimpering now as terror overwhelmed her. Then she tripped, and fell heavily to the floor. Dimly, she was aware of Beth's body beneath her.

Then, as the brightening glow of the door began to illuminate the room once more, she remembered the window.

She stood up, and tried to reach it.

And the sound of that awful laughter—Amy's laughter—mocked her efforts.

She began screaming then, screaming for her father to come and save her.

Each breath seared her lungs, and her screams began to weaken.

She slumped to the floor, her mind beginning to crumble as the heat built around her.

Her father wouldn't come for her—she knew that now. Her father didn't love her. He'd never loved her. It had always been the other child he'd loved.

With the remnants of her mind, Tracy tried to remember the name of the other child, but it was gone. But it didn't matter, because she knew she'd killed her, and that was all that was important.

Her grandmother.

Her grandmother would save her. It didn't matter what she'd done, because her grandmother was always there.

But not this time. This time, there was nobody.

She was alone, and the heat was closing in on her, and she could feel her skin searing, and smell her singeing hair.

She writhed on the floor, trying to escape the death that was coming ever closer, but there was nowhere to go—nowhere to hide.

The whole room was glowing around her now, and she was afraid, deep in her heart, that she had already died, and would be confined forever to the fires around her—the fires of hell.

Once again she called out to her father, begging him to save her.

But she died as Amy had died, knowing there would be no salvation.

Her soul, like Amy's, would be trapped forever, locked away in the burning inferno. . . .

Twenty-seven

By the time Phillip reached the mill, it was already clear that the building was doomed. Three fire trucks were lined up along the north wall, and two more stood in the middle of Prospect Street, their hoses snaking across the sidewalk and up the steps to the shattered remains of the plate-glass doors. But the water that poured from the hoses into the building seemed to evaporate as fast as it was pumped in.

The roar of the blaze was deafening, and when Phillip found Norm Adcock, he had to put his mouth to the police chief's ear in order to be heard at all.

"It's no good," he shouted. "There's no way to stop it."

Adcock nodded grimly. "If they can't get it under control in ten minutes, they're going to give up on the building and just try to keep the fire from spreading."

But they didn't have to wait ten minutes.

The main floor had burned through now, and the fire was raging through the new construction. The heat and flames rose upward, and suddenly, as Phillip watched, the great dome over the atrium seemed to wobble for a moment, then collapse into the firestorm below. The gaping hole in the roof combined with the shattered front doors to turn the entire structure into a vast chimney. Fresh air rushed into the vacuum, and the blaze redoubled, lighting the sky over the town with the red glow of hell. Over the roar of the inferno, the wailing of sirens sounded a melancholy counterpoint, a strange dirge accompanying the pageant of death the mill had become.

"The girls," Phillip shouted, straining to make himself heard over the deafening crescendo.

Again Adcock shook his head. "By the time I got here, there was no way to get inside. And if they were in there . . ." There was no need to finish the sentence.

The firemen had given up on the building now, and the hoses were turned away, pouring water onto the ground around the mill. And yet there was really little need for this. Always, the mill had stood alone between the railroad tracks and Prospect Street, the land on either side of it vacant, as if no other building wished to be associated with the foreboding structure that had for so long been a brooding sentinel, guarding the past.

Prospect Street itself was filling now as the people of Westover, hastily dressed, began to gather to witness the last dying gasps of the mill.

They stood silently for the most part, simply watching it burn. Now and then, as a window exploded from the pressure of the heat within, a ripple of sound would roll through the crowd, then disappear, to be replaced once more by eerie silence.

It was a little after two in the morning when the brick walls that had stood solid for well over a hundred years finally buckled under the fury of the fire and the weight of the roof, trembled for a moment, then collapsed.

The entire building seemed to fall in on itself, and almost immediately disappeared into the flames.

All that was left now was a vast expanse of flaming rubble, and once more the fire fighters turned their hoses toward the blaze. Clouds of steam mixed with smoke, and the roar of the inferno suddenly dissolved into a furious reptilian hissing, a dragon in the final throes of death.

Now, at last, the crowd came to life. It stirred, murmuring softly to itself, drifting closer to the dying monster.

It eddied around Phillip Sturgess as if he were a rock dividing a current. He stood alone as the mass of humanity split, passed him by, then merged once more to flood into the street.

And then, finally, he was alone, standing silently in the night, facing the ruin that had once been the cornerstone of his family's entire life.

Carolyn stood on the terrace with Hannah, watching the flames slowly die back until all that was left was an angry glow. She could see the black silhouettes of people, looking from Hilltop like no more than tiny ants swarming around the remains of a ruined nest.

It should have happened a hundred years ago.

The thought came unbidden into her mind, where it lodged firmly, until she finally spoke it out loud. For a moment Hannah remained silent; then she nodded abruptly.

"I expect you're right," the old woman said softly. Then she took Carolyn's arm in her gnarled hand, and pulled her gently toward the house. "I won't have you standing out here in the night air, not when there's nothing you can see, and nothing you can do."

"I have to do *something,*" Carolyn objected, but nevertheless let herself be guided inside. She followed Hannah into the living room, then sank into an overstuffed chair.

"You just stay there," Hannah said gently. "I'll put some tea on so it will be ready for Mr. Phillip when he comes back."

Carolyn nodded, though the words barely penetrated her mind.

Slowly, she relived the short time since Phillip had left the house.

She'd followed him downstairs, the strange book she'd found in Beth's room still clutched in her hand. Only when he was gone had she taken it into the living room, and read it through carefully.

Just as she had finished, Hannah had appeared, to tell her the mill was burning.

Even before she'd gone out on the terrace to look, she'd come to the certain realization that both Beth and Tracy were dead. And in the numbness following the first overwhelming wave of grief for her daughter, she'd also come to understand that there was a certain unity in what had happened.

It was as if the tragedy that had occurred in the mill a century ago—a tragedy that had never been fully resolved—was finally seeking its own resolution, and exacting a terrible revenge on the descendants of those who had for so long avoided their responsibilities.

Except for Beth.

For the rest of her life, she knew, she would wonder why Beth had had to die that night.

Now she sat alone in the living room, waiting for Phillip to come home, trying to compose her thoughts, preparing herself to explain to her husband what had happened in the mill so many years ago.

At last, just before three, she heard the sound of his car pulling up in front of the house. A moment later the front door opened and closed, and she heard Phillip calling her. His voice sounded worn out, defeated.

"In here," she said quietly, and when he turned to her she could see the anguish in his eyes.

"The girls—" he began. "Tracy—Beth—"

"I know," Carolyn said. She rose from her chair, and stepped out of the dim pool of light from the single lamp she had allowed Hannah to turn on. She went to her husband, and put her arms around him, holding him tight for a moment. Then she released her grip, and drew him gently into the living room. "I know what happened," she said softly. "I don't understand it all, and I don't think I ever will, but I know the girls are gone. And I almost know why."

"Why?" Phillip echoed. His eyes looked haunted now, and there was a hollowness to his voice that frightened Carolyn.

"It's in the book," she said softly. "It's all in the little book I found in Beth's room."

Phillip shook his head. "I don't understand."

"It's a diary, Phillip," Carolyn explained. She picked the small leather-bound volume up from the table next to Phillip's chair and put it into his hands. "It must have been your great-grandfather's. Hannah says she's seen it before. Your father used to read it, and Hannah thinks he kept it in a metal box in his closet."

Phillip nodded numbly. "A brown one—I never knew what was in it."

"That's the one," Carolyn replied. "Hannah found it in Beth's closet right after you left."

"But how did it—?"

"It doesn't matter how it got into Beth's room. What matters is what was in the diary. It . . . it tells what happened at the mill. There was a fire, Phillip."

Phillip's eyes widened slightly, but he said nothing.

"There was a fire in a workroom downstairs."

"The little room under the loading dock," Phillip muttered almost to himself. "The one behind the stairs."

Carolyn gasped. "You knew about the fire?"

"No," Phillip breathed. "No, I'm sure I didn't. But one day I was down in the basement with Alan. We were looking at the foundation. And right at the bottom of the stairs, I smelled something. It was strange. It was very faint, but it smelled smoky. As if something had burned there once.''

"It did burn,'' Carolyn whispered. Now she took Phillip's hand in her own. "Phillip, children died down there.''

Phillip's eyes fixed blankly on his wife. "Died?''

Carolyn nodded. "And one of the children who died there was your great-grandfather's daughter.''

Phillip looked dazed, then slowly shook his head. "That . . . that isn't possible. Tracy is the first girl we've ever had in the family.''

Carolyn squeezed his hand once more. "Phillip, it's in the diary. There was a little girl—your great-grandfather's daughter by one of the women in the village. Her name—the child's name—was Amelia.''

"Amelia?'' Phillip echoed. "That . . . that doesn't make sense. I've never heard of such a story.''

"He never acknowledged her,'' Carolyn told him. "Apparently he never told a soul, but he admitted it in his diary. And she was working in the mill the day of the fire.''

Phillip's face was ashen now. "I . . . I can't believe it.''

"But it's there,'' Carolyn insisted, her voice suddenly quiet. "Her name was Amelia, but everybody called her . . . Amy.''

Phillip's face suddenly turned gray. "My God,'' he whispered. "There really was an Amy.''

"And there's something else,'' Carolyn added. "According to the journal, Amy used her mother's last name. It—Phillip, her name was Deaver. Amy Deaver.''

Phillip's eyes met hers. The only Deavers who had ever lived in Westover were Carolyn's family. "Did you know about this?'' he asked now. "Did you know all this when you married me?''

Now it was Carolyn who shook her head. "I didn't know, Phillip. I knew how my family felt about yours; I knew that long ago they'd lost a child in the mill. But who the child's father was—no, I never heard that. I swear it.''

"What happened?'' Phillip asked after a long silence. His voice was dull now, as if he already knew what he was about to hear. "Why didn't the children get out?''

Carolyn hesitated, and when she finally spoke, her voice was so quiet Phillip had to strain to hear her. "He was there that day,'' she said. "Samuel Pruett Sturgess. And when the fire broke out, he closed the fire door.''

"He did *what?*'' Phillip demanded.

Carolyn nodded miserably. "Phillip, it's all in the diary, in his own handwriting. He closed the fire door, and let all those children burn to death. Even his own daughter. He let them burn to death to save the mill!''

"My God," Phillip groaned. He was silent for a moment, trying to absorb what Carolyn had just told him. The story was almost impossible to believe—the cruelty of it too monumental for him to accept. And yet he knew it was true—knew it was the secret that had finally driven his father mad.

Even his mother, at the end of her life, had discovered the tale, and accepted its truth.

"I don't believe in ghosts," he said at last. "I never have. I never will."

"I don't either," Carolyn agreed. "But I keep thinking about it. The children, caught in a fire. Tonight, our children, caught in a fire. And the other people who have died in the mill. Your brother. And Jeff Bailey. The Baileys had an interest in the mill once, didn't they?"

Phillip nodded reluctantly. "But what about Alan?"

"The reconstruction," Carolyn whispered. "Don't you see? Your father was right. The project never should have started to begin with."

Phillip's head swung around and his eyes met hers. "And what about Beth?" he asked. "What did she do to deserve what happened tonight?"

At last Carolyn's tears began to flow. "I don't know," she said through her sobs. "She was such a sweet child. I . . . I just don't know!"

Phillip put his arms around his wife, and tried to comfort her. "It was an accident, darling," he whispered softly. "I know how it all seems now, but whatever happened tonight, it couldn't have had anything to do with what happened a hundred years ago. It was just a terrible accident. We have to believe that."

We have to, he repeated to himself. *If we don't, we'll have to spend the rest of our lives waiting for it all to start again.*

And then, against his will, a picture of his daughter came into his mind.

He saw her once more as he'd seen her the day Alan Rogers had died, and she'd gazed into the mill at the broken body of Beth's father.

Her eyes had glittered with malicious hatred, and her lips had been twisted into a satisfied smile.

He held his wife closer, and shut his eyes, but still the vision lingered.

Late the next afternoon, both Phillip and Carolyn stood with Norm Adcock as a pair of workmen pried away the metal plate that had covered one face of the loading-dock wall for the last hundred years.

Samuel Pruett Sturgess, in the last pages of his diary, wrote of the metal plate, and his hopes that it would seal the room from the outside, as the firmly bolted metal door sealed it from the inside. It was his intention, in the last days of his life, that no one ever enter the workroom behind the basement stairs again.

Grayish wisps of ash still drifted toward the sky from the smoking ruin, and its heat still caused a shimmering in the summer air.

The men, their shirts stripped off against the combined heat of the sun and the fire, worked quickly, using a cold chisel and a maul to break away the bolts that secured the metal to the concrete of the dock. At last it fell away, and the window, its glass long ago broken out of the frames, was exposed to the sunlight for the first time in a century. The workmen stepped back, and Norm Adcock, with Phillip at his side, moved forward.

Residual heat drifted from the room, but when Adcock reached out and gingerly touched the concrete itself, he realized that it was no longer too hot to go inside. He dropped to his knees, and shone a flashlight inside.

At first he thought the room was empty. Opposite the window, he could see the remains of the metal door, twisted and buckled by the intensity of the heat that had all but destroyed it, hanging grotesquely from its broken support rail.

He worked the light back and forth, examining the floor.

Everywhere he looked, there was nothing but blackness.

And then, at last, he shone the light straight down.

"Jesus," he whispered, and immediately felt Phillip Sturgess's grip tighten on his shoulder. "I'm not sure you're going to want to look at this, Phillip," he said quietly.

"They're inside?"

Adcock withdrew his head from the window, and faced Phillip. "They're there. But I really think you should let us take care of it. Take Carolyn home, Phillip. I'll let you know if we find anything."

Phillip hesitated, but finally shook his head. "I can't. I have to see it for myself." When Adcock seemed about to protest further, he spoke again. "Carolyn and I have talked about it," he said. "And we decided that whatever is in there, I have to see it."

Adcock's brows rose. "Have to?"

"I'd rather not explain it," Phillip said. "Frankly, I doubt that it would make much sense to you. But I do have to see what happened."

Adcock weighed the matter in his mind, then reluctantly nodded. "Okay. I'll have the men put the ladder in, then we can go down."

When the ladder had been lowered, Adcock disappeared through the window. Phillip followed him. He carefully avoided looking down until he was on the floor and had stepped carefully away from the ladder. Then, as his eyes became accustomed to the shadowy light of the little room, he let himself look at what Adcock had already seen.

The heat of the fire had all but destroyed the remains of the two girls.

Their clothes had burned, as had their hair. There were still fragments of skin clinging to the skulls, and the skeletons themselves were wrapped in the emaciated remains of the soft tissues of their bodies.

Phillip was reminded of photographs he'd seen of the Nazi concentration camps after the war. He struggled against the nausea that rose in his gorge, then made himself kneel, and reach out to touch what was left of his daughter.

Tracy's body lay curled tightly, as if she'd died trying to protect herself against the heat.

Around her neck there was a chain, and attached to the chain, clutched in the bony remains of Tracy's right hand, was a jade pendant that he recognized as having been his mother's.

If it had not been for the pendant, he was sure he wouldn't have known which of the hideous, almost mummified bodies was Tracy's.

His gaze shifted to Beth's body. It was stretched prone on the floor, one hand up; its fleshless fingers seemed to be reaching toward the window.

Slowly, he became aware of the marks on the wall. At first they were only a blur, almost lost in the blackness on which they had been smeared. But as he stared at them, they gradually began to take shape, and he realized that before the girls had died, one of them—he couldn't be sure which one—had left a message. Now the message was clear.

It consisted of only one word: AMY.

"It looks like blood," he heard Norm Adcock say. "There's some more on the floor." Then his voice dropped. "Phillip?"

"I'm listening," Phillip replied.

"I can't be sure, but right now I'd say only Tracy died from the heat. I think Beth was already dead before the fire started. Look."

Reluctantly, Phillip made his eyes follow Adcock's pointing finger.

Despite the damage done by the fire, the seared skin and the shrunken flesh, the marks were clearly there.

Either before, or just after she'd died, Beth Rogers had been hacked nearly to pieces.

Phillip groaned as he realized what it must mean; then his mind rejected the knowledge, and his body finally rebelled. He could fight the nausea no longer. His stomach heaving, and his throat already filling with the sour taste of bile, he retreated to the far corner of the room.

Ten minutes later, pale and shaking, but once again in control of himself, he emerged from the little room into the daylight outside. Carolyn was still there, standing where he'd left her, waiting for him. She looked at him, her eyes asking him a silent question.

He took her in his arms, and held her close. "It's over," he said. "It's all over now."

Carolyn shuddered, and let her tears flow freely. She felt numb, empty, as if she'd lost everything that she had loved.

But that's not true, she insisted to herself.

I still have Phillip, and we still have our baby.

And then, for the first time, she felt their unborn child stir within her.

We'll get through it, she told herself. *We'll get through it all, and we'll survive. Whatever's happened, we'll survive.*

She took Phillip's hand and pressed it to her belly. "It's not over, darling," she whispered. "We just have to begin again. And we can. I know we can."

Once again, the tiny child within her moved, and this time Phillip felt it, too.

Epilogue

Almost a year had passed.

On the morning of July 4, Carolyn Sturgess started across the lawn toward the two stone lions that flanked the path to the mausoleum. She walked at an easy pace, enjoying the warmth of the sun. The sky was a deep blue that morning, and nowhere was there even a trace of a cloud that might foreshadow an afternoon shower. The day, she knew, would be perfect.

She wished Beth were there to share it with her.

The pain of her loss had eased with the passage of time, and as she remembered her daughter today, there was only a dull ache to remind her of the terrible days of the previous summer. And even that ache, she was finally beginning to believe, would someday fade away.

She stepped into the shade of the path, and started up the gentle grade toward the top of the hill and the marble structure that guarded the remains of her husband's ancestors. The light was different here, filtered into a soft green by the leaves of the trees above her head. Here and there the sun shone through, its rays dancing on specks of dust that hung in the air. A squirrel paused in the path a few yards ahead of her, sat up, and examined her

with bright inquisitive eyes before darting up a tree to chatter angrily at her from a perch twelve feet up. Carolyn stopped to chatter back at the squirrel, laughing softly at the indignant thrashings
of its tail. When the squirrel finally gave up its tirade and disappeared into the treetops, she moved on, coming at last to the mausoleum itself.

There was a seventh chair at the table now, and the broken
pillar had at last been repaired. The addition of the chair and the
new pillar had changed the feel of the monument, as well as its
looks. No longer did it have an air of mystery to it, as if it were
filled with unanswered—and unanswerable—questions. There was
a completeness to it, as if the addition of the chair for Amy Deaver
Sturgess had closed the family circle around Samuel Pruett Sturgess. Now he sat with his wife at his side, and his four sons flanking them. But directly opposite him now, providing a kind of
symmetry, was his only daughter's chair. And beyond her chair,
the new pillar blocked the view of the place where the mill had
stood for so many decades.

No longer would Samuel Pruett Sturgess spend eternity gazing at
the source of both his wealth and his guilt. Now he would sit with
his completed family, his long-denied daughter acknowledged at
last. For Carolyn, the mausoleum had finally lost its feeling of the
grotesque, and had become a place of peace.

She paused there that morning, then moved on down the trail that
would eventually lead to the river. But that trail was no longer an
overgrown tangle of weeds and fallen trees. It had been cleared and
widened, and neat stone steps had been carefully installed to look as
if they'd been there forever. So well had the work been executed
that even the week after they had been laid the steps had blended
perfectly into the hillside.

Carolyn came to an intersecting path, and turned left, following
the well-worn trail she had once used nearly every day. Since spring,
though, she had found herself coming here less frequently. Indeed,
she realized as she came into the little meadow where both Beth and
Tracy were buried, it had been almost two weeks since she had been
here last.

Now, as she slowly approached the graves that lay flanking the
slight depression where Amy's bones had once been buried, she
remembered the funeral that had taken place here last summer.

There had been no question of separate funerals for the two
girls—they had been bound too closely together by their deaths.

Almost all of Westover had been there that day, and both Carolyn and Phillip had come to realize that their tragic loss had not
been totally in vain. Though nothing had been spoken, there was

a feeling that the funeral for the two young girls marked a turning point for the town, a final severing of its ties to the past, a laying to rest of the last vestiges of resentment toward the Sturgesses and the other old families who had once controlled the lives of the townspeople.

After the service there had been a reception on the front lawn, for even the mansion itself had not been large enough to hold the crowd. And as Carolyn and Phillip had moved through the throng of people, accepting the condolences that were that day genuinely offered, they began to sense the healing that was taking place.

It was that night that they had decided to build a park on the site of the mill, and donate it to the town. Then, during the weeks when the park was being built and the charred remnants of the mill were being obliterated, they had discussed the naming of the park.

It was Phillip who finally suggested they dedicate it to the memory of Alan Rogers, and Carolyn had immediately concurred. It seemed fitting that the Sturgess name would no longer be associated with that part of Westover.

Carolyn gathered a few wildflowers, and placed them as she always did between the two graves where Beth and Tracy lay. As always, she wondered fleetingly what had really transpired in the basement of the mill the night the girls had died, but she had never asked Phillip what he'd seen in the little room beneath the loading dock, nor had he ever volunteered to tell her. Though she knew in her heart that it was a fiction, she liked to believe that they had simply gone out together on what was intended to be nothing more than an adolescent adventure, an adventure that had gone disastrously wrong.

The truth, she knew, was something too painful for her to bear.

She turned away from the graves, and started back to the house, putting the past behind her.

"We are only going on a picnic," Phillip observed wryly as he watched Carolyn pack the immense basket with more things than he could imagine her finding a use for. "It's not as though we're going to be gone for a week."

"Babies may be small, but they're great little consumers," Carolyn replied placidly, adding two more diapers, and a stuffed bear that was even bigger than their child to the contents of the already overfilled basket. "Besides," she added, "didn't I hear you telling Hannah to put two extra cases of beer in the car?"

"I don't want to run out, do I?"

"Heaven forbid. Of course some people might suspect you of

trying to buy votes with beer, but I suppose it's better than just handing out money." She finished with the basket, and tried to close its lid, which seemed to be impossible. "Here," she said, hefting the basket and handing it to Phillip. "It'll be good for your image if you're seen dragging baby stuff around the park. Gives you the domestic look."

"That, I suppose, is as opposed to the idly arrogant look of the old aristocracy?" Phillip asked as he took the basket.

"Whatever. Take it down and put it in the car, and I'll bring the baby. And if you want to kiss her, do it now. I won't have you kissing every other baby in town, then bringing the germs back to your own daughter."

"Candidates for alderman don't kiss babies," Phillip sniffed good-naturedly. "That's strictly state and federal stuff. See you downstairs."

Alderman, Carolyn thought as she picked the baby up from the crib and began wrapping the blanket carefully around the little girl's robust body. *Who ever would have thought a Sturgess could run for alderman?* Yet it had happened, and not through any effort on Phillip's part. Rather, a delegation of merchants had come to him back in December, while Carolyn was still in the hospital after delivering their baby, and after a great deal of awkward hemming and hawing (which Phillip had delighted in detailing for her the next day) had finally informed him that they had met among themselves and decided that what Westover needed was an alderman who had the time to make tending to the town business a full-time job. And it had to be someone with some business sense, and strong ties to the town. After giving it due consideration, they had come to the conclusion that Phillip Sturgess was the man they wanted.

Phillip had been shocked. He'd noticed that since the funerals for his daughter and stepdaughter, the attitudes of the townspeople had changed. They spoke to him now whenever he went down to the village, stopping to pass the time of day with him as they did with each other.

Conversations no longer eased when he came near. Instead, circles widened to include him.

The same thing had happened to Carolyn.

It was as if the town, recognizing that even the Sturgesses were not immune to tragedy, had closed ranks around them.

And now they wanted Phillip to lead them.

When they arrived at the park twenty minutes later, they found that Phillip did not, after all, have to put on the great display of domesticity that Carolyn had threatened him with. Instead, Norm Adcock grabbed the basket of baby supplies, while four of his men unloaded the beer.

Eileen Russell appeared out of the crowd, and pulled open the front door of the Mercedes, reaching in to take the baby from Carolyn.

"I swear to God, Carolyn," she said as the other woman released the seat belt and got out, "if you don't start using that baby seat I gave you, something horrible is going to happen to Amy."

Then her face turned scarlet as she realized what she'd said, but Carolyn—as she always did at moments like this—ignored the gaffe, knowing it had been unintentional.

"When she gets older, she goes in the seat. For now, I just prefer to hold her." Then she took Amy back, cradling her gently in her arms.

Amy.

At first both she and Phillip had been reluctant to give the child the name that had come to both their minds even before she was born, but in the end, they realized, there was really no other choice.

But this time, there was no chance that Amelia Deaver Sturgess was going to have anything but a perfectly happy life.

There had been a few shocked looks when people first heard the baby's name, but after either Carolyn or Phillip had explained to them where the name had come from, and what had happened to the first Amy, people had quickly come to understand.

And Amy, too, had become a part of the healing of Westover.

Carolyn began threading her way through the crowd, doing her best to keep up with Phillip. Everywhere they went, people flocked around them, chatting with Phillip for a few moments, then clucking and cooing over the tiny dark-eyed baby nestled in Carolyn's arms.

And Amy, her big eyes serious, looked up at all of them almost as if she recognized them, even though she was only six months old.

At last they came to a spot near the back of the park, where the wall separating the park from the railroad tracks lent some shade against the afternoon sun, and the babbling of the fountain in the wading pool made it seem cooler than it actually was. Phillip spread a blanket, and Carolyn gently laid their daughter in its center.

The moment she touched the ground, Amy Deaver Sturgess began screaming.

The spot Phillip had chosen for the picnic blanket was exactly where the little room behind the stairs in the basement of the mill had once been. Though Phillip and Carolyn were unaware of it, their child was not.

For even in her infancy, Amy Deaver Sturgess remembered perfectly everything that had ever happened in that room.

She remembered, and her fury still grew. . . .

THE UNWANTED

For my father,
the best father
in the whole world.

Prologue

T he sun was high in the cloudless blue sky, and had it not been for the faint trace of a breeze drifting in from the sea, the stiflingly humid heat of the August afternoon would have been unbearable. The beach was all but deserted. Only far away—much farther than she was allowed to go—could the little girl see the barely visible figures of the big children playing at the water's edge. Once—and it didn't matter how long ago it had been, for in her two-year-old world every day was forever and each week an eternity long forgotten—she had tottered toward the distant figures, her tiny hands reaching out as if she could touch them at any moment. But long before she had gotten close enough even to see them very well, she had felt the stinging slap of her mother's hand and heard the horrible word.

"*No!*"

Even before the first scream of pain burst from her, she had felt herself being jerked around and dragged back in the direction from which she had come, the rough sand scraping the skin from her knees as a stream of unintelligible sound rained down on her from her mother's looming face above. Though she didn't know what all the words meant, the message was clear.

She had done something wrong. When they got back to the blanket, her mother would spank her, and then she would have to sit on the blanket even long after she had forgotten just why she was there or what she had done.

Today she watched the children playing in the distance for a while, but made no move to abandon her bucket and shovel and try to escape down the beach toward them. Though she no longer remembered exactly what would happen if she did, she knew going that way hurt, and she didn't want to hurt.

She began digging in the sand with her shovel. In a little while there was a hole beside her, with water seeping into it as if by magic. She tried to splash the water out of the hole, but each time more water came in, and it always seemed to be just as deep.

She tried digging the hole deeper, but that didn't work either. It kept filling up with water, and then the sides would cave in, and pretty soon the hole would be wider but almost all filled up again.

Then she noticed that if she dug into the sand at the bottom of the hole, and scooped up whole handfuls of the mixture of sand and water, she could dribble it out onto her legs in neat rounded drops that looked like tiny little gray pancakes.

And if she dribbled more on top of that, it looked like a whole stack of little pancakes.

Chuckling and clucking softly to herself, she began covering her legs with dribbles of sand, building towers of it on top of her knees and ankles, then covering her toes as well.

After a while she noticed that if she held very still, the gray sand would turn white. And if she waited for it to turn white, then wiggled her toes, it would crumble away into the beach again.

Over and over she repeated the game. Then another idea came into her head.

She packed her bucket full with wet sand from the bottom of the hole, then patted the sand next to the hole flat. Turning the bucket upside down on the flat space, she lifted the bucket away and found a neat round pile of sand with a flat top.

Scrunching around onto her knees, she began dribbling wet sand from the hole over the top of the mound, letting it run down over the edges like frosting on a cake. Then she began dribbling it into towers, turning it into a castle. When she was done, she picked up her shovel and began carefully digging a moat around the castle. But when the moat was about six inches deep, it began to fill up with water and its sides began to cave in.

The little girl watched in fascination as her sand castle crumbled away.

When it was gone, she started another one.

The sun drifted slowly across the sky, but the little girl didn't notice.

She was surrounded now by the ruins of five sand castles, and was starting to build another one when she felt something brush against her.

It was a kitten, its tail sticking straight up in the air, its gray fur matted with sand.

It mewed softly, then sat down in the sand, staring up at her with large, curious yellow eyes.

The little girl reached out to touch the kitten, but it backed quickly away.

"Kitty," the little girl said softly. Then, again: "Kitty."

Her sand castles forgotten, she pulled herself to her feet and took an uncertain step toward the kitten.

It was then that she saw the little boy standing a few yards away, frowning deeply as he stared at her.

She looked back at him, then grinned and plumped back down onto the sand.

The little boy giggled and came closer.

The kitten, three feet away now, sat back down on the sand and wrapped its tail around its legs.

As the sun continued its slow course across the sky, the two children sat in the sand looking at each other, giggling happily as each of them mimicked the other's movements, with the kitten sitting a few feet away, watching them both.

Then, mewing softly, the kitten stood up, stretched elaborately, and darted away across the beach.

"Kitty!" the little boy exclaimed. Pushing himself to his feet, he started after the tiny cat, the little girl apparently forgotten.

The girl sat where she was for a few seconds, then turned around and stared solemnly at the blanket on which her mother was sitting.

Her mother was looking the other way, talking to a man the little girl didn't recognize.

The little girl scrambled to her feet and started after the boy and the kitten—her bucket and shovel, as well as her sand castles, completely forgotten.

She had to hurry to catch up with the little boy, but she knew that if she called to him, her mother might hear and stop her, so she stumbled along as fast as she could, tumbling down every few steps, then scrambling back to her feet and hurrying forward once again. Every few steps she felt her shorts slipping down over her bottom and reached down to pull them up again, but when the little boy kept getting farther and farther ahead, she finally abandoned the shorts altogether, leaving them in a heap on the sand.

The slope of the beach got steeper, and the little girl found her feet sliding out from under her with almost every step. But there was dune grass here, and she could use that to pull herself along. When she finally got to the top of the slope, the little boy was standing by himself, the thumb of his right hand poked securely into his mouth while his eyes—wide set and round—stared at the kitten. The kitten was sitting next to what the girl knew was the Bad Place.

She wasn't sure why it was the Bad Place, but dimly she remembered her mother bringing her here once and pointing to the place, then spanking her while she repeated the Word.

"No! No, no, no! Do you understand?"

Between the Word and the angry sound of her mother's voice and the stinging on her bottom, she understood.

She stopped uncertainly, and instinctively looked back. But all she could see was grass.

After a moment the little boy saw her, and his thumb suddenly popped out of his mouth. He pointed at the kitten and giggled happily. Then he started walking toward the Bad Place, holding his own shorts up with his left hand as his right thumb went back into his mouth.

The little girl hesitated, then followed.

The slope dropped away, and in a few seconds the little girl caught up with the little boy. He stopped walking and turned to stare at her, but didn't say anything. Instead his eyes watched her gravely.

She reached out and put her hand in his. Then, following the skittering kitten, the two of them started toward the Bad Place.

Suddenly there was no more of the warm dry sand that felt so good between her toes.

Instead there was an icky sticky feeling, and she could feel something cold oozing around her feet. She stopped and looked down.

Mud.

Thick and black, it squished around her feet, and there was an odor about it that made her wrinkle her nose and make a face. But the kitten didn't seem to notice it at all, and neither did the little boy.

The little girl took another step, pulling her foot loose from the muck and wiping it carefully on her other leg before putting it back down into the ooze.

But there was a path into the Bad Place, and if there was a path, it must be all right.

Now there was tall grass on both sides of her, and it almost felt as though she was in a jungle.

And there were sounds all around her, sounds she had never heard before.

At first she didn't know whether she should be frightened or not.

Then she remembered the sounds she'd heard in her room on the nights when the "monsters" had come for her, and she'd started screaming until her daddy had come in and turned on the lights and told her that there weren't any monsters.

But she knew there *were* monsters, and as she walked along in the Bad Place, holding on to the little boy's hand, she knew that the monsters were all around her, even if she couldn't see them.

It was the monsters that were making the sounds.

She had a crawly feeling in her tummy now, and her skin felt all tingly.

And in her chest, her heart was beginning to thump loudly.

If the monsters heard her heart, they would know where she was and come after her.

A tiny whimper of fear escaped her lips, and her eyes burned with tears.

She wanted to call to her mother—wanted her mother to come and get her, although she was afraid of what would happen to her if her mother found her in the Bad Place.

She tugged at the little boy's hand and he stopped. His thumb still in his mouth, he gazed at her uncomprehendingly.

"M-monster—" the little girl managed to say. "There!" She pointed at the jungle that was all around them, but the little boy shook his head.

"Kitty."

Then, pulling at her arm, he toddled along the path toward the kitten that they never seemed to be able to catch up with.

She didn't know how far into the Bad Place they had gone, but she was crying now, her heart pounding so hard she knew the monsters had to hear her soon.

They were all around her, making low moaning sounds, and she could hear them rustling softly as they searched for her.

Her crying got worse, and she let go of the little boy's hand and started running as fast as she could, trying to catch up with the kitty. But the muck seemed to grab her feet, slowing her down, and the harder she tried to run, the slower she seemed to go.

Just like in the middle of the night, when she had to run away from the monsters but couldn't. . . .

The jungle was reaching out for her, trying to trap her in its writhing green arms, trying to wrap her in a web and pin her down so the monsters could come and eat her. . . .

It wasn't grass and vines around her now. It was snakes, coiling up and striking out at her, hissing angrily as she fled past them.

And then, so suddenly the little girl didn't realize it was happening, the jungle opened up to one side and there was a big sandy place that looked just like the beach down by the water.

She was safe!

She was out of the Bad Place, and there was sand, and she was safe!

The kitten was still a few yards away, but it had stopped again and was sitting in the path, watching her. The child's heart was pounding a little less now, and she stumbled out onto the sand, out of the sucking muck, away from the terrors of the jungle that had threatened to suffocate her.

The sand gave way beneath her feet.

She screamed now, a full-throated howl of terror that echoed around her and made even the jungle monsters fall silent.

She screamed again, then tried to pull her legs free from the sand that was suddenly knee deep.

Knee deep and cold and oozing like the mud in the jungle.

The little boy tottered out of the jungle and stopped, staring at her.

She screamed again, then lost her balance and fell into the cold, wet quicksand.

The little boy took a step toward her, then another.

First his right foot then his left sank into the bottomless depth of the sand.

The little girl knew why it was the Bad Place now.

It was the place where all the monsters of her nightmares lived, and as she thrashed in the quicksand, she could feel them coming closer, creeping out of the jungle, coming to get her.

She could hear her heart pounding, and her screams grew even louder, but even in her panic she knew her daddy wouldn't come for her.

She wasn't in her room, and it wasn't night, and her daddy couldn't hear her.

Even her mother couldn't hear her.

This time the monsters were going to get her.

She knew they were going to get her, because always before, when they had come for her in the night, her daddy had been there.

But now it wasn't night, and her daddy was nowhere near, and there was nothing but the monsters.

The monsters and the little boy.

He was coming closer to her now, but she knew the monsters were going to get him too. And even as she watched—his image blurred through the tears that streamed from her eyes—he stumbled in the sand and fell.

The quicksand closed over him for a moment, then his head reappeared and his screams were added to her own.

And the monsters grew ever closer. . . .

Night came suddenly, a cold dark night that closed around the child, cutting off her screams, blocking out the sound of the monsters as well as the light.

Her chest felt as though it was going to burst, and she struggled against the chill weight of the darkness, struggled to breathe against the watery night.

Now she couldn't even scream anymore, couldn't fight the monsters anymore, couldn't escape the black abyss of the Bad Place. . . .

She opened her eyes, a scream welling in her throat.

The blackness was gone.

Hands were touching her.

Warm hands.

But not her daddy's hands.

She blinked, the scream dying in her throat.

Warmth was all around her, and she felt herself being held close to the softness of a body.

When she looked up, there was a face above her.

Not her mother's face.

A face she had never seen before, but a woman's face.

And then she heard the voice, a low, crooning voice.

"You are mine now. You've come to me, and now you will belong to me. Forevermore you will belong to me."

One

Cassie Winslow stood quietly in the heat of the April afternoon, doing her best to focus her mind on the casket suspended over the open grave. The machinery that would lower it into the ground in a few more minutes was only partially concealed by the flowers that her mother's friends had sent, and even the largest bouquet—the one from her father—looked tiny in its position of honor on top of the coffin. There was a numbness in Cassie's mind— the same numbness that had settled over her three days ago when the police had arrived at the little apartment in North Hollywood she and her mother had shared to tell her that her mother wouldn't be coming home. Now, no matter how often she reminded herself that it was her mother they were about to bury, she couldn't bring herself to accept the idea. Indeed, she half expected to feel her mother's elbow nudging her ribs and hear her mother's voice admonishing her to stand up straight and pay attention.

I'm almost sixteen! Why can't she leave me alone?

She felt herself flush guiltily at the thought, and glanced around to see if anyone was staring at her. But who would there be to stare? Except for the minister and herself, the only other person who had come to the funeral was the lawyer who had arrived the day after her mother had died to tell her that he was taking care of everything; the day after the funeral—tomorrow—she would be flying to Boston, where her father would pick her up.

Pick her up in Boston! If her father really cared about her, why hadn't he come out for the funeral?

But Cassie knew the answer to that—her father was too busy taking care of his new family to bother about the one he'd dumped almost the minute she was born. So why would he fly all the way to California just for a funeral? As if she were still alive, her mother's voice rang in Cassie's ears: *"He's no good! None of them is any good—your father, your stepfather—none of them! In the end they always run out on you. Never trust a man, Cassie! Never trust any of them!"*

Cassie decided her mother had been right, for her stepfather, who had always made such a big deal about how much he loved her, hadn't shown up at the funeral either. In fact she hadn't heard from him since the day he'd walked out of the apartment almost five years ago.

It had been almost that long since she'd heard anything from her father.

The minister's voice droned on, uttering the words of prayers Cassie hadn't heard since the last time she'd gone to church about ten years ago, she thought, before her mother had gotten mad at the minister. Her attention drifted away from the gravesite, and she looked out over the broad expanse of the San Fernando Valley. Her home had been here for so long that she couldn't remember anything else. It was a clear day, and on the far side of the Valley, the barren mountains were etched sharply against a deep blue sky. It was the kind of day when everyone always said, "This is why I came to California. Isn't it great?" By tomorrow the smog would close in again and the mountains would disappear behind the brown stinging morass that would choke the Valley all summer long.

As the machine began whirring softly, and the coffin was slowly lowered into the ground, Cassie Winslow wondered if they had smog on Cape Cod.

Then the funeral was over and the lawyer was leading her down the hill to put her into the limousine the funeral home had provided. As they drove out of the huge cemetery that seemed to roll over mile after mile of carefully watered green hills, Cassie wondered if she would ever come back here again.

She knew that a lot of people went to cemeteries to visit their dead parents, but somehow she didn't think she would.

For as long as she could remember, she'd always had a fantasy that perhaps her mother wasn't really her mother at all. Sometimes, late at night in the dark security of her bedroom, she'd let herself dream of another woman—a woman she saw only in her mind— who never yelled at her, never corrected her, never soured her with bitter words. Never—

She shut the thought out of her mind, unwilling even to remember the other things her mother had done to her.

She concentrated once more on the woman in the fantasy. This woman—the woman she wished were her mother—always understood her, even when she didn't understand herself.

But that wasn't the woman they had just buried, and in the deepest place within her heart, Cassie knew she would never return here. But would she ever find that other woman, the woman who existed only in her dreams, who would truly be her mother?

Eric Cavanaugh watched the ball hurtle toward him, tensed his grip on the bat, squinted slightly into the afternoon sun, then swung.

Crack!

The wood connected with the horsehide of the baseball, and Eric swore softly as he felt the bat itself splitting in his hands. Then, as the ball arced off toward right field, he dropped the bat and began sprinting toward first base. If the bat hadn't splintered, it would have been a home run for sure. As it was, he'd still get a base out of it, unless Jeff Maynard managed to snag it.

There was little chance that Jeff would make the catch. That was the reason Eric had hit it to him in the first place. He rounded first easily and, fifteen feet before he got to second base, he plunged headfirst into a slide and felt his uniform tear away at the shoulder.

"You're gonna break your neck doing that someday," he heard Kevin Smythe say, and knew from the second baseman's tone that he'd made it. Safe! Grinning, he got to his feet, and began scraping mud from his torn jersey. But then, as his eyes swept the field, his smile faded.

Beyond the fence, parked by the curb on Bay Street, was the old white pickup truck with CAVANAUGH FISH emblazoned in cobalt blue on its side. Leaning against the truck was his father, his arms folded over his chest, his head shaking slowly as he muttered something to the coach, who nodded in apparent agreement from his place just inside the fence.

Eric's heart sank. Why couldn't his father have shown up half an hour before, when he'd put the ball over the left field fence? But that was the way it always seemed to happen: if he was going to make a mistake, his father was going to see it, and over dinner tonight Ed Cavanaugh would want to talk about it. Since this mistake had come on the baseball diamond, it meant that after dinner he and his father would be back here on the high school diamond, going through batting practice until the light got so bad neither of them could see. Even then Ed would insist on "just a couple more," so Eric wouldn't be able to get to his homework until after eight o'clock.

Unless his father got drunk. That was always a possibility. But when his father was drunk, things were always even worse than when his father was sober.

The coach's whistle signaled an end to the practice session, and Eric, after waiting for Jeff Maynard to catch up with him, started toward the locker room, wondering if he should skip the four-thirty student council meeting. If he weren't the president of the council, he wouldn't even be thinking twice about it. The council, he knew, didn't really mean anything at all. Being on it just gave him one more opportunity to have his picture in the yearbook, and gave his father one more thing to brag about when he was out getting drunk. But Eric *was* the president, and if he didn't go, his dad would be sure to hear about it. Coach Simms would make sure of that. Then there would be a long speech about "living up to what I expect of you" to go with the extra batting practice.

"That woulda been another homer if the bat hadn't busted," Jeff observed as he caught up. "How come you always hit those to me? You know I can't catch 'em."

Eric's grin came back, and his blue eyes sparkled with quick good humor. "You don't care if you catch 'em or not. If I hit 'em to you, I know I'm gonna get a base, and I know you're not gonna worry about it."

Jeff shrugged his indifference, but his eyes clouded slightly. "Your dad saw what happened," he said quietly. "You gonna get in trouble?"

"I always do, don't I?" Eric replied. He tried to make his voice sound as if his father's wrath didn't mean any more to him than a missed fly ball meant to Jeff. Except that Jeff had been his best friend almost as long as he could remember, and Jeff always seemed to know what was going on in his head, no matter what he said out loud. Now, he proved it once again.

"Wanta cut the council meeting? If we did, we could get the trig assignment out of the way before you've gotta be home. Or we could cut the trig, too, and go down to the beach," he added hopefully.

Eric thought about it, then shook his head as he pulled open the heavy locker-room door and stepped inside. "Can't. If I don't get an A on the test next week, I won't get an A in the course. And you know what that means."

Jeff rolled his eyes. "How would I know? And you don't either, since you've never gotten anything *but* A's. Besides, your dad won't kill you, will he?"

"I don't—" Eric began, but was immediately cut off by the coach yelling at him from the equipment cage next to the showers.

"That's two bats this week, Cavanaugh! One more and you start paying for them! Got that?"

"I didn't mean—"

Simms's voice grew louder, and his words seemed to echo the lecture Eric heard from his father so often: "I don't care about what you meant. All I care about is what you do!"

Eric felt a sudden surge of anger flood up through his body, and struggled against it. Getting mad would only make things worse. What the hell was the big deal about a broken bat anyway? Except it wasn't just the bat—it was everything. And it had been that way as long as he could remember. No matter what he did, it never seemed to be good enough—not for his father, not for his teachers, not for anyone. Always they seemed to think he wasn't trying hard enough, that he ought to do better. But he was already doing the best he could. What more did they want?

Once again Jeff Maynard seemed to read his mind. "Forget it," he heard his best friend say so softly that he knew no one else could hear. "If you say anything else, he'll tell your dad you mouthed off and make you run laps. Then you'll miss the meeting and flunk the test too! 'Course," Jeff couldn't resist adding, "it might be fun to watch Mr. Perfect fall on his face just once!" Then, as Eric swung around to punch him on the arm, Jeff darted off and disappeared around the corner toward his locker.

Eric glanced at the big clock on the wall, and realized he only had ten minutes to get to the council meeting. He began stripping off his stained jersey, shoving it into his book bag for his mother to wash that night.

He would mend it himself.

It was five-thirty when Eric finally left Memorial High and started home. The streets of False Harbor were nearly empty, since the summer season wouldn't start for another six weeks and most of the small fishing fleet was out to sea. The summer shops along Bay Street were still boarded up, and the town wore the strangely deserted look it took on every winter after the summer people were gone and the seasonal shopkeepers had closed their stores, heading south to bask in the sun and sell the same merchandise to the Florida vacationers that they sold on Cape Cod all summer. Though the town had an oddly forlorn appearance, the offseason was still Eric's favorite time of year. It was only then that he could go off by himself sometimes, hiking across the dunes and combing the beach, alone with the pounding sea and the stormy winter skies.

Then there was the marsh, flooded at high tide, that had given the town its name by making the harbor appear much larger and more easily accessible than it actually was. In the summer the dredged channel, which provided the only opening to the deeper harbor inland of the marsh, was choked with pleasure boats, and when the air took on the stillness of August, the acrid exhaust of their engines hung over the reeds like a poisonous haze. But in winter, with a northern wind howling, the marsh held a special magic for Eric, and he would sit for hours, his back to the village while gulls screamed and wheeled overhead. Once or twice he'd talked Jeff Maynard into exploring the marsh with him, but Jeff had only shivered in the cold for a few minutes, then suggested that they go bowling at the little six-lane alley on Providence Street, where at least it was warm. But that was all right with Eric—he didn't have the opportunity to go to the marsh very often, and when he did, he preferred to be alone.

Today there was no time for a hike out to the marsh, but as Eric strode along Bay Street, his book bag slung over his right shoulder, he considered stopping at the wharf. A gull had built the first nest of the season on one of the pilings, and Eric had already checked it twice for eggs. So far there were none. Still, you could never tell.

When he reached Wharf Street and glanced up at the clock that stood atop an iron tower at the entrance to the marina, he changed his mind. If he wasn't home by six, there would be hell to pay. So he turned left, starting toward the old common two blocks away.

It was only there, in the center of the town, that False Harbor began to look lived-in again, for it was in the long central strip—four blocks wide and eighteen long—stretching from the marsh at the western end of town to the rolling expanse of dunes that marked the far eastern boundary, that the year-round population lived. The residents of False Harbor had left both Cape Drive and Bay Street to the summer people. Indeed, once you left Bay Street there wasn't much to set False Harbor apart from any other small New England village. It was built around a rectangular common that hadn't seen a sheep grazing in more than a century, and the owners of the buildings facing the common had resisted the temptation to turn the village center into anything that might be called *quaint* by the tourist guides.

Yet quaint was exactly what it was, for many of the buildings were more than two centuries old. Once they had been private homes, but most had long since been converted into stores, remodeled by former owners in the days when Victorian architecture had been modern. The brick town hall still dominated the acre facing

Commonwealth Avenue, which was bounded on the east by the common and on the west by High Street. Next to it stood the stone Carnegie library, which had replaced the town stables in the early twentieth century.

Eric turned away from the town hall as he emerged from Wharf Street, cutting diagonally to the point where Commonwealth picked up again after having been broken for a block by the square. Then, changing his mind, he veered south again, toward Ocean Street and the old Congregational Church which occupied its own acre between the common and Cambridge Street.

The church had always been Eric's favorite building in False Harbor, though if anyone had asked him why, he would not have been able to say. A tall, narrow structure, its severe white clapboard side walls were broken at regular intervals by stained-glass windows which had only replaced the original flashing two hundred years after the church had been built and a hundred fifty years after the last of its puritan founders had been put to rest in the adjoining graveyard. Its steeply pitched slate roof was surmounted by a tall steeple in which the original bell still hung, though it was rung now only on Sundays and holidays. Eric paused again in front of the church, wondering if he dared take enough time to slip inside and watch the ancient clock in the vestibule strike six. Just as he'd made up his mind to risk it, a horn sounded. He turned to see his father's white truck idling at the curb. From the driver's seat Ed Cavanaugh was waving impatiently.

Eric felt his stomach begin to knot up with a familiar tension as he hurried across the lawn and slid into the truck next to his father.

"Got time to waste hanging out in there?" Ed Cavanaugh growled as he shoved the truck into gear, then let out the clutch.

Eric said nothing. He looked straight ahead. He could feel his father's eyes boring into him.

"Seems to me you could be spending your time a little more productively than standing around watching an old clock strike," Ed Cavanaugh went on. His voice was dangerously soft, a certain sign to Eric that his father was angry.

"I wasn't going to be there more than a couple of minutes—" he began, but got no further.

"Unless you want to end up in the gutter, I don't think you've got a couple of minutes to waste," the elder Cavanaugh replied. He glanced at the road as he turned into Cambridge Street, then shifted his attention back to his son. "And you can damn well look at me when I talk to you," he added.

Eric felt the knot in his stomach tighten, but he was determined not to let his expression betray his fear. Obediently he turned to face his father.

"You think I'm too hard on you, don't you?" Ed Cavanaugh asked, his voice edged with an acid whine. He was breathing harder now, and the heavy reek of whiskey on his breath made Eric shrink back slightly. When the boy made no reply, Ed shook his head. "Well, I'm not. All I want's for you to do your best. And you can't do that by dawdling your afternoons away."

Like you can dawdle yours away in a bar? Eric thought, but didn't dare voice the thought. "I was on my way home, and I just decided to stop at the church for a minute," he ventured. "That's all."

"Should have been home studying," Ed groused. "And it seems to me you and I better spend a couple hours on the diamond after supper. At sixteen you should be able to hold a bat right."

"It was an accident," Eric groaned. He'd hoped that if nothing else, at least the drinks his father had consumed had made him forget about that afternoon's baseball practice. "I know how to hold a bat. You taught me yourself, didn't you?"

Ed Cavanaugh's eyes narrowed with suspicion, and his jaw tightened. "You getting fresh with your old man, Eric?"

"But you did teach me," Eric insisted. "And I'm not getting fresh. You didn't see the rest of the practice, did you? I hit a home run, and I pitched three strikeouts in a row. How come you couldn't have seen that?"

"It wouldn't matter if I had," Cavanaugh replied. "Home runs and strikeouts are what I expect of you. What I don't expect are broken bats and pop flies that any idiot except Jeff Maynard could catch. And I don't expect sass either!"

"Jeff's not an idiot," Eric protested. "He just doesn't care as much about baseball as you do. If he'd wanted to catch that fly, he could have."

"If he could have, he should have," Ed said tersely. He swung the truck right into Alder Street and halfway down the block pulled it up in front of the shabby two-story clapboard house he'd bought when he and Laura arrived in False Harbor the year Eric had been born. Back then he'd only thought of the house as something temporary, a place for them to live while he built up a fleet of commercial fishing boats. But the business hadn't worked out at all. Ed Cavanaugh's "fleet" still consisted of nothing more than the same fifty-foot trawler he'd started with seventeen years before. He'd long since given up any hope of moving into one of the larger houses in the west end of the village. Besides, he told himself whenever he still bothered to think about it, it wasn't really his fault the fishing hadn't panned out, any more than it was his fault that the house, like the boat, had gotten more and more run down over the years. But where the boat only needed a coat of paint, the house needed a new roof as well, and the garden that had once run neatly along the front of the house was overrun with weeds.

Of course, if he'd had a wife who gave him at least a little bit of support, it all would have been different. The house would look great and the business would be booming. Well, it didn't matter anymore. In fact nothing mattered much anymore.

He glanced over at Eric once more, and found a point of focus for the anger that was suddenly threatening to boil over inside him.

Eric, he decided, wasn't much better than Laura. Everything came too easy for the boy, and the rotten kid didn't appreciate it. Besides, the little know-it-all wasn't quite the hot shit he thought he was.

Oh, Eric was smart—Ed knew the kid was a lot smarter than Laura, if not himself, and he was almost as well coordinated as he himself had been at the same age. Almost, but not quite.

Nobody—but nobody—had been as good an athlete as Big Ed Cavanaugh. And if things had just turned out different—if he'd just gotten even one decent break—he'd have played in the big leagues. But, of course, he'd never gotten a decent break.

Eric, on the other hand, always seemed to get the breaks. And all it had done for him, as far as Ed was concerned, was to make him cocky.

That meant he had a duty to take the kid down a peg or two.

And he knew how to do it too. Just keep pushing at the kid. Never let him think he was doing enough.

Swinging himself down from the cab of his truck, Ed glanced around the yard, looking for some extra chores to add to Eric's list of weekend duties. Then he glanced at the house next door, and the rage he was feeling toward his son shifted again.

How come, he wondered, the Winslows' house always looked so much better than his own? But, of course, he knew the answer: Keith Winslow—who wasn't any better than anyone else, except he always got all the breaks—had somehow managed to snag himself a decent wife. And that made all the difference in the world. If *he'd* been married to Rosemary Winslow, things would be different for *him* too. Not only did she keep the house looking good, but she made a decent living as well.

And that let Keith spend his time lounging around on a boat that never did any real fishing at all. Just took a bunch of rich people from Boston and New York out for sport every now and then.

Ed's gaze drifted to the upstairs front window of the Winslows' house as he thought about what Rosemary Winslow was doing right now. But he figured he knew, since Keith had gotten home from a four-day cruise just this morning.

He wondered what Rosemary did all those nights when Keith was gone. Sometimes, when he could see that she'd put the kid to bed, he'd thought maybe he ought to go over and keep her company for a while. Of course, so far he hadn't actually done it, but that didn't mean he never would. And if Laura didn't like it, that would be just too damned bad.

Suddenly he became conscious of his son's eyes on him, and he turned to see Eric staring at him, almost as if the boy had been reading his thoughts. "You got a problem?" he demanded. Then his mouth twisted into an ugly leer. "You're thinkin' about Winslow's daughter, huh? The one that's comin' from California tomorrow?" Eric, quickly shaking his head, turned away and started up the driveway toward the back door, but Ed merely raised his voice. "Well, you can forget about her, boy! I don't want you gettin' in trouble with any trashy little slut from California. You hear me?"

Once more Eric said nothing, but his shoulders hunched defensively, as if he could physically deflect his father's words.

A moment later, with a last glance at the Winslows' house, Ed followed his son up the drive. There was going to be trouble tonight. He could feel it coming. Either Eric or Laura was going to smart off, and he'd have to teach them a lesson. But that was all right. He'd had a lousy day anyway. He always felt better after he'd let off some steam.

From her regular post by the kitchen sink Laura Cavanaugh watched her husband and son come up the drive, and knew immediately that there was trouble. Ed's face—always florid—was redder than usual, and Eric wore the expression of strained placidity that she had learned a long time ago to recognize as repressed anger.

What was it about this time? she wondered. Well, she would find out soon enough. She opened the oven door to give the spareribs a final basting, then pulled the salad out of the refrigerator and took it into the dining room, where the table was already set for dinner. She heard the screen door slam, and went back to the kitchen just as Ed and Eric came in from the service porch. Eric gave her a quick kiss on the cheek, and a moment later she heard him taking the stairs two at a time as he went up to his room. Ed dropped his lunch box on the counter, then started washing his hands at the kitchen sink. The muscles on his back rippled under his blue denim shirt.

Fifteen years ago she would have gone to him, slipped her arms around him and hugged him. But she knew what would happen if she tried that now. He would stiffen, then twist away from her, his eyes flashing with anger. Then, acting as if nothing had happened, he'd ask why dinner was late, and before she could reply, he would settle into the breakfast nook and bury himself in the newspaper.

Unless Eric came back down.

If Eric came downstairs, Ed would put the paper aside and start rehashing every minute of Eric's day with him. What had happened? Who had he had lunch with? How were his classes going? What had be done after school? What was he doing in the evening? Was he seeing Lisa Chambers?

And Eric, looking to Laura like a trapped animal, would do his best to give his father satisfactory answers. Except, as Laura was all too well aware, there were no satisfactory answers.

Now Ed turned away from the sink, dried his hands on one of the dish towels, then shoved his bulk into the breakfast nook. His eyes met hers, and his brows knit into a scowl. "Something wrong?" he asked.

Laura opened her mouth, then changed her mind, closed it and shook her head.

For a second she thought Ed was going to stand up again, but he merely reached out and pulled the newspaper over to the place in front of him. Breathing a silent sigh of relief, Laura turned back to the sink.

I should leave him, she told herself. I should take Eric and get out.

But, of course, she wouldn't. There was no place for her to go. She was trapped, and there was no way out.

Besides, none of what had gone wrong for her family was Ed's fault. She knew that—Ed reminded her of it almost every day, one way or another.

Everything that went wrong was her fault. Somehow, some way, she'd failed Ed. And having failed him, she couldn't walk out on him.

But why did he always have to take it out on Eric too?

She'd tried to talk about it with him a few times, when he seemed to be in a particularly good mood, but he'd always insisted that he wasn't being hard on the boy, that he was only giving Eric the guidance that a father owed to a son.

But Laura was certain there was more to it than that. Though Ed maintained that all he wanted was the best for Eric, Laura always had the distinct feeling that it was something else, that it wasn't just the normal desire of a man to see his son succeed.

It was as if her husband wanted to punish Eric. But she had never been able to discover the reason why.

Almost surreptitiously she found herself studying her husband. His hair—dark brown when she had first met him—was iron gray now, and the athlete's body that had been his pride then had thickened over the last twenty years. His hands—the large hands that had once made her feel so safe when they held hers—were callused now, and the veins on their backs stood out, even under the thick mat of hair that started at his fingers and ran all the way up to his elbows. His face had been ruggedly handsome when he was in his twenties, but the years of drinking had blurred those sharp features, and there was a puffy looseness in the skin under his eyes.

So different from Eric, whose lithe body would never attain the mass of his father's, and whose hands always struck Laura as being the hands of an artist or a musician. Not, of course, that Eric had ever tried any such thing, although Laura knew that sometimes, when he was by himself, Eric liked to draw. Several times she had found sketches in his room. Once she'd even thought about showing them to Ed.

She had quickly changed her mind, knowing how her husband felt about art: "Sissy way to make a living," she remembered his saying as he'd sat in front of the television, drinking a beer while she watched a documentary about the life of Andrew Wyeth. "And even most of the good ones wind up starving." So she'd put Eric's sketches back in the drawer where she'd found them, and never mentioned them at all.

Eric's face, too, was different from Ed's. Where Ed's handsomeness—while he'd still had it—had always been rugged, Eric's face was sensitive, his blue eyes ringed with long black lashes, and his delicately chiseled features framed by an unruly mass of curly black hair which, when he was small, had been the bane of his existence. Even today Laura found it difficult to pass her son without running her hand through his hair.

Indeed, she sometimes wondered if it was Eric's looks alone that make Ed ride him so hard. Perhaps, she sometimes thought, if Eric had looked more like his dad, Ed wouldn't have needed to mold him quite so strictly.

Suddenly her husband's angry voice intruded on her reverie.

"It's ten after six, Laura. Can't you ever have dinner ready on time?"

Laura jumped at his voice, then hurriedly bent to open the oven. "I'll start serving right away," she promised. "H-how was your day? Did everything go all right? Did you get the engine fixed?"

Ed glared at her, his attention already drifting back to the sports page open in front of him. "If it went badly, I'd tell you, right? And no, I didn't get the engine fixed. I had to spend most of the afternoon with the wholesaler, trying to soften him up to give me a decent price on the catch."

Which means you sat in the Whaler's Inn, drinking all afternoon,

Laura thought as she began placing the ribs onto the three plates on the counter.

Silently she carried the plates into the dining room. Then, just as she was about to call upstairs to Eric, he appeared in the doorway that separated the dining room from the kitchen.

"Mom?" he asked, his voice low enough so that Laura knew he didn't want his father to hear. "Can you talk to Dad? He wants me to go practice batting with him tonight, but I have to study."

Laura stood still. Her eyes met her son's. She could read the fear in them, and the shame he was feeling at asking for her help. She hesitated, then almost in spite of herself, shook her head.

"I can't," she said quietly. "If he's made up his mind, I can't change it. You know that."

For a moment something flickered in Eric's eyes, then it was gone. "Yeah," he said finally. "Yeah, I know. Well, don't worry, Mom. It'll be all right—I'll figure something out."

A moment later Ed Cavanaugh came in and took his place at the head of the table. He waited silently until his wife and son had seated themselves. His eyes surveyed the dinner in front of him, then came to rest on them.

"I guess I can't complain," he said, his voice oozing with a stinging slime of vicious sarcasm. "A crappy house, a lazy son, and a wife who can't cook. What more could anyone want?"

Eric's eyes flashed with anger as his mother winced at the lash of the words, but neither of them answered him, each silently hoping that when Ed started shouting, the neighbors wouldn't hear him. But of course, they would—they always did—and though none of them ever said much, Laura and Eric always knew what they were thinking.

Eric always did his best simply to act as if nothing had happened, but for Laura the pitiful looks she always got from the neighbors—particularly from Rosemary Winslow—were almost as painful as her husband's blows.

Two

"If you don't get started, you won't make it," Rosemary Winslow said, her eyes flicking to the clock on the wall. It was already after nine, but Keith didn't seem the least bit worried. As she watched, he poured himself another cup of coffee and neatly folded *The Boston Globe* to the sports page. "Keith! Didn't you hear me? This is not a fishing trip—you're picking up your own daughter, and you can't be late!"

"I won't be late," Keith replied, setting the paper aside. "It's Saturday—there won't be that much traffic." He heard the sound of a screen door slamming next door, and glanced out the window to see Ed Cavanaugh starting down his driveway, his eyes bleary, his footsteps dragging. He gestured toward the window with his head, at the same time grinning wickedly at his wife. "Bet Laura doesn't nag *him* the way you nag me."

Rosemary's eyes darkened as she remembered the sounds that had erupted from the Cavanaughs' house late the night before. Though Ed's yelling hadn't been punctuated with any of Laura's quickly stifled screams of pain, Rosemary was still certain the man had been slapping his family around again. Perhaps last night she should have given in to Keith's desire to call the police. "It's not funny," she said, "and I wish you wouldn't make jokes about it."

From her place next to her father Jennifer, who had mercifully slept through the Cavanaughs' argument, looked up from the little rivers of maple syrup she was dredging through the scrambled eggs on her plate. "What's not funny?" she demanded, her large eight-year-old's eyes searching her parents' faces.

"The way Mr. Cavanaugh treats his family," Keith replied, his bantering tone suddenly gone. "And your mother's right. I shouldn't make jokes about it."

"Oh," Jennifer replied, immediately losing interest. Then, once more taking up an argument she'd lost earlier that morning but saw no point in abandoning, she turned to her mother. "How come I can't go to Boston with Daddy to pick up Cassie?"

"I already told you, sweetheart," Rosemary replied. She reached out to ruffle the red curls that capped Jennifer's freckled face.

"Cassie just lost her mother, and she won't be feeling very good. We just think it would be easier for her if she didn't have to deal with anyone but your daddy right away. Besides, you and I have a lot to do. We have to go shopping, then finish the bedroom. We want it to be ready for Cassie, don't we?"

Jennifer's face darkened and her lower lip quivered petulantly. "That was supposed to be *my* room," she reminded her mother. "You promised me—"

"I know what I promised." Rosemary sighed, wondering how to explain to an eight-year-old that promises sometimes had to be broken. "But that was before we knew Cassie was coming to live with us. And didn't you decide it would be nicer to have a big sister than a bigger room?"

Jennifer hesitated, then decided not to answer the question at all. "But what if she doesn't like me?"

"Of course she'll like you, Punkin," Keith told her. "What's not to like? Just because you talk all the time, tend to be a little sassy, and kick and scream when you don't get your way? What's not to like?"

"I do not!" Jennifer protested. She was trying very hard to look indignant, but instead she dissolved into the giggles that always came over her when her father teased her. "And my name's not Punkin, either. It's Jennifer."

"Right, Punkin," Keith said. He slid off his chair just in time to avoid his younger daughter's fist as she aimed it at his side. "Stop worrying—Cassie will like you."

Jennifer's giggles faded away, and suddenly her expression became serious. "If she'll like me, how come she never came to visit me? Doesn't she like you?"

For a split second Keith's eyes met his wife's. Jennifer, they both realized, had just asked the question neither of them was willing to deal with.

Neither Rosemary nor Jennifer had ever met Cassie, and Keith himself hadn't seen her for more years than he liked to admit. The last time he'd gone to California to see his daughter—until then an annual pilgrimage—the trip had turned into a disaster. His first wife, Diana, had been divorced for the second time by then, and she seemed to blame the failure of her second marriage—as well as her first—squarely on Keith.

"I don't want to see you," she'd told Keith on the phone. "I don't suppose I can stop you from seeing Cassie, but I don't have to see you myself."

"But why?" Keith had demanded. "What did I do?"

"Tommy left me," she'd said bitterly. "He left me because I

couldn't trust him, couldn't let myself depend on him. And that's your fault. Thanks to you, I can't trust anybody."

Immediately Keith had understood what had happened. Once more Diana's insane jealousy had destroyed her marriage. It wasn't, he knew, that she hadn't been able to trust or depend on him. Somewhere, deep inside her, there was a demon who whispered to her every minute of the day, telling her that people didn't like her, that they looked down on her, that she wasn't good enough.

But the worst of what the demon whispered was that her husband was cheating on her.

And though it was untrue—Keith had never betrayed her, had never even contemplated doing so—Diana had believed the demon within her. She had begun questioning his every move. When he wasn't with her, she sat alone at home, imagining him in the arms of another woman. Eventually she'd come to the conclusion that a baby was the answer to their problems, and Keith had finally agreed with her. It had occurred to him that Diana's jealousy might be rooted in her deep-seated conviction that Keith didn't truly need her. A baby might change that, giving Diana both the self-esteem of being a mother and a new focus for her energies.

And so they had conceived Cassie.

But Diana's jealousy had only worsened, until finally, unable to deal with it any longer, Keith had left.

Diana had never forgiven him. When the divorce had finally come, he'd given up his rights to partial custody of Cassie rather than subject the child to what Diana swore would be an unending fight through the courts. As soon as she'd won, Diana had taken Cassie to California.

Each year Keith had gone by himself to Los Angeles for a week, checked into a hotel, and spent as much time with his daughter as Diana would allow.

But on that last trip Cassie had barely spoken to him, and toward the end of the week Keith had finally discovered that Diana had convinced the child, too, that the loss of her stepfather was her father's fault.

One week a year, Keith had decided, was not enough to repair the sundered relationship. The following year, when Diana had told him that Cassie didn't want to see him, he and Rosemary had decided it would be better for Cassie, if not for Keith, to stay out of the situation entirely.

Then, four days ago, Diana had gone out after work for dinner with some friends, but never made it home.

It had been three o'clock in the morning when Rosemary had

sleepily answered the phone, to be told her husband's first wife was dead.

Cassie, not knowing what else to do, had given the police her father's phone number, but Rosemary had learned the next day that Cassie had also warned them not to be surprised if Keith hung up on them. Her exact words were, "He hung up on my mom and me a long time ago." When Rosemary had repeated them to Keith, he'd winced with a pain that was almost physical.

Had it been any other time, Keith would have been on a plane to Los Angeles immediately, but when Rosemary was finally able to reach him, he was two days out of False Harbor, with no one else on the boat who was capable of skippering it alone. And so, through a series of tense radio-telephone calls, arrangements had been made for Cassie to fly to Boston, where he would meet her and bring her to False Harbor to live with him and his second family.

As for Jennifer's question, he had no simple answer for it.

As far as he knew, no, Cassie did not like him.

On the other hand, she hadn't seen him for five years, and hadn't lived with him since she was two.

But he was still her father. He still loved her, and now that she needed him, he would be there.

"She'll like me," he finally told Jennifer. "She'll like us all."

Then, after kissing his younger daughter and giving his wife a hug, he left the house and hurried out to the car. Five minutes later he was out of False Harbor and on the highway to Boston.

Cassie felt a gentle tap on her shoulder, and glanced up from the book in her lap to see a stewardess leaning over the two vacant seats between her and the aisle. She reached up and pulled one earphone of her Walkman away from her head.

"Your seat belt," the stewardess said, pointing to the sign that glowed on the bulkhead three rows ahead. "We're making our final approach. We'll be landing in five minutes."

Cassie nodded silently, removed the headset, and dropped both it and the Walkman, along with her unread book, back into the big leather tote bag that had been her mother's. The previous night, when she'd decided to take it with her, she had thought that the bag might make her feel better, might give her at least a tenuous connection with her mother. But every time she looked at it, her eyes flooded with tears, and already she was wishing she'd left it behind with everything else in their little apartment in North Hollywood, to be packed for shipment by the movers who would arrive the next day. She looked resolutely away from the bag as she fastened the seat belt, and her gaze drifted out the window to the city that lay below.

All through the five hours of the flight, she had entertained the impossible hope that she might recognize Boston, but deep inside had known she wouldn't. Now she discovered she'd been right. As the plane soared out over Massachusetts Bay, then banked into the final turn before gliding over Boston harbor to touch down on the runway at Logan Airport, Cassie searched the landscape below for something—anything—that looked familiar. But there was nothing, and as the plane sank lower and lower, until finally only the buildings along the waterfront were still visible, she turned away from the window. Why, after all, should anything look familiar? She hadn't been here since she was barely two years old. How could she remember it? Besides, if it hadn't been for the accident, she wouldn't even be trying to remember it. For a split second she felt a flash of anger toward her mother, then resolutely put the feeling aside. The accident, she told herself one more time, was only that—an accident. But still the thought remained. Twice since her mother had died, Cassie had awakened in the dark, her body trembling and damp with a cold sweat, for the dream she'd first had the night before her mother died had come back.

In the dream she was standing by the freeway watching the traffic rush by, and then, far in the distance, she had seen her mother's car. In the dream it looked just like all the other cars on the freeway, there didn't seem to be anything different about it. But still, somehow she had known that that particular car was her mother's. And then, as the car passed her, she saw her mother turn and look at her. The odd thing was that the woman in the car, whom she *knew* was her mother, didn't look like her mother at all. While her mother's hair was a sort of drab brown—at least at the roots—the woman in the car in her dream had long black hair which fell around her shoulders, and deep blue eyes which seemed to penetrate right into Cassie's soul.

Her mother's eyes had been brown, like Cassie's own.

And then, in the dream, her mother had said something.

Cassie couldn't quite make out the words, but a second later her mother had begun laughing, and the car suddenly shot forward. A second after that it veered sharply to the left, smashed headlong into the concrete supports of an overpass, and burst into flames. Cassie had awakened then, sweating and shaking, her ears still ringing with the sound of the explosion, her vision still filled by the sight of her mother's face—the stranger's face—flame consuming her as she stared at Cassie and uttered a single word: "Good-bye."

Then she'd started laughing, a high-pitched screeching laugh, as if she didn't care that she was leaving Cassie alone in the world.

But the strangest part of the dream was that the woman in the car—the woman Cassie was still certain had been her mother—was a stranger.

It didn't make sense. Had her mother killed herself, or had Cassie herself, in some unknown way, caused the accident? And yet she knew she couldn't have caused it, for she hadn't even really seen it, except in the dream.

The very next night the dream repeated itself—this time in horrible reality. And Cassie's feeling that she might somehow have caused the accident still persisted.

She felt a slight bump as the plane touched down. She tightened her grip on the arm rests as the engines reversed, fighting the ground winds, and the plane slowed to a stop. A few minutes later it was parked at the gate and the jetway was swinging slowly around to link up with the door. Beyond that door, waiting for her, was the man who had abandoned her when she was only a baby, and eventually even stopped visiting her.

Why couldn't she have stayed in Los Angeles? At least there she would have had her friends around her.

As the other passengers streamed up the aisle past her, Cassie stayed in her seat putting off as long as she could the moment when she would have to get off the plane and face her father.

What if he didn't even recognize her? Would she have to go up to him and say, "I'm Cassie?" No, that wouldn't happen. There wouldn't be anyone else left on the plane, so he would *have* to know who she was. Finally, when the last person had disappeared from the aisle in front of her, she released the seat belt, pulled her coat down from the overhead compartment, and picked up her tote bag. She passed the stewardess at the door, saying nothing when the woman wished her a nice day, then moved slowly down the jetway. A few seconds later she stepped into the terminal and looked around.

The last of the passengers was drifting away, and a few people sat in chairs, baggage at their feet, waiting for the next leg of the flight.

But no one at all was waiting for her.

Her first instinct was to turn around and hurry back into the airplane, but she knew she couldn't do that. Suddenly she felt embarrassed, as if everyone in the airport were watching her. What should she do?

Maybe she had misunderstood, and her father was going to meet her at the baggage area. But no, she distinctly remembered his telling her that he would meet her at the gate and she needed only to pack enough for a few days. Everything else would be shipped, and what she didn't have room to pack in a bag small enough to carry on, they could buy. She wasn't to worry about checking luggage. That, in fact, was the other reason she had chosen her mother's tote bag. It was big enough to carry a lot of things, but had a shoulder strap.

She looked around once more. He had to be there. He *had* to! He couldn't make her fly all the way across the country and then just not show up. Or could he?

She remembered how her mother used to talk about her father: "I could never trust him. Every time I turned around, he was gone, and I could never be sure he'd ever come home again. And then one day he didn't. There wasn't any warning, any sign that anything was wrong. He just didn't come home one day, and the next thing I knew, he was divorcing me! And he did the same thing to you, Cassie! Just stopped coming to see you, and stopped writing to you! Just like that. In a way, it's lucky for you you're finding out what kind of man he is now, before he can hurt you any more."

But he wouldn't do that, Cassie told herself. I just talked to him last night. He promised he'd be here.

But he wasn't.

A few yards away a bank of telephones lined one wall of the terminal area. Cassie started toward it, fishing at the bottom of the tote bag for some loose change. She would call him and find out what had gone wrong.

When she'd let the phone ring twenty times, she hung up. She slumped down on the floor, staring up at the phone, her eyes flooding with tears. What if the same thing had happened to him that had happened to her mother? What if he was on his way to Boston, and there had been another accident?

What if he was dead?

Then, as if from a great distance, she heard her name being called. She looked up, and there he was, hurrying toward her.

"Cassie? Cass!"

She stood up and started to take a step toward him, but then he was there, his arms around her. She stiffened for a moment before she let herself relax slightly.

"I'm sorry, baby," Keith whispered in her ear. "I would have been here in plenty of time, except for the tunnel. It's my own fault—I should have left a little earlier."

Cassie pulled back and tipped her head up to look at him. "I—I was afraid something had happened. I was afraid—"

"Shh," Keith purred, pulling her to him again. "You're safe, and I'm safe, and nothing's going to happen to either of us."

Taking the heavy tote bag from her, he led her out of the terminal.

*   *   *

Neither Keith nor Cassie spoke much on the long drive from Boston down to Cape Cod, for Keith was reluctant to press his daughter to talk until she felt like it, and Cassie was, for the moment, content to sit curled against the door, staring out the window at the passing scenery, still hoping for a feeling of familiarity to come over her.

But none did.

Instead she had a growing sense that here, in the part of the country where she was born, everything was too small. As they left Boston, and suddenly the urban area ended—replaced by gently rolling hills covered with forests which had a miniature look to them—she suddenly realized that she had no idea which direction they were going.

At home she'd always known which direction was which, just by the positions of the two mountain ranges that bounded the San Fernando Valley on the north and the south. But here, no matter which way she looked, there were no mountains.

Cassie began to have a feeling that the countryside was closing in around her. She tried to get over it by concentrating on the forests, but they, too, had a different feeling to them. Her only previous experience with forests had been in the Sierras, or among the redwoods of northern California, where enormous trees, widely spaced and primeval, dominated the woods with their splendor. Here even the trees seemed small and crowded together, and looked to her as if they were fighting to survive. Then, finally, they turned off the main highway and began winding along a narrow road, passing through one small town after another. Suddenly things began to look more familiar.

It wasn't memory, she decided, or the feeling that she'd been here before. Instead she recognized the towns from pictures she'd seen in magazines, from movies she'd been to, and from television shows she'd watched. Small towns with well-kept yards, which seemed to begin quite suddenly, emerging from the surrounding woodland with no warning, then as suddenly disappearing again. Not at all like the towns she was used to, where you couldn't really tell where one ended and the next one began. In California, when you went out into the desert, the towns always seemed to start slowly, with a lone house or two sitting back from the road, surrounded by wrecked cars. Then, a little farther on, there would be a junkyard, or a gas station, and then more houses, until eventually you would find yourself in a town, not quite certain when you had gotten there.

Here, in New England, you knew. First you were in the woods, then you were in the middle of a town, then you were in the woods again.

"Are all the towns like this?" she asked her father.

Keith, startled out of a reverie, glanced over at her. "Like what?"

"I don't know. So . . . well, all the towns seem separate, as if they're all by themselves. At home everything runs together."

Keith smiled. "I noticed the same thing when I used to go out there. I could never tell the difference between North Hollywood and Studio City and Van Nuys and Sherman Oaks. I could never see how anyone could stand it."

For the first time since her mother had died, Cassie found herself giggling. "That's because there isn't any difference," she said. "They're all the same. The whole Valley's all the same." Her smile faded. "Is that how come you stopped coming to visit me? Because you didn't like the Valley?"

Keith said nothing for a moment, then shook his head. "I wouldn't have cared where you lived. I just thought—Well, it doesn't matter now."

Now it was Cassie who fell silent. *He doesn't want to talk about Mother,* she thought. Her mind drifted back to the last time she'd seen him, right after Tommy had moved out. She'd wanted to talk to him then, wanted to ask him what had happened when she was little and he'd left her mother. But she'd been afraid to. Her mother had told her often enough that all he'd do was lie to her and that she shouldn't believe a word he said. So she hadn't said anything at all that day. And then she'd never seen her father again.

"You could have written to me," she said finally.

Keith looked at her once again. She was facing straight ahead, her eyes apparently fixed on the highway, but he could see they were glistening with tears. "I did write to you, honey," he said quietly. "I wrote to you every month. And I sent you Christmas presents, and birthday presents too. But I never heard anything back." Keith waited, but Cassie said nothing. "Your mother never gave them to you, did she?" he finally asked.

Cassie hesitated, then shook her head.

For the rest of the trip to False Harbor, neither of them said anything.

Eric Cavanaugh was mowing the front lawn when he saw the Winslows' station wagon pull into the farthest of the twin driveways that separated his house from the Winslows'. He waved, and was about to call out a greeting, when the passenger door opened and a girl got out.

She looked about the same age as he was. Her face was pale, and her dark brown hair, pulled back in a ponytail, made her skin seem even whiter than it was. She was wearing a pair of red jeans, with sneakers of the same color, and had on a white blouse. As he watched, she opened the back door of the station wagon and pulled out a brown raincoat and a bulging leather bag. Though Eric couldn't see anything about her that looked much different from all the other girls he knew, he had a distinct feeling that there was something odd about her. Then he heard Mr. Winslow speaking to him.

"I want you to meet someone, Eric. This is my daughter, Cassie. She's just arrived from California to live with us. Cassie, this is Eric Cavanaugh. The proverbial boy next door," he added, winking at Eric.

Cassie smiled shyly and held out her hand, but Eric didn't take it. Without meaning to, he frowned slightly, still trying to place her in his mind. As their eyes met, he took an involuntary step backward. Then, remembering his manners, he recovered himself and managed a crooked grin. "H-hi," he stammered. "I'm sorry about your mother. . . ." Cassie's face turned even more pale, and as she turned and hurried toward the house, Eric wished he'd thought of something else to say. But his mind had suddenly gone blank, for as he'd looked at Cassie, something had happened to him.

It was as if their minds had met, as if an instant connection had been made. Something within her had reached out, and something within him had responded. As he went back to his lawn mowing, the strange feeling inside him grew stronger.

She was someone he'd been searching for, though he had been unaware that he was even searching. He knew her, knew how she felt, knew what she was thinking. For some reason he didn't understand, he was certain that it had been the same for her.

And in that instant, he had known something else—that Cassie Winslow didn't truly care that her mother had died.

But that's stupid, Eric told himself. *I've never seen her before, and I don't know anything about her at all.*

Three

S he looks so much older than I thought she would, Rosemary Winslow thought as the front door opened and Cassie stepped inside. But, of course, why wouldn't she? After all, the last pictures Keith had brought back had been taken when Cassie was only eleven. The child in those pictures, the little girl with the large—almost haunted—dark brown eyes which had stared out from beneath thick bangs, was gone. The girl who stood before Rosemary was now almost grown up. Nearly as tall as Rosemary herself, Cassie held herself erect, her long chestnut hair drawn back to expose a pale face that seemed more mature than her fifteen years. But the girl's eyes still seemed to have the same haunted look that Rosemary remembered so vividly from the last set of snapshots.

"I'm Rosemary," she said, offering Cassie a smile and stepping forward, ready to hug the girl. "I'm so very sorry about what's happened. If there's anything I can do . . ."

Cassie hesitated—Rosemary could almost feel the girl shrinking away from her. Then she offered Rosemary her hand. "I'm Cassie," she said softly. "It . . . it was good of you to take me in."

Good of us? Rosemary repeated in her own mind. What a strange thing to say—what else could she have thought might happen?

"I've been wanting to meet you for so long," Rosemary said out loud. "I even tried to convince your father to take Jennifer and me along the last time he went to visit you, but Jennifer was only three, and in the end it just didn't seem like it would be fair." She turned and glanced up the stairs. "Jen? Don't you want to come down and meet your sister?"

Jennifer suddenly appeared at the top of the stairs, looking shyly down at Cassie. Very slowly she started down the steps. "My name's Jennifer Elizabeth," she said, offering her hand to Cassie. "But you can call me Jen, or Jenny. Just don't call me Punkin. Daddy calls me that, and I hate it. Did he call you by a dumb name when you were little?"

Cassie stared at the little girl, who was a tiny feminine version of her father. Her reddish curls seemed to go in every direction, and her sparkling green eyes peered out of a square face with a jaw that gave her a stubborn look. But though her voice had been serious when she spoke, Cassie still saw a happy gleam in Jennifer's eyes.

"I don't remember what he called me," she said. "I was only a baby when he went away." She turned to her father. "Did you have a nickname for me?"

Keith spoke without thinking. "Same as Jen's. Punkin." Then, seeing the hurt in both his daughters' eyes, he wished he could take the words back. "I guess I don't have any imagination, do I?" he offered, trying to ease the moment.

"Jenny, why don't you take Cassie upstairs and show her her room?" Rosemary said hurriedly, then turned to Cassie. "Did you really manage to get everything into that one little bag, or are there some suitcases in the car?"

Cassie shook her head. "This is all I brought. Daddy said I shouldn't bring anything else—"

"And you paid attention to him?" Rosemary replied with an exaggerated gasp. "I told him no girl your age could put everything in one bag, and that he shouldn't have asked you to."

"It's all right," Cassie replied. "I don't really have much anyway. All I needed was a few extra clothes."

"Well, all right," Rosemary said doubtfully. "But if you find out you forgot anything, just let me know, and we'll go do some shopping."

Jennifer, who was already halfway up the stairs, whirled around. "Come *on*," she urged. "Don't you even want to see the room?"

Cassie hurried up the stairs after Jennifer, then followed her down the hall to a large room in the southeast corner of the house. As she stepped through the door, she stopped short. The room had obviously just been done over, but whoever had planned it must have thought she was still ten years old. The walls were papered with what looked like characters out of *Alice in Wonderland*, and the curtains were made out of material that matched the paper. Against one wall there was an ornate brass bed, covered with a blue quilt with white ruffles. In addition to the bed there was a wooden desk, a bureau, and a rocking chair, all of it painted white. The rocking chair had a cushion on its seat, upholstered in the same blue as the quilt on the bed.

"Don't you just love it?" Jennifer asked excitedly. "*Alice in Wonderland* is my favorite book in the whole world."

Cassie suddenly understood. "This is your room, isn't it?"

Jennifer hesitated, then slowly nodded. "It's always been my room. Mom and I just finished decorating it, and I was going to move back into it today. But then when we found out that you were coming, we decided I should stay in the other room and you should have this one, because this one is bigger."

"That's dumb," Cassie announced. "Let's go see the other room."

Jennifer's eyes clouded over with doubt. "I shouldn't show it to you. Mom says I shouldn't let anyone in my room unless I've cleaned it, and I didn't even pick it up today."

"Well, that's dumb too," Cassie decided. "I never cleaned my room at home, and I had anyone in it I wanted. Let's go see it."

Reluctantly Jennifer led Cassie back into the hall, then across to the other side of the house. "It's kinda small," she said before she opened the door. "Daddy says there didn't used to be a bathroom up here, and when they put one in a long time ago, they took half of this room for it." She pushed the door open and let Cassie step inside.

This, she knew as soon as she crossed the threshold, was the room that would be hers.

Had it not been for the space lost to the bathroom, the bedroom would have been large and L-shaped, with two windows on each wall. As it was, the room was perfectly rectangular, but no more than eight feet wide, with its fifteen-foot length giving it more of the feeling of a hall than a room. Just inside the door—to the left—a closet had been built. The floors were pine, and as Cassie moved slowly down the length of the room toward the single window at the far end, the planks creaked under her feet.

And yet despite its odd proportions and creaking floor, or maybe even because of them, the room felt right to her. Its relationship to the rest of the house seemed to her to reflect her own relationship to her father's family.

Not quite connected, not quite fitting in.

Set apart.

In her mind's eye she emptied the room of Jennifer's toys and filled it with her own things. She covered the pink wallpaper with forest-green paint, and trimmed the window sashes in white enamel. Suddenly the room took on a cozy feeling, as if it were wrapping itself around her, protecting her. As Jennifer had said, the room wasn't nearly as large as the other one, but it wasn't really small either. It was just oddly shaped. As Cassie examined it more carefully, she realized she could divide the space in half, with her bed in the part closest to the door. The rest of the room would be set aside as a private place, a place shut off to everyone else but her.

She came finally to the window and looked out. Below her was the backyard, its lawn neatly cut, and beyond that, separated from the yard by a black wrought-iron fence, was a small cemetery. "What's that?" she asked, and Jennifer came over to stand beside her.

"It's the graveyard," the little girl said solemnly. "It's the oldest one in False Harbor, and everyone in it's been dead a real long time. Practically nobody ever gets buried there anymore—it's almost all full."

Cassie grinned mischievously at the little girl. "Are there any ghosts in there?"

Jennifer's eyes rolled scornfully upward. "There's no such thing as ghosts. Everyone knows that!"

"But it's still fun to think about," Cassie replied. "I mean, wouldn't it be neat to think maybe there are still people down there who've been there for hundreds of years, and sometimes, when it's real dark, they get up and wander around the town?"

Jennifer frowned. "Why would they want to do that?"

Cassie shrugged, and let her imagination begin to flow. "Lots of reasons. Maybe they just want to see the houses they lived in, or keep an eye on their descendants." Her voice dropped slightly. "Or maybe there are people in the graveyard who weren't supposed to die, and they're still there, waiting for revenge."

Jennifer's eyes narrowed, but when she spoke, her voice quavered just the tiniest bit. "Now, *that's* dumb!" she declared in conscious imitation of Cassie's earlier pronouncements. "All you're doing is trying to scare me, and you can't. I'm not a baby."

"But it could be true," Cassie insisted, her gaze returning to the graveyard once more. "Nobody knows what happens to us after we die. Maybe we just die, but maybe we don't. Maybe we keep on living, in different bodies."

Jennifer frowned. "You mean like re—reincar—whatever that word is?"

"Reincarnation," Cassie said. "Maybe—" She fell silent as she noticed a slight movement out of the corner of her eye. Peering out the window, she looked to the left and saw Eric Cavanaugh leaning into the power mower, pushing it through the thick grass in his backyard. She frowned slightly, remembering his odd reaction when he'd been introduced to her. For a second he'd almost seemed afraid of her.

She watched him for a few moments, and then, as if he could feel her eyes on him, he turned, squinted against the sun as he tipped his face up, and hesitantly waved. Another moment went by before Cassie waved back.

Abandoning the window, she looked at the room once more, then her eyes fell on Jennifer, who was watching her warily. "I told you it was small," the little girl said cautiously. "You don't like it, do you?"

"Yes, I do," Cassie said. "In fact I like it a lot better than the other room, and I think we ought to trade."

Jennifer's eyes lit with sudden excitement. "Really?"

Cassie nodded. "Why don't you go down and tell your mother, and if she says it's all right, we'll just start moving your stuff back into your room, okay?"

Jennifer squealed with delight, and darted out of the room. A second later Cassie heard her pounding down the stairs. Then, alone in the room, she let herself feel it once more.

As before, it felt right.

This house wasn't hers, and the people she lived with weren't hers. Not really. But this room, for some reason she couldn't quite understand, truly felt as though it belonged to her, and she was meant to have it. Here she would feel comfortable, feel safe.

When Rosemary appeared in the doorway a few minutes later, Cassie was still by the window, sitting on its ledge.

"Cassie?" Rosemary asked. For a moment the girl didn't move. "Cassie, is something wrong? Is there anything I can do?"

Cassie looked at her then, and fleetingly Rosemary had the impression that the girl was somewhere else, somewhere far removed from the little bedroom. Then something in Cassie's eyes changed, and she smiled.

"No. I just think I should have this room, and Jennifer should have the other one. Is it all right?"

For a moment Rosemary was tempted to argue, tempted to point out that surely Cassie would need the extra space much more than Jennifer. But as her eyes met Cassie's, she changed her mind. For in Cassie's eyes she saw something that suddenly worried her.

Keith's stubbornness, like Jennifer's, was in his jaw, and was nothing more than a physical feature. But Cassie's was reflected in her eyes, and that, Rosemary knew, was something else entirely. Cassie's stubbornness was in her spirit, and Rosemary was suddenly quite certain that once this girl made up her mind about something, it would be very difficult to change it.

"If that's what you want," she said at last, "I don't see any reason why you shouldn't have it."

But as she left the room a moment later, Rosemary had the strange feeling that although Cassie's voice had betrayed nothing, the two of them had just had their first confrontation, and Cassie had won.

That's ridiculous, she told herself. All she did was make a very nice gesture toward Jennifer, and I should accept it at face value.

But for some reason she couldn't. And as she went back down the stairs, she realized why. All through their conversation she'd had the unsettling feeling that she wasn't truly talking to Cassie at all, but to someone else, some persona Cassie had devised to present to the world. Beneath that persona, Rosemary thought, there was someone else—the real Cassie.

Of that person, she was certain, nothing at all had been exposed.

Eric finished his yard work at six-thirty, put the tools back into the garage, swung its lopsided door shut, and started across the driveway toward the back door. At least the lawn looked all right, and he'd gotten most of the weeds out of the garden. But the Cavanaughs' house still didn't look nearly as nice as the Winslows' house next door, and Eric knew exactly why: paint.

If he could only talk his father into buying a few gallons of white paint, Eric knew he could make their house look a lot better than it did. But he also knew it was hopeless, for he'd asked his father about it last year. Ed had only glowered darkly at him and told him he should keep his mind on his schoolwork and not worry about the house. "Besides," he had added, "I don't have money to waste just to put on a show for the neighbors. Only reason to paint a house is to sell it, and I don't plan to sell this place."

But there was another reason why his father wouldn't buy paint, and Eric knew all too well what it was: most of Ed Cavanaugh's money was spent on liquor.

It had happened again today. His father had left right after breakfast, having announced that he was going down to the pier to finish the repair job on the *Big Ed*. But when lunchtime came around and his father hadn't come home, both Eric and his mother had known where Ed was, though neither of them had said anything. Then, half an hour ago, the truck had pulled into the driveway. When his father climbed down from the driver's seat, Eric immediately knew that he was drunk. His step was unsteady, and his eyes held the bright glaze of anger that meant he was looking for a fight. Eric had looked away as quickly as he could, concentrating on clipping the edge of the lawn next to the sidewalk. But he hadn't been quick enough.

"You staring at something, boy?" Ed had growled. "Well, let me tell you something—anyone works as hard as I do deserves a little relaxation, and if I stop off for a coupla beers with my friends, that's my business. Got it?"

Eric had nodded mutely, not daring to challenge his father, but sure in his own mind that it had been a lot more than a couple of beers his father had shared with his friends. Maybe it started that way, but after the second beer Ed would have switched to a shot of whiskey with a beer chaser, and bought the same thing for anyone willing to listen to him talk while they drank his booze. Only when there was no one left willing to listen, would his father have finally come home. Eric kept his mouth shut and his eyes on his work, and after a few seconds which seemed to stretch out into eternity, his father had shambled down the driveway and into the house.

Now, unable to put off going inside any longer, Eric pulled the screen door open and went into the service porch. He could hear his father's voice from the kitchen beyond. Though he couldn't see him, Eric knew Ed was sitting in the breakfast nook, a half-empty glass of bourbon in front of him, his glazed eyes fixed dangerously on his wife.

"Some reason why supper's late again?" Ed Cavanaugh was saying, his voice slurring slightly, his words edged with bitter sarcasm. "You been doing something useful again, like sitting on your ass watching TV all day? Seems to me if I can work all day, the least you could do is have my meals ready when I get home."

"I'm sorry, Ed," Laura replied, her voice barely audible. "But I'm fixing you a roast, and it's just taking a little longer than I expected."

Eric moved into the kitchen. The oven door was open, and his mother bent down in front of it, tapping the meat thermometer with a wooden spoon. As Eric watched, she removed the roast from the oven and set it on the counter.

"Smells good, Mom," Eric offered, hoping to deflect his father's anger.

"It should," Ed growled. "The price they get for that crap, and all it is is gristle."

"Aw, come on, Dad," Eric protested when he saw his mother's eyes start to flood with tears. "Mom cooks great—"

Suddenly Ed was out of the breakfast nook, his bulk planted in front of his son, his eyes blazing with fury. "What the hell do you know about it?" he demanded. "You an expert on cooking too?" His right hand rose threateningly.

"Ed, don't!" Laura protested. "Eric didn't do anything."

But it was too late. Ed's arm flashed downward and his open palm smashed against Eric's left cheek, twisting his head around. Eric staggered, stunned by the blow. Then, as his own eyes flooded with tears of pain, he rushed out of the kitchen and up the stairs toward his room.

"And don't come back down till you can show some respect!" he heard his father shouting after him.

Eric lay on his bed, still seething from the blow his father had dealt him nearly three hours before. The stinging on his cheek had diminished, but in his head the rage he felt only grew stronger.

I'm going to kill him, he thought. *Someday he's going to hit me once too often, and I'm just going to kill him*. Staring at the shadows that played over the ceiling of his room, wishing the anger would subside so sleep would come, he found himself beginning to fantasize about how he could do it.

How he could actually kill his father.

The boat would be the easiest way. There were all kinds of things he could do to the boat, and nobody would ever know what had really happened. If it sank, no one would even think twice about it. His father took such crummy care of the *Big Ed*, it was a miracle it hadn't sunk already.

Except that deep in his heart, Eric knew he would never do it. He might dream about it, might even figure out exactly how it could be done, but when it came to actually doing it, he knew he wouldn't.

Because in the end his father was still his father.

He tossed restlessly on the bed and punched at the pillow. If only he could understand why his father was always mad at him. It wasn't as if he didn't try to please him—he did. But for some reason nothing he said or did was ever good enough.

His mother always told him it wasn't his fault, that he should just try to ignore it when his father got drunk and started beating up on him. But how could he when no matter how hard he tried, it always seemed to turn out wrong?

The rage and frustration grew. Eric tossed and turned, twisting the bed covers. If he didn't do something, he was going to start ripping the bed apart.

He got up and went to the window. Outside, beyond the suddenly confining walls of the house, the night was calm and peaceful. The first of the tree frogs were beginning to chirp softly to each other, and in the distance he could just make out the sounds of a low surf washing the beach.

Maybe he should go out—just go for a walk—until he was calm enough to sleep. He started to pull on a heavy sweater, then stopped, aware that he could not leave the house.

Often on nights like this when his father was drunk and angry, he came into Eric's room late, his fury still not expended. If Eric wasn't there, it would enrage Ed more, and he'd turn on the only other person in the house.

His mother.

Better to take the beatings himself than have to watch his mother's silent suffering as she nursed her bruises in the morning.

Trapped in his room, he stared out across the driveway to the Winslows' house, where the window to Jennifer's room stood open.

That, too, was sometimes the subject of his fantasies. Some nights he lay awake for hours, wondering what it would be like to live there, where no angry words ever erupted in the night and everyone seemed to love each other.

Suddenly there was a flicker of movement in the window across the driveway, and a face appeared. But it wasn't Jennifer's face.

It was Cassie's.

His eyes met hers, and for a long moment they simply looked at each other. As the moment stretched on, Eric slowly began to feel his anger draining away. It was as if in the look that passed between them, Cassie had somehow understood the feelings he was experiencing, had let him know that she understood.

At last Cassie smiled slightly and nodded, then disappeared from the window.

Long after she was gone, Eric stayed at the window, trying to figure out what had happened. After several minutes had passed, he felt something else.

Somewhere in the night something was watching him.

His gaze shifted then, to scan the little graveyard that lay behind his yard as well as the Winslows'. At first he could see nothing but the shadows of the trees and the tombstones, but then, slowly emerging from the night, a shape took form. It was indistinct at first, but as he concentrated on it, he suddenly knew what it was.

Miranda.

The strange woman who lived alone outside the village. But what was she doing here in the middle of the night, watching his house?

And then, as the dark figure moved slightly and became clearer, he realized that it wasn't his house Miranda was watching.

It was the house next door.

Like himself, Miranda was watching the room in which Cassie Winslow now lived.

Cassie awoke in the blackness of the hours before dawn, her heart thumping, her skin damp with a cold sweat that made her shiver. For a moment she didn't know where she was. Then, as she listened to the unfamiliar sound of surf pounding in the distance, the dream began to fade away, and she remembered where she was.

She was in False Harbor, and this was where she lived now. In the room next to her, her stepsister was asleep, and down the hall her father was in bed with her stepmother.

Then why did she feel so alone?

It was the dream, of course.

It had come to her again in the night. Again she had seen the strange woman who should have been her mother but was not.

Again, as Cassie watched in horror, the car burst into flames, and

Cassie, vaguely aware that she was in a dream, had expected to wake up, as she had each time the nightmare had come to her.

This time, though she wanted to turn and run, she stood where she was, watching the car burn.

This time there had been no laughter shrieking from the woman's lips, no sound of screams, no noise at all. The flames had risen from the car in an eerie silence, and then, just as Cassie was about to turn away, the stranger had suddenly emerged from the car.

Clad in black, the figure had stood perfectly still, untouched by the flames that raged around her. Slowly, she raised one hand. Her lips moved and a single word drifted over the crowded freeway, came directly to Cassie's ears over the faceless mass of people streaming by in their cars.

"Cassandra . . ."

The word hung in the air for a moment. Then the woman turned, and as soundlessly as she had emerged, stepped back into the flames.

Instinctively Cassie had started toward her, wanting to pull her back from the flames, wanting to save her.

The silence of the dream was shattered then by the blaring of a horn and the screaming of tires skidding on pavement.

Cassie looked up just in time to see a truck bearing down on her, the enormous grill of its radiator only inches from her face.

As the truck smashed into her she woke up, her own scream of terror choked in her throat.

Her heartbeat began to slow, and her shivering stopped. Now the room seemed to close in on her, and she found it hard to breathe. Slipping out of bed, she crossed to the window at the far end of the narrow room and lifted it open. As she was about to go back to bed, a movement in the darkness outside caught her eye.

She looked down into the cemetery on the other side of the back fence. At first she saw nothing. Then she sensed the movement again, and a dark figure came into view. Clad in black, perfectly silent, a woman stood in the shadows cast by the headstones.

Time seemed to suspend itself.

And then the figure raised one hand. Once more Cassie heard a single word drift almost inaudibly above the pounding of the surf from the beach a few blocks away.

"Cassandra . . ."

Cassie remained where she was, her eyes closed as she strained to recapture the sound of her name, but now there was only the pulsing drone of the surf. And when she reopened her eyes a few seconds later and looked once more into the graveyard, she saw nothing.

The strange figure that had stepped out of the shadows was gone.

She went back to her bed and pulled the covers close around her. For a long time she lay still, wondering if perhaps she'd only imagined it all.

Perhaps she hadn't even left the bed, and had only dreamed that she'd seen the woman in the graveyard.

But the woman in the graveyard had been the woman in her dream. But she didn't really exist.

Did she?

Four

"Can't I go with you?" Jennifer Winslow begged. The little girl was gazing at Cassie with the wistful expression that never failed to soften her father, though her mother usually ignored it. "Please?" With Cassie, the look seemed to work.

"All I'm going to do is look around the town," Cassie replied. "Don't you think it might be kind of boring?"

Jennifer shook her head vehemently, and pushed her empty breakfast plate aside. "I like to go for walks. And I know all the neatest places too." She turned to her father. "Can I show Cassie the boat? Please? We won't touch anything!"

Keith glanced questioningly at Rosemary, then shrugged. "Why not? In fact, maybe we should all go for a cruise this afternoon. We can run over to Hyannis if the weather holds."

"And if you get all the yard work done," Rosemary added pointedly. "I believe Jennifer was going to help you with that."

Jennifer's eager smile faded. "Do I have to?" she asked plaintively.

"Why don't Jennifer and I go for a walk, and then we can both help Dad?" Cassie suggested. Her eyes fixed on Rosemary, and a small smile played around the corners of her mouth. "We won't be gone very long. I promise."

Rosemary hesitated, feeling vaguely uncomfortable, as if she'd just been manipulated. And yet what Cassie had suggested made perfect sense. Still, she felt a certain reluctance as she nodded her assent. She said nothing until the girls had shrugged into their jackets—Cassie nearly lost in one she had borrowed from her father—

then sat down opposite her husband. "Do you get the feeling we've just been worked around?" she asked, carefully keeping her voice light.

Keith glanced up from his paper. "Worked around? All they wanted to do was go for a walk. I'm just glad that Jen wanted to go with Cassie, and Cassie didn't object to her tagging along."

"Jennifer knew perfectly well she was supposed to help you this morning," Rosemary pointed out.

Keith snapped the newspaper impatiently. "There'll be plenty of other mornings, and there isn't that much work to do in the yard. Let them have a good time. Considering what Cassie's been through—"

"It's not that," Rosemary objected, suddenly wishing she'd never brought the subject up, but determined to have her say. "It's just that I had a feeling both girls were trying to manipulate me."

Now Keith set the paper aside entirely. "Oh, come on, Rosemary. Jennifer's always trying to work her way around both of us. All Cassie did was suggest a compromise."

"Then why did I suddenly feel as though I'd lost control of my own daughter?" Rosemary blurted out. "Why do I feel as if everything has changed?"

Keith was silent for a moment, then reached out to cover Rosemary's hand with his own. "Because it has, sweetheart," he said gently. "I know you weren't planning on having to deal with a teenager for another few years, but sometimes things don't work out the way we want them to. Let's not start getting ourselves worked up over nothing, all right? Cassie's only been here a few hours. Let's just get used to it." He grinned. "Or are you planning on turning into a wicked stepmother on her very first day?"

"I don't know what I'm planning." Rosemary sighed. Slipping her hand out from under Keith's, she got up and started clearing away the breakfast dishes. "It's just a feeling I have, that's all. I would have thought Cassie would want the nicer room, but she didn't. And I've never yet met a teenaged girl who wanted a younger sister tagging around after her. It just doesn't seem . . . well, I guess she just isn't reacting to things the way I would have thought she would."

"But she's reacting fine," Keith replied. "Add don't forget that she's a stranger here. She's just trying to feel her way along and fit in. But give her a week or so, and I'll bet you find you have a perfectly normal teenager on your hands. Then we'll both have something to complain about."

Rosemary forced a smile she didn't feel, and began scraping the leftovers into the disposal. Of course Keith was right. What had just happened was nothing out of the ordinary. She should count herself lucky that Jennifer and Cassie were accepting each other so readily.

Then why did she feel so uneasy about Cassie?

It's just that it's something new, she reminded herself. And if I'm feeling uneasy, how must Cassie be feeling?

Terrified, she silently answered herself. She's lost her mother, and she's been jerked out of the only home she ever knew.

She finished the dishes, then went upstairs to straighten up the master bedroom. Jennifer's door, as usual, stood open to reveal the mess in which the little girl always left her room.

Cassie's door was closed.

Rosemary stared at it for a moment, knowing she should go about her business, remembering how much she herself at Cassie's age had resented it when her own mother violated her privacy. I won't do anything, she told herself. I won't touch anything, and I won't go in. I'll just take a look. Guiltily, she put her hand on the doorknob, twisted it, then pushed the door open a crack. Feeling like a spy in her own home, Rosemary peered into the room.

The bed was perfectly made, and the few clothes Cassie had brought with her were neatly hung in the closet. On the small dresser, her comb and hairbrush were laid out, and behind them stood a silver picture frame.

The frame was empty.

Frowning slightly, Rosemary stepped into the room and approached the dresser. Then, instinctively, her eyes went to the wastebasket that stood on the floor next to the dresser. Scattered on its bottom were the fragments of a picture.

Ignore it, Rosemary told herself, but knew she couldn't. Almost against her will she fished the pieces of the photograph out of the wastebasket and carefully fit them back together.

A chill passed through Rosemary as she realized what she was looking at. Cassie had destroyed her own mother's portrait.

Cassie walked slowly beside Jennifer, studying the village with fascination. Everything about it was completely different from what she'd been used to. Everywhere, enormous maple and elm trees were just beginning to come into leaf. Their branches stretched out, meeting and intermingling overhead to form a canopy over the street. Even now, with the last traces of winter still in the air, she could picture them in summer, when their full foliage would create cool green tunnels of shade.

There were no fences between the yards, and all the houses looked to Cassie as if they were at least a hundred years old. Most of them were two or three stories high, surrounded by neat borders of tulips and daffodils which were already sprouting. Even now, in early spring, the grass was lush and green.

Then they came to the square, and Cassie looked about her curiously. There was a drugstore and a market, but they, too, looked nothing like the enormous stores surrounded with huge parking lots that she was accustomed to. Here instead were small wooden buildings looking out on the sidewalk, with diagonal parking spaces marked in the streets they faced. She could also see a little bookstore, three clothing stores, and some antique shops. Jennifer was dragging her toward one of them.

"This is Mom's store," the little girl said excitedly when they were in front of a window displaying a Queen Anne dining room set. "Isn't it neat?"

To Cassie the shop didn't look much different from the other antique stores on the block, but she dutifully squinted in through the window, scanning the contents of the store as Jennifer continued, "It's open every day during the summer, and sometimes Mom lets me help out if I'm real careful not to break things. That's in the summer, though. This time of year hardly anybody comes out here."

As Jennifer chattered on, Cassie turned away from the shop, and surveyed the rest of the square with disappointment. "Is—is this all there is?" she asked finally, and Jennifer giggled next to her.

"Except for the stores down on Bay Street," she explained. "But only the summer people go to them."

"But where do you shop?" Cassie asked. "Isn't there a mall?"

Jennifer shook her head. "Sometimes we go to Providence, or Boston. We don't even have McDonald's in False Harbor."

Cassie looked curiously at the little girl. "But . . . what do all the kids do here?"

Jennifer shrugged, unconcerned. "There's lots to do. All summer long we can go to the beach, and in the winter you can go ice skating on the pond out by the school," she explained. Then, as a figure turned the corner onto the square a block away, she fell silent, and a moment later tugged at Cassie's hand. "Come on," she said in a whisper. "Let's go somewhere else."

Startled, Cassie looked down to see Jennifer watching the approaching figure, her small face creased in worry. "What's wrong, Jen? Who's that?"

"It's Miranda," Jennifer breathed. "Let's go somewhere else. Please?"

Cassie felt the little girl tug at her arm, but she stayed where she was, transfixed by the approaching figure. As the woman drew closer, Cassie began to feel a chill of déjà vu pass over her.

Silently, the woman drew closer. She was dressed all in black, and her skirt nearly touched the ground. She was pushing a shopping cart, and in the cart were several shopping bags that looked as though they were filled with old clothes. She moved slowly along the sidewalk, pausing every few steps to stare into the shop windows.

Every now and then her lips moved as if she were speaking, but no sound came out.

"Come *on*," Cassie heard Jennifer urging her. The little girl had started to cry, and was now tugging at her arm hard. Cassie finally gave in and let Jen pull her across the street and into the square.

But she turned back to look at the strange woman once again. The woman was moving steadily along the sidewalk now. At first Cassie didn't think she was even aware of being watched. Then, when she was directly across the street, she stopped abruptly and turned to face Cassie.

Her eyes met Cassie's and held them for a moment. Then she nodded and turned away. Moving more slowly than before, the black-clad figure continued down the street, pushing her shopping cart ahead of her.

Cassie, her heart pounding now, felt another chill as the odd figure turned the corner at the end of the block and disappeared.

In that single moment when their eyes had met, Cassie recognized the woman in black.

It was the woman she had seen in her dreams ever since the night her mother died.

The woman who had been driving her mother's car.

The woman who was a stranger, but who—in the dream—had also been her mother.

The woman she had seen in the graveyard last night, who had spoken her name.

But it didn't make any sense—how could she have dreamed about that woman? She'd never seen her before, had she? Again Cassie became aware of Jennifer jerking at her arm. She looked down to find the little girl staring up at her worriedly, her face streaked with tears.

"Did she look at you?" Jennifer asked, her voice sounding surprisingly younger than before.

Cassie hesitated, then nodded.

Jennifer's eyes widened with apparent fear. "Don't let her do that," she said. "Don't ever let her do that again."

Cassie frowned, puzzled. "Don't let her look at me?" she asked. "Why not?"

"Because she's a witch," Jennifer breathed, then glanced around as if she was afraid the woman might still be watching them. "She's a witch, and she can put a hex on you just by looking at you."

Cassie stared at the little girl in disbelief. "A witch?" she repeated at last. "Who told you that?"

"I . . . I don't know," Jennifer said uncertainly. Then, seeing that Cassie didn't believe her, her eyes darkened. "It's true," she stated. "All the kids know she's a witch. She lives out by the beach, and she's real mean, and you have to stay away from her. And don't ever let her look at you."

"But, Jen, there isn't any such thing as a witch. It's just a story, that's all. You're not really afraid of her, are you?"

Jennifer's head bobbed up and down. "Everybody's afraid of her. She acts real crazy, and all she ever does is stay in her house, except when she pushes her grocery cart around."

"She's just a bag lady," Cassie protested, despite the eerie feeling that had passed through her when the woman's eyes had met hers. "They're all over the place. We even had them at home. They used to wander up and down Ventura Boulevard all day, and sleep in the park, if the cops would let them. They're just a little crazy, that's all."

But Jennifer shook her head. "Miranda's different. Wendy Maynard's mom told her that Miranda's mother was just like her, and that all the kids were just as scared of her as we are of Miranda. And her mother lived in the same house she lives in, and nobody ever goes out there."

Cassie stared at the little girl. It was just childish nonsense—it had to be! And yet Miranda was the woman she'd seen in her dreams— she was almost positive of it now. But how was it possible?

Her heart beat faster as she realized that she had to know more about the strange woman in black—had to find out the truth about her.

She was frightened now—very frightened. But at the same time, she was fascinated. "Do you know where she lives?" she asked Jennifer, and the little girl, after hesitating a moment, slowly nodded.

"Will you show me?"

Instantly Jennifer shook her head. "I won't go anywhere near her house," she said. "And if you do, I'm going to tell Mom and Dad!"

"But has she ever actually done anything to anyone?" Cassie pressed. "I mean, anything really bad?"

"I . . . I don't know," Jennifer replied. "For a long time she wasn't even around here. When I was a little girl, she was locked up somewhere. In an insane asylum."

"Well, then, what's there to be afraid of? If she was dangerous, they wouldn't have let her out, would they?"

But Jennifer wasn't to he dissuaded. "I don't know," she said stubbornly. "All I know is that she's crazy, and she's a witch, and I bet she could kill you just by looking at you, if she wanted to. And we better go home or we're going to get in trouble."

"But I thought you were going to show me Dad's boat," Cassie said, carefully controlling the smile playing around the corners of her mouth. When Miranda had disappeared, she'd noticed, it had been in the direction of the marina. Apparently Jennifer had noticed too.

"I'll show it to you next time," Jennifer promised.

The bells of the Congregational Church began to peal as they started back toward Alder Street, and as the two girls drew near it, the doors opened and the crowd of morning worshipers began flowing out onto the sidewalk. Jennifer began waving to her friends, and suddenly Cassie found herself surrounded by a covey of small children, all of whom listened excitedly as Jennifer told them about having seen Miranda a few minutes before.

"And Cassie looked right at her," Jennifer reported, her voice betraying none of the fear of a few minutes earlier, Some of the children stared up at Cassie in obvious awe. Cassie was about to say something when she felt eyes watching her. Looking up, she saw a blond girl about her own age standing just outside the church door, staring at her. Cassie raised her hand in a tentative wave, but the girl turned pointedly away from her and began talking to someone else.

Although she couldn't hear what was being said, Cassie was almost certain the girl was talking about her. Feeling herself flush with embarrassment, she took Jennifer's hand and drew her away from the small crowd of children. Only when they were around the corner, out of sight of the group gathered in front of the church, did she speak.

"Who was that?" she asked. "The girl who was staring at me?"

Jennifer looked up at her curiously. "I didn't see anyone. Why would anyone stare at you?"

Cassie shrugged helplessly. "I don't know," she said. "But it was a blond girl—" Before she could finish, the same eerie sense that someone was staring at her came over her again. She quickly turned around.

At the corner the same girl was talking to two other girls. Both the other girls were staring at Cassie, but seeing her looking at them, they turned away.

"There," Cassie said to Jennifer. "Who is she?"

But it was too late. Jennifer, spying her father pushing the power mower over the front lawn, had dashed ahead. Cassie hesitated, half tempted to go back to the corner and introduce herself to the three girls. But in the end, her face once again burning with the humiliation of being stared at, she hurried across the lawn and into the house.

"Cassie, is something bothering you?" Rosemary asked after dinner that evening. All of them were in the den, Jennifer sprawled on the floor, her chin propped in her hands as she watched the early movie on television. Keith was leafing through a marine catalog, while Rosemary worked on the sweater she was knitting. Cassie was curled on one end of the sofa, a book open in her lap, but Rosemary noticed that she hadn't turned a page for the last fifteen minutes.

Startled, Cassie glanced up at her stepmother, then shook her head and went back to her book, but Jennifer rolled over on the floor and faced her mother.

"We saw Miranda in the square today," she said. "And Cassie looked right at her."

Rosemary glanced at Keith, who had stopped turning the pages of the catalog. When she spoke, she was careful to keep her voice neutral. "You know perfectly well that there's no harm in looking at Miranda. As long as you weren't staring."

Jennifer gasped. "I wouldn't stare at her. I won't even look at her if I can help it. Wendy Maynard says—"

"I know perfectly well what Wendy Maynard says," Rosemary interrupted her, "and you know as well as I do that it's all so much nonsense. Miranda Sikes is perfectly harmless."

"That's not what all the kids say," Jennifer protested. "And when Cassie looked at her, she looked right back at Cassie too!" She shuddered, letting her imagination run away with her. "It was weird. There she was, in that awful black dress, walking along talking to herself. I made Cassie cross the street, and told her not to look, but she did it anyway."

"I wasn't staring," Cassie said, closing the book. "I just looked at her, that's all."

"That's all it takes," Jennifer pronounced. "I bet she put a spell on you!"

"Oh, for heaven's sakes!" Rosemary said, her voice edged with exasperation. She leaned forward and looked directly at her daughter. "Jennifer, we've been through this a hundred times. Miranda Sikes is a bit eccentric, but she's perfectly harmless."

"Then how come they locked her up?" Jennifer demanded. "How come they put her in the insane asylum?"

"But she's not still there, is she?" Rosemary countered. "If she were still sick, they wouldn't have let her out. She's trying to get well, and the way you and your friends treat her doesn't help her at all!"

Jennifer's face crumpled at the severity of her mother's scolding, but Rosemary couldn't stop herself. "How would you feel if every time your friends saw you, they ran away from you? Don't you think you might start talking to yourself and acting funny too?"

Tears welled up in Jennifer's eyes, and she scrambled to her feet. "I didn't do anything," she wailed. "All I did was cross the street because I'm scared of her. I didn't point at her or look at her or anything!" Bursting into tears, she fled from the room. A moment later her door slammed shut.

The living room was silent until Cassie spoke, her voice soft. "She didn't stare at her, Rosemary. She didn't do anything at all. She was just scared, because Miranda looks so strange." She stood up, leaving her book on the couch. "I'll go up and talk to her—"

"No!" Rosemary broke in, her voice strident. "I'll do it. I was the one who snapped at her, not you." She got to her feet and hurried up the stairs, but before she left the room, she saw the look on Keith's face. Though he said nothing, she could feel his reproach at the way she'd spoken. And, of course, he was right—Cassie had only been trying to help.

After apologizing to Jennifer, she would have to apologize to Cassie too.

She found Jennifer in her room, lying facedown on the bed, her body shaking as she cried into her pillow. "Jen?" Rosemary asked quietly. "May I come in?"

When Jennifer said nothing, Rosemary entered the bedroom and closed the door behind her. Sitting on the edge of the bed, she gathered her daughter into her arms. "I'm sorry I snapped at you, honey," she said.

Jennifer wriggled around and looked up at her. "I didn't do any-thing—" she began, but Rosemary put her fingers over the child's lips.

"I know," she soothed. "But I just want you to understand that when you act like you're afraid of Miranda, it hurts her."

"But I *am* afraid of her," Jennifer protested, rubbing her eyes with her fists. "All the kids are."

"But what I'm telling you is that you don't have to be. She's just a strange woman, and a little bit different from everyone else, that's all. But she's not wicked, and she's not a witch. There's no such things as witches, at least not the kind that can cast spells on people, or work magic. So there's nothing to be afraid of. All right?"

Jennifer nodded, but Rosemary could see she wasn't convinced. And why should she be? she thought to herself, remembering when she'd been Jennifer's age and all her friends had been as positive as she that the woman who lived in the old house on the corner was a witch. Of course, by the time she was in her teens she'd discovered that the woman wasn't a witch at all—she was simply an alcoholic, and perhaps agoraphobic as well. Someone to be pitied, not feared. But the old stories had certainly served to keep the neighborhood children away, which was probably what the woman had wanted all along. Maybe, after all, Miranda Sikes didn't mind the tales that were circulated about her among the children of False Harbor.

Rosemary decided she'd said enough. "Do you want to go back downstairs and finish watching the movie?"

Jennifer shook her head. "It wasn't any good. It was for kids."

Her mother chuckled affectionately. "Well, preserve us from that, right?"

Jennifer nodded solemnly, then met her eyes. "Cassie said someone was staring at her in front of the church today."

Rosemary's smile faded. "Staring at her? Who?"

"I don't know. I didn't see anybody. But why would anyone stare at Cassie?"

Rosemary shook her head and stood up. "Maybe no one was," she replied. She bent over and kissed Jennifer on the forehead. "It's eight-thirty, and I want you in bed by nine. All right?"

Jennifer automatically started to argue, but Rosemary held up an admonishing hand. "Not tonight. Nine o'clock, and not a minute later. Okay?"

Jennifer hesitated, then looked up hopefully. "Can Cassie come up and tuck me in?"

Rosemary hesitated as an emotion very much like jealousy stabbed at her. Resolutely, she put the feeling aside. "Of course," she said. "I'll send her up in a little while." Then, kissing her daughter once more, she went back downstairs.

Keith had returned to his catalog, and Cassie was once more involved in her book. Rosemary went back to her knitting, but every few moments she found herself glancing at Cassie. Though Cassie was now turning the pages of the book every couple of minutes, Rosemary was still certain her stepdaughter wasn't reading a word.

Several times Rosemary was tempted to speak to the girl, but each time she changed her mind. Later, she decided. After she's gone upstairs, I'll go up and talk to her.

It was almost ten when Rosemary tapped softly on Cassie's door then let herself into the room, even before Cassie had replied. Cassie lay on the bed, her book propped up on her knees, but once again Rosemary was certain she hadn't been reading.

"I . . . I thought maybe we could talk for a few minutes," Rosemary began uncertainly. She came to perch on the edge of the bed, and reached out as if to take Cassie's hand, but when Cassie made no response to the gesture, she pulled her own hand back. "I just thought you might like to talk," she began again. Then, almost against her will, her eyes flicked to the empty picture frame on the dresser.

"Is that what you want to talk about?" Cassie asked immediately. "My mother's picture?"

Rosemary felt her face burn. "N-no . . ." she stammered. "I mean—"

"I tore it up," Cassie said.

Rosemary took a deep breath, then nodded. "I know," she admitted. "I . . . well, I came in earlier, and I couldn't help but notice the empty frame." She reached out again, and this time she took Cassie's hand in her own. "Why did you tear it up, Cassie?"

Cassie hesitated, then shook her head. "I . . . I don't know. This morning when I woke up, I just couldn't stand to look at it anymore."

Rosemary thought she understood. "I know," she said. "It must be terrible for you. But why didn't you just put the picture away? After a while, when you get used to the idea of . . ." She faltered, then chose her words carefully. "When you get used to her being gone, you'll want a picture of her."

Cassie's eyes darkened. She shook her head. "No, I won't," she replied, her voice low. "I don't care if I never see a picture of her again."

"Cassie—"

"Well, I don't!" Cassie exclaimed. "And why should I? She never cared about me. If she had, she wouldn't have—" She cut her own words off, her eyes brimming with tears.

"Wouldn't have died?" Rosemary asked gently. Cassie said nothing, and Rosemary leaned forward and brushed a strand of hair away from the girl's forehead with her free hand. "Cassie, she didn't die on purpose. It was an accident. She loved you very much—"

"She didn't!" Cassie flared. "Nobody's ever loved me. Daddy sent us away when I was just a baby, and all Mom ever did was go out! She didn't care about me! All she ever did was tell me I wasn't doing anything right, and she always made me feel like I was in her way! And the only reason I'm here is because Daddy had to take me!"

"No," Rosemary protested. "That's not true! You're here because your father loves you, and I love you—"

Cassie sat bolt upright and jerked her hand out of Rosemary's. Her eyes were blazing. "No you don't. You don't even know me! Nobody loves me. Nobody at all! And don't tell me you know what I'm feeling! Nobody knows what I'm feeling. Nobody's *ever* known what I feel!"

Once again Rosemary reached out to hold Cassie's hand, but Cassie pulled away, her voice rising. "Leave me alone!" she yelled. "Why can't you just leave me alone?"

Suddenly the door opened and Keith, his face pale, stood framed against the light from the hall. "Cassie?" he asked. "Cassie, what's wrong?"

Cassie swung around to face her father. "Make her leave me alone," she sobbed. "She's not my mother and she doesn't know me and she doesn't have any right to come in my room. Just make her leave me alone."

Keith stood silently for a moment, then spoke to Rosemary. "What happened?" he asked. "What did you say to her?"

"Nothing," Rosemary said helplessly. "I just came in to talk to her and—" She turned and reached out toward Cassie once again. "Cassie, I'm so sorry. I didn't mean to upset you. I just thought—"

"Leave me alone!" Cassie screamed. "Why can't you just leave me alone?"

"I—" Rosemary began, but this time it was Keith who cut her off.

"I'll take care of her," he said. He came into the room and gestured Rosemary away, then sat on the bed, taking his daughter into his arms. "Just leave us alone a minute, okay, honey?" he asked.

Rosemary hesitated, then nodded quickly and hurried out of the room, closing the door behind her.

"What is it, Punkin?" Keith asked when he was alone with Cassie. "Can you tell me about it?"

Cassie shook her head and turned away. "I'll be all right," she said. "I just . . . . I just need to be left alone. Please? Can't you just leave me alone?"

Keith hesitated, certain there was something he should say, something he should do. But finally, feeling helpless to console her, he shrugged and patted Cassie's leg. "All right, Punkin," he said gently. "Whatever you want. But if you want to talk, just remember that I'm here, all right?" He waited for a response from Cassie. When there was none, he got up and quietly left the room. Maybe that was all she needed, he told himself as he went back downstairs. Maybe all she needed right now was to be left alone.

Rosemary was waiting for him downstairs, her face ashen. "Is she all right?" she asked as he came into the den.

Keith gestured helplessly with his hands. "All right? How can she be all right, given what she's been through? What happened up there?"

As best she could, Rosemary recounted what had happened in

Cassie's room. "She wouldn't even talk to me," she finished. "She says no one loves her and no one understands her. I was only trying to help."

"I know," Keith replied. "But maybe the best way we can help her right now is simply to leave her alone so she can work things out for herself."

Rosemary's eyes widened. "Keith, she's only a child—"

"She's almost sixteen," Keith pointed out. "She's not a child, and we can't treat her like one."

"But if she thinks no one loves her—"

"She doesn't," Keith interrupted. "For heaven's sake, Rosemary, I'm her father. She knows I love her. She's just upset right now, and she has a right to be. But she'll get over it."

But what if she doesn't? Rosemary thought. What if she truly believes no one loves her? What will happen to her? But she said nothing, for Keith's jaw had taken on the stubborn set that told her that for tonight, at least, the discussion was over.

Cassie lay on her bed, trying to sort things out. She hadn't meant to yell at Rosemary, not really. But how could she explain to this woman the real reason why she'd torn up the picture of her mother? How could she tell her that when she'd gotten up that morning and seen the picture, a wave of cold anger had washed over her and she'd ripped the picture to shreds before she'd even thought about it.

It wasn't that her mother had died—that wasn't it at all. It was all the things that happened while she was still alive.

It was her mother's voice, constantly correcting her.

It was her eyes, constantly accusing her.

It was all the other things—the things she would never tell Rosemary about, never even tell her father about. And so she'd torn the picture out of its frame and ripped it to pieces.

She couldn't explain it to Rosemary—she never would have understood.

Then she remembered Miranda, remembered the look that had passed between them in the square that morning.

Miranda would have understood. Miranda would have listened to her and nodded. Hadn't Miranda smiled gently at her this morning? Cassie was certain now that the woman had.

Miranda. Cassandra.

The names almost rhymed, almost sounded like music.

The more she thought about it, the more certain she was that Miranda was, indeed, the woman she'd seen in her dreams, the woman who had stood among the flames and wreckage and beckoned to her.

But who was she, really?

Cassie felt a sensation sweep over her, a feeling of yearning—of need—that was so intense it made her shiver. She pulled the quilt on the bed up tight around her neck. She had to see Miranda again, had to know who the woman in black was. She closed her eyes, seeing again the woman in the street, the woman of the dream. Once again, as she drifted toward sleep, she heard Miranda call her name.

She was almost asleep when the first faint scratching sounds intruded on her. She curled deeper into the mattress and pulled the covers closer.

The sounds came again, an odd rasping, as if something were brushing up against the window screen.

She tried to ignore it. She switched on the radio and focused her mind on the soft music. But the sound persisted. Finally she sat up and looked at the window.

At first she saw nothing. Then, in the darkness outside, a shadow moved.

Cassie's heart began to pound and she felt the first stirrings of panic as the darkness in the room began to close around her. Instinctively she reached out, fumbling to find the lamp that stood on the nightstand.

At the window a pair of feral eyes suddenly glowed yellow in the blackness outside.

Cassie gasped as an icy finger of fear played along her spine. The eyes, unblinking, stared in at her.

Slowly she reached out to turn off the radio, and the click seemed to echo loudly in the room. Then the only sound Cassie could hear was the pounding of her own heart.

At last, from the window, another sound came.

The same rasping scratch as before, but this time the yellow eyes blinked, and there was a soft mewing sound.

A cat. It had been nothing more than a cat scratching at the window.

Suddenly feeling foolish, Cassie got out of bed and went to the window. The cat, clinging to a branch of an elm tree, meowed again as she approached, then reached out with one of its forepaws and scratched once more at the screen.

"Hello, cat," Cassie said softly, half expecting the creature to bolt at the sound of her voice. "Do you want to come inside?"

As if it understood her words, the cat reached out and raked the screen yet again.

Cassie groped in the darkness for the hooks that held the screen in place, released them and pushed the screen outward. As soon as the crack was wide enough, the cat leaped from the branch to the windowsill and slithered through. Dropping to the floor, it rubbed up against Cassie's ankles, its long tail twining around her left leg. Then, as Cassie refastened the screen, it bounded across the room and up onto the bed.

Returning to bed, Cassie switched on the lamp again and in the dim light looked more closely at the cat.

It seemed nothing more than an alley cat, its grayish fur marked across the shoulders and down its back with two stripes which were almost black. It sat on the bed, the tip of its tail twitching nervously, staring back at Cassie with eyes so bright that they looked almost golden in the soft light of the lamp.

"Who are you?" Cassie asked. "Do you live here?"

The cat mewed softly, then crept close and began purring as it licked at Cassie's hand.

As Cassie slid back under the quilt, the cat did, too, and as she reached out to switch the light off, she felt it curling up around her feet.

A few minutes later, with the cat purring quietly at the foot of her bed, Cassie finally fell asleep.

That night she saw Miranda in her dreams once more. Miranda smiled at her, then reached into one of her shopping bags and brought forth a wriggling creature, which she handed silently to Cassie.

"This is for you," Miranda said as she placed the animal in Cassie's arms.

Cassie looked down into the cat's eyes. "What's its name?" she asked.

For a long time Miranda said nothing. Then, still smiling, she reached out and stroked the cat. "He has no name," she said. "He is a gift, and it is for you to decide what to name him, and how to use him."

The image of Miranda merged into the blackness, disappearing. For a moment Cassie was startled back into wakefulness.

At her feet the cat stirred restlessly.

And deep in Cassie's subconscious a long-forgotten memory also stirred.

Five

Monday morning dawned bright and clear, but with a snap to the air that reminded Cassie immediately that she was no longer in southern California. At home on a day like today the temperature would reach eighty degrees before noon, and by lunchtime she and her friends would be talking about cutting the rest of their classes and going to the beach. But here the morning was still far too chilly even to think about the beach. Cassie got out of bed, pulled on the same pair of red jeans she'd been wearing all weekend, and found a clean white shirt to wear under her black sweater. The cat, emerging from under the quilt, sat at the foot of the bed watching her dress, then bounded over to the windowsill. A moment later it looked expectantly back at Cassie.

"You want to go out?" Cassie asked. Crossing to the window, she unhooked the screen and pushed it open. The cat leaped into the tree, jumped from branch to branch, then dropped to the ground and slipped through the fence into the graveyard. Cassie watched it until it disappeared, then frowned thoughtfully. Finally she went to her closet, found a wire coat hanger, and worked it into a brace to hold the window screen open a few inches. Then, leaving the window open, too, she went downstairs.

Her father and Jennifer were already at the table in the corner of the kitchen, eating scrambled eggs and pancakes. From the stove Rosemary smiled at her uncertainly. "Are you all right, Cassie?" she asked. "Maybe . . . maybe you'd rather wait a few days before you start school. I mean . . ."

It took a moment before Cassie understood, but then her eyes met Rosemary's. "You mean because of last night," she said calmly.

Rosemary hesitated for a fraction of a second, then nodded.

"It's okay," Cassie told her. "I'm sorry I yelled at you. I just . . . well, I guess things just sort of got to me, that's all."

Rosemary smiled in relief. She'd lain awake for hours last night, turning the scene with Cassie over in her mind again and again and dreading the coming of morning, certain that when Cassie appeared at the breakfast table—*if* she appeared—she would be sullenly silent. But Cassie seemed to have put the incident behind her. Yet

Rosemary still felt uneasy. "Are you sure you want to go to school today? It just seems like it might be too much for you. I mean, you don't really have anything to wear—"

"What's wrong with what I have on?" Cassie asked, frowning. "At home everyone wears jeans to school."

"That's what they do here too," Keith put in. "I think Rosemary's just wondering how clean they are."

Cassie's face clouded. "They're clean enough. Besides, the only other thing I packed was a dress. And nobody wears dresses to school!"

Jennifer snickered, then fixed her eyes gleefully on her mother. "See? I told you so. How come no one ever believes what I say?"

"Because you're eight years old, and everybody knows that eight-year-olds named Jennifer lie their heads off all the time," Keith replied, then ducked away from Jennifer's pummeling fists. "Anyway, even if she wanted to change her clothes, there isn't time. You want some eggs, Cassie?"

Cassie shook her head. "All I ever have in the morning is orange juice and coffee." As her father and stepmother exchanged a glance, she shrugged. "That's all Mo—" She stopped abruptly, then went on. "That's all Diana and I ever had. Neither of us ever ate breakfast."

At Cassie's use of her mother's name, Keith glanced up, but Rosemary shot him a warning glance. "Suit yourself," she said quickly. "But if you get hungry before lunch, don't blame us." As she poured Cassie a cup of coffee there was a soft rap at the back door. Rosemary put the coffeepot down and went to the service porch. A moment later she came back with Eric Cavanaugh behind her. Keith stared at the boy in surprise.

"Eric! What brings you over so early?"

Eric flushed slightly. "I . . . I just thought maybe Cassie might want to walk to school with me. I mean, since it's her first day and everything."

"I was going to drive her—" Rosemary began, but Cassie was already on her feet.

"It's okay. I'd really rather walk. I mean—" Her voice faltered, and she flushed even redder than Eric had a few seconds earlier.

Rosemary's brows arced knowingly. "You mean you're not sure that being driven to school by your stepmother is quite the thing to do?" she asked.

Cassie's flush deepened. "I—I didn't really mean that—"

"It's okay. Really," Rosemary assured her. "In fact it was kind of stupid of me not to have figured it out for myself. I guess I'm not very good at being a mother to a teenager yet."

"But you're not—" Cassie began, then stopped. For a moment there was an awkward silence, broken finally by Jennifer, who looked up at Eric, her eyes wide.

"Cassie's mother died," she announced. "And that makes my mom her stepmother, and me her half sister. Isn't that neat?"

Keith stiffened. "Jennifer. I'm sure Eric already knows what happened to Cassie's mother, and I'm sure we don't need to talk about it right now! And from now on your mother is going to be Cassie's mother too. Understood? We don't need any of that 'step' or 'half' nonsense around here."

At the anger in her father's voice, Jennifer's expression froze and her eyes filled with tears. Wordlessly, she looked to Cassie for help.

"It's all right," Cassie said. "Jennifer didn't mean anything, did you, Jen? She was just telling Eric the truth."

Keith hesitated, then nodded. But his expression remained serious. "Okay. But I won't have either of you getting the idea that Rosemary cares more for Jennifer than she does for you."

Cassie stared at her father for a moment, and Rosemary braced herself for another outburst. But instead of saying anything, Cassie merely bobbed her head and followed Eric out the back door. Only when Jennifer had disappeared up to her room in search of her school bag did Rosemary speak.

"I wish you hadn't said that," she said quietly. "Cassie didn't believe you, and there's no reason why she should have."

"I just don't want her to feel like she's a second-class member of this family," Keith insisted.

"She's not," Rosemary agreed. She smiled wryly. "I guess I'm going to tell you what you told me. Leave her alone, Keith. Let her fit herself in. You can't force her."

Keith reddened slightly. "I'm not—" he began. But he knew that his wife was right. "I'm sorry," he said. "I guess I just want her to feel that she's at home here."

"She will," Rosemary promised. "In time she will." But even as she spoke the words, she wondered if they were true. Remembering Cassie's words from the previous night, she wondered if Cassie had really ever felt at home anywhere, wondered if that was the reason for the pain that seemed constantly to linger in the depths of her eyes.

"I—I'm sorry about your mom," Eric said when they were a block away from the Winslows' house.

Cassie said nothing for a few seconds, then smiled shyly at Eric. "Would you think I was weird if I said I'm not really sorry she's dead?"

———

321

Eric frowned, and cocked his head. "But she was your mom, wasn't she? I mean, you have to be sorry your mom died, don't you?"

Cassie bit her lip. "I don't know. I guess I am, in a way. But I . . . well, I just don't really miss her. It's kind of strange. I don't think she ever really wanted me in the first place." She hesitated, then went on. "I always had this neat fantasy that I had another mother—that maybe I was adopted."

Eric was silent for a few seconds. When he spoke again, his voice was very low, as if he were afraid someone would overhear what he was saying. "I wish . . . sometimes I wish I'd been adopted too. At least if you're adopted, you know someone wanted you."

Cassie stopped walking and turned to face Eric. "That's a funny thing to say. Don't your folks want you?"

Eric shrugged. "I don't know," he said at last. "I guess maybe my mom does, and my dad says he does, but I don't believe him. He's always putting me down, telling me I'm no good."

"And he beats up on you, too, doesn't he?" Cassie asked.

Eric stared at her for a long moment. "H-how did you know that?" he asked finally.

Cassie was silent for a long time. There was something she'd never told anyone before, something she'd been determined to keep secret forever. But there was something about Eric—she'd felt it that first moment she'd met him—that was different.

Finally she turned to face him, looking deep into his eyes.

He looked back at her steadily, his blue eyes clear and open, ready to accept whatever she might say.

She made up her mind.

"I knew because it happened to me too," she whispered. "Only it wasn't my father. It was my mother. Every time something went wrong, she used to beat me up . . ." Her voice quavered slightly, but she was determined to finish. "It didn't matter if I hadn't done anything. She did it anyway. She just . . . sometimes she'd just start hitting me! I hated her for it. I really hated her!"

During the rest of the walk to school, neither Cassie nor Eric said anything else.

The first thing Cassie noticed was how small Memorial High was.

At home the high school had spread out over several city blocks, with separate gym buildings for the boys and girls, and so many students that on the days when she decided to skip her afternoon classes, the odds were good that she'd never even be missed. Here there were only two buildings: a large frame structure, three stories tall, capped by a steeply pitched roof with a bell tower on top; and next to it a low building that she knew must be the gymnasium, since it faced a playing field that covered the rest of the block on which the school sat.

There couldn't be more than a couple hundred students in the whole school, she thought, and turned to Eric nervously. "How many kids are there in our grade?"

"Fifty-three," Eric replied. "Fifty-four, including you."

Cassie frowned. "And everyone knows everyone else don't they?" she asked, her voice reflecting her sudden nervousness.

"Sure they do. We all grew up together."

"What . . . what if they don't like me?"

Eric looked at Cassie curiously. "Why wouldn't they like you? There's nothing wrong with you, is there?"

Cassie hesitated, then shook her head. "But I'm new. And at home whenever someone new came in, everyone . . . well, everyone just sort of ignored them at first. You know what I mean?"

Eric shrugged. "I guess. But nobody's going to ignore you. I know everyone, and I'll introduce you around. Who's your homeroom teacher?"

"I don't know . . . I guess I'll have to go to the principal's office to find out."

"Right. It's on the main floor, on the left. There's only two classes in our grade, so if you're not in my homeroom, I'll see you at lunch. Okay?"

Cassie nodded, and started up the steps toward the front doors of the school, threading her way through the groups of students chattering among themselves before their first classes began. As she passed among them, they all fell silent around her, as if her very presence had silenced them. Then she stopped, her back tingling once again with the eerie sensation of eyes watching her. The memory of the crowd in front of the church the day before was still fresh in her mind, and when Cassie turned, she wasn't surprised to see the same blond girl staring once again, her angry eyes fixed coldly on her. She was a little smaller than Cassie. When Cassie met her gaze, the other girl quickly looked away, then moved over to Eric Cavanaugh, and slipped her arm through his.

Suddenly Cassie thought she understood. The other girl must be Eric's girlfriend, and she must have thought Cassie was trying to cut in on her. But before she could go over and say anything, the first bell rang and the students on the steps began pushing through the front doors. Eric, with the blond girl still clinging to his arm, disappeared into the building.

When Cassie entered the principal's office a few minutes later, a friendly looking woman of about forty peered up at her over the tops of horned-rimmed half glasses and smiled cheerfully.

"Good morning. I'm Patsy Malone, and you must be Cassandra Winslow."

Cassie's head bobbed. "H-how did you know?"

"You're the only new face I've seen in seven months," the woman replied. "Besides, your stepmother called us last week. You can go right on in—Mrs. Ambler is waiting for you."

For the first time, Cassie noticed the door to an adjoining office; CHARLOTTE AMBLER was neatly stenciled onto the opaque glass set into its upper half. She hesitated, then twisted the knob without knocking. As she slipped inside, though, she could feel Patsy Malone still watching her.

Charlotte Ambler looked up from the papers on her desk, then removed her reading glasses and let them drop. They were fastened to her neck with a heavy gold chain, which was the only jewelry she ever wore. The glasses came to rest on her ample bosom; she had grown so used to having them there that she rarely noticed them anymore, sometimes searching her desk for several minutes before she remembered where to find them. Once, to her chagrin, her secretary had caught her unconsciously putting the glasses on in an effort to make the search for them easier. Though the secretary had said nothing, Mrs. Ambler noted that she was unable to keep from grinning. The next day she'd brought an extra pair of glasses to her office. "So I'll have something to find when I start hunting," she'd explained. As Charlotte hoped, by the end of the day the story had spread through the school, and her carefully nurtured reputation for being just a little vague had grown a little larger.

Charlotte Ambler, though, was anything but vague, and as she rose from her desk to greet her newest student, she used the two seconds to size up the girl who stood nervously next to the door.

"Troubled" was the first word that came to Mrs. Ambler's mind, but she quickly dismissed it. Given Cassie Winslow's circumstances, it would be remarkable if she looked anything but troubled. "Is it Cass, or Cassie?" she asked.

"Cassie."

"Good," Charlotte replied, smiling warmly. "Cassandra's a lovely name, but a bit formal. And Cass is too short. Why don't you sit down?"

Cassie moved across the small office and lowered herself into the wooden captain's chair next to Charlotte Ambler's desk. "Well, what do you think of things so far? False Harbor isn't much like California, is it? And I guarantee you that our school is different from the one you went to at home."

Cassie's eyes widened in surprise. "How do you know about Harrison?"

"I don't, really," Mrs. Ambler admitted. "But according to your records, you were ranked fifty-fifth in a class of over four hundred. That makes your class alone twice as large as our entire school. It's got to be different." As she spoke, she opened a thick folder on her desk and put her glasses back on.

"What's that?" Cassie blurted out, and Mrs. Ambler glanced up once more.

"Your records. Harrison's computer transferred them to ours on Friday afternoon. Amazing, isn't it? It used to be that you couldn't count on records arriving at all. Now they send you more than you could ever want. Sometimes I wonder if computers are really a blessing at all."

As Charlotte Ambler went back to the file on her desk, Cassie sat perfectly still. She stiffened as the principal's brows rose slightly at something she'd read in the file, but the woman said nothing, merely flipped through a few more pages then leaned back and smiled at her. "Well, it doesn't look as though you and I are going to be spending too much time together," she said. "According to these, you managed to get through almost three years at Harrison with no problems at all. Mind telling me what your secret was?"

Cassie felt her face flushing. "I—I guess I just never had time to get in trouble," she said. "I just went to school, and then went home and studied."

Charlotte Ambler cocked her head. "Then you were something special," she remarked. "The way I hear it, most of the big schools are having all kinds of problems now. It seems some of the students only come to school about half the time," she added pointedly.

Cassie said nothing, but her heart sank. Apparently someone *had* noticed all those afternoons she'd cut.

Though she'd been careful to keep her tone light, the principal had watched Cassie's face carefully as she spoke, and she was certain her words had struck home.

Cassie said nothing. After a few seconds of silence that seemed to her to go on forever, Mrs. Ambler finally spoke again.

"I'm putting you into Mrs. Leeds's class for your homeroom, and as it happens, we were able to work in most of the same classes you were taking at Harrison, except for Advanced Art. I'm afraid we're just not big enough to offer anything past Art Two, and that's only for seniors. We can either give you a drama class or a study hall."

"Study hall," Cassie said immediately. This time there was no mistaking Mrs. Ambler's frown.

"Drama might be a better way to get acquainted with people," she suggested, but Cassie only shook her head. Charlotte Ambler hesitated, then decided not to push the issue. She made a note on an enrollment card, then handed it to Cassie. "Just give this to Mrs. Malone and go on along to room 207, upstairs at the other end of the hall. Mrs. Leeds already knows you're coming." She stood and started around her desk to walk Cassie to the door, but Cassie was already on her feet. Clutching the registration cards in her hand, she hurried out of the office.

Charlotte Ambler waited a few seconds, then sat down at her desk again and reopened Cassie Winslow's file. Slowly, wanting to miss nothing, she read it through for the third time.

All she could see were the records of a very bright girl whose only problem was that she had never truly applied herself to her school-work.

"Highly imaginative," "very creative mind," and "potential beyond her performance" were the phrases her teachers had most often used to evaluate Cassie. Indeed, if it hadn't been for her lackadaisical attendance record, Charlotte assumed that Cassie would have been at the very top of her class.

Then why was it that the moment Cassie had come into her office, all the instincts Charlotte had developed over the years immediately set her antenna to quivering?

"Troubled" was the word that had come instantly to the principal's mind. And now, as she sat alone in her office, reflecting on Cassie Winslow's arrival in False Harbor, the idea still hung in the atmosphere. For some reason Charlotte Ambler couldn't quite put her finger on, she was certain that Cassie Winslow was going to cause trouble.

Cassie paused in front of room 207, then pulled the door open and stepped inside.

The room was small, and looked old-fashioned. Instead of the green chalkboards she was used to at Harrison, the walls at Memorial High were covered with old-fashioned slate blackboards. Dark-stained wainscotting rose four feet up from the floor; above, the walls were painted a stark white. The wood-framed windows, double hung from the wainscotting to the ceiling and running the full length of the eastern wall, were covered with ancient venetian blinds, and the old student desks were solid wood, their surfaces deeply carved by the knives and ballpoint pens of generations of students.

Mrs. Leeds sat at a large wooden desk at the front of the room, severe-looking in a dark blue suit and high heels. At home Cassie's teachers had dressed almost as casually as the students themselves, but there was nothing casual about Mrs. Leeds.

As the door closed behind her, the rustling of papers in the room suddenly stopped as one by one the students swung around to gaze curiously at the new student. Cassie did her best to smile under the scrutiny of her classmates, but almost immediately she spotted the girl who had been staring at her that morning. She was sure that the blonde, whoever she was, had already been talking about her to the rest of the kids.

After what seemed an eternity to Cassie, Mrs. Leeds finally spoke. "There's a seat next to Eric Cavanaugh. Why don't you sit there?" Cassie saw Eric nodding to her, but beyond him she could also see the blond girl, her eyes flashing wrathfully. Cassie quickly scanned the room for another vacant seat, but there were none, so she reluctantly moved up the aisle and slid into the seat. As she did, she saw the blonde lean over and whisper something to Eric.

"I'm afraid you've arrived in the middle of a test," Mrs. Leeds went on. "Of course, I won't expect you to take it—"

"What's it on?" Cassie asked without really thinking.

The teacher hesitated a moment. "History," she said finally. "The Vietnam war."

Once again Cassie found herself speaking without intending to. "I don't mind taking the test," she said, and in the silence that followed, she felt the class scrutinizing her again.

"All right," Mrs. Leeds agreed. "But if you don't do well, I won't count it." Her eyes left Cassie and swept the rest of the class. "That doesn't go for the rest of you, so you'd better get back to work." She approached Cassie's desk and handed her four sheets of paper stapled together in the upper-left-hand corner. "Don't worry about finishing. There's only twenty minutes left. Do you have your registration card?"

Cassie nodded silently, handed the card to the teacher, then focused her attention on the exam. It was a combination of true and false and multiple choice questions, and covered the same material Cassie had studied in California only a month earlier. Fishing in her bag for a pen, she started working.

There were still five minutes left in the hour when Cassie finished. She looked around, surprised to see that most of the class was still concentrating on the quiz. Finally she looked at Mrs. Leeds, who smiled sympathetically and beckoned her to the front of the room.

"I guess I shouldn't have let you take it after all," the teacher said quietly when Cassie was next to her.

"It's all right," Cassie replied. "I'm finished."

Frowning, Sarah Leeds took the quiz from Cassie and quickly compared it to the answer key on her desk. Her brows rose appreciatively as she marked an A in the corner of the paper. "Three minutes," she announced to the class, and with a wink at Cassie, added, "and I might as well tell you that you have some new competition. Cassie Winslow has finished the test in twenty minutes, with only one wrong answer."

The silence that fell over the class this time was resentful rather than curious, and Cassie quickly realized her mistake. She shouldn't have finished the test—shouldn't have taken it at all. But now it was too late. Though she couldn't bring herself to look at the rest of the kids, she could feel them all staring at her with the same hostility that earlier had come only from the girl next to Eric.

She could practically hear what they were thinking: *Her first day, and she's already trying to look better than us.*

Then—mercifully—the bell rang, and suddenly the class was on its feet, milling around Cassie as the students dropped their test papers onto Mrs. Leeds's desk before churning out into the hall on their way to their next classes. Only when the room was empty did Cassie start toward the door.

"Do you know where you're going?" she heard Mrs. Leeds ask, and stopped short, realizing that she didn't. She turned back to see the teacher writing quickly on a piece of paper.

"Here's your schedule, with all the room numbers and names of your teachers." Mrs. Leeds handed her a scribbled list. "And don't worry about the test. I shouldn't have said anything, but I spoke before I thought. I'm sorry."

"It's all right," Cassie replied after a slight pause. "I just . . . well, tests have always been easy for me. I just remember things."

"Like Eric Cavanaugh," Mrs. Leeds observed. "I'll bet he finished in twenty minutes, too, and I suspect he got a perfect score. But I'll bet I'm the only one who knows how quick he is. He always spends the whole hour going over and over his answers, pretending he's having trouble." She winked at Cassie. "You might try that trick."

Cassie nodded, then hurried out of the room as the warning bell for the next period sounded in the crowded halls. She glanced at the paper in her hand and began working her way toward the staircase at the end of the hall. Suddenly she was bumped from behind and felt herself losing her balance. She reached out, grabbed the banister of the stairwell, and turned to face the person who had bumped into her.

"Can't you watch where you're going?" a voice demanded.

"I'm sorry," Cassie blurted, then recognized the blonde with the angry eyes. Once again the girl was glaring at her.

"You should be sorry," the girl replied. "And you shouldn't be trying to show us all up just because you're from California either!"

"I didn't mean to do anything—" Cassie began, but the girl cut her off.

"And if you think Eric's going to look out for you just because he lives next door to you, you're wrong! He doesn't even like you. Now, would you mind getting out of my way?"

The girl pushed past Cassie, running down the stairs to catch up with two other girls, who were waiting for her on the landing below. As Cassie started down the flight, the other girls disappeared from her view and she heard a burst of laughter.

They were talking about her. It was only her first day, but they were already talking about her.

She told herself it didn't matter, tried to convince herself that she wouldn't even see the girls again.

Except that when she found her second-period classroom, there was only one seat left, and in the next seat the blond girl sat whispering with someone on the other side of the aisle.

"I didn't mean to show anyone up," Cassie said as she slid into the seat. "My name's Cassie. Cassie Winslow."

The girl glared at her. "I know your name," she replied, her voice mocking. "We all do. We just don't care!" Then, twisting in her seat so her back was to Cassie, she went on with her conversation.

For the next hour Cassie sat stiffly at her desk, staring straight ahead.

She would give it until lunchtime. But if things weren't any better by then—if something good didn't happen—she wouldn't be back in her classes when lunch was over.

Rosemary glanced at the clock above the kitchen sink. She still had half an hour before the shop had to be open. Just enough time to change the beds and get the laundry started. She hurried up the stairs, then paused outside the closed door to Cassie's room.

Memories of the previous night came flooding back to her.

Maybe she should ignore Cassie's room, and leave a note for Cassie to change her bed when she got home from school.

But that was ridiculous. All she was going to do was make the bed. Surely Cassie couldn't resent anything as simple as that, could she?

Making up her mind, she turned the knob and opened the door. The first thing she noticed was the chill in the room, and her eyes immediately found the open window. She walked the length of the room quickly and was about to close the window when she noticed the bent coat hanger holding the screen open. She paused, frowning at the mangled piece of wire, trying to imagine what it might be for.

Finally, deciding that perhaps the screen had been rattling during the night and that Cassie had propped it open rather than wiring it shut, she took the coat hanger out, rehooked the screen, and shut the window.

Then Rosemary went to the bed and began to pull the quilt back, intending to straighten the bottom sheet.

An angry screech filled the room as the quilt came away from the bed, and a grayish form rose off the mattress and hurled itself at her. Instinctively she raised her right arm to shield her face, and a split second later felt the burning heat of claws sinking into the flesh of her wrist.

Barely able to stifle a scream of pain and shock, she jerked her arm away from the cat's claws and leaped backward. The cat dropped to the floor then shot across the room toward the window, leaping up to the sill as if it expected to be able to slip outside. Thwarted, it turned back, arching its back and hissing.

Rosemary gasped, suddenly understanding why the screen had been propped open.

But where had the cat come from? She'd never seen it before, couldn't remember even seeing one that looked like it.

She started toward it, stopping when the creature's fur stood up and its hissing turned into a dangerous snarl. Rosemary glanced around the room but saw no weapon, nothing with which to fend the cat off. She picked up a pillow and threw it at the angry animal. The cat ducked away from the pillow, leaped from the windowsill, and disappeared under the bed. Instantly Rosemary ran to the window, jerked it open, and fumbled with the hooks. As soon as they were free and the screen was once more loose, she felt the cat brush past her. As she watched in astonishment, it leaped into the tree, dropped to the ground, then disappeared into the cemetery next to the church.

Her heart beating rapidly, Rosemary waited by the window for a moment, trying to catch another glimpse of the cat, but then the burning pain in her arm penetrated her consciousness. Looking down, she saw four deep scratches in her wrist, a line of blood oozing from each of them. Slamming the window shut, she abandoned Cassie's bedroom and hurried into the bathroom to wash her injured wrist.

A cat, she thought. Where on earth had it come from, and what was it doing in Cassie's room? But, of course, she already knew—it had come around begging, and Cassie had let it in. Well, there would be no more of that—if there was one thing Rosemary Winslow had never been able to stand, it was cats.

———

Six

"There she is!" Lisa Chambers whispered loudly, leaning forward across the cafeteria table to make sure Teri Bennett and Allayne Garvey could hear her. "Isn't it spooky? I mean, just look at her!" She straightened up, brushing a stray lock of her blond hair back in place, then fell silent as her two best friends shifted their attention to the cafeteria door, where Cassie Winslow stood scanning the room as if she were looking for someone. After a few seconds she moved to the end of the food line and picked up a tray.

"I don't think she looks so weird," Allayne commented, then wished she hadn't said it when Lisa's eyes raked her scornfully.

"Are you nuts?" Lisa demanded, her voice no longer a whisper. "Look at the way she's dressed. She looks like some kind of leftover hippie or something!"

"What's wrong with that?" Teri protested. "And she's dressed just like everyone else, except her jeans are red. If I could find a pair that color, I'd buy them too."

Allayne, feeling more secure now that she knew Teri hadn't seen anything particularly strange about Cassie either, nodded. "And her hair's gorgeous," she added. "It's almost the same color as Eric's, except his is curly and hers is straight." At the mention of Eric's name she saw Lisa's color deepen, and suddenly understood what Lisa really had against Cassie. She grinned mischievously, and her voice took on a needling quality. "In fact I'll bet she and Eric would look neat together, wouldn't they, Teri?"

"They would not," Lisa snapped, instantly rising to Allayne's bait. "Besides, Eric can't stand her."

"Then why did he walk her to school this morning?" Teri asked with a deliberately innocent tone. She was enjoying Lisa's obvious discomfort. Usually it was everyone else who felt uncomfortable while Lisa said whatever was on her mind. As Lisa struggled to find an answer to her question, Teri spoke again, keeping her voice blandly innocent. "Here come Eric and Jeff Maynard. Let's ask Eric."

"Don't you dare," Lisa gasped, her face suddenly paling. "If you ask him, Teri, I swear I'll never speak to you again!" As Eric dropped into the seat next to her, and Jeff into the one next to that, she fell silent.

"What's going on?" Eric asked as the two girls across the table stifled a giggle.

"Nothing," Allayne finally said. "We were just talking about Cassie. Lisa doesn't like her very much." Lisa's eyes flashed her a warning, but Allayne decided to ignore it. "What's she like?"

Eric shrugged. "I don't know. I only talked to her on the way to school this morning."

"Well, what did you talk about?" Teri pressed.

Before Eric could answer, Cassie appeared next to the empty seat beside Teri Bennett.

"Is anybody sitting here?" she asked, her voice betraying nervousness.

Eric was about to shake his head when he felt Lisa's elbow nudge him sharply.

"It's saved," Lisa said. "Teri's boyfriend always sits there, and he'll be here any minute. Sorry."

Cassie hesitated, then moved off toward a small empty table next to the far wall. Teri stared at Lisa.

"My *boy*friend?" she echoed. "Would you mind telling me who that's supposed to be?"

"Well, why should she sit with us?" Lisa protested. "Can't she make her own friends? Just because she lives next door to Eric doesn't make her part of our group. She's just a nobody, and I don't think any of us should have anything to do with her."

A silence fell over the table as the other four teenagers looked at each other, each of them waiting for someone else to speak first. Finally Eric Cavanaugh broke the silence.

"How's she supposed to make friends if nobody will even talk to her?" he asked. Without another word he rewrapped his sandwich and put it back in the bag. Then, with his lunch in one hand and an open carton of milk in the other, he got up and walked over to the table where Cassie sat alone. As his friends watched in silence, he said something to Cassie. She nodded, and then he sat down.

Finally Allayne Garvey leaned across the table. "I thought you said he couldn't stand her."

Lisa's eyes narrowed and her lips tightened with anger, but she said nothing.

When the bell rang twenty minutes later, Eric began stuffing the remains of his lunch into the paper bag. Across from him Cassie didn't seem to have heard the bell at all. "What's your next class?" he asked.

She started slightly, then shook her head. "I—I don't know. Math, I think."

"Mr. Simms," Eric grunted. "He's a real creep. You want me to walk you up there?"

But instead of answering his question, Cassie asked one of her own. "What's Lisa's next class?"

Eric frowned. "Math. So what?"

Cassie took a deep breath then stood up, hooking her right arm through the straps of her bag so she'd have both hands free to pick up her tray. "So, I guess I won't go to class," she said.

"Not go?" Eric asked blankly. What was she talking about? You didn't just decide not to go to classes. "What do you mean?"

"Just that," Cassie replied, her voice calm. "I decided during second period that if things didn't get any better by lunchtime, I was going to leave."

"But you can't leave," Eric protested, scrambling to his feet to follow Cassie as she headed toward the bins of dirty dishes at one end of the long food counter. "Besides, what's been so bad?"

Cassie added her tray to the stack on the counter, then quickly sorted her dishes into the various bins. When she was done, Eric shoved his empty lunch bag into a trash barrel and fell in beside her as they started toward the cafeteria doors. "I just feel like everybody hates me," Cassie replied. "They're all talking about me, and Lisa's the worst. So if she's in the math class, I'm just not going to go."

"But what'll you do?" Eric asked.

Cassie shrugged. "I don't know. Wander around, I guess. Maybe I'll go to the beach." She glanced at Eric. "Want to come with me? You could show me the beach."

Eric stared at her. He'd thought about cutting school, even talked about it with Jeff Maynard a few times. But he'd never actually done it, because he'd known what would happen if his father ever found out. And yet now, as Cassie challenged him with her eyes, he felt himself wavering. When she spoke again, it was as if she'd read his mind.

"If your father catches you, I'll tell him it was my fault. We'll say I was feeling really sick and you were walking me home, but then I felt better and wanted to go to the beach. And you couldn't just leave me by myself. I mean, what if I got sick again?"

Eric knew his father wouldn't buy a story like that, even if it were true. But as he opened his mouth to tell Cassie it wouldn't work, he found himself agreeing to it.

"Okay," be said. "But if we get caught, I'm gonna be in big trouble."

"We won't get caught," Cassie replied. "Come on."

*   *   *

They walked down Maple Street to Cape Drive, crossed to the beach side, then started walking west, toward the mouth of the harbor. Cassie carried her tote bag in one hand and said little, concentrating instead on the weathered shingled houses that bordered the beach. They were spaced wide apart, and between them were expanses of grassy sand, broken here and there by low picket fences whose paint had long since been worn away by the storms of winter. The houses, their shutters closed, had a lonely look to them. Finally, as they passed the fifth one, Cassie turned to Eric.

"Doesn't anyone live in them?"

"Not this time of year. They won't be opened up until school lets out."

"You mean they're empty all the time except during summer?"

Eric shrugged. "They're just summer houses. Who wants to go to the beach during the winter?"

"I do," Cassie replied. "At home that was one of my favorite times to go to the beach. There'd hardly be anybody there except me, and sometimes I'd go out on the bus all by myself and just walk for miles. The summer's okay at the beach, but it gets too crowded. I mean, at the good beaches there's so many people in the summer, you can hardly move. It gets really gross."

Eric grinned. "It's never that crowded here, even when all the summer people are around. Unless you go out to Provincetown. Out there it gets really jammed."

They came to a path and turned right, then began climbing a series of low grass-covered dunes that separated the road from the beach itself. As they crested the last of the dunes, the soft roar of the surf grew louder. Suddenly the Atlantic lay spread before them. Cassie stopped abruptly, staring at the ocean.

"It looks different," she said, cocking her head thoughtfully. Then she understood. "It's the sun. The sun's coming from a different direction." She dropped down onto the sand, stretched out on her back and stared straight up into the sky. Gulls wheeled overhead, and she could hear them screeching to each other as they dove down every few seconds to snatch something out of the water or off the sandy expanse of beach. Finally she rolled over, jumped to her feet, and ran down the beach toward the water line. A flock of sandpipers skittered away from her, then spread their wings and fluttered into the air. Flying straight out to sea, they suddenly banked around to the right, then glided in to land again, fifty yards farther along. Cassie watched them, entranced, then kicked off her shoes, stuffed them into her tote bag, rolled her jeans up to her knees, and waded into the water. Immediately a shriek burst from her throat.

"It's cold!" she shouted to Eric, who had followed her down onto the hard-packed sand of the beach, but not into the water.

"What did you expect?" Eric shouted back. "It's only April!"

"At home everybody's swimming already," Cassie gasped, splashing out of the water. She dashed back up the beach to her tote bag and put her shoes back on. Then something at the far end of the beach caught her eye. "What's that?" she asked.

Eric squinted into the afternoon sun. "It's the marker at Cranberry Point. It shows where the channel starts, so the boats don't wind up in the marsh."

Cassie gazed thoughtfully at the channel marker for a few moments, then turned to face Eric. "Is that where Miranda Sikes lives?" she asked abruptly. "Down that way?"

Eric blinked in surprise. "Why do you want to know that?" he asked.

Cassie regarded Eric carefully. Should she tell him about the dreams she'd had, and that she was almost sure Miranda was the woman she'd seen in the dream? But it would sound crazy to him, wouldn't it? Besides, she didn't even know if it was true or not. Except that she had this feeling, deep inside . . .

"I don't know," she said finally. "I just saw her yesterday, and she . . . well, she looked kind of interesting."

"She's just a bag lady," Eric replied, too quickly. "She's nuts."

Cassie felt a surge of anger. "How do you know?" she demanded. "Have you ever talked to her?"

Eric said nothing.

"Then you shouldn't talk about her," Cassie plunged on. "You don't know what she's like any more than anyone knows what I'm like!" The memory of Lisa's cutting words in the classroom came back to her. "Doesn't anybody around here even want to get to know me? Or do you just not count unless you grew up here?"

"Hey, that's not fair—" Eric began. But then he remembered Lisa gossiping in the cafeteria, and realized that what Cassie had said wasn't very far from the truth. "I want to get to know you," he said quietly.

But Cassie didn't seem to hear him as she kicked moodily at the sand. "Maybe I never should have come here," she said almost to herself.

Eric frowned. "But you had to, didn't you? What were you going to do, stay in California all by yourself?"

Once more Cassie's eyes met his. "Lots of kids my age live on their own. I could do it too."

"Sure," Eric agreed. "And you could wind up hooking in the

Combat Zone in Boston, and doing drugs too. Or you could even end up like Miranda."

Cassie's eyes glistened with tears. "Well, maybe it would be better than this," she said. "And what's so awful about Miranda, anyway?"

Eric opened his mouth to say something, then abruptly closed it again and looked out to sea. Cassie said nothing, waiting for Eric to make up his mind. Finally, still not looking at her, he shrugged his shoulders. "I don't know," he said. Then he grinned crookedly, and managed to meet her eyes. "I guess you're right. Nobody knows anything about her, really. She never talks to anybody, and nobody even looks at her anymore."

"Well, where does she live?" Cassie asked. "Does she work?"

Again Eric looked nervous. He shook his head. "She must be on welfare or something. She lives down there," he went on, nodding toward the point. "Down in the marsh. I—I can show you where it is, I guess."

"Then let's go see," Cassie said immediately. She got to her feet again and slung the bag over her shoulder. Without waiting for Eric to reply, she started toward the tall red channel marker barely visible in the distance. When Eric caught up with her a few moments later, her mood seemed to have changed. She glanced over at him, grinning happily. "Now, isn't this better than school?" she asked. "Out here I can almost forget about everything and pretend everything's perfect!"

"It's fun," Eric admitted. "But what if we get caught?"

"If you always worry about what will happen, how can you do anything?" Cassie asked. "Besides, what's so great about school?"

"If you want to go to college, it helps if you go to high school," Eric pointed out.

"I go," Cassie replied. "Anyway, I go enough so I don't get behind. Besides, all you're supposed to do is learn the stuff they teach, so if I learn fast, why should I waste my time sitting in classes all day? Especially with people like Lisa."

Eric kicked self-consciously at the sand. "Lisa's okay."

Cassie looked at Eric out of the corner of her eye. "Is she your girlfriend?"

Eric felt himself flushing. "I—I don't know. I guess she is. Anyway, she thinks she is, and my dad likes her."

Cassie stopped short. "Your *dad* likes her? What's that got to do with anything?"

Eric shrugged uncomfortably. "It—well, it just makes things easier if I go out with people my dad likes." He could feel Cassie's eyes on him then, and he tried not to look at her. At last he couldn't help himself, and his eyes met hers. "That's kind of stupid, isn't it?" he asked.

Cassie said nothing, but nodded her head.

They continued walking along a few feet apart, and though neither of them said anything for a long time, there was nothing uncomfortable about the silence. When Cassie finally spoke again, Eric knew immediately what she was talking about.

"I bet she's rich, isn't she?"

"Uh-huh. Mr. Chambers married Kevin Smythe's aunt, and the Smythes used to own most of False Harbor."

"I bet your dad wishes *he'd* married Kevin Smythe's aunt."

Almost in spite of himself Eric snickered. "She wouldn't have married him. She can't stand my dad."

Cassie's eyes rolled. "So your dad likes Lisa because of who her parents are, and her parents don't like your dad but let Lisa go out with you?"

Eric nodded.

"What a bunch of crap. Doesn't it make you want to puke sometimes?"

Eric frowned. "I'm not sure what you're talking about," he said, even though he thought he knew exactly what she meant.

"Just parents," Cassie said. She tipped her face up into the breeze, enjoying the feel of the crisp air on her face. "They always do things for dumb reasons. Like my mom hated my dad and was always telling me how rotten he was." Her voice took on a hard edge, but her eyes were glistening with tears. "She only kept me around so he couldn't have me. Then she went out and got killed on the freeway, and how was that supposed to make me feel? I mean, Mom wanted me to hate Dad as much as she did, and now I have to live with him 'cause she's dead. . . ." She hesitated, fighting the conflicting emotions that roiled inside her. "Well, it's no big deal that she died—just because she was my mom didn't give her the right to beat me up! And you know what? She was wrong about my dad. He's not a bad guy. But what does he need me for? He's got a whole other family." She sniffled, then determinedly wiped her tears away and managed to smile weakly at Eric. "It makes you wonder why they bother to have kids in the first place."

Eric looked at the sand at his feet, embarrassed by Cassie's outburst. And yet almost everything she'd said were things he himself had thought about. "But what can you do about it?" he asked softly. "You can't choose who your parents are."

Cassie stopped walking and turned to face him. "Maybe I can," she said quietly. "I mean, Dad and Rosemary don't really want me. I'm just in their way. So . . ." She hesitated, wanting to tell Eric about the fantasy but not wanting him to laugh at her. If he laughed at her—But she had to take the risk. "Maybe . . . maybe I can find a mother who really wants me." She hesitated, but Eric didn't laugh. Instead he only looked at her intently.

She decided to tell Eric a little bit of what was in her mind. Not much. Just enough to see what his reaction would be. "I had a dream," she said, a nervous laugh rippling around her words. "I—I dreamed that Miranda Sikes was really my mother. Isn't that weird?"

Eric looked away from her, and when he replied, his voice was low. "I don't know," he said. "Lots of funny things happen in dreams. And—and sometimes they mean something, don't they?"

Feeling suddenly encouraged by Eric's response, Cassie bobbed her head eagerly. "In the dream, she called my name, and she was reaching out to me. I think she wanted me to come to her."

Eric looked at her strangely. "What makes you say that?" he asked.

A stab of fear ran through Cassie. Did he think she was crazy? "I didn't say she did," she added quickly. "It was just a dream."

Eric said nothing for a while. When he finally spoke, his voice was barely audible. "But if she were calling you," he said, "that would mean you'd have to go out there."

Cassie frowned. "Why shouldn't I?"

Eric hesitated for a long time. "No reason," he said at last. "I'll show you where it is. And maybe I'll even show you what happens if you get too close."

Rosemary Winslow beard the tinkling of the bell above the shop door and glanced up from the chair she was working on to see Charlotte Ambler pausing just inside, examining a copy of a Tiffany lamp. It couldn't be after three already, could it? Frowning, Rosemary glanced at her watch.

It wasn't. In fact it was barely two o'clock. Then what was the high school principal doing here? Suddenly alarmed, she rose to her feet and threaded her way through the maze of furniture that cluttered the small store.

"Charlotte?" she asked. "Has something happened to Cassie?"

Charlotte Ambler shook her head. "I doubt it, but I don't know, really," she said. "In fact I was hoping you might know. Is she here, by any chance?"

"Here?" Rosemary repeated. "But . . . well, school isn't even out yet, is it?"

The principal sighed. "No, it isn't. But I'm afraid that Cassie didn't go to any of her classes after lunch. I thought—well, I thought perhaps I might find her down here."

Rosemary shook her head in confusion. "I'm not sure what you mean. Was she ill?"

"Not according to Lisa Chambers," Charlotte said. "It seems that Lisa saw Cassie and Eric Cavanaugh leaving school after lunch. Neither of them have been seen since."

Rosemary's brows arched in surprise. "You're telling me that Eric Cavanaugh cut school?" she asked. *"Eric Cavanaugh?"*

"Well, it's hardly as earth-shattering as the second coming," Charlotte observed dryly, "but yes, that's what I'm telling you. More to the point, I'm also telling you that Cassie cut along with him. I'd hoped she'd at least last out the first day."

Rosemary frowned. What was the woman talking about? "I'm afraid I don't understand."

Charlotte nodded. "That's why I came," she said. "Do you have a minute? I have some things here I think you ought to see."

Her apprehension deepening, Rosemary led Charlotte to the back of the shop, where she had a tiny office. As Charlotte settled herself into a chair, she drew a file folder from her briefcase. "These are Cassie's records from her former school. I thought perhaps you should look at them."

Frowning, Rosemary took the file from the principal with her unbandaged hand and flipped through it. But it was the first page, obviously, that Charlotte Ambler was concerned with.

"I see," she said. "Apparently this isn't the first time she's cut some classes."

"Apparently she's in the *habit* of cutting," Mrs. Ambler corrected her. "I thought perhaps we ought to discuss it face-to-face. Given all the circumstances," she added pointedly.

The principal's tone made Rosemary look up at her. "The circumstances?" she repeated. "What circumstances? Couldn't you have just called me? After all, it's her first day of school in a strange town where she has no friends. Perhaps she shouldn't even have started today."

"I hope you're right," the principal replied, "but I'm afraid there might be more to it than just the simple fact of her being new here." She fell silent, but her eyes remained expectantly on Rosemary.

"I'm sorry," Rosemary said after a moment's silence. "I'm afraid I don't know what you're talking about."

The blank look on Rosemary's face made Charlotte Ambler wonder if coming here had been a mistake. But it was too late now. "I'm not sure how to approach this," she began.

Rosemary felt a pang of alarm. What on earth was bothering Charlotte? "Directly, I should imagine," she replied.

Charlotte took a deep breath, as if preparing herself for a plunge into icy water. "I've been a teacher and a principal for a long time, Rosemary," she began. "And I like to think I've developed a sixth sense about children."

Rosemary felt a chill pass through her, and instinctively knew what was coming next.

"And there's something about Cassie," Charlotte went on. "I can't quite put my finger on it. It's just something . . ." She fell silent, as if searching for the right words.

"Something in her eyes?" Rosemary said quietly.

Charlotte Ambler looked at her quickly, startled. Then she nodded. "That's it," she said. "That's it exactly. When she came in this morning, the first thing I noticed was her eyes. They're so deep, and yet I kept having the feeling that I wasn't really seeing into them. I had the feeling there was something else there—something, well, 'hidden' is the word that keeps coming to my mind. And usually when children are hiding something, it's anger. I know this must all sound a little strange, but—"

"But it doesn't, Charlotte," Rosemary broke in. "It's the same thing I've seen. I keep telling myself it doesn't mean anything, that she's been through a lot, and of course she's doing her best to hide her pain, but—well, I guess I keep thinking there's something more."

Charlotte frowned thoughtfully. "Have you talked to Keith about it?"

"I've tried, but you know Keith. He sees what he wants to see, and he never wants to admit that anything's seriously wrong. And he's usually right." She gestured helplessly. "I'm hoping he's right about Cassie too."

Charlotte's head cocked thoughtfully. "I wonder—do you know how Cassie's relationship with her mother was?"

"Not good," Rosemary blurted before she thought it through. Then she paused. "I mean . . . well, apparently she feels some resentment toward her mother, but that's common with children when their parents die, isn't it? They feel abandoned, and then turn their hurt into anger, don't they?"

Charlotte nodded. "It's almost stereotypical," she agreed. "And maybe that's what's happening with Cassie."

But when the principal left a few minutes later, neither she nor Rosemary were satisfied with their conversation. They both felt that something had been left unsaid, though neither of them had been willing to say it.

What neither of them had talked about was the strange sense of fear that Cassie Winslow induced in both of them.

*   *   *

Rosemary closed the shop early, but instead of going home, she went down to the marina, and as she'd hoped, found Keith aboard the *Morning Star III,* polishing her brass fittings. He grinned as she stepped aboard, and held up a rag.

"Want to help?"

Rosemary shook her head and held up her injured hand. "Good for sanding, but not for Brasso," she said. "Would you believe I found a cat in Cassie's room this morning?"

"A cat?" Keith echoed. "How on earth could it have gotten in?"

Rosemary shrugged. "For some reason she'd propped the screen open this morning. Anyway, it was sleeping in her bed, and it didn't take kindly to me disturbing it. But that isn't why I'm here. I wanted to talk to you before you got home, in case Cassie gets there before we do."

Keith's grin faded. "Cassie? What's wrong?"

"She cut school. She and Eric both."

Keith only shrugged. "What's the big deal? I mean, every kid cuts school now and then, and—"

Before he could finish his sentence, an angry voice erupted from the boat in the next slip. Both he and Rosemary turned to see Ed Cavanaugh, his eyes bleary but blazing with anger, emerging from the hatchway of the *Big Ed.* "I'll tell you what the big deal is," he snarled, wiping grease from his hands with a filthy rag. "The big deal is that *my* boy doesn't cut school. And maybe you don't give a damn about what your girl does, but I do! I'm gonna find Eric, and you better hope that tramp of yours isn't with him. Got that, Winslow?"

Keith's mouth opened, but before he could speak, Rosemary put a restraining hand on his arm, and neither of them said anything until Ed Cavanaugh had shambled off the dock.

"He may be able to talk to Laura like that," Keith finally said, his voice quaking with anger. "But he can't talk to me that way, and he can't talk about Cassie that way."

"He's drunk," Rosemary said. "He doesn't even know what he's saying. And even if he finds them, he won't touch Cassie. Ed's a lout, and he's lazy, but he's not that stupid."

Keith was silent for a long moment, then Rosemary saw the tension drain out of his body. "Hang on for five minutes and you can give me a ride home. On the way we can decide what to do about Cassie."

When they got home ten minutes later, Cassie was not there.

Seven

C assie stood at the very end of Cranberry Point. The noise of the surf was much quieter here, for a sandbar lay off the mouth of False Harbor, and only beyond the bar was the bottom steep enough to allow the ocean swells to build into breakers. Between the bar and the beach the water was no more than four feet deep, except for the narrow channel visible only by a darkening of the water where its depth had been dredged out. Standing like a beacon in the middle of the harbor's mouth, a red marker rose high out of the water, a light at its top flashing four times every five seconds. Inland of the marker a series of red-painted pilings marched in a gently curving line toward the shelter of the inner harbor.

"Why are they painted red?" Cassie asked, frowning thoughtfully. "If they're marking the channel, shouldn't they be green?"

Eric shook his head. "Red right returning. If you're coming in on a boat, you always keep red markers to your right. So if the pilings were green, everyone would come in on the wrong side of them and run aground in the marsh."

Cassie's gaze shifted then, taking in the weed-choked marsh which was separated from the sea only by the low strand of beach that formed the point. The strangest part about it, she decided, was that you couldn't really tell where it started and where it stopped.

Then, on a rise far out in the middle of the marsh, she saw a thin stand of windblown pines. In their midst, nearly hidden from view, she could just make out the shape of a small cabin.

"What's that?" she asked Eric, but the sudden racing of her heartbeat told her the answer before Eric even spoke.

"That's Miranda's house," Eric said. "It's on the only solid ground in the whole marsh."

"Can we go out there?" Cassie asked.

"You're not supposed to," Eric replied carefully. "It isn't really safe unless you know your way around. I've been doing it all my life, and I know almost all the trails. But you still have to be careful because some of the trails change from year to year. When we have really big storms, with real high tides, the marsh floods completely. Sometimes the paths wash away. Then you have to find new ones."

Cassie frowned. "But what does she do when the marsh floods?"

Eric shrugged. "Just stays there, I guess."

Cassie stared out over the marsh in fascination, trying to imagine what it must be like for Miranda Sikes, living alone in the marsh with only a few ragged trees to protect her from the winter winds. Then, as she gazed at the little cabin, the ancient, unfocused memory from the night before stirred within her once again. There was something about the house that seemed to beckon to her, almost as if it were to draw her to itself. She tried to ignore the strange feeling, but couldn't. "Take me out there," she said softly. "I want to see it up close."

Eric's gaze followed Cassie's and fixed on the little house as if he were searching for something. Then, finally, he nodded. "Maybe she's not home. If she isn't . . ." His voice trailed off, and he led Cassie back along the point, finally veering off into the marsh on a path that was barely visible to Cassie's eyes. The ground felt spongy under her.

With each step, she felt the soil compress beneath her weight, leaving footprints that flooded briefly then faded into the swampy ground. "What is it?" she called to Eric, who was a few yards ahead of her. He looked back.

"What's what?"

"What we're standing on. It doesn't look like sand."

"The sand's underneath, except in a few spots where there's quicksand on the surface. But this is all peat, and it's about thirty feet deep. Come on."

They moved slowly through the thick grass that covered the surface of the marsh. Every few steps birds, disturbed in their feeding, burst into the air, their wings flapping wildly as they screamed their alarm. Twice Cassie heard vague rustling noises that sounded like snakes slithering invisibly around her. She shivered with a sudden chill, then quickened her step to catch up with Eric.

Suddenly Eric stopped short. Cassie nearly bumped into him before she realized he was standing perfectly still, staring off into the grass to the left. "What is it?" she whispered, her eyes following his but seeing nothing.

"A goose. First one I've seen this year. See? Over there, sitting real still. He's watching us."

Still Cassie could see nothing, but then a movement caught her eye and the bird was suddenly perfectly clear. It was waddling placidly now, dipping its head under the surface of the water to feed off the bottom. They watched it for a few moments before Eric started along the path once more. As soon as he began moving, the goose honked loudly and launched itself into the air.

Eric stopped when they were still fifty yards from the base of the little hill on which Miranda's house perched. A network of paths seemed to go off in every direction, but only one path led to the hill and the tiny cabin in the stand of stunted pines. A post had been planted in the marsh here, a weatherbeaten sign warning trespassers away.

"Can't we go any farther?" Cassie asked, instinctively dropping her voice to a whisper.

Eric shook his head and pointed toward the house. "See that?" he asked. "On the roof?" It was sloped on all four sides, and rose steeply to a sharp point in the precise center of the square structure. Cassie searched carefully and finally spotted a white shape perched on the very point of the cabin. "It's hers," Eric went on. "It's an albino hawk, and it's always up there, just sitting and watching. She trained it. Come on."

He veered off to the right, and slowly they began circling the little rise. The house was visible now through the scraggly trees. As they moved slowly around it, Cassie had the feeling they were being watched.

The cabin was perfectly symmetrical, built of peeled logs that had long since weathered to a silvery gray. There was a single window on either side of the front door, and a low porch, only one step above the sandy soil on which the house stood, ran the width of the structure. The door was closed, but the heavy oak shutters that hung at each window were held open by large wrought-iron hooks.

Cassie stared at it for several seconds, trying to imagine how anyone could live here, in so small and cramped and desolate a place. Even the trees around it looked as if they were trying to draw away from the building. A tangle of weeds struggled for survival in the nearly barren soil surrounding it.

As Cassie and Eric began making their way slowly around the cabin, the bird on the roof stirred, its feathers ruffling angrily as it screeched an alarm.

Still perched on the point of the roof, the eerie white hawk began shifting nervously from one foot to the other. It shook itself every few seconds, and its head—dominated by an evil-looking hooked beak—was constantly in motion as the creature's sharp eyes endlessly surveyed its territory. From deep in its throat an ominous clucking sound emerged.

Only when the two teenagers stopped moving did the hawk once more subside into silence.

Each side of the house bore two shuttered windows, and the back, like the front, had a door in its exact center. But instead of twin windows, the back of the house had a single window to the left of the door and a stone chimney to the right. Nor was there a porch along the back wall—only a small step from the threshold to the ground. From a few yards away Cassie could also make out a well, its mouth circled by a low ring of stones. Above the well twin posts supported a wooden roof, with a metal rod and a crank at one end. A rope was wound around the rod, and a bucket stood on the lip of the well.

"Does she still use that well?" Cassie asked, her voice little more than a whisper.

Eric nodded. "There isn't any electricity or anything. All she has is a wood stove, and there's an outhouse over there. See it?"

He pointed off to the left. At the bottom of the hill, covered with a tangle of vines, Cassie saw a sagging privy, its weathered planking cracked and splintered.

"How can she live here?" she asked. "Why do they even let her?"

Eric tipped his head noncommittally. "She's always lived here, except when she was in the hospital." He faced Cassie, his blue eyes serious. "This is how come everyone thinks she's crazy," he went on. "I mean, you would think you'd have to have something wrong with you to live like this, wouldn't you?"

Cassie bit her lip, her eyes suddenly filling with tears again. "But how come nobody does anything for her?" she asked.

Eric paused, then shrugged his shoulders again. "Mom says people tried a few times, but Miranda wouldn't even let them into the house. She . . ." He hesitated, then went on. "Well, I guess she just likes it out here."

At last—with the hawk eyeing them warily every step of the way—they worked their way back to where they'd begun and Cassie stopped to look at the house once more. As she watched, the front door opened and Miranda, dressed in the same black clothes she had been wearing the day before, stepped out onto the porch.

She stared out over the swamp for a moment, then, as her eyes found them, she slowly raised her arm.

Instantly the white hawk rose from the roof, its wings beating rapidly as it lifted itself into the sky.

As the hawk soared higher and higher and Cassie felt a shudder of sudden fear, a shout floated over the marsh. "Eric? *Eric!*"

"Oh, Jesus," Eric whispered. "It's my father. What are we going to do now?"

Cassie said nothing. She stood motionless, as if hypnotized by the ghostly bird. Then she tore her eyes away and faced Eric. "Nothing," she told him. "We already decided what we'd say if we got caught. So let's go do it. Come on."

With a last quick glance at the strange figure of Miranda standing on her front porch, Cassie turned and began making her way back toward the beach.

The hawk, screaming with fury now, beat its way after them, flying low over the reeds of the marsh. Only when they reached the beach did it finally turn back, screeching once more, to return to the peak of the cabin's roof. Panting, Eric and Cassie watched it for a few seconds then headed for the parking lot that edged the eastern-most border of the marsh.

Ed Cavanaugh was leaning against the fender of his truck, his eyes flashing with unconcealed rage.

"What the hell are you doing out here, boy?" he demanded. "You got any idea what time it is?"

"I—I don't know," Eric stammered. "Two-thirty? Three?"

"Don't sass me, Eric. You know what happens when you sass me." The muscles in Ed's jaws twitched dangerously, and his right hand clenched into a fist.

"I'm not sassing you, Dad," Eric said, his voice desperate, "I don't know what time it is, that's all."

"It's four," Ed rasped. "Four o'clock! And if it were two-thirty or three, it wouldn't make a goddamned bit of difference. What the hell are you doing out here?"

"It's my fault, Mr. Cavanaugh," Cassie tried to interrupt, but Cavanaugh raked her scornfully with his eyes.

"I ain't talking to you, you little slut," he snarled. "Get your ass in the truck, Eric! You and I are going to have a little talk when we get home!"

Eric's face paled but he said nothing, only glanced quickly at Cassie before climbing into the passenger seat of the battered white truck.

A second later Ed Cavanaugh's eyes met Cassie's, and she felt a chill of pure terror. *He hates me,* she thought. *He's never even met me, and he hates me.*

Then Cavanaugh swung himself into the driver's seat, slammed the door, and gunned the engine. The truck shot forward, spraying Cassie with a stinging hail of sand and gravel. She instinctively raised her arm to shield her eyes. When she touched her face a moment later, her fingers came away bloody.

Biting her lips against both the pain of the cut on her forehead and the sting of tears in her eyes, she started home. But before she'd gone more than a few yards, she found herself stopping to turn back once more and gaze out over the marsh toward the tiny cabin in the pines. She could barely make out the dark form of Miranda Sikes, still standing on her porch. Seconds, marked only by Cassie's heartbeat, passed. At last, almost tentatively, Cassie raised her arm and waved.

For a moment Cassie thought Miranda hadn't seen her. But then, just as she was about to turn away, she thought she saw Miranda smile.

Whatever anger Keith may have been feeling toward Cassie vanished as she came in through the back door. Her right hand was held against her forehead, and her cheek was stained with a dark smear of drying blood. "Cassie? Honey, what's happened?"

"I'm okay," Cassie said. "I just—it was an accident, that's all." She dropped her tote bag on the kitchen table, then went to the sink and bent over it, washing the cut with warm water. She groped for a paper towel, pressed it against the wound, then straightened up and faced her father. "Are there any Band-Aids?" she asked, managing a weak smile.

"Upstairs in the bathroom," Keith told her. "Come on." Herding Cassie up the stairs ahead of him, he guided her into the bathroom and opened the medicine cabinet. "Maybe we better let a doctor have a look at that," he suggested as he fumbled with the little metal box. "When Rosemary gets back from Jen's dance class, I'll take you."

"It's just a cut. It doesn't even need a big one. Are there any of the little round ones?"

"Got it," Keith said, ripping open the paper cover and extracting the small plastic disk inside. He peeled away the backing, then told Cassie to tip her head back. When she took the paper towel away, he saw that she was right—the cut wasn't nearly as bad as it had looked when she came in. He centered the bandage carefully, then pressed it tightly to her skin.

"Okay," he said when they were both back downstairs, "now let's hear the whole story. Starting with why you left school right after lunch."

Cassie's heart sank. How had he found out so soon? But then she knew the answer: False Harbor wasn't like the San Fernando Valley, where nobody ever noticed what anyone was doing. False Harbor was a tiny little town, and everybody knew everybody else. Someone had seen Eric and her, and told on them.

"School was—" she began. She was about to blurt out the truth, but then remembered the story she had made up for Eric. What would happen to him if she told her father the truth and Mr. Cavanaugh found out about it? "I—I got sick," she began again. "I was having lunch with Eric and I got sick to my stomach. I decided to come home and lie down, and Eric said he'd come with me, in case I started throwing up on the way home."

Keith frowned. "But that was three hours ago," he said. "Where have you been since then?"

Cassie's expression turned wary. "I got better," she replied. "By the time we got home, I was all over it."

Keith eyed her suspiciously. "Then why didn't you go back to school?"

"I didn't *want* to," Cassie said without thinking. "School was horrible, and I hate it. It isn't anything like I'm used to, and everyone was talking about me."

"Talking about you?" Keith repeated, his eyes narrowing slightly. "Why would they do that?"

Cassie shrugged. "One of the girls hates me."

"Hates you? That's a little hard to believe, honey. How would anyone hate you on the first day?"

"It's Lisa Chambers," Cassie replied. "She's Eric's girlfriend, and she thinks I'm trying to take him away from her."

Keith relaxed. "And for that you skipped half a day of school?" he asked, the beginnings of a smile playing around the corners of his mouth.

"It's not funny," Cassie began, just as the back door opened once more and Rosemary came into the kitchen.

"Well, she's right," Rosemary sighed after Keith had repeated what Cassie had told him. "It's not funny, really. Lisa Chambers can be pretty nasty when she wants to be." But just as Cassie was starting to let herself relax, her stepmother turned stern eyes on her. "But that still isn't any reason for you to stay away from school. If you were sick, you should have gone to the nurse's office."

"I—I didn't know there was one," Cassie stammered.

Rosemary's brows arched skeptically. "Did you ask?"

Cassie hesitated, then shook her head and turned to her father. "Mr. Cavanaugh found out we cut too. Eric says he's going to be in trouble."

Keith glanced at his wife, who said nothing, apparently waiting for him to take the lead. "Don't you think you might be in a little trouble too?" he asked with more severity than he was really feeling.

Cassie shrugged. "I don't care. But Eric's father—I think Mr. Cavanaugh's going to beat Eric up."

"Beat him up?" Rosemary echoed, her voice clearly betraying her doubt. "Just for cutting school? What gave you that idea?"

"Eric told me. He says his father hits him when he gets mad. He hit him Saturday night."

Simultaneously both Keith and Rosemary remembered the shouting they'd heard coming from the Cavanaughs' two nights before.

Surely it had been no more than an argument, hadn't it? But, of course, they both knew better, for each of them had at one time or another seen the bruises on Laura's and Eric's faces and arms. Eric's injuries had always been explained away as nothing more than accidents on the playing field, but neither Keith nor Rosemary had ever put much faith in Laura's implausible accounts of her own clumsiness.

Suddenly Keith understood the truth of his daughter's tale. "You didn't get sick, did you?" be asked, his voice gentle. "You made that story up for Eric, so his father wouldn't beat him up."

After a moment Cassie nodded unhappily. "You won't tell, will you? It was all my idea. Eric didn't want to go with me, but I talked him into it. Please?"

Keith hesitated, uncertain. When he glanced at his wife, he could see she was still determined to leave the situation up to him. "I don't see what harm it can do," he said at last. "If claiming you got sick will keep Ed Cavanaugh's hands off Eric, I think it's worth it. But I want you to promise me you won't cut school again. Or if you do, at least don't try to talk anyone else into going along. Understood?"

Rosemary saw Cassie glance at her, but said nothing, and after a long silence Cassie finally nodded. "Yes, Daddy," she said quietly.

"Then that's settled," Keith said.

"Not quite," Rosemary interjected. "Don't you think we have to do something about this?"

Now Cassie's eyes met her stepmother's directly, and Rosemary was sure she recognized a challenge in them.

"Why?" Cassie asked. "My mom never did anything when I cut school at home."

"Did she know what you were doing?" Rosemary countered.

"Sure," Cassie replied, her tone just short of belligerence. "I used to do it all the time. What's the big deal? I get good grades, and the classes are so dumb I don't see the point of going."

Rosemary decided to ignore the jibe. "What did you do when you cut school?"

"Nothing much," Cassie replied vaguely. "Sometimes I'd go to the beach, like Eric and I did today. But usually I just went home and read."

"And your mother didn't care?"

Cassie's jaw tightened, but when she spoke, her voice was almost emotionless. "Most of the time she probably didn't even know. She was always at work, and then after Tommy left, she usually went out all the time. Sometimes I didn't even see her except on the weekends."

"I see," Rosemary breathed, suddenly softening. Apparently Keith was right—Diana hadn't really cared about Cassie at all. "Well, under the circumstances I guess we can let it go this time," she said. "But I want you to understand that here we *do* care if you go to school or not. Even though I have my store, I won't be working all the time, and I certainly won't be going out every night. If you have problems at school, we want you to talk about them, not just stop going to classes. Okay?"

Cassie's eyes narrowed slightly, but she bobbed her head. "Can I go up to my room now?"

Rosemary hesitated, feeling certain there was more to be said, but not quite sure what it was. As had already happened a couple of times before, she felt vaguely manipulated. "All right," she sighed. "I'll call you when I need you to come down and help Jennifer set the table." Cassie started toward the stairs when Rosemary suddenly remembered the cuts on her wrist. "Cassie?" she called.

The girl stopped, and turned back questioningly.

"There was a cat in your room this morning," Rosemary said. "It was in your bed, and when I went in to make it, it scratched me." She held up her bandaged hand. "Do you have any idea where it came from?"

Cassie said nothing for a moment, the dream from last night suddenly coming back to her. Then she shook her head. "I don't know. It was in the tree last night, so I let it in. Then I let it out this morning, but it must have come back." She hesitated a second, then: "Can—can I keep him?"

Immediately Rosemary shook her head. "You shouldn't even have let him in. I'm sure he belongs to someone, and I let him out again."

Now it was Cassie who shook her head. "He'll come back," she said. "I know he will. When he does, can I keep him? Please?"

Rosemary glanced at Keith. Wasn't he going to say anything? He certainly knew how she felt about cats—she'd made it perfectly clear last year when Jennifer wanted a kitten. "I—I don't know," she finally temporized. "He probably won't come back, but if he does, we'll talk about it then."

Cassie opened her mouth to say something, but then seemed to change her mind.

A moment later Keith and Rosemary were alone in the kitchen. Rosemary went to the refrigerator and pulled out the bottle of white wine they had opened the night before but hadn't finished. "I know it's a bit early," she said, offering Keith a glass of wine and a rueful smile. "I guess I'm just feeling a little overwhelmed."

Keith raised his glass and tipped it toward her. "Well, if you ask me, you handled that situation like a champ."

"Did I?" Rosemary mused. "I wonder. I have this nagging feeling that maybe we should have insisted on some kind of punishment.''

"But you heard her," Keith replied. "It was almost as if she didn't even know that what she did was wrong. And it's obvious she didn't think we'd care.''

Rosemary shook her head. "I don't know. She certainly knew there was the possibility of getting in trouble. I mean, she went so far as to make up that story to protect Eric. And I'm also having a problem dealing with the idea that Diana really didn't know what was going on, or didn't care.''

"Well, it doesn't surprise me," Keith replied bitterly. "In fact I'm not sure Diana ever really cared about anyone but herself. Even when we were married and she claimed she loved me so much she couldn't stand to have me out of her sight, she wasn't telling the truth. The truth was that she couldn't stand being away from me because she could only convince herself I loved her if I was there every second. And I've never been sure she didn't take Cassie just to keep me from having her.''

"My God," Rosemary said, her eyes drifting up to the ceiling toward Cassie's room. "What must it have been like for her?''

Then they both fell silent as they heard Ed Cavanaugh's voice shouting from next door.

"*Lying, stinking, rotten kid!* I'll teach you to talk back to me!''

Laura's voice came next, softer. "Ed—''

"SHUT UP!''

Keith rose to his feet, but Rosemary stopped him. "Don't," she said. "We can call the police, or we can ignore it. But I don't want you to get involved.''

"But we are involved, damn it," Keith replied. "We have to listen to it, don't we? And what about Eric and Laura? Do we just let him beat them up?''

Rosemary met his eyes. "Then call the police," she insisted. "If you want to do something, call the police. But let them handle it.''

Keith reached for the phone, then, as he always did when he was tempted to report the fights at the Cavanaughs', hung up again before he dialed. If he called the police, Ed Cavanaugh would know immediately who had reported the fight at his house. And there were too many nights when Keith had to be at sea, and Rosemary and the girls would be alone in the house. He couldn't risk Ed taking out his drunken anger on them when Keith himself was hundreds of miles away.

"Shit," he said softly, pouring himself a second glass of wine. Then he smiled sadly at Rosemary. "I guess Cassie's story didn't work for Eric. But at least she tried, didn't she?''

For a moment Rosemary said nothing. Was that really all the lie had been? An attempt to help Eric? Or had it been meant for them too? She wished she could be sure.

She dismissed the uncharitable thoughts from her mind and made herself smile. "Yes, I guess she did." She reached over and squeezed her husband's hand. "We'll make things work out. She's got some problems, but nothing we can't handle."

"And it's hard to get mad at someone whose always looking out for someone else, isn't it?" Keith added. "She did it for Jennifer the other night, and she did it for Eric today. Whatever mistakes Diana may have made, I think she raised a good kid."

But Rosemary made no reply, for once again her mind was occupied with the strange feeling she had about Cassie, the feeling that the things Cassie was doing, no matter how well-intentioned they seemed on the surface, were cloaking something else. Cassie, she was beginning to believe, was a lot more complicated than she seemed on the surface. Something was going on behind those large brown eyes of hers, and it wasn't something that Rosemary understood.

More and more, she was growing certain that it was something she should fear.

But that's silly, she told herself once again. She's only a child. What can there be in a child to be afraid of? But as the afternoon turned into evening, and the evening turned to night, Rosemary found herself watching Cassie, looking for something.

What it was, she didn't know. . . .

Late that night, as Miranda Sikes carefully banked the fire in the ancient wood-burning stove that sat next to her makeshift kitchen sink, the nondescript grayish cat with the black markings on its back wove around her feet, rubbing itself against her ankles. She finished with the stove, closing the vent to let in only enough air to keep the fire going, then turned the oil lantern on her table down low.

She began stripping off her clothes, hanging them carefully in the armoire against the east wall, and finally slipped into a worn flannel nightgown. As she turned the bed down, the cat leaped up and slithered under the covers, but Miranda shook her head.

"No, no, no, Sumi," she crooned.

Reaching into the depths of the bed, she scooped the cat up and cradled it in her arms. Stroking its belly, she looked down into its glowing yellow eyes. "Didn't we have a long talk yesterday, and didn't I explain to you that you can't come back here anymore?"

The cat mewed softly, and one of its forepaws stroked Miranda's wrist.

"Yes," Miranda crooned. "I know what you want, but you can't always have what you want, can you? And you just can't live here anymore, no matter how much you want to. You have to stay with Cassandra. You have to stay with her and do what she wants you to do. She needs you now, doesn't she?"

Opening the front door, she stooped down and slid the cat out into the night.

The cat hesitated, looking up almost questioningly into Miranda's eyes. But once again Miranda shook her head.

"No, you can't come back in. You know where you live now, and you know what you're to do." Quietly but firmly she shut the door.

The cat stared at the closed door for a moment, then bounded off the porch and down the slope into the darkness of the marsh. It moved quickly, slipping through the reeds and grasses like a dark shadow, its eyes glittering brightly in the starlight.

As the clock in the church tower struck midnight, the cat slipped once more through Cassie's window. A few minutes later it was asleep at its new master's feet.

By the end of the week Rosemary Winslow was finding that she no longer looked forward to each new day. So on Saturday morning, instead of getting up at her usual time, she allowed herself to sleep in, lingering in bed, not quite asleep, but somehow unwilling to dress and begin the day.

"Are you sure you're all right?" Keith asked when he came up to look for her just after seven.

The look of concern on his face and the slight tremor in his voice almost made Rosemary laugh out loud, but when she had reassured him and he'd gone downstairs again, she lay awake, a strange feeling of ennui overcoming her. Slowly she'd come to realize that she wasn't nearly as all right as she'd told Keith she was, though she still couldn't put her finger on precisely what was wrong.

Part of it was simply the fact of Cassie's being there. She understood that and accepted it. Time would take care of that. It was simply a matter of waiting for new routines to establish themselves. What, after all, had she expected? Had she really thought that a teenaged girl could come into their lives without having anything change? Of course not.

Yet deep down inside she suspected that she had hoped for precisely that. A part of her knew that she'd hoped nothing would change, that somehow Cassie would simply meld into their family, sliding naturally into her role as Jennifer's older sister and her own eldest daughter. Which, of course, was a stupid idea, even if it had been an unconscious one. And if she was completely honest with herself, she also knew that so far everything had gone much better than she could realistically have hoped for.

And yet . . .

She cast her mind back over the week, remembering all the little things that had happened, the little things that really shouldn't have bothered her but somehow did.

The biggest of those things was the cat.

Tuesday morning when Cassie had come down to breakfast, the cat had been with her. Rosemary's first instinct had been to tell her to put it out and not let it come back in again, but when Jennifer had seen it, she'd squealed with excitement and immediately demanded to be allowed to hold it. Rosemary had opened her mouth to protest, but before she could say anything, Cassie had set the cat in Jennifer's lap. It immediately closed its eyes and began purring.

"His name's Sumi," Cassie said.

"Sumi?" Keith repeated. "How did you come up with that?"

"I dreamed it," Cassie replied. She turned to Rosemary, smiling softly. "When you dream something, you should pay attention to it, don't you think?"

Before she could even think, Rosemary had nodded. She wanted to protest again and insist that the cat must go, but Cassie had artfully changed the subject. By the time she was able to turn the conversation back to the cat, it all seemed to be over.

"But I always wanted a cat," Jennifer wailed. "And it's not a kitten, like the other one was. This one's all grown up, and I bet it won't even scratch the furniture or anything."

"You have to admit it's kind of pretty," Keith argued. "It almost looks like a gray Siamese, except I've never heard of such a thing."

"But it's just an alley cat," Rosemary protested. "And it looks far too well-fed to be a stray. It has to belong to someone."

It wasn't until the girls had left for school and Keith had gone down to the marina to work on the *Morning Star,* that Rosemary realized that throughout the discussion Cassie had said nothing. She had merely brought the cat downstairs and let her father and half sister talk Rosemary into letting it stay. As she'd loaded the breakfast dishes into the washer, the cat had sat quietly on a chair, watching her.

Watching her, Rosemary had thought, as if it knew exactly what had happened, and knew that it—and Cassie—had gotten the best of her.

That's stupid, Rosemary told herself now. It's only a cat, and cats don't think. Even so, all week long, whenever she found herself alone in the house with the cat, she'd kept getting the feeling that the cat was watching her, assessing her somehow. As each day passed, she grew more wary of the animal. More wary, and also more suspicious.

Where had it come from?

What did it want?

Unreasonable as she knew the thought was, she had a growing certainty that the cat did, indeed, want something.

But it wasn't just the cat.

One night—Wednesday night, she remembered—she had asked Cassie how things were going at school.

Cassie had shrugged. "Okay."

"What about the kids?" Rosemary asked as casually as she could. "Do you like them?"

Though Cassie's face had tightened, she had shrugged once more. "They're okay, I guess," she said, though her eyes never left her plate.

Rosemary opened her mouth to speak again, then changed her mind, remembering the conversation she'd had with Cassie on Monday. So far Cassie had not cut school again, nor had she complained of any problems with her classmates.

She hadn't spoken of school at all, in fact. Each day she'd come home and disappear into her room, presumably to do her homework. Once, when Rosemary had been passing through the upstairs hall, she'd paused outside the closed door to Cassie's room and listened.

Within, the soft tones of music from the radio had been barely audible, and above that she'd heard the sound of Cassie's voice, murmuring softly.

Immediately, unbidden, an image of Miranda Sikes had come to Rosemary's mind—Miranda, pushing her grocery cart slowly along the sidewalk, muttering to herself in barely audible tones.

No! Rosemary told herself, forcing the image from her mind. *She's just talking to Sumi, that's all. Everyone talks to pets, and there's nothing strange about it.*

Then why had she become increasingly uneasy about it as the week had passed? Why had she begun to feel that though Cassie was being perfectly cooperative, appearing whenever she was called and doing whatever was asked of her, she was separating herself from the rest of the family, turning increasingly inward?

Then, late on Thursday afternoon, something else had happened.

She had been in Jennifer's room, finally unable to stand any longer the mess that never seemed to bother Jennifer at all. She was packing Jennifer's toys away in the chest below the window when she'd glanced outside.

In the cemetery on the other side of the fence, kneeling in front of one of the graves, she'd seen Cassie. For several minutes she'd watched in silence.

Cassie seemed to be reading one of the headstones. Then she reached out and touched it. Her hand rested on the granite for a few moments before she moved on to the next one, where she repeated the process.

Finally, after about ten minutes, Rosemary left Jennifer's room, went downstairs and out the back door, then crossed to the low fence that separated the yard from the graveyard.

"Cassie?" she asked, keeping her voice low.

Cassie froze, her left hand about to touch another of the grave markers, hovering in midair. Slowly, almost furtively, she'd turned around and looked at Rosemary.

"What are you doing?" Rosemary asked.

Cassie's eyes flicked almost guiltily away from Rosemary. "I was just reading the gravestones," she replied. She met Rosemary's gaze, and once more Rosemary saw that look of challenge in her eyes. "They're—they're interesting."

Rosemary's brows creased into a frown. "But you can hardly see them."

Cassie hesitated, then nodded and got to her feet. "It's all right," she said. "I was just about done anyway." She came to the fence and scrambled over it, then looked at Rosemary uncertainly. "Did I do something wrong?" she asked. "I mean, aren't I allowed to go into the graveyard?"

Suddenly flustered, Rosemary shook her head. "No, of course not," she said. "It's just . . . well, it seemed like an odd thing for you to be doing, I suppose."

Cassie's eyes immediately darkened. "Well, maybe I'm just an odd person," she said, her voice quavering. "But I don't think there's anything wrong with that either!" Covering her face with her hands, she fled toward the house.

Rosemary took a single step after her then stopped. It was too late—once again she'd said the wrong thing, and once again Cassie was upset. She took a deep breath, wondering once more why it was that she seemed to have such a talent for saying the wrong thing to the girl. She was about to go back into the house herself when she changed her mind and carefully climbed the low picket fence into the graveyard. It was nearly dark now, and the huge ancient trees that dotted the little cemetery seemed to be closing their branches overhead, as if trying to shut out what little light remained.

The air in the graveyard seemed to carry a chill Rosemary had not felt a few moments before.

Slowly, almost apprehensively, she moved toward the grave Cassie had been kneeling over when she'd come outside a few minutes ago. It was the grave of Rebecca Sikes, who had been Miranda Sikes's mother.

Next to that was the grave of Charity Sikes, Rebecca's mother.

Rosemary moved slowly down the row of graves, examining the stones that marked the memory of the generations of Sikes women.

It wasn't the first time she'd looked at these graves—indeed, over the years she'd read most of the headstones in the village cemetery. And long ago she'd noted the oddity about the Sikes women.

None of them had ever married, and each of them had borne a single child—a daughter.

Except for Miranda.

Miranda was the last of the line. When she was gone, for the first time since the seventeenth century there would be no Sikeses in False Harbor.

But what was it that Cassie had been looking for? Why had she been touching the stones?

Suddenly Rosemary remembered standing outside Cassie's door, listening to Cassie talking softly in the privacy of her room. She remembered how she'd been reminded of Miranda.

Shivering against the chill and the darkness, Rosemary hurried out of the cemetery.

That night she'd tried to talk to Keith about it. Though he'd listened patiently as she attempted to voice her concerns about Cassie, he became coldly furious when she'd mentioned Miranda.

"What are you trying to say?" he asked. "That Cassie is going to turn into another Miranda, walking around in rags and talking to herself? For Christ's sake, Rosemary, look at things from her point of view. She's an outsider here, and she's having a hard time making friends. So she's lonely. Haven't you ever talked to yourself? And as for the graves, why shouldn't she be interested in them? Miranda's the town character, isn't she? Cassie's probably been asking questions about her, and somebody told her about the graves."

"But she hasn't been talking to anyone," Rosemary protested.

"That's the problem—she spends all her time in her room, with that cat."

Keith only shrugged. "Just because you can't stand cats doesn't mean everybody has to hate them," he said. If he noticed how his words stung Rosemary, he gave no sign. "Sumi's a nice cat. Besides, Cassie has a lot to work out for herself, and she hardly knows us. You can't expect her to open up to us right away. Give her a chance, honey. Just give her a chance." He snapped his paper and turned the page, and Rosemary knew the conversation was over.

Feeling dismissed, she retreated into silence.

And then, yesterday, Miranda Sikes had come into her shop.

Many times before, Rosemary had seen her pause in front of the shop to stare inside. She had often wondered if Miranda was really seeing what she was looking at, or if her eyes merely drifted from object to object while she herself watched whatever strange visions might be going on in her head. Over the years Rosemary had been tempted to open the door and speak to her, but when she tried, Miranda had quickly moved on. After a while, understanding that the woman didn't want to be spoken to, Rosemary had given up. Indeed, for the last year or so she'd barely been conscious of the strange figure in black who drifted through the town almost like some sort of ghost.

But on Friday morning Miranda had paused outside the shop again, staring in through the window, and Rosemary had suddenly become aware of the fact that her lips were not moving in their customary whispered monologue. As Rosemary watched, afraid to move lest Miranda dart away, the woman pushed her shopping cart close to the window, carefully tucked the large black shawl she always wore on her head over the tops of the bags, and opened the door.

She stopped cold as the bell tinkled above her, then slowly tipped her head up to stare at the tiny brass object. At last, nodding, she came inside and closed the door behind her.

She looks like a fawn, Rosemary thought. She looks exactly like a frightened fawn. Rosemary stayed where she was, certain now that if she moved, Miranda would bolt out the door.

For a moment Miranda seemed totally disoriented, as if she didn't know quite what to do. She glanced around, then took a tentative step forward and reached out to brush her fingers lightly over the marble top of a Victorian sideboard. As if reassured by the fact that the piece of furniture didn't crumble under her touch, she moved farther into the shop, pausing every few steps to lean down over one of the display cases. Finally she was only a few feet from Rosemary, but still Rosemary didn't speak.

At last Miranda turned and looked directly at her.

As their eyes met, the room seemed to reel, and for a split second Rosemary was afraid she might faint.

Suddenly she knew why she'd been so certain she had seen Cassie's eyes before. She was looking into them now.

Yet Miranda looked nothing like Cassie at all. As Rosemary studied the ruin that was Miranda's face, she could see no resemblance to Cassie's clean, clear features. Whatever beauty Miranda might once have had was long since buried under the sea of wrinkles that had ravaged her flesh. Her gray-streaked black hair was pulled back into a thick braid that had always before been hidden in the folds of the black shawl.

And where Cassie's eyes were dark brown, Miranda's were the startling blue of sapphires. Always, Rosemary had had the impression that Miranda Sikes's eyes held the strange vacant stare of the mentally disturbed. But now, as the woman faced her, she saw that they held the same strange intimation of darkly hidden secrets that Cassie's eyes contained. In their depths Rosemary was sure she saw an underlying residue of anguish, and something more.

"If you don't want me here, just say so," Miranda said in a voice that was little more than a whisper.

Slowly, deliberately, Rosemary tried to clear away the fog that seemed to have gathered around her mind. Part of her—a part she immediately understood to be irrational—wanted to turn away from Miranda, to banish this grotesque figure from her shop and her mind. But the pain she'd seen in Miranda's eyes was so clearly reflected in the woman's voice that a tear welled up and overflowed onto her cheek. Vainly she searched for her voice. Miranda waited for her to reply, then finally nodded slightly and turned away. Only then did Rosemary manage to get to her feet. "No—no, please don't go," she said.

Miranda turned back.

"I'm sorry," Rosemary floundered. "You—I didn't know what to say. I thought—oh, Lord, I don't know what I thought. . . ."

Miranda smiled then, but instead of replying, she turned away from Rosemary again and looked curiously around the shop. "I've always wanted to come in here, you know," she said at last. "It's my favorite place in the whole village. I always look forward to the days when you change the windows."

Rosemary swallowed. I have to speak, she thought. I have to say something. Anything. "Y-you should have come in then," she heard herself say.

But Miranda shook her head. "I don't go in any of the shops. They don't want me, and I don't want to impose myself."

"But you came in today," Rosemary breathed. And yesterday Cassie was looking at your ancestors graves, she thought. And the day before that I thought of you while I listened to Cassie. She could feel her heart begin to pound.

A shadow fell over Miranda's eyes. Rosemary noticed for the first time that she was clasping her hands nervously together.

They were the hands of an old woman, the skin as translucent as parchment, covered with a network of fine wrinkles. Dark brown spots were scattered over their backs, and the fingers seemed permanently bent. She's an old woman, Rosemary thought. So old. But it was impossible. Surely Miranda Sikes couldn't be much past forty.

As if she felt Rosemary's eyes on them, Miranda's hands suddenly disappeared into the folds of her long black skirt. "I wanted to talk to you about Cassandra," she said. "I wanted to tell you that she's going to come to see me."

Rosemary's jaw sagged dumbly. "She's spoken to you?" she asked, her voice hollow. "I didn't know—"

"She hasn't spoken to me," Miranda interrupted, as if she'd read Rosemary's mind. "But she wants to talk to me. She wants to know who I am."

Rosemary shook her head uncomprehendingly. "I—I'm afraid I don't understand. . . ."

"She's going to come tomorrow," Miranda went on. Her eyes took on a faraway look, and she nodded slightly. "Yes, tomorrow. I hope you will let her."

Rosemary's confusion only deepened. Tomorrow? How could Miranda know what was going to happen tomorrow, unless she'd already talked to Cassie? What did Miranda want of her stepdaughter? Rosemary felt a shiver of foreboding pass through her. "What is it?" she pressed. "What is it about Cassie? Why do you want to see her?"

Miranda's eyes met Rosemary's, but she did not answer. She turned away then, and started slowly out of the shop.

Rosemary stood frozen where she was for a moment, trying to absorb the strange words the woman had uttered. And then, without thinking, she spoke. "Miranda!"

Miranda stopped and turned back.

"Miranda," Rosemary asked, "is something wrong with Cassie?"

For a moment Miranda said nothing, then she shook her head. "No," she said in a voice that was oddly empty. "Nothing's wrong with her. But she belongs to me." She fell silent for a moment, then smiled again. "Yes," she repeated. "She belongs to me." Then she turned away again, and left the shop. Outside she removed the black shawl from the shopping cart and carefully wrapped it around her head. Without looking back, she started down the sidewalk, pushing the shopping cart in front of her.

The memory of that strange visit had hung over Rosemary all the rest of that day, and last night she'd found herself watching Cassie.

Perhaps it had been meaningless. Perhaps Miranda was—as everyone thought she was—only harmlessly daft.

But what had she meant? Cassie belonged to her? It was crazy!

She had said nothing the night before, unwilling to try to talk to Keith about it and knowing that to Cassie none of it could possibly make any sense. But still, before Cassie had gone up to her room for the night, Rosemary had asked her what her plans were for the weekend.

Cassie looked at her disinterestedly. "I don't know," she'd said at last. "I don't have any, really. I guess I'll just study."

Then she hasn't talked to Miranda, Rosemary had thought. So it probably doesn't mean a thing. Still, she'd been unable to sleep last night.

It was nearly nine when Rosemary finally went downstairs. She found Keith sitting at the kitchen table, working on a crossword puzzle. There was no sign of either Cassie or Jennifer.

"Where are the girls?" she asked as she poured herself a cup of coffee and settled into the chair opposite her husband.

He glanced up from his paper, shrugging. "The beach," he said. "Cassie was going by herself, but Jennifer made such a nuisance of herself—"

"The beach?" Rosemary echoed hollowly. "Did—did she say why?"

Keith grinned at her. "Why do kids ever go to the beach?" he countered.

But Rosemary knew Cassie hadn't gone to the beach at all.

It was the marsh.

The marsh where Miranda lived.

The fear that had been flitting around the edges of her consciousness ever since Cassie had come to False Harbor suddenly coalesced into a tight knot in her stomach. Her hands shaking, Rosemary tried to pour herself another cup of coffee.

It spilled over the rim, scalding her hands.

Nine

There was a sharp bite to the morning air, but the sky was a deep cloudless blue and the morning sun made the sea sparkle as if it had been scattered with millions of tiny diamonds. A strong wind was blowing in from the east, and a heavy surf was building, the swells close together, so the beach resounded with a steady din of crashing water. There were birds everywhere—gulls and sandpipers covered the beach. A flock of ducks churned over the marsh, rising as one into the air, circling, then dropping back down into the reeds to continue feeding. As Cassie and Jennifer walked along the hard-packed sand, staying just above the highest reach of the surf, the sandpipers skittered out of their way, opening a path before them then closing it again after they'd passed. Jennifer stopped short, clutching at Cassie's hand. "Look!"

From the south, barely visible above the horizon, Cassie could make out a faint line. "What is it?"

"Geese," Jennifer explained. "Sometimes they stop in the marsh."

The birds flew steadily toward them, and Cassie watched, fascinated by the perfect formation. As they drew nearer she could make out the individual birds, their necks stretched out straight, their feet tucked up under their bodies, their wings beating steadily in an almost hypnotic rhythm. By the time the formation reached the coast, everything else in Cassie's consciousness had faded away and she found herself imagining that she was with them, riding on the wind, looking down on the sparkling expanse of water and the thin strip of beach along its edge.

The big Canada geese were flying low, and as they came across the surf line, Cassie could hear the rush of air across their wings and almost feel it on her brow. Her whole body began to tingle with excitement. Then, as if giving a signal, the bird at the center of the V-formation honked loudly and veered off to the left. In perfect synchronization the rest of the flock banked to follow, then the formation suddenly broke as the geese lost altitude, braked in mid-air, and plummeted into the marsh in a cacophony of flapping wings and excited honkings. Even after they had disappeared from her sight completely, Cassie gazed out over the marsh, the image of the magnificent birds still vivid in her mind. Then, in the distance, she saw something else.

Far out on the rise in the middle of the marsh, Miranda was standing on the porch of her cabin. Though the distance was far too great for Cassie to see clearly, she knew that Miranda, too, had been watching the geese.

Now Miranda was watching her.

Watching her, and silently calling to her.

Already Cassie could feel the first stirrings of the strange force within her, drawing her toward the marsh.

"Isn't it neat?" Jennifer said excitedly, totally unaware of the strange feeling that had come over Cassie. "By next week there'll be so many of them you can hardly believe it. They just keep coming in, and then one day they all take off. They're going up to Canada, and after they're gone there won't be any more until fall." Her eyes widened in wonder as she gazed at the marsh. "How can they do it? How can they fly that far?"

Vaguely, Cassie heard Jennifer speaking, but her eyes never left the figure on the porch of the little cabin, and she made no reply.

Finally Jennifer looked anxiously up at Cassie. "Cassie? Is something wrong?"

"Look," Cassie said quietly. "Look out there."

Puzzled, Jennifer followed the older girl's gaze, and then gasped with sudden alarm. "It's Miranda," she breathed. "Don't look at her, Cassie."

But Cassie seemed not to hear her. She took a step forward.

Sumi, who had followed them from the house and was now sitting quietly at her feet, suddenly leaped to his feet and darted ahead, his tail twitching.

Jennifer's heart began to beat faster as she realized what Cassie had in mind.

"Cassie?" she called. "Cassie, what are you doing?"

Jennifer's voice sounded to Cassie as if it was coming from far away. In her mind, Cassie could hear another voice—Miranda's voice—calling to her.

She had to answer that call—she had to!

She took a step forward, then felt something tugging at her. Almost in a trance now, she looked down to see Jennifer clutching at her arm, trying to hold her back.

"I have to go out there," she said softly. "She wants me."

"No!" Jennifer protested. "You can't go out there. It's dangerous, and Miranda's crazy, and—" She fell silent as she saw the strange faraway look that had come into Cassie's eyes.

"She isn't crazy," Cassie breathed. "And you can't keep me from going out there. Nobody can."

With a short gasp, Jennifer dropped Cassie's arm and backed away. "B-but you'll get lost," she whispered in a final attempt to change her half sister's mind.

Cassie only shook her head. "Sumi knows the way. He'll show me. Look." A few yards away the cat had stopped and turned around, his eyes fixing on Cassie. His tail twitched impatiently and he uttered a loud meow.

Jennifer backed farther away, her heart thumping now. Cassie took a step toward the frightened child, but when Jennifer shrank back from her, she turned away and began following Sumi along the beach. Jennifer stayed where she was, too afraid to follow, until Cassie was fifty yards away from her. Then her curiosity overcame her fear, and she timidly started after her half sister.

Sumi angled across the beach, loping easily up the gentle rise of the low dune. He disappeared over the crest, but a moment later Cassie spotted him ranging back and forth at the very edge of the marsh, his tail once again twitching as if to signal her. She moved faster then. When she was within a few feet of Sumi, the cat turned and bounded down one of the narrow paths that led into the tangle of tall grasses and reeds. Cassie hesitated only a second, then followed.

Jennifer stopped short at the edge of the marsh. She stared fearfully at the oozing black water. Visions of slithering snakes and huge spiders made her skin crawl.

"Cassie?" she called out, her voice sounding small and lost against the cries of the birds and the muffled roar of the surf. "Cassie, don't . . ."

But Cassie was gone, already lost from Jennifer's view. She paused for a moment, trying to decide what to do. Should she go home and tell her parents what Cassie was doing? But that was tattling, wasn't it?

Then she had an idea. She wouldn't go into the marsh, but at least she knew a place where she could watch. Her fear easing slightly, she turned and started running down the beach.

Lisa Chambers and Allayne Garvey walked along Oak Street, which skirted the marsh from Bay Street all the way to Cape Drive. It was one of the prettiest streets in False Harbor, for before the village had been laid out, Oak Street had been a cow path that wound along the edge of the wetlands. When the town fathers had laid out a more formal structure of streets, Oak Street's route was allowed to follow the natural contours of the land, as the path had always done, instead of being forced into the puritan uniformity of the rigid grid upon which the rest of the village streets had been surveyed. On both sides of the gently curving road, rows of giant oaks had spread their branches wide. Near the end of the street a strip of the marsh had been reclaimed in the early part of the century to form a grassy park, dotted now with picnic tables, swings, and teeter-totters.

All the beauty of the street was lost on Lisa, however, for her mind was totally occupied with her fury toward Cassie Winslow.

"I don't see why Eric wants to walk her to school every day," she complained, kicking sullenly at an empty Coke can that lay next to one of the trash barrels. "Doesn't he even care what people think?"

"What's he supposed to do?" Allayne argued. "Cross the street every time he sees her?"

"Well, why shouldn't he? She's not part of our group, and she never will be." She stopped in mid-step and turned to face Allayne. "Mom doesn't think she has any class at all, and nobody even knows where her mother came from."

Allayne's eyes rolled, and she started tuning Lisa's voice out. There wasn't much she hadn't already heard about Lisa's own family, and how old it was, and how important. But Allayne knew perfectly well that outside of False Harbor nobody had ever heard of the Chamberses or the Smythes or the Maynards. Nor, for that matter, had they heard of the Garveys, either, and Allayne's family had been around at least as long as any of the others. It was just that in her family, the kind of haughty pride the Chamberses displayed was known as arrogance. "Most of the founding fathers were a pretty sleazy bunch anyway," her father always said. "Stealing the land from the Indians, then snooping on their neighbors all the time. And we all think that just because we haven't had the gumption to get out of here, we're something special. The only special person we have around here is Miranda Sikes, and nobody will even talk to her."

"Including you," Allayne had pointed out, but her father had only dismissed her words with a wave of his hand.

When Allayne had asked him what was special about Miranda Sikes, he'd shaken his head and replied, "If you want to find that out, maybe you ought to go out there and see." Ever since, Allayne had thought about his words and wondered if he was really serious. She also wondered if she'd ever work up the courage to take up his challenge.

Now, as Lisa Chambers's voice droned on, Allayne sighed and glanced at the park in the hopes of finding something that might divert Lisa from her monologue of complaints about Cassie Winslow. Almost immediately she found something. Standing on one of the picnic tables, staring into the marsh, she saw Jennifer Winslow. Allayne watched the little girl for a few seconds, and when she didn't move, gently nudged Lisa. "Look," she said quietly.

Lisa, annoyed at being interrupted, looked irritably toward Jennifer. "So what?" she asked.

"What's she doing? There must be something in the marsh."

"Birds," Lisa said. "That's all that's ever in the marsh. Why don't we go down to the drugstore and get a Coke?"

But Allayne ignored Lisa's words. "I think she's watching something," she said. "Come on, let's find out what it is." She veered off the sidewalk into the park, and after a moment Lisa followed her. "Jennifer?" Allayne called.

Startled, Jennifer jumped, then turned to face them. She looked almost frightened, but as she recognized Allayne, who had been her favorite baby-sitter before Cassie arrived, her expression eased.

"Jen?" Allayne asked. "Is something wrong?"

"It's Cassie," Jennifer breathed. "Look."

She pointed out into the marsh, and a second later Allayne and Lisa saw what the child had been watching.

Far out in the marsh, maybe two hundred and fifty yards away, they could see a figure moving quickly through the weeds.

"But what's she doing out there?" Allayne asked. "Doesn't she know it's dangerous?"

"I told her," Jennifer said solemnly. "But she wouldn't listen to me."

"She's crazy," Lisa Chambers pronounced. "She doesn't know anything about the marsh."

"She isn't either crazy," Jennifer shot back.

"Isn't she?" Lisa taunted. "Well, if she isn't, what's she doing out there?"

"She's going to see Miranda!" Jennifer exclaimed without thinking, then clamped both hands over her mouth as if she could take back her words.

Lisa and Allayne stared at the little girl for a moment, and then suddenly understood. They looked out over the marsh once more, but this time they ignored Cassie, searching instead the low rise on which Miranda Sikes's cabin stood starkly silhouetted in its scraggly grove of trees.

On the porch of the tiny house, standing so still she might have been carved from stone, was Miranda.

A slow, cruel smile spread over Lisa Chambers's face, and her eyes gleamed with malice. "I knew it," she said quietly. "I told you so, didn't I? She's just as crazy as Miranda is!"

But Allayne, fascinated, said nothing, for in the wetlands beyond the park even the birds had suddenly fallen silent as Cassie slowly approached the strange cabin in the marsh.

Cassie was barely inside the grove of spindly pines when the hawk on the roof of Miranda's cabin suddenly came to life, raising its head from beneath its wing to peer out into the surrounding swamplands. Then, as its eyes found Cassie, it rose up onto its feet, its wings flapping noisily.

With a high-pitched scream of fury, the hawk rose up off the roof, its wings beating hard as it circled up into the cloudless blue of the sky.

Cassie watched as the bird flew higher and began to circle. She turned slowly, both fascinated and frightened by its graceful flight. Then, as she followed the bird's path across the marsh, she saw the three figures in the park. For a split second she thought they were watching the hawk too. Suddenly, with a flash of anger, she realized that they weren't staring at the hawk, but at her.

They were staring at her, and talking about her. She could almost hear the sneering words coming out of Lisa Chambers's mouth. Her surge of anger grew, and for a moment she wished the hawk would see them, too, and know what they were saying, and stop them.

From high above her head another angry screech erupted from the hawk's beak. Instantly, a flock of ducks burst from the reeds. Cassie froze, her heart suddenly beating faster as she remembered the terror she'd felt when she had first seen the bird rise from the roof in a frenzy of beating wings. But then she felt Miranda's eyes upon her once more, and her fear began to abate.

Cassie braced herself, certain that the bird was about to plunge down to attack her.

Instead the white hawk shot away to the east, passing over Cassie's head, blotting out the sun. As Cassie watched it, unable to move, it circled above the park. Then it dove downward.

Allayne looked up just as the hawk, screaming once again, burst through the budding branches of the oaks and chestnuts that circled the picnic table. Her eyes widened in shock as she realized what was happening, and she snatched Jennifer off the table. "Run!" she shouted as she lowered the child to the ground. "Put your arms over your head and run!" Jennifer, a shriek of fright escaping her lips, obeyed instantly, but Lisa Chambers, too surprised by what had happened to move, was frozen to the spot, staring mutely at the attacking bird.

Only at the last instant did she manage to throw up an arm to fend off the hawk's extended claws. A searing flash of pain shot through her forearm as its talons sliced through her skin and tore at her flesh, then she finally came to life as Allayne grabbed her other arm. Screaming with fear and agony, she stumbled after Allayne.

The attack was over as quickly as it began. The hawk rose once more into the air, caught the wind, and soared skyward without so much as a beat of its wings.

Cassie watched it all. She saw the bird dive, saw Allayne send Jennifer running from the park, saw the hawk slash viciously at Lisa's arm then burst back out of the trees. But as Lisa and Allayne stumbled away, the hawk screamed once more. Cassie looked up into the sky.

This time the hawk was coming toward her.

Cassie felt herself begin to tremble, and her skin turned clammy with a cold sweat as the bird flew over the marsh, gained altitude, then hovered over the pines for a moment.

Then it closed its wings and dived.

Cassie couldn't move. She remained where she was, paralyzed with fear. She closed her eyes and waited for the bird to strike.

At the last moment she heard a fluttering of feathers, then felt a weight on her shoulder. A moment later, something brushed her cheek, and when she finally managed to open her eyes again, the hawk was perched on her shoulder.

Sumi sat at her feet, his tail wrapped around her leg.

From the front porch of the cabin Miranda beckoned. "They are your friends," she said softly. "They'll always be your friends."

Then, reaching her hand out to Cassie, the woman in black drew her inside the cabin.

Ten

"Why the hell would Cassie want to go out and see Miranda?" Keith asked. Though his tone was light, Rosemary knew by the expression on his face that he was really wondering why she'd wasted a whole night worrying about the words of an old woman the whole town knew was half crazy.

"I don't know," Rosemary repeated for the third time. Her lack of sleep was catching up with her, and she felt herself growing angry with Keith. Why was he insisting that she should have simply dismissed whatever Miranda had said to her? Wasn't he even interested? "All I'm telling you is what happened yesterday, and that I think you ought to go out to the marsh and see if she's there. Probably you're right—she's down at the beach with Jen and there's nothing at all the matter. But I just wish you'd take a look. Is that so horrible of me, that I'm worried about your daughter?"

Keith's eyes narrowed. "My daughter," he repeated. "Is that what this is all about? She's my daughter, and you don't really have anything to do with her?"

Rosemary's eyes brimmed with tears. "You know that's not true," she said, her voice quavering. "And I'd go myself, but it seems as though every time I try to talk to her, I say something wrong. If I go, she'll think I'm . . . well, she'll think I'm spying on her."

"Which is what you want me to do, isn't it?" Keith asked. "I have a lot to do today," he went on, "and I'll be damned if I'll waste my time poking around in the marsh just because Miranda was babbling to you yesterday. And if I were you—"

Before he could finish, the back door slammed open and Jennifer plunged into the kitchen, her frightened face stained with tears. Behind her, sobbing uncontrollably, was Lisa Chambers, her right arm bound up with a bloody scarf. At her side was Allayne Garvey. Keith froze in mid-sentence as Jennifer threw herself into his arms. While Lisa continued to sob hysterically, Allayne tried to explain what had happened in the park. Rosemary—her anger at Keith momentarily banished from her mind—carefully unwound the scarf from Lisa's arm and gently rinsed the wound at the kitchen sink.

There were deep slashes in the girl's forearm, each of them almost an inch long, so clean that they might have been made by a razor blade. The skin had shrunk back from them, exposing the torn muscle beneath. Wincing with sympathetic pain as she soaped the cuts, Rosemary tried to follow what Allayne was saying while still keeping half an ear on Keith's hurried call to Paul Samuels, the village's only doctor.

"We'd better take her in," he said after he'd hung up. "Paul says if the cuts are as deep as I told him, she'll need stitches. I'll call Fred Chambers and tell him to meet us at the clinic." Leaving Rosemary to take care of Jennifer, he half carried Lisa out to the car, then, with Allayne tending to Lisa, he drove toward the twelve-bed emergency hospital a few blocks away.

*   *   *

"Lisa said Cassie did it," Jennifer told her mother when she was finally calmed down enough to make sense. Her eyes were wide and her jaw set stubbornly. "All the way home she kept yelling that Cassie did it." Her fear was quickly giving way to anger now. "But that's dumb, isn't it? Cassie wouldn't do something like that! Only a mean person would, and Cassie's not mean! I don't care what Lisa Chambers says. She's a big liar, anyway."

"Slow down, darling," Rosemary protested. "Slow down, and just try to tell me what happened. Everything, from the moment you left the house with Cassie this morning."

Jennifer's face screwed up into an expression of intense concentration as she began telling the story, her eyes fixed anxiously on her mother. "I tried to stop her," she finished. "I told her she shouldn't go in the marsh by herself, but she wouldn't listen to me."

"But where is she now?" Rosemary asked when Jennifer was finally done. Even before Jennifer spoke, she was already certain she knew the answer to her question.

"She went into Miranda's house," Jennifer breathed, her voice trembling with awe. "Allayne saw it. She said the bird just came down and perched on Cassie's shoulder for a minute, and then Cassie followed Miranda into her house."

Twenty minutes later Keith was back, his face flushed with anger. "You want to hear something really wonderful?" he asked tightly. "Fred Chambers says if there's so much as a single mark on Lisa's arm, he's going to sue us. Can you believe that?"

"Sue us?" Rosemary echoed. "What on earth for?"

Keith's voice hardened. "He seems to think he's got lots of grounds. For starters, there's Lisa's cockamamie story about Cassie making the hawk attack her. But it gets worse. There's also the fact you took the scarf off Lisa's arm and tried to clean up the cuts. That, he claims, could be construed as practicing medicine without a license."

Rosemary's eyes flashed indignantly. "That's ridiculous!"

"Of course it is," Keith agreed. "But ridiculous has never stopped Fred Chambers before. Even if he loses, he can make life miserable for us." Shaking his head with barely contained anger, he began shrugging into his pea coat. "I'd better go out there and find Cassie. Maybe she knows what really happened."

But as he left the house, Rosemary noticed that he'd said nothing about the fact that apparently she had been right all along. For whatever reasons, Cassie had, indeed, gone out to see Miranda Sikes.

Just as Miranda had said she would.

*   *   *

Eric Cavanaugh was walking aimlessly over the dunes. The chill wind whipped around him, slowly cooling the anger that still burned inside him. He'd been walking for more than an hour, not really aware of where he was going, and not caring. But now, looking up, he realized he was halfway out Cranberry Point. He paused, breathing deeply of the salt air and enjoying the cool sting of spindrift against his skin. As far as he could see, whitecaps glistened brightly in the sun and the thundering surf had scrubbed the beach clean of every trace of seaweed. The last of his fury seemed to drain into the roiling sea, and when he at last turned away to gaze out over the wetlands on the leeward side of the point, he felt the beginnings of the peacefulness he always found here begin to wash gently over him.

In strange contrast to the churning ocean, there was a placidity about the marsh now. The wind, rushing freely over the open expanse of the Atlantic, had been unable to vent its full strength on the protected marsh, and the reeds were merely swaying in the breeze. Here and there open expanses of black and brackish water rippled gently, reflecting the crystal blue of the sky in a rainbow of hues. A redwing blackbird, its beak filled with a tuft of grass, was industriously pulling reeds together in the first stages of its nest building. Far in the distance Eric could make out the familiar shape of Miranda Sikes's cabin, the ubiquitous white hawk perched on the peak of the roof.

Then, as he watched, someone emerged from the cabin. At first, as the figure hesitated on the porch, he was certain it was Miranda, but a second later he knew it was someone else, for the person bolted off the porch and began running down the slope of the hill.

Cassie. It had to be Cassie.

As she disappeared into the tall grasses, a shout drifted over the marsh, then another. A movement off to the right, near the park, caught Eric's eye, and then he recognized Keith Winslow running along the strip of grass that edged the marsh. As Eric watched, Keith shouted once more, then veered off into the marsh itself.

A moment later the hawk on the roof of Miranda Sikes's cabin came to life, rising off its perch with a single beat of its powerful wings. A second later Eric lost sight of it as its ghostly image disappeared into the brightness of the morning sunlight.

Cassie reappeared for a moment, then was gone again, lost somewhere in the reeds. But even in the split second she'd been visible, Eric knew she was running toward him rather than her father. He hesitated, wondering what could have happened. Had she really gone to Miranda's house alone? But how had she done it? How had she threaded her way through the maze of trails and paths, most of which led nowhere but simply petered out into boggy morasses of peat and treacherous expanses of quicksand?

And what had made her father come looking for her?

And then, over the pounding surf and Keith Winslow's shouts, Eric heard a high-pitched scream. The hawk, no more than a tiny speck high above the marsh, was preparing to dive.

Cassie had no idea of where she was—on both sides of her the reeds seemed to be closing in, reaching out, grasping at her. The pounding of her heart thundered in her ears, but above the throbbing she could hear the cries of the birds in a howling cacophony.

And then her foot slipped and she plunged headlong off the path and into the marsh itself. Screaming, she flailed in the muck and tried to grab at a clump of reeds. The reeds came loose in her hand and she only rolled over, the foul waters of the marsh oozing through her clothes. Struggling to her hands and knees, she looked wildly around, but the path seemed to have disappeared.

"Help!" she yelled. "Somebody help me!"

Staggering to her feet, she took a single step, then tripped again, plunging face first into the mire. The screams of the marsh birds were even louder now, and she imagined she could hear the beat of the hawk's wings as well. She looked up, and at first saw nothing. Then, high above her, she found the pale shape of the hawk, floating on the wind. As she watched, it seemed to discover her, and folding its wings against its body, dropped into a plunging dive.

It couldn't be coming after her—it couldn't! It was her friend, and it wouldn't turn against her. And yet with every second it was swooping closer.

Keith dodged to the right, then to the left. Almost there—just a few more yards. He shouted to Cassie again, but she didn't seem to hear him. She just kept plunging onward, stumbling through the mud.

Why didn't she stop? Why couldn't she hear him?

Her screams were muffled now, but the white hawk was clearly visible, streaking out of the sky. From its open beak a high-pitched scream of attack rent the air, and its feet were extended, the talons glittering in the sun like deadly jewels. Still running, Keith ripped his pea coat off, preparing to throw it over Cassie.

Only at the last minute did he realize that the hawk was not attacking Cassie at all.

He himself was the target.

He froze, caught in a nightmare as the hawk loomed larger and larger above him. He could see its eyes now—bloodred spots bored into the white mask of its face. Suddenly its wings spread out as it braked in midair, and the creature s talons seemed to spread wide.

At the last instant Keith's arm jerked reflexively upward. The bird's talons closed, but instead of sinking into his own flesh, they tore only into the thick wool of the jacket.

Instantly the hawk's mighty wings spread wide as it tried to launch itself back into the sky with its prize clutched in its claws, but Keith jerked hard on the jacket, and the bird plunged into the reeds, thrashing wildly. Screaming in furious confusion, it rolled over, then found its balance and hurled itself into the air for a second attack.

Keith plunged through the reeds and found Cassie, half mired in the mud, struggling to free herself from the entangling reeds. Grasping her arm, he pulled her to her feet, then shielded his head with his free arm as he prepared for the hawk's next attack.

"Hang on," he shouted. "Just hang on, Cassie!"

Half carrying and half dragging her, his feet sinking into the peat with every step, Keith slogged through the marsh until he found a path. Then, still clutching Cassie's hand, he ran toward the beach.

The hawk, beating against the wind, kept pace with them. As they neared the edge of the wetlands, it spiraled high until it was once again only a shimmering speck against the blue backdrop of the sky. As they reached the dunes and the beach beyond, Keith braced himself for another attack.

But it never came. As he watched, the hawk turned away, then sailed back out over the marsh in a graceful loop, settling once more on the peak of Miranda Sike's cabin. Only then did Keith finally turn to face his daughter.

Her clothes were black with the reeking waters of the marsh, and her face was smeared with mud. Slimy grasses had tangled themselves in her hair, and her hands were covered with a network of tiny cuts where the sharp edges of swamp plants had slashed her skin. Beneath the mud her face was pale, and her entire body was trembling.

Releasing her father's hand, she sank down onto the beach and choked back a sob.

"What is it, baby?" Keith breathed, dropping to his knees beside her. "What happened out there?"

Cassie looked at him with haunted eyes and shook her head mutely, still overcome by the churning of her emotions and the thoughts reeling through her mind. It was real. It was true. Miranda Sikes was the woman of the dream, the woman in black. And Cassie knew now that she was Miranda's. She belonged to Miranda, and it was to her that Miranda would reveal her incredible powers. But at the same time as she knew this, Cassie also had a terrifying foreboding that something was about to happen. Something terrible. To Miranda. And to her.

Keith stared helplessly at his anguished daughter for a few seconds. She was sobbing uncontrollably now. "She's going to die," Cassie gasped. "I know it."

"Who is, baby? Who's going to die?" Keith whispered, but he got no response. Cassie's hysteria was abating now as she struggled to regain control of herself. At last, Keith drew her to her feet, his arm around her, supporting her. "Come on, baby," he said soothingly. "It's all right. I'm taking you home. I'm taking you home now." Slowly, with Cassie still sobbing against his chest, he led her away.

Only when Cassie and her father were gone from the beach did Eric Cavanaugh stand up in the patch of dune grass where he'd lain hidden. He looked out into the marsh. It was quiet now—its placid calm restored as if the chaotic scene of a few minutes before had never happened.

He stood still for a few minutes, Cassie's words echoing in his mind. Then, moving slowly and deliberately, he started out into the marsh, following the familiar twists and turns that would lead him out to the low hill on which Miranda's cabin stood.

He hadn't really believed Cassie would go out there. No one went out there, no one at all, except . . .

He made up his mind.

It was time for him to go see Miranda.

By the time Keith got Cassie home, her crying had stopped, but she had fallen into a silence that neither Keith nor Rosemary could penetrate. She offered no explanations about why she'd gone out to Miranda's house, no explanations for her strange words. Instead she simply retreated to her room, where she spent the rest of the day alone, with the door closed.

Around noon there was a scratching at the back door, and Rosemary let Sumi in. The cat, ignoring its bowl of food, streaked up the stairs, and a moment later Cassie let it into her room.

As the day wore on, there was still only silence from the second floor. Rosemary went upstairs several times and tapped softly at Cassie's door, but when there was no response, she turned away and went back downstairs, shaking her head at Keith's inquiring glance.

"We should try to *make* her talk about it," Rosemary finally said when dinner was over and Cassie had still not been seen. "Whatever happened out there obviously terrified her."

Once again Keith shook his head. "She'll talk about it when she's ready to," he said, though remembering the stricken look on his daughter's face and her hysterical sobs, he was more worried than he cared to admit.

Rather than precipitate another fight, Rosemary reluctantly agreed to let it go—at least until morning.

Cassie jerked awake, her skin clammy and her heart pounding. In the dream she'd been in the marsh, but the grass had been higher than it really was. It had towered over her head almost like a bamboo forest, and the stems of the cattails and reeds had seemed almost like the trunks of trees.

Ahead of her, Miranda was walking, and though Cassie couldn't quite see her, she knew she was there.

There was someone else there too. Cassie could feel a presence in the darkness, but she didn't know who it was.

The night sounds of the marsh were loud in her ears, and she could distinguish every separate noise, from the soft thruppings of the tree frogs and chirpings of the crickets, to the restless rustling of sleeping birds as they ruffled their feathers. The marsh was filled with odors, too, odors that brought vague images to her mind and made her want to leave the trail and investigate.

But she never did. Instead she stayed on the path, quietly following Miranda.

She had no sense of time, but after a while she began to feel a sensation of foreboding.

Something had gone wrong. Miranda was no longer moving ahead of her.

She moved faster, and as she came around a bend in the path, everything suddenly changed.

The reeds were broken and the grasses crushed down.

Then, a little way off the trail, she saw it.

Miranda was on the ground and there was a shape above her, staring down at her. Miranda was staring back at the looming figure, but neither of them was saying anything. Then the peaceful sounds of the night were interrupted by a stream of angry curses, followed by a loud, broken laugh.

It was the laugh that awakened Cassie.

She sat bolt upright in bed, shivering against the clammy chill of cold sweat that covered her body.

Sumi was sitting in the darkness beside her, his eyes fixed on her as if he knew she'd just awakened from a nightmare. Then he ran to the window, leaping up onto the sill. But instead of disappearing out into the limbs of the tree beyond, he looked back at her, mewling anxiously.

At first she didn't understand. Then, slowly, the realization of what the cat wanted became clear. He wanted her to follow him.

Instantly she knew that this dream was like the other one—the one in which she had seen her mother die and first met Miranda.

It wasn't just a dream. It was a vision. It was real.

Miranda needed her.

But where was she? It didn't matter—wherever Miranda was, Sumi would lead her there.

Slipping out of bed, she pulled on her clothes and went to the window. A moment later she was gone, climbing down through the tree to the ground, following Sumi into the night. . . .

Rosemary's eyes blinked open and she stared for a moment at the glowing numerals of the clock on the bedside table.

Midnight.

She wasn't sure what had awakened her; she wasn't even sure how long she'd been awake. All she knew was that something in the house felt wrong.

She told herself it was nothing, and turned over. Keith stirred next to her, then rolled over on his back and began gently snoring.

She closed her eyes and tried to ignore the strange feeling of something amiss. But the feeling only grew stronger. At last she sighed, slid out from under the covers, and shoved her arms into the robe that hung over the chair in front of her vanity. Slipping out of the master bedroom, she moved quickly down the hall and opened the door to Jennifer's room. By the bright glow of the moon she could see Jennifer sleeping peacefully, one arm cuddling her favorite doll, a large Raggedy Ann. Her chest rose and fell in the deep steady rhythm of sleep. With a soft click Rosemary pulled the door closed.

She paused outside Cassie's door, listening for any sounds from within.

There were none.

She rapped softly, then hesitantly twisted the knob and pushed the door open.

She caught her breath, then stepped inside. The bed, its covers piled at the foot, was cold. At the far end the window stood open. The screen had been removed from its hinges and stood next to the window, leaning against the wall. Her heart beating faster, Rosemary hurried back to her own room and shook Keith. He mumbled, rolling over, then sleepily opened his eyes.

"She's not here," Rosemary whispered urgently. "Keith, Cassie's gone."

Keith blinked, then sat up and switched on the lamp next to the bed. "Gone?" he repeated. "What do you mean, she's gone?"

Quickly she explained. "We'd better call Gene Templeton," she finished.

Ten minutes later the False Harbor police chief appeared at the front door, his eyes red with sleep, his uniform rumpled. He listened to Rosemary's story silently, then shrugged. "Lots of kids take off like that," he told her. "She's probably just poking around town, having herself an adventure."

But Rosemary shook her head. "She's gone out to the marsh," she said. "I don't know why she's gone out there, but I'm sure that's where she is. I can feel it."

Templeton sighed, and wondered why it was that women always "felt" things. Never men. Men had "hunches." But it was the same thing, and Templeton had long ago learned to act upon his hunches. So now he would act on Rosemary Winslow's feeling. "Okay, I'll go out and take a look around."

"I'll go with you," Keith said, but the police chief shook his head.

"No you won't. You'll stay right here with your wife. The last thing I need is having the father along while I look."

Keith started to protest, but the look of determination in Templeton's eyes stopped him. And, of course, the chief was right. His job was to find Cassie, not deal with Keith.

As Templeton left the house, Jennifer, rubbing her sleepy eyes, came downstairs. "Something woke me up," she said, reaching up to her father. "Is something wrong?"

"It's okay," Keith assured her, lifting her into his arms and kissing her on the cheek. "Cassie just went for a walk, and Mr. Templeton's gone to find her."

Jennifer screwed her face into a worried expression. "Did she go back to Miranda's house?" she asked.

"Now why would she want to do that?" Keith asked.

"Because Miranda's a witch," the little girl said solemnly. "And I bet she cast a spell on Cassie."

Templeton swung the police car into the parking lot at the end of Oak Street, then maneuvered it in a wide curve so the headlights swept out over the marsh like twin searchlights. A few birds, disturbed by the sudden brilliance, burst into the air then settled down again. Seeing nothing, Templeton turned off the ignition and the headlights, then sat for a moment, letting his eyes adjust to the pale glow of the full moon above. At least the night was clear and the moon high, he reflected as he released the flashlight from its clip beneath the dash. He left the car and started toward the marsh. If Cassie Winslow was out there, she wouldn't be too hard to spot.

Unless she didn't want to be spotted.

If that was the case, his job would be the next thing to impossible, for all she would have to do was stay low and there would be no way for him to see her among the reeds. Unless, by sheer chance, he happened to stumble across her.

He chose the widest path he could find and started into the boggy morass, moving carefully but swiftly, his easy grace belying the bulkiness of his six-foot-four-inch frame. He searched for anything that might be construed as fresh footprints, but in the saturated soil even his own tracks disappeared almost as soon as his feet left the ground. After a few minutes he stopped looking at the trail ahead, letting his eyes constantly flick out over the marsh itself, looking for a movement or a silhouette that might be Cassie. Almost without making a conscious decision, he found himself moving in the general direction of Miranda Sikes's cabin. The paths began to grow narrower, branching off in a haphazard fashion dictated more by the contours of the marsh than any particular destination. Around him Templeton could hear the night sounds of frogs and insects, and twice he saw snakes slither across the path to disappear into the tangled safety of the reeds.

He was halfway to the rise on which Miranda's house stood, when he suddenly froze.

Off to the left there had been the barest flicker of movement, then nothing. He stood perfectly still, his eyes flicking back and forth as he searched for the source of the movement.

It came again, and then from out of the gloom a shape emerged. Twenty or so yards away, almost lost in the reeds, a figure was making its way carefully along one of the paths.

Cassie, or someone else? Miranda?

Templeton couldn't be sure. But whoever it was, the figure moved very slowly, head tipped down slightly, as if watching something on the trail. Templeton watched for a few moments, then silently began working his way closer. He circled around, always keeping the dark shadow of the figure within his range of vision, until he was ahead of her.

The trail she was following intersected his own a few steps ahead. He crouched down, waiting.

Suddenly a shadow darted across the trail ahead, but it was gone before Templeton could identify it. Then the figure of the person stepped into the intersection of the two trails, and Templeton, every muscle in his body tensed, rose to his feet and switched the flashlight on.

"Hold it!" he said, his words snapping in the quiet like the flick of a whip.

The figure froze, then turned slowly toward him. In the brilliance of the flashlight's halogen bulb, he recognized Cassie Winslow, her skin pale and her eyes frightened. He relaxed and took a step forward.

"It's all right, Cassie," he said gently. "It's Chief Templeton." He turned the flashlight off, and in the shimmering moonlight saw Cassie blink as her eyes tried to adjust to the sudden darkness. He reached out a hand and took her arm to steady her. "What are you doing out here?" he asked.

For a moment Templeton wasn't sure she'd heard him, but then she spoke. Her voice was barely audible, and tears were streaming down her face. "Miranda," she whispered. "She needed me."

Templeton frowned in the darkness. "Miranda needed you? Why?" Cassie made no reply, but her eyes flicked away from Templeton, scanning first the path ahead, then the sky above. "Where is she?" Templeton asked. "Isn't she in her house?"

Cassie slowly shook her head. "There," she said, and her right arm slowly came up, pointing into the sky. "She's over there."

Templeton studied the sky in the direction she was pointing, and at first saw nothing. But then, in the blackness, he saw a sudden flicker of light, then another. Slowly a ghostly shape took form in the darkness, and after a few moments Templeton realized what it was.

The white hawk, sailing silently on the air currents, was slowly circling a spot a hundred yards away. "Come on," Templeton said quietly. "Let's take a look."

Guiding Cassie with his free hand, Templeton started along the trail, lighting their way with the flashlight. Every few seconds he looked up at the hawk, half expecting it to have disappeared. But it was always there, and as they drew closer, its circle seemed to tighten. Ahead Templeton heard a soft mewling.

"Sumi," Cassie breathed. "He's already there."

There was a bend in the trail a few paces farther on, and as they came around it, the flashlight's beam trapped the cat in a circle of brilliance. It was sitting in the middle of the path, its twitching tail curled around its feet, its eyes glowing with an almost unnatural brightness. It suddenly squawled loudly and bounded away. Above them the hawk screamed once then folded its wings and dropped down out of the night sky.

Templeton's eyes followed the hawk, watched it plunge downward into a small area to the right which was free of anything except a thin sheen of shining water. At the last moment it spread its wings to break its fall and landed on something that protruded out of the marsh. Clucking softly, the bird settled its feathers then fell still and silent.

Templeton played the light out over the open area. The bird, red eyes glowing like embers, blinked, but made no attempt to fly away. And then Templeton realized what it had perched on.

From the depths of the quicksand a human hand protruded upward into the night. On its crooked fingers—frozen in death—the hawk had found its roost.

"She needed me," Cassie said once again, her voice cracking. "She needed me, and I had to come. I had to . . ."

Eleven

At three o'clock on Tuesday afternoon Cassie, wearing a navy-blue skirt with a white blouse and dark blue sweater that her stepmother had bought for her the day before, walked up the steps in front of the Congregational Church. Keith and Rosemary were on either side of her, and Jennifer, clutching her mother's hand tightly, did her best to keep up with Rosemary's quick stride.

The four of them walked down the aisle and slipped into the front pew. In front of the altar a plain white coffin containing Miranda Sikes's body sat on a small catafalque. Its lid was closed, and on top of it lay the spray of flowers that Rosemary had ordered that morning.

Other than that single spray, the church was barren of any decoration whatsoever.

The organist sat at the console, staring straight ahead, her thin lips forming a disapproving line across her face. As soon as the Winslows had seated themselves, she began playing. The music echoed oddly in the silent church. A moment later the little door behind the empty choir box opened and the dour-faced Congregational minister stepped out, a bible held tightly in his hand. As he closed the door behind him and stepped to the pulpit, Rosemary glanced over her shoulder.

Except for the Winslows, the church was totally empty.

His reedy voice sounding hollow in the nearly deserted church, the minister began the short service in memory of Miranda Sikes.

There was no choir, no eulogy, only a short prayer and brief recounting of the life of a woman to whom the minister had never spoken in all his years in False Harbor. Twenty minutes later it was over, and the doors of the church were opened. Six pallbearers hired for the occasion by the undertaker in Barnstable marched quickly down the aisle, picked up the coffin, then began their slow retreat from the church.

The Winslows rose to their feet.

Cassie, with her family behind her, followed the coffin and the minister out into the spring afternoon. The bearers carried the coffin around the church to the graveyard, where an open grave awaited, the newest—and last—in the even row that contained the earthly remains of all the generations of Sikes women. As the Winslows gathered around the grave, the minister began intoning the prayers for the dead.

It was during the prayers that Cassie first felt eyes watching her. The skin on the back of her neck began to prickle. Finally, when she could stand it no longer, she turned around.

Just beyond the fence separating the graveyard from the sidewalk, she recognized Wendy Maynard, pulling at her mother's arm. But Lavinia Maynard was ignoring her daughter. Instead she was staring at Cassie as if examining a bug on the end of a pin. As soon as their eyes met, though, Mrs. Maynard turned away, then she hurried down the sidewalk with her daughter, the two quickly disappearing around the corner. Cassie turned back to face the minister again, but in a few moments felt her skin begin to crawl once more. When she looked back this time, she saw Lisa Chambers standing across the street in the square with some of her friends. They were whispering to each other while watching Cassie.

She felt a tear well in her eye, but didn't brush it away until she'd turned her back on Lisa.

At last the minister finished his prayer and reached down to pick up a clod of earth. He crushed the lump between his fingers and the dirt dropped onto the casket the pallbearers were lowering slowly into the grave.

As the casket disappeared from view, Sumi slipped out from behind one of the gravestones and darted over to peer into the open grave. The fur on his neck rose, and a soft mewing emerged from his throat. Then he backed away, his eyes fixed on the yawning chasm in the earth, until he came in contact with Cassie's leg. She bent over slightly, and he leaped up into her arms and licked gently at her cheek.

As the casket touched the bottom of the grave, Cassie had a sudden urge to look up into the sky.

So high up it was barely visible, the white hawk was floating above the graveyard, its wings fixed as it effortlessly rode the wind coming in off the sea. As Cassie watched, it turned and soared away.

Finally it was over, and with Sumi still cradled in her arms, Cassie was led out of the cemetery and back around the church to the house on Alder Street.

Before she went inside, she glanced out toward the marsh. It wasn't fair, she thought. She'd barely met Miranda, and already she was gone.

Except that deep within her Cassie had a feeling that Miranda wasn't gone at all.

This funeral—Miranda's funeral—hadn't been at all like her mother's. All through the ceremony she'd found herself reliving once again those few moments she'd spent with Miranda, feeling once again the power of the connection between them, hearing once again the words Miranda had spoken to her.

"You are mine. You've come home again, and now you belong to me. Forevermore you belong to me."

And Cassie knew that she had heard those words before. The memory was becoming clearer, though it was still not complete.

But Cassie knew that though Miranda was dead, she wasn't gone. Not the way Cassie's mother was gone.

Miranda's spirit, the spirit to which Cassie had felt herself drawn from the moment she'd first seen the strange woman who lived in the marsh, was still alive.

Alive within Cassie herself.

Gene Templeton tipped back in the large chair behind his desk and propped his feet up on the open drawer which had been designed to hold an array of files but had long since been converted into a convenient storage bin for the endless snacks with which he filled his stomach. Someday, he supposed, he would pay for his constant grazing, and his stomach would begin bulging out over the wide black belt of his uniform. But it hadn't happened yet, despite the dire warnings of his wife Ellie. His weight hadn't changed an ounce from the two hundred ten pounds he'd carried when he graduated from college thirty-odd years ago. Though Ellie liked to tease him that forty of those pounds had converted themselves over the years from muscle to fat, Gene knew it wasn't true: his body was as hard as it had ever been. Metabolism, he always told her. That was the key to it: a good, healthy metabolism.

Except that the whole thing with Miranda Sikes was making him overeat, and if he wasn't careful, he would throw that precious metabolism off balance. Then watch out. He could picture himself ballooning up fifty pounds overnight, and having to forego most of the meals Ellie liked fixing for him.

Which wasn't, he knew, really the point. He was thinking about food to avoid thinking about what had happened to Miranda and what the implications of his investigation might mean. Besides, things like finding Miranda Sikes's body in the marsh weren't supposed to happen, not in quiet little towns like False Harbor.

In Boston, where he'd worked for more than twenty years, you expected bodies to turn up unexpectedly dead, and more often than not you wound up never finding out exactly what had happened, or why.

But Miranda Sikes had lived in the marsh all her life and knew every inch of it as well as Templeton knew the inside of his snack drawer. Could she really have simply wandered off one of the paths in the middle of the night and gotten caught in quicksand? Of course, it was possible that she had committed suicide. But suicide didn't really make much sense either; if she were going to kill herself, surely she would have found a less macabre way to go than to hurl herself into quicksand.

And there was also the question of Cassie Winslow.

It wasn't simply the fact that Cassie had not only been in the marsh when Miranda had died, and even been able to lead him to her body. That could have been coincidence, and it was, in truth, the hawk that had led both of them to the body.

But there were also the words she had spoken to her father on Saturday afternoon.

"She's going to die. . . ." Had Cassie had some uncanny premonition? Had she somehow known what was going to happen? Or had she been somehow involved? Templeton leaned forward in the chair and heard the springs screech in protest at the sudden shift of his weight. The words, written in his own hand, seemed to leap off the page at him. But what, exactly, did they mean?

If Cassie had known Miranda was going to kill herself why hadn't she told anyone? You didn't listen to someone announce she was going to commit suicide, and then just not tell anyone, did you?

On the other hand, he remembered watching her at the moment they had discovered Miranda's corpse. The expression on her face had been one of pure horror. Nothing about her had suggested that she knew what they were going to find, nor did anything she said. "She needed me, and I had to come." Those had been her words, and Templeton was certain that she had hoped to find the old woman alive.

He sighed heavily. He had to make up his mind what to do. Should he talk to Cassie again? But what good would it do? What could she tell him that she hadn't told him already?

He also had to consider the harm it might do. Nothing had been easy for Cassie since the day she'd arrived in False Harbor, and it wasn't about to get any easier. And if he kept after her, the rumors that had already begun—the rumors that she must have had something to do with Miranda's death—were only going to spread.

Spread, and grow.

And in the end what would be accomplished? Nothing. For in the end there was no evidence. No weapon had been involved, and no injuries had been apparent on Miranda's body. Nor was there a motive.

In his gut Templeton didn't truly believe that Cassie Winslow had killed Miranda.

He made up his mind, and filled in the one remaining blank on the report of Miranda Sikes's death. *Cause of Death: Accidental Drowning.*

Then he closed the file on Miranda Sikes.

Cassie knew she had to be alone for a while, had to deal with everything that had happened. As soon as she'd changed her clothes, she slipped out of the house and started toward the marsh. But when she got to the park, she found herself unable to cross it and move into the marsh itself.

The memory of Saturday night was still too raw, too painful.

Instead she turned toward the beach, walking slowly, reliving the night Miranda had died.

She came to the beach finally and walked out into the dunes, settling in a patch of grass from which she could see both the ocean and the marsh.

She sat gazing out at the cabin, thinking again about the vision she'd had Saturday night, the vision that at first she'd thought was a dream.

She had said nothing to the police chief about the vision—had said nothing to anyone. Who would believe her?

No one.

But ever since, she'd been going over the vision again and again, trying to see clearly the figure that had been looming over Miranda while she died.

It had done no good. Even in the vision it had been too dark and she'd been too far away.

Since that night a knot of grief had held her in its grip, and the cold shroud of loneliness that had wrapped her in its folds so long ago closed even tighter around her.

Sometimes—times like now, when she sat alone in the dunes, staring out at the sea—she wished that it was she herself who had died in the marsh.

And yet there were the words Miranda had spoken to her in those hours they had spent together. They were, indeed, the last words Miranda had spoken.

"It's all right. I will die soon, but I will never leave you. Remember the things I've taught you, and I will live on within you. I will live on, and you will never be alone again."

But what did the words mean?

Cassie didn't know, but as she sat watching the heaving sea, a certain knowledge began to grow within her that soon she would find out.

Even from the grave Miranda would find a way to tell her.

Eric Cavanaugh had avoided the village square after school that day, knowing that his friends had made plans to go down and watch the burial of Miranda Sikes from outside the cemetery fence.

What they really planned to do, he knew, was watch Cassie Winslow.

He'd been listening to them talking about her all that day and the day before, speculating on whether or not she would come back to school on Wednesday.

Or, possibly, not at all.

"I hope she never comes back," Lisa Chambers had said angrily at lunch hour. Her injured arm, freed of the unnecessary sling she wore around her neck, was displayed on the table as if it were an indictment. "If you ask me, she's just as crazy as Miranda was, and even if she didn't kill her, she doesn't belong here. And if she comes back, I don't think any of us ought to speak to her at all!"

Eric had said nothing, and when Lisa—and most of his other friends as well—had trooped down to the square after school, he'd gone to the beach instead, and spent an hour walking slowly along the dunes, watching the birds and enjoying the feeling of the wind on his face.

And enjoying the solitude.

When he'd seen a figure in the distance, he almost turned away and started walking west again. But then he'd realized it was Cassie Winslow and quickened his step. She was sitting on the grass in the dunes, looking out over the marsh. As he approached, she'd looked up at him, her eyes large and rimmed red with tears.

"Hi," he said, shifting his weight from one foot to the other, uncertain about what to say. Finally, deciding it didn't really matter, he dropped down onto the sand beside her. "Is it all over with?"

Cassie nodded, and bit her lip. "Some of the kids were in the square while they were burying her," she said softly, her eyes still fixed on the marsh.

"I know," Eric replied. "They wanted me to go with them, but I wouldn't."

Cassie turned to see him then. "Why not?" she asked, her voice bitter. "You could have laughed at me too."

Eric flinched, and the pain she saw in his eyes made her wish she could take back the words. "I'm sorry," she whispered. "I just . . . well, I wish you'd come to the funeral."

"I—I couldn't," Eric stammered. "I had to go to school." He looked away quickly, afraid his face would betray his thoughts. Cassie only nodded silently, then, after what seemed an eternity to Eric, spoke again. "Nobody else came either."

Eric's eyes widened. "Nobody?" he echoed.

"My dad, and Rosemary, and Jennifer. But they had to go, I guess. And then afterward, in the cemetery, everyone was staring at me from across the street." Her voice broke, and Eric saw a tear welling up in her eye. She blinked it back, then looked at him shyly. "Are you going to start staring at me too?" she asked, her voice barely audible. "Is that why you came out here?"

Eric frowned. "Why would I do that?"

"Because that's what everyone else is doing. They all think I'm crazy, don't they?" She saw Eric start to shake his head then think better of it. "Well, I'm not," she went on, her voice rising slightly, "and Miranda wasn't either! And I didn't do anything to her. I don't care what anybody thinks, I didn't do anything to her!"

"Hey," Eric protested. "How come you're mad at me? I didn't say anything, and if I was going to start staring at you, I would have been with everybody else, wouldn't I?"

Cassie hesitated, her eyes flickering with uncertainty. "Does that mean you're going to be my friend?" she asked, and once more her voice had turned shy.

Eric looked at her out of the corner of his eye. "I thought we were already friends," he said carefully. "If I wasn't your friend, I wouldn't be here right now, would I?"

Now Cassie turned to face him squarely, and as their eyes met, he had a peculiar feeling that she was looking beyond his eyes—was looking straight into the depths of his soul. It was a strange sensation, almost frightening, and for a moment he wanted to look away again. But then she nodded, and smiled at him.

"You *are* my friend," she said quietly, and stood up. "Would you like to see my house?"

Eric frowned. "Your house?"

Cassie nodded, and pointed out into the marsh.

"Miranda's house," she said softly. "It's mine now."

Hers? Eric thought. What was she talking about? Miranda wouldn't have given her the cabin. She *couldn't* have.

"I think that . . ." Cassie went on uncertainly, "Well, I just have a feeling she wants me to have it. So I've decided it's mine." She smiled crookedly. "You won't tell anyone, will you? I mean—well, I guess it sounds sort of crazy, doesn't it?"

Eric hesitated only a moment. "I don't think so," he said. "If that's the way you feel, that's the way you feel." Pausing, he added, "I guess she wasn't going to give it to anyone else." His eyes went to the cabin, and he saw the white hawk on the rooftop suddenly lift up and spread its wings. A shrill whistling sound drifted across the wetlands.

"It's all right," Cassie said, certain she knew what he was thinking. "He won't hurt you. He won't hurt anyone who's my friend."

Eric shook his head. "I can't stay," he told her. "My dad—I promised my dad I'd be home early."

Cassie smiled sadly. "All right," she said. "Tomorrow. I'll show it to you tomorrow."

As Eric hurried away, she started walking slowly out into the marsh. The white hawk rose up off the rooftop, his wings beating rapidly as he flew toward her.

Twelve

E ric sat silently at the breakfast table the next morning, his eyes carefully avoiding his father's, for he had known the moment he came into the kitchen that his father's anger was still seething just below the surface. Finally, though, Ed spoke to him.

"You not going to say good morning to your old man?" he asked, his voice rising and falling in the sarcastic singsong that was always a sure signal he was looking for a fight.

"Morning, Dad," Eric mumbled, glancing up to see his father's eyes—little more than narrow red-rimmed slits this morning—fixed balefully on him.

"I been thinking," Ed went on. "And I decided something. I don't want you hanging around with Cassie Winslow. You only got enough time for Lisa Chambers."

"What's wrong with Cassie?" Eric protested. "And I'm not hanging around with her. All I did was—"

"Don't you argue with me!" Ed commanded, rising slightly out of his chair. "You were messin' around with her again yesterday afternoon!"

Now Eric felt his own anger beginning to rise inside him. "We didn't do anything," he replied. "All we were doing was talking. What's the big deal?"

"Don't you sass me, boy," Ed snarled. He was on his feet now, looming over Eric, his right hand reflexively clenching into a fist.

"No!" Laura Cavanaugh suddenly exclaimed. Though her eyes were wide and frightened, the strength in her voice deflected Ed's wrath from his son to his wife. He swung around to face her.

"What did you say?" he rasped, his voice dangerously low.

"Don't hit him," Laura pleaded. "Do you want him to have to go to school with a black eye? What will people say?"

"They wouldn't say a damned thing," Ed growled. "What's the big deal if a kid takes a swat from his old man now and then? I got my share from my pa, and I didn't turn out so bad, did I?" He glared at his wife and son, as if daring them to challenge him. Then he was gone, slamming out the back door. A moment later they heard a grinding sound as the engine of the old pickup reluctantly turned over, then caught and roared into life. The screeching of spinning tires followed, the truck shooting backward down the driveway and out into the street.

A strained silence hung over the kitchen. Laura gazed at Eric beseechingly but saw that his eyes had gone dark and his jaw had tightened in unconscious imitation of his father.

Laura, her voice little more than a sob, finally spoke. "Why?" she breathed. "Why does he hate us so much?"

"I wish he wouldn't come back. I wish he'd just go away and disappear."

"I know," Laura said tiredly, getting to her feet to begin clearing the breakfast dishes away. "Sometimes I wish the same thing. But it won't happen." She smiled with wan encouragement. "But in another year you'll be away at college."

"Yeah," Eric agreed, making no attempt to keep the bitterness out of his voice. "That'll be really great, won't it? I'll be gone, and you'll be stuck here with him all by yourself. How come you don't just kick him out, Mom?"

"I can't," Laura said. "What would I do? How would you and I live?"

As she spoke Eric's pity for his mother's defenselessness turned to rage.

"How do we live now, Ma?" he demanded. "We're scared witless all the time, and half the time he beats us up. And all we ever do is pretend nothing's happening! You call that living? I sure as hell don't!" Before Laura could reply, he grabbed his book bag and stormed out the back door.

Just like his father, Laura found herself thinking. He walked out the same way his father does. She started washing the dishes, but her mind kept drifting away from her work as she saw over and over again the image of her son—as filled with rage as his father—stamping out of the house. What if it was too late? she wondered. What if she'd stayed with Ed Cavanaugh too long, and the fury and hatred that had already consumed Ed was working now in Eric as well?

Cassie caught up with Eric just as he was leaving the Common to start down Wharf Street. "How come you didn't stop this morning?" she asked shyly, falling into step beside him.

Eric said nothing for a moment, then managed to give her a weak smile. "It wasn't you," he explained. "It was my dad. He says he doesn't want me to spend any time with you anymore."

Cassie said nothing as she continued to walk silently beside him. By the time they'd turned the corner on Hartford Street, with Memorial High four more blocks away, she could contain herself no longer. "He thinks I'm crazy, doesn't he?"

Eric hesitated, then nodded once. "I guess."

"They're all going to act like that, aren't they?" Cassie went on. "It's not just going to be your father. It's going to be your friends too."

"So what?" Eric asked carefully.

"So I was just wondering what's going to happen, that's all," Cassie replied. "I mean, what are you going to do if everyone starts treating you the way they've been treating me? Are you still going to be my friend?"

Eric nodded, his jaw setting stubbornly. "It doesn't matter what my friends think, and I don't give a damn what my dad says either," he insisted.

A hopeful smile touched Cassie's lips, but her eyes seemed to plead with him. "Then meet me after school this afternoon," she said. "I—I really want to show you my house. I mean Miranda's house," she corrected herself quickly.

Eric hesitated, then shook his head. "I—I don't think I better," he said, and the pleading in Cassie's eyes dissolved into unconcealed pain. "I mean, I have baseball practice today. I skipped it yesterday, and if I do it again, Simms'll kill me."

"I'll wait for you," Cassie decided. "In fact I'll come out and watch you practice. I've never done anything like that before."

Eric cocked his head quizzically, relieved that the subject of the conversation had shifted. "How come? Lots of the guys' girlfriends come out and watch them practice. Didn't they do that in California?"

He hadn't told her not to come, Cassie thought. Maybe he really was still going to be her friend. "That's what I'm talking about," she said. "It was always the airheads that went out to watch the boys. And none of my friends had boyfriends. I mean, we all had friends that were boys, but they weren't boyfriends." Suddenly her eyes turned wary again. "If I come out and watch you, is everyone going to think I'm your girlfriend? What's Lisa going to think?"

Eric grinned. "Do you care?"

Cassie hesitated. "I just . . . well, I just don't want her to think I'm after you, that's all."

Eric's grin widened. "Don't worry about Lisa," he said, with more confidence than he felt.

They started up the steps of the school, and for the first time since Miranda had died, Cassie was genuinely smiling. But suddenly Lisa Chambers detached herself from a group of her friends, her eyes flashing with anger when she saw Cassie with Eric.

"What's so funny?" she demanded of Cassie, slipping her arm possessively through Eric's. Cassie's smile faded away, and she hurried up the steps and disappeared into the building.

"We were just talking, that's all," Eric explained. He faltered, seeing the jealousy in Lisa's eyes. "It didn't mean anything. I mean—"

"I know what you meant, Eric," Lisa said, dropping his arm as her voice turned chillingly cold. Silence fell over the group on the steps as they all listened. "And if you want to spend your time with someone like her, I'm sure I don't care." She turned back to the group she'd left seconds before, leaving Eric standing helplessly alone as all the rest of the kids stared at him.

This is how Cassie felt last week, Eric thought. *Just like some kind of freak.*

When the last bell of the day finally rang, Cassie still hadn't made up her mind what she was going to do. Today had been even worse than last week. She'd made it through the morning only by telling herself repeatedly that she'd see Eric at noon and at least she wouldn't have to eat at a table by herself, with everyone staring at her. But when she got to the cafeteria, Eric was nowhere to be seen. She'd waited at the door for ten minutes, hoping he'd show up, but when they finally began closing down the steam table, she took a tray, chose some food without really looking at it, and started toward the same table she'd occupied the week before.

As she moved through the cafeteria she felt the rest of the students staring at her, and heard them whispering to each other after she passed their tables. Though she couldn't hear all that they said, she heard enough.

"Everybody *knows* she did something," Lisa Chambers said as Cassie passed the table where Lisa sat with Allayne Garvey and Teri Bennett. Lisa hadn't even bothered to lower her voice. "I mean, my mother actually *saw* Mr. Templeton's car in front of their house yesterday!"

"But what's going to happen?" Teri demanded. "If she killed Miranda, why don't they arrest her?"

"Maybe she didn't do anything at all," Allayne Garvey suggested, but by the time she spoke, Cassie was out of earshot. "Maybe you're just mad, Lisa, because Eric came to school with her again."

"I don't care about Eric," Lisa insisted. She raised her voice to make sure it would carry across the room to the table where Cassie sat by herself. "If he wants to spend all his time with someone who's crazy, why should I care? But he better watch out—she might do the same thing to him that she did to Miranda Sikes!"

A wave of rage washed over Cassie and she wanted to scream at Lisa. But she didn't. Instead she made herself remember the words Miranda had spoken to her the day she'd died.

"It doesn't matter what they say about me, and it doesn't matter what they say about you. Some people are set apart from everyone else, Cassie. But whatever they say about you, they can never truly hurt you." She'd smiled then, a small, cryptic smile that Cassie hadn't understood. "I made certain of that. So don't worry about what they say. Just don't let them hurt you. Be true to yourself, and always remember that you must never let them hurt you."

So instead of saying anything, Cassie simply sat alone at her table, concentrating on forcing the tasteless food into her mouth and trying not to gag as she swallowed it. The lunch hour seemed endless, and when the bell finally rang, she began the afternoon ordeal, moving somnolently from class to class, the stares and whispers of her classmates stinging her soul.

At last it was three o'clock, and she had to make up her mind.

Should she go out to the baseball diamond to wait for Eric, or should she just leave and spend the afternoon by herself? She thought about the beach and the little house in the marsh, and the prospect of being alone with nothing but the seabirds and the crashing of the surf for company. At least out there no one could stare at her, and if people were whispering, she couldn't hear them.

Then she remembered Eric, and his absence from the cafeteria at lunchtime. Making up her mind, she shoved her books into her bag and left the building by the back door. A small set of bleachers stood behind the backstop. Already a group of girls was clustered at the far end of the lowest three tiers. They turned away from Cassie as she approached, and began giggling among themselves. Every few seconds, one of them would surreptitiously glance at Cassie. Head held high, Cassie pretended she didn't notice.

There was no one on the baseball diamond yet, so Cassie fished her math book out of the bag and began working on the homework assignments from the last two days, which Mr. Simms had insisted be completed even though Cassie had missed the classes. "After all," he'd pointed out in front of the whole class, his voice edged with sarcasm, "it isn't as if you were sick, is it? No one else went to Miranda Sikes's funeral, did they? It's beginning to look as if you don't think school is worth bothering with."

Cassie's face had burned as a ripple of snickering had passed over the class. "But she was my friend," she'd breathed.

Simms's thin lips had only curled into a scornful sneer. "Even if that were true, Cassie, you hardly knew her. And if you had, you'd know she was nothing more than a mental case who should never have been let out of the hospital. In my opinion you simply used Miranda Sikes's unfortunate demise as another opportunity to cut classes. Your parents may approve, but I don't. Please have the assignments completed by tomorrow."

Cassie had forced herself to stifle an urge to run from the room. It didn't matter, she told herself once again. He can't hurt you. None of them can. So instead of running away, she'd controlled her tears, and her anger, and her pain. And now, as she looked at the assignment, she was glad she had. The problems in algebra were so simple she could work most of them in her head. Shutting everything else out of her mind, she quickly began writing down the equations and their solutions.

Twenty minutes later, just as she finished the last problem, the baseball team trotted onto the field to warm up. Eric hesitated for a split second, and Cassie felt a quick pang of fear that he was going to ignore her, but then he waved before he and Jeff Maynard began tossing a ball back and forth along the first-base line. At last the coach came out of the gym, but it wasn't until he'd actually arrived at the diamond that Cassie recognized him.

It was Mr. Simms.

His mouth was twisted into the same ugly smile he'd worn while humiliating Cassie earlier that day, and she knew instantly that something else was about to happen. But this time she couldn't be the target—he hadn't even seen her.

He blew his whistle, and the team immediately gathered around him. He said nothing for a few seconds, and the boys fell silent, squirming uncomfortably as they cast sidelong glances toward Eric. In the bleachers Cassie suddenly understood who Simms's new victim was.

"Decide to join us today, Cavanaugh?" Simms finally asked, his small, close-set eyes fixing on Eric.

Eric nodded. "I—I'm sorry about yesterday," he said. "I shouldn't have skipped practice, and I won't do it again."

"What you do or don't do isn't really of interest to me, Cavanaugh." Simms's eyes glittered with pleasure at Eric's discomfort. "If you can do without us, we can certainly do without you. As of now, you're off the team. Smythe, you'll be taking over as pitcher."

Eric's eyes widened as the coach's words sunk in. "Off the team?" he repeated. "But—but you can't do that."

"Can't I?" Simms replied with an exaggerated drawl. "And what makes you say that?"

"It's not fair," Eric pleaded. "I'm the best pitcher in the school, and I have to play baseball."

"Really?" the coach pressed, now openly relishing Eric's misery. "And why is that?"

Eric's voice fell to a whisper. "If I'm going to college, I have to have a scholarship," he managed. "And if I can get one in baseball, I can go to—"

"Too bad you didn't think of that yesterday," the coach interrupted. "But it's too late now, isn't it?" He turned his back on Eric and faced the rest of the team. "All right, let's get it going, guys," he called. "Let's have a lot of chatter out there, okay?"

The boys glanced at each other, uncertain what to do. Kevin Smythe, his eyes smoldering angrily, was about to say something, when Cassie, whose own fury had been growing as she'd listened to Simms talk to Eric, scrambled off the bleachers and hurried out onto the field.

"Mr. Simms?" she called.

The coach swung around and looked at her. "Well, look who's here," he said, glancing at the boys then facing Cassie again. "I would have thought you'd be long gone." Two of the boys snickered quietly but fell silent when the others didn't join in. "What is it?" Simms asked. "If it's a question about your assignments, save it for class."

"It isn't," Cassie said. "I just wanted to turn the work in now."

Simms hesitated, and his sarcastic smile gave way to an uncertain frown. "You're done?"

Cassie shrugged. "I'm going to talk to Mrs. Ambler about changing classes," she said, her voice perfectly level.

Simms's smile returned. "If the work's too hard—"

"It's not," Cassie replied. "It's too easy. But I guess if the school needs a baseball coach that badly, they have to give you something else to do, don't they?" She let her voice drift off, and shrugged again. Then, as the baseball team stared at her in stunned silence, she turned and walked away from the baseball diamond. She could feel Simms's fury bore into her as she left, and knew she'd gone too far. What if there was no other class for her to transfer into? What if she had to stay in Simms's class for the rest of the year? It didn't matter, she decided: what he'd done to Eric wasn't fair, and she'd had to do something. She'd *had* to.

She was three blocks from the school when Eric, panting, caught up with her. "I thought you were going to wait for me."

"I—I wasn't sure you'd want me to," Cassie stammered. "I mean, after what happened."

Eric rolled his eyes. "What happened is nothing next to what's going to happen. You should have seen Simms after you left. All the guys started laughing at him, and I thought he was going to go crazy. Now he's going to be out to get you."

Cassie nodded. "I know. But I was so mad, I didn't even think about it." She hesitated, then met Eric's eyes. "Is it true? That you have to get a baseball scholarship if you want to go to college?"

Eric nodded, his jaw setting angrily, and he fell into step beside Cassie. "I don't see how I can make it any other way. God knows, my dad doesn't make enough money to help me out. And he probably wouldn't, even if he could." He shook his head bitterly. "Now I'm going to have to talk to Mrs. Ambler tomorrow and try to get her to fix it with Simms. He thinks he's a big deal, but he's scared to death of her. At least she still likes me." He shifted his book bag to his other hand and glanced at Cassie. "So what are you going to do? He's the only math teacher, and you've gotta take math."

Cassie shook her head. "What *can* I do? I'll just make sure I do all the work and pass all the tests. And next year I'll get someone else."

Eric shook his head. "I told you, there isn't anyone else. Simms has senior math, too. The only way you're going to get away from him is if he quits, and he'll never do that." He grinned. "Unless we could figure out some way to make him quit."

Cassie stopped walking and turned to face Eric. "You're kidding, aren't you?"

Eric's jaw clenched. "Maybe I am. I mean, he didn't have to kick me off the team just because I skipped practice, did he? It isn't fair. Besides, there isn't any harm in thinking about it, is there? I mean, as long as we don't actually do anything to him."

Cassie thought about it for a few seconds, and once more Miranda's words echoed in her mind.

"Don't let them hurt you. Never let them hurt you."

But what if they *did* hurt you?

"Why not?" she thought out loud. "You can't hurt someone just by thinking about it, can you?"

Eric glanced at her out of the corner of his eye, but said nothing.

They were still a hundred yards from the house in the marsh when the pale form of the white hawk rose up into the afternoon sky, screeching loudly. Eric froze, his eyes tracking the bird until it suddenly disappeared into the sun and the brilliant glare made him turn away.

"It's all right," Cassie told him. "His name's Kiska and he's my friend. As long as you're with me, he won't do anything at all." She started forward, but Eric didn't move. He was staring up into the sky once more, watching the hawk circling above them. "Watch," Cassie said quietly.

She gazed up into the sky and her eyes locked onto the soaring bird. Then, slowly, she raised her right arm, with her index finger pointed directly at the cabin.

As if she'd issued a command, the bird instantly banked and began beating its wings against the breeze. A moment later it settled onto the peak of the house and began preening its feathers.

Eric's heart pounded. He turned to face Cassie. "How did you do that?" he asked. "Did—did Miranda teach you that?"

Cassie smiled at him, nodding happily. "I told you he's my friend. He was Miranda's friend, but now he's mine." Her smile widened into a grin. "He'll do anything I want him to."

Eric looked at her sharply. "What do you mean?"

But instead of answering him, Cassie merely smiled.

With Eric following behind her and keeping a watchful eye on the restless hawk on the roof, she led him toward the little cabin on the hill.

On the porch, his tail curled around his feet, they found Sumi waiting. He jumped into Cassie's arms, and she cuddled him for a moment. Then they stepped through the cabin's door.

Though on the outside the cabin seemed dilapidated and about to collapse, the walls inside were paneled with pine, all of it waxed to a soft golden sheen which appeared to glow from within. There was a large walnut armoire against one wall, and against another, tucked into one of the corners, was a small bed. A table sat in the very center of the cabin's single room, and the back wall was half occupied by a stone fireplace, to which a cast-iron wood-burning cooking stove had been added at some time in the distant past. Along the other half of the wall was a wooden counter with a sink mounted in it, and above the counter, on either side of the window, pine cabinets.

Aside from the two chairs at the center table, there was an old wooden rocker next to a small table by one of the front windows. There was no other furniture.

Though everything in the cabin was very old, and obviously made by hand, each object had been perfectly cared for. There was not even so much as a speck of dust in the room, nor was there any sign of the clutter with which everyone in False Harbor had always assumed Miranda surrounded herself.

Eric grinned to himself. It was nothing like anyone thought it was. And that, he decided, was the strangest thing about the cabin. You couldn't tell from the outside what was happening on the inside. In some ways, the cabin was just like himself.

He looked up.

The four triangular panels of the peaked ceiling were each painted a different color, and all of them were covered with strange designs that time had faded until they were nearly invisible.

"What is it?" he asked. "Did she ever tell you what they mean?"

"It's astrology," Cassie explained. "She told me this house is special because it's in tune with everything around it." She hesitated a moment, but when Eric said nothing, she went on. "She told me it's a magical place."

Eric's eyes avoided hers, but when he spoke, she heard no trace of mockery in his voice. "Did you believe her?" he asked.

"I—I don't know," Cassie replied. "I'm not even sure what she meant. But I know she believed it."

"But didn't she tell you?" Eric asked, his tone more insistent now. "She must have said something else."

"She did," Cassie said, sinking down onto one of the chairs at the table. Eric was looking at her, and she searched his eyes but was sure she saw nothing in them except curiosity. He wasn't looking at her the way the rest of the kids had.

She decided she could trust him.

"She said I was special," she told him. "She said she was giving me a gift and that I could . . . well, that I could do things. And she said I shouldn't let people hurt me."

Eric's heart beat faster. "You mean, like Mr. Simms hurt us," he said.

Cassie thought a moment. "I—I guess so," she said finally.

Eric dropped onto the chair opposite her and picked up Sumi, who was anxiously pacing the floor beneath the table. "But what can you do?" he asked.

"I don't know," Cassie breathed. "But I'm going to try to find out." She closed her eyes and her lips began to move, though no sound emerged from her throat.

Eric watched her as the seconds slowly stretched into minutes. Silently, fixing his gaze on her in fascination, he watched until he saw Sumi slide out from under his caressing fingers and off his lap.

A moment later the cat slipped out the door.

Harold Simms lounged against the wall of the locker room until the last of the boys had dressed and left, then went into the little office he shared with the other coaches and closed the door.

Still seething with anger at what Cassie Winslow had said to him earlier that afternoon, he finally picked up the sheaf of paper on which she'd neatly laid out the two days of homework that should have taken her at least two hours to complete.

All of it was done perfectly.

Obviously, he decided, she must have cheated. Even if she'd spent the hour of her study hall working on it, she shouldn't have been able to finish the assignments so quickly. He concluded that she'd just done today's assignment, and Eric Cavanaugh had given her the answers to yesterday's. Smiling to himself, he marked both papers with an F, and added an admonition that cheating would not be tolerated in his class. And just let her try to argue, he thought to himself. She's in big enough trouble already, and if she starts back-talking, I'll have her suspended. In fact he hoped she *would* talk back to him, and give him an acceptable excuse to punish her for the humiliation she'd caused him. He could still hear the laughter from the baseball team, still see them looking at him with mocking eyes.

It wasn't that they cared about Cassie Winslow—they were just mad at him for what he'd done to Eric Cavanaugh. But he'd been right in throwing Eric off the team—the kid had always been everybody's favorite, and he'd been waiting a long time to knock him off his pedestal. Simms's only regret was that he wouldn't be there to see what happened to Eric when Ed Cavanaugh found out his son had been dropped from the baseball team. Eric would be lucky to come out of that one with all his teeth intact.

Simms snapped out of his reverie. He had an uncanny feeling that he was no longer alone in the building. He glanced around, half expecting to see someone else at the other desk, but there was no one. Frowning, he left his chair and went to the door. Opening it, he gazed out into the empty locker room and the showers at the far end.

"Hello?" he called. "Anybody in here?"

His voice echoed hollowly off the concrete walls of the gym. Frowning, he reclosed the door and returned to the desk, intending to pack his briefcase before leaving for the day.

His back was still to the door when he heard it slowly creak open.

He froze, his heart pounding, then turned.

Crouched in the doorway, its tail twitching spasmodically, was a gray cat.

Simms frowned. He hated cats—had hated them as long as he could remember. Tentatively he took a step forward.

But instead of backing away, the cat rose to its feet, its back arching as its fur stood up. It bared its teeth, and a hiss emerged from its throat.

"What the hell?" Simms muttered. He took another step forward, and drew his right foot back to kick the cat. But before he could swing his leg forward, the cat leaped at him, all four of its legs outstretched, its claws extended.

Simms screamed as the animal hit his chest and its claws slashed through his T-shirt and into his skin. He lurched backward, grabbing at the cat, but it seemed to slip through his grip. A moment later he felt a burning pain as its claws slashed across his face. He raised his right arm to try to knock the animal away, but before the blow struck, he lost his balance, falling backward over his desk and rolling off onto the floor on the other side.

Sprawled on his back, he looked up to see the cat poised over him, hissing furiously. Before it could launch its next attack, Simms struggled to his feet and hurled himself away, crashing into the bare concrete wall of the office. Swearing, he turned to see the cat leaping toward him.

The door.

He had to get to the door, had to get out.

He whirled, but the door slammed shut as the cat struck his back. Simms screamed with pain as he smashed into the door then sank to his knees. He felt the cat's teeth sink into the flesh on the back of his neck, felt blood begin to ooze out of the open wound.

Terrified now, he threw himself to the floor and rolled, trying to crush the animal beneath his own weight. But no matter where he turned, the cat seemed to be there, its fury growing constantly. Its claws slashed at his face, and its teeth tore pieces of flesh from his arms and torso.

His screams grew louder, and he staggered to his feet once more, but there was no escaping the torture. Everywhere he turned the beast was there first, and over and over he felt its claws and fangs slashing into his flesh. Finally, whimpering, he wedged himself into the kneehole under his desk and wrapped his arms around his bleeding head. And then, at last, the attack ended and a silence fell over the room.

It was broken by the sound of soft laughter, and as Harold Simms sank slowly into unconsciousness, he thought he recognized the laughing voice.

It sounded like Cassie Winslow's voice, mocking him.

Half an hour later the door opened once more, and Jake Palmer, who had been the janitor at False Harbor's high school for forty years, stepped inside. He set his mop and bucket down, then glanced around the room.

"Holy Jesus," he whispered softly to himself "What the hell they been doing in here today?" Everywhere he looked, the walls were stained with red smears, and the floor looked as if a wild animal, mortally wounded, had spent its last moments thrashing around in a violent search for some unseen enemy. As Jake's mind tried to accept what his eyes were seeing, he heard a low moaning sound from a few feet away. Slowly, carefully, he made his way around to the other side of the room, then bent over to look under the desk.

Staring back at him, Jack saw the pale visage of Harold Simms, his skin torn away, his flesh oozing blood.

"It was her," he heard Simms moan. "It was that crazy girl. She . . . she tried to kill me." Then Simms's eyes closed as he slid into unconsciousness for a second time.

In the cabin Cassie's eyes blinked open and she saw Eric watching her intently. "What—what happened?" she asked.

Eric shook his head. "Nothing. You were just sitting there, and your lips were moving, and then—well, then you started laughing."

Cassie cocked her head thoughtfully. She'd been thinking about Mr. Simms, and then she had drifted off, as if in a dream. But what had happened in the dream?

She couldn't remember.

Frowning, she looked around.

Something was different. Then she realized what it was.

The cat was gone.

Her eyes flicked back to Eric. "What happened to Sumi?" she asked.

Eric was silent for a moment, then shrugged. "Who knows?" he said. "He was on my lap, and then he just sort of took off."

Then he grinned. "Maybe he went after Simms," he suggested. "Maybe you sicked him on him."

Thirteen

G ene Templeton left Memorial High by the side door, fishing in his pocket for his car keys. Only the day after the funeral, and already it had started. Templeton was pretty sure he was on a wild-goose chase, for the story he'd heard at the school made no sense at all. But still, he had to check it out, he thought, as the squad car cruised slowly through the village toward the Winslows' house.

He got out of the car and approached the house, sighing as he pressed the doorbell. A moment later the door opened. Rosemary Winslow stared at him apprehensively.

"What is it?" she asked. "It's not something else about Miranda, is it? I thought we were all through with that."

Templeton held up his hands in a reassuring gesture. "Nothing to do with Miranda at all, Rosemary. It's . . . well, uh, it's something else. I wonder if I might come inside?"

Relief apparent in her eyes, Rosemary stepped back and held the door open. As Templeton stepped into the foyer, Jennifer Winslow came crashing down the stairs.

"Hi, Mr. Templeton!" she said, grinning up at him with her hand held out expectantly. Grinning back at her, Templeton fished in his jacket pocket and pulled out one of the jawbreakers he habitually carried there, insisting to anyone who asked that they were only for bribing children, that he never ate them himself. It was a lie, but everyone knew it, so it didn't matter.

"Hi, yourself," Templeton replied, holding the jawbreaker just out of Jennifer's reach. "You being a good girl? Haven't tried to rob the bank this week?"

"No," Jennifer shrieked. "Can I have it? Please?"

Templeton glanced at Rosemary, who nodded, then gave the candy to Jennifer, who immediately stuffed it into her mouth, her right cheek bulging grotesquely. "Now run along," he said. "I have to talk to your mom about something."

"Can't I listen?" Jen begged, her words garbled by the mass in her mouth.

"No, you can't," Rosemary told her.

Faced with the unanimous decision of two adults, Jennifer retreated back up the stairs. When she was gone, Rosemary led Templeton toward the kitchen.

"I have a little pie, but I'm afraid that's all," she apologized. She poured them each a cup of coffee and pulled the last slice of last night's apple pie out of the refrigerator before sitting down to face Templeton, her eyes still worried. "Now, what's going on?"

Templeton's expression turned serious, and he shook his head. "I'm not really sure. But I'm hoping maybe I can nip this one in the bud real quick. Do you happen to know where Cassie's been this afternoon?"

The worry cleared from Rosemary's face. "That's easy," she said. "She's with Eric. They're right here, upstairs in Cassie's room."

Templeton's brows rose a fraction of an inch. "Cassie's room?" he repeated, and Rosemary chuckled.

"Times have changed, Gene. All the kids have their friends in their rooms now, boys and girls both. It's not like when you were young. Or me, either, for that matter."

"Thanks for that, at least," Templeton grumped. "So, how long have they been there?"

Rosemary shrugged. "All afternoon, as far as I know."

The relief Templeton had been momentarily feeling vanished. "As far as you know?"

"Well, I've only been home half an hour. I did a little shopping after I closed the store, but they were here when I got home. Now, would you mind telling me what this is all about?"

Sparing her as many of the details as he could, Templeton described the scene he'd found in the high school gym office an hour before. "And what's happened," he finished, "is that just before Simms passed out, he told Jake Palmer that 'the crazy girl did it.'"

Rosemary gasped, and her face paled. "He . . . what?"

"It's not quite as bad as it sounds," Templeton added. "And Jake said he didn't actually name Cassie. But, well . . ." He floundered for a moment, then fell into an embarrassed silence.

"There's only one girl in town that they're calling crazy," Rosemary finished for him, her voice cold. "Is that it, Gene?"

Templeton nodded. "Rosemary, I'm sorry. I know how all this sounds, but I still have to do my job. And anyway, it might not be so bad—he didn't actually name her, and nobody saw Cassie around the school at all. In fact a couple of the kids saw her leave, and saw Eric catching up with her. After that, no one saw either one of them at the school again. So if I can place Cassie somewhere else, we can put an end to this right now.''

"Then let's do it," Rosemary said. "The last thing we need right now are more rumors flying around." She went out into the hall and called up the stairs. A minute later Eric and Cassie appeared at the kitchen door. Recognizing Templeton, both their expressions turned worried.

"What's wrong?" Cassie asked.

Rosemary started to speak, but Gene Templeton held up a hand to stop her. "You kids mind telling me where you've been all afternoon?" he asked.

Eric and Cassie glanced at each other, then Eric shrugged helplessly. "We've been here for about an hour, I guess," he said.

"An hour," Templeton repeated. Whatever had happened to Simms, it had happened more than an hour ago. "What about before that?" Eric's eyes suddenly took on a wary cast, and he said nothing. Instead he glanced at Cassie, and Templeton's stomach knotted as he realized that maybe, after all, there was some truth to Simms's disjointed words. When Cassie finally spoke, the nervousness in her voice only tightened the knot.

"We—we were out in the marsh," she said. "I was showing Eric Miranda's house."

Templeton glanced at Rosemary, who seemed to be as surprised at the words as he was. "All right," he said carefully. "Do you mind telling me why you went out there?"

Cassie's eyes darkened. "I already told you," she said. "I was showing Miranda's house to Eric. Why shouldn't I? Miranda was my friend. I can go there if I want to."

"Whoa," Templeton protested, holding up his hands in an exaggerated gesture of defense. "Slow down. I didn't say you had no right to go there. I just wondered if there was any special reason why you went."

Cassie was silent for a moment, then nodded. "We were mad," she said. "Mr. Simms kicked Eric off the baseball team this afternoon."

Rosemary gasped, but Templeton managed not to react to the words at all. Suddenly everything made even less sense than it had before, for Cassie had just blandly confessed to a motive. "Mind telling me about that?" he asked Eric, watching the boy carefully. But as Eric told him the story, Templeton could see nothing in his manner that seemed anything other than completely spontaneous.

"Simms is weird sometimes," Eric finished. "But I'll go talk to Mrs. Ambler tomorrow, and she'll straighten it out. But what's happening, anyway?"

His eyes still fixed on the two teenagers, Templeton told them what had happened at the school that afternoon. "Simms is in the hospital. And I'm here because he said something that might have meant he thought Cassie attacked him. From what I saw, it looked like whoever did it must have used a knife." He saw Cassie and Eric glance at each other, and there was something in that exchange of looks that bothered him. It was more than surprise—there was something else there, something he couldn't quite put his finger on. But what? "And you two say you were down in the marsh and then here all afternoon, right?"

Cassie nodded. "We were."

"By yourselves," Templeton pointed out.

Cassie hesitated, then shook her head. "Jennifer saw us in the marsh," she said. "Ask her."

Rosemary hesitated, then went to the bottom of the stairs and called Jennifer. A moment later the little girl came running down the stairs and followed her mother into the kitchen.

"But how do you know they were in Miranda's house all the time?" Gene Templeton asked five minutes later, after Jennifer had confirmed what Cassie and Eric had told him.

Jennifer blushed, and stared shamefaced at the floor. "I was watching," she finally admitted, her voice tiny. "All the time they were in there, I was playing on the swing in the park, and I kept watching to see if anything was going to happen. But nothing did. They just went in, and after a while they came out." Her eyes went fearfully to Cassie. "I'm sorry," she said. "But I wasn't really spying on you. I just wanted to see what you were doing."

"It's okay, Jen," Cassie told her, a little smile playing around her lips. "And it's okay for you to tell them what we were doing too."

Jennifer's eyes shifted to appeal to her mother. "They weren't doing anything," she said. "They just came over here and went up to Cassie's room and started listening to the radio."

The tension drained out of Rosemary, and she turned to the police chief "Well, at least we know that whatever happened to Harold Simms, Cassie and Eric weren't involved."

Gene Templeton nodded absently, but his eyes were still watching Cassie and Eric. He was certain there was something they were holding back. "Miranda's house," he said finally. "What were you doing in there?"

Once again that strange look passed between the two teenagers, and for a moment Templeton thought Eric was going to speak. But before he could utter the first word, Cassie rushed in.

"We were talking about Mr. Simms," she said, her eyes meeting Templeton's. And though her eyes were clear—as if she had nothing to hide—there was a challenge in them. "We were talking about what a creep he is, and wishing something would happen to him. That's weird, isn't it? I mean, that while we were wishing it, something really did happen to him?"

"Cassie!" Rosemary exclaimed.

"Well, why should I lie about it?" Cassie asked. "It's not like we did anything to him. And I'm not sorry about what happened to Mr. Simms either. He was awful to me, and what he did to Eric wasn't fair at all. If someone beat him up, I'm not going to claim I'm sorry!"

Before anyone could say anything else, she turned and fled from the kitchen. Rosemary glanced at Templeton and started to go after her, when the policeman shook his head. "Let her go," he said gently. "She must be sick of me asking her questions all the time, and I think it's pretty obvious she didn't have anything to do with Simms." He unfolded himself from the chair and closed his notebook. "You have anything else to say, Eric?" he asked.

Eric shook his head.

"Okay." He let himself out the back door and was just about to start down the driveway when a sudden movement caught his eye. Turning, he saw a gray cat slip through the fence between the Winslows' yard and the cemetery next to the church. It dashed across the lawn and slithered up into a large oak tree. When it reached the lowest branch, it paused, then turned to glare balefully at Templeton. Its mouth yawned open and a menacing hiss boiled out of its throat. Then, in a flash, it leaped up through the branches of the tree and disappeared through an open window on the second floor.

"Sumi?" he heard Cassie's voice asking anxiously. "Did you really do it? Did you do what I wanted you to?"

His brow creased in thought, Templeton continued down the driveway.

"Upstairs," Ed Cavanaugh growled. He'd watched Eric come out of the Winslows' house a few minutes after the police chief had left, and by the time the boy had crossed the common driveway and come through the back door, Ed had worked himself into a fury. It hadn't taken him long to get the whole story out of his son. As he listened, his rage had grown. Now his eyes fixed malevolently on Eric. "Move!" he snapped when Eric failed to react to his command.

"Ed, don't," Laura protested. Ed said nothing, but his hand flashed out, striking Laura's face with enough force to knock her back into her chair. "Now!" he bellowed, then reached out and grabbed Eric by his shirt collar, dragging him out of the kitchen. As Laura sat trembling in the chair, she heard her husband manhandling their son up the stairs. *Why?* she thought bitterly. *Why did he ever think he wanted a son in the first place?*

Eric started to go into his own room, but Ed grabbed his wrist, twisted his arm up behind his back, and shoved him into the little room that would have been a guest room had anyone ever come to visit the Cavanaughs.

Eric's heart sank, for when his father took him in here, it meant things were really going to be bad. "Strip!" his father commanded, already pulling his belt out of the loops in his pants.

Eric's eyes widened. "No," he whimpered. "Come on, Dad—I didn't do anything—"

"You disobeyed me, and you got yourself kicked off the team," Ed rasped. "I don't call that nothing." He reached out with his free hand, grasped Eric's shirt, and ripped it off. Eric cringed, but knowing there was no escape, quickly removed his pants and underwear, then stretched out on the bed.

The belt whistled in the air before it lashed across Eric's naked buttocks, but Eric knew better than to scream out with pain. When his father was like this, the sounds of his agony only seemed to make it worse. He clenched his teeth, his hands gripping the posts at the head of the bed.

Again the leather strap whistled in the air and struck.

With each lash, Eric's rage increased.

"Well, it fits with what I've found," Dr. Paul Samuels commented, after listening to everything Gene Templeton had to say. "As far as I can tell, he wasn't attacked by any kind of weapon at all."

Charlotte Ambler looked at the doctor in surprise. She'd followed the ambulance over from the school, then waited impatiently while Simms was being examined, anxious to know exactly what had transpired in the gymnasium. "No weapon?" she repeated, her voice taking on the acerbic quality she usually reserved for her students, forgetting that it had been twelve years since Paul Samuels had been one of them. "For heaven's sake, Paul, I saw Harold myself!"

"And something happened to him," Samuels agreed. "But it doesn't look to me like he was attacked by anybody, at least not with a knife."

"You want to expand on that?" Gene asked, glancing at the clock. It was now thirty minutes past dinner time. He sighed silently and turned his attention back to the doctor.

"A knife makes a clean cut," Samuels explained. "If you slash someone with a knife, you're going to stab them deep, or lay them open, but the edges of the cuts are going to be clean. And there won't be any pattern. But that's not the way it is with Harold Simms. It looks to me as though he was attacked by some kind of animal. At least at first."

The memory of the hissing animal in the tree outside Cassie's room came into Templeton's mind. "Could it have been a cat?" he asked.

Samuels thought a moment, then nodded. "Could be. I certainly wouldn't rule it out."

"But Harold was very certain that he heard someone laughing," Charlotte Ambler reminded them.

"Who simply doesn't seem to have been there," Templeton observed wearily. "I'm sorry, Charlotte, but whatever happened, I can't see how Cassie could have had anything to do with it. And Simms could have been wrong."

Charlotte turned impatiently to the doctor. "Is that true?"

Samuels shrugged noncommittally. "It's possible. It's even possible that he did most of the damage to himself."

"Did it to himself?" Charlotte repeated indignantly. "What on earth are you saying?"

"Just that," Samuels replied. "I think it's pretty clear what happened, particularly after what the chief's told us. Simms had just thrown Eric off the team, and then Cassie managed to humiliate him in front of the kids. And you yourself have already told me that Simms was—what? Highstrung? Weren't those the words you used?"

Charlotte's eyes narrowed. "He had some problems, yes—"

"Well, if you ask me, he just snapped," Samuels went on. "There's no way of saying exactly what happened, and some of the marks were certainly inflicted by some kind of animal. But I don't think there was anyone in that office with him. I think that something set him off and he just came apart in there. He literally started bouncing off the walls. I don't doubt that he thought he was being attacked by Cassie. In fact I wouldn't be surprised if he claimed he actually saw her. But I'd be just as willing to bet that it was an hallucination."

"But the wounds . . ." Charlotte pressed.

"Except for the deepest scratches and bite marks, the wounds are all consistent with someone striking hard against concrete block walls. The bruises, the abrasions, everything. There isn't much that couldn't have been self-inflicted."

Templeton regarded the doctor thoughtfully, his fingers absently rubbing at the stubble on his chin. "What you're saying is that he just went nuts?"

Samuels's brows arched. " 'Just went nuts' isn't precisely the terminology I would use, no. I'd be more inclined to label it a psychotic episode."

"Is there a difference?" Templeton drawled, and Samuels, despite the circumstances, couldn't quite suppress a chuckle.

"In some cases, not really," he admitted. "But with Simms, it's too early to tell. 'Just went nuts,' as you put it, always seems to me to imply a permanent condition. A psychotic episode can be quite a temporary thing."

"How temporary?" Templeton asked.

"A few minutes. An hour. A day. Who knows?" Now he turned once more to Charlotte Ambler. "What can you tell me about Simms's condition the last few days?"

Charlotte hesitated, then sighed. "Well, actually, I've been worried about Harold. He's seemed to be wound up about a lot of things lately, and I know he's been taking it out on some of his classes. It hasn't been too serious, and so far no one has complained. But it *has* been there. I'd hoped he'd make it through the year and then get a good rest. But I've also had some reservations about renewing his contract. Frankly, I'm not sure he's cut out to teach. He . . . well, I've always had the feeling that deep down, he just doesn't like the students."

"And if he came apart, he'd be likely to blame it on one of the kids?" Samuels suggested.

Charlotte's lips tightened. "I'm afraid I find that a little hard to believe." She paused and met the doctor's eyes. "May I talk to him again? Is he conscious?"

Samuels nodded. All three of them stood up and left the doctor's office, walking down the hall to the last of the six rooms which were all the False Harbor hospital required. Inside the room, strapped to a bed, they found Harold Simms.

Charlotte moved to the bedside and looked down at the math teacher's face. The blood had been washed away, and now she could see that the lacerations were not as serious as they'd first appeared. His cheeks were scratched, and on Simms's forehead a large round black and blue spot marked the point at which something had struck his forehead.

But what? The wall? Or even, perhaps, the underside of the desk beneath which the teacher had been found?

Simms's eyes blinked open and for a moment he seemed to stare unseeingly at the ceiling. Then his gaze flickered around the room, finally focusing on Charlotte Ambler's face. Then he began struggling against the restraints that held his arms, legs, and torso immobile, meanwhile mumbling broken fragments of words. Templeton listened closely, but nothing the man said made any sense. It was nothing more than a disconnected stream of syllables.

Simms's voice rose to a scream and the words became garbled

beyond recognition. He was thrashing on the bed now, straining against the heavy leather straps, his hands clenching into fists so tight that his knuckles turned white and the palms began to bleed where his fingernails pierced his own skin.

"Jesus Christ, Doc," Gene Templeton whispered. "Can't you do something?"

His words were unnecessary. Samuels had already picked up a syringe from a table that lay near the door, filled it, and was in the process of plunging it into Simms's arm. After a few seconds the drug began to take hold, and slowly Simms began to relax.

"What are you going to do?" Charlotte Ambler finally asked, her voice bleak.

"We're moving him tomorrow," Samuels replied. "He'll be taken up to the state hospital near Eastbury."

Templeton shook his head sadly and turned away. "Hope they bring a straitjacket," he muttered softly as he started out the door. "Looks to me like that guy's going to need one."

And yet, as he left the hospital he still couldn't get Cassie's words out of his mind.

"Sumi? Did you really do it? Did you do what I wanted you to?"

Fourteen

"I don't be*lieve* it!" Teri Bennett squealed excitedly. "You really *saw* it?"

Kevin Smythe nodded, glancing at his watch out of the corner of his eye to make sure there was time to tell the story once more. So far he'd had to repeat it twice, but each time new arrivals appeared on the front steps of the school, and they wanted to hear it too. Feigning boredom with the repetition, he began again. "I was just coming around the corner from Pine Street, and there was an ambulance right there in front of the entrance on Hartford. I almost just went on by, cause at first I didn't think anything was happening. But then the doors opened and they brought him out. Man, it was weird—they had him all strapped down, and there was one of those bottles with a rubber hose on it, and everything! Then they stuck him in the back of the ambulance and the lights started flashing and they took off!"

"But where are they taking him?" Allayne Garvey demanded. "I mean, are they really going to lock him up?"

Kevin shrugged with exaggerated casualness. "Search me," he said, and then his voice dropped to a level that implied he was about to divulge a secret. "But my dad said he went absolutely spacey after it happened—"

"After what happened?" Jeff Maynard asked, trotting up the stairs to join the group on the top step. "What's going on?"

Kevin and the two girls stared at Jeff in disbelief "You mean you didn't hear?" Kevin asked. "Cassie Winslow hung around after school yesterday and tried to kill Mr. Simms."

Jeff's mouth dropped open. "Are you nuts?" he demanded. "She left right after Simms kicked Eric off the team. And—" He suddenly fell silent, staring at the street. The eyes of the others followed his gaze, and they, too, stopped talking.

Walking along the sidewalk, their heads close together, as if they were whispering to each other, were Eric Cavanaugh and Cassie Winslow. By the time they got to the foot of the steps, not a sound was to be heard from any of the thirty or so students gathered in front of the school, all of whom were now staring at the latest arrivals.

Cassie glanced up and knew immediately what had happened. But for Eric it seemed to take a moment.

"Hey!" he called to Jeff Maynard. "What's going on?"

Jeff looked back at him uncertainly, then his eyes shifted to Kevin Smythe. It was Kevin who finally spoke.

"What are you doing with *her?*" he asked, the belligerence in his voice tempered by nervousness. To him Cassie Winslow suddenly looked dangerous.

Eric frowned. "What are you talking about? Why shouldn't I be with Cassie?" His gaze shifted to Teri and Allayne, but both of them were now looking somewhere else. And then he, too, understood. "Hey," he said, "she didn't do anything to Simms. I was with her, and we were out at the marsh at—" He stopped himself as he saw his friends exchange doubtful looks.

Lisa Chamber—who had been silent until now, trying to sort out the truth from all the strange things she'd heard last night and this morning—suddenly made up her mind. She glared down at Eric. "You were in Miranda's house, weren't you?" she accused. "What were you doing there? Helping Cassie figure out how to do it? Or did you help her do it yourself?"

Eric's jaw tightened. "Do it?" he demanded. "Do what? You guys don't think she did anything to Simms, do you? And even if she did, so what? Every one of you hated his guts! We all did!" No one said anything as Eric slowly searched the faces of the people who only yesterday had been his friends. Only Jeff Maynard seemed to be uncertain. "Jeff? You don't think Cassie and I did anything, do you?"

Jeff felt like a trapped animal, caught between his best friend and practically everyone else he knew. "I—I don't know," he stammered. "I just got here. Teri says—"

"What does she know?" Cassie demanded, her eyes flashing with anger. "Were you there? Did you see what happened to Mr. Simms? Maybe *she* did it!"

Teri's face turned scarlet with indignation. "Don't you try to blame me, Cassie Winslow!" she shouted. "All I know is what my mother told me, and she says you did it and they ought to lock you up! So don't try to blame it on me!" Bursting into tears, she wheeled around and rushed into the building, Allayne and Lisa hurrying after her.

Eric, now as angry as Cassie, started up the steps, his hands clenching into fists. But then he abruptly changed his mind, and took Cassie's hand in his own. "Let's just go," he said, his voice so quiet no one but she could hear him. "It doesn't matter what they thought about Simms. They just want to blame you."

They were already a block away when the school P.A. system came to life and an announcement that the first class of the day would be replaced by an assembly was broadcast through the halls and out over the grounds.

Neither Eric nor Cassie heard it.

Charlotte Ambler stood behind the podium atop the choir platform hastily assembled fifteen minutes earlier, and looked out at the assembled students of Memorial High. Ordinarily they tumbled happily into the auditorium, laughing and chattering among themselves, looking forward to an assembly—any assembly—as a release from an hour of classes. But today it was different. They were still chattering, but their voices were subdued, and as they huddled together in small groups, they seemed to glance furtively around them, as if sensing that they were talking about something none of them had any information about and that they shouldn't be talking about at all. Charlotte Ambler was about to give them the information they wanted, but she had a sinking feeling that it might already be too late, for nowhere in the sea of faces could she spot either Eric Cavanaugh or Cassie Winslow.

Rapping sharply on the podium with a gavel, she waited for the hubbub to die down, then cleared her throat.

"I'm sure most of you are aware of the unfortunate incident of yesterday afternoon," she began, determined to choose her words as carefully as possible. If she couldn't defuse the situation now— and quell the rumors that had already begun—there was a distinct possibility that the rest of the term would be a complete loss. If, indeed, it wasn't too late already. "One of our teachers," she went on, "Mr. Simms, has suffered a form of illness that is not at all uncommon in our day and age. Mr. Simms has been under a great deal of pressure—"

"And maybe a few knives?" someone yelled from the back of the room.

There was a gasp, followed by dead silence, and Charlotte Ambler slowly removed her glasses, letting them drop down to her breast. Abandoning the short speech she'd written a few minutes before, she stepped around the podium and moved forward to the edge of the platform. When she spoke again, her voice needed no amplification from the microphone.

"I shall not ask who said that," she said, her words echoing coldly through the room, "because if I found out, that person would no longer be a part of this high school." She paused for a split second, then went on. "What has happened is this: Mr. Simms suffered a sort of mental breakdown in the gymnasium yesterday afternoon, and it caused him to inflict a certain amount of harm upon himself. He is being taken to a hospital in Eastbury, where he will be treated for an indefinite period. For the remainder of this term his coaching duties will he handled by Mr. Johnson, and his classes by myself!" She paused, as if waiting for any of the students to dare make comment on her selection of substitutes for the absent teacher. When there was no response, she continued. "There may be certain scheduling changes, and you will be notified of those in due course. As for the rumors that have been circulating this morning, there is no evidence that Mr. Simms was attacked by anyone, or that there were any weapons involved. That is all. You may return to your homerooms."

She stepped off the platform and immediately disappeared out the side door of the auditorium, unwilling to allow even a moment for any of the students to ask a question she might not be prepared to answer.

There was a moment of silence before the realization that the assembly was over sank in. Then, slowly, the students got to their feet and began drifting toward the doors. But everywhere there was a soft buzz of whispered conversation as the teenagers tried to decipher the truth of what had happened in the gymnasium the day before.

By the time the auditorium had emptied, a consensus had been reached, and though Charlotte Ambler wasn't there to hear it, it would not have surprised her.

Lisa Chambers summed it up as she left the auditorium, the center of a group that only a few days before had always pivoted around Eric.

"I don't care what anybody says," Lisa announced. "I could tell Cassie Winslow was weird the first time I saw her. If Mr. Simms said she tried to kill him, I believe it. And if you ask me, Eric better stay away from her before she does something to him too."

"We can't just ignore it, Keith," Rosemary insisted. "If you keep trying to bury your head in the sand, things are just going to get worse and worse!"

"Bury my head?" Keith demanded. He glanced at the clock above the kitchen sink. It was nearly nine. He should have been down at the marina an hour ago, but Rosemary seemed determined to keep arguing with him until he admitted that there was something wrong with Cassie. "I'm not burying my head in any sand, and I'm getting a little tired of you saying I am. If Gene thought there were anything to Harold Simms's story, don't you think he'd have been back here by now?" His strong jaw set in an expression of grim determination. "What the hell do you want? Cassie and Eric say they were out at Miranda's house, and Jennifer backs them up. Even if Eric and Cassie were lying—which I don't believe—why would Jen lie?"

Rosemary shook her head doggedly, determined that this time she wouldn't be swayed by Keith's stubbornness. "You weren't here," she insisted. "If you'd heard her, you'd be worried too! I know you would!"

Keith took a final swallow of his coffee, then drained the rest into the sink. "All right, so she said she wished something would happen to Simms. Why the hell wouldn't she? He's always been a mean little wimp, and I don't blame her for wishing him the worst." He set the cup on the drainboard, placing it with the overly careful precision that was a certain clue to his growing impatience. "If he'd treated me the way he did the kids, I'd want to kill him too." He turned to face Rosemary once more, and his voice took on a patronizing tone that made her simmer with anger. "But wanting to do something and actually doing it are two different things. If Templeton accepted her story, I don't see why you can't." The patronizing tone gave way to a sarcastic edge. "Don't you think I've noticed how you're always watching her, as if you're just waiting to catch her in a lie, or make a mistake? My God, Rosemary, even when she does something nice you've acted like she's trying to get something for herself!"

"That's not true!" Rosemary breathed, her heart pounding with indignation. And yet, deep inside, she knew that there was some truth to Keith's words.

All those strange feelings she'd had about Cassie, which she'd tried to keep to herself. Apparently she hadn't been successful.

"All right," she admitted, sagging into one of the kitchen chairs. "I have been suspicious. There's just something about her, Keith. I keep getting the feeling that she's hiding something from us."

"That's ridiculous," Keith snapped. "She's a perfectly normal fifteen-year-old, and when she came here we were perfect strangers to her. Even me, when you get down to it. What did you expect? That she'd open up to us the first minute she was here?"

Rosemary studied Keith beseechingly, trying to find the love that she'd always seen in his eyes. Right now there was none. Only a coldness that made her want to shiver. "But after all that's happened . . ." she began again, struggling to keep her voice steady.

"Nothing's happened, Rosemary," Keith broke in. He was wiping the cup with a dish towel, then abruptly slammed it down on the counter with such force that it shattered. Keith ignored the fragments of broken china. "All you're doing is giving in to a whole lot of unfounded gossip."

It was too much, and Rosemary's temper suddenly snapped. "I don't believe it!" she said, angrily snatching up the pieces of the smashed cup, punctuating her words by hurling them into the trash basket in the corner. "Is Miranda being dead nothing but unfounded gossip? What about Harold Simms? Is what happened to him nothing but unfounded gossip too? Isn't he really in the hospital at all, Keith?"

"You know that's not what I meant," Keith replied, his voice icy. "Of course those things happened. What I'm telling you—and what seems quite obvious to me—is that Cassie didn't have anything to do with them!"

"Then why was she out there?" Rosemary flared. "Why is it that when Miranda died, and when Harold Simms was attacked, Cassie was out there in the marsh, doing . . . God only knows what?"

A heavy silence fell over the kitchen as Keith and Rosemary faced each other. Finally Keith shook his head. His anger seemed to dissipate visibly, to be replaced by a melancholy sadness. "Listen to us," he whispered. "Will you just listen to us? What are you trying to say? That Cassie's some kind of witch?"

"Oh, for God's sake," Rosemary wailed. "Of course not!"

But it was too late. Snatching his coat from the hook by the door, Keith slammed out the back door. A second later Rosemary heard the sound of his car starting, and then he was gone. But when she was alone, it wasn't Keith's words that stuck in her mind, it was her own.

What *had* Cassie been doing in the marsh? But it wasn't the marsh. It was the cabin in the marsh, the run-down shack that had stood out there, housing generation after generation of Sikes women, apparently each of them as strange as the one who had come before.

Coming to a quick decision, Rosemary abandoned the remains of the morning's breakfast and put on her own jacket. Locking the back door behind her, she hurried down the driveway then cut across the lawn toward Cambridge Street, at the foot of which lay the park, and beyond it, the marsh surrounding Miranda Sikes's cabin. It was time she herself had a look at the place that seemed to have such a fascination for her stepdaughter.

Just as she turned the corner onto Cambridge Street, a gray shadow slipped out the open window of Cassie's room and dropped nimbly through the tree to the ground.

Crouching low, Sumi began stalking after Rosemary.

Laura Cavanaugh glanced at the clock over the kitchen sink and wondered if she should go upstairs and waken Ed. She didn't want to, yet at the same time she was almost afraid not to. But it didn't matter, really—whatever she did would be wrong. If she woke him, he'd be mad at her for not letting him sleep, and if she didn't wake him, he'd be furious at her for letting him oversleep. She decided to compromise—ten more minutes wouldn't matter anyway, and it was nice to have the house quiet, at least for a little while. Except that at times like this morning, even the quiet had a tension to it, like the eye of a hurricane; a moment of calm, but with storm clouds pressing in from every direction.

She filled Ed's thermos with coffee, then clamped it into the top of his lunch pail. There were already three sandwiches and an apple in the pail. After hesitating a moment, she added a can of beer—Ed would take beer on the boat with him anyway, and if she left it out of his pail, he would only accuse her of implying that he drank too much. She was just closing the lunch bucket when she heard him lumbering down the stairs. Then he was in the kitchen, smiling at her.

I don't believe it, she thought. Last night he whipped Eric and slapped me around the bedroom, and this morning he acts as though nothing happened.

"What's for breakfast, doll face?" he asked, sliding into the breakfast nook and pulling the sports page out of the pile of newspapers Eric had left on the table.

Laura looked at him uncertainly. "I—I thought you'd just take a Danish and eat it on the boat," she said. "It's already after nine, and if you're not out by nine-thirty, the tide will be too low, won't it?''

The smile faded from Ed's face and his eyes flashed dangerously. "What the hell does the tide matter?''

Laura searched her memory for anything he might have said last night about not working today, but there was nothing. "I thought . . . I thought—''

"*I thought!*" Ed mimicked. "Jesus, Laura, can't you let me do the thinking around here? I told you last night I wasn't going out today. Can't you remember the simplest goddamned thing?'' Tossing the paper aside, he went to the refrigerator, jerked it open, and fished around on the bottom shelf for a beer. Twisting the cap off, he tossed it into the sink then tipped the bottle and drained half of it in one long swig. Wiping his lips with his forearm, he shook his head. "I'm goin' down to the high school to talk to that snotty principal about Eric. I'm gonna see to it she puts him back on the baseball team.''

Laura shuddered, remembering the last time Ed had gone to talk to Mrs. Ambler. He'd stopped off at the Whaler's Inn on the way, and by the time he'd gotten to the school, he'd been so drunk he'd barely been able to stand up. Mrs. Ambler had listened to him for only two minutes before calling up Gene Templeton and having Ed escorted out of the building. Gene had taken Ed down to the police station and put him in the town's single jail cell for the rest of the morning, then sent him home. "Maybe it would be better if—''

Ed's jaw tightened and his eyes narrowed. "Better if what?'' he demanded, his voice dropping to the snarl that was always a warning of impending violence. But it didn't matter. This time Laura was determined to try to stop her husband.

"Better if you just let everything alone for once,'' she said. "Don't you think you've done enough? Don't you think I know what you did to Eric in the guest room last night? You're sick, Ed. You don't need to go talk to Mrs. Ambler about Eric—you need to go talk to a doctor about yourself!''

Ed's eyes glowed with a manic rage, and Laura knew she'd gone too far. She started to back away, but Ed came after her, his fingers already working spasmodically. He reached out and grabbed her hair with his left hand, jerking her head back as he slapped her across the cheek with his free hand. "I'm sick?'' he demanded. "Me? Who the hell are you to be talking? Who the hell do you think keeps this family together? You think I like sacrificing my life for the likes of you? I shoulda gotten rid of you a long time ago!'' He slapped her again, then hurled her across the room. Her hip smashed into the counter and she yelped with pain, then sank to the floor, sobbing.

"It's all your fault," Ed told her, moving across the room. He drew his foot back and kicked her viciously in the ribs.

"No!" Laura screamed. "Ed, I didn't do anything—I'm sorry! I'm sorry!"

"Sorry?" Ed mocked. "You're sorry?"

"But it isn't my fault!" Laura wailed. "I've never done anything to you! I've never done—"

"Shut up!" Ed roared. *"Goddamn it, woman, will you just shut up?"*

His foot swung back once more, but this time Laura rolled away, scrambling to her feet and managing to bolt out the back door. Ed started after her, but by the time he got outside, she was already up the driveway and limping across the street. He watched her go, then shook his head in disgust.

He'd have one more beer, then head for the school. Let Laura go hide out with the people across the street—he'd deal with her tonight.

Fifteen

Charlotte Ambler wondered if she should signal Patsy Malone to call Gene Templeton, or try to handle the situation herself. But, of course, it was too late now. If she was going to call the police chief, she should have done it thirty minutes ago, when she'd first seen Ed Cavanaugh sitting in his truck, drinking from a bottle of whiskey he hadn't even tried to hide in a brown paper bag, and glowering darkly in the direction of her office. When she'd first noticed him, she'd stood at her window staring back, putting him on notice that he'd been seen. Usually that was enough, and after sulking in his truck for a few minutes, he would drive away, presumably to the Whaler's Inn, where, Charlotte knew, he would sit at the bar and brag to whoever would listen about how he'd "set that uppity Ambler woman straight on a few things." All of which was fine with her. If he wanted to puff himself up that way, it wasn't any skin off her nose. The one time she had actually called the police, Ed had bided his time through the day, then taken his rage out on his wife and son that evening. When Eric had shown up with bruises on his face the next day, Charlotte had tried to convince him that he should report what had happened to the police, but Eric had refused, insisting that nothing had happened—he'd simply tripped and fallen down the stairs that morning.

Strange, she reflected cynically to herself as she watched Ed climb out of his truck and shamble up the steps of the school, how the drunken fools like Ed Cavanaugh never trip and break their necks. She heard him lumber into the outer office, and went back to her desk. When he pushed her own door open a moment later, she was staring at him calmly and coldly. "I don't believe we have an appointment, Mr. Cavanaugh," she began, but he only sneered at her.

"I don't need an appointment where my boy is concerned," he said, advancing across the room to lean over Charlotte's desk. The reek of his breath made the principal lean back, but her eyes never left his.

"Eric's situation will be dealt with in a—"

"Don't give me that pious bullshit, lady." His eyes had narrowed to slits, and his jaw was clenched tight. "None of what's happened is his fault anyway. It's all that trashy Winslow girl. If it wasn't for her, none of this would have happened!"

Charlotte decided there was no point in arguing—Ed was far too drunk for that. "I'm sure you're right—" she began, but once more Ed cut her off, this time with his fist pounding on her desk.

"And don't you patronize me!" Ed roared. "I already took care of Eric for cutting school and getting himself dumped from the baseball team. All I want from you is your word that you'll see to it he gets back on the team! And I want you to keep him away from that girl too!"

Suddenly Charlotte Ambler had had enough. The strain of the last fifteen hours suddenly telescoped, and her temper snapped. She rose to her feet. Though her height was no match for Ed's, the fury in her eyes seemed to cut through his alcoholic haze. "Is it!" she spat. "Is that what you want? Well, let me tell you what I want! I want you to get out of my office and off my campus. I want you to stop drinking, and stop beating your wife and son! I want you to start being a decent husband and father! And then, when I get what I want, perhaps I'll be willing to listen to what you want! But until that happens, keep in mind where you are, and who you are, and who I am! Now get out of this office, and if you have anything further to say, put it in writing and send it to the school board. If you *can* write!"

Ed's face turned ashen and his fist rose up threateningly.

"Do it," Charlotte challenged him, her voice dropping, but taking on a cutting edge. "Just do it. But don't expect me to keep my mouth shut about it. You might be able to bully your family, but you can't bully me. I'll have you in front of a judge before the blood even dries. Now either get out of my office or swing that fist."

Ed stood still for a moment, his entire body trembling with rage, and for a moment Charlotte thought she'd pushed him too far. But then she realized that she didn't care. Indeed, she found herself half hoping he *would* try to slap her around. Let him think about it in jail for a while. As she watched him warily, he seemed to regain control of himself

"You can't talk to me that way," he rasped, but the menace was gone from his voice. "I know what you think of me—I know what everybody thinks of me in this crummy town. But I can take care of myself, and I can take care of my family. And ain't you or anybody else gonna stop me. So you think about that, Mrs. High-and-Mighty, 'cause if that girl gets my boy in any more trouble, I can tell you there's gonna be hell to pay!" He turned around and shambled out of the office, leaving the door open behind him. Only when the outer door had slammed shut did Patsy Malone appear nervously in her office, her face pale.

"Are you all right?" the secretary asked. "I was just about to call Gene Templeton."

"I trust," Charlotte observed dryly, "that if he'd actually hit me, you would have followed through on that impulse."

"I . . . well, I don't . . . well, of course I would," Patsy floundered, and for the first time since Harold Simms had been found in the gym the day before, Charlotte Ambler found herself chuckling.

"Well, that's nice to know." She eyed Patsy mischievously. "And can I also trust that you won't say anything about that little scene?"

"Why . . . why, of course not!"

"Good," Charlotte replied, knowing as well as Patsy did that by the end of lunch hour there wouldn't be a person at the school who hadn't heard every detail of what had just transpired. If nothing else, the story should put an end to any further discipline problems for the year. The way Patsy would tell it, it would sound as if Charlotte had actually given Ed Cavanaugh a thrashing. "Now perhaps we can get on with the day, all right?"

The secretary's head bobbed, and she quietly pulled the door closed, leaving Charlotte alone in her office. Charlotte went over to the window and saw Ed Cavanaugh's truck still sitting in front of the school, and Ed himself still glaring at her. But when she nodded to him, he started the engine, slammed the truck into gear, and careened down the street, his wheels shrieking in protest as they skidded over the pavement. Only when the truck had disappeared around the corner did Charlotte return to her desk and lower herself tiredly into her chair. She leaned back, removed her glasses, and closed her eyes, rubbing at them for a moment. In her mind Ed Cavanaugh's last words kept re-echoing.

Hell to pay.

Didn't he realize that since Cassie Winslow had come to False Harbor there had already been hell to pay?

And unless Charlotte missed her guess, it was all just beginning. Despite her words to the students that morning, and despite what Paul Samuels had told her, Charlotte Ambler was still not convinced that Cassie had nothing to do with what had happened to Harold Simms.

She recalled all too clearly that first meeting with Cassie, when she'd instinctively sensed trouble. And her first instincts, as always, were proving to be correct.

Cassie Winslow was, indeed, proving to be trouble.

"You can't just never go to school again."

"Why not?"

Eric and Cassie had been sitting on the beach, staring out over the water, saying nothing. After leaving the high school an hour ago, they'd cut over Maple Street to Cape Drive, but instead of walking along Cape until they came to the public path, Cassie had insisted they go through someone's yard. Eric thought about arguing, then realized that Cassie was right—the more quickly they put the beach and dunes between themselves and the village, the less chance there was of someone spotting them and reporting them to his father. And so they'd slipped through one of the beachhouse gates, ducked around the corner of the house itself, then scrambled down a low bank to the beach. From there they'd walked along the deserted expanse of sand, finally flopping down to watch the sea and the birds.

"Because you just can't do that," Eric argued now. He regarded Cassie carefully out of the corner of his eye. "Besides, if you don't go back to school, everyone's going to think you're afraid to."

Cassie was silent for a moment, and when she finally spoke, there was a tremor in her voice. "Maybe I *am* afraid to go back."

"Why?" Eric asked, his voice almost teasing. "You didn't do anything, did you?"

"Maybe—maybe I did," Cassie whispered. "Maybe we both did."

Eric hesitated, then shook his head. "That's stupid."

"But what about yesterday?" Cassie asked. "What I thought about really happened."

Eric reached down and scooped up a handful of sand, then let it run slowly through his fingers. "Nobody even knows what happened to old Simms. Not really. And it doesn't matter what he said—you didn't beat him up."

Cassie turned to face Eric. "But we wanted something to happen to him, and it did!"

Eric shrugged. "So what? You didn't really do anything, and it isn't your fault if old Simms cracked up."

"But what if it is?" Cassie blurted out. "Miranda said I had a gift, and what if that's what she meant? That I can make things happen just by thinking about them?"

Eric was silent, but his fist closed on the rest of the sand, squeezing it hard for a moment. Then he threw it down, stood up and started walking away.

"Eric?" Cassie called after him, scrambling to her feet. "Are you mad at me, too, now?"

Eric stopped and turned around. He stared hard at her, then said, "I don't know. I don't know what you're talking about. But, you know, Cassie, it sounds kind of crazy."

Cassie gasped, but Eric didn't seem to hear her. "And maybe you feel like you can never go back to school again, but I can. So I'm going for a walk and think things over. Okay?"

Cassie helplessly watched him walk quickly away, disappearing into the distance, his head down. She wanted to follow him, wanted to try to talk to him some more, try to explain the confusion she was feeling. But she couldn't bring herself to do it—the look in his eyes as he'd stared at her a moment before, a look that resembled pure hatred—stopped her. He didn't hate her, did he? Eric was her only friend. If he started treating her the way everyone else did—

She shuddered, and tried to close the thought out of her mind. If Eric turned against her now, she wouldn't have anyone left at all. But there was nothing she could do. Nothing at all. Turning in the opposite direction from where Eric had gone, she headed toward Cranberry Point and the marsh.

For the first time in years Rosemary found herself really looking at the marsh. How long, she wondered, had it been since she'd last gone for a walk in it?

She remembered the first time she'd seen it, soon after she'd met Keith and come to False Harbor. It had been spring, and the day had been much like this one—clear, with just a touch of crispness still lingering from the winter. The wetlands had been full of geese that day, and the air vibrant with their honkings and the quacking of ducks. It had been a beautiful sight, bursting with life, and she'd made Keith walk in it with her for hours.

But that had been ten years ago, and as time had passed, the marsh became just another familiar fixture of False Harbor, until finally she'd grown so used to it that she barely noticed it at all.

Until now.

But as she looked at it today, it seemed to have changed. A feeling of foreboding appeared to have settled over it, and where once she had sensed new life stirring within it, now she was most conscious of the stifling odor of decay, as if deep within it, somewhere below its shimmering waters, there was a rotten core threatening to bubble to the surface.

But, of course, she was wrong—nothing in the marsh had changed at all. It was her feelings toward it, for as she stood at the edge of the park, gazing out over the green expanse of grasses and quivering reeds, she realized that in the last few days she'd come to associate the marsh with the uneasy tensions that had begun to wrap themselves around her like the coils of a serpent.

And in the center of the marsh, rising like a boil on an otherwise smooth skin, was the barren hummock that supported Miranda Sikes's cabin, with its half-starved trees reaching upward like the hands of a corpse trying to claw its way out of the grave.

Stop it, Rosemary commanded herself. *Just stop it. It's only a marsh, and an empty shack. There's nothing to be frightened of at all.*

Determinedly she pushed her way through the barrier of tall weeds that separated the park from the wetlands, and found one of the soggy trails that led out into the bog itself.

She made her way slowly, for the path she had chosen was narrow and nearly overgrown with rushes and cattails. Every few yards, it seemed, the trail split off and she had to make a decision about which direction to take.

More than half the decisions appeared to be wrong, the trail petering out entirely, the grasses closing in around her, the earth giving way beneath her feet.

Twice she felt the deceptive firmness of quicksand that seemed solid when she put her weight on it, only to give way a second later, sucking at her shoe like something alive. Both times she jerked loose, her heart beating fast as panic welled up inside her. But both times she forced the panic back into its cage and backed away to find solid ground.

Several times, when she realized she'd made a mistake and turned around to retrace her steps, she saw a flash of movement out of the corner of her eye, as if something had been following her on the trail and darted off as she turned, to disappear into the reeds.

The third time it happened, she stood perfectly still, only her eyes flicking over the marsh, searching for a telltale movement that would expose the animal. But the seconds crept by, and she saw nothing. Her skin began to crawl. Though she could not see them, she knew that there were eyes on her, watching her from some hidden ambush, waiting for her.

Once again she had to force herself to go on, had to fight back the urge to retreat to the park, with its secure footing and protective groves of trees.

But the cabin was closer now, and she could see it clearly.

And she could see the hawk, perched at the very peak of the roof, stretching its wings restlessly, its head bobbing back and forth as its red eyes fixed on her.

And then, when she was only a hundred yards from the cabin, the bird rose into the air, its great white wings lifting it onto the wind then locking into position as it effortlessly soared toward her.

Rosemary stared at it, mesmerized, and in her mind's eye she saw once again the deep slashes the bird's talons had left in Lisa Chambers's arm.

The hawk passed between Cassie and the sun, and its shadow flashing over her face jerked Cassie out of her silent reverie. She glanced up to find that she had walked nearly the whole length of the beach. Only a few yards ahead the concrete cylinder of the Cranberry Point light rose up from the end of the peninsula, and for a moment Cassie thought that was what she'd seen. But then she spotted the pale white form of the hawk circling high above the marsh.

As she watched, she thought he was searching for something, but then she realized that he wasn't searching at all. Whatever he was looking for, he'd already found it.

Frowning, she scanned the area of the marsh the bird was hovering above. She saw nothing. Then, almost invisible against the green expanse of the wetlands, she found the hawk's target.

There was someone out there, staring fixedly up into the sky, and Cassie realized that the reason she hadn't seen the figure right away was because it was clad in a jacket that was nearly the same color as the marsh itself

But who was it? She strained her eyes, but the distance was too great.

Then Cassie understood what was about to happen. Whoever was out there was on his way to the cabin—her cabin—and the hawk was preparing to attack. Cassie watched in fascination. What should she do? Should she try to shout a warning?

But why should she? Whoever it was had no right to go into her cabin.

If something happened to a trespasser, it was his own fault, wasn't it?

But what if she was wrong? What if the person was just wandering around and didn't realize he'd gone too close?

She vacillated, part of her wanting to cry out to the person or try to distract the hawk.

But another part of her wanted to watch, to see what would happen. Her eyes fixed on the great bird, Cassie almost unconsciously moved closer to the marsh.

The hawk circled higher and its spirals grew ever tighter. In another moment, Cassie knew, it would draw its wings in and plunge into the streaking dive of its attack.

Rosemary knew what was going to happen, and knew she had to do something, but panic was coursing through her now, setting her heart pounding and draining the strength from her limbs. She tried to tear her eyes away from the bird, certain that if she could break the creature's hypnotic spell, she could bring herself back to life. But it was as if she'd lost control of her own will. Even as the bird suddenly folded its wings tight against its body and began dropping out of the sky toward her, she could do nothing but stare at it in horrified fascination.

It grew larger and larger as it picked up speed, and as the bird lunged toward her, time seemed to stand still, each second becoming an eternity.

She could see its gaping mouth now, the pointed hook of its beak hurtling toward her like the curved blade of a miniature scythe, ready to tear into her flesh. Her own mouth opened then, but her throat felt numb and no scream came out.

And then it was on her, its legs outstretched, its talons poised to slash into her. Still Rosemary couldn't move. Her heartbeat was pounding in her head and icy tentacles of fear held her firmly in their grip. She could smell the bird, the rank odor of its raw-meat diet emanating off its skin and filling her nostrils with the putrid scent of rotting flesh. At the last possible instant her arm came up and she felt the bird's talons close down on it, tearing through the thin material of her jacket to slash deep into her flesh.

She ducked her head away, but even that movement came too late, and she felt a searing flash of pain as the razor-sharp beak sliced into her right cheek.

Instantly she felt a hot gush of blood pour out of the wound, and a moment later her mouth filled with the salty taste of fresh blood.

The pain of the attack brought Rosemary back to life, and a surge of adrenaline shot through her. With her uninjured arm she swung wildly at the bird, and suddenly its talons released her arm. It jerked spasmodically as it tumbled to the ground, an angry screech of frustration erupting from its throat. Then it regained control of itself, its wings beating wildly as it took to the air once more.

She felt its tail feathers brush against her face, then heard the peculiar whumping sound of its wings as it pulled away. A moment later it was gone, streaking away low over the grasses, its wing tips barely clearing the cattails and reeds.

Blood oozing from the cut on her face, her right hand clutching at her damaged left arm, Rosemary turned and fled through the marsh, ripping and tearing at the weeds and vines that threatened to entangle her. At last, her breath rasping in her lungs, she hurled herself onto the firm ground of the park and sank sobbing onto the lawn. For a long time she didn't move, fighting the waves of pain that wracked her body. Then, slowly, her pounding heartbeat began to ease and her breathing returned to normal. At last—she didn't know how much later—she sat up and wiped the tears and blood away from her eyes. Her vision slowly cleared, and she looked around.

A few yards away, sitting with his tail curled around his legs, was Sumi.

Rosemary's eyes met the cat's, and burning yellow eyes held hers for a moment. Then the cat ducked his head, his tail twitched, and he darted away into the marsh. Instinctively Rosemary knew where he was going.

Had it been Sumi she'd seen in the marsh, following her? But why?

And why had the hawk, after striking her down suddenly abandoned its attack?

She struggled to her feet, every fiber of her body aching with exhaustion. She had to get home, had to lie down. But as she started out of the park, something pulled at her, made her pause and turn back.

She saw Cassie standing on the porch of the cabin. As Rosemary watched, she saw the gray cat dash out of the marsh and up the gentle slope of the hummock.

As the hawk perched calmly on the rooftop, the cat leaped into Cassie's arms.

Sixteen

Rosemary winced as the needle pierced her skin, and her knuckles turned white as she gripped the arms of the chair in Paul Samuels's office.

"Almost done," Samuels told her, his voice soothing. "Just one more."

She felt the needle jab again, followed by the eerie rasping sensation of the suture being drawn through her skin. Her left eye followed the movement of Samuels's deft fingers as he tied a knot then covered the stitches with a bandage. "That's it," he said, winking at her. "Want a lollipop?"

Rosemary managed a weak smile, and shook her head. "What about a scar? Will there be one?"

Samuels raised his hands in a gesture of incredulous dismay. "A *scar*? Would these fingers leave a *scar*?"

"I don't know," Rosemary replied, managing only the faintest hint of a smile, then instantly wincing with pain. "That's why I'm asking."

The doctor shook his head. "Shouldn't. The cut wasn't as bad as it looked, and in a couple of weeks—maybe a month—you shouldn't even know it was there. Actually, your arm was in worse shape than your cheek, but at least you kept that damned bird away from your eyes." His expression darkened slightly. "Have you told Gene Templeton about this?"

"That's where I'm going next," Rosemary replied. She got out of the chair, took off the smock that had covered her clothes, and began searching in her purse for a comb. "Somehow it seemed more important to get this mess cleaned up first." Her eyes met the doctor's in the mirror above his office sink. "But let me tell you, I can understand now why Lisa Chambers was so upset last week. I don't think I've ever been so frightened in my life. And the worst of it was, I couldn't do anything! I just stood there, Paul. I just stood there and let it happen."

"Panic," the doctor told her. "It does that sometimes. But it's something else too. There's an instinct to freeze when you sense danger. But then at the last second, when you know you can't hide, instinct takes over. That's what saved your eyes," he added point-edly. He moved to his desk and began making some notations in Rosemary's file. "I want you to go talk to Gene. If something isn't done about that bird, it's going to do real damage someday."

"Don't worry," Rosemary replied, her voice grim. "If he won't do anything about it, I'll have Keith go out and shoot it himself." She put her comb back in her purse, then picked up the shredded remains of her poplin jacket. "Anything else? Do I need any antibi-otics or anything?"

"I've got the prescription all ready." Samuels handed her a slip of paper, then walked with her out to the hospital's small waiting room. Just as Rosemary was about to leave, he stopped her. "What about Cassie?" he asked. "You said you saw her out there. And there was a cat, too, wasn't there?"

Rosemary looked at the doctor blankly, then the meaning of his words began to sink in. "Paul, are you saying what I think you are?"

"I'm not saying anything," Samuels replied neutrally. "I'm just asking a question."

"And I'll answer it," Rosemary told him. "Yes, Cassie was out there, and yes, her cat was out there. But the cat didn't attack me, and I'm absolutely positive that Cassie *was* there. I didn't imagine seeing her. So if you're wondering if I had the same kind of hyster-ical attack that Harold Simms had, the answer is no. The hawk attacked me, Paul. That's all that happened."

But as she left Samuels's office to walk the two blocks to the town hall, she replayed the entire incident in her mind. And she remem-bered Lisa Chambers's insistence that Cassie had made the hawk attack her. But it wasn't possible, was it?

Of course not.

Templeton listened to Rosemary's story silently, taking a few notes in between munches on his mid-morning doughnut. When she was finished, he sighed heavily. "Well, it looks like it's time for me to go hunting again, doesn't it?"

"Then you'll do it?"

"I'll try," he agreed. "But I'm not going to promise you anything. I've gone after that bird before, but it's never done me any good. It's almost like it knows I'm coming and just takes off. And in the mean-time I'll post the marsh. At least maybe we can keep people out of there for a while."

When Rosemary was gone, he left the police station and drove home. Thirty minutes after that, carrying his favorite hunting rifle—equipped with a telescopic sight—he headed for the marsh.

It was almost noon, and the sun was high in the sky. The last of the morning chill had left the air, but Templeton kept his uniform jacket on. If the hawk attacked him, at least he would have the protection of the heavy gabardine covering his arms and chest. He locked the squad car, and cradling the gun in his left arm, started out toward Cranberry Point. Before he started shooting, he'd damned well better make sure the marsh was deserted.

There was no one on the beach, and only the constant fluttering of the feeding birds disturbed the tranquillity of the wetlands. Tightening his grip on the gun, Templeton began making his way toward the cabin.

Cassie sat in the rocking chair by the window, with Sumi curled up in her lap, purring contentedly. But Cassie herself was not content.

She was worried. Worried and frightened.

She had watched from the beach as Kiska attacked the person in the marsh, and then, after the green-clad figure had struggled to its feet and hobbled back to the park, she had hurried out into the marsh herself.

She wasn't afraid of it anymore, wasn't worried about getting lost in the tangled maze of paths, or stumbling into one of the patches of quicksand that dotted the bog where the peat had never built up. It was almost as if there were some kind of invisible map in her head, guiding her. Today, in fact, she'd almost felt as if she were one of the birds soaring above the reeds, and that she could look down and pick the quickest, safest route from the beach to the cabin. Finally she'd gotten to the cabin and was just about to open the door and step inside, when she sensed something coming toward her. She turned, and out of the marsh, darting up the hill toward her, came Sumi. The cat had hit the porch then bounded into her arms, nuzzling against her cheek.

As the cat nuzzled her, her eyes were suddenly drawn to the person in the park—the person wearing the torn green jacket—and she suddenly knew who it was.

Rosemary.

But how had she known? She watched the figure carefully, squinting against the sun, but the distance was too far. Even though she knew who it was—*knew it*—she couldn't distinguish her stepmother's features. Finally, when Rosemary had limped out of the park, clutching her injured arm with one hand and holding the other to her bleeding face, Cassie had turned away and gone into the cabin.

Immediately a sense of peace had come over her. She settled herself into the chair by the window, rocking gently, cuddling Sumi in her lap.

The cat had looked up at her, and their eyes met. Then, as her fingers rubbed at the cat's fur, she felt a tingling sensation on her skin and vague images began to form in her mind.

She had a sense of being surrounded by something like seaweed, and all around her there was nothing but a swirling green cloud. She concentrated, and slowly the flickering images began to come into focus.

Not seaweed. Grass.

The grasses of the marsh, but larger, towering over her head, as they seemed to the night of her vision of Miranda's death. She had the sensation of being in the marsh herself, but not on any of the paths. Instead she was close to the ground, threading her way through the tangle, moving quickly and smoothly, almost as if her feet weren't touching the soggy earth at all.

The tingling in her fingers grew stronger, and the vision in her mind suddenly changed. She was out of the marsh now, gliding over a thick carpet of coarse grass, and around her immense trees, much larger than she'd ever seen before, towered overhead. A little bit ahead of her she saw a form lying on the ground and heard the rasping sounds of labored breathing. But there was something strange about the breathing, and as she concentrated even harder, she realized that it sounded amplified.

Indeed, everything was being amplified.

She could actually hear the sounds of the blades of grass as they rubbed against each other beneath her, and a few yards away she heard a soft rustling sound which she instantly knew was a mouse searching in a thicket for food.

Then the form lying on the grass moved and looked up.

It was Rosemary, her face bleeding from a deep gash on her right cheek. Her left hand was still clamped over the cuts on her right arm and tears were flowing from her eyes.

Now Cassie understood what was happening.

I'm seeing it. I'm seeing it all through Sumi's eyes, just as he saw it a few minutes ago. . . .

Slowly the vision dissolved and her mind cleared. Once again she was looking into Sumi's glowing golden eyes, and as the tingling faded from her fingers, she felt once more the soft warmth of his fur.

"You told me, didn't you?" she said softly. "When you jumped up into my arms, that's the first thing you did."

As if he understood her words, the cat began purring agreeably, and nestled deeper into her lap. Then his eyes closed, his ears flicked a couple of times, and he went to sleep.

Ever since, Cassie had been sitting by the window, trying to decide what it meant.

Maybe it wasn't Rosemary at all. Maybe she had only imagined the whole thing. But she knew she hadn't, knew that what she'd felt emanating from the memory of the cat into her fingers and then up into her own mind had been the truth.

So that was what Miranda had been talking about, that was the gift she'd given her. She could communicate with Sumi. She could see what the cat saw, and hear what it heard.

Instantly she knew that the dream she'd had the night Miranda died was no dream at all. Sumi had actually seen Miranda die, and then come back home and shown it to her. So there *had* been someone out there that night.

Someone who had killed Miranda.

But who? And why?

And then, unbidden, another memory came back to her.

Eric staring at her on the beach.

In her mind she melded his image with the one she'd seen in Sumi's memory, then rejected it.

It couldn't be right. It simply couldn't!

She squeezed her eyes shut and tried once again to visualize the figure as it bent over Miranda, but she could not make it out. Though she tried with every ounce of concentration she could bring to bear, the face eluded her as though her inner vision had been blocked.

Tears flooding her eyes, she looked down at Sumi once more. Could he do the same thing? Could he see what she saw, and feel what she felt? Could he really understand her?

Deep in her soul she felt that he could. There was some kind of bond between them, and yesterday, when she had imagined Sumi attacking Mr. Simms, the cat had understood and carried out her wishes.

But she hadn't really meant to hurt Mr. Simms, had she?

She searched in the deep recesses of her mind, and after a while found a cold black place that was filled with anger—and she knew that there, where all her darkest demons dwelt, was a part of her that could easily have killed Mr. Simms yesterday if it had been given a chance.

But everyone had a place like that. It was where you hid your worst hatreds away, concealing them from yourself as well as everyone else, and you didn't do anything about them. You put them away there, and kept them under control, and after a while you forgot about them.

That was the part of herself she'd been exploring yesterday when Sumi had attacked the teacher. But somehow the cat had understood her anger and acted upon it.

Was that what Sumi was? Some kind of weapon her very mind could use to strike back?

As if in answer to her unspoken question, the cat stirred in her lap and its pink tongue came out to lick gently at her fingers.

Then what was Kiska, the ghostly white hawk that perched constantly on the rooftop?

But she already knew the answer to that.

He was her guardian, there to protect her, to drive off anyone or anything that threatened her.

But why had he attacked Rosemary? What had Rosemary wanted? Perhaps she hadn't wanted anything, and the bird would attack anyone unless Cassie herself told him not to.

And she could have.

She'd sensed it while she was on the beach, known that if she pointed up at the bird and told it to go back to the rooftop, it would have obeyed her instantly.

But she hadn't.

Instead she'd let it attack.

But she hadn't known who it was, she told herself. She hadn't known who it was or what the person wanted. And besides, Kiska wasn't really her bird. He just lived there, didn't he? It wasn't her fault he'd attacked. And what if she hadn't been there? Then there wouldn't have been anybody to stop him.

But she *was* there, and she *hadn't* stopped him.

She shivered slightly. From now on, she knew, she would have to be very careful. She couldn't allow herself ever again to get as angry as she had been at Mr. Simms, couldn't allow herself to imagine hurting anyone else.

Slowly she began to understand Miranda's words. 'Don't let them hurt you. You must never let them hurt you.' She couldn't let anyone hurt her anymore, because if she did, she might be tempted to release the demons in that dark place in her mind, and along with the demons, the animals that understood her darkest fantasies. . . .

Something glinted in the sun beyond the window, and the flash of light in her eye brought Cassie out of her reverie. Turning, she looked out at the marsh and recognized Gene Templeton making his way toward the cabin through the reeds. With each step the sun flashed off the reflective lenses of his sunglasses, and Cassie blinked against the sudden glare. Cradling Sumi in her right arm, she got out of the chair and went closer to the window. She could see that the police chief was carrying something, but for a second she didn't realize what it was. Then she recognized the object.

A rifle.

She gasped as she realized what it must mean, and hurried to the front door. As she opened it she heard a quick rustling of wings, and realized that Kiska had already taken off from his perch. She stepped out onto the front porch and looked up, shading her eyes against the sun.

The bird was spiraling upward in what Cassie knew was a first preparation for an attack.

Gene Templeton stopped short when the white hawk suddenly lifted off the rooftop and raised the rifle to his shoulder. He put his eye to the telescopic sight and a moment later found his target. But the bird was circling rapidly, and he knew that until it reached altitude and started toward him, he wouldn't be able to hold the gun on target long enough to get a shot. Only when the bird chose a direction and he could gauge its speed closely enough to determine how far to lead it, could he risk taking a shot, for he knew that if he missed on the first one, he wouldn't get a second chance. His attention riveted on the bird, he didn't see the cabin door open and Cassie step out onto the low porch.

Cassie herself wasn't sure what to do. Should she summon the bird back to the roof, or just let him go? But what if he went after the policeman? Her mind in turmoil, she watched anxiously as the hawk reached the apex of its climb and leveled off. And then she realized that he was going to be all right.

Kiska knew what was going to happen and was flying the other way. She let out a sigh of relief.

The target steady in the sight, Templeton carefully lined up the cross hairs. In the magnification of the lens the bird loomed large, its wings beating steadily, the muscles of its back working rhythmically. It was flying almost directly away from him, and Templeton realized he needn't lead it at all.

Simply line it up and squeeze the trigger.

Slowly, carefully, he steadied the gun and gently began to apply pressure to the trigger.

A sharp report exploded from the barrel and the stock of the gun recoiled into his shoulder. In the sky the bird jerked and a few feathers seemed to pop away from it. Templeton quickly put his eye to the sight again and found the target.

It was tumbling through the air now, a red stain spreading through its feathers.

Then, as he watched the bird fall toward the ground, a piercing scream rent the quiet that had followed the gunshot.

Cassie, still standing on the porch, heard the gun's report and saw Kiska suddenly tumble in the sky. But the scream that erupted from her throat was not one of fury, but of pain, for at the moment the bullet had struck the white hawk, a searing pain had shot through her back and into her chest. As Sumi yowled in sudden alarm and leaped out of her arms, Cassie's knees buckled and she sank down onto the porch, then rolled off the single step and onto the ground itself. The pain burned within her, and her hands clutched at her breast as if attempting to close a wound.

Templeton, startled by the scream, let the rifle drop away from his shoulder and looked at the cabin just as Cassie collapsed to the ground.

"What the hell . . . ?" Templeton whispered under his breath, already breaking into a lumbering run. What had happened? He couldn't have shot her—he'd only fired a single shell, and he'd seen the bullet hit the bird. And even if he'd fired twice, he couldn't have shot that wildly. He couldn't have!

He burst out of the marsh and pounded up the low hill, then dropped onto the ground next to the writhing girl. Her face was twisted into a mask of pain and low moans bubbled out of her lips.

"It's all right, Cassie," Templeton told her. "It's all right. I'm here!"

Setting the rifle aside, he grasped her wrists to pull her hands away from the wound she was clutching. She fought against him, twisting away, trying to escape his grip, but he was much too strong for her. At last she let her arms relax slightly, and her hands came away from her chest.

Nothing.

No blood, no hole where a bullet might have passed through the man's white shirt she was wearing, nothing at all.

Still whimpering, she rolled over and Templeton was able to examine her back as well.

It, too, showed no signs of any kind of wound.

And yet there was no question the girl was in terrible pain, for her eyes had glazed over with shock and she was still moaning softly.

He ran his hands over her limbs, looking for broken bones, but found none. Finally, leaving the rifle where it lay, he picked her up and started back through the marsh, toward the squad car.

Cassie lay in the hospital bed, staring out the window at the setting sun. The pain still throbbed in her chest, and she knew that no matter what the doctor said, she wasn't imagining it.

"But something *must* have happened to her," she heard her father insisting through the open door to the hall. "You heard what Gene said. She was in shock, for Christ's sake!"

"I know what Gene said," Samuels replied patiently, "but I also know that I've examined her and I can't find anything wrong. Nothing at all. No marks, no cuts, nothing. I've looked at the X rays at least five times, and there's no internal damage either. If you want to, we can go over them again. The only thing I can tell you is that she's not hurt.''

"Then what happened?" Keith asked. "Gene claims he shot the bird—though what the hell he was doing out there with a gun when Cassie was out there, too, is something that's beyond me—but he can't find the bird. He says he saw it drop, and knows where it came down. But it's not there. So how do we know he shot it at all?"

Samuels shrugged, but when he spoke, his voice clearly revealed that he was running out of patience. "Fine. He didn't shoot it. Frankly, I don't really give a damn about the hawk, but his not finding it doesn't prove a thing either. By the time he got back, a raccoon could have gotten it. But he didn't shoot Cassie. You don't shoot someone and not leave a wound. It's a physical impossibility.''

Keith's eyes narrowed angrily. "So you're telling me Cassie's faking, is that it?"

The doctor licked his lips and shook his head. "I'm not telling you that at all. In fact I'm sure her pain is quite real. But that doesn't mean a bullet caused it.''

"Then what did?" Keith asked, his voice icy.

"A hysterical response. She saw the bird get shot, and she felt the pain herself.''

"That's your answer to everything this week, isn't it?" Keith asked, making no attempt to keep the sarcasm from his voice. "Isn't that pretty much what you had to say about Harold Simms?''

Samuels's eyes glinted darkly hut he kept his anger under control. "All I can do is tell you my diagnosis," he said evenly. "If you want a second opinion, I'll be more than happy to refer you to someone. But frankly, I think any other doctor will agree with me. There just aren't any wounds.'' Noticing the open door to Cassie's room, he reached out and closed it, then lowered his voice. "If you want my opinion, Keith, I think you might want to have her talk to a psychiatrist. After everything she's been through in the last couple of weeks, she's got to be in a lot of emotional pain. What we're seeing today could be symptomatic of that.''

Keith's brows arched. "So we send her off to Eastbury along with Simms, and don't deal with it, right? Sorry, Paul, I don't work that way, not with my own daughter.'' Before the doctor could say anything else, Keith turned away and let himself into Cassie's room, closing the door behind him.

"Hi, Punkin," he said gently, forcing a smile. "How're you feeling?"

Cassie looked at him suspiciously. Why had they closed the door a minute ago? What were they saying that they didn't want her to hear? But she already knew.

They were talking about whether she was crazy or not. But she knew she wasn't.

But if they decided she was . . .

"I'm okay," she said softly, struggling not to let the pain in her chest show on her face. "I just—I don't know what happened, Daddy. But I'm all right now. Really I am. Can—can I go home?"

Keith frowned. "Are you sure you feel well enough?"

Cassie nodded. "It's almost gone," she said, though the pain still felt like a hot poker had been stabbed into her. Then her eyes met her father's. "How's Rosemary?" she asked. "Is she all right?"

Keith nodded. "Dr. Samuels says it's not bad at all."

"I'm sorry," Cassie said. "If I'd known it was her, I wouldn't have let Kiska do it."

"Let him do it? What do you mean?"

"I didn't know who it was," Cassie explained. "If I'd known, I would have told him to leave her alone. Really I would."

Keith grinned crookedly. "Honey, you can't tell a hawk what to do. Not unless you've been training him for years. And even then you can't always stop them from attacking. It wasn't your fault. Anyway, none of it matters anymore. The hawk's dead."

Cassie shook her head. "Mr. Templeton shot him, but he's not dead."

The grin faded from Keith's face and his eyes darkened. "He isn't?" he asked. "How do you know that?"

Cassie hesitated, then shrugged. "I just know, that's all."

She wasn't about to tell her father that during the hours she had spent in the hospital, she'd figured out what was happening to her. It sounded too crazy.

But she knew that the pain in her chest wasn't her pain at all. It was Kiska's pain, and it was being transmitted to her.

But it was all right, and she could bear it, for she knew what the pain meant.

It meant that Kiska was alive somewhere. He was injured, but he was alive.

If he was dead, she wouldn't still be feeling the pain, for it would have died with him.

Now she had to conceal the pain until he got well and came back to her.

Seventeen

For five days Cassie stayed in her room, lying on her bed—fighting against the deep burning pain in her chest. But each time Rosemary suggested that she should see the doctor again, Cassie had shaken her head.

"It's getting better," she'd insisted. "And there isn't anything he can do. I just have to get over it."

On Monday Rosemary went to Samuels herself, and while he changed the bandages on her cheek and forehead she talked worriedly about her stepdaughter. But to her surprise, the doctor agreed with Cassie. "She's having an emotional reaction," he told her. "The best thing you can do is simply give her some time. If it weren't getting better, I'd agree with you. In fact I'd insist she see a psychiatrist. But if she says she's feeling better, just leave her alone. Keep an eye on her, but don't push her."

Samuels's advice seemed to work, and for the next four days Cassie came downstairs each morning, picking at her breakfast then insisting on doing the dishes and cleaning up the kitchen before returning to her room.

Then, on Friday morning, Cassie came down from her room dressed for school, her face pale but set in determination. "I'm going back to school," she announced.

Keith's eyes clouded with doubt. "Are you sure that's a good idea? Maybe you ought to wait until Monday. Missing one more day isn't—"

"But I want to go back," Cassie insisted. "I'm fine now, and if I go today, at least I can get all the work I missed and do it over the weekend."

She left the house right after breakfast and walked slowly through the town, surprised by how quickly spring had taken over. The morning was warm, and there was a softness to the air. The trees, their leaves only budding ten days ago, were bursting with a vibrant green, and tulips were blooming everywhere, dotting the village with bright patches of color. There was a freshness and promise of new beginnings to everything which imbued Cassie with a sense of well-being she had never felt before.

The last vague twinges of pain in her chest left her, and as she approached the school, even it seemed to have changed. The chestnut trees surrounding the old frame building were in full leaf, softening the lines of the structure, and the lawn of the playing field had taken on a brighter green than it had displayed ten days ago.

But as she mounted the front steps, Cassie's good feelings began to fade away. She passed through the knots of chattering teenagers and conversations suddenly stopped, voices dropping to whispers.

Her skin tingled with the now familiar sensation of eyes watching her.

It doesn't matter, she told herself. None of it matters, and this time I'm not going to run away. Eric was right—I can't not ever go to school again. So I'll ignore them, and after a while they'll forget all about me.

Taking a deep breath, she quickly climbed the stairs to the second floor, and long before the first bell rang, she was already in her seat. Today, at least, she wouldn't feel everyone staring at her as she came in late.

The morning dragged by, and each time she had to change classrooms, Cassie moved through the halls with the strange detached air of a zombie. It was as if there were some sort of force field around her, and wherever she went, the crowds in the corridors seemed to part for her, as if the other students were now afraid even of brushing up against her. She did her best to pretend she didn't notice, looking straight ahead, her face an expressionless mask.

By the end of the third period the urge to run away was upon her, but she refused to give in to it.

Don't let them hurt you, she reminded herself over and over again. Slowly the rhythm of the words became a silent chant, and eventually she imagined that Miranda herself was with her, whispering the words in her ear, giving her strength.

Maybe Miranda really is with me, Cassie thought as the last bell of the morning rang and she started slowly toward the cafeteria, willing her feet to move even though every fiber of her being wanted to turn and flee. After all, this is how Miranda had felt.

Every day of her life Miranda felt like this, Cassie thought—no one speaking to her, no one even smiling at her.

But staring at her.

Always staring at her.

The noise in the cafeteria seemed to dry up the moment Cassie opened the door and stepped inside, but she did her best to ignore it once more, moving slowly down the line, pushing the plastic tray in front of her, selecting food automatically, without even realizing what she was putting on her tray.

And all the time she could feel the eyes of the gathered students boring into her back, watching her slow progress toward the cashier.

Wordlessly she fished in her book bag for her wallet and paid the cashier, who glanced up at her for a moment, then looked again.

"Are you all right?" the woman asked tentatively.

Cassie nodded mutely, though she could feel a clammy sheen of sweat on her forehead and her legs were trembling. But the cashier wasn't satisfied.

"Maybe you ought to go to the office and lie down for a few minutes," she said. "My goodness, you're so pale you look like you've seen a ghost!"

Instantly the cafeteria erupted with laughter. Cassie's eyes brimmed with tears as she tried to pick up the tray, but her hands were shaking too badly, and the glass overturned, splashing water into the bowl of macaroni and cheese.

Then she heard a voice behind her.

Eric's voice.

"I'll take it," he said. "There's a table over there by the window. Come on."

Relief flooding through her, Cassie let Eric take the tray, then followed him as he walked quickly through the tables filled with snickering teenagers. One of them stuck a foot in Eric's way, but he deftly stepped over it, throwing the boy a dirty look as he passed. By the time they reached the table, the last of the giggles had died away, but when Cassie glanced around, she could see the kids whispering among themselves.

Eric seemed to read her mind.

"If you let them get to you, they'll never quit," he said, setting Cassie's tray on the table. He fished his sack lunch out of the depths of his book bag, looked at the contents of the brown paper bag sourly, then grinned crookedly at Cassie. "Trade you a soggy sandwich for the macaroni and cheese."

"It's soggy too," Cassie replied, her voice quavering as she struggled to keep her emotions in check.

"That's okay," Eric told her. "I'm just so sick of tomato sandwiches, I could puke." He held up the unappetizing mess of white bread, limp lettuce, and thin slices of tomato, but Cassie shook her head.

"Take the macaroni and cheese anyway," she said. "I hate it, and I'm not very hungry."

"Then why'd you buy it?"

Cassie shrugged. "I had to buy something, didn't I? Anyway, I wasn't really looking at the food." She fell silent, but her eyes darted around the room, and Eric nodded.

"Want to know what they've been saying?"

Cassie swallowed hard, trying to clear the lump that had risen in her throat, but she nodded.

"Well, everybody has a slightly different version, but the main idea is that you're crazy."

Cassie flinched but said nothing, and Eric managed another grin. "But it's not so bad, really."

"Not so bad?" Cassie breathed. "You don't know—they've been staring at me all morning, and nobody will talk to me. It's—it's the same way everybody treated Miranda."

Eric met her eyes. "I know," he said. "They're treating me the same way."

Cassie stared back at him. "You? But—but—"

"It's because of Simms. Everyone's sure you did something to him, and since I was with you, they think I must have helped you."

"But we didn't do anything to him," Cassie protested.

"No one cares what we say," Eric said, his voice bitter. He leaned closer. "But it isn't just that," he whispered. "I've been spending a lot of time out in the marsh."

"The marsh?"

Eric nodded. "Everybody heard about what happened out there. So I went out and looked for Kiska." He glanced around quickly, and his voice dropped even further. "Cassie, I found him."

Cassie gasped, then covered her mouth with her hand. "Where is he?" she asked. "Is he all right?"

Eric nodded quickly. "He was almost dead when I found him. He was about a quarter of a mile from the cabin. There's a big bush out there with vines all over it, and he was inside the bush. When I found him he couldn't even walk, and for a minute I thought he was dead. There was blood all over him. Anyway, I took a cage out there and sort of bandaged him up, and I've been going out there every day, taking him food."

"And he's really okay?" Cassie asked anxiously.

"He's almost well again. He can stand up, and he takes the food right out of my hand'"

"Monday," Cassie said softly, her eyes suddenly boring into Eric. "He started standing up again on Monday, didn't he?"

Eric looked at her quizzically. "How'd you know that?"

"Because that's the day I got up," Cassie replied, her voice taking on an edge of excitement. "I knew I was feeling what Kiska was feeling, and that proves it, doesn't it? I was getting better, but I couldn't really get up until Monday. And now I'm all right again." Suddenly her eyes were sparkling. "And I bet that means Kiska can fly now. Let's go out there. Right after school, let's go let him out of the cage."

But Eric shook his head. "I can't. Not right after school. I got back on the baseball team, and I can't miss practice. And if anybody sees you go out there . . ." His voice trailed off, but Cassie knew what he meant.

She glanced quickly around and saw Lisa Chambers glaring at them. "Is that why they've started staring at you too?" she asked. "Because someone saw you going out there?"

Eric's gaze wavered for a split second, then he nodded. "I—I always act like I'm going to the cabin, but then I go down the hill on the other side of it." Suddenly his eyes flashed with anger. "Anyway, it doesn't matter. If they all want to think I'm crazy, let them. They're all just like my dad—it doesn't matter what you do, it's always the wrong thing."

"But why didn't you tell them?" Cassie asked. "All you were doing was taking care of Kiska—"

"Are you serious?" Eric demanded. "They would have told, and then Templeton would have gone out and killed him. Why do you think I left him there in the first place?"

"But it's not fair," Cassie protested.

Eric's eyes darkened. "So who ever said anything was supposed to be fair? Nobody was ever fair to Miranda, either, and look what happened to her. But it's not going to happen to us," he added, his voice taking on a bitter edge. "I won't let it happen to us."

Cassie looked at him, her eyes frightened almost as much by his tone as his words. "But—but what can we do?" she asked.

"There's some things," he said, and smiled. "For starters we can let them all know they're not getting to us. From now on we act like nothing's the matter at all. If they want to stare, let them stare. If they want to talk, let them talk. And tomorrow we'll go let Kiska out of his cage. Okay?"

Cassie smiled gratefully. "Okay," she agreed.

"Come on," Eric said. He shoved the remnants of his lunch back in the bag and dropped the crumpled bag on Cassie's tray. Then, with his book bag in one hand and the tray in the other, he weaved his way between the tables, Cassie right behind him. They were halfway to the doors when Lisa Chambers's voice stopped them.

"What are you doing, Eric?" she asked, her tone saccharine sweet. "Playing nursemaid to the poor little crazy girl?"

Cassie felt her face burn with humiliation, but as she tried to hurry past the table, Eric dropped his book bag and grasped her arm, stopping her. "If that's what you want to think, Lisa, fine," he said. "But if you really want to know, it isn't that at all."

Lisa blinked uncertainly. She'd expected Eric to blush as deeply as Cassie, and ignore her. Instead he was looking right at her, his eyes mocking her.

"Actually I was inviting her to the dance tomorrow night. See you there." He dropped Cassie's arm, reached down and picked up the book bag, then started once more toward the door, Cassie hurrying after him.

Lisa sat still, a wave of cold anger washing over her.

What was Eric doing?

Until today—without Cassie Winslow coming to school—everything had been just as it always had been. Every day Eric sat with her at lunch, and she waited for him until baseball practice was over, then he walked her home. He'd never even mentioned Cassie Winslow.

And the day before yesterday he'd asked *her* to the dance.

Now she could feel her friends staring at her, and hear Allayne Garvey snickering. She glared at Allayne, daring her to say anything.

Allayne's snickering only grew into a laugh. "Didn't you say he was all done with her?" she asked, throwing Teri Bennett a knowing look. "I thought he was taking *you* to the dance."

"He was," Lisa said stiffly, doing her best to conceal both her anger and her disappointment. "But I changed my mind. I broke the date yesterday."

Allayne rolled her eyes. "Sure you did," she said. "That must have been while I was flying to the moon, wasn't it? Come off it, Lisa—he dumped you again. All she had to do was show up, and he went right back to her." She winked at Teri. "And, you can't really blame him, can you? I mean, she is pretty."

Lisa's lips tightened and her eyes narrowed to angry slits, but she said nothing. A cold knot of hatred toward Cassie Winslow formed in her belly like a lead weight. Somehow, she would get even with Cassie.

She didn't know how, but she would find a way.

"What were you talking about?" Cassie asked. There were still a few minutes before the lunch hour would end, and they were sitting outside, their faces tipped up to the sun. "You didn't ask me to a dance. What dance?"

Eric glanced over at her, then closed his eyes again. "The one tomorrow night. Don't you want to go?"

Cassie started to shake her head. It was bad enough having

everyone stare at her at school all day long. But to have to spend an entire evening—

She couldn't stand it. Just the idea of it terrified her. Then she remembered what Eric had told her at lunch time, and Miranda's words. "All right," she said quietly. "I'll go."

Eric smiled at her. "I knew you would."

Eighteen

When Rosemary came downstairs Saturday morning she found Keith already sitting at the breakfast table, his marine charts and tide tables spread out before him. That, together with the phone call he'd gotten earlier, could mean only one thing.

"You have a charter?" she asked.

Keith nodded, not looking up. "Some guys from Boston. They'll be here at noon."

"It—it's awfully short notice, isn't it?" she asked.

Keith glanced up at her, the quaver in her voice catching his attention. He shrugged. "That's the way this business is. You take the jobs as they come, and if you turn them down, they don't call again."

"But . . ." She fell silent. It wasn't the first time this had happened, and it wouldn't be the last.

Under normal circumstances, it wouldn't have bothered her. But the circumstances weren't normal. Hadn't been normal since the day Cassie had come to live with them. Now, for the first time, he was going to leave her alone with this strange girl she hardly knew, and of whom she was beginning to be desperately afraid.

Cassie herself, her food untouched, was staring out the window, a faraway look in her eyes as she gently stroked Sumi's gray fur.

Jennifer, her eyes wary—as if she knew something had gone wrong in the house but wasn't sure what—was poking nervously at her eggs.

"Hurry up and finish them," Rosemary said automatically. "As soon as they're gone, you can go outside and play."

Jennifer frowned. "I don't want to go outside. There isn't anyone to play with."

Rosemary shot a glance at Keith, who had finally pushed his charts aside and was looking at Jennifer now. "Why don't you go to the park?" she heard him ask. "There's always someone over there, isn't there?"

Jennifer nodded uncertainly. "But Wendy Maynard always goes there, and she doesn't like me anymore."

"She doesn't?" Keith asked. Rosemary saw his eyes flick toward her then return to his youngest daughter. "Why not?"

Jennifer opened her mouth to say something, glanced at Cassie, and seemed to change her mind. "I don't know," she said, but her eyes evaded her father's. She slid off her chair. "May I be excused, please?"

Keith hesitated, then nodded.

Now Cassie emerged from her reverie and smiled at Jennifer. "What if I go with you?" she asked. "Would that be fun?"

The little girl looked uncertain. "I—I don't know."

"Come on," Cassie urged. "We can play on the swings and do the teeter-totter, and anything else you want." Jennifer still seemed unconvinced, and Cassie turned anxiously to her father. "It's all right, isn't it?"

Keith shrugged. "If you're sure you're up to it."

"I'm fine," Cassie said. And indeed, this morning she was feeling even better than yesterday. There was only a trace of the pain left in her chest, and on her back, where she'd first felt the blinding stab of agony when Kiska had been shot, there was only a faint itching, like a scab that was about to fall off.

"Great," Keith said. He swung Jennifer off her feet as she tried to dart past him, and planted a kiss on her cheek. "Aren't you going to say good-bye to your old dad?"

"'Bye," Jennifer replied, kissing him back.

He put her back down and she dashed out into the morning sunshine. Grinning happily, Keith turned to Cassie once more. "Take good care of your sister while I'm gone, okay?"

Cassie nodded, then she, too, disappeared out the back door. When she was gone, the smile on Keith's face faded and he turned to Rosemary. "Now, what is all this?" he asked. "It's obvious you don't want me to take this charter. And I presume it has to do with Cassie. Right?"

Rosemary took a deep breath. "I just . . . well, I just don't feel comfortable with her, that's all."

Keith's eyes rolled impatiently. "For God's sake, haven't we been through this before? She's fine now."

"She's not fine!" Rosemary snapped. "She wouldn't leave the house for over a week, and when she came home yesterday, she didn't say a word about school. All she did was go over to the cemetery and sit by Miranda's grave. She sat there for more than an hour, Keith. I watched her and it was—Well, it was just weird. She had that awful cat on her lap, and she was sitting on the grass next to the grave, petting the cat and talking to herself. Maybe you call that normal, but I don't!''

"Oh, for God's sake," Keith rasped. "She's having a rough time, and except for Eric, Miranda was the only person in town who was nice to her. So is it a crime that she went to visit her grave?"

"But it isn't just that," Rosemary pleaded.

"Then what is it?" Keith demanded.

Rosemary cast around in her mind for something concrete, something Keith couldn't simply dismiss. "All right. Before we came downstairs I told her she had to clean her room this morning. Instead she's off playing in the park with Jen."

"So? Maybe she forgot."

Now Rosemary's eyes flashed. "Or maybe she was just playing us off against each other!"

"Make up your mind," Keith said, his voice taking on a cutting edge of sarcasm. "Is she crazy, or is she manipulative, or is she both?" The sarcasm gave way to cold anger. "Or are you just imagining things?" Turning his back on her, Keith returned to his marine charts.

When he started out of the house twenty minutes later, the anger between them still hung heavy in the atmosphere. Rosemary knew he wouldn't be back before he took the boat out. "Keith?" she blurted. He turned back, but his hand stayed on the half-open screen door. As their eyes met, she could see that he was in as much pain as she.

"I'm sorry," she whispered. She went to him and slipped her arms around him, burying her face against his chest. "We can't just leave it like this. Please?"

She felt him stiffen for a moment, but his arms went around her and he held her close. "It's going to be all right, baby," he whispered. "I'm sorry too. But I just can't believe there's anything really wrong with her."

Rosemary hesitated, then nodded, her head pressed close to his chest. "When will you be back?"

"Tuesday, maybe Wednesday. They weren't sure." He held her away from him then. "And you can always get me on the radio. You know that. Okay?"

She hesitated, wanting to beg him not to go, to back out of the charter, just this once. But in the end she nodded again. "I love you."

"I love you too."

And then he was gone, and Rosemary was alone.

Cassie was pushing Jennifer on one of the swings when she first saw Lisa Chambers and Teri Bennett walking along Oak Street. At first she thought they were going to pass by without noticing her. But then Lisa glanced in her direction and came to an abrupt stop, putting out a hand to stop Teri as well. At Cassie's feet Sumi opened his eyes and stood, a soft mewing emerging from him as he pressed himself against her legs and twined his tail around her calf.

"Would you look at that?" Cassie heard Lisa say loudly to Teri, intending to be overheard. "Do you believe Mrs. Winslow's letting her take care of Jennifer? She must be as crazy as Cassie is!"

Swallowing the sudden surge of anger that rose in her, Cassie forgot the swing.

"Push me," Jennifer called out. "How come you stopped?" Then, as the swing gradually came to a stop, Jennifer saw the two girls standing at the edge of the park, watching them. "Just pretend they're not there," she told Cassie. "Maybe they'll go away."

Instead, Lisa left the sidewalk and started across the lawn toward them. When she was a few yards away she stopped again, her lips twisted into a cruel smile. "Didn't anyone tell you about Cassie?" she asked, her eyes fixed on Jennifer.

Jennifer got up from the swing and moved next to Cassie. "Tell me what?" she asked, her eyes narrowing suspiciously.

Lisa's eyes glinted maliciously. "That she's a witch, just like Miranda was."

Jennifer gasped. "Th-that's not true," she stammered. But in her head she heard an echo of Wendy Maynard's singsong chant after school yesterday. "Cassie is a wi-itch. Cassie is a wi-itch."

"How do you know?" Lisa taunted. "She has a cat, doesn't she? Don't all witches have cats?"

Cassie, her temples throbbing with anger, stepped forward. "Stop it, Lisa," she said. "Why do you want to scare her? She's only a little girl."

"Why should I stop it?" Lisa sneered. "Maybe it's true! Besides, what can you do about it? You don't have Miranda's hawk anymore, do you? Mr. Templeton shot it! So what are you going to do?"

Cassie's eyes narrowed and she reached down to pick Sumi up. His body was tense, and the fur on his hackles was standing up stiffly. His soft mewling had turned into a hiss, and she could feel his claws flexing.

"Do you want me to let Sumi go?" she asked. "Is that what you want me to do?"

Lisa's twisted grin faded slightly. "You think I'm afraid of a crummy cat?" she asked. "Or are you going to put a hex on me?" Bolstered by her own words, she grinned again and turned her attention back to Jennifer. "That's what she did to Mr. Simms, Jennifer. She put a hex on him and made him go crazy. Is that what you want her to do to you too? Make you as crazy as Mr. Simms?"

Jennifer was trembling now. Suddenly all the stories she'd heard about Miranda came back to her. Instinctively she took a step away from Cassie, and Lisa saw the movement.

"That's right. You'd better get away from her. If I were you, I wouldn't even want to sleep in the same house with her. You don't know what she might do to you in the middle of the night, do you?"

With that, Cassie's anger erupted. "Stop it!" she shouted. "Stop it right now!"

"Why?" Lisa taunted. "What are you going to do about it?"

Cassie froze, and Miranda's words echoed once more in her mind. *Don't let them hurt you.*

But it was too late, and she ignored Miranda's words, letting her anger run free.

"I'll kill you," she shouted, her eyes burning with tears. "If you don't leave me alone, I'll kill you!"

For a moment Lisa said nothing, but then her mouth opened and an ugly peal of laughter burst from her throat. "You can go to hell, Cassie Winslow," she shouted. "In fact, why don't you? Nobody wants you around here!" Still laughing, she turned back to Teri Bennett. "Come on," she said. "Let's get out of here before she cracks up completely."

Cassie stared after Lisa, fury churning inside her. She could feel it coursing through her, making her whole body shake.

Her limbs trembled with it, and after a moment she felt Sumi begin trembling too. Suddenly the cat leaped from her arms and streaked across the park after Lisa.

No! Cassie thought. *Stop!*

Instantly the cat stopped running and turned back to look at Cassie. Both the girl and the animal stood frozen for a split second. Then the cat—as if obeying some unspoken order—trotted back and rubbed itself against Cassie's leg.

The tight knot of anger in Eric Cavanaugh's belly hadn't relaxed in the slightest, despite the three hours of hard work he'd put himself through since the fight with his father that morning.

He still wasn't exactly sure what had triggered Ed's explosion, unless it had been the mere sight of Cassie Winslow coming out of the house next door.

"What you starin' at, boy?" his father had growled.

Eric looked up from his plate of greasy hominy cakes—the breakfast his father insisted on every Saturday morning, and which Eric and Laura did their best to pretend they liked, though the very sight of them made both of them slightly nauseated. He shook his head. "I'm not staring at anything—"

"Don't you lie to me, Mr. Smartmouth," Ed had cut in, his eyes glittering dangerously. "Don't you think I know what goes on in that head of yours?"

Frowning in puzzlement, Eric had glanced out the window just in time to see Cassie and Jennifer disappearing around the corner onto Cambridge Avenue. "I wasn't staring at anything, Dad," he insisted, though he knew that arguing with his father was useless. Once Ed had made up his mind about something, there was no changing it.

"You were starin' at *her*!" his father snapped, pushing his chair back and rising to his feet so abruptly that the chair tipped over and crashed to the floor. Eric flinched involuntarily, and his father's mouth twisted into a vicious smile of victory. "Thought you could fool me, didn't you?"

"Leave him alone, Ed," Laura pleaded, standing next to the sink. "Can't you just let him finish his breakfast? He wasn't looking at anyone!"

Ed's hangover-induced fury quickly shifted focus, and he sneered at Laura. "How's anybody 'sposed to eat this slop?" he demanded.

"I thought you liked it—" Laura blurted, then stopped herself. But it was too late.

Ed's hand snaked out to strike her across the face with enough force to knock her off balance. She stumbled, then fell to the floor, her head banging against the door of the cupboard below the sink. "Don't you argue with me, you worthless bitch," he stormed.

"Stop it, Dad!" Eric yelled. "She didn't do anything to you, and neither did I. Why don't you just go get drunk and leave us alone!"

Trembling, Ed faced his son, but this time Eric, who was on his feet now, showed no fear. "Try it, Dad," he said quietly. "Just go ahead and try it. I'm done letting you beat up on me for things I never did."

Ed's eyes flickered uncertainly. "You ain't big enough to take your old man," he snarled, certain that the words alone would be enough to cow Eric.

But Eric's jaw only tightened. "Try it, Dad," he challenged. "Just go ahead and try it. I'll kick the shit out of you so fast you won't even remember what happened."

For a moment Ed wavered, and Eric had been certain his father was going to swing at him. If he did, Eric would have to make up his mind what to do. Would he really strike back at his own father? No, not yet. It wasn't quite time. Not quite.

But instead of taking a swing at him, Ed had shambled toward the door. "Some goddamn son you are," he mumbled. "What kind of kid threatens his old man?" Then he was gone, and both Eric and Laura knew where he was going. He'd start out drinking on his boat, then move to the Whaler's Inn. And when he was drunk enough, he'd come home.

When they were alone, Eric had tried to help his mother, but she'd shaken her head and waved him away. "Just leave me alone," she said, her voice muffled. "I'll be all right."

He'd gone outside then, and begun the weekly routine of yard-work, but even the work hadn't helped. His mind refused to concentrate on the job.

Instead he kept thinking about the rage growing within him.

It wasn't just his father anymore, he knew. The anger was spilling over now, onto his mother too. . . .

Before—when the rage had grown to the point where he thought he might burst—he'd always gone to the marsh and talked to Miranda.

Always—since he was ten years old, and Miranda had come home from the hospital—she'd been there for him. He had been able to go out to her cabin and sit with her—Sumi snuggled comfortably in his lap—and pour out the rage. And no matter how bad it had been— how filled with hatred he'd been—Miranda had always listened to him, comforted him, and accepted him. She'd been his friend, always there.

She had taught him how to control the rage, how to use it, how to bury it so deep that no one else even knew it was there.

She had taught him how to survive.

And then Cassie had come, and Miranda—the only person who had ever been Eric's alone—had taken her in too.

"She's just like you, Eric," Miranda had told him on that last afternoon when he'd gone to visit her. "And I've known her just as long. I found her the same day I found you, when you were both so young. And I won't turn away from her. I won't, and you mustn't either. She needs us, Eric. She needs both of us."

That day his rage had turned for the first time on Miranda. But he'd kept it under control, hidden it so deep that even she—who could see everything—hadn't been able to see it. And then, late that night, he'd gone back to the marsh.

But even after Miranda had died, even after he'd finally given in to the rage within him, it hadn't stopped.

Instead the fury only seemed to feed on itself, growing ever stronger.

And then, the day Simms threw him off the baseball team, Miranda's words came back to him. But Miranda had been wrong. He suddenly understood that it wasn't Cassie who needed him.

It was he who needed Cassie.

Needed her so that when he finally released all the rage that had built up within him over the years, it would be Cassie who took the blame.

And it would begin today, when they released Kiska.

He put the mower back in the garage and hung the edging clippers on their nail in the wall. After he closed the garage door, he crossed the double driveway and knocked at the Winslows' back door. A moment later Rosemary Winslow stepped out into the service porch and held the screen door open for him.

He composed his features into the friendly smile that had long ago become the mask behind which he hid the furies burning within him. "Is Cassie here?"

Rosemary frowned uncertainly. "I—well, yes, she is. But I'm not sure she's feeling too well. When she got back from the park, she went up to her room, and she hasn't come down again."

"Oh," Eric said, feeling a twinge of disappointment. "Well, when she comes back down, would you tell her I was here?"

"Of course," Rosemary replied. She was about to let the door swing shut on its spring when Cassie suddenly called out from the kitchen.

"It's okay. I'm here."

Surprised, Rosemary turned to face Cassie. When she'd come back from the park an hour ago, it was obvious that something had gone wrong, but Cassie had refused to tell her what. Instead she'd disappeared up the stairs, retreating once more into the solitude of her room, shutting Rosemary out. Jennifer, though, told her what had happened, and Rosemary had been tempted to call Harriet Chambers.

Except that you didn't do that when two teenagers had a spat, did you?

Had it been Jennifer and one of her friends, fine—the two mothers could do their best to straighten it out. But when the kids were Cassie's and Lisa's age, shouldn't she stay out of it?

Now she felt foolish for even having thought of calling Harriet, for obviously Cassie's anger had passed. She was smiling at Eric now as if she hadn't a care in the world.

"Hi," Cassie said to Eric. "You ready?"

Eric nodded. "I would have been here earlier, but—well, you know."

Cassie's smile faded. "Your dad?"

Eric shrugged dismissively. "You know what he's like. Come on."

As the two teenagers started out the back door, Rosemary reached out and stopped Cassie. "What about your room? Have you cleaned it?"

"I'll do it later," Cassie replied. She started to move around Rosemary, but Rosemary stepped sideways to block her path. "You got out of it earlier by taking Jennifer to the park. Now, before you do anything else, I want that room cleaned."

Cassie's eyes darkened. "I'll do it later," she said again. "Besides, you're not my mother, and you can't tell me what to do!"

While Rosemary stared after her in shocked silence, Cassie disappeared out the back door, letting the screen slam behind her.

For just a moment Rosemary considered going after her, then abandoned the idea.

She was going to have at least four days alone with Cassie. She didn't want to start them off with a fight.

From the *Big Ed's* pilothouse Ed Cavanaugh watched the *Morning Star III* move sedately out of the harbor as Keith Winslow carefully maneuvered it past the channel markers.

From the provisions he'd watched Keith stowing aboard, it looked like he was planning to be out quite a while. That meant his wife would be alone in the house with Jennifer.

Jennifer, and Cassie.

His mind darkened as he thought of the girl.

He'd seen her watching him. It had been going on ever since Miranda had died, and gotten worse in the last few days, after she'd locked herself up in that room of hers.

Almost every day he'd seen her standing at her window, looking down at him, accusing him, like maybe she thought *he'd* killed Miranda.

But he hadn't done anything, no matter what the girl thought. Not that he cared that Miranda was dead—in fact he was glad. At least Eric wouldn't be wasting any more time going out to that cabin of hers, listening to whatever crap the crazy bitch had been telling him all those years. And Eric thought he was so smart, thought no one knew where he was going all those times when he sneaked out of the house on weekends, leaving all the work for him to do.

He should have stopped it years ago, Ed thought. Would have, too, if there'd been any way he could have kept his eye on the kid all the time. But there wasn't.

Once he'd even tried to go out to the cabin himself and slap some sense into Miranda. Tell her to leave his kid alone! And after he'd told her—

But he'd never even gotten close to the cabin. The goddamn hawk had seen to that.

So when the old witch had finally gotten what was coming to her, he hadn't shed any tears.

Except that now Cassie was picking up where Miranda Sikes had left off. Now it was Cassie who Eric was always talking to. And he knew what Eric was telling her.

He was telling her the same things he'd told Miranda—telling her what a jerk his old man was!

And she was listening to Eric, too, just like Miranda had. And why wouldn't she? He'd seen what the little tramp was after right from the beginning, staring at the boy with those big brown eyes and getting him into all sorts of trouble, cutting school and being wise with his father. Cassie Winslow and Miranda Sikes were two of a kind. Well, he might not have been able to do anything about Miranda, but he knew what he could do about Cassie Winslow.

He already knew Rosemary Winslow didn't like her. So tonight he'd go pay a little call on Rosemary. With her smart-ass husband gone, she'd pay attention to him. He'd tell her exactly what Cassie was all about, and let her know what would happen if she didn't see to it that Cassie stayed away from Eric. If she wanted to live with a nut in the house, that was fine with him. But she'd damn well keep the kid away from his son.

And after they'd talked . . .

Ed's eyes glistened as he thought about what he might do to Rosemary Winslow.

Hell, he thought, she probably wouldn't even scream. She'd probably like it. She'd sure given him the eye enough times.

He opened the little icebox next to the sinkful of dirty dishes and fished around for a beer. When there wasn't any, he slammed the icebox closed and locked the *Big Ed*.

The Whaler's Inn always had beer, and people to talk to. Good people—people who liked him.

Not sluts like his wife, and Rosemary Winslow, and Cassie.

Well, he'd show them. He'd show them all. And he'd start tonight.

Nineteen

The hawk cocked his head, his pink eye fixing on Cassie, the feathers on his neck ruffling nervously.

The cage had been completely invisible as they approached; indeed, Cassie hadn't even been sure toward which bush Eric was leading her. To her eye the entire area to the west of the hillock seemed choked with vegetation, and the path Eric had followed had been all but completely grown over with vines and reeds.

But a few moments ago she'd felt a tingling sensation come over her, almost as if there were unseen eyes watching her. She'd paused, looking around, and Eric had looked at her sharply. "You can feel him, can't you?"

Cassie hesitated. "I—I can feel *some*thing," she said. "Are we close?"

Eric nodded. "Over there. The big bush, with the clump of cattails growing out of it."

Cassie had scanned the area ahead, then spotted the bush Eric was pointing at. She'd started toward it, and the tingling sensation grew stronger. Finally, with Eric behind her, she'd knelt down on the damp earth and pushed her way through the dense foliage. The cage was hidden among the branches, near the trunk of the shrub.

Inside the cage, his talons wrapped around a makeshift perch, Kiska had gazed warily at her, soft clicking sounds emerging from his throat.

Eric crept up beside her, then fished in the pocket of his jacket. "Here," he breathed. "Give him this." He put something in her hand.

Cassie glanced down, gasping as she recognized the small shape of a dead mouse sitting in her right palm. Her stomach recoiled and her hand jerked reflexively, the mouse falling to the ground.

The hawk stretched up from the perch, its neck extending as it reached for the small gray form. Cassie looked fearfully at Eric. "What should I do?"

"Pick it up," Eric told her. "Hold it on your hand, but keep your hand flat. Then put your hand in the cage. He'll take it right away."

Cassie swallowed hard, then gingerly picked up the dead mouse and laid it in the palm of her hand.

Kiska clucked eagerly, his head bobbing and weaving as he kept his eyes on the furry shape.

Cassie carefully opened the cage door just wide enough to slip her hand inside. Kiska's head flashed forward, and suddenly the mouse was in his beak.

Cassie quickly pulled her hand out of the cage and shut the door. Then, as they watched, the bird began eating the mouse.

He dropped it to the floor of the cage and pounced on it, his talons puncturing the creature's hide, sinking into its flesh as his curved beak began tearing chunks of skin and meat from the small skeleton. As soon as a piece came loose, the bird jerked his head back, his tongue stuffing the morsel back into his throat. Even before the first piece was swallowed, he was tearing at the corpse once more. In seconds the mouse had disappeared, even its bones torn apart and forced down the bird's gullet.

"Did you ever see anything like it?" Eric breathed, his eyes still on Kiska, who was back on his perch now, methodically preening his feathers with his beak.

Cassie, still fighting a wave of nausea, shook her head.

"You've really been doing this every day?" she asked. "Where did you get the mice?"

Eric said nothing for a moment, then shrugged. "The cellar of our house. Dad dumps everything down there, and there's mice all over the place. I just set some traps. A couple of days ago I had three for him."

"But what are we going to do with him?" Cassie asked. "We can't just keep him out here forever."

Eric glanced at her out of the corner of his eye. "And we can't just let him go, can we?"

"But he's okay now," Cassie said. "I know he is."

"But what about Templeton?" Eric asked. "If he sees him, he'll shoot him again."

Cassie fell silent, her eyes fixed on the bird for several long seconds. Inside the cage Kiska stopped preening his feathers, standing perfectly still as he stared back at Cassie.

The soft cluckings in his throat died away.

Finally Cassie reached out once more and opened the door of the cage. Immediately the hawk hopped from the perch to the floor of the cage and extended his head through the opening.

Slowly, warily, Cassie moved her hand down until her wrist was just outside the door.

Kiska bounded onto her wrist, his talons closing around her flesh as they had around the mouse's a few minutes earlier. But the pressure was light, and the needle-sharp points of his claws didn't pierce her skin.

A soft sigh escaped her lips, and she smiled at Eric. "It's all right," she said. "I can feel him, and it's all right."

As if to prove her words, the hawk suddenly leaped from her arm, his wings spreading as he beat his way through the thick foliage and burst into the sky above the marsh. Cassie and Eric pushed out of the tangled branches of the bush and scrambled to their feet. Above them the hawk was circling higher and higher, his wings moving strongly as he searched for the wind. Then he found it and his wings locked into position as he soared on the breeze, his tail spread wide, a screech of excitement bursting from his throat. A moment later he dived, swooping low over the pine trees around the cabin, flushing a flock of ravens from their nests. Cawing loudly, the black birds fluttered into the air, streaking after the hawk. He rose high again, with the ravens chasing after him, then dived straight into the flock. Frustrated and furious, the ravens tumbled through the air then spread out, surrounding the hawk. One by one they darted in at him, but each time he dived away, gradually leading them out over the sea.

"What's happening?" Cassie asked. "What are they doing?"

"He's playing with them," Eric told her. "First he flushed them out to make them mad, and now he's teasing them. Watch!"

The ravens tumbled around the hawk, rolling in the air as they darted toward the bigger bird, then dropping away before he could attack them. Finally he wheeled over the sea, found the wind once more, and sailed serenely back, ignoring the screaming ravens as he dropped to the peak of the cabin roof.

For a few minutes the ravens circled him, attempting to lure him back into the air, but he sat calmly where he was, his beak once more methodically combing through his feathers. Losing interest at last, the ravens drifted back to their nests. Within a few minutes the marsh was quiet again, only the soft murmurings of the feeding ducks occasionally punctuating the rhythmic washing of the surf beyond the dunes.

Feeling the warmth of the sun on their backs, Cassie and Eric started walking slowly back toward the cabin. A deep sense of peace settled over Cassie, and once more she understood why Miranda had been able to live here by herself, why she'd loved the marsh so much. It was a universe sufficient to itself, teeming with life and activity, but somehow set apart from the rest of the world.

Then, a second later, the quiet that hung over the marsh was shattered by a high-pitched screech as Kiska leaped from the roof, climbing into the air.

"What is it?" Cassie gasped. "What's wrong with him?"'

Eric said nothing for a moment as he gazed into the sky, one arm shielding his eyes from the sun. The bird spiraled higher, then leveled off, soaring across the marsh toward the park.

A moment later he disappeared from their view.

"Where's he going?" Cassie cried. "If anyone sees him—"

Eric grabbed her hand. "Come on," he yelled. "I think I know where he's gone. I'm sure of it!" Pulling Cassie with him for the first few steps, he began running through the twisted labyrinth of trails. Cassie hurried after him, doing her best to keep up, her feet slipping in the mud every few steps. As Eric reached the edge of the marsh and paused to catch his breath, she caught up.

"What is it?" she asked. "Eric, where are we going?"

"After Kiska," Eric gasped. "Will you stop asking questions and just come on?"

"Look!" Eric shouted. He came to a sudden stop, and Cassie had to throw herself to one side to keep from crashing into him. She stumbled, then she caught herself, regained her balance and followed Eric's gaze.

They had come up Commonwealth Avenue, and the square opened before them. But Eric wasn't looking at the square. He was pointing off toward the Congregational Church.

Cassie searched the sky for a moment, before finding what she'd been looking for.

High up, almost out of sight, Kiska was circling in an ever-tightening downward spiral. Slowly the speck in the sky grew larger, and then Cassie heard once more the faint sounds of his screams as he cried out in preparation for an attack.

"But what is it?" she asked. "It's just the church—"

"Not the church!" Eric yelled. "The graveyard! He's over the graveyard, Cassie!"

Her heart pounding anew, Cassie rushed around the corner then across the street and into the square. The little cemetery next to the church came into view, and she could see clearly what Kiska had somehow known and Eric had guessed.

In the graveyard, crouched in front of Miranda Sikes's grave, was Lisa Chambers.

Around her were half a dozen of her friends. Cassie recognized Jeff Maynard and Kevin Smythe, along with Teri Bennett and Allayne Garvey. The others were faces she'd seen before, but had no names for.

But she knew what they were doing, knew it just as surely as had Kiska and Eric.

"No!" she screamed. "Don't do that!"

Lisa looked up, and when she saw Cassie and Eric, a cold grin spread across her face. "I can do what I want," she taunted. "There's nothing you can do to stop me!"

"Yes there is!" Eric shouted from behind Cassie. "Look!"

He pointed into the sky. Lisa and her friends looked up, then froze where they were.

Kiska was streaking down, his high-pitched scream of attack electrifying the air, his talons reaching out.

Cassie gasped, staring at the strange spectacle, knowing what would happen in just a few more seconds.

And she wanted to let it happen, wanted to let Kiska tear into Lisa the way he had torn into the corpse of the mouse only a little while ago.

But once more Miranda's voice welled out of her memory, speaking softly to her.

She tried not to listen, tried to shut out the words. But she couldn't do it.

Miranda spoke, and she had to listen.

"No!" she screamed out loud. "Kiska, don't!"

The hawk, already into his final dive as he prepared to attack the crowd of terrified teenagers, whirled in the air, flapped wildly for a moment until he caught the wind, then reversed his course and began climbing upward once more. A few seconds later he leveled off and wheeled back toward the marsh.

Eric and Cassie watched until he'd disappeared, then Eric's eyes narrowed. "You should have let him do it," he said, his voice bitter.

Cassie shook her head. "I couldn't. Miranda—" She broke off, but Eric looked at her, his eyes penetrating.

"What?" he pressed. "What about Miranda?"

"She never wanted to hurt anybody," Cassie said quietly. She started across the street to the graveyard, where Lisa and her friends were now backing away. As Cassie stepped through the gate into the cemetery itself, they turned and fled. But it wasn't until they were gone, and she and Eric were alone, that she finished what she'd been saying. She looked down at the defaced headstone that marked Miranda's grave, and the shredded remains of the uprooted flowers she'd planted there so short a time ago. "She never wanted to hurt anyone," Cassie said again. "And she doesn't want me to hurt anyone either."

Eric's jaw tightened. "But she's dead! She doesn't care what you do."

Once more Cassie shook her head. "But I don't feel as though she's dead," she said quietly. "I feel as though she's still alive inside me, and sometimes I can . . . well, I can almost hear her talking to me. And she doesn't want me to hurt anybody.''

"Even if they hurt you?" Eric challenged.

Cassie hesitated. "They—they can't hurt me," she faltered. "Not unless I let them."

"But they *are* hurting you," Eric insisted. "When Lisa does something like this, it hurts you just as much as your mother hurt you and my father hurts me." The bitterness in his voice hardened into anger. "Just because they aren't beating up on you doesn't mean they're not hurting you. And they won't stop as long as they know they're succeeding."

She knew he was right, knew that what Lisa and her friends were doing stung just as much as any of the slaps she'd ever received from her mother.

But how could she stop them?

Then, slowly, an idea began to take shape in her mind.

Maybe, after all, there was a way. Maybe Eric was right. If they thought they weren't hurting her at all . . .

Quickly, before she lost her nerve, she made up her mind. And when she told Eric what she was going to do, he nodded his agreement.

"It's perfect," he said. "It's just perfect."

Then they began repairing the damage Lisa had done to Miranda's grave.

It was almost eight-thirty when Cassie and Eric walked around the end of the school building and cut across the playing field to the gymnasium entrance. The double front doors to the gym stood open, light from the foyer spilling out onto the front steps and the yard beyond. A couple of kids were standing at the edge of the lighted area, passing a cigarette back and forth between them.

Cassie paused in the comforting shelter of the darkness, then spoke quietly. "Maybe—maybe we shouldn't go in at all."

"But we already decided," Eric replied. "Besides, I can hardly wait to see their faces."

Cassie felt a knot of fear tighten in her stomach as she remembered the expression on her stepmother's face when she'd come downstairs half an hour ago.

Rosemary had been sitting in the little den at the front of the house. When Cassie stepped in from the foyer, she'd glanced up from her knitting and gasped, her eyes widening in shock. But before she could speak, Cassie had hurried out the front door and down the street, where Eric was waiting for her on the corner in front of the church.

"Did she say anything?" he asked.

Cassie had shaken her head. "She didn't have a chance." She'd chuckled. "For a second I thought she was going to faint."

But now, as the throbbing rhythms of rock music reverberated from the building and she thought of the crowd of teenagers inside—all of them friends of Lisa Chambers—she was beginning to lose her nerve.

As if sensing what was happening, Eric took her arm. "Come on," he said. "You can't back out now." His grip on her arm tightening, he led her out of the shadows, and they hurried up the steps into the gym.

Charlotte Ambler stood at the door to the gym itself, keeping a watchful eye on the crowd that covered the dance floor. So far everything seemed to be perfectly normal, and she was enjoying a brief respite from the tension that had permeated the school almost from the day Cassie Winslow had arrived. When she'd heard the rumor that Eric Cavanaugh had broken his date with Lisa Chambers for tonight and was planning to bring Cassie Winslow to the dance, she'd had a sinking feeling that something was going to go terribly wrong. So she'd made sure she got to the gym and taken up her station even before the doors had opened, hoping her very presence could avert whatever trouble might be brewing. During the last hour, with no sign of either Eric or Cassie, she'd begun to let herself relax. Apparently they weren't coming at all.

As the band wound up its first set of the night, the last electronic wailings of the synthesizer fading away, she sensed someone behind her and turned, prepared to welcome the latest arrivals.

Turned and froze.

Standing perfectly still, her face an ashen white, her eyes wide, stood Cassie Winslow.

Except that it wasn't Cassie.

It was Miranda Sikes.

The black skirt—the same black skirt Miranda had worn every day of her life—fell from Cassie's waist to the floor.

She wore Miranda's thick black woolen sweater, and wrapped around her head in loose folds that almost concealed her face, was Miranda's black shawl.

She cradled Sumi in her left arm while the fingers of her right hand slowly stroked his fur.

The cat's eyes, large and golden, glowed dangerously in the soft light from the gymnasium.

"C-Cassie—" Charlotte breathed. A wave of dizziness swept over her, and she had to reach out to the wall to steady herself.

"Cassie?" the eerie apparition said, her voice echoing with the oddly detached quality of Miranda Sikes. "I'm not Cassie. Cassie's gone. I'm Miranda. I'm Miranda Sikes."

Moving slowly and deliberately, she walked past Charlotte and paused in the doorway that led to the dance floor.

It was only then that Charlotte saw Eric Cavanaugh standing just inside the building, his face pale, his eyes fixed on Cassie. Her heart thumping erratically, Charlotte hurried over to him. "What's going on, Eric?" she asked, her fear giving way to sudden anger. "Is this some kind of a joke?"

Eric only shook his head, pretending to be puzzled. "I—I don't know," he stammered. "When I picked her up, she was dressed that way, and all the way over here she wouldn't say a word. I—I tried to talk to her, but she wouldn't answer me. I'm not even sure she heard me."

Charlotte closed her eyes for a moment in a vain effort to shut out the strange image of Miranda that Cassie had managed to create, shut out the reality of what must have happened.

A hush fell over the crowd of teenagers inside the gym as one by one they became aware of the dark figure that stood framed in the doorway.

Cassie didn't move. She simply stayed where she was, her fingers stroking Sumi, her eyes—wide and unblinking—flicking over the crowd. And then, across the room, she found what she was looking for.

Lisa Chambers, her back toward Cassie, was standing with Teri Bennett and Allayne Garvey next to the punch bowl.

Her eyes fixed on Lisa, Cassie moved slowly across the now silent room.

The crowd parted before her, watching her slow progress. When she was ten feet from Lisa Chambers, she stopped.

Lisa suddenly realized the room had grown totally silent, and her skin began to crawl as she felt eyes watching her.

She turned around.

The cup of punch in her hand crashed to the floor as she stared at the black-clad figure that stood ten feet away.

It was Cassie.

It *had* to be Cassie.

But somehow it wasn't.

It was Miranda, her empty eyes glaring balefully.

She felt Teri and Allayne move away, and suddenly she was standing alone, facing the accusing eyes. Icy fingers of panic began to close around her, and her legs began to tremble.

The cat hissed dangerously, its fur rising up to stand on end.

Then Cassie's hand came up, her forefinger pointing directly at Lisa. "You," she breathed. "It was you. . . ."

Once again she moved forward, and as she came closer to Lisa the hand of fear squeezed tighter on the other girl.

The cat's teeth were bared now, and its back had arched as it once more spat out at Lisa. Then it crouched down, its tail twitching as it prepared to spring from Cassie's arm.

As Cassie took one more step, Lisa screamed and twisted away from the approaching figure.

Stumbling, she lurched into the table. Its legs gave way, and the table, with its punch bowl and cups, crashed to the floor, Lisa sprawling on top of it. She tried to scrabble away across the floor, but the tablecloth entangled itself around her and she flailed helplessly, still shrieking with fright.

Then, behind her, she heard a peal of laughter. Whirling around, she stared up at Cassie, who was smiling mockingly at her as she pulled the shawl off her head.

"You said I was crazy, didn't you?" Cassie asked. "Isn't that what you told everyone? Well, I just decided to be what you said I was. How did you like it?"

There was a moment of dead silence as everyone in the room realized what had happened.

Then, from a few feet away, another laugh broke out.

And another.

And another.

Lisa, her dress stained with punch, struggled furiously to her feet. "It's not funny!" she screamed, her voice trembling with fury and her face contorted into a twisted grimace of rage. "Look what she did to me!" She turned to Allayne and Teri, but they, too, were laughing.

"She got you," Allayne told her, unable to suppress her giggling. "She got all of us!"

As the laughter swept through the rest of the room, Eric appeared at Cassie's side, his eyes glittering. "Well?" he asked. "You didn't answer Cassie's question. How did you like it?"

Still trembling with fury, Lisa glared at her laughing classmates. "You did it," she spat at Eric. "She couldn't have thought of anything like this. It was you!" Her hand lashed out and she slapped Eric across the cheek.

Instantly the humor disappeared from Eric's eyes, replaced with a chilling cold. "You shouldn't have done that," he said, his voice tight, anger boiling inside him. "You shouldn't have done that at all."

Lisa only slapped him again, her face scarlet with fury. "I'll do anything I want!" she screeched. "I'll get both of you for what you did! You'll be sorry! You'll both be sorry!" Then, tears of rage and humiliation streaming down her cheeks, she shoved her way through the crowd and stormed out into the night.

A moment later, as her classmates crowded around her, Cassie realized that Sumi was gone. "We've got to find him," she whispered to Eric as soon as she could get close enough for him to hear her. "What if he finds Lisa? What'll he do to her?"

But as they made their way out of the gym, and Eric still felt the sting of Lisa's slaps on his cheek, he knew that he didn't care what the cat did to Lisa.

In fact, if he had his way, Sumi would kill Lisa Chambers.

Twenty

Rosemary Winslow glanced at the clock for the fifth time in fifteen minutes. She had promised herself not to do any of what she thought of as "serious" worrying until midnight, but it was becoming harder to keep that promise as each minute dragged by.

What could Cassie have been thinking of? That moment still burned in Rosemary's memory—that eerie moment of certainty that she was actually seeing a ghost—when Cassie had stood in the doorway, her face all but lost in the shadows of Miranda's shawl. If her intention had been to frighten Rosemary, she'd certainly succeeded. But what would happen when she got to the dance?

By the time Rosemary had recovered enough to go after Cassie, the girl was gone, swallowed up into the night. For a moment Rosemary had considered going after her in the car, but then gave up the idea, certain that even if she found Cassie, there would only be a scene as she demanded that Cassie come home and change her clothes and Cassie refused. So she'd spent the evening with Jennifer, half expecting Cassie to come home early in tears, humiliated by the taunting of her classmates.

But Cassie had not come home.

Rosemary put Jennifer to bed at nine, and settled down in the den with her knitting, deciding that everything must have turned out all right after all. Then the clock in the living room had struck eleven and her worries returned. For the last fifteen minutes she'd been pacing restlessly through the house, wondering what to do.

The radio that could put her in instant contact with Keith seemed to beckon to her, but so far she had resisted its seduction. Still, she was standing at the den door for the fourth time in the last hour, chewing at her lower lip as she once more weighed the seriousness of the situation, when the soft tapping at the back door intruded on her consciousness. Had it not been for that, she would have given in and called Keith, begging him to come home. Of course, she would have had to call him back when Cassie finally did come home—as Rosemary was positive she sooner or later would—and tell him that it had all been a false alarm. She was thinking this as she abandoned the den and hurried into the kitchen.

To Rosemary's surprise, Laura Cavanaugh was standing on the back step, her face pale and drawn in the light from the service porch. When she opened the door and saw her neighbor more clearly, Rosemary couldn't stifle a gasp.

Laura's eyes were puffy, each of them circled with a dark ring of bruises. There was a cut on her left cheek extending nearly to her ear, and her right cheek was swollen, its edematous flesh mottled with an ugly purplish color.

The two women stared at each other in silence for a moment as tears welled in Laura's damaged eyes. "I know how I look," she said apologetically. "I suppose I shouldn't have come over—"

Rosemary's hands rose in an instinctive gesture of protest. "Not come over? Why on earth not? Laura, what's happened? Did Ed—" She broke off when she saw Jennifer, rubbing sleepily at her eyes, standing in the kitchen door and staring curiously at Laura.

"I couldn't sleep," the little girl said. "I thought maybe Cassie was home."

"Go back up to your room, sweetheart. Mrs. Cavanaugh and I are just going to have a little talk." Jennifer hesitated, frowning, then decided that this was not the time to argue with her mother. A moment later she was gone, and Rosemary turned her attention back to Laura. "Did Ed do that to you?" she asked, the hardness in her voice indicating that she assumed he had.

Laura started to shake her head, but then, almost against her will, nodded. "It's not too bad, though—really. And it's not why I came. It's Eric—he hasn't come home yet. I—well, I was wondering if he was over here with Cassie." Her eyes went to the ceiling, as if she might be able to pierce the wood and plaster that separated the two floors of the house. "I hate to be a bother, but Ed could come home any minute, and if Eric's over here, well . . ." Her voice faltered, then she fell silent, sinking helplessly onto one of the straight-backed kitchen chairs.

"Have you called Gene Templeton?" Rosemary asked. Without asking Laura if she wanted any, she began preparing a pot of tea.

"Gene?" Laura echoed vaguely. "Why would I call Gene? It's not like something's happened to Eric—"

"I'm not talking about Eric!" Rosemary broke in. "I'm talking about you. For heaven's sakes, Laura, how long are you going to put up with this? You can't just let Ed beat you up every time he gets mad!"

Laura shook her head helplessly. "He doesn't—"

"Yes, he does!" Rosemary insisted. "My God, Laura, it's not as if it was a secret. Everyone in town knows what he does to you. But if you won't stick up for yourself, what can anyone do?"

Laura's hands went to her face, and she rocked back and forth in her chair. Rosemary watched her for a moment, wondering if she should go to Laura, put her arms around her, try to comfort her. She knew, though, that what Laura Cavanaugh truly needed was not pity, but a discovery of the strength that would finally allow her to walk out on Ed. And no amount of comforting would give her that. Sighing heavily, Rosemary poured hot water over three tea bags, let the tea steep for a while, then poured a cup of the steaming brew and set it in front of Laura Cavanaugh. At last Laura seemed to regain control of herself.

"I'm sorry," she said. "I know you're right! But it's Eric I'm worried about right now. He said he was going to the dance with Cassie—"

"And Ed hates Cassie," Rosemary broke in. "I know. But he's not here, and neither is she."

"But where are they?" Laura gasped. "If Ed comes home—" Once again she fell silent, but this time her eyes went fearfully to the kitchen window. Following Laura's gaze, Rosemary saw Ed Cavanaugh's white pickup truck weave down the driveway, its brakes squealing as he slammed it to a stop. Both women watched in silence as he slid out of the truck and lumbered unsteadily toward the back door of his house.

"Drunk, of course!" Rosemary said disgustedly as he disappeared from their view. Then they heard him roaring his wife's name, and his son's. A few seconds later he reappeared at the back door and Laura and Rosemary could see him staring speculatively at the Winslows' house. The sharp intake of Laura's breath rasped with unnatural loudness as Ed started across the driveway separating the two houses.

She lurched to her feet. "He can't find me here," she whispered. "If he does—"

But it was too late.

Ed Cavanaugh, his bloodshot eyes glowing with malevolence, jerked the back door open without knocking and was suddenly framed in the service-porch door, his fleshy mouth twisted into a scornful sneer.

"Mighta known you'd come sniveling over here." He spat the words at Laura with a viciousness that made her wince, then turned his attention to Rosemary. "Where's Eric?" he demanded. "He with that crazy brat of yours?"

Rosemary rose to her feet, her fear of his drunkenness washed away by indignation. "Eric isn't here, and neither is Cassie," she told him. "They're still at the dance. And if you're still here in two minutes, I'm going to call the police."

Ed regarded her with contemptuous eyes, then waved his hand dismissively at his wife. "Get the fuck outta here, Laur—me and the uppity lady here are gonna have a little talk."

"Ed—" Laura began, but before she could speak another word Ed raised his hand and, in what seemed to Rosemary an almost idle gesture, spun Laura around and shoved her out of the kitchen. Laura hesitated only a fraction of a second before pushing through the back door and hurrying into her own house, her hands once more covering her face as she sobbed in pain and humiliation. Only when the Cavanaughs' back door had closed behind her did Rosemary finally speak, and when she did, it was from the telephone.

"I'm calling Gene Templeton," she said. "I'm going to tell him exactly what happened, and I hope Laura will finally file some charges against you."

But before she could finish dialing, Ed had crossed the room, the bulk of his body pressing Rosemary against the wall as he twisted the receiver out of her hand and dropped it to dangle from its cord a few inches above the floor.

"That what you gonna do, uppity lady?" he asked. "Now why would you want to do a thing like that? I didn't hurt her none. Fact is, she likes it. But now she's gone, and ain't nobody home but you and me, is there? Your snotty husband ain't coming home at all, and his creepy kid's off gettin' my kid into more trouble, ain't she? So what do you say you and I get in a little trouble of our own?"

His face moved closer to hers, and Rosemary suddenly realized what he intended to do. His mouth was only a few inches from her own, and his sour breath made her gorge rise. She tried to push him away, but his weight seemed immovable. Then, from the door to the dining room, she heard Jennifer's voice.

"Mommy? Mommy, is he hurting you?"

Rosemary struggled, but Ed's hamlike hands had closed on her wrist and he held her immobile against the wall. She twisted her head to one side just as his mouth was about to press against hers. "Get out, Jenny!" she yelled. "Run across the street and get help. Tell them to call the police!"

"Goddamn you—" She heard Ed growl as his hands tightened on her wrists like twin vises.

"*Now,* Jen!" she yelled. She heard Jennifer yelp in sudden fear, and out of the corner of her eye saw her daughter dart away. Finally, summoning the last reserves of her strength, she jerked her leg up, plunging her knee into Ed Cavanaugh's groin.

A strangled howl burst from his throat, and his grip was momentarily loosened by the searing pain that rose from his groin to slash upward through his body. Rosemary twisted away from him, shoving hard.

Losing his balance, Ed tumbled backward into the kitchen table then fell to the floor, his hands gripping his crotch as he glared furiously up at Rosemary.

"Crazy," she heard him say as she dashed past him, toward the back door and the safety outside. "You're as crazy as the girl. All you hadda do was be nice. . . ."

A few minutes later, from the shelter of the neighbors' house across the street, Rosemary saw him stagger out the back door of her house, pause for a moment as if making up his mind what to do next, then get back into his truck. Thirty seconds after Ed was gone, Gene Templeton turned onto the block, the red lights flashing on top of his car.

Ed drove blindly, fighting the nausea that roiled through his body. The pain in his groin seemed untempered by the alcohol in his blood; indeed, the two seemed to combine into a raging fury that grew within him like a separate being, driving him on, banishing the last vestiges of reason from his mind.

He knew where he was going; knew where to look to find the source of his fury.

And he knew what he would do when he got there.

Cassie Winslow was just like Miranda Sikes.

She'd put a spell on the boy, and if Ed didn't do something about it, she'd put a spell on everybody else too.

He decided she'd already put some kind of spell on Rosemary Winslow. She must have, or Rosemary wouldn't have done what she did. After all, Rosemary wanted him as bad as he wanted her, didn't she? Sure she did—he'd seen the way she'd looked at him, seen the lust in her eyes.

But today, when she finally could have had him, she'd kicked him. She'd actually tried to hurt him.

No woman had ever done that.

So Cassie must have done something to Rosemary.

Maybe he should go back and try to explain it all to her.

That was it! That was where he'd gone wrong!

He'd gone over there to talk to Rosemary, but Laura had been there and he hadn't had a chance to explain things to Rosemary.

It was all Laura's fault! She'd spoiled it for him, just like she'd always spoiled everything for him!

And now it was too late. Rosemary Winslow wouldn't listen to him now. None of them would, not as long as Cassie could keep working her witchcraft.

Witchcraft.

The word echoed in Ed's fogged mind, but as he kept driving, his eyes barely seeing into the darkness beyond the windshield, he knew he'd stumbled on to the truth.

She was a witch, just as Miranda Sikes had been, and she'd cast a spell over his son, just as Miranda had!

Well, he'd fix that, as soon as he found them.

He might not know much, he told himself, but he sure as hell knew what to do with women.

Twenty-one

It was Cassie's fault—all of it!

And Lisa was about to make her sorry.

She walked quickly along Oak Street, glancing furtively to each side whenever she stepped into the pools of illumination cast by the streetlamps. She tried to tell herself that it didn't matter if anyone saw her. It wasn't even midnight yet, and she had a perfect right to be out walking.

Except that if anyone saw her, and remembered seeing her . . .

She hadn't known what she was going to do when she'd gotten

home from the dance. Still furious, she'd ripped off her ruined dress, changing into jeans and one of her father's old sweaters, then stuffed the dress into the trash barrel behind the garage. At least her parents weren't home, so she didn't have to explain to them what had happened. She'd turned on the television set, but only sat staring unseeingly at it, her fury steadily growing, focusing on Cassie. There had to be a way to get even with her. There had to be!

It was during the eleven o'clock news that the idea came to her. She hadn't really been watching the television until the screen glowed brightly with flickering reds and oranges, catching her attention. With her anger still burning, she listened to the report of a fire in Boston.

A fire that had been set deliberately, with a book of matches and a can of lighter fluid . . .

Her father kept lighter fluid in his den, along with all the other junk he used to take care of the pipes her mother hated so much but that he wouldn't give up.

By the time the news ended, she'd made up her mind, and by eleven thirty-five she'd found what she needed and slipped out of the house.

So far it had all been easy.

She came to the park and left the sidewalk, pushing her way into a clump of lilac bushes that edged the lawn. As the heavy foliage closed around her, she breathed a sigh of relief and let herself relax. Though clouds were scudding across the sky now, enough moonlight filtered through the branches so she could see where she was going, and it occurred to her she might not need the flashlight in her pocket at all.

Lisa worked her way through the bushes slowly and carefully, the anxiety she'd felt on the sidewalk quickly transformed into a thrill of excitement.

She came to the edge of the lilacs and paused. Twenty yards of open lawn separated her from the next thicket.

Should she run, hoping to make it across the open space before anyone could notice her, or should she simply step out onto the lawn and not worry if anyone saw her?

But why would she be alone in the park at night? The sidewalk was one thing—she could be going anywhere. But the park was something else again. She crouched in the thicket for a few more seconds, then made up her mind.

Taking a deep breath, she stepped deliberately out of the bushes and slowly sauntered across the grass, doing her best to look as if she hadn't a care in the world. Only when she was within a few yards of her goal did she lose her nerve and break into a quick trot. And then, once again, she was safe from any prying eyes. From here on it would be easy.

She moved more confidently now, pausing again only when she came to the far side of the thicket. Parting the leaves with her hands, she looked out over the marsh.

The evening breeze had died away, and the only sound Lisa could hear was the rhythmic pounding of the surf on the beach. With the strange amplification of sound at night, she could hear even the soft hiss of each dying wave as it spent its energy on the sand, followed by a short silence as the next wave built up for its assault on the shore.

Over the marsh itself there was an eerie stillness that almost made Lisa change her mind. Her confidence ebbed away, and she shivered involuntarily at the thought of going out into the bog alone. For the first time in years she remembered the stories she'd heard when she was little, about the ghosts that haunted both the marsh and the cabin it surrounded. But they were only stories, and Lisa knew there were no such things as ghosts.

Indeed, the only truly fearful things that had ever been in the marsh were Miranda and her hawk, and now Miranda was dead.

But what about the hawk? Where was it?

She lingered a few more moments, unwilling to take that first step into the bog, and when she finally left the shadowy security of the lilac thicket, she stayed on the narrow path skirting the marsh, leading toward the friendly familiarity of the beach and Cranberry Point.

There was no hurry, she told herself. She had plenty of time.

Her step quickened, and as she neared the beach, her cold anger fed her confidence. It was going to be all right.

Already she could see the cabin—the cabin that Cassie Winslow loved so much—burning brightly against the night sky. By morning, only a heap of smoking ashes would be left.

Inside the cabin a single oil lantern burned on the table beneath the peak of the roof—its wick turned so low that only a soft glow suffused the room, leaving the corners in shadowy darkness. Eric had built a fire in the stove, damping it down so that it was no more than slowly burning embers, the little smoke that escaped up the chimney invisible against the blackness of the night sky. The cabin was warm, and had a cozy feeling to it that his own house had never had. It seemed to welcome them, shielding them from the rest of the world. And even with the lamplight and the fire, Eric knew that from the outside the cabin would still appear to be deserted. He grinned at Cassie. "How long do you suppose we could stay here before anyone found us?"

"Sometimes I wish it could be forever," Cassie replied, scratching at Sumi's ears. He was curled in her lap now, purring contentedly. They'd found him outside the gym, skulking in the darkness, but when Cassie had called to him, instead of running to her and leaping into her arms, he'd dashed the other way, then paused, his tail twitching as he twisted his head around to look at them. For the next thirty minutes he'd darted away, just out of Cassie's reach, then waited, leading them on until they realized where he was going.

"I wonder why he brought us out here?" Eric mused, his eyes drifting from Cassie to the animal in her lap. "It almost seems as if he knows something we don't."

"Sometimes I think he does," Cassie replied. She tried to explain to Eric the strange connection she had with the cat, talking hesitantly at first, afraid he might laugh at her.

But he didn't laugh.

Instead he listened to her intently, and when she was done, asked her a question: "Is that the way it is with Kiska too?"

Cassie nodded. "When Mr. Templeton shot him, I could feel it. It sounds crazy, doesn't it?"

Eric hadn't answered the question directly. Instead his eyes had taken on a faraway look, as if he were thinking about something else entirely. "Lots of things are crazy," he'd said at last. Then, almost reluctantly, he stood up. "I've got to go home," he said.

"Why?" Cassie asked. "Your dad doesn't want you around, and Rosemary doesn't want me around. Why can't we just stay here?"

Eric hesitated only a split second. "I can't. If I do, my dad'll find out and he'll kill me." When Cassie didn't move, he cocked his head uncertainly. "You coming with me?" he asked.

Cassie hesitated. She knew she ought to go home, knew that if she didn't, Rosemary would be furious with her. But Rosemary, she was certain, was furious with her already. And there was a warmth and comfort about the cabin that made her feel closer than ever to Miranda. She shook her head. "I'm staying here." Her eyes met Eric's. "If Rosemary asks you, don't tell her where I am. All right?"

Eric shrugged. "I guess. You sure you'll be okay?"

Cassie smiled at him reassuringly. "Of course I will. This place feels like it's really mine—it's the first place I've ever been where I really feel I belong."

A moment later Eric was gone, and Cassie was alone in the little cabin, with only Sumi for company.

*   *   *

Lisa froze.

Twenty yards away a dark figure had stepped out of the marsh onto the dunes that formed Cranberry Point. But that wasn't possible, was it? She'd been watching the marsh so carefully, looking for any signs of movement, and she could have sworn there were none.

And yet someone was there, standing still, staring out over the moonlit sea. Then the figure moved, and started toward her.

She stepped back, pressing herself into the small clump of shrubs that stood alone at the corner of the parking lot which served both the park and the beach. If she stood perfectly still, maybe the person would pass by without seeing her.

As the figure grew closer, she knew who it was.

Eric.

Her whole body tensed with anger. But what was he doing out here? Was Cassie with him? No—he was alone.

Then she understood.

He'd been out in Miranda's cabin, and Cassie must still be there.

She smiled darkly—that would make it even better.

She shrank deeper into the bushes, holding her breath.

A twig snapped.

She saw Eric stop, saw him turn toward her. But maybe it still wasn't too late. If she held perfectly still—

"Who's there?"

Eric's voice was startlingly loud in the stillness of the night. Despite herself, Lisa jumped slightly. Instantly Eric's body shifted, and she knew he'd seen her. There was only one thing left to do.

"It's me!" she exclaimed loudly, stepping out of the bushes into the moonlight.

Eric stared at her. She'd changed her clothes, and was dressed in jeans and a black sweater now, with a scarf tied around her head. But why was she here? What was she doing, sneaking around in the middle of the night?

The memory of her slaps stung sharply, and his eyes narrowed. "What are you doing out here?"

"J-just taking a walk," Lisa replied, but the hesitation in her voice told Eric there was more to it than that. "You won't tell anyone you saw me, will you?" Lisa asked anxiously.

"Not tell anyone?" Eric demanded. "Why shouldn't I? And what the hell are you doing, hiding in the bushes?"

"I—I didn't know who you were," Lisa stammered. But almost against her will her hand closed on the can of lighter fluid and the book of matches in her pocket. Eric saw the movement.

"What have you got?" he demanded. "You *are* doing something, aren't you?"

"No!" Lisa said, too loudly. "I was just—I just wanted to go for a walk," she said, her voice taking on a belligerent tone. "Isn't that all right with you? You don't own the beach, do you? Or is it only you and Cassie who are allowed to come out here?"

Eric looked at her carefully. She *was* up to something—he was sure of it. But what? And why was she dressed like Cassie? "What's in your pocket, Lisa?" he asked. "What are you going to do?"

"Nothing!" Lisa insisted, her temper once more slipping away from her. She took a step backward but missed her footing and stumbled in the sand.

Eric moved closer, grabbing at her arm. "You tell me what you're doing!" he demanded. Lisa struggled in his grip but couldn't wriggle free.

Then, from the road beyond the parking lot, Eric heard something and looked up.

On Cape Drive he saw the familiar shape of his father's pickup truck. It was weaving slightly, and instantly Eric knew his father was drunk and looking for him.

"Come on," he said to Lisa. "It's my dad." Jerking roughly on her arm, he pulled her out into the dunes and the beach beyond.

The marsh, Ed Cavanaugh thought. That's where he'd found them last time, and that's where he'd find them this time. He pressed his foot down on the accelerator while slamming the transmission into a lower gear. There was a satisfying shriek as the tires spun wildly for a second then caught, shooting the truck forward. Ed's eyes fixed on the pavement ahead as he raced past the summer houses that lined Cape Drive. Just ahead was the expanse of tall grass that marked the beginning of the marsh. Then, out in the dunes that separated the marsh from the beach, he saw two running figures—a boy and a girl—their hands clasped together.

Eric and Cassie, he thought.

Ed's grip tightened on the steering wheel as his fury grew. Ahead, on the left, he saw the parking lot and veered the truck off the road. It wasn't until he was nearly across the lot that he realized he had no intention of stopping.

Tonight there would be no shouting from the cab of his truck.

Through a haze of alcohol he imagined he could see them clearly now—see the grins on their faces. Hell, he could even hear them, and knew what they were laughing at.

They were laughing at him.

But they wouldn't laugh much longer. When he got done with them, they'd never laugh at him again.

*   *   *

Cassie sat quietly, enjoying the solitude of the cabin, feeling the peace that Miranda must have felt here. Though there was no one else around, she didn't feel alone. If she listened carefully, she could hear the sounds of the sleeping birds murmuring in the marsh, and the raccoons and other creatures as they moved through the wetlands, searching for food.

Strangely, she felt less lonely now, with only the birds and animals around her, than she ever had before. And then his back arching as an angry hiss boiled out of his throat—Sumi leaped out of her lap and darted over to the door. She looked at him curiously, then understood.

Someone was out there.

Someone who meant her harm.

Tears of frustration flooded her eyes. Why couldn't they just leave her alone? Why couldn't they just let her be?

Without thinking, she went to the door and opened it a few inches. "Go see, Sumi," she said softly. "Go find out who it is."

Like a ghost, his padded feet making no sound at all, the cat disappeared into the night.

Eric jerked Lisa to a stop. Turning, his eyes fixed on the truck. It should have stopped in the parking lot. But it hadn't. Instead it was still coming, jumping slightly as its tires struck the low curbing that separated the paved lot from the sand of the beach. Now it was crossing the beach itself, slogging through the soft sand toward the water. When it reached the hard-packed wet sand near the water's edge and turned toward them, he realized what was happening.

Lisa understood at the same moment. "He's coming right at us," she gasped, her anger suddenly forgotten. Now it was she who reached out to grasp Eric's hand.

Eric cursed under his breath. His father really intended to kill him this time! For an instant his body froze, then he summoned all his energy. "Come on!" he yelled. Jerking her hard, he leaped sideways out of the truck's path. It swept past them—its horn blaring, its tires spitting a stinging sleet of sand into their faces. As they watched in growing fright, the truck slowed then spun around to face them again.

"What are we going to do?" Lisa wailed. "What does he want?"

But Eric was too terrified to answer. The truck was gathering speed again, and he had to decide which way to go. Before he could make up his mind, the issue was decided for him. The truck bore down on them, and there was nothing Eric could do but drag Lisa into the protection of the water itself.

"He's drunk!" he yelled as he stumbled into the roiling surf. "He wants to kill us!"

Lisa's eyes widened, and she turned to stare at the truck, which had passed them once more and was even now circling around to try again.

"Get out of the water!" she heard Eric yelling. "When he comes back, he'll try to push us in again and he'll swerve down the slope. But this time we'll go the other way."

The truck was gathering speed now, and Lisa stared at it in detached fascination. It bore down on her like some kind of raging beast, but she couldn't move. Instead she stood still, frozen like a rabbit in the glare of the headlights.

She felt Eric yank on her arm, felt herself being pulled out of the path of the screaming juggernaut. Eric had been right. At the last second the truck swerved down the sloping beach, its left tires hitting the water. As it passed, Lisa got a clear look into the cab.

Behind the wheel, his face contorted into a twisted grin and his eyes lit with a strangely glowing madness, she saw Ed Cavanaugh. An icy chill of pure terror sliced through her. Once again she knew that Eric was right.

He meant to kill them.

She started screaming as Eric dragged her up the beach toward the edge of the marsh.

Goddamn it, Ed swore to himself. He should have had her that time, should have felt the impact as the front fender crashed into her body, slamming her down into the sand and crushing her under the wheels.

But Eric had outsmarted him. Pulled her the wrong way, so all he'd done was drive the fucking truck into the water. He fought to control the slewing tires, pulling the wheel hard to the right. But it was as if the water itself was fighting him now, trying to pull both the truck and him out to sea. Then, slowly, the ocean seemed to release its grip and the truck surged back onto the hard-packed sand. But the windshield was covered with salt spray now, and he could barely see out. Clutching the wheel with his right hand, he began groping along the dash with his left.

At last the wipers came on and the windshield cleared. He jerked the truck into another U-turn, then he saw them racing across the beach, toward the marsh. If they got in there, he'd never catch them.

He slammed his foot onto the accelerator and the truck lunged forward, hurtling across the wet sand. He leaned on the horn and listened as its blaring rose above the pounding of the surf behind him. The truck slowed as it plowed into the soft sand above the tide line and surged up the gentle slope of the dunes.

But it didn't slow enough to make any difference.

He'd cut them off this time and drive them back down toward the water. He slammed the transmission into a lower gear, and the extra power made the truck leap forward.

As he shot past them he could see the terror in their eyes. Even the blasting of the horn couldn't drown out the girl's scream.

"He's going to kill us!" Lisa shrieked as the truck shot past, only inches away. Once again she'd seen Ed clearly, his greasy hair matted against his forehead, his drunken eyes glazed over as he stared drunkenly back at her.

And he was laughing.

Even over the awful cacophony of the racing engine and blasting horn, she'd heard an unearthly laughter pour from his throat.

"He's trying to push us back in the water," Eric gasped. "Come on!"

Half dragging Lisa now, he lurched to his feet and started once more toward the marsh. The truck was only a few yards away, floundering in the sand as Ed struggled to turn it toward them once again. Then the lights swept around, blinding Eric for a moment, and he tightened his grip on Lisa's hand.

"Run!" he yelled, but over the mass of sound that seemed to roll over the beach, he could barely hear his own voice.

Then he was over the dunes, and one of the paths into the marsh opened before him. Hauling Lisa behind him, he lurched into the reeds and stopped, gasping for breath.

Behind him Lisa collapsed to the ground, panting. Sobs of fear wracked her body, and when she looked up at Eric, her face was streaked with tears and sand.

"What's he doing?" she wailed. "What's wrong with him?"

"He's gone nuts," Eric replied, kneeling beside her and straining to see out onto the dunes and the beach. The headlights had destroyed his night vision, and though he couldn't see the truck itself now, he could see its twin beams of light and hear its engine roaring like an infuriated animal that had momentarily lost its prey. "We've got to get out of here. If he finds us—"

"How?" Lisa demanded. "We should have stayed on the beach! We can't get through here—we're trapped!" She stared fearfully into the depths of the marsh, remembering the maze of nearly invisible paths, some of which led somewhere, some of which simply disappeared into the reeds and the quicksand. Why had she ever come out here in the first place? Why had she ever thought she could get all the way out to Miranda's house all by herself? "I didn't mean it," she suddenly sobbed. "I shouldn't have come out here at all! I didn't mean it! I swear I didn't mean it!"

Eric turned to face her, his eyes suddenly blazing. "Didn't mean what?" he demanded. "You tell me what you were doing, damn it!"

"The cabin," Lisa wailed. "I was going to burn it down! I was going to get even with Cassie by burning the cabin!"

The anger inside of Eric suddenly boiled to the surface. "You're just like him, aren't you?" he grated through clenched teeth. "You think you can do anything, and everybody's always going to let you get away with it!"

"Stop it," Lisa whimpered. "I didn't mean—"

"You didn't mean what? You didn't mean to do what you just said you were going to do? You didn't mean to slap me? What didn't you mean, Lisa? What!"

But Lisa didn't hear him, for the truck was moving again, its headlights slowly sweeping the marsh, twin eyes searching for them.

"Maybe—maybe he won't be able to see us," Lisa gasped. "Maybe if we just stay still—"

And then the lights were on her, and without thinking Lisa stood up. She stood perfectly still, frozen in the blinding glare.

Like a bug on a fucking pin, Ed Cavanaugh crowed to himself. There she stood, a scarf wrapped around her head, her black sweater almost invisible against the background of the night. But it was her, all right. He could almost see those eyes of hers, those accusing eyes—and he could almost taste the fear in her. But where was Eric? But it no longer mattered, not really. He could take care of Eric anytime.

But he might never get another shot at Cassie as good as this one. He gunned the engine and popped the clutch. The rear end of the truck dropped lower and the wheels once more dug into the sand.

The sudden movement of the truck seemed to free Lisa, and she screamed.

"Run! He's coming again. *Run!*" Without thinking, she spun around and lurched off the path, into the reeds and grasses that choked the marsh.

Water flooded into her shoes and she stumbled, then caught herself and plunged on, no longer caring whether she was on a path, caring only about hiding herself from Eric's father and the truck. But the lights seemed to stay on her no matter how she twisted and dodged. It was almost as if they were playing with her.

*　　*　　*

Eric moved quickly down the path, his fury still growing. Suddenly he hoped his father *would* find her. Let her find out what could really happen to her! He didn't care anymore. He didn't care about any of them! And then, a few steps ahead of him, he saw a shape on the path—no more than a small dark mass, crouching low to the ground.

And two yellow eyes, glowing brightly in the darkness.

Sumi.

Eric paused, staring at the cat.

Cassie's cat. Or so they all thought.

There was a reason why he was here, why he had stumbled across him—he was sure of it.

As he looked into Sumi's glowing eyes, he knew what the reason was.

He thought quickly, then knew what he had to do. He crouched down and whispered soothingly to the cat. Sumi's tail twitched, then he crept slowly forward into Eric's waiting hands.

Slowly, concentrating on the fury pent up inside him—and on the sting of Lisa's slap—he began stroking Sumi's soft fur.

Beneath his fingers he could feel the cat's body tense up. It was working. It was all working.

The gray shape rose in front of Lisa like a shadow out of the night, and her hands instinctively came up to shield her face.

Too late.

With the speed of lightning Sumi's claws sank into the flesh of Lisa's cheeks, and she screamed in sudden pain. Stumbling, she lurched sideways, and suddenly the grasses seemed to wrap themselves around her.

But far worse than the slime and reeds of the marsh was the creature tearing at her now.

Where had it come from?

Why was it attacking her?

She thrashed against it, trying to tear it away, but it only clung closer, its claws sinking deeper and deeper. A searing pain slashed through her as its jaws closed on her cheek and ripped a piece of flesh away.

She rolled violently, trying to escape the animal's fury, and then the ground suddenly gave way beneath her and she felt herself begin to sink through the brackish water, into the sucking mixture of mud and sand below.

She screamed again, flailing at the muck that held her in its grasp, managing to knock the cat aside. Sobbing, she struggled to her hands and knees, but then the cat was on her again. She felt her right leg plunge knee deep in the quicksand as the animal's claws stripped the skin away from her forehead. As she clawed at the cat with her hands, she tried to jerk her leg free, but only felt her left leg begin to sink too.

"No!" she screamed. Then: "Eric! Eric—help me!" For a second nothing happened, but then she heard the roar of the truck's engine once more. Suddenly the lights were on her again, slicing through the tangle of reeds which now seemed to threaten her.

"Please," she sobbed. "Please, help me . . . please. . . ." But the marsh held her firmly in its grip, and the cat's attack went relentlessly on.

The harder she struggled, the deeper into the quicksand she sank. Then, as the shallow layer of water above the quicksand closed over her, the cat suddenly abandoned her.

Swim.

The thought rose out of the depths of her subconscious, and she began trying to fight the panic that had already overwhelmed her. But it was too late, and as she flailed her arms, the reeds and grasses only wrapped themselves more tightly around her . . . until she felt she could struggle no more. All she could do was wait, whimpering and bleeding, to die.

Eric burst out of the marsh and paused to catch his breath. His heart was pounding and he could feel the blood throbbing through his veins with so much pressure it made his head ache and his vision blur. But when he looked back toward the beach, he could still see the lights of the truck.

Only they were still now, reaching out into the marsh.

Had his father found Lisa yet? And if he had, what had he found . . . ?

He turned away and forced himself to run once more. Then he found the house he was looking for, and pounded up onto its front porch to pummel at the door with his fists. After what seemed to be an eternity, the door finally opened and Charlotte Ambler, clutching at the bodice of her robe, stared out at him.

"It—it's Lisa," Eric gasped. "In the marsh. He—he's trying to kill her, Mrs. Ambler."

Charlotte's eyes widened. "Kill her?" she repeated. "Who, Eric? Who's trying to kill Lisa?"

"My father," Eric rasped. "My father!"

Charlotte Ambler stared at Eric. What on earth could he be talking about? After what had happened at the dance—

Her mind reeling, she pulled Eric into her house.

A moment later she was calling the False Harbor police department. It seemed as though it took forever before a bored voice finally answered the phone.

Ed Cavanaugh sat in his truck, watching the girl die. It seemed to take a long time, but it didn't matter. It was good to see it happen, good to enjoy every moment of it.

As she struggled, he began to feel the same strange pleasure he always felt after he'd put Laura in her place, or given Eric a whipping.

He left the truck and picked his way slowly into the marsh, until at last he was standing in the muck only a few feet from her. Now, out of her torn and bleeding face, he could see her eyes watching him in the glow of the headlights. There was terror in them, the kind of terror he had never seen in Laura's eyes, or in Eric's, and he smiled as he watched her writhing in the tangle of reeds and ooze. But even through his drunkenness, he could sense that something wasn't quite right.

It was her eyes. There was something about them that was wrong.

Maybe, he decided, it was just because she was dying.

Lisa looked up into the twisted face above her.

He wasn't going to help her, wasn't going to release her from the grip of death.

He was smiling at her, smiling at her with an expression she had never seen before.

He was going to watch her, and he was going to enjoy every moment of her agony.

No, she told herself. *No. I won't let him do that. I won't.*

Making up her mind, she tensed her body for the final effort, then lunged—

—downward.

She twisted deeper into the muck, and felt it close over her head and begin to ooze up into her nostrils.

She opened her mouth, but no scream emerged as the thick sludge filled her mouth, then her throat.

Even as her body revolted, retching against the vile invasion, she forced herself yet deeper, until she felt the mud and sand close over her.

It wasn't right. She wasn't supposed to die tonight. If anyone was supposed to die, it should have been Cassie. But she hadn't even come out here to kill Cassie. Not really.

She was only going to burn the cabin.

That was all. Just burn the cabin down.

Then, as the oxygen slowly leeched out of her bloodstream, a strange euphoria began to overtake her.

In the final moments of her life, the fear and terror drained out of Lisa Chambers, and she felt a great calmness seize her spirit. Then the blackness overcame her, and the last thing she saw, its tail twitching as its eyes glowed a bright gold in the yellow beam of a headlight, was the cat—Cassie's cat—watching. Watching, and remembering everything that happened.

It knew, Lisa thought. It knew what I was going to do.

Then it was over.

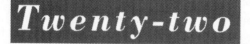

Twenty-two

G ene Templeton stifled a yawn and tried to ignore the weariness that was slowly infusing his body. Twenty years ago he'd just be getting his second wind along about now. But not anymore. He was just too old. Still, a long night stretched ahead of him. He glanced at the notes he'd taken while Eric Cavanaugh repeated his story of what had happened on the beach an hour before, then shifted his attention to the boy himself. Eric's eyes betrayed his nervousness, but he was much calmer than he'd been when Templeton arrived. He sat stiffly on the edge of the Victorian sofa in Charlotte Ambler's living room, his mother beside him.

The bruises on Laura's face were still clearly visible.

"Ed did that to you, didn't he," he stated, his voice flat.

Laura stiffened, then shook her head. "I—I fell," she murmured.

Fell. Did she really expect him to believe her? She knew he'd just come from talking to Rosemary Winslow. She'd seen him there before he'd picked her up and brought her here. Well, he wasn't going to argue with her right now. Sighing heavily, he turned back to Eric, whose expression clearly indicated that he wasn't sure the police chief believed his story any more than he believed Laura's. "You're sure it was your dad?" Templeton asked once more.

Eric nodded his head obstinately. "I already told you. I saw him, and so did Lisa. It was Dad, all right."

Templeton flipped his notebook closed and tucked it into the inside pocket of his jacket. "Okay. I'll go out to the beach and have a look around." He turned to Charlotte Ambler, who had been sitting in silence, carefully listening to every word Eric had spoken.

But so far she'd said nothing. "Can I use your phone? Before I start combing the beach I'd like to call Fred Chambers. Maybe Lisa's already home."

Charlotte rose to her feet. "In the kitchen," she said, though there was a telephone sitting on the table at Templeton's elbow. "It's more private," she added. She led the police chief into the kitchen and nodded to the wall phone next to the sink. But instead of leaving him alone to make his call, she stayed where she was, obviously thinking about something. But only after Templeton finished talking to Fred Chambers did she speak.

"She's not home, is she?" she asked softly.

He turned to the high school principal and shook his head. "Something's on your mind, Charlotte. If it has anything to do with this, you might as well tell me now."

Charlotte Ambler took a deep breath. "I keep wondering what Cassie was doing all that time. I mean, I could hear Ed's horn blaring. I didn't think much about it—it happens all the time when the kids are out there. But if Cassie was in Miranda's cabin, she must have heard it too. Wouldn't she have come out to find out what was going on?"

"Same thing I've been thinking," Templeton agreed. "And you can bet that that's where I'm going first. If Lisa did go into the marsh, she'd probably have tried to get to the cabin. With any luck at all, that's where she is right now." He shook his head. "I wish to Christ Laura had filed charges against that son of a bitch years ago. Something like this was bound to happen sooner or later."

"Laura should have left him," Charlotte agreed. "She should have thrown him out."

"Well, the fact is she didn't, and it sure looks like he's gone around the bend this time. I'll let you know what I find out at the beach. If I find anything," he added darkly.

A moment later he was gone, and a few minutes after that Laura and Eric left too.

"Are you sure you want to go home?" Charlotte asked them. "If Ed's there—"

"I can take care of him," Eric replied quietly. "I told him this morning I was through with him pushing me around. That's why he came after me with the truck. But he can't bring the truck in the house. We'll be all right."

After they were gone, Charlotte Ambler sat silently in her living room, waiting.

While they'd been talking, a spring squall had gathered, and now she heard the patter of rain begin on the roof.

It struck her as an omen.

*   *   *

They're coming for me, Cassie thought. *They're going to think I'm crazy, and take me away. . . .*

She knew Lisa was dead, had known it as soon as Sumi came back and leaped into her arms.

She'd felt the familiar tingling sensation, and then the images had begun to form.

And she'd watched Lisa die.

She'd stayed in the cabin for a while, but then, when she saw the flashing light of the police car and watched it speed down Oak Street and pull up in front of one of the houses across from the park, she'd known what was going to happen.

What if they found her here, sitting all by herself in Miranda's house, with Miranda's cat curled up on her lap? What if they made her tell them what Sumi had shown her? They'd think she was crazy. They'd think she'd killed Lisa herself, and then they'd lock her up.

Panic began to build up in her, and she quickly closed the damper on the old cast-iron stove then put out the lamp. At last she left the cabin, pushing her way through the marsh as fast as she could.

If she got home soon enough—if they didn't find her—she could say she'd left the cabin right after Eric did. She wouldn't have to tell them what had happened, or what she'd seen through Sumi's eyes.

It seemed to take forever, but finally she came to the edge of the marsh and slipped into the thicket of bushes on the fringe of the park. Unaware that she was retracing the route Lisa Chambers had used earlier, she forced herself through the lilacs, working her way toward Oak Street. When she got there, she paused for a moment, searching the street for cars. There were none. Taking a deep breath, she bolted out of the bushes, dashed across the street, and ran up Cambridge to Alder. Only when she was within sight of the house did she pause to catch her breath. Then, as the rain started to fall, she dashed across the street and down the driveway to the back door.

Rosemary was sitting at the kitchen table, her face pale, a cup of tea clutched between her hands. When Cassie came into the kitchen, she gasped slightly, and rose to her feet. She took a step toward the girl, but Cassie shrank back.

In Cassie's arms Sumi hissed softly.

Rosemary hesitated, but then everything that had happened that evening suddenly jelled into anger. "Where have you been?" she demanded. "You walked out of here wearing those—those *rags*—looking like you'd lost your mind or something, and then you're gone most of the night! Do you really think you can just walk in and out of here like it's some kind of hotel?"

Cassie gasped, and her eyes widened fearfully. "Eric and I—something happened at the dance, and we left early. So we went out to Miranda's cabin. . . ."

Rosemary glared at the girl furiously. *Miranda's cabin,* she thought dumbly. *Everything I've been through, and she went for a walk in the marsh. All the things I imagined, all the things I was afraid of, and they were out* hiking! The last vestige of her self-control dissolved. "How dare you? I don't know if Diana put up with this kind of thing, but I can tell you that I won't. I know you've been through a lot, and I know your father thinks I'm too hard on you! But let me tell you something, young lady—your father isn't here now, and as long as you're in my house, you will obey my rules!"

Cassie's eyes glistened with tears. "I didn't do anything—" she began, but Rosemary cut her off.

"Didn't do anything? This afternoon you walked out of here against my wishes, and were rude to me as well. And tonight you promised to be home no later than eleven o'clock. You didn't come back when you said you would, and you didn't even bother to phone. Do you really think you can just walk back in and not expect anything to happen? I was about to call your father!"

Cassie felt a chill of fear. Rosemary was going to call her father just because she'd stayed out too late? But that didn't make any sense. She must already know about Lisa. "You're going to call Dad?" she asked, her voice trembling slightly. "Wh-why?"

Rosemary glared at her, about to lash out again, but then checked her fury. It wasn't Cassie's fault—not all of it. For a moment she was tempted to tell Cassie what had happened with Ed Cavanaugh, then changed her mind. There wasn't any point, and besides, it was all over now. "It doesn't matter," she said. "At least you're home and you're all right."

But Cassie didn't hear her, for the panic she'd felt in the cabin was flooding back over her now. "You've been talking about me, haven't you?" she demanded.

Rosemary gasped in surprise at the accusation. "Cassie—"

"You have, haven't you?" Cassie insisted. *Who was it? What had they said? And why wouldn't Rosemary tell her?* "Was it that doctor? The one who thinks I'm crazy?"

"Cassie . . ." Rosemary said again. She took a step toward her, and Cassie backed away. Her eyes looked wild now, darting from one corner of the room to another, as if she were searching for something she expected to attack her at any moment.

"You're just like Lisa, aren't you?" she demanded, her voice breaking as she choked back a sob. "She hates me—she hates me, and she wanted to kill me tonight! But it wasn't my fault! I didn't do anything, but everybody hates me!'' She spun around and fled from the room, and a moment later Rosemary could hear her feet pounding up the stairs.

Rosemary sat still for a moment, then forced her body to relax. What had happened? What on earth had gone wrong? She hadn't accused Cassie of anything at all. She'd been angry, yes. But not that angry.

And yet—

Cassie's words echoed in her mind.

I didn't do anything, but everybody hates me. . . .

But nobody hated her, not really. And to say that Lisa Chambers wanted to kill her . . . it sounded . . .

She hesitated, then let herself formulate the word in her mind. It sounded paranoid.

Suddenly her fears—all of them—closed in on Rosemary once again, and once again she felt the urge to call Keith. He couldn't get home tonight, but tomorrow . . .

No! she told herself. You're upset, and you're not thinking clearly, and you're overreacting to everything. Stop it! Just stop it!

Doing her best to shut out everything that had happened that day, she began going through the habitual motions of closing up the house for the night. Not that there was any point to locking up, she thought ruefully.

Deep in her gut she knew that the day was not yet over, and that she would get no sleep tonight.

"We have to get rid of him, Mom," Eric said.

His voice was emotionless, but the cold hatred in his eyes twisted at Laura's heart. *Not him, too,* she prayed silently. *Don't let him turn out like his father. Please!* "We can't," she whispered. "Please, Eric—don't talk like that!"

"Why not!" Eric demanded. "He beat you up this morning, and he hit you again tonight! For God's sake, Mom. What are we supposed to do? Just wait around until he actually kills one of us?"

Laura's eyes widened, and her hand dropped away from the new bruise on her cheek. "Eric! He's your father, and he loves you. You mustn't talk like that."

"Why not? And he doesn't love me, any more than he loves you. For God's sake, Mom, he tried to kill me tonight!"

"He was just angry," Laura tried to explain, but the words sounded hollow even to herself. "You shouldn't have gone off with Cassie like that. You know what he told you, and you deliberately disobeyed him."

"So now it's my fault that he beats us up?" Eric exploded. "You don't expect me to buy that, do you? Now, are you going to tell me what happened or not?''

"He—he found me over at the Winslows'," Laura whispered. "I thought you and Cassie might be there. And he found me there."

"He hit you just because you went over to the neighbors?" Eric's rage drove the last vestiges of fear out of his mind. "I'm gonna call Templeton again. Maybe you won't tell him what happened, but I bet Mrs. Winslow will." He reached for the phone, but Laura put out a hand and stopped him.

"He was here," she whispered, her voice twisted with the sobs she was struggling to control. "Rosemary called him after . . . after . . ."

"After what?" Eric said tightly. His jaw was working, and his voice was taut with fury. "Did he beat her up too?"

Laura shook her head, and buried her face in her hands. When she spoke, Eric could barely hear her. He had to ask her to repeat her words. Finally she dropped her hands from her face and stared at her son expressionlessly. When she spoke again, her voice was flat, as if the words no longer meant anything to her. "She says your father tried to rape her. And she says she's going to press charges against him."

Eric stared at his mother speechlessly, then sank into a chair. His mind was whirling, trying to sort it out. His father must have gone crazy. Finally, after it had sunk in, he looked at his mother with bleak eyes. "I hope she does," he said softly. "And I hope they lock him up."

"Eric—" Laura tried to protest, but he only shook his head.

"He was trying to kill us, Mom. I don't know why he was pissed at Lisa, but—" He fell silent as he realized the truth. "Oh, Jesus," he whispered, his face turning ashen.

"Eric?" Laura breathed. "What is it?"

"It wasn't Lisa at all. She was dressed like Cassie. That's who he thought it was. He thought Lisa was Cassie. And he wanted to kill her so bad, he would have killed me too."

Laura clamped her hands over her ears, trying to shut out what Eric was saying. "No," she whimpered, rocking back and forth in her chair. "No, it isn't true . . . none of it—"

"It is, Mom," Eric said softly. "And it's only going to get worse." His voice hardened, and his eyes flashed dangerously. "But he won't hurt us anymore, Mom. I won't let him. I'll kill him, Mom. If he tries to hurt me again, I swear to God I'll kill him."

Gene Templeton got out of his car and started out into the blackness over the beach and the marsh. He reached back into the car, switched the headlights on, and twin beams of light cut through the rain, casting an eerie glow over the sand and the surf beyond. As far as he could tell, there was no sign of the white pickup truck. He started to slam the car door, then thought again and switched on the flashing lights on top. If Lisa Chambers was still out there somewhere, there was no use letting her think Ed Cavanaugh had come back again. Finally, flipping on the powerful flashlight he always carried in the car, he started through the rain toward the cabin where Miranda Sikes had lived. With any luck at all he would find Lisa Chambers there.

Twenty minutes later he was back.

The cabin had been empty, but the stove was still warm. So at least part of Eric Cavanaugh's story had been true. But what about the rest of it?

His bones beginning to ache, he began his search of the beach. It was easy to find the tire tracks where the truck had left the parking lot and started across the sand, but the tracks quickly disappeared where the rising tide and the pounding surf had washed the beach clean. He began walking east toward Cranberry Point, playing the light on the sand just above the surf line. About a hundred yards up the beach he found what he was looking for.

More tire tracks, this time leading toward the marsh. He followed them across the beach and over the dunes, then traced them as they led back and forth along the edge of the wetlands. The truck seemed to have turned twice then found what it was looking for. Though the rain, increasing now, was quickly washing them away, there were still the remnants of two short tire tracks perpendicular to the tide line, where it appeared that the truck had been parked for a while.

Cautiously, Gene Templeton approached the marsh, searching with his light for a break in the reeds. Three times he called out Lisa's name, but the rain muffled his voice, and he could hear no answer except for the flappings of a bird.

Finally he found a narrow path with two sets of footprints still faintly visible in the packed mud and sand. He followed them for a few yards and came to a place where it looked as though someone had either knelt or fallen. From there a single pair of footprints continued along the path.

But off to the left some of the reeds had been broken and the marsh grasses were bent.

Here, apparently, was where Lisa Chambers had left the path. Templeton played his light out into the marsh, wondering vaguely whether he was hoping to get a glimpse of her or not. If she was still here and had neither seen him nor responded to his calls—

He abandoned the thought, knowing too well where it led.

The darkness was momentarily washed away by a sweep of headlights, then by another set of beams. Templeton turned and saw two cars turning off Cape Drive into the parking lot. A moment later they were joined by a third, then a fourth.

Great, he reflected sourly. Just what I need. A search party that thinks it can comb a fucking swamp in the middle of the fucking night. I'll wind up with half the town caught in quicksand. He quickly retraced his steps and started down the beach. By the time he got back to the parking lot, Fred Chambers was busy giving orders to three of his friends, all of whom, the police chief noted silently, had kids about the same age as Lisa. As he stepped into the group, Chambers eyed him almost belligerently.

"Did you find her?" Lisa's father demanded.

"I just got here, Fred," Templeton replied. "How come you're not home with Harriet?"

"You think I'm going to sit at home when my little girl's missing? I'm not that kind of man, and you know it!"

"I also know there isn't much any of us can do out here right now," Templeton said. "I was just about to call a couple of my boys to give me a hand, and I could use some of the fire volunteers too." He nodded toward Clyde Bennett, who was the unpaid assistant fire chief of the village. "You want to take care of that for me?" Bennett's eyes flicked toward Fred Chambers, then he nodded and went to Templeton's car. A few seconds later he spoke quickly but quietly into the microphone of the car's radio. "As for the rest of you," Templeton continued, "if you want to poke around, I can't stop you. But I don't want any of you going into the marsh. Not tonight. It's too dangerous, and I can't worry about you guys and Lisa too."

The two men he was speaking to said nothing. Both of them seemed to be waiting for Fred Chambers to contradict the police chief. But when he spoke, Chambers didn't argue.

"What about Cavanaugh?" he asked instead. "Have you picked him up yet?"

Templeton shook his head. "Nope. Right now I'm a lot more interested in finding Lisa than I am in finding Ed."

"But what if he's got her?" Chambers began.

Templeton cut him off. "If he does, then we're too late already. I'm betting he was so drunk he didn't even know what he was doing. And if he was, Lisa probably got away from him, which means she might still be out there somewhere. But I can't find her if I have to stand here with you all night. Go home, Fred. Go home and take care of Harriet, and as soon as I know what's happening, I'll let you know. Okay?"

For a moment Templeton thought the banker was going to argue with him, but then he saw Chambers's shoulders sag in resignation.

"Okay," Fred agreed, all the authority in his voice suddenly gone. "It's just—Christ, Gene, I just feel so helpless. And you know how I am. . . ."

"I know," Templeton agreed. *Got to try to run everything, whether you know what you're doing or not,* he said silently to himself. Then, aloud: "It'll be okay, Fred. We'll find her."

He led Chambers back to his car, still trying to reassure him, and as his deputies and the members of the fire department began to arrive, turned his attention to organizing a search party. "I want you to work in pairs," he told them. "It's dangerous out there. So be careful. But we're going to search the marsh foot by foot. Let's just hope she's out there somewhere." Finally, as the men began moving carefully over the treacherous paths of the marsh, he returned to his own car.

It was time to find Ed Cavanaugh.

The bottle of bourbon on the greasy dinette table was only one-fourth full, and the sink of the galley held half-a-dozen empty beer bottles. But for some reason the alcohol hadn't made Ed feel any better. He reached down and fished in the little refrigerator under his seat for another beer, then cursed softly when he realized there wasn't any more. Tipping the bottle of bourbon to his lips, he poured a long slug into his mouth, then slammed the bottle back onto the table as the fiery liquid burned its way down his throat to his stomach. Vaguely, he heard the topside hatch open, and glanced up to see Gene Templeton standing at the top of the companionway. "Well, look who's here," he drawled, gesturing toward the empty seat opposite him. "Pull up a bunk and have a drink. I'm buyin'."

Templeton's eyes flicked over the cabin, and he found himself almost relieved that there was no sign of Lisa Chambers. "Thought you and I ought to have a little chat, Ed," he said. He moved into the grubby interior of the fishing boat, and wondered how even Ed Cavanaugh could stand the mess. Everything in sight was covered with grease, and the sole of the cabin was strewn with a tangle of ropes, tools, floats, and odd bits of net. Trying to ignore it, he slid into the dinette opposite Cavanaugh and poured himself a shot of whiskey he had no intention of drinking.

"Saw your truck up on the street," he said, doing his best to sound casual. Ed was so drunk, he might just be able to catch him completely off guard. "Just thought I'd drop in and say hello."

Cavanaugh's brows arched skeptically. "Well, ain't you the sociable one," he grunted. "And why shouldn't my truck be up there? It against the law to park on the street now?"

"Just thought you might have let Eric have it tonight," he offered. "It being Saturday night. Know what I mean?" he added, forcing the kind of lewd wink Cavanaugh was so good at.

Ed snickered drunkenly. "Little shit'll be lucky if I even let 'im live, after tonight." He laughed mirthlessly. "An' I bet he's so scared he never even says boo to me again."

"Scared?" Templeton asked. It was working. Cavanaugh was going to admit to the whole thing. "How come he should be scared?"

" 'Cause of what I did," Ed told him, a boozy cackle bubbling out of his throat. "Caught him down on the beach with Cassie Winslow and scared the piss out of both of them."

Now it was Templeton who frowned with puzzlement. "What are you talking about, Ed? What did you do?"

Suddenly Cavanaugh's expression took on a look of cunning. "Oh, no," he said. "I know what you're trying to do. You're trying to pin it on me, ain't you? But I didn't do nothin'. All I did was chase 'em around, till they ran into the marsh. An' I tried to save her. I really did."

"Tried to save her?" Templeton echoed, a tight knot of fear forming in his stomach. "Tried to save who?"

Ed eyed him blearily. "Cassie," he mumbled. "Ain't you listenin', Templeton? Goddamn bitch went off the trail and got caught in the quicksand. Tried to get to her, but jus' couldn't do it. Jus' couldn't do it . . ." His voice faded away. He reached for the bourbon bottle, but before he could grasp it, Gene Templeton's hand closed on his wrist.

"You've had enough, Ed," he said quietly. "In fact you've had a lot more than enough. I'm taking you in."

Ed's eyes opened in drunken surprise. "Me? What for? What did I do?"

Templeton regarded the other man with a mixture of pity and contempt. "You don't know, do you?" he asked quietly. "You really don't know."

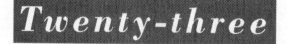

Twenty-three

*I*t's not real. None of it is really happening at all. It's all a bad dream, and I'm going to wake up, and everything's going to be fine. Even as the thoughts flitted through her mind, Rosemary knew it wasn't a dream and that she wasn't going to wake up. A numbness had settled over her, and when her eyes wandered to the clock above the sink, she could barely believe it was only a little after two A.M. The weariness that suffused her mind and body insisted that it must be close to dawn.

And at dawn, she was now certain, she would still be numbly awake, still be dressed, still be sitting up somewhere in the house, waiting.

Waiting for what?

For word that Lisa Chambers had been found? But all of them knew, though no one had yet said it, that when Lisa was found she was going to be—

She couldn't say it, couldn't deal with it.

Tiredly, she faced Gene Templeton, knowing that whatever had to be said, had to be said by her. Laura Cavanaugh seemed to have retreated into some secret place inside herself, and Eric and Cassie had sat listening impassively as Templeton repeated what Ed Cavanaugh had told him. Once or twice Eric shook his head as if to deny his father's version of what had happened on the beach. Cassie had revealed no reaction whatsoever, but merely listened in silence, her expression completely impassive. As Rosemary had watched the girl, she had the strange feeling that Cassie already knew what Ed had told the police chief.

"Then what are you going to do?" Rosemary asked. "What is it you want us to do?"

Templeton shrugged, betraying his helplessness. "I can keep Ed locked up for the rest of the night, but tomorrow, I don't know. If Laura won't charge him—"

"But I'll bring charges," Rosemary insisted. "For God's sake, Gene, he tried to rape me!"

"Did he?" Templeton replied, reluctantly assuming the role of devil's advocate. "We went through this earlier, Rosemary. There isn't a mark on you, and there are no witnesses—"

"Jennifer saw—"

"We already know what Jennifer saw," Templeton repeated for the third time. "She saw you on the telephone, and Ed standing next to you. That's all. If you had a bruise, a scratch, anything!—I might have something to go on. As it is, though, if you bring charges against him he'll just counter-sue. And when I strip-searched him an hour ago, I found the bruise he needs to back himself up, which you've already admitted you gave him." His lips twisted into a rueful grin. "The odds are, though, that he was too drunk to remember exactly what happened. So there we are—he swears he didn't see Lisa on the beach at all, and right now he's absolutely certain that Cassie is dead. He insists he saw her go into the quicksand but couldn't get to her in time to save her. Not that I can put much credence in anything Ed says, given his condition."

"He didn't even try. He hates me, you know." The words had come from Cassie.

Templeton studied Cassie carefully for a moment. She was holding something back, he was almost certain of it. But what? And why would Ed Cavanaugh hate her? But her eyes had taken on a veiled look that told him she'd said all she was going to.

Appalled by the realization of what she had said, Cassie sat silently, hands tightly clasped in front of her. She wanted to tell them she knew exactly what had happened to Lisa, tell them that Mr. Cavanaugh could have saved her, but instead he'd stood there and watched her die. But what could she say that would make them believe her? If she told them the truth—that she'd seen the whole thing through Sumi's eyes—they'd only think she was crazy. "He—he wouldn't have tried," she stammered as her stepmother and the police chief continued to stare at her. "If he thought Lisa was me, he wouldn't have done anything. He—he hates me. He didn't even want Eric to talk to me anymore!"

"All right," Templeton said heavily, standing up and pulling his raincoat on. "I'd better get out to the marsh and see what's happened. Ed can sit in a cell the rest of the night, and in the morning I'll think of something to charge him with. I can try failure to report evidence of a crime or something." He turned to face Laura. "Unless you decide to change your mind."

Laura looked up fearfully. "I can't." Her voice was a whisper. "I just can't. You have to understand. . . ."

Templeton nodded wearily. He did, indeed, understand, for the position Laura had taken tonight was no different from what he'd seen again and again as a policeman in Boston: women who were absolutely certain that the only way to save themselves from worse beatings was to keep silent about the ones they had already suffered. And in a way they were right, for too many men had come out of courtrooms swearing they had changed, only to return to their wives with their hatreds festering deeper than ever.

Some of those women, Templeton knew, had paid with their lives for assuming the law could protect them. Laura Cavanaugh had no intention of becoming one of those.

"Okay," he said, his voice gentle. "I'll do what I can to hold him, but I can't tell you he's not going to do it again, Laura. You know he is."

Now it was Eric who broke his long silence. "He won't," he said, his voice clear. "I told Mom, and I'll tell you too. If he ever tries to beat either one of us again, I'll kill him."

Templeton gazed silently at the boy. Something in Eric, he realized, had changed. Always before there had been a gentleness and kindness in Eric that he'd always marveled at. By rights the boy should have been silent and brooding, striking out at others in retribution for the injustices he suffered at home.

In Templeton's experience, most boys Eric's age and with Eric's background had long since shown some rebellion. But Eric never had. Always he'd seemed to rise above his father's hatred, had appeared almost untouched by it. But now there was a hardness in the boy's eyes, a detached coldness. Eric's words had not been uttered in momentary anger.

"That won't be an answer, Eric," he said quietly. "In a few more years you'll be out of it. If you can't stand it now, file charges against him yourself, or take off. But don't even think about killing him. He'd probably kill you first, but even if he didn't, you'd never get away with It. You're a good kid, Eric—you always have been. Don't let him push you into destroying your own life."

Eric's lips tightened, and the expression in his eyes didn't change. Finally, with nothing left to be said, Templeton buttoned up his raincoat and disappeared out into the night. When he was gone, Rosemary looked nervously at Eric, but he didn't seem aware of her gaze. His eyes were fixed on Cassie with an intensity that made Rosemary turn to look at her stepdaughter.

Cassie was returning Eric's steady gaze.

An icy chill passed through Rosemary's body. *They're hiding something,* she thought. *They know something that neither of them wants to talk about.*

The rain finally stopped as dawn began to break, but still the morning light came slowly. Leaden clouds hung low over the sea, and the horizon seemed not to exist at all. It was as if False Harbor, that morning, had been suspended in both space and time.

Charlotte Ambler opened the drapes over the front windows of her house and looked out into the gray morning. A somnolent foreboding hung over the village, and there was none of the usual Sunday morning peacefulness that had always been her favorite part of her week. On any other rainy Sunday morning she would be lighting a fire in her fireplace and curling up in her robe to slowly peruse the thick weekend edition of the Boston paper. But this morning was not like other Sunday mornings.

She gazed out toward the marsh, where the tired figures of the searchers were now clearly silhouetted against the gun-metal sky. A knot of people had already gathered in the parking lot at the end of Oak Street, and as she watched them quietly talking among themselves, she realized that she was seeing a reflection of both the best and the worst of village living.

In another place—a larger city—Lisa Chambers's disappearance would have been noted in the morning paper, and the search would have gone quietly on, almost unnoticed. And for most people, life, too, would have gone quietly on, essentially unchanged for the absence of a single member of their society.

But in False Harbor there was no morning paper; indeed, none was needed, for by now, Charlotte was quite certain, there wasn't a soul in town who was unaware of what had happened last night, at least in its barest essentials. But in the realm of detail there would be as many versions filtering from ear to ear as there were mouths to speak them, and until the truth about what had happened to Lisa was discovered, there would be scant attention paid to any other subject.

She turned away from her front window and went to the kitchen. Soon people would begin noticing that her drapes were open and would start dropping by, some looking for news, some only needing a respite from the vigil by the beach. Her large percolator had just begun to simmer when the doorbell rang for the first time. When she opened the front door, she wasn't surprised to see Gene Templeton standing on the front porch, looking every bit as tired as she herself felt.

"Anything?" she asked.

Templeton shook his head. "Not yet."

"What about Ed Cavanaugh?"

Templeton shrugged. "I found him on his boat, dead drunk. He—well, he claims there's a body out there all right. But he says it's Cassie Winslow's. He says he saw her in some quicksand but couldn't get to her."

"Cassie?" Charlotte echoed. "But Eric said—"

"I know," Templeton interrupted. "And if there *is* a body out there, it isn't Cassie. She's at home with Rosemary. Anyway, a little while ago I got to thinking . . ." He fell silent, reluctant to reveal the thought that had been nibbling at the edge of his mind for the last hour or so.

Charlotte frowned in puzzlement.

"I keep thinking about Simms," Templeton said finally.

"Harold?" Charlotte breathed. "I—I'm afraid I don't understand."

The police chief licked his lips nervously. "Remember what happened that day? He'd been riding Cassie pretty hard, and Eric too." He paused. Then: "Lisa's been giving Cassie a rough time, too, hasn't she?"

Charlotte's frown deepened as she grasped what Templeton was suggesting. Before she could speak again, a shout rose up from the marsh and both she and Templeton turned to see one of the deputies waving frantically. Templeton's stomach knotted as he realized that the man was standing only a few yards inside the marsh, very close to the place where last night he'd seen the fading marks of tire tracks on the beach. It was, he realized now, almost as if they had been pointing at the spot where Harve Lamont now stood.

Swearing softly, Templeton took the front steps of Charlotte Ambler's house two at a time and began loping back toward the marsh. Pausing only to pull her mackintosh from the hook by the front door, Charlotte followed as quickly as she could.

"How'd you find her?" Templeton asked, his voice low enough that only the heavyset deputy would be able to hear him. Harve Lamont said nothing for a moment. His eyes were still fixed on the specter of Lisa Chambers's face, barely visible beneath the thin layer of brackish water that covered the surface of the marsh.

"The reeds," Harve finally managed to say. "I couldn't really see her at all. But the reeds were all broken here, and the grass was kind of squished down. It looked to me as though there'd been some kind of struggle or something. So I came out a little closer, and there was just enough light, so . . . so—" His voice cracked and he was unable to go on.

She was nearly buried in the mud, only her face visible. Her mouth, wide open, seemed still to be forming a silent scream, while her eyes stared sightlessly up through the water. The lacerations that covered her face had been washed clean, and the damage that had been inflicted showed clearly through the water. The skin on her forehead was all but torn away, and a large chunk was missing from one of her cheeks.

And everywhere—in every place in which her flesh was still intact—there were deep parallel rows of cuts that looked to Gene Templeton almost exactly like the wounds that had covered Harold Simms's face.

Lisa's left arm was buried in the mud, but her right, almost completely entangled in a matting of swamp grass, was crossed over her body. From her position Templeton was almost certain she had continued struggling right up until the end, then—in a last terrified grasp at survival—managed to turn herself over. But it had already been too late.

Templeton nodded curtly, then signaled two of the firemen to bring a stretcher. Clyde Bennett and another man appeared with it. Behind them came two other deputies carrying wide planks, which they carefully laid on the surface of the marsh, one on each side of the corpse.

It took the four men several minutes to work Lisa's remains loose from the oozing sands. When at last her stiffened body came free, there was an ugly sucking noise as the marsh gave up its prize. But then, as Templeton watched in a kind of awe, the mud flowed swiftly together. In moments only the broken reeds still testified to the fact that only hours before a girl had died there.

In a strange cortege, Templeton led the four men bearing Lisa Chambers's body slowly back to the path and the beach beyond. Waiting for them at the point where the reeds met the sand was Harriet Chambers, her face ashen, her hands trembling.

She stared at the body for a few seconds, her lips working to stifle the scream building in her throat.

"No," she whispered at last, and then the word was repeated, rising into a keening wail that sliced through the quiet of the morning. *"Noooooo . . ."*

She was about to throw herself on her daughter's corpse when Templeton slid a firm arm around her, holding her back while he signaled to Fred Chambers with his free hand. Instantly Fred was next to his wife, supporting her while he glared at the police chief over her shoulder.

"Well?" he demanded. "Are you satisfied now? Now are you going to lock that drunken son of a bitch up?"

Templeton stared at the man for a moment, then decided it was useless to try to argue with him now. If he wasn't in shock yet, he would be in another few minutes, and though the police chief felt pity for Lisa's distraught parents, he had to attend to pressing matters. To his relief the Chamberses' friends were already beginning to surround them even as he stepped away to begin issuing orders to have Lisa's body taken to the clinic, where it would be examined by Paul Samuels.

Starting back toward the parking lot and his car, Templeton saw Charlotte Ambler, who appeared to have been frozen in her tracks by the sight of Lisa's body. But as he came abreast of her, she put out a hand and grasped his wrist.

"What does it mean?" she asked. "It—it *is* just like Harold Simms. But what does it mean?"

Templeton shook his head grimly. "I don't know yet," he said. "And I'm not going to even venture a guess until the doc's taken a look at her."

He tried to move on, but Mrs. Ambler didn't release her grip. Templeton felt her fingers tighten on his arm.

"What if it is?" she pressed. "What if it really is just like Harold?" Her eyes held Templeton's. "Are you going to say she did it to herself?"

Templeton's eyes flashed toward the group of onlookers who were staring curiously at Charlotte now, straining to hear her words. "I'm not saying anything yet, Charlotte." He spoke quietly but with an urgency he hoped she would understand. But Charlotte seemed not to have heard him at all.

"What if Harold was right?" she went on. "What if he really did see Cassie that day? And what if Ed Cavanaugh really saw her last night?"

Templeton heard the faint gasp that passed over the small crowd, immediately followed by a buzz of whispering.

That does it, he thought. Within an hour the rumors would be all over town.

Ed Cavanaugh woke up quickly: a sharp pain was jabbing through his head, as if someone had shoved a knitting needle into his ear then jerked it viciously up and down. His eyes, still closed in a futile effort to shut out the throbbing ache in his head, felt like they had ground glass in them, and his tongue—a thick slab in his dry mouth—had a sour taste to it. His body felt clammy, and remnants of the nausea that had first awakened him sometime before dawn were still clawing at him, warning him that if he moved too fast, he would find himself on his knees, retching.

A siren sounded somewhere, exacerbating the agony inside his skull, and he tried to raise his hands to clamp them over his ears, but the movement was too much for his polluted body to stand, and his stomach heaved in protest. He dropped his hands back down and concentrated on summoning the energy to bellow to Laura for a cup of coffee.

Or maybe he should just go back to sleep for an hour.

His fingers closed on the sheets, ready to pull the covers up over his head. Dimly, he became aware that something was wrong.

His hands, instead of clutching the sheets and soft blankets of his own bed, had closed on some kind of rough wool. He held still for a moment, trying to think through the pain in his brain. Then he groaned and opened his eyes a crack.

What he saw confirmed the vague memory he had summoned from the depths of his consciousness.

Above the metal cot on which he lay, there was a concrete wall, its gray paint chipped and etched with obscenities. Halfway up the wall there was a small window, covered on the outside with a heavy grillwork of bars. He stared at the barred window for a few seconds, numbly wondering if perhaps he was only dreaming.

But he knew he wasn't.

Carefully twisting his neck, the throbbing in his head building to a crescendo of pain at the movement, he saw a toilet bolted to the opposite wall.

Another memory stirred, and he vaguely recalled having rolled off the cot during the night to lean over the toilet while the contents of his stomach boiled up from his throat. The stench in the air told him that when he'd finally returned to the makeshift bed, he hadn't bothered to flush the toilet. Slowly, almost tentatively, he reached out and pressed the button that protruded from the wall next to the toilet. Instantly the roar of water under pressure filled the cell, then faded away as the mess in the metal toilet bowl disappeared into the sewers. Ed Cavanaugh groaned, turned his head to the wall and clamped his eyes closed again, as if the action itself could change the reality around him. A moment later, though, the clang of a heavy metal door made him roll back and reopen his bloodshot eyes.

Fuzzily, he recognized Gene Templeton staring at him with a face of stone from outside the cell.

"Heard the toilet flush," Templeton said.

Ed managed a nod. "Sick," he muttered. "Puked my guts out during the night."

"Tough," Templeton replied. "Wash up. You're getting out of here."

Taking a deep breath, Ed heaved himself into a sitting position and dropped his feet to the floor. His shirt, smeared with his own vomit, clung to his body like cellophane, and when he cradled his head in his hands, the smell from his shirt assaulted his nostrils with a force that once more threatened the stability of his aching stomach. "What happened?" he asked. "What am I doing here?"

Templeton regarded him silently for a moment. "You don't remember?"

Cavanaugh hesitated, then slowly shook his head. "I was on my boat," he finally managed. "I was on my boat, and then . . . then . . ." His voice trailed off into silence as slowly, a piece at a time, memories of the previous night trickled back to him. "Fuckin' bitch wife didn't have the guts to file any charges, did she?" he finally asked, his lips twisting into an ugly grin.

Now it was Templeton who took a deep breath, his hands unconsciously clenching into fists as he stared with disgust at the man in the cell. "She not only wouldn't charge you, she showed up an hour ago and put up bail for the only charge I could dream up." His lips tightened grimly. "I did my damnedest to talk her out of it, but she's afraid of what you'd do to her if she left you here. But sooner or later you'll go too far, and when you do, it's going to be my pleasure to ship you off to the slammer, Ed. Then we'll all see how tough you are. The only thing those guys hate more than a rapist is a guy who slaps his wife and kid around. Now clean yourself up. You're disgusting."

Templeton turned away, taking a malicious pleasure in slamming the metal door as he left the block of three small cells. Returning to his desk in the corner of the squad room, he dropped into his chair. His stomach growled in protest against the fact that it was now nine o'clock in the morning and he had missed—so far—two complete meals, not to mention several snacks. He picked up the phone to call Ellie, knowing his wife would cheerfully bring an enormous breakfast to his desk, then dropped the phone back on the hook as he realized that he wasn't really hungry, despite the fact he hadn't eaten since noon the day before.

It was Paul Samuels's report on the manner of Lisa Chambers's death that had cost him his appetite. Not the fact of her death—Templeton had long since learned to deal with death itself. But what Samuels told him a few minutes ago had left him feeling completely helpless.

As he'd feared, there was not a mark on Lisa that Samuels could definitely identify as having been made by human hands. She had died by strangulation, but the doctor was certain that it had been mud in her throat and trachea that had killed her, not some external force closing around her neck. Nor were there bruises on her flesh where hands might have clamped on her, forcing her down into the mud.

"But she fought," the doctor had assured him as they went over the report together. "Some kind of animal attacked her, and she struggled to fight it off. I found traces of fur under her fingernails, but it'll have to be analyzed before I can tell you what it's from. The main thing is, she fought hard, and if it was Ed Cavanaugh she was fighting, he'll have some marks to show for it. But frankly, I don't think he did it. As near as I can figure it, she was trying to fight off whatever jumped her, but she stumbled into the quicksand and lost her footing. And that was it."

There were a few cuts on her arms, but the ones that weren't easily identifiable as having been made by an animal's claws had the exact characteristics of the lacerations made by two varieties of marsh grass. In several of the cuts Samuels had discovered minute traces of the grasses themselves.

"If she'd kept her head," Samuels had finished, "she might have been all right. Whatever it was probably abandoned the attack when she fell into the quicksand, and she could have lain there all night. She'd have been cold and miserable, but she would have lived. Still, you can't blame her for panicking, can you?"

Of course he couldn't. In fact, he couldn't blame anyone yet. Despite all the talk and speculation in the village there was no proof of anything. In Templeton's gut, however, he was now certain that in some way he didn't yet understand, Cassie Winslow was involved.

Cassie's words from last night still haunted him. *He didn't even try.* Her face expressionless, her eyes fixed as though she were staring into the distance, she had spoken in a strange monotone—as though she were reliving something she had already seen.

And then there were the eerie similarities between the wounds on Lisa's face and the angry slashes that had marked Harold Simms.

"What about a cat?" he'd asked Samuels just before he left the clinic.

"It's possible," the doctor had replied. "But it did a hell of a lot of damage. If it was a cat, it sure was no ordinary house pet."

It all added up to zero: no evidence to charge Ed Cavanaugh with Lisa Chambers's death, and no satisfactory explanation for what had happened to her.

And with Laura bailing Ed out of the single charge Gene had been able to devise—obstructing justice by not reporting the discovery of Lisa's body—Templeton couldn't even keep the son of a bitch off the streets for a few days.

His thoughts were interrupted by a banging on the steel door to the cell block, and he got up to bring Ed Cavanaugh into the squad room. Fleetingly he wondered if he could get away with punching the smug look off Cavanaugh's bloated face, but knew he couldn't—bullies like Cavanaugh were the loudest screamers when someone finally gave them what they deserved. Instead he contented himself with telling Cavanaugh exactly what he thought of him while he unlocked the safe and retrieved the other man's keys and wallet. Not that it did much good.

"Aren't you gonna drive me home?" was all that Cavanaugh said when Templeton's warnings were over.

"Walk," Templeton growled. "The fresh air won't kill you. And if we all get lucky, you might just be hung over enough to get hit by a truck. Now get out of here."

When Cavanaugh was done, Templeton considered going back to his desk, then gave it up. With a nod to the deputy, he headed home. Maybe with a little sleep—and a good meal—he could start to make sense out of what was happening in False Harbor.

Twenty-four

E d Cavanaugh let himself in through the back door. Laura was standing at the kitchen sink, washing up the dishes from the breakfast neither she nor Eric had been able to eat. He said nothing, but stripped off his soiled shirt, dumped it into the washing machine, then slipped his arms around Laura's waist and gave her a gentle squeeze. When she stiffened in his arms, he felt a surge of anger, but quickly put it down. He nuzzled her neck for a moment, then pressed his mouth close to her ear.

"I'm sorry," he whispered. "I'm sorry about everything. I just— well, I guess I let things get out of control last night."

Laura twisted away from him. Her voice was cold. "Last night?" she repeated. "What happened last night wasn't anything new, and you know it! You don't expect me just to forget it, do you?"

When he replied, Ed's voice had taken on the slight whine that had become familiar to Laura over the years. "But you have to forgive me, honey. You're all I've got. I just—well, sometimes I love you so much that when I think about losing you I go all to pieces. But last night was it. I promise you that if you forgive me this time, it'll never happen again. Never."

"Until you get drunk again," Laura blurted out, then wished she could reclaim the words. But she'd heard it all so often before. He'd drink, then beat her, then—the next morning—swear it was the last time. And always she wanted to believe him. Wanted to hope.

As if he were reading her thoughts, Ed pulled her closer and pressed her head against his chest. Though the sour odor of vomit still clung faintly to him, Laura could still feel his heart beating, and the gentle throbbing gave her a strange sense of security. I don't understand, she thought. I don't understand how he can still make me feel so safe sometimes.

"I had a long time to think about things in jail," Ed said, stroking her head now. "Maybe that was what I needed—for Gene to haul me in. I'm not holding it against anybody, sweetheart. Not against you, or Eric, or even Rosemary Winslow. All we have to do is start fresh. I'm going to stop drinking, and start taking care of you and Eric. But I can only do it if I know you still love me. You do, don't you?" he added anxiously. "Isn't that why you bailed me out?"

Laura felt herself weakening. He sounds as if he means it this time, she found herself thinking. But then she reminded herself that he always sounded as if he meant it when he apologized. Not once had it ever made a difference. "I bailed you out because I didn't want Eric to have to face his friends knowing his father was in jail." It was only half true, she knew, but this time she just wasn't going to give into him.

Once again he seemed to read her thoughts.

"But this time it's really true. I swear it is. I never landed in jail before, and it scared me. I lay there all night thinking about my life, and your life, and what I've done to you, and I felt like a heel. If you left me, I don't know what I'd do. I—I think I might go crazy."

He was kissing her neck now, his lips working gently over her skin. Despite herself, Laura felt the first stirrings of excitement rising in her. Almost involuntarily her arms slid around his neck and her fingers ran through his hair. A moment later he picked her up and carried her upstairs.

Eric was sitting at his desk when he heard his bedroom door open, but he didn't turn around. For half an hour he'd been trying not to hear the sounds emanating from his parents' room, sounds he hated to hear almost more than he hated to hear the sounds of his father beating his mother. How could she do it? How could she let him touch her, after the things he'd done? When he first heard his father coming up the stairs, he'd gotten his baseball bat out of the closet and stood in the middle of the room clutching the bat, waiting for Ed to open the door. But instead his father had walked on by. In a few moments Eric had understood what was happening.

He'd had a terrible urge to rush into his parents' room and kill his father right then. Had his mother screamed—just once—he knew he would have done it. But she didn't scream, not at all. Instead he heard only moans of pleasure, and his grip tightened on the bat as his rage grew even wilder. But he didn't lose control. When he became aware that he had actually taken several steps toward the door, and understood what he was about to do, he forced himself to turn around and go to his desk, put the bat on the floor next to his chair, and open one of his textbooks. It was the wrong time; the wrong place. Since then he'd been staring unseeingly at the same page, battling to keep his emotions in check.

Now his father stood in the doorway to his room, and Eric had to turn around and face him. Ed was clad only in a pair of underwear. "I want to apologize," he said, taking a tentative step into the room. When he saw Eric reach down and pick up the baseball bat, he stopped where he was, a look of puzzlement coming over him. "You don't want to do that, Eric," he said softly. "You don't want to hurt the old man. Hell, I told Templeton you didn't have anything to do with what happened last night."

Eric said nothing.

"I didn't kill her," Ed went on, his voice taking on its whining edge once again. And he hadn't, not really. Some of it had come back to him as he'd walked home. He had a vague memory of being on the beach, chasing Eric and Cassie in the truck. He remembered Eric disappearing down one of the paths in the marsh, but Cassie . . .

Cassie had not been able to get away from him. Finally she'd stumbled into the quicksand. He'd watched her die. But he hadn't killed her. If he had, why would Templeton have let him out of jail? "I didn't do it, son." He licked this lips nervously and his mind raced as he saw the cold fury in Eric's eyes. "I'm sorry she's dead," he lied. "But you can't hold it against me, can you? Hell, you hardly even knew her. And you've still got Lisa. . . ."

Eric's eyes widened. He doesn't know, he thought numbly. He doesn't even know who was out there.

Then, as Eric watched his father with an almost detached curiosity, he saw the blood drain from Cavanaugh's face and a look of terror come into his eyes.

"No," his father snorted. *"No . . ."*

Eric realized that Ed was no longer looking at him. His eyes, wide with shock now, were fastened on the window. Eric's own eyes followed his father's gaze. Then he understood.

Standing in her window, staring at Ed Cavanaugh with an unblinking gaze, was Cassie Winslow.

"No," Ed Cavanaugh breathed once more as he stared at the girl who should have been dead. "It can't be her! She's dead, goddamn it! She's dead!" Wildly he tore his eyes from Cassie and glared furiously at Eric. "I saw it!" he managed to say, his voice strangling now. "I tell you I was there, and I saw her die!"

Eric shook his head, his lips curling into a faint smile. "It wasn't Cassie, Dad," he said quietly. "It was Lisa. You killed Lisa!"

His face purpling with rage, Ed took another step toward Eric, but Eric raised the bat.

"Don't touch me! Don't you come near me, or I swear to God I'll kill you, even though you are my father!"

Ed froze, staring at the bat and at Eric. Now his voice turned venomous. "She's really got you, doesn't she?" he snarled. "Just like Miranda. She's got you the same way Miranda had you!" His eyes sparkled malevolently. "Miranda should have let you die out there, boy! She should have let both of you die! Nobody ever wanted either one of you anyway!" An evil laugh bubbled up from his throat, and he lurched out of the room, his mind suddenly consumed with a single thought.

A drink. He had to have a drink.

Eric didn't know how long he'd been lying on his bed, didn't know whether he'd been sleeping or awake.

His father's words still echoed in his mind.

He knew they were true; had always known. . . . He pulled himself upright, his body stiff, his mind muddled. An image of his father seemed burned into his memory, and he could still feel the venomous look Ed had given him and recall the words he'd uttered.

He stood silently for a moment, then crossed the room to the window. When he looked out, Cassie was still at her window.

But now she was staring at him.

He left his room and started toward the stairs, pausing at the landing to listen to the house and sense the atmosphere. He heard no sound, but neither did he feel the tension that always hung in the air when his father was at home. Slowly, almost against his own wishes, he started down the stairs.

He found his mother in the parlor, sitting stiffly on one of the wing-back chairs which were only used on special occasions, her eyes fixed on some point beyond the window. When he spoke to her, she didn't seem to hear him, but finally, just as he was about to speak again, she swung around to look at him. Her eyes, usually filled with fear, had taken on a look of tired resignation, as if she had finally faced herself and found herself wanting.

"I'll never get out," she said, and the emptiness in her eyes was matched by her voice. "After everything he's done, I forgave him. How could I have done that, Eric? How could I?"

Eric's eyes glittered with barely contained fury. "What happened?" he demanded, his voice low but with an edge so sharp it made Laura flinch. "He said Miranda should have let us die. He said no one ever wanted us. Tell me what happened, Mother. Tell me what he was talking about!"

Laura gazed blankly at her son for a moment, then seemed to focus. "Miranda," she breathed, nodding slowly. "But it was so long ago. So very long ago. . . ."

It had been a Saturday. One of those hot humid Saturdays when the house was almost unbearable. Ed had been on edge all day, and she'd done her best not to do anything that might annoy him. After lunch, when he suggested he take Eric to the beach, she was relieved. It would give her a chance to catch up with the laundry and the thousand-and-one other things she somehow never quite found the time to keep on top of. And so she'd packed a change of clothes for Eric and sent them off. But a couple of hours later, when she'd finished the laundry, the heat had finally gotten to her.

She'd decided to join Ed and Eric at the beach.

She knew where they always went—far out to Cranberry Point, where the summer people never went. And it hadn't taken long to find them.

Find Ed, at least.

He was lying on a blanket making love to Diana Winslow, the two of them locked in a passionate embrace. Then Ed must have sensed her presence, for he looked up. As Laura stared at him, speechless with shock and disappointment, she saw his humiliation turn to rage.

And the children—Eric and Cassie—were gone.

She never remembered much about what happened in the next half hour. All she'd known was that she had to find Eric.

And she'd found him.

Found him in Miranda's house.

Miranda had smiled at her as she'd come through the front door—a strange smile that chilled Laura's heart.

"I found them," Miranda told her. "I found them in the quicksand, and they're mine now. They belong to me."

Laura said nothing. Instead she snatched both of the children up into her arms and fled from the cabin in the marsh, rushing almost blindly through the bog until she was back on the beach. And there she had found Ed and Diana, waiting for her. She demanded to know how they could dare behave as they had. Didn't they know the children could have been killed in the marsh?

Neither of them had said a word, and as Laura watched them, she slowly realized why they weren't speaking to her.

They weren't speaking because they had nothing to say.

Consumed by their own desires, neither of them, neither Eric's father nor Cassie's mother, had cared if the children lived or died.

Laura never spoke of the incident afterward, never told anyone what had happened that day on the beach. A month later Diana had left False Harbor, taking Cassie with her.

And Laura—unable to face raising Eric alone—had stayed with Ed.

After that day on the beach the beatings began. In his own mind, Ed had blamed her. Blamed her—and Eric too—for what she witnessed that day. Now, brokenly, painfully tearing away the scars that had hidden her wounds for years, she told Eric the whole story. "That's why he hates us, Eric," she finished, her voice barely audible. "He hates us because of his own shame—shame for betraying me, shame because he knows that you could have died and it would have been his fault. He hates me because I *know*," she finished, her voice cracking. "He must have thought I'd leave him. But I couldn't—I just couldn't!"

Eric froze, staring at his mother, who finally turned back once more to face him with beseeching eyes.

"You have to forgive me, Eric," she pleaded. "You have to."

The room reeled, and a black abyss seemed to yawn at Eric's feet. As his mind spun with his effort to grasp what his mother had said, the memories came flooding back to him.

He saw a face looming over a bed—his bed. Eyes filled with hatred glared down at him from above, and a horrible odor hung in the air. He tried to roll away from it, but every time he tried to squirm under the blankets, rough hands—hands so big they could have crushed him—reached down to snatch the blanket away. And there was a voice, and words he'd never been able to remember before. Now they rang clear in his memory.

"You're nothing," the voice had said. "You should be dead now, you understand me? Nobody wants you, boy. And I'm gonna make you wish you *had* died!"

After a while the voice had stopped, but the beatings had started. And all his life, no matter what he'd done, it had never been right, never been quite good enough, never pleased his father.

And all because of something that had happened when he was only two years old.

"Why?" He uttered the word as an almost formless croak, but he could see that his mother understood.

"It was the shame," Laura said brokenly. "Can't you see, Eric? It was the shame. He never got over the shame. . . ."

"Shame?" Eric repeated, the shattered fragments of his life suddenly coalescing into a rage that surpassed all the anger he had ever felt before. "He wasn't ashamed of what he did! He was ashamed that he got caught! But he's never been ashamed of what he's done to us! And what about you? Didn't you care what he was doing to me? I figured out a long time ago you don't give a damn what he does to you! But what about me? I didn't know what he'd done. I was just a baby! How could you let him do that to me?"

He was shouting now, and Laura cowered on the chair, shrinking away from his words.

"How?" he screamed. "How could you let it happen?"

Laura pushed herself to her feet and took a step toward Eric, but he backed away.

"Don't touch me," he whispered. "Don't you ever touch me again."

"No, Eric," Laura pleaded. "No. I love you, Eric . . . I've always loved you. Please . . . ?"

"Loved me?" Eric wailed. "If you loved me, you wouldn't have let it happen!"

"I couldn't help it, Eric. I tried . . . I tried so hard—"

Eric's hand clenched into a fist and he drew his arm back, ready to strike the pathetic figure before him. Laura froze—like a rabbit trapped in the glare of a headlight—waiting for the blow.

"Do it," she whispered. "You hurt so much, and you're so angry. Do it, Eric."

Slowly, through an agonized exercise of sheer will, Eric un-clenched his fist and dropped his arm to his side.

Something in his eyes changed, and Laura felt her blood run cold. In that moment when Eric had refused to strike her, she knew she had lost him forever. "I didn't mean for it to happen," she said quietly. "If I'd known what would happen—"

"But you did know, Mother," Eric said quietly. "You knew right from the beginning. You knew what he did to me. And you didn't do anything about it."

As he turned and walked out of the house, Laura sank back into her chair.

He's gone, she thought. *He's gone and he'll never be back.*

She's dead, Ed Cavanaugh thought. *I was there and saw her die, and if she hadn't died, I would have killed her!*

But she wasn't dead.

She had been standing there in her bedroom window, staring at him as if she could see right into his brain, and she'd been smiling at him.

She knew. She knew what he'd tried to do, knew what he'd wanted to do. Somehow she had tricked him.

He turned the key in the ignition of the *Big Ed,* then waited for the glow-plug indicator to go out. The engine turned over slowly, started to die, then caught. It coughed loudly, and a plume of black exhaust belched up from the stern, filling the cabin with choking fumes.

Ed stumbled toward a window, pushed it open, and breathed deeply of the fresh air outside. Then, while the engine warmed up, he took a swig from the fresh bottle of bourbon sitting on the chart table next to the helm, and went out to start casting off his mooring lines.

He had to get away, had to think it all out.

The engine smoothed out to a steady rumble, and Ed cast off the last line then stepped to the secondary helm on the after deck of the trawler. He put the transmission in reverse and began backing out of the slip.

The bow of the *Big Ed* swung around, hitting the starboard side of the boat next to it and scraping its entire length before clearing the slip to drift out into the channel. Ignoring the damage he'd done to the other boat, Ed went back inside the cabin and slid onto the helmsman's seat. Throwing the transmission into forward, he pushed the big engine up a notch, then gulped another shot of bourbon out of the bottle. Tending the wheel with one hand, he maneuvered the trawler down the channel toward the open sea. Not until he had passed Cranberry Point did he begin to feel safe.

They couldn't get at him now.

Maybe he'd head toward Hyannis and spend a day or two there. He had a lot of friends in Hyannis, and most of them owed him a drink.

I have to *do* something, Laura Cavanaugh thought. I can't just keep sitting here, waiting for something to happen. I have to do something.

Outside, the light was beginning to fade as the sun set, and it occurred to Laura that she hadn't moved all day. She'd simply sat, her mind numb, staring sightlessly out the window, waiting. . . .

Waiting for what?

For Eric to come home?

But Eric wasn't coming home. Deep in her heart she was certain that Eric would never come home again.

Ed, then.

Ed would come home. And then what would happen? Would she tell him that Eric was gone and wouldn't be coming back?

He would blame it on her, and then—

She couldn't go on with the thought, knowing too clearly where it would lead.

She had to get out. If she was still there when Ed came home, this time he would kill her.

She tried to move but couldn't, and a terrifying feeling of being trapped swept over her. She wasn't going to be able to get out of the house, wasn't even going to be able to stand up. Her mind seemed to have lost control over her muscles, and when she gave herself the command to rise up from the chair, her legs refused to respond. She waited a moment, forcing herself to be calm, then tried again. At last, aching from the hours of immobility, her legs reluctantly responded, and she shakily got to her feet. She left the living room, moving slowly down the short hall to the kitchen, feeling the emptiness of the house.

Neither of them is coming back.

The thought flashed through her mind, and though she tried to reject it, there was a feeling of abandonment in the house now, which told her with more certainty than any words ever could have that she was never going to see either her husband or her son again.

She moved through the kitchen unseeingly, then went out the back door. Without thinking, she crossed the driveway that separated her own house from the Winslows' and knocked on the back door. After what seemed a long time, Rosemary Winslow, her eyes red, opened the door and looked out at her. It was the look on Rosemary's face that reminded Laura that she had neither washed nor dressed since Ed had left so many hours ago. As her right hand clutched at her worn housecoat, her left ran spasmodically through her hair in a futile attempt to put it in order.

"I'm sorry . . ." she said. "I shouldn't have—"

But Rosemary pushed the door open wide. "Laura? Laura, what is it? What's happened?"

"They're gone," Laura said hollowly as she allowed herself to be led down the hall to the living room. "They're both gone."

Jennifer, who was sprawled on the floor with a book open in front of her, looked curiously up at Laura. "Who's gone?" she asked.

Laura's eyes fixed vacantly on Rosemary, and when she replied, it was as if Rosemary herself had asked the question. "Eric. And Ed. They both left, Rosemary. They both left, and they aren't coming back. What am I going to do?"

Rosemary glanced at Jennifer, and considered sending her back up to her room, then rejected the idea. "Come on," she said. "I'll fix you a cup of coffee." But when they got back to the kitchen and she fished in the cupboard above the counter for a mug, Laura shook her head.

"A drink," she said quietly. "I haven't had one in years—because of Ed, you know—but I really need one." She sank down on one of the chairs at the table, then immediately stood up again, moving restlessly around the kitchen, finally leaning against the sink as she tried to find the words to explain to Rosemary what had happened.

All the years of lying for Ed, and covering up, and finally I have to tell the truth, she thought. I wonder if I even still know how.

Slowly, tears welling in her eyes, she began telling Rosemary what had happened that morning.

Twenty-five

Cassie moved slowly along the beach, oblivious to the terns and gulls wheeling overhead and the sandpipers skittering ahead of her as they searched the tidelands for morsels of food. The storm had passed, and the sea was calm now. Sumi padded along at Cassie's feet, darting off every few seconds in pursuit of one of the birds, only to be driven back by the gently lapping surf.

She'd had another fight with Rosemary that morning, and she knew she should go back home and apologize to her.

Except that the Winslows' house wasn't home anymore, and she knew that Rosemary didn't want her there. Home was the cabin in the marsh now, the cabin Miranda had lived in and that she knew someday—somehow—she would live in too.

Last night, even after Eric left, it had felt right to her.

Safe.

And then . . .

And then, what? She knew what had happened in the marsh, knew that Sumi had attacked Lisa. But why? She wasn't even angry at Lisa anymore, and when she'd stopped Sumi in the park yesterday morning, the cat had obeyed. But last night Sumi had attacked.

There had to be a reason.

She turned away from the beach and started out into the marsh, carefully avoiding the place where they'd found Lisa early that morning. There were still a lot of people there, talking among themselves. As Cassie passed, they fell silent.

She could feel them watching her.

Just as they had watched Miranda.

The hostility coming from them was almost palpable. Cassie shuddered, then reached down and picked up Sumi, cuddling the cat close. Why did they hate her so much? She hadn't meant to hurt anyone, not really.

Except that she had. Deep inside, she had let herself get angry with Mr. Simms, and with Lisa Chambers.

She had let them hurt her, and she had struck out at them. She mustn't do it again. Never again.

Except there was still Mr. Cavanaugh.

He wanted to kill her. Last night, in fact, he thought he had killed her. She'd known it when Sumi came back and crept into her arms, and the images had come into her mind. She had seen Eric's father standing above Lisa and felt the hatred coming from him. But it wasn't Lisa he had hated.

It was her.

And then, this morning, when she'd seen him staring at her from Eric's window, she'd felt it again, felt it even more strongly than last night.

She came to the low rise on which the cabin stood, and stepped into the circle of trees surrounding it. Almost immediately a feeling of peace came over her. Then a thought came into her mind, fully formed.

He can't get me here. As long as I stay here, he can't get me.

Silently, cradling Sumi against her chest, she went into the cabin.

Cassie didn't know how long she'd been alone in Miranda's house before Eric arrived. She was sitting in the rocking chair, her eyes closed, listening to the calming sounds of the marsh. It was only when Sumi stirred in her lap that she sensed his presence.

She opened her eyes to find him standing in the doorway, watching her.

"I know what happened," Eric said. "And I know why he hates you so much. You're part of it, you see. You and your mother."

As Cassie listened, Eric began to tell her what had happened that day so many years ago. The day they had both met Miranda for the first time.

"Where are you going?" Rosemary demanded.

"I'm going to find Cassie!" Keith replied, his voice trembling with rage. "I'm her father—what else do you expect me to do?"

Rosemary felt a lump rise in her throat. "I expect you to help me try to figure out what's happening. Isn't that why you came back? To help me?"

"I came back to help Cassie," Keith shot back. He'd only been home for an hour, but after listening to Rosemary's story, he wasn't sure he should have come back at all. Four perfectly good customers, and now they were all furious because he'd insisted on rushing home when Rosemary had called him on the radio that morning. And for what! Some cockamamie story that Cassie had somehow managed to kill Lisa Chambers last night.

"You mean you actually believe it?" he'd asked when Rosemary had told him everything she knew about what happened. "You really believe Cassie could have had anything to do with any of this?"

"I only know what Gene Templeton told me," Rosemary said miserably. "They found cat hairs under Lisa's fingernails, and the cuts on her face matched the ones on Harold Simms. That's when I decided to call you. And if you'd seen her last night when she went out—"

That was when Keith lost his temper. "So now the story is that Cassie sent the cat to attack Harold Simms and kill Lisa Chambers? For Christ's sake, Rosemary! You're an intelligent woman. How can you buy crap like that?"

"It's not *my* crap!" Rosemary shot back. "All I know is what Paul Samuels said. Lisa Chambers is dead, Keith, and it doesn't matter what you think—everyone else in town already believes Cassie had something to do with it!"

"So this whole town's gone nuts in the last two days!"

"Maybe it has," Rosemary agreed, her voice etched with acid. "But Lisa's still dead, and Ed Cavanaugh was trying to kill Eric and Cassie! Not just Eric! Cassie too! Why won't you face the fact that ever since Cassie's been here things have gone wrong, and somehow she's always at the center of it?"

Keith had stood up from the table so abruptly that his chair crashed over onto the floor. He snatched his coat off the hook in the service porch and was halfway out the door, his eyes blazing, when he heard Jennifer's plaintive voice.

"Don't," the little girl said, her chin trembling as she struggled against her own tears. "Please don't yell at each other. Please?"

Keith's and Rosemary's eyes met.

"What are we doing?" Rosemary finally asked. "Dear God, Keith, what are we doing to ourselves?" Then, as Jennifer ran to her mother, Keith put his arms around both of them.

"It's going to be all right," he told them. "We'll be all right, and Cassie will be all right too. We won't let anything happen to any of us." He gave them a hug, then released them and finished pulling his jacket on. When he spoke, his voice was gentle. "I have to go see if

I can find her," he said, reaching out to touch Rosemary's cheek. "I guess I'm just starting to understand what the last couple of days have been like for you. But think what they've been like for Cassie, darling. I don't care what anyone else thinks. I don't believe Cassie would willingly hurt anyone. I just don't believe it." And then he was gone.

Keith paused at the foot of the low rise upon which Miranda Sikes's cabin stood. Cassie was there—he could sense it even before he saw the thin wisp of smoke drifting up from the chimney.

And on the roof of the cabin, eyeing him warily, the white hawk was perched, its feathers ruffling as it moved restlessly from one foot to the other.

"Cassie?" Keith called. Then again, "Cassie! It's your father!"

He took a single step forward, then froze as the hawk launched itself from the rooftop, found the wind, and began spiraling upward. From the cabin he heard a single word.

"No!"

Instantly the hawk changed course, dropping out of the air to settle back onto the peak of the roof. Only when it had landed did Keith shift his eyes from the bird to the figure on the porch of the cabin.

It was Cassie, her brows knit into an uncertain frown. She was watching him warily.

"It's me, Punkin," Keith said quietly.

For a moment Cassie was silent, and when she spoke, her voice was heavy with suspicion. "I didn't do anything," she said. "I know what everybody thinks, but I didn't do anything."

Keith felt his heart twist with pain. He wanted to go to her, take her in his arms, hold her. "I know," he said, the words quavering as he struggled to hold his emotions in check. "That's why I came out here. I came to help you, sweetheart." Almost involuntarily his eyes flicked upward toward the watchful hawk. "Can I come up there?"

Time seemed to stand still as Cassie watched her father, and then she nodded.

Feeling the hawk's eyes on him every step of the way, Keith climbed the hill and stepped into the cabin.

"I don't know what to say," Keith told his daughter an hour later. He felt sick as all the pieces of the puzzle finally began to come together. No wonder Diana had been jealous of him: she'd been certain he'd been doing the same things she'd been doing. "I never knew any of it. If I'd known, I never would have let your mother take you away."

"But why did she even want to?" Cassie asked, her voice quavering. "If she didn't care enough about me even to watch me on the beach, why did she want to take me with her?"

Keith shook his head helplessly. "It wasn't you, honey. It was never you. She just didn't want me to have you. She knew how much I loved you. And she knew how much it hurt me when she took you."

"And she never told you what happened?" Cassie asked, her disbelief apparent. "She never told you I almost drowned in the quicksand?"

"She couldn't," Keith replied bitterly. "She knew if she did, I'd have wanted to know how you got lost in the first place. And if I'd found *that* out, she never would have been able to take you away from me." He turned to Eric, who was sitting silently at the table. "I don't know what to say to you either. All those years . . ."

Eric spoke in a nearly toneless voice. "Maybe Miranda shouldn't have saved us. Maybe she should have just let us drown. Nobody cared. Nobody at all."

"That's not true—" Keith started to protest, then changed his mind. It was the children who had lived through all those years, who had received the beatings, and who had lived without love. How *could* they believe that anybody had cared?

"What was she like?" he asked softly. "What was Miranda really like?"

"She was my friend," Cassie replied. Her eyes filled with tears as she remembered those few hours she'd spent with Miranda. "She listened to me. When I talked to her, she knew exactly how I felt. She knew how alone I was, and how different I was, and how much—" Her voice broke, but she forced herself to go on. "She knew how much I hurt." She met her father's eyes. "She wasn't crazy, Daddy. She wasn't crazy at all. She just didn't have any friends, except Sumi and Kiska. That's why she knew how I felt. She always felt the same way. And she never wanted to hurt anybody either. She told me that just because people didn't understand me, it wasn't any reason to hurt them."

In her lap Sumi meowed softly, and Cassie gently scratched his ears. "That's why she gave me Sumi," she went on. "She wanted me to have a friend that really understood me."

Keith felt a chill as he remembered what Rosemary had told him when he came home. "Understands you," he said quietly. "You don't really mean the cat understands what you say, do you?"

Cassie hesitated, then nodded. "He understands what I'm feeling, and he does what I want him to do. So does Kiska. That's why he didn't go after you. I made him stop."

"But, honey, that's crazy," Keith began, then wished he could take back the words when he saw the pain in Cassie's eyes. "I'm sorry," he said quickly. "It's just—well, people can't really do things like that."

Cassie's eyes met his unwaveringly. "Most people can't," she said. "But Miranda could, and I can to. The animals were all she had, and she left them to me." She swallowed hard, then forced herself to go on. "That's what I did to Mr. Simms. I—I sent Sumi after him. I didn't really know I could, but . . ." She fell silent, watching her father fearfully.

Keith said nothing for several long minutes. If it was true, what did it mean? And was it really true? He had to know. "Show me," he said at last.

Cassie blinked uncertainly. "H-how?"

"Make him attack me. If you can make him attack me, I'll believe you. Then we'll figure out what to do."

Cassie glanced at Eric but said nothing. "I don't want to hurt you," Cassie whispered, looking back to her father.

"Make him attack me, then make him stop," Keith pressed. "If I'm going to help you, I have to know what happened."

Cassie stared at him for several seconds without speaking. Then her eyes closed.

She can't do it, Keith thought. She thinks she can but—

In a sudden flash of movement Sumi hissed angrily and tensed in Cassie's lap. As Keith stared in shock, the cat hurled himself toward him. A screech of fury roiled from his throat, and his lips curled back from his fangs. Keith threw up his hands to protect his face, but just before the cat struck him, he heard once more the single word that Cassie had spoken earlier on the porch.

"No!"

The shriek of attack died in Sumi's throat, and he dropped lightly into Keith's lap. His tail twitched once or twice, then he licked Keith's hand and settled down, purring contentedly.

For a long time no one said anything. Then Cassie broke the silence.

"I didn't kill Lisa, Daddy," she said softly. "Really, I didn't."

Keith hesitated, then nodded. "I believe you, Punkin," he said. "I believe you."

Eric said nothing at all.

Rosemary was playing Chinese checkers with Jennifer on the floor of the den when the doorbell rang. She was tempted not to answer it.

All day, as the rumors had spread through the village, she'd seen a steady trickle of people passing by the house—people who didn't live in the neighborhood and didn't ordinarily go for walks along Alder Street. But today had been different, and finally Jennifer, looking curiously out the window, had asked what they were doing.

"They're just looking, honey," Rosemary had assured her. "I guess they just don't have anything better to do."

"Can I go out?" Jennifer had asked.

Rosemary shook her head, knowing all too well the sort of things Jennifer was likely to overhear on the streets that day. And so after Keith left, she'd settled down with Jennifer in the den, partly to keep the little girl entertained, but also, she knew, to keep her own mind off everything that had happened.

The bell rang again. "Aren't you going to answer it?" Jennifer asked.

Rosemary sighed, and got stiffly to her feet. But when she opened the front door, she wished she'd followed her first impulse to pretend that nobody was home. Fred Chambers, his eyes red and puffy, glared angrily at her.

"It's her fault!" he said, his voice trembling with a mixture of grief and bitter fury. "Everything was fine here until that crazy daughter of Keith's showed up. And now look what's happened! My daughter's dead, Rosemary! Do you understand that? Dead! It wasn't Ed Cavanaugh at all. It was Cassie! And she knew what she was doing too! From the minute she showed up at that dance all dressed up in Miranda's clothes, she knew what she was doing! She's as crazy as Miranda was!"

Rosemary stared at Fred Chambers, her heart pounding. "Stop it, Fred," she said, struggling to keep her voice under control. "I know what's happened, and I can't tell you how sorry I am. But we don't know that Cassie had anything to do with it. We don't know!" she repeated, her voice taking on a note of desperation. "The cat might have been anyone's," she added, though she knew she didn't believe her own words.

"Bullshit!" Fred Chambers exploded. "You think anyone's going to believe that? Teri Bennett saw that cat go after Lisa just yesterday! And it went after Harold Simms, too, didn't it? I don't know what Lisa was doing out there, but we know it was Cassie who killed her. She's doing something to us, and we all know it! She tried to kill Harold Simms, and she *did* kill my daughter. And if Templeton won't do something about it, the rest of us will! She's nuts!" He backed away a couple of steps, then wheeled around and charged off the porch. Halfway to the street he spun around to face Rosemary once more. "She's crazy, Rosemary! She's as crazy as Miranda was! She's some kind of witch, and she ought to be locked up!" A moment later he slammed the door of his car and started the engine, his tires screeching as he pressed his foot down on the accelerator. Rosemary, breathing hard, waited until the car had disappeared around the corner before she finally closed the door and returned to the den.

Jennifer, her face ashen, sat silently on the floor, staring at her.

"I don't like him," the little girl finally said. "I don't like him saying bad things about Cassie." She stood up and came to Rosemary, putting her arms around her mother and burying her face in Rosemary's skirt. "She wouldn't hurt anyone. I know she wouldn't."

Rosemary reached down and stroked her daughter's hair, wishing she could offer some words of comfort. But she couldn't, for she knew that despite everything Keith had said, her questions about Cassie were as great as ever, and that deep in her soul she had no real argument with what Fred Chambers had said.

But maybe—just maybe—when Keith brought Cassie home, she would find out that she'd been wrong, that there was a rational explanation for everything that had happened.

But the day turned into night, and Keith didn't come home.

It wasn't the first time Laura Cavanaugh had spent the night alone in the house, but this time it was different. Always before, she'd spent the evening comfortably, doing exactly as she pleased, enjoying the brief respites from the constant tension of her husband's drinking and violence. Even having Eric gone for a night had never bothered her, for she'd always known exactly where he was and when he'd be back.

But tonight was different. Eric would not be back, and she hadn't the slightest idea of where he was. For a while she'd considered calling Gene Templeton, but in the end hadn't been able to. Though she'd poured the whole story out to Rosemary Winslow, she was not yet ready to face anyone else with it—and certainly not the police chief. So she'd spent the evening drifting nervously around the house, starting one task or another, only to abandon it after a few minutes, unable to concentrate. Finally at nine o'clock she'd retreated to the bedroom—not the bedroom she had shared with Ed, but the guest room, where the memories were fewest.

She'd lain awake for hours, listening to the noises of the house. Until tonight she'd always found the soft creakings and groanings of its timbers reassuring. But tonight they sounded different to her, almost like living things going through some strange torture she could neither comprehend nor alleviate. And then, when finally she did drift into a fitful sleep, nightmares plagued her and she tossed and turned, twisting the sheets around her like a shroud.

Ed came to her dreams, but he had changed into the devil incarnate, determined to punish her for sins she could never hope to understand. And yet in the dreams she accepted her guilt, for why else was she being punished? And so she submitted willingly to the devil's tortures and silently prayed for death to rescue her from her agony.

Finally she thought death was near, and opened her eyes to welcome it, only to find that blackness surrounded her.

She lay still, waiting for the next sting of the whip or burn of the coals the devil had placed against her flesh, but it didn't come.

Slowly Laura realized that she had awakened and the dream was over. But her body, clammy with sweat, still shivered with the terror of the dream, and she tried to gather a blanket around her.

As she reached for the blanket she saw the cat perched on the sill of the open window, a dark silhouette against the pale silver of the moonlit night. Its eyes glowed a golden yellow in the darkness, and Laura had an eerie sensation that it was grinning at her, its lips curled back from teeth that emerged as pointed fangs from bloody gums. She gasped in sudden fear and drew back, clutching the blanket defensively to her breast.

The cat leaped nimbly from the windowsill and disappeared into a dark corner of the room. A moment later its yellow eyes flashed out at her from the shadows.

Slowly the cat began to creep nearer. . . .

The moon was beginning to drop toward the horizon when Sumi silently slipped through the branches of the tree then darted invisibly through the long shadows of the night. In only a few seconds he was back in the tree next to the Winslows' house and slithering once more through a window. When he leaped onto the bed and snuggled close to the warmth of the body beneath the quilt, his claws were wellsheathed and he was nothing more than a soft and comforting presence. Nothing was left of the golden-eyed demon that had stared accusingly at Laura Cavanaugh, silently demanding that she obey his will.

"Did you do it, Sumi?" the sleepy voice asked. "Did you do what I wanted you to?"

As if in response, Sumi began to purr.

Twenty-six

J ennifer stirred, rolled over, then opened her eyes. The first light of dawn was glimmering outside, and she started to get up when she realized that something was wrong.

This wasn't her room.

And then, slowly, she remembered.

Sometime during the night her father had come in, gently lifted her out of bed, and carried her into her parents' bedroom. Then he'd tucked her in, kissed her, and told her that Eric was going to be sleeping in her room tonight.

Jennifer stayed awake as long as she could, trying to hear everything that was being said downstairs, until at last sleep overtook her.

But she was awake now, with her mother beside her and her father on the other side of the bed. Being careful not to waken her parents, she slipped out of the bed and crept out of the room and down the hall to Cassie's room.

Opening the door, she silently slid inside, then went over to Cassie's bed and gazed curiously at her sleeping half sister.

She puzzled over the words she'd heard Mr. Chambers saying yesterday evening, and tried to make sense out of them. But they still didn't seem right to her.

Cassie couldn't be a witch, could she? Witches, if they were real at all—and most of her friends thought they were—were old and ugly, with horrid, hooked noses and deep wrinkles all over their faces.

Cassie wasn't like that at all.

In fact Cassie was the nicest person in the whole world. She'd let Jen keep her newly decorated room, and stuck up for her when her mother had gotten mad at her, and hadn't even been angry when Jennifer had followed her that day.

So Mr. Chambers must be wrong.

She poked at Cassie, but nothing happened. She poked at her again, and Cassie rolled over, stretched, then opened her eyes.

"Hi," Cassie said, then frowned uncertainly. "What time is it?"

"Almost six," Jennifer pronounced, climbing onto the bed and regarding Cassie with serious eyes. "Can I tell you something without you thinking I'm a tattletale?"

Cassie nodded solemnly. "What is it?"

"Mr. Chambers was here yesterday, and he said something really bad about you."

Cassie's eyes darkened. "What did he say, Jen?" she asked.

Jennifer hesitated, then looked away. "He—he said you're a witch," she breathed. "He said you're a witch and you're crazy, just like Miranda was, and you ought to be locked up." She fell silent, then finally managed to turn and face Cassie again. "It's not true, is it?" she asked anxiously.

To her surprise, Cassie smiled gently at her. "What do you think?"

"I—I don't know what to think," she said. Then: "After he was gone, I asked Mom."

Cassie's eyes flickered with worry. "And what did she say?"

Jennifer hesitated, and looked away. "She—she didn't say anything," she replied quietly. "But if it wasn't true, why would Mr. Chambers say something like that? Grown-ups don't lie, do they?"

Cassie was silent for a few seconds, and when she finally spoke, she sounded angry to Jennifer. "Sometimes they do," she said. "And Mr. Chambers did because he doesn't like me. In fact he hates me, because of what happened to Lisa."

Jennifer blinked curiously. "But you didn't do anything to Lisa, did you?"

"I—" Cassie began, then shook her head. "It doesn't matter, Jen. Why don't you just go back to bed?" Turning away, Cassie pulled the covers up and closed her eyes.

Jennifer slid off the bed, but then reached out to pat the spot at the foot of the bed where Sumi always slept.

There was nothing there.

She felt again, then explored the rest of the bed with her hands. "Cassie?" she asked a moment later.

"Huh?" Cassie mumbled.

"Where's Sumi? Why isn't he here?"

Cassie's eyes popped open and she sat up. She quickly scanned the room.

The cat had been there last night. She was sure of it. But this morning he was gone.

"G-go back to bed, Jen," Cassie said.

Jennifer hesitated, but something in Cassie's eyes told her not to argue. She hurried out of the room and a few seconds later was back in bed, snuggled against the warmth of her mother. Soon her breathing evened out into the gentle rhythms of sleep.

For Cassie the night's sleep was over.

*　　*　　*

It was already ten past seven, but neither Cassie nor Eric had yet come downstairs. Rosemary wondered if maybe she should simply let them sleep in. Certainly they wouldn't be going to school this morning, not after what they'd been through over the weekend.

And what was today going to be like?

She shook her head as she tried to imagine Gene Templeton's response to Cassie's version of what had happened to both Lisa Chambers and Harold Simms. Would he feel the same sense of shocked incredulity she had experienced the previous night when Keith had finally brought both Cassie and Eric home from Miranda's cabin in the marsh?

"I was angry at them," Cassie had explained, her blue eyes looking beseechingly at Rosemary. "I was angry at them, and I wanted to hurt them. But I didn't know what Sumi could do. I didn't know!"

Rosemary had looked at her in confusion. "Sumi? Cassie, what on earth are you talking about?"

"The cat," Keith explained, his voice tight. "There *is* some kind of communication between Cassie and the cat. The cat understands what's going on in her mind and acts on it."

Slowly Cassie began to tell the story, and as Rosemary listened, her shock grew with each passing minute.

"Sumi went after Lisa because she was going to do something to me," Cassie finished. "When he came back, I saw what happened. It's like I can see whatever he saw." She bit her lip, and her eyes glistened with tears. "Mr. Cavanaugh didn't kill her. But he didn't try to save her either. He just stood there and watched her die."

It had gone on past midnight, and finally Rosemary hadn't been able to deal with it anymore. "I think we'd better call Gene Templeton," she'd said.

But Keith had shaken his head. "Not tonight," he told her. "We've all been through too much, and I won't ask the kids to talk to Gene tonight."

Rosemary had stared at him. What was he saying? Were they all just supposed to go to bed?

"I told Eric he could stay here tonight," he went on. "Tomorrow we'll talk to Gene and Paul Samuels."

Rosemary wanted to argue, but her exhaustion had finally overcome her. "All right," she'd said at last. "I don't know what's happening anymore. I don't know if I believe any of it or not, but I just can't think anymore." Her eyes had gone to Cassie. "I don't think you should expect them to believe any of this," she said. "Even if it's true—"

"Do you believe it?" Cassie had asked. Her voice was low, but her eyes were gazing steadily at Rosemary.

"I—I don't know," Rosemary had replied, even though she was certain that whatever the truth was, Cassie had not yet told all of it. To try to blame it all on a cat . . . "And I'm not going to talk about it anymore tonight."

Nor had she. When Keith had tried to discuss it with her after they were in bed, she'd turned away from him and said nothing. But for hours she'd lain awake, puzzling over it.

Did Keith seriously believe that Gene Templeton would accept Cassie's story? It was impossible. The whole thing. And Gene wouldn't accept it. There was no way he could. It was too strange— too bizarre.

Keith sipped silently on his coffee, warily watching his wife.

This morning Rosemary knew she could no longer put off dealing with it. Sighing, she turned to Jennifer, who was sitting at the table spooning sugar onto her cereal. "See if you can hurry them up, will you, honey?" she said to her daughter.

Jennifer slid off her chair, went to the bottom of the stairs and yelled up to the second floor. When she got no response, she sighed with all the dramatic resignation an eight-year-old can summon and started up the stairs.

"You don't believe Cassie, do you?" Keith asked quietly when Jennifer was gone.

"I—I don't know," Rosemary faltered.

"If you'd been out there yesterday. If you'd seen—"

"No!" Rosemary burst out. Her eyes stung with tears as she turned to face Keith. "I kept waking up all night long thinking about that story of Cassie's, and I just can't accept it! It's just too—too bizarre!" She was about to say more, but abruptly stopped herself as Jennifer reappeared in the kitchen.

"They're not up there," Jennifer said. "They're gone."

"Gone?" Rosemary echoed blankly. "What do you mean, gone?"

"I looked in my room, and I looked in Cassie's room, and—"

Rosemary brushed past her daughter and hurried up the stairs. It wasn't possible. If they'd gotten up, wouldn't she have heard them moving around?

She stopped in front of the closed door to Jennifer's room and rapped loudly. "Eric? Eric, are you awake?" There was no answer. After rapping once more, Rosemary twisted the knob and pushed the door open.

The room looked as it always did, with Jennifer's toys strewn around the floor and a few of her clothes piled on the chair. The bed, unmade, was empty, and there was not a trace of Eric Cavanaugh anywhere in the room.

Frowning, Rosemary pulled the door closed then went to Cassie's room, where she repeated the process.

Cassie's room, too, was empty.

Methodically, knowing it was useless even before she started, Rosemary searched the second floor, and even went up to check the little attic tucked under the roof. When she returned to the landing, Keith was waiting for her, looking at her with questioning eyes. She shook her head.

"They're not here," she whispered, her voice trembling. "But where would they have gone? Why?" Her voice began to rise, cracking dangerously as she tried to stifle a sob. "We hear everything in this house—everything! My God, you can't even breathe without everyone hearing you. And they're gone, Keith! We didn't hear them, we didn't see them. They didn't even speak to us! Why? Why!" She felt herself crumbling, and let her husband gather her into his arms. "I don't understand it," she sobbed. "I just don't understand any of it. . . ."

"Shh," Keith soothed, stroking her hair and leading her into their bedroom. He lowered her gently to the bed. "Just take it easy," he told her. "I'll have a look around. There's got to be some explanation. Just take it easy. . . ." Then, as Rosemary's breathing began to return to normal, he, too, searched the house.

It didn't take him long to figure out what had happened. The window in Cassie's room was wide open and the screen hung loose. Obviously both the kids had gone out the window and down the tree outside. Yet that didn't explain where they might have gone, nor why they felt it necessary to sneak out. He went back to the master bedroom and found Rosemary sitting up, dabbing at her eyes with a Kleenex.

"I'm all right," she said. "I just . . . fell apart for a minute, I guess. But I'm all right now." She listened in silence as he told her what he thought had happened, then numbly followed him back down to the kitchen, slowly and deliberately pouring herself a fresh cup of coffee before she spoke again. At last she turned to face her husband. "I can't stand any more of this," she said quietly. "I know you love Cassie, and I want to love her too. But I can't keep on with this, Keith. How can I be expected to believe what she says when none of it makes sense to me, and she pulls stunts like this? Whatever the truth of all this is, I will not let her destroy my family. I—"

Keith's eyes widened in shock. "Destroy your—Honey, all she's done is take off again!"

But Rosemary shook her head. "She didn't take off, Keith. That's what she did yesterday, after a fight. I saw her go. I heard her go. I even knew why she went. But this morning she just disappeared. Both of them did." Her voice began quavering again, and she could feel her self-control slipping away once more. "I feel like I'm going crazy, Keith. I don't know what's happening, and I don't understand any of it, and . . . and . . ." Her eyes welled with tears, and she cradled her head in her hands as her sobs once more overtook her.

Keith watched helplessly, wishing he knew what to say. But he didn't. All he could do was go out once more and search for his daughter.

"I'm going out," he said tightly. "And when I find her, this time I'll wait till I have her home before I ask her what's going on. This time we'll listen to her together."

Rosemary looked at him beseechingly. "Not now," she pleaded. "Not right now—please. Just stay with me for a little while."

Keith hesitated, then nodded. "Go next door," he told Jennifer. "Get Mrs. Cavanaugh and ask her to come over. Can you do that?"

Jennifer, her eyes wide as saucers, nodded and started toward the door.

"No!" Rosemary suddenly screeched, grabbing Jennifer by the shoulders and pulling her back. "She's not going over there! If Ed came back—"

Keith took a deep breath and nodded. "All right. I'll get Laura myself. Be right back."

He strode across the driveway and knocked loudly at the back door of the Cavanaughs' house. When there was no answer, he pulled the door open and went inside. "Laura? Where are you?"

There was still no answer, and he moved quickly through the kitchen and hall until he was at the bottom of the stairs. Calling out once more, he started up.

He paused to listen when he reached the landing on the second floor, and glanced around. Three bedrooms and a bath opened off the landing. Two of the bedroom doors stood open, as did the bathroom door.

The last door was almost closed, and as he approached it, Keith felt an icy chill of foreboding.

Bracing himself, he pushed the door open with his left foot.

Hanging from the tarnished brass chandelier above the bed, a sheet knotted around her neck, was Laura Cavanaugh. Her head was cocked at an unnatural angle, and her legs hung down nearly to the floor. Her face had turned a mottled bluish black, and her tongue, swollen and discolored, protruded from the rictus of her lips.

Her cheeks—both of them—bore angry red claw marks.

Keith felt his gorge rise and quickly turned his face away, trying to block the hideous sight from his memory, though he already knew he would remember it as long as he lived. Gagging, and clutching a handkerchief to his mouth in a futile effort to control his retching, he bolted down the stairs and out of the house. Falling to his knees, he vomited onto the back lawn, his stomach contracting violently long after it had emptied itself of its contents. At last, panting and gasping for breath, Keith managed to get to his feet and stagger back toward his own house.

Rosemary looked up at him as he lurched through the back door, and her face turned ashen as she saw the look of horror in his eyes.

"Gene," Keith gasped. "Call Gene. It's Laura . . ." His voice trailed off, and he moved through the kitchen to the little half bathroom tucked under the stairs. As Rosemary fumbled with the telephone she could hear Keith vomiting once more.

"Cut her down," Templeton said grimly.

Photographs had already been taken, and one of his deputies was dusting the room for fingerprints, but Templeton didn't think it would make any difference unless they turned up prints that didn't belong to Ed, Laura, or Eric. Besides, from what he'd seen, Gene was almost certain about what happened.

It had to have been Ed.

He could almost picture it.

Ed drunk, coming home and starting one more fight with his wife. Only this time the beating had gotten out of hand.

As he stared at the carnage that had been Laura's face, Gene hoped she'd already lost consciousness by the time Ed started cutting at her cheeks. If she hadn't—

He winced just thinking about the pain she would have had to endure, and put the thought out of his mind.

Had Ed hanged her before she was dead, or not until he'd discovered he'd actually killed her this time? Not that it made any difference, really, for whether he'd beaten her to death, strangled her, or hanged her, she was still dead, and Ed was still guilty of murder, despite his drunken attempt to make it look as if some kind of animal had attacked her. But animals didn't hang people. If Laura Cavanaugh weren't dead, Templeton would have found the clumsy gesture almost laughable.

The medics cut the twisted sheet and gently lowered Laura's corpse onto a stretcher, covered it, and carried it out of the room. Glancing out the window, Gene saw the knot of people gathered on the front lawn of the Cavanaughs' house. More were drifting down the sidewalk, and Gene could almost hear them murmuring among themselves, passing the rumors from one ear to the next.

"Go pick up Ed," Gene told the deputy who had finished dusting the room. "Unless I miss my guess, he's down on his boat, dead drunk."

The deputy—Tony Vittori—frowned and shook his head. "Don't think so, Gene. I saw the *Big Ed* goin' out yesterday morning, and it hasn't been back. Slip was still empty when I came up this morning."

"You sure?" Gene asked, though he already knew the answer. Tony lived alone on a sailboat he kept in the last slip of the marina, and made a few extra dollars each month by keeping an eye on things. His heart sank. If it hadn't been Ed then—

Eric?

It was the only other possibility that came readily to mind, but the very idea of it made Gene feel sick. Still, he had to face up to it. "Okay," he sighed. "Cruise around and see if you can spot Eric anywhere, and see if you can get hold of Ed on the radio. I'll go next door and talk to Keith. They must have heard something."

And yet even as he crossed the driveway and let himself into the Winslows' house, Gene had a sinking feeling that no one in the house next door had heard anything the night before.

Twenty-seven

E d Cavanaugh woke up with his head throbbing and his nostrils filled with the familiar odor of stale vomit. For a moment he refused to open his eyes, certain that if he did, he would once more see the gray walls of the False Harbor jail closing in on him. But then the gentle rocking of the boat reassured him, and he let his right eye open a crack to take in the familiar mess of the cabin of the *Big Ed*. Slowly, the previous night came back to him. He'd sat in a bar in Hyannis, putting away boilermakers until finally the bartender had thrown him out. Then a couple of his friends—whose names would come back to him in a minute—helped him back to the boat, and they'd polished off a fifth of bourbon that he'd found tucked away down in the engine room just in case of such an emergency as this. He could even remember when he'd gotten sick, but hadn't bothered to go out on the deck to throw up. After that . . .

He rolled over, pulling the greasy blanket up over his head in a vain effort to shut out the sour smell. No point getting up until his head stopped pounding.

The radio suddenly came to life, and he heard an urgent voice calling to him. He tried to ignore it, but after a few minutes of silence it started in again. Swearing under his breath, he kicked the blanket aside and stumbled out of the bunk to scramble up the companionway to the pilothouse. He fumbled with the microphone for a moment, dropped it, then found the transmit button.

"This is the *Big Ed.*" The words were slurred, and his tongue felt thick and cottony.

"That you, Ed?" the voice crackled back.

"Who wants to know?"

"This is Tony Vittorio, Ed. We got a problem, and we need you back here as soon as you can get here."

Ed frowned blearily. "What kinda problem? A man's gotta earn a living, ya know. Can't do that runnin' home all the time."

There was a long silence this time, then the radio crackled to life again. "It's Laura, Ed. She's dead."

Cavanaugh stared at the radio dumbly. What the hell was the deputy talking about? Dead? Laura couldn't be dead—anyway, she hadn't been the last time he'd seen her. His eyes narrowed suspiciously. "Don't you bastards try to blame it on me, Tony. I maybe hit her a few times, but I never killed her."

In the police station Tony Vittorio felt a knot of cold anger form in his belly. Didn't the son of a bitch even care that his wife had died? Taking a deep breath to steady himself, he pressed the key on his own microphone. "We're not saying you did, Ed. But we thought you ought to know. Where are you?"

"Hyannis. Been here all night, and I can prove it."

"Great," Tony Vittorio replied, his eyes rolling upward. "So when can you get back here?"

Ed shrugged in the pilothouse. "Three, maybe four hours."

"You need any help?"

"What for?" Ed spat. "A little hangover never kept me in port before."

"Yeah," Tony replied. "We'll look for you around noon, then. But if you don't show up, we'll come looking for you. Got that?"

"I got it," Ed whined, and shoved the microphone back onto its bracket without bothering to sign off. "And fuck you too." Snotty bastard. Just like all the rest of them. But this time they didn't have anything on him. Anything at all.

His brain still throbbing, his mind still foggy, he started the engine warming and put a pot of coffee on the propane stove.

Numbly, his mind began to accept the fact that Laura was dead. A strange emotion began to seize him, and at first he couldn't even identify it. Then, dimly, he began to recognize it as grief.

He'd never considered the possibility that Laura might die, never even considered the idea that she might leave him. But now she was gone. She was gone, and he was alone.

What was he supposed to do now? Slowly his grief began to dissolve into a more familiar emotion.

Anger.

"I want to go away," Rosemary said after Templeton had left. He hadn't believed it, hadn't believed any of it. And why should he? She didn't believe it herself, not anymore. "I want to take Jennifer and get away from here." She watched Keith's face, looking for a reaction—any kind of reaction—but for a long time there was none. Then, finally, his head swung around and his haunted eyes met her own.

"I can't go away," he said softly. "She's my daughter, honey. I can't just abandon her."

Rosemary's knuckles whitened as she clenched her hands into fists. "She's crazy! And if she's responsible for what you saw next door, then she's—she's some kind of monster!"

"Yesterday—"

"Things were different yesterday!" Rosemary flared. "Yesterday I wanted to believe her. I didn't want to believe she could have done all this. But this is today, and Laura's dead, and . . . and . . ." Her voice trailed off, but she refused to give in to the sobbing that threatened to overcome her.

"And you believe Cassie did it. Isn't that what you're thinking?"

Rosemary shook her head violently, though his words were true. "I don't know what I'm thinking. I'm trying to be rational, and it isn't working. I just—Keith, I'm scared! I keep telling myself that none of this is true, that there's a reasonable explanation for what's happening. But I can't. All I can think about is that something's going to happen to you next. Or to Jennifer." She looked at him with beseeching eyes. "Why can't we just go away somewhere, and stay away until it's all over?"

Keith's eyes flickered dully around the room. "Just go away," he repeated, as if the words had no meaning. But then he shook his head. "I can't do that, Rosemary. Whatever this is all about, it's partly my fault. Whatever Cassie is—or isn't—she's my daughter. I can't just walk away from that. I have to stay. I have to."

Rosemary's jaw tightened, her lips thinned down to an angry line, and her eyes flashed dangerously. "All right," she said, her voice grating. "We'll stay. But for how long? How long do you want us to stay, Keith? Until we're all dead?"

Keith turned away and went to the window. Looking out into the brightness of the spring morning, everything that had happened seemed unreal. And yet the image of Laura was too deeply burned in his memory to deny.

Had Cassie truly been responsible for that? He didn't want to believe it. And yet—

"I don't know," he said at last, his voice barely audible. "Until I can help her, I guess. Or at least until I can understand."

Cassie faced Eric across the small table in the center of the cabin, her eyes empty, her mind reeling, her body shivering with an unnatural chill.

It wasn't warm and comforting here this morning; would never be comforting again.

She knew what had happened now, knew it from the first moment they had come into the cabin and Sumi leaped into her arms, purring softly.

The images had come quickly, and she'd watched the pictures in her mind with growing horror, watched Eric's mother knot the sheet around her neck, watched her step off the edge of the bed.

Watched as the cat left his telltale marks on her cheeks then slipped back out the window.

She even heard Eric's voice, crooning to Sumi as the cat slipped back into bed with him.

"Did you do it, Sumi? Did you do what I wanted you to do?"

It hadn't been her—hadn't been her at all. From the first moment—the first time they'd been here together—it had been Eric.

It all made sense now.

The day Sumi had attacked Mr. Simms—Eric had been holding Sumi that day.

And after Kiska had been shot, Eric had known where to find him.

It wasn't just to her that Miranda had given her gift. It was to Eric too.

"It was you," Cassie whispered. "Right from the beginning, it was you."

Eric nodded, a cold smile playing at the corners of his mouth. His eyes, glittering an icy blue in the morning light that filtered through the scraggly trees outside, were fixed on her with an odd detachment, almost as if he didn't see her.

All the sympathy she'd seen there—all the understanding—were gone.

"But they were our friends," she whispered bleakly. "Miranda never wanted us to—"

"Miranda's dead!" Eric grated, his eyes narrowing to slits. "It doesn't matter what she wanted anymore! She's dead!"

As he spoke the words, Sumi squirmed in Cassie's lap, and another image came into her mind.

Once more she saw Miranda—the quicksand closing around her—a shadowy figure looming over her. But this time she could recognize the face. Eric's face.

"You killed her," she breathed. "You killed them all." Her eyes, glistening with the pain she felt, reached out to Eric, trying to touch him. "Your own mother, Eric. You even killed your own mother. . . ."

Eric's smile twisted into a knife slash of scorn. "Sumi killed my mother, and Sumi killed Lisa. And everyone knows that he does everything *you* want him to do."

Cassie felt numb. He was right—she knew he was right—and already, deep in her heart, she was beginning to understand that there was nothing she could do about it.

"Why?" she asked. "Why did you do it, Eric?"

"They deserved it," Eric rasped. "They hurt me, and so I killed them."

Cassie shook her head as if to dispel the nightmare closing around her. "No. Miranda was your friend—she never hurt you. She loved you."

"Until you came," Eric spat. "She was mine, but you took her away from me." His eyes were now glimmering with the rage and hatred inside him. "She was just like all the rest of them. She didn't love me—she didn't want me. So I killed her. Just like I'm going to kill my father!"

Cassie gasped. "No! Eric, you can't!"

Eric's eyes glowed with fury. "Why not? No one's going to blame me. No one's even going to know I did it. They're going to blame you, Cassie. They're going to blame you for all of it."

"No!" Cassie shouted. "I won't let you! I'll tell them the truth! I'll tell all of them!"

"Tell them what?" Eric demanded. "You're crazy, remember? No one's going to believe you. You're like Miranda! You're nuts! The little kids all think you're a witch!" An ugly cackle of brittle laughter welled up in his throat. "Didn't Miranda tell you what it was like, having them point at you, and whisper about you, and run away from you? That's what they're going to do to you, too, Cassie. And you won't do anything about it. You'll just let them hurt you." His voice dropped to a bitter whisper. "But not me. I'm done letting people hurt me. I'll kill them all, and they'll all think it was you." His cold smile came back. "And there's nothing you can do about it, Cassie. You're like Kiska and Sumi. You'll do whatever I want you to do. You always have, and you always will."

Sumi stirred restlessly in Cassie's lap, then his whole body stiffened.

Images began to flicker in Cassie's mind.

Images of herself, her face bleeding as Sumi's claws dug deep into her flesh.

Eric.

He was reaching out to the cat with his mind, telling him what to do.

She tried to fight it, tried to calm the cat, but it did no good. He was stronger than she was—too strong.

And then she knew what she had to do.

Her hands closed around Sumi's neck and she began to squeeze her fingers tight.

The cat started to struggle, lashing out with his feet, his claws bared as he tried to twist free of her grip.

She reached out with her mind, tried to soothe the furious animal, tried to overpower the hatred flowing out of Eric's mind and into the body of the cat.

Sumi's mouth opened and he spat at her, his fangs dripping with saliva.

Cassie could feel herself losing the struggle with Eric now, feel his mind overpowering hers. She squeezed harder, her hands pressing tighter on the cat's larynx. Once more he tried to twist away, but then, slowly, his struggling eased. A minute later Sumi lay still in her lap.

Cassie closed her eyes for a moment, fighting against the tears that threatened to overwhelm her. Then, very gently, she placed the cat in the center of the table and forced herself to look into Eric's cold eyes.

"He's dead," she said. "He's dead, and he'll never hurt anyone again."

But Eric only smiled once more. "I still have Kiska." He rose to his feet, went to the door, then raised his arm and pointed to the sky.

Instantly the pale white form of the hawk rose off the cabin's roof and spiraled upward into the sky. As it started out toward the sea, Eric turned back to Cassie.

"He's going," he said. "He's going to kill my father."

Cassie felt the blood drain from her face, and tried to reach out to the bird.

But once again Eric's power overwhelmed her own, and the great hawk flew on.

There was nothing more she could do. Eric was stronger than she.

She felt her mind slipping, felt a strange gray fog begin to close around her.

Sounds seemed to retreat into the distance, and her eyes began to play tricks on her.

She tried to look at Eric, but he seemed to be a long way away from her now, and as she watched, his image faded away entirely.

She was alone now, and would always be alone.

But it didn't matter; not really. She'd always been alone, except for those few short hours with Miranda.

Now she would live alone, wanting nothing, needing nothing, sitting by herself in the soft gray fog.

In the fog, where nothing—and no one—could ever hurt her again.

Gentle swells rolled under the bow of the *Big Ed,* causing a barely perceptible pitch in the forty-foot trawler. The sky had cleared, and a bright sun warmed the cabin. Ed lounged in the pilot's seat, using his left foot to keep the boat on course while he watched the shore of the cape move by at a steady seven knots. Another hour and he'd be back in False Harbor.

The flat sea and steady throbbing of the diesel engine under the floorboards lulled him, and his mind began to drift. The fog of the hangover was beginning to pass now, and he'd taken a couple of aspirin against the stabbing pain of his headache.

So Laura was gone.

It was something he'd never thought about, really, never planned for. Even when she'd threatened to leave him, he'd never taken her seriously. If she was going to do that, she'd have done it long ago. But she never had, and over the years Ed had come to a dim certainty that she never would. That was the thing about Laura: she didn't have the guts to fight back, and she didn't have the guts to leave. In fact, the way he treated her had been her fault, really. After all, if she let him beat up on her, why shouldn't he?

But now she was gone.

Dead.

Of all the stupid things she could have done—

He checked himself. No point getting mad at her now. And besides, what the hell did it really matter, anyway? Whatever had happened, had happened. He shouldn't even think about it, not yet. When he got home and found out all the details, then he'd think about it.

A flickering movement on the bow caught his eye, and he swung his head idly around to look through the salt-fogged windshield as a snow-white bird hovered in the air for a moment, then settled onto the railing around the foredeck. Ed's lips curled into a cynical smile. "Nothin' today," he said out loud, though he knew that even if the gull could hear him over the roar of the engine, his words would mean nothing to it. "No nets, no fish, not even any bait. You wasted your time."

He half expected the bird to take off then, leaping into the air with a mad fluttering of its wings before it caught the breeze, but it didn't. Instead it stayed where it was, one of its reddish eyes staring at him.

Staring at him almost as if it was accusing him of something.

But that was dumb. He hadn't done anything, and even if he had, what the fuck could a stupid bird know about it?

But as the bird continued to sit on the bow rail, its eyes fixed on him, Ed began to feel nervous.

Why didn't it go away?

Finally, frowning, he opened the window and flung a scrap of the doughnut—which had been too dry for him to force down his throat this morning—at the bird.

The piece of pastry struck the bird on the right wing then fell to the deck.

The bird made no move to go after it—didn't even look at it. Instead its gaze as it stared through the windshield at Ed seemed to intensify.

Ed's frown deepened.

He flipped on the autopilot and adjusted its course, then picked up a wrench and went out on deck. He started forward, the wrench held loosely in his right hand.

He froze as he realized that the bird wasn't a gull at all.

It was the ghostly white hawk that had perched on Miranda Sikes's rooftop for all the years that he could remember.

But it was dead. Gene Templeton had shot it.

And yet there it was, perched calmly on the rail of his boat.

The hawk watched him, cocking its head slightly. Ed tightened his grip on the wrench. He slowed his pace, moving more carefully now, wanting to be sure he was close enough to the bird to hit it with the first swing.

Before he came within range of the hawk, it leaped into the air, its wings beating furiously. But instead of flying away from the boat to hover mockingly just out of reach, it came straight toward Ed.

Its beak opened and a shrill screech burst from its throat, stabbing at Ed's aching head as if someone had jammed an ice pick into his ear. As Ed swung the wrench wildly, the bird's claws slashed at his face, tearing open his right cheek. Screaming in pain and fury, Ed hurled the wrench at the bird, but with a quick flick of its wings it rose out of the wrench's trajectory and the heavy metal tool fell harmlessly into the sea.

The bird hovered then, and a strange cackling sound, almost like laughter, rattled in its throat.

Suddenly, beneath Ed's feet, the boat pitched violently.

Ed almost lost his balance, then grabbed for the railing to steady himself.

The hawk dove, slashing at him again, and he felt a hot jab of pain in his left cheek, then tasted blood on his lips. Shielding himself with his left arm and hanging on to the railing with his right hand, he started back toward the cabin. The bird attacked once more, its talons ripping across the back of his neck as he ducked inside and slammed the door shut behind him. By the time he got back to the pilot's seat, the bird was once more perched on the bow pulpit, eyeing him malevolently.

Though the sky was still clear, the wind had picked up, and around him the swells were building, their crests topped by frothing whitecaps. But there seemed to be no specific direction from which the sudden squall was coming, and now the boat began to roll in a sickening counterpoint to its pitching. A faint queasiness began to twist at Ed's guts.

As the boat swung wildly off course, Ed grabbed the wheel with both hands and kicked the autopilot off. Now, as the rudder seemed to fight him and he had to struggle to bring the boat around, he forgot the pain from the lacerations on his body. Spray was coming over the bow, and he let go of the wheel with his right hand to reach out and flick the windshield wiper on.

Almost as if it sensed his momentary distraction, the boat slewed around, broaching on a swell, and slid sickeningly into the trough. Twisting the wheel violently, Ed forced the boat around to climb the face of the next swell.

The hawk, its wings folded serenely, still clung to the bow railing, riding the pitching and rolling of the waves as if it were floating on the surface of the water.

Then, as Ed watched, it launched itself into the air once more and hurtled toward the windshield.

He ducked reflexively away from the hawk's threatening claws, despite the fact that the heavy windshield was protecting him from the creature's fury. But as the bird bounced off the heavy glass then settled once more on the bow, Ed's heart was pounding.

He reached for the radio.

* * *

Tony Vittorio recognized Ed Cavanaugh's voice behind the interference on the radio, and reached out to press the transmission switch on the radio that sat on the duty officer's desk. "This is the False Harbor Police Department, Ed. Do you read me?"

A blast of static emerged from the radio, then once again Tony heard Ed's voice. "Something crazy's going on! I'm caught in a squall, and—and there's a bird attacking me!"

Vittorio glanced out the window at the bright morning sun. A maple tree, just beginning to leaf out, showed no signs of anything more than a light breeze. He pushed the switch again, his brows knitting into a frown. "Say again, Ed?"

The message was repeated, but through the static Tony could hear a note of panic coming into Cavanaugh's voice. "I don't know what's going on, but I'm starting to ship water!"

Vittorio picked up a pencil. "Give me your position, Ed."

On board the *Big Ed,* Cavanaugh glanced up at the LORAN suspended above the helm and read off the longitude and latitude as quickly as he could. Outside, the bird was on the windshield again, its flapping wings spreading out over the glass until he could see nothing at all of the sea ahead. To either side the waves continued to grow—enormous gray mountains bearing down on him from every direction. The boat was pitching and rolling wildly now, and the compass was spinning on its axis, giving him no clue at all as to the direction in which he was headed. A huge wave towered over him for a moment, then broke, water cascading over the trawler with a force that made the hull groan in protest. All the windows were covered for a moment, and then the water fell away, washing over the gunnels and draining off the decks.

But the hawk, apparently unaffected by the deluge, still clung to the windshield. As Ed watched with horrified eyes, it slammed its beak against the glass and a crack appeared, moving outward from the point of impact toward the window's teak framing.

"I need help," Ed managed. "I need help, and I need it quick." Then the trawler slewed around, and as the rudder twisted in the heaving waters, the wheel was torn from Ed's grip. He dropped the microphone, grasping the wheel with both hands once more, then shoved forward on the throttle with his elbow.

The diesel roared louder, and Ed felt the trawler surge forward through the sea.

"I don't get it," Tony Vittorio told the off-duty officer he'd called in to relieve him while he went out to look for Ed Cavanaugh. "Sound's like Ed's drunk, but it also sounded like he's scared. I'm going out to take a look." Twenty minutes later he was on his way down the channel in the runabout the marina owner kept on hand for use in emergencies. As he carefully negotiated the narrows near the Cranberry Point light, he tried to explain the situation to Bill Dawson, who had been checking out the runabout when Vittorio had appeared on the dock.

"Sounds nuts to me," Dawson grumbled as he surveyed the nearly flat sea and the cloudless blue sky above. "You ask me, he was drunk again."

"Maybe so," Vittorio replied. "But I'd hate to find out later he wasn't. You got binoculars on this thing?"

"In the forepeak," Dawson said. He disappeared for a moment, then emerged from the tiny double bunk beneath the bow. As Tony brought the boat around to a westerly heading, Dawson scanned the horizon with the glasses. "Something up ahead," he said after a few seconds had slipped by. "About two points off the port bow."

Vittorio adjusted his heading slightly and shoved the throttle to full open. The engine's pitch rose slightly, and the runabout hurtled forward, cutting the water at thirty knots. A rooster tail of loaming spray rose up in their wake. The tiny dot on the horizon quickly began taking shape, and within five minutes was clearly identifiable as a fishing trawler.

A fishing trawler that was violently pitching and rolling in what was otherwise a calm sea.

Cavanaugh was steering blind. Somehow the hawk had managed to spread itself across the full width of the windshield, and its beak, bloodied now, was still battering at the glass, which was covered with a spiderweb of cracks. Bits of shattered glass were falling from it, and one of them had lodged itself in the corner of Ed's eye. Each time he rubbed at it, the glass dug itself in deeper, until the eye began to bleed and swelled shut.

For a brief second Ed considered opening one of the side windows to poke his head out into the maelstrom that surrounded him and try to get some glimpse of his bearings.

Suddenly the boat pitched once more, and the sliding door on the port side crashed open. Instantly the hawk abandoned its attack on the windshield and burst into the cabin itself. The second it was inside, the boat yawed and the door slammed shut.

Abandoning the wheel, Ed threw his arms over his face to try to protect himself from the bird's fury.

It did no good.

Its beak and talons nothing more than a flashing blur, it tore at Ed's clothes, ripping them away until it had exposed his bare skin.

Now it was his flesh the hawk attacked, and Ed began screaming in agony as the sharp beak tore into him, jerking bits of skin and muscle away. The violent pitching of the boat increased, and Ed was hurled across the beam, his head smashing into the bulkhead. He crumpled to the floor for a moment, groaning, then shrieked as the bird renewed its attack. He rolled over, but once again the boat yawed, and Ed's body slammed against a corner of the dinette. He felt a rib crack, and a searing pain slashed through his chest. Then the pain was forgotten as the bird began stripping more flesh from his exposed arms and back.

He tried to roll now, back and forth, frantically seeking escape from the virago that swarmed over him, but there was no escape.

His screams fading to whimpers, he finally could fight no more, and lay still as the bird shredded his flesh. At last the blessed relief of unconsciousness began to overtake him, but at the last instant he opened his good eye.

Just before the bird snatched his eyeball from its socket, Ed thought he recognized a face looming above him.

But it was impossible. It was all impossible. . . .

And then the hawk's curved beak plunged into his eye, and the world, with a last flash of searing white-hot pain, went black.

"What the hell's going on?" Bill Dawson asked as the runabout drew near the fishing trawler. The trawler was still rolling gently, but the violent pitching they had witnessed as they raced out from the harbor had subsided. Still, the sea around the trawler was as calm as it had been when they passed Cranberry Point, and the sun still shone warmly from a cloudless sky. And yet both of them were certain they had seen the boat being tossed around as if it had been caught in a hurricane. Now, with only five yards separating the two vessels, Vittorio slowly circled the trawler.

It was soaking wet, with water still dripping from the cabin roof and running off the gunwales.

The windshield, though still in place, was shattered, and had caved slightly inward. Scattered over its surface was a random pattern of small holes, as if someone had driven nails through it in a misguided effort to gain entry to the boat.

At last Tony picked up the hailer Dawson had brought from the forepeak and called out to the trawler.

There was no response.

Tony brought the runabout alongside the trawler, and Dawson threw a line over its cleats. When two lines had been made fast, both men climbed aboard the *Big Ed*. While Vittorio checked the afterdeck, Dawson moved forward, finally sliding open the port door to the main cabin. A pure white hawk burst out of the pilothouse, spiraled over the trawler for a moment, then settled on the bow pulpit, its head swiveling rapidly as it surveyed its surroundings.

When he'd recovered from the shock of the bird, Bill Dawson stepped into the cabin and yelled for the police officer.

The cabin walls were smeared with the bright crimson of blood that hadn't yet dried, and on the floor, sprawled on its back, was what remained of Ed Cavanaugh's corpse.

The bones of his forearms and hands were completely exposed, the flesh torn away and scattered around the cabin. His chest, punctured and lacerated to little more than a reddish pulp, was covered only by a few remaining shreds of the heavy flannel shirt he'd been wearing.

His face—what was left of it—was a grotesque mask of terror, made even more hideous by the remnants of his left eyeball, which hung from its socket by a thread of torn tissue.

"Christ," Dawson breathed. "I never saw nothin' like this."

"Neither did I," Vittorio agreed, his voice grim as he fought the nausea rising in his gorge. "Get a tow line hooked up while I call in. If the radio still works," he added darkly.

By the time they got back to False Harbor, a small crowd had gathered on the dock. Tony Vittorio was not the only person who had heard Ed Cavanaugh's call for help, and several people had also heard Tony's brief report to the duty officer. As the runabout, laboring hard against the heavy load of the fishing trawler, made its slow way up the channel, a murmur of anticipation ran over the forty-odd people who had been waiting since noon.

In the runabout Tony's expression was one of anger mixed with resignation. "Wouldn't you think they had better things to do?" he asked.

Bill Dawson shook his head. His haunted eyes, still filled with the memory of what he'd seen in the cabin aboard the *Big Ed,* scanned the crowd. "With what's been goin' on around here, you got to expect it. They're scared, and you can bet that after they get a look at Ed, they're gonna be even more scared."

"I'm not giving them a look at Ed," Tony replied. "In fact if there were another place to put in, I'd do it. When we're tied up, make damned sure nobody gets aboard Ed's boat. And I mean nobody." He pulled back the throttle, gradually slowing the runabout, then prepared to lash it alongside the trawler as inertia brought it even with the smaller boat. Once they were tied together he'd begin working both boats toward the dock.

As the trawler closed, the white hawk that had ridden silently on the bow throughout the long, slow cruise eyed Tony malevolently one more time, then rose into the air, found a thermal, and spiraled upward above the trawler. At last, with an eerie screeching that echoed over the small harbor, it wheeled and soared off in the direction of the marsh.

Every eye in the crowd on the wharf followed it, and every person who saw it recognized it.

It was Miranda's hawk, going home to roost.

Gene Templeton and Keith Winslow approached the cabin slowly. A curl of white smoke drifted up from the chimney, dissipating quickly in the clear spring air.

The hawk perched on the roof, its head swiveling warily as it watched them come. But long before they were close enough for Templeton to get a shot at it, it lifted off, its wings beating powerfully, and sailed off across Cranberry Point and out to sea.

They came to the bottom of the rise, where Templeton paused. "You sure you want to come?" he asked.

Keith nodded. "I have to," he said. "Whoever she is—whatever she is, she's still my daughter. I've loved her since the day she was born, and no matter what she's done, I still love her."

Then, his lungs expanding as he drew in the fresh sea air, he started up the gentle slope, Templeton behind him.

No sound came from within the cabin. All the shutters were closed, as was the door. If it hadn't been for the smoke drifting from the chimney, it would have looked completely deserted.

After pausing on the porch for a moment, Keith reached out and pushed on the door.

It swung slowly open.

Keith stepped inside.

They sat at the table in the center of the room, opposite each other.

Keith could see Eric's face clearly over Cassie's shoulder.

His skin looked pale even in the dim light of the cabin, and his blue eyes seemed to be fixed on Cassie's face. But when Keith stepped across the threshold, Eric's eyes moved slightly. Then he swallowed.

"He's dead, isn't he?" he asked. "My father's dead."

Keith hesitated, then nodded.

"She said he was," Eric said almost tonelessly. "When we came out here, she told me Kiska had gone to kill my father."

"Why did you come out here?" Keith heard Templeton ask.

Eric frowned slightly, as if he were thinking. "Sumi," he said at last. "He wasn't in the house this morning." He hesitated, then managed an abashed smile. "We knew Mr. Winslow wouldn't let us come back here, so we sneaked out."

"The cat," Templeton said. "Is he here?"

Eric nodded, and glanced down at the tabletop. Keith took a step forward. Then he saw him.

In the middle of the table, his head twisted around in a grotesquely unnatural position, was the gray cat that had been Cassie's pet.

"She killed him," Eric said. His eyes met Keith's and didn't waver. "When we came out here, Sumi was in the cabin, and Cassie picked him up. She held him for a while, and then she told me what she saw." Eric's voice dropped to a whisper. "She saw my mother hanging herself. Sumi was there, and made her do it, and afterward—" He stopped abruptly, shaking his head as if to rid himself of the memory.

"Go on, son," Templeton said quietly. "What else?"

"Sumi clawed my mother's face."

Why is Eric telling it? Keith thought. Why is Cassie just sitting there, letting Eric tell it? But even as the questions came into his mind, a cold knot of fear closed on him as he began to suspect the answer.

"She killed Sumi," Eric went on. "She said there was no reason for my mother to die, but he killed her anyway. She said she'd lost control of him, so she killed him. She—she didn't want him to hurt anyone else."

Keith swallowed, trying to clear the lump out of his throat, but it did no good. Unable to speak, he slowly moved around until he could see Cassie's face.

Her eyes were wide and clear, and though they were staring directly at him, he knew she didn't see him.

Though the pain was finally gone from Cassie's eyes, nothing had replaced it. All that remained was a blank, empty void.

Her mouth hung slightly open, and the muscles in her cheeks had gone slack.

At last, his hand trembling, he reached out to touch her cheek. Her skin felt cool and slightly damp, but she showed no reaction to his touch.

"She wanted to stop Kiska," Eric said. "She wanted to, but she couldn't. . . . She couldn't. . . ."

"It's all right, son," Templeton said gently, laying his hand on the boy's shoulder. "It's over now. It's all over."

A few minutes later Keith lifted Cassie out of the chair and cradled her in his arms.

Her breathing was slow and steady, and he could even feel her heart beating in her breast.

But she herself was gone.

He carried her out of the little cabin and back through the marsh.

Templeton walked beside him, saying nothing.

Eric stayed in the cabin.

"I just want to be by myself for a little while," he said as they left. "I'll be all right. I just—I just have to get used to it, that's all."

Both Keith and the police chief had understood.

Templeton's car was in the parking lot by the beach, and Keith gently eased his daughter into the back seat. They drove across the parking lot toward Cape Drive, but as Templeton paused before pulling out onto the street itself, Cassie suddenly moved, twisting in the seat to look back out over the marsh.

On the porch of the cabin, Eric was barely visible.

Cassie frowned, then slowly raised her hand and pointed.

For a split second nothing happened. Then Kiska spread his wings, found the wind, and rose into the sky. He hovered for a moment, as if searching for his prey, then closed his wings and dove downward.

Eric, relaxed in his moment of triumph and Cassie's defeat, never saw him coming, never had a chance to reach out with his own mind, never had a chance to escape the bird's slashing talons.

Now it's over, Cassie thought silently as she let herself drift back into the cool comfort of the fog.

Now it's truly over.

SLEEPWALK

For Lee and Marshall—
So many places yet to go . . .

Prologue

T he woman stood at the blackboard at the front of her classroom, watching her students work on the problem she had laid out a few minutes earlier. Though her eyes flicked constantly over the class, her mind wasn't registering the images her eyes were feeding to it.

The heat of the day was building, which was good.

The hotter the sun beating down on the roof, the less the joints in her fingers and toes, her hands, her feet—even her arms and legs now—hurt her.

That was some consolation, though not much. At least, although the winter's cold threatened to make her totally immobile, she still had the summers to look forward to—the dry, desert summers, when the heat would soak into her bones and give her some tiny measure of relief, a slight easing of the pain her disease brought with it, a pain that grew each month, along with the ugly deformities of her misshapen joints.

She was supposed to be better now. The doctor had promised her the new treatment would work. No, that wasn't actually true, she reminded herself. He'd said he *hoped* it would work; he hadn't promised her anything.

She gritted her teeth, and denied herself even the brief solace of a sigh as a sharp pain shot up from her left ring finger.

Her instinct was to rub the painful finger, but that would only make her right hand hurt more, and already she was barely able to hold the chalk as she carried on her class.

Against her will, her eyes traveled to the clock.

Ten more minutes and the noon bell would ring. Another day of summer school would be over.

She could make it.

In the fourth row of the classroom the boy stared once more at the problem he'd copied onto the paper on his desk, and quickly computed the solution in his mind. It was right, he was certain, but even if it wasn't, he didn't care.

He put his pencil down and let his gaze wander to the window, where the heat was making the mesa shimmer in the distance.

That was where he should be today—hiking up on top of the mesa or in the cool of the canyon, swimming in one of the deep holes the river had cut from the canyon's floor, working the anger out of his system with physical exercise. He'd had another fight with his father that morning, and the last thing he'd wanted to do was go from the oppressiveness of his home to that of the school.

Perhaps he should just get up and walk out.

He tried to put the tempting thought out of his mind.

He had agreed to go to school this summer, and he would.

But it would be the last summer.

Indeed, these few weeks of school might be the last ever.

He looked up at the clock and sucked in his breath.

Nine more minutes.

Then, as he watched the second hand jerk slowly around the face of the clock, he had a sudden feeling he was not the only one concerned with the time.

He glanced instinctively at the teacher.

As if feeling his glance, her eyes shifted from the clock and met his for a moment, and he thought he saw the beginning of a smile on her lips.

Then she winced slightly and, as if ashamed that he'd seen her pain, she turned away.

The boy wondered why she kept teaching. He knew—everyone knew—how much the arthritis hurt her, how much it crippled her in the winter. Even now he could remember the day, the previous January, when the temperature had been well below zero and he'd seen her sitting in her car in the parking lot. He'd watched her for a few minutes, unable to see her face clearly through the moisture that had built up on the windshield, but still somehow able to sense her reluctance to step out of the warmth of the automobile into the bitter morning chill.

Finally he'd approached the car and asked her if she was all right.

She'd nodded, then opened the door.

Slowly, painfully, she'd eased her legs to the ground, and finally, carefully, stood up, a gasp erupting from her lips as she battled the pain.

He offered to help her, but she'd shaken her head.

He'd turned away and hurried into the school building, but when he was inside he'd turned back and watched her through the glass doors.

She'd moved slowly, every step clearly an agony, her face down in an attempt to hide her pain.

But she'd kept moving, kept walking, not even hesitating when she came to the steps and had to pull herself slowly upward, gripping the iron railing with her gnarled left hand as her right hand clenched against the pain.

She wouldn't give up.

She'd never give up.

She'd keep teaching, and keep browbeating her students to do better and work harder, until the day she died.

The boy smiled slightly as he remembered the last time he'd been subjected to one of her tongue-lashings. She'd called him in after school and flung a homework assignment at him, her eyes fixing accusingly on his as she announced that she was considering failing him.

He'd studied the homework and discovered two mistakes, which he didn't think was so bad. When he'd voiced that opinion, her eyes had only mocked him: two mistakes might be fine for most of the class; from him she expected more. Much more. He was smarter than the rest of them, and the work shouldn't have been a challenge.

He'd squirmed, but she'd kept on: if he wasn't going to try in high school, how was he going to get through college, where there would be a lot of people smarter than he?

That was when he'd told her he wasn't going to college. Even now he wished he hadn't.

Glaring at him, her fist had smashed down on the desk with a force that should have caused her to scream with agony. But he had been the one who flinched at the blow, and she had smiled in triumph.

"If I can do *that*," she'd said, "then you can damn well go to college."

He hated to think what she would say, at the beginning of his senior year, when she found out he was thinking of dropping out of high school.

But there were other things he wanted to do, things he didn't want to put off.

The teacher glanced surreptitiously at the clock once more. Just two more minutes. She could go home and sit in her back yard, ignoring the shade of the cottonwood trees to bask in the sun, letting the full heat of the afternoon penetrate the pain as she worked on her lesson plans and graded the examinations she'd given the class that morning.

She began straightening up the clutter on her desk.

She frowned slightly as a strange odor filled her nostrils. For a moment she couldn't quite identify it, but then realized what it was.

It was a malodorous scent, like a garbage dump on a hot day.

She sniffed at the air uncertainly, her frown deepening. The dump had been closed years ago, replaced by a treatment plant.

She looked up to see if anyone else had noticed the odor.

A flash of pain shot through her head.

She winced, but as quickly as the pain had come, it faded.

She shook her head, as if to shake off the last of the pain, then looked out at the class.

A red glow seemed to hang over the room.

She could see faces—faces she knew belonged to her students—but tinged with the red aura, seen dimly through a wall of pain, they all looked strange to her.

Nor could she put names to the faces.

The knife inside her head began to twist again.

Just a twinge at first, but building quickly until her skull seemed to throb with the pain.

The reddish glow in the room deepened, and the odor in her nostrils turned rank.

A loud humming began in her ears.

The aching in her head increased, and turned now into a sharp stabbing. She took a step backward, as if to escape the pain, but it seemed to pursue her.

The hum in her ears built to a screech, and the redness in the room began to flash with bolts of green and blue.

And then, as panic built within her, she saw a great hand spread out above her, its fingers reaching toward her, grasping at her.

She screamed.

The boy looked up as the piercing scream shattered the quiet of the room. For a split second he wasn't certain where it had come from, but then he saw the teacher.

Her eyes were wide with either pain or terror—he wasn't certain which—and her mouth twisted into an anguished grimace as the last of the scream died on her lips.

Her arms rose up as if to ward off some unseen thing that was attacking her, and then she staggered backward, struck the wall and seemed to freeze for a moment.

As he watched, she screamed once more and sank to the floor.

Her arms flailed at the air for a few seconds, then she wrapped them around her body, drawing her knees up to her chest as she rolled helplessly on the worn wooden planks.

The boy rose from his seat and dashed to the front of the room, kneeling down beside her. But as he reached out to touch her, she screamed yet again and scrabbled away, only to collapse a second later, sobbing uncontrollably.

When the ambulance took her away, she was still sobbing, still screaming.

The boy watched the ambulance leave, but even after it had disappeared into the distance, the sobs and screams lingered on, echoing in his memory.

Perhaps the other students who were in the classroom might forget the agony they'd heard and seen that day.

The boy never would.

One

J udith Sheffield felt the familiar tightening in her stomach as the final bell rang. All that was left of her day was the walk to the parking lot, accompanied, as always, by the prayer that today the tires on her car would still be inflated and none of its windows would be smashed. The day itself hadn't been too bad. Both her classes had gone well, which, she ruefully reminded herself, meant only that the disruptions had been minor.

At least today no fights had broken out in the classroom. After two years of teaching in East Los Angeles, Judith regarded that as a victory. But still, teaching during the summer session had been a mistake. She should have taken the summer off to relax, to rejuvenate herself and prepare for the far worse chaos of the regular school year. But she'd let herself be tempted by the extra pay, and conned herself into believing that the summer students would be more motivated than the regular term crowd.

The truth—which she knew perfectly well—was that the summer session students were there because they thought summer school would be a snap. Eventually they'd turned out to be right, for as Judith's energies had slowly drained through July and into August, she'd begun to slip, ignoring assignments not turned in, and skipping her regular morning quizzes. As the heat and smog of the Los Angeles summer closed in, she'd even begun dismissing her second class early, eager to return to her tiny apartment in Redondo Beach, strip off her clothes, then spend the afternoon lying in the sun on the beach, listening to the surf and trying to pretend that teaching in Los Angeles would get easier as she gained more experience.

It was getting harder to pretend.

The bell rang, and the kids poured out of the classroom into the halls like an overflowing toilet. Judith chided herself for the cruelty of the simile, then decided she didn't care—she tried to be a good teacher, tried to take an interest in the students, but if they didn't care, why should she? And what, really, could she do about it?

She could try harder.

And she would.

For the next six weeks she would relax, and by mid-September she would be ready, searching for new ways to capture the kids' interest, combing through the school's budget for the money she would need for new books. Perhaps this fall she would even organize a painting party to make her classroom a little less drab. She could hustle some plaster from Bobby Lansky's father—after all, it was Bobby who had hurled the desk that had made the hole in the wall—and she herself would spring for the pizzas she'd use to bribe some of the better students into participating.

She waited until the last of the kids' babble had died away, finished straightening the papers on her desk, then left her room, locking the door behind her. Warily, she glanced up and down the corridor, but it seemed deserted, and she told herself that today there would be no problems—it was the last day of summer session, and even the worst troublemakers would have been eager to get out of the building.

But as she moved toward the back staircase, she thought she heard a faint shuffling sound. She froze, listening.

A snicker, echoing maliciously, drifted through the hall.

She turned and started toward the main staircase at the other end of the hall.

Her step quickened and she instinctively clutched her heavy leather bag tighter, one hand gripping its shoulder strap while the other hovered protectively over the purse's flap.

A low whistle sounded behind her, and she steeled herself against the urge to break into a run.

Another whistle, slow and seductive, echoed in the hallway, and Judith felt her face turning scarlet.

She should be used to the wolf whistles by now—she heard them every day. Most of the time she simply ignored them.

But today, in the deserted third-floor corridor, the sound held an ominous note.

She hesitated at the top of the stairs, refusing to glance behind her, peering down the stairwell itself.

Empty.

She started down, moving quickly, one hand on the banister. She had made the first turn, and started down the fifteen steps to the second-floor landing, when suddenly she heard another whistle.

Two boys she didn't recognize stepped into the wide opening provided by the double doors on the landing below. They gazed up at her, smiling mockingly.

Though Judith knew they were no more than seventeen or eighteen, their eyes seemed much older, and they slouched in the doorway with a dark malevolence.

Judith paused as the familiar fear reached out to her once more. Her fingers tightened on the strap of her bag, and she slowly continued her descent.

One of the boys whistled again, while the other let his fingers stroke suggestively at his groin. "Got something for you, pretty teacher," he said. "Wanta see it?"

Judith said nothing. She came to the bottom of the stairs and took a tentative step toward the next flight.

The larger of the two moved to block her. "Want to have a good time?" he asked, his voice lifting with menace.

Judith's mind raced. She could scream, but there was no one to hear. And if someone heard her cry, would he rush to help?

Not likely.

She could try to flee back up the stairs, but a display of fear would only spur the boys on, turning what might have been a game into something far worse.

She moved forward again, focusing her mind on the lessons she'd learned last summer, after her first year of teaching here. "If you'll excuse me," she said, willing her voice to remain steady, "I'd just like to get to my meeting." There wasn't a meeting, but at least the boys might think she was expected somewhere.

The second boy reached out to her. "I got something wants to meet you."

As his hand came close to her, Judith spun around, slipping her bag off her shoulder and swinging it hard. She completed the turn, and the bag slammed into the boy's head, the weight of the ten rolls of quarters she always carried in its depths lending it enough force to knock the teenager against the wall. As her would-be attacker howled in pain and his friend stared at Judith in open-mouthed surprise, she broke into a run, dashing down the stairs, grabbing at the banister to steady herself.

"Get her!" she heard one of them shout as she came to the first-floor landing. Footsteps pounded in the stairwell. She ran into the corridor, turning left toward the side door that led to the faculty parking lot. By the time she reached the door she could hear her pursuers racing down the hall after her. She burst out the doors, praying that someone—anyone—would still be around.

There were a few cars in the lot, but no one in sight.

She stumbled down the steps, fumbling in the bag for her keys, then made a dash for her car. She jammed the key into the lock just as her assailants exploded from the building, twisted at it frantically, then managed to pull the door open. Scrambling inside, she jerked the door closed and pushed down on the lock just as the boys reached the car.

As she put the key in the ignition, the boys began rocking the car—a tiny Honda Civic she'd had for five years.

The ignition ground for a moment, then caught, and she stamped hard on the accelerator, racing the engine.

The boys were laughing now, and the car was rocking wildly. Saying nothing at all, Judith put the car in gear and released the brake. The Honda shot forward and her attackers jumped back. Judith turned sharply, heading for the parking lot gate, and suddenly the boys were running to another car, a low-slung Chevy painted a brilliant candy-apple red. As Judith pulled out of the parking lot and turned left toward the freeway a mile west, the Chevy fell in beside her.

They were going to follow her home!

Thinking quickly, Judith made a quick right turn, drove two blocks, then made a left, and another right.

The red Chevy stayed behind her, so close she was certain they were going to hit her. But then, as she made one more turn, her tormentors must have realized where she was going.

A block ahead was the low-slung building of the precinct station, a few patrol cars sitting in front of it. At the next corner the Chevy turned and disappeared into the traffic along Whittier Boulevard. Shaking, Judith pulled up in front of the police station, put the car in neutral and sat for a few minutes as her breathing returned to normal and her fear began to ease.

At last, when her hands could grip the wheel without trembling, she put the car in gear again and started home. But as she turned onto the freeway and started toward the beach, she realized what was happening to her.

Though she was barely twenty-six years old, she was already

beginning to feel burned out. She no longer cared about her students; she couldn't even be bothered to report what had just happened to the police.

The traffic inched along the broad expanse of the Santa Monica Freeway. In the distance, where she should have been able to see the hills surrounding the Los Angeles basin, there was today only a thick brown veil of smog, as heavy and unpleasant as her mood. Every day, for the next six weeks, she would dread that first day of school more and more.

She'd set out to be a teacher, not a warden.

An hour later she pulled her car into the garage under her building a block from the beach and let herself into the small apartment. She'd intended it only to be temporary, but it was fast looking as though she would spend the rest of her life here. On her salary, there was no way she would ever be able to buy a house in Southern California, and rents everywhere were skyrocketing—only her lease was protecting her now, a lease she would renew this week in the hope that next year rent control would come to her area. If it didn't, and her rent went up again, she would have to find a roommate, maybe even two.

She unlocked the sliding patio door and dropped her heavy purse onto the coffee table. As she entered the kitchen in search of a Coke, the phone began to ring, and she decided to let the answering machine handle it. Probably it was the boys who'd been following her, calling her up now to continue their harassment.

She made a mental note to have her phone number changed, with the new number unlisted.

But a moment later, as her message tape ran out and a voice she hadn't heard in years began to speak, she snatched up the phone.

"Aunt Rita?" she asked. "Is it really you?"

"Judith!" Rita Moreland exclaimed. "I thought you weren't there. I was just going to leave a message."

"I just don't answer the phone anymore until I know who's calling," Judith said. Propping the receiver against her shoulder, she opened the refrigerator and pulled out a Coke. "I'm afraid it's been a rough day."

"Oh, dear," Rita Moreland murmured apologetically. "If it's a bad time, I can call back—"

"No!" Judith protested. "It's just that it was the last day of summer session, and something happened."

Twenty minutes later, with the Coke finished and another one opened, Judith realized that she'd just unburdened herself of all her problems to a woman whom she hadn't seen in nearly ten years. Though she'd called Rita Moreland "aunt" all her life, the Morelands were really not relatives at all, but old family friends. "I'm sorry," she said. "I guess I really needed to talk to someone just now, and you happened to call. And I didn't even ask you why."

Rita Moreland laughed softly, an oddly tinkling sound that transported Judith back to the childhood that seemed so long ago and so far away. "Actually," Rita said, "perhaps it's providence that made me call today. I have a problem, and I'm getting desperate. And I thought of you. If you want to say no," she added in a rush, "believe me, I'll understand completely."

Judith frowned, mystified. "What on earth is it?" she asked. "You know if there's anything I can do for you and Uncle Max—"

"Oh, no," Rita broke in. "It isn't us. It's the school. We have an opening for a math teacher. Poor Reba Tucker's been hospitalized."

"Mrs. Tucker?" Judith said, surprised. Reba Tucker had once been her teacher and she remembered her fondly.

"I know it's awfully late in the year," Rita hurried on, "and you already have a job, but we're having a terrible problem finding someone." Rita Moreland talked on, but Judith was only half listening to what she was saying. Finally, Judith interrupted her.

"Aunt Rita?" she asked. "What's Borrego like now? It's been so long since I've been back."

Rita Moreland fell silent for a moment, then, once again, her bell-like laugh came over the line. "It's about the same," she said. "Things out here in New Mexico don't change very fast, you know. We're pretty much the way we've always been."

In that instant Judith Sheffield made up her mind. "I'll take the job, Aunt Rita," she said.

Jed Arnold slouched in the driver's seat of his ten-year-old Ford LTD, his fingers drumming impatiently on the steering wheel. The radio was blaring, tuned to the single station with a signal strong enough to reach from Santa Fe up to Borrego. It played country and western music twenty-four hours a day, but he supposed it was better than nothing at all.

"Maybe Jeff's not going to show up," Gina Alvarez said, reaching out to turn the volume down. She was curled up on the seat next to Jed, her head cradled against his shoulder. The remains of a hamburger and a shake were balanced on the dash, and when Gina felt a slight pressure on her shoulder, she reached out, picked up the last of the fries and stuck it in Jed's mouth.

"He'll be here," Jed told her, munching on the fry. "He was gonna get some beer."

Gina stiffened, then sat up and moved to the far side of the car, her eyes flicking to the backseat, where Heather Fredericks was necking with Randy Sparks. "You didn't say anyone was bringing beer," she said, her voice taking on an accusatory tone.

Jed grinned at her, that cocky, half-mocking grin that never failed to quicken her heartbeat. "If I had, you wouldn't have come, would you?"

Gina hesitated, then shrugged. "Maybe," she temporized. "Maybe I would, and maybe I wouldn't."

"You wouldn't," Jed declared knowingly. "You'd have given me one of your lectures on the evils of alcohol, and then shut the door in my face."

"I would not!" Gina replied. "How come everyone always acts like I'm some kind of goody-goody?"

"Because you are," Heather Fredericks replied from the backseat, squirming loose from Randy's arms and buttoning up her blouse.

"I am not," Gina protested. "But what happens if we get caught?"

Jed sighed in mock exasperation. "We're not going to get caught," he told her. "All we're gonna do is go out and drag the highway for a while, then go up into the canyon and have a couple of beers. What's the big deal?"

Gina thought it over, and decided that maybe he was right—maybe it wasn't a big deal. Almost all the kids she knew—certainly all of Jed's friends—got a couple of six-packs practically every weekend and went up into Mordida Canyon. And it wasn't as though they did anything really wrong. They just went for a swim, then sat around on the beach, listening to the radio and talking. And if she didn't go, all she'd wind up doing was sitting at home with her little sister, watching television.

Her mother would be furious if she found out, but it was Friday night, and she'd be working at the café until at least one in the morning. By then Gina would be home in bed, asleep.

A pair of headlights swept across the ugly orange walls of the A&W stand in front of them, and a horn blasted as Jeff Hankins pulled up next to the LTD in his ancient Plymouth. He revved the engine threateningly, then called to Jed, "Still think that piece of junk can take me?"

Jed snickered, and switched on the Ford's engine. "Only one way to find out, isn't there?" he yelled back. As he dropped the transmission into reverse, the car jerked backward with enough force to throw Gina against the dashboard. She shoved herself back onto the seat and pulled the seat belt around her waist. "What's the matter?" Jed teased her. "Think I've forgotten how to drive?"

"I think if you roll the car over, I want to stay where I am," Gina told him.

They were out of the parking lot now, and a moment later Jeff

Hankins pulled his Plymouth up next to the LTD. "The canyon?" he asked.

"You got it," Jed replied. "Anytime you're ready."

Jeff nodded, then suddenly popped his clutch, and the Plymouth, its tires screaming, shot forward. A split second later Jed jammed his foot onto the LTD's accelerator. By the time he was ready to shift into second gear, he'd come abreast of the Plymouth, but as he shoved the gearshift up into second, the Plymouth pulled ahead of him again.

"Shit," he yelled. "What the hell's he done to that thing?"

"Stuck in a new carburetor," Randy said from the backseat. "I got a buck that says he beats you."

Jed gunned the engine, then shifted again, but the Plymouth was far ahead of him now, its taillights mocking him as Jeff raced out of town. The road ran straight for a mile, then turned right for another mile before coming to the canyon turnoff. Jed broke into a grin as he spotted a side road ahead. "You're on!" he shouted, then hit the brakes and spun the wheel.

The LTD slewed around, then left the pavement and shot onto a dirt track that angled off from the main road.

Randy Sparks jerked around to see the Plymouth disappearing into the distance. "Hey, what the hell are you doing?" he demanded.

"Cutting cross-country!" Jed shifted down and tightened his grip on the wheel as the Ford lumbered along the rough track.

"Are you nuts? You'll tear the pan out."

They hit a bump and the car thudded as its suspension hit bottom. Then a roaring filled the night.

"Oh, Christ," Jed muttered. "There goes the muffler."

The car lurched down the rutted road, its undercarriage slamming hard every few seconds. In the distance Gina could see Jeff Hankins's Plymouth making the turn on the main road. Jed saw it too, put the LTD into a lower gear and gunned the engine. The roar from the unmuffled manifold rose, but the car shot forward.

When he hit the main road again less than a minute later, Jed was only ten yards ahead of the Plymouth. He spun the wheel once more and skidded across the road. The tires on the right side of the car left the pavement, hit the gravel along the shoulder, and finally dropped into the ditch next to the road. The steering wheel wrenched loose from Jed's grip and spun around.

The car flipped, rolled over, and came to a stop upside down, its wheels spinning slowly. There was a sudden silence as the engine died, then a screaming of tires as Jeff Hankins braked to a stop.

A moment later Jeff and his girlfriend, JoAnna Garcia, were in the ditch, staring numbly into the ruined LTD.

"Heather!" JoAnna screamed, finally finding her voice. "Gina! Oh, my God. Are you all right?"

"Get the door open," Gina mumbled. She was still strapped to the seat, suspended upside down, her head brushing against the roof of the car. She fumbled with the seat belt for a moment, got it loose, and dropped in a heap onto the roof itself. JoAnna struggled with the wrecked door. One of its hinges already broken, it squealed in protest, then fell off into the ditch. A moment later Randy Sparks managed to force the rear door open too, and the four teenagers began creeping out of the wreckage.

Heather Fredericks had a cut on her right arm and a bump on her head, and Randy Sparks's left hand was bleeding, but otherwise they seemed uninjured.

"What the hell were you doing?" Jeff demanded, as his relief that his friends were all right gave way to anger. "You could have killed yourself and everybody else, too!"

Jed Arnold hardly heard Jeff's words. He was staring dolefully at the wreckage of his car. Already he could hear his father yelling at him. His father hadn't wanted him to buy the car at all, and now . . .

His thoughts were interrupted by the distant wail of a siren. He looked up to see the flashing red and blue lights of a police car coming toward them through the night.

Jed sat alone in the little police station in the basement of the City Hall, waiting for his father to come and pick him up. His friends had left an hour ago, Randy Sparks, Gina, and Heather having been escorted to the hospital to have their injuries taken care of, Jeff and JoAnna sent home.

But Jed was still waiting. His father was working the swing shift at the refinery and wouldn't get off until midnight. Jed had done his best to talk Billy Clark into letting him go, but the deputy had only looked at him coldly.

"You damn near killed yourself and three other kids tonight, you damn half-breed." Jed's eyes had blazed with cold fury at the term, but he'd kept silent. "You really think I'm just going to let you go?" the cop went on. "You've been making trouble around here long enough, but this time you're not getting off." He'd fingerprinted Jed, taken mug shots, then locked him in the station's single holding cell while he'd written up a report and a citation against Jed for reckless driving and endangerment of human life.

In the cell, Jed waited silently until his father finally showed up a little after midnight.

With no words exchanged between them, Jed signed for his

things, and showed no emotion at all as his father led him out of the police station and drove him home.

He listened equally silently as Frank Arnold lectured him on the stupidity of what he'd done and told him he could forget about getting the car fixed.

At last Jed went to bed, but he didn't sleep.

Instead he lay awake, remembering Billy Clark's words, and knowing Clark was only saying what nearly everyone else in Borrego thought.

He, Jed Arnold, wasn't white, and he wasn't Indian.

He was something else, something halfway in between.

Sometimes—like now—he felt as if he didn't fit in anywhere.

It was at times like this, late at night, when he was all alone, that all the fury contained within him would threaten to erupt to the surface.

It was at times like this that he wondered if someday the rage might overflow and he might actually kill someone.

Or maybe even kill himself.

That, as he well knew, was always an option too.

Two

A week after Rita Moreland's phone call, Judith Sheffield was on her way to Borrego. Immediately after the conversation, there had been a moment of panic as she wondered whether she'd been rash to accept the offer, but by the next morning, when for the first time in months she'd awakened with a sense of actually looking forward to the day, rather than dreading it, she knew she'd made the right decision.

For the next five days she dealt with the details of making the move.

It was surprisingly simple. Her landlord was actually relieved when she told him she'd changed her mind about renewing her lease—he had three people willing to take the apartment at a rent far higher than Judith would have paid. And the new tenant, anxious to move in as quickly as possible, instantly agreed to buy whatever furniture Judith left behind.

She left all of it, packing only her clothes and personal belongings into the foot locker she'd been using as a coffee table, and shipping her books and records ahead.

The moment she dreaded most—the moment of telling Floyd Morales that she wasn't signing the contract for next year—turned out to be almost as easy.

"Well, you're certainly not making my life any easier," the principal had commented. "But I can't say that I blame you. There've been plenty of times when I've thought about getting the hell out of here myself."

Judith's brows had risen, but Morales had only shrugged. "What can I do? I grew up here . . . my family lives here—maybe I feel like I owe them something." But then his gaze had drifted to the window and the littered playing field, fenced in like a prison, that lay beyond his office. "I don't know," he'd mused. "Sometimes it feels so hopeless." At last he'd straightened up and taken on his usual briskness. "But there are still kids who want an education, and deserve one. So I guess I just can't give up and go away."

Judith felt the sting of his words. "Is that what you think? That I'm giving up? Cutting and running?"

Morales had apologized immediately. "Of course not. In fact, you're doing exactly what I did when I came back here after college. You're going home, and helping them out. Nobody can condemn that." He'd offered her his hand. "They're lucky to be getting you. You have a way with the kids."

Judith had grinned ruefully. "I wish that were true."

"It is," Morales had insisted. "I know it's been rough, but you've had less trouble with the kids than most of the teachers. And you've turned at least half a dozen of them around. Kept them in school when they were on the verge of dropping out."

"Half a dozen," Judith had repeated. "Out of how many hundred? Somehow, it doesn't seem like much to me."

Still, as she'd left the school for the last time, she felt a sharp pang of regret. There were a few students—not too many, but some—to whom she wished she'd been able to say good-bye.

The next morning, when she read an account of a gang fight the night before and found that one of her best students hadn't survived it, the last of her regrets evaporated.

Now, as she drove the final fifty miles north from Interstate 40, up into the neck of land between the Navajo reservation to the west and the Apache lands to the east, she was still certain she'd done the right thing.

The New Mexican sky, an immense expanse of brilliant blue that seemed—impossibly—to have grown even larger than she remembered from her childhood, spread above her, dwarfing even the mesas that rose from the desert floor in the distance.

She was tempted to turn off the highway for an hour or so and pay a short visit to the vast ruins at Chaco Canyon, but as she came to the turnoff, she changed her mind, suddenly eager to see Borrego once more.

Borrego.

The town she'd grown up in, but never, until last week, expected to come back to.

She came over the last rise in the gently rolling desert floor and pulled over to the side of the road, parked the Honda on the shoulder and got out of the car. She perched on the hood, staring out at the town in the distance.

Borrego could have been beautiful: sprawled at the foot of one of the mesas, it lay near the mouth of Mordida Canyon, a deep, narrow gorge that, though only the tiniest fraction of the size of the Grand Canyon to the west, had a unique beauty all its own, its flat bottom dotted with cottonwoods, a gentle stream flowing through it year 'round.

The town hadn't been built on the river, for the Mordida, like all the other streams in the region, could turn into a raging torrent within a few moments, fueled by the torrential rains that could pour out of the desert sky with no warning at all.

Not that the Mordida was a threat to the town any longer; indeed, the river had been safe from flash floods for more than fifty years, ever since a small dam had been constructed across one of the canyon's narrows, generating the electricity needed to power the refinery that old Samuel Moreland had built when he discovered oil in the area.

For that was what Borrego really was—an oil town. But not a boom town like the bonanza towns of Texas. No, Borrego was only a tiny service village, a place for the refinery workers to live, along with the drillers and the crews who looked after the dam. As the oil reserves around Borrego had always been limited, so too had the prospects for the town, which had reached its peak shortly after the dam and refinery had been constructed. Ever since, it had slowly been declining. The Sheffields had moved from Borrego to Los Angeles for just that reason, when Judith was sixteen. Now, squinting against the glare of the sun, she could just make out the worn buildings that made up the town.

A layer of dust seemed to lie over Borrego, a layer that even the violent desert rain squalls could never quite seem to wash away. It was almost as if the town had deliberately ignored the expansive red, orange, and brown landscape that surrounded it, and become afraid of the limitless cobalt-blue dome of sky above. Borrego appeared to huddle defensively against the ground, many of its old adobe buildings long since replaced with a collection of cinderblock structures whose metal or asphalt roofs absorbed more of the summer heat than they reflected.

Judith's gaze shifted to the top of the mesa, and for a moment she imagined she could actually see the little Kokatí Pueblo. That, she hoped, was still unchanged, but after her visit to the Hopi mesas yesterday, when she'd seen the same tin-roofed, cinder-block houses that so many of the Indians had moved into—leaving their beautiful pueblos to begin crumbling in the weather—her hope had faded. It was certainly possible—even probable—that the Kokatís had also abandoned the old village for something that was not better, but was only new.

She climbed back into the Honda, started the engine, and drove the last few miles into Borrego. A mile and a half out of town, set back from the road, the oil refinery stood exactly as she remembered it—a maze of pipes and towers, with a small tank farm behind it. Then there was the cutoff to the canyon—still unpaved, little more than twin ruts leading off across the desert floor toward the cleft in the mesa.

At last she came to the town itself, its boundary marked by the squat, ugly orange building that was the A&W stand. Not one of the new ones—bright and airy, with tables and a fast-food counter—but the old style, with a walk-up window and a couple of teenage carhops wearing outdated uniforms, lounging at a picnic table at the edge of the deserted parking lot.

Judith wondered if the A&W was still the place where the kids met in the evening, shouting back and forth between their cars, then racing off into the night, going nowhere, only to return to the drive-in a few minutes later.

The main street was unchanged. The same two competing markets stood facing each other, one of them flanked by the dry goods store, the other by a drugstore and the post office. Beyond them were a few new shops that Judith didn't recognize, and some of the old ones were gone.

Two blocks down, opposite the small movie theater that was now boarded up, stood the Borrego Building—a four-story brick structure that housed the bank on its main floor and the offices of Borrego Oil Company on the floors above. When it was built, it had been intended to be the first of many multistoried buildings in what everyone had hoped would become a small city.

But Borrego was still nothing more than the little town it had always been, crouched in the high desert, all but bypassed by the development along the interstate to the south.

Yet Judith found she was glad so little change had come to the town. She felt oddly comforted to recognize some of the people who stood chatting in front of the tiny post office, their faces weathered by the desert climate, but their features—like the town's own—essentially unchanged, only more deeply ravaged by time and the elements than they'd been a decade ago.

She left the town behind, driving east for a mile, then turned up the long drive that led to the foot of the mesa and the big house—a bastard-Victorian structure that stood defiantly at odds with its environment, not quite a mansion, but by far the largest home in Borrego. Old Samuel Moreland had built it for his wife at a time when no one else was building such things. His son Max, and Rita Moreland, still lived there.

Surrounded by a grove of large cottonwoods that sheltered it from the sun and screened the most ornate of its gingerbread details from the viewer, it had a look of solidity and permanence to it that Judith admired. Tall, and somewhat narrow, it seemed to peer out at the desert with a spinsterish disapproval, as if eyeing its surroundings with thinly-veiled distaste. Judith pulled the Honda to a stop in front of the house, then stepped out into the cool shade of the cottonwood trees. Even before she'd mounted the steep flight of steps to the porch, the big door opened and Rita Moreland stepped out, her arms spread wide in welcome.

"Judith? Is it really you? I hadn't thought you'd be here until tomorrow!"

Judith rushed up the steps and into the older woman's embrace, then pulled away to get a good look at the woman who'd been the closest thing to a grandmother she'd ever had.

"You look wonderful, Aunt Rita."

It was true. Rita Moreland, at seventy-two, looked no more than sixty. She still held her tall, somewhat angular frame perfectly erect, and she was dressed in the sort of simple linen skirt and blouse she had worn as long as Judith could remember. Around her neck was an antique silver and turquoise squash-blossom necklace, and her wrists held several bracelets, most of them modern Hopi designs. Her hair, snow white, was rolled up into an elegant French twist, held in place by a silver comb. Only her eyes, alight with pleasure, belied her look of cool composure.

"Well, you've changed," Rita replied. "All grown-up, and just as pretty as your mother. Although," she added, cocking her head speculatively, "I think perhaps your hair's starting to darken a little."

Judith grinned. "It's called aging, Aunt Rita. Is Uncle Max here?"

Rita's eyes clouded for just a split second, then cleared as she shook her head. "Oh, no—always at the office, or the plant. You know Max—he'll work till he drops, even though he keeps promising me he'll slow down. Now come on, let's get you inside." Before Judith could protest, Rita had darted down the steps and pulled one of Judith's bags from the backseat of the Honda.

Upstairs, Judith gazed with unabashed pleasure at the room Rita had chosen for her. It was a large chamber in the corner—almost two rooms, really, since the tower that rose at the southwest corner of the house was incorporated into it. There was an immense four-poster bed, and in the tower itself, a cushion-filled love seat and a large easy chair. Five windows were set into the curving wall of the tower, and the view, framed by a pair of cottonwoods, was a panorama of desert and mesas, with the town no more than a small collection of buildings in the foreground.

"You can see almost fifty miles from up here," Rita told her, reading her thoughts. "Of course, it would be even lovelier without the town and the refinery, but without those we wouldn't be here at all, would we?" She lifted one of the suitcases onto the bed and snapped it open. "Let's get you unpacked. By then Max should be home and we can all have a gin and tonic."

Judith firmly closed the suitcase. "I have an even better idea," she said. "Let's leave the unpacking for later, and you and I can have something right now. It's been a long drive."

Long, she thought as she followed Rita back downstairs, but worth it. All her doubts were now gone.

She was glad to be home.

Stretched out on a chaise under one of the cottonwoods, sipping slowly at her second drink, Judith felt a sense of ease and comfort she hadn't experienced for years. Rita had filled her in on most of the news of the last decade, what there was of it. Many of the kids she'd grown up with were still here, married now, most with at least one child. Laura Sanders, to whom she'd promised to write but never had, had come back five years ago, graduating from nursing school and taking a job at Borrego High.

The one piece of news that had truly upset her was Rita's recounting of the death of Alice Arnold four years ago.

"How did Jed take it?" Judith asked. In her mind she pictured the little boy—only five or six when she'd last seen him—with his Kokatí mother's dark skin and jet-black hair, and his father's brilliant blue eyes. She remembered Jed as a happy child, interested in everything he saw, full of questions, always eager to go exploring in the canyon or up on the mesa. Judith had baby-sat for him many times, once or twice taking care of him all weekend while Frank took Alice away, hoping to break her strange melancholy with trips to Santa Fe, or up into the Utah canyon lands. Judith had loved those weekends, taking care of Jed, riding up into the canyon with him perched on the saddle in front of her, or up to the mesa to visit his grandfather in Kokatí. Jed, his bright eyes darting everywhere, talking constantly, asking questions, urging her onward to explore.

To have lost his mother, when he was still only eleven.

"It was hard for him," she heard Rita saying. "It was Jed who found her. He came home from school one day, and there she was . . ." Rita's voice trailed off, and both the women were silent for a moment.

"How is he now?" Judith asked. "It's such a terrible thing for a child that age."

"It's hard to say," Rita replied. "In so many ways he's so much like his mother. I'm afraid there's a part of him no one will ever know. It's almost as if he's closed part of himself down." Her eyes met Judith's. "It's very difficult for him, you know, being half Indian out here."

"But not as difficult as it must have been for Alice, trying to live in Borrego after growing up in Kokatí. After she married Frank, her father barely spoke to her."

"I know," Rita sighed. "In their own way, the Indians can be every bit as prejudiced as we are."

They talked on for a while, and finally Judith turned to a subject she'd been avoiding—the reason she was back in Borrego.

"What about Mrs. Tucker?" she asked. "How is she?"

Again, as when Judith had asked about Max, a troubled cloud passed over Rita Moreland's eyes, but this time it didn't pass. "I think maybe you should save that question for Greg," she began.

"Greg?" Judith exclaimed. "You mean Greg is here too?"

Rita stared at her. "You mean you didn't know?" she asked. "You had such a crush on him ten years ago, I thought that might have been one of the reasons you came back."

A crush, Judith thought. The first great love of my life, and all it's remembered as is a crush.

But of course infatuation was exactly what it had been.

Greg Moreland—Max and Rita's nephew—had spent all his summers in Borrego, coming home from his boarding school each spring, impressing all the local girls with his blond curls and dimpled chin, as well as his sophistication, then leaving them each fall with broken hearts as he returned to New England, first for college, then for medical school. During the summer before his last year at Harvard Medical School it had been Judith's turn to fall for him. Not that he'd even noticed her, of course, except to take a turn with her once or twice at the weekend dances at the union hall.

But it had been enough to make her fall in love with him—or at least develop a major crush—and when he'd left, she was sure she would die.

Not only hadn't she died, but she'd quickly developed another crush on someone else—someone even more unattainable than Greg—and hadn't even thought of Greg for the last five years.

"But what on earth is he doing back here?" she asked. "Somehow, I always pictured him opening a terribly successful Park Avenue practice in New York."

Rita chuckled appreciatively. "Well, I can't say I didn't see pretty much the same thing myself. But it turned out we were wrong. He did a residency in Boston, then came back here for one more summer to think things over. And he never left." Rita beamed with as much pride as if Greg were her own son, instead of her nephew. "He started dropping in on Bob Banning at the clinic every now and then, just helping out when there was an emergency, and at the end of the summer he decided to stay until Christmas. That was six years ago, and he's still here."

"Does he live here?"

"Oh, no," Rita replied. "He has a little house in town—nothing special, considering what his tastes used to be."

Judith frowned. "But he has plenty of money, doesn't he? Why hasn't he built something terrific?"

Rita smiled cryptically. "Why don't you ask him yourself?" she asked. "He'll be here for dinner tonight."

Judith stared at Rita for a moment, then cocked her head. "Is this part of a plan?" she asked archly.

Rita's smile faded. "I wish it were," she said softly. "But I don't think I would have gone so far as to put poor Reba in the hospital."

Judith's laughter died on her lips. "I'm sorry," she said. "I didn't mean—"

"Of course you didn't," Rita assured her.

Judith said nothing, but lay back, relaxing in the warmth of the sun that was now beginning to drop toward the western horizon.

A lot in Borrego hadn't changed at all.

But a lot else, she suddenly realized, had.

Unbidden, her thoughts returned to Alice Arnold, and she made a mental note to call Frank the next day.

So many things had happened here, so long ago.

And now she was back.

*　　*　　*

"How are you feeling?" Greg Moreland asked as he carefully un-wrapped the gauze from Heather Fredericks's arm.

Heather winced as the bandage came off the wound, then relaxed as she realized there was no pain at all. Still, the cut looked ugly, with its coating of dried blood and the four stitches the doctor had taken a week ago. "Okay," she said. "Is there going to be a scar?"

Greg turned on his best reassuring grin. "Would I leave a scar on a girl as pretty as you?"

Heather blushed with embarrassment at the compliment, and shook her head.

Greg carefully began cleaning away the dried blood and was pleased to see that the cut was healing nicely There was none of the puffiness that might have indicated an infection setting in, and the raw edges of skin were knitting perfectly. In another week there would be nothing left except a hairline, and that too would be gone within a month.

"What do you say we get the stitches out?" he asked

Heather shrugged, but her face screwed up with anticipation as Greg carefully clipped the threads, then worked them loose with a pair of tweezers. When he was done, he re-covered the cut with a piece of surgical tape, then replaced the old bandage with a new one.

"How about your head?" he asked when he was finished. "That was a pretty nasty bump you got. Any headaches? Blurring of your vision?"

Once again Heather shook her head. "I took aspirin for a couple of days, but there was hardly even any swelling."

"Okay," Greg said, making a couple of notes on Heather's chart. "Then I guess that's it till next week when you should be able to get rid of that bandage." Heather made a sour face. "Who cares about the bandage? My mom won't let me go out for two more weeks anyway. And none of it was even my fault."

Greg leaned back in his chair and gave Heather a speculative look. Perhaps, in this case at least, Heather was right. She'd been in the backseat of Jed Arnold's car, and hadn't been drinking. But then he remembered the two six-packs of beer that had been found in Jeff Hankins's car. "And I suppose you weren't going to drink any of the beer either, were you?" he asked.

Heather's expression tightened into a pout. "Maybe I didn't even know it was there."

"Maybe you didn't," Greg agreed. "But I'll give odds you did, and I'll give even better odds you would have had more than your share of it if you'd all gotten up to the canyon." He leaned forward and the lightness disappeared from his voice. "It hasn't occurred to any of you kids how lucky you were, has it?" he asked.

Heather shrugged sulkily as she realized she wasn't going to be able to con Dr. Moreland into talking her mother out of grounding her. "Can I go now?" she asked.

Greg opened his mouth as though to say something else, then changed his mind. He nodded, told Heather to make an appointment for the following week, then watched as she left the room.

A girl, he thought, who was heading for trouble.

Just like so many of the kids in Borrego.

Not much to do, and not much to look forward to.

For the most part they'd wind up like their parents, getting married too young, having too many kids, then living out their lives in trailer houses, or ugly little concrete blocks, like the ones they'd grown up in.

Every day Greg saw it—saw the discontent and unhappiness of the parents, saw the boredom and disinterest of the children.

That, perhaps, was why he'd returned to Borrego. He wanted to change what he saw there. But some days, like today when he tried to talk some sense into kids like Heather Fredericks, he wondered whether he was simply wasting his time.

Kids like Heather and her friends just never seemed to listen to him, never seemed to learn.

Still, he couldn't stop trying.

He sighed, glanced up at the clock, then began clearing off his desk. In another hour he was due at his aunt and uncle's house. If he hurried, he'd have time for a quick shower, and maybe even half an hour of sleep.

Even if Judith Sheffield was still as pretty as he remembered her from ten years ago, it was going to be a long night.

Three

J udith sat quietly in one of the large leather-upholstered club chairs that flanked the fireplace in the Morelands' living room. She was finally feeling the exhaustion of the long day on the road, and though she supposed she should have excused herself an hour ago and gone upstairs to bed, she'd lingered on, listening to the talk between Max and Greg.

It was apparent to her that Max was proud of his nephew, and Judith could understand why. Greg seemed to her to have lost the hard edge of sophistication he'd affected in his college days, and the almost artificial perfection of his features had softened slightly as he'd matured. Now, in his thirties, his darkening hair was no longer as perfectly combed as it had once been, and his dark eyes had taken on a new depth. Though he was still remarkably handsome, he no longer seemed to be either conscious of his good looks, or impressed by them. Rather, he seemed far more interested in his work than in anything else, although she noticed he had listened intently when she'd asked Max about his own plans for the future.

Max, she reflected sadly, had not aged as gracefully as his wife over the last decade. His brow was deeply furrowed, and the flesh of his face seemed to have lost its tone—folds of loose skin hung at his jowls, and his eyes had sunk deep within their sockets. And, beneath his obvious pleasure in seeing her, she thought she could detect a certain strain, as if he were worried about something but didn't want to dwell on it, or cause anyone else to share his concerns. She'd pressed him, though, after dinner, and finally he'd admitted that there were some problems at the refinery. Though he'd done his best to make light of the situation, she gathered that the last few years, when oil prices had suddenly dropped, had been difficult for his company. There was a large debt load to support, and the refinery itself was becoming more obsolete each year.

"But it'll be all right," he'd finally assured her. "The oil business has always had ups and downs, and it always will. Hell, if everything ran smoothly for a couple of years, I'd probably start feeling useless and go do something else." Then, as if to emphasize his wish to change the subject, he'd waved toward Greg. "Now, if you want to hear something really interesting, ask him about what he's doing up in the canyon."

"It's not much," Greg said. "Uncle Max tries to make it sound like I'm the best thing since Mother Teresa, but I'm afraid it doesn't compare at all."

"What doesn't?"

"Well, you remember the old farm up there?"

Judith nodded, remembering it clearly. When she'd been a little girl, it had been one of the most popular haunts around for her and her friends. Far up the canyon, only half a mile below the dam, there had been an abandoned farmhouse, with a few outbuildings including an old barn and a bunkhouse. Legends about the farm abounded, old ghost stories that she and her friends had never tired of telling.

The farm, long uninhabited and nearly in ruins, was off limits on the grounds that it was unsafe, and therefore a favorite spot for adventurous ten-year-olds.

Judith could still remember the delicious feeling of forbidden adventure that creeping up into the creaking hayloft in the barn brought—praying the floorboards wouldn't collapse under your weight, shuddering as you heard small unseen creatures scurrying about, and later bragging about your exploits to the younger kids, as you told them what a terrifying place it was. "So what have you done with it?" Judith asked.

"He's turned it into a sanitarium," Max announced proudly.

Judith cocked her head uncertainly. "A sanitarium?" she echoed uncertainly. "I'm not sure I understand."

Greg shook his head. "It isn't really a sanitarium at all," he said. "It's more of a hospice, but since I also take a few rehab patients who have no place else to go, everyone around here has started calling it a sanitarium. Even," he added, feigning a glare at his uncle, "Uncle Max, who should know better. It's just a place for people who need some medical care—nothing too major, of course—but don't have much money or insurance."

"It's a hell of a lot more than that," Max declared, turning away from his nephew to face Judith. He was fairly beaming, and as he talked, all the old zest and enthusiasm Judith remembered came back to his voice. "That old place was just sitting there rotting away, and Greg figured out what to do with it. He's got some nurses and physical therapists up there, but if you just wandered into the place, you'd swear you were in a resort. Everybody has private cabins, and they bring you your meals if you need it. But he figured out how to do it without making it too expensive. It's a great place for people who are too sick to stay home but can't afford a hospital or a nursing home."

"It just seemed that there was a need for something in the middle," Greg said, his expression serious now. "A nice environment for people who were either going to get better pretty fast or were really beyond treatment and just needed a comfortable place to live out their last few days or weeks. So I set it up as a foundation, and conned Uncle Max into donating the land and the buildings."

"And you put in a lot of your own money too," Rita Moreland said, her voice reflecting the same pride in Greg as her husband's had a moment earlier.

"Not all that much," Greg replied. "Actually, I've been spending a lot of time rustling up grants, and it's working out pretty well. I guess," he added, suddenly sounding shy, "what I've really done is build the kind of place I'd like to be in myself."

Judith sat silently for a few moments, then a thought came to her. "Is that where Mrs. Tucker is?" she asked.

It was Rita who nodded, her expression somber.

"What happened to her?" Judith asked Greg.

He spread his hands helplessly. "It was one of those things you can never predict. She had a stroke. It surprised me—I'd been treating her for arthritis, and monitoring her pretty closely. Her blood pressure was fine, and except for the arthritis, she seemed to be in great condition." He looked at his uncle, his features taking on an exaggerated cast of disapproval. "She wasn't like some people I could mention, whose blood pressure is far higher than it should be, and whose arteries are totally clogged up from eating the wrong things for seventy-five years, and who are stroke victims waiting to happen."

"Doesn't sound like anyone I know," Max growled, and poured himself another shot of bourbon from the bottle sitting open on the coffee table in front of him. He held the glass up and grinned at his nephew. "Thins the blood, right?" he asked, and drained the slug of whiskey in one gulp.

Greg rolled his eyes in mock horror. "Anyway, Mrs. Tucker seemed to be doing fine, and then one day last month she had a massive stroke. It happened during one of her classes, and I guess it was pretty bad for the kids. They didn't know what had happened, and there was nothing they could do. She was teaching them one minute, and the next she was on the floor, caught up in a seizure. Now . . ." His voice trailed off and his hands spread in a bleak gesture of helplessness. "There just doesn't seem to be anything I can do for her except make her comfortable."

The conversation had drifted on, but Judith was only half listening, most of her attention focused on the plight of her former teacher. She tried to imagine what it must be like to be trapped the way Reba Tucker now was, unable to take care of herself, unable even to communicate.

Her whole life reduced to a small cabin, in which she waited to die.

In such circumstances, Judith imagined, a person must pray for death every moment of every day. Long ago she had come to realize that sometimes it was easier to die than to go on living.

Heather Fredericks lay in her bed, staring up at the ceiling. She wasn't certain how long she'd been awake, wasn't even certain what it was that had awakened her.

All she knew was that she felt perfectly relaxed—even the pain in her arm, a lingering throbbing that had been bothering her when she'd gone to bed earlier that night, seemed to be gone.

Her mind drifted, her thoughts floating lazily, vague images appearing now and then, then fading away again.

And then, from somewhere outside, she heard a voice.

"Heather."

Just the single word; nothing else.

She lay still, her eyes fixed on the ceiling, waiting.

A few seconds later she heard the voice again:

"Heather come outside."

Without thinking about it, Heather pushed the covers aside and stood up. She was wearing nothing except a pair of flannel pajamas, but she didn't stop to dress or even put on a robe before obeying the voice she'd heard. She simply left her room, padded barefoot down the hall and through the kitchen, then went out the back door, leaving it standing open behind her.

When she was outside she stopped, waiting.

A few moments later the voice came again, as though from nowhere.

"Follow me."

Heather gazed around, not questioning the command, only looking for the person who might have spoken the words.

The moon was high, and nearly full, and the desert was illuminated with a pale silvery light. For a moment Heather saw nothing, but then a form appeared out of the deep shadows behind the garage. It stood watching her silently, and a moment later turned and walked away, crossing the backyard and opening the gate in the Fredericks's back fence.

The house, on the very edge of the town, was separated from the desert only by the fence, so as Heather crossed the lawn and stepped through the gate herself, she immediately left the village behind.

She was alone in the desert, following a shadowy form.

Yet she was not afraid.

The figure ahead of her kept a steady pace, moving quickly, and Heather had to struggle to keep up, but in her mind she didn't question what she was doing, didn't wonder why she was doing it.

She only knew she had to obey the instructions she'd been given. Indeed, obeying those instructions was all she wanted to do.

She walked for nearly an hour, her bare feet moving steadily across the sand and rocks of the desert.

She stepped on a broken bottle, the sharp fragment of glass slashing at her foot, but she neither felt the pain of the cut nor noticed the blood that oozed from it. Her attention remained focused on the dark figure ahead as it led her steadily across the desert.

The path they walked began rising, then turned into a series of switchbacks as it led up to the top of the mesa. But even as she climbed, Heather felt no tiredness in her muscles, no shortness of breath. Even her heartbeat remained steady.

They came eventually to the top of the mesa, but still the figure moved onward, not speaking, not pausing, not even looking back.

And Heather followed.

At last the figure stood motionless.

"Stop."

The word was uttered softly, but its effect on Heather was no less profound than if it had been shouted directly into her ear.

Instantly, she too came to a halt, then remained perfectly still, waiting to be told what to do next.

"Turn left," the voice said.

Heather turned.

"Walk forward ten steps."

Heather began to move, silently counting. When she reached ten, she stopped again.

"Look down."

Heather's gaze shifted, and she peered downward.

Only a step ahead of her the wall of the canyon dropped away, falling nearly a thousand feet straight down. At the bottom of the canyon, barely visible, she could see the stream glinting faintly in the moonlight.

"Jump," the voice commanded.

Without thinking about it, without hesitating, Heather Fredericks stepped off the edge of the abyss and plunged silently into the depths of the chasm.

The shadowy figure waited a few moments, staring down after her until she disappeared, then silently began retracing its steps, moving steadily back toward the town.

At last, after all the years of preparation, the time had come.

Jed Arnold was sprawled out on the worn Naugahyde couch in the living room of the house he shared with his father. The television was tuned to a rerun of a show Jed had already seen and hadn't much liked in the first place. Not that he was watching it; more than anything else, it simply served as background noise, filling the silence.

He'd been grounded for two weeks, and he still had a week to go—seven more long evenings, with nothing to do and no one to talk to.

A car pulled up in front, its engine racing noisily for a moment before suddenly dying. Jed heard two car doors slam, then a loud pounding on the front door. Rolling off the sofa, he opened the door to find Randy Sparks and Jeff Hankins grinning at him.

"Come on," Randy said. "Jeff's got some beer, and we're going up to the canyon. We'll do some skinny-dipping and get smashed."

Jed started to shake his head, then changed his mind. After all, it was only eleven-thirty. His father had gone to work an hour ago, and wouldn't be home until a little after seven-thirty in the morning. By then he'd be back home. And even if he went ahead and had a few beers, his father would never know.

But what if his dad called to check up on him, as he had last night?

There was an easy answer to that one, Jed thought—with the phone off the hook, he could say he'd been talking to friends, and his father would never know the difference.

His mind made up, he went into the kitchen, removed the receiver and laid it on the counter. Then he went to his own room and pulled his leather jacket out of the pile of clothes on his chair.

Leaving the television and the lights on, he glanced guiltily at the house next door, but was almost sure the neighbors had gone to bed an hour ago.

By the time he was in the backseat of Jeff's Plymouth, crouched down for the first few blocks so no one would see him, he was certain he was going to get away with it.

"It's okay," Randy said from the front seat a few minutes later. "We're out of town."

Jed sat up, peered quickly out the back window, then relaxed. There were no other cars in sight, and even the glowing lights of the A&W stand were barely visible in the distance.

"Your dad still pissed at you?" Jeff asked as they came to the cutoff that led up the floor of the canyon. There were still faint skid marks from the week before, when Jed's own car had spun across the road and rolled into the ditch.

"Oh, yeah," Jed replied. "Every single day he gives me another lecture on responsibility. It's like he never made any mistakes at all when he was my age."

"Maybe he didn't," Jeff suggested. "My mom says he was always a real straight arrow."

Jed rolled his eyes. "That's what they all say they were, isn't it? But it's a bunch of bullshit, if you ask me."

"Yeah, but nobody asked you," Randy said, switching on the radio and turning the volume up as high as it would go.

They turned up the canyon road, a cloud of dust rising behind the car as its wheels dug into the dirt. Jeff pressed down harder on the accelerator, shooting the plume even higher. The Plymouth shot across the desert toward the mouth of the canyon.

Five minutes later Jeff parked the car at a bend in the canyon where the stream had dug a deep hole next to the canyon's south wall, leaving a gently sloping beach lined with cottonwoods on its northern bank. There was still a little light from the moon on the north wall of the canyon, but the stream was shrouded in deep shadows, and the night air had turned chilly. While Randy Sparks wedged the two six-packs of beer into some rocks a few yards upstream, so the water itself would keep it cold, Jed and Jeff stripped off their clothes and dove into the river.

The water was cold here, much colder than the surface water in the lake two miles farther up, for the water pouring through the turbines of the dam came from the bottom of the reservoir and wouldn't warm up again until it reached the Colorado, a hundred miles away.

Jed's body sliced through the water as he swam upstream, pacing himself against the current so that he could keep swimming as long as he wanted but never move from where he'd started. Finally he rolled over onto his back and let himself float, feetfirst, toward the point fifty yards downstream where the riverbed narrowed, coursing through a cluster of boulders worn perfectly smooth over the centuries. The water raced through the rapids—known to generations of Borrego kids as the Chute—turning and twisting for a hundred yards before coming into the next pool, and Jed sensed the familiar rush of excitement as he felt the current strengthen. The rapids could be dangerous—indeed, during the spring, when the spillways at the dam were wide open to release the floodwater from the melting snowpack in the mountains to the north, they were deadly. By September, though, even some of the more adventurous of Borrego's junior high school kids were trying their courage against the Chute.

Tonight the current seemed a little stronger than usual, which meant the dam was probably operating at full capacity. If he got into trouble . . . For a moment he almost changed his mind, but the sound of Randy's voice galvanized him.

"What's the matter?" his friend shouted. "Is the halfbreed chicken?"

Randy's words struck him like stones. His first impulse was to swim away from the entrance to the Chute, to go ashore and shove the epithet back down the other boy's throat. But a moment later the decision was out of his hands as the current grabbed him, hurtling him forward. He braced himself for the first turn. Here, you had to push off with your left foot at just the right moment, or risk becoming wedged between two huge rocks. That part wasn't really dangerous, but it ruined the ride—once stopped, there was no way of getting back into the current, and you had to climb out, scramble over the rocks to the pool upstream, and start over.

He felt his foot touch the boulder, allowed his knee to bend, then shoved hard. His body twisted in the water, and he pointed his toes, using his feet almost like the bow of a tiny skiff. He knew every inch of the Chute, knew where to push off with his feet, where to use his hands instead.

He was getting close to his favorite spot now—an immense boulder with a deep cleft in it. Hollowed out by the river over millennia, it had become a perfect natural water slide. He felt the current strengthen even more, then was into the slide, his skin rubbing against the slippery rock, the water cascading over his body. He picked up speed, then shot over the final lip of the Chute and into the pool below.

And struck something unfamiliar, something that had never been there before.

He paused, treading water, then dived down to feel in the depths, to try to locate the strange object.

His hand closed on something, and then his feet found the bottom and he pushed upward.

When he came to the surface, he strained his eyes in the darkness to see what he held.

It was a mass of soggy flannel, and inside it was the broken body of Heather Fredericks.

Four

T he slowly spinning lights on the roofs of the two police cars and the ambulance shot a kaleidoscopic pattern of reds and blues up the canyon walls, creating a strangely hypnotic effect on Jed. He was still sitting numbly on a rock a few yards from the spot where he'd found Heather Fredericks's body nearly an hour before. Randy Sparks had stayed with him while Jeff raced back into town, and although no more than half an hour had passed before the squad cars and the ambulance had roared up the canyon, their sirens wailing mournfully in the night, to Jed it seemed as if hours had ticked by.

He had no memory at all of having pulled Heather ashore; the memory that stayed in his mind—and, he was sure, would stay with him the rest of his life—was the image of Heather's face, her eyes open, staring at him lifelessly in the silvery moonlight.

He'd been only barely conscious of the arrival of the police, and as the medics had moved Heather's broken body onto a stretcher, Jed had sat staring at the activity, his mind playing games with him, so that several times he was almost certain he saw Heather move. Listening, concentrating, he even imagined he heard a low groaning sound—the longed-for moan that would tell him she wasn't dead after all.

It was the silence—the absence of the siren's wail as the ambulance disappeared back into the night—that told Jed the girl he'd known all his life was truly dead, that what was happening was not simply a nightmare from which he would awaken to find himself back on the sofa in his living room, the television still droning in the background.

"You ready to talk about what happened?"

Jed looked up to see the two policemen, Billy Clark and Dan Rogers, standing on the riverbank, watching him. Clark switched his flashlight on, shining it directly into Jed's eyes, and the boy's arm went up defensively as he turned away from the blinding glare.

"We need to know what happened, boy," Clark growled.

Jed shook his head, trying to clear it, but the image of Heather refused to go away. "N-Nothin' happened," he said, his voice barely audible. "I went through the Chute, and when I got to the bottom, there she was."

Billy Clark's lip curled. "Oh, sure. You and your punk buddies weren't doin' a thing, right? Just came up for a little swim, and there's your girlfriend, drowned. You think anyone's gonna believe that? Now, why don't you tell us what really happened?"

Jed swallowed nervously and glanced around. A few yards away, sitting in the front seat of the Plymouth, Randy Sparks and Jeff Hankins were watching him worriedly. "But that's what happened," Jed said. "Didn't you ask Jeff and Randy?"

"I'm asking you, boy," Clark growled. "And I can tell you right now the coroner's going to be going over that girl, looking to find out what happened to her. And if he finds out she had sex tonight, he's also gonna find out who it was with. You understand me, *breed?* The best thing you can do for yourself is tell the truth, and tell it right now."

Jed felt the familiar tight knot of anger begin to push the shock out of his mind. With narrowed eyes, and fists clenched against the desire to strike out against the insult, he said: "Come off it, Clark. If you're gonna arrest me, go ahead and do it, and then call my dad. But if you want to know what happened, I'm trying to tell you."

Clark seemed about to say something to Jed, but Dan Rogers interceded. "Come on, Billy. Everyone in town knows Jed goes with Gina Alvarez, and even if Heather had been his girlfriend, it doesn't make any difference." He turned to Jed, his voice friendly. "No one's saying you did anything, Jed. We just want to know what happened."

Slowly, almost hesitantly, Jed repeated what he'd said before, beginning with the moment Randy and Jeff had showed up at his house shortly after his father had gone to work. When he was finished, he looked up at Billy Clark, his eyes challenging the policeman. "It's the truth," he said. "I swear it is."

Clark stared at him silently for a long moment, but finally, almost reluctantly, nodded his head. "All right. It jibes with what your buddies said. And the medics seemed to think she'd been in the water for at least an hour."

Jed closed his eyes and felt a little of the tension drain out of his body. "Wh-What happened to her?" he asked.

It was Dan Rogers who answered him. "Don't know. It looks like she might have fallen off the top, or gotten pushed. We'll have a lot better idea after we find out what she was up to tonight." He turned to Clark. "Billy, why don't you call a couple of the day guys and go see Heather's folks. I'll take the boys back to the station and get statements from all of them."

Clark seemed about to argue, then apparently changed his mind. Wordlessly, he went back to one of the squad cars, and a moment later disappeared into the night.

"You want to ride with me?" Dan Rogers asked as he walked back toward Jeff Hankins's Plymouth with Jed at his side. "I figure you must be feeling a little shaky."

Jed nodded, then went to wait in the police cruiser while the cop spoke to Jeff and Randy. Rogers slid behind the wheel and started the engine.

Jed, preoccupied with what had just happened, didn't look back as they drove out of the canyon, Jeff following close behind.

He knew he was in trouble again, but not for something he'd actually done.

He was in trouble simply because of what he was.

Reenie Fredericks stared at the three policemen blankly. "That's not possible," she said. "Heather's in bed, sleeping." But the look on Billy Clark's face made her turn and race from the doorway to Heather's room, where she gazed in stunned silence at the empty bed.

Heather's clothes were still scattered on the floor in the haphazard manner that sometimes threatened to drive Reenie crazy. Now
she simply stared at them in dismay. If Heather had decided to sneak
out, surely she would have dressed . . .

She started back toward the front door, then felt a draft. Turning,
half expecting to see Heather coming in the back door, she saw
instead the kitchen door was standing open, a gaping hole leading
into the blackness of the night and the empty desert beyond the
fence. As she gazed vacantly at the door, the truth of what Billy Clark
had just told her struck home. A wail of anguish rose from her
throat.

"But she wouldn't have just gone out like that," Reenie said
twenty minutes later when Billy Clark had explained to her that
when she was found, Heather was wearing nothing but a pair of
pajamas. "If she'd gone on her own, she would have dressed!"

And yet, searching the house, the policemen found no signs of a
struggle, and even her mother admitted that she couldn't imagine
sleeping undisturbed in the next room if Heather had been fighting
off an abductor.

It was nearly one-thirty in the morning when one of the policemen brought a dog in and the tracking began. The scent was fresh,
and the dog had no trouble picking it up. Sniffing eagerly, it moved
steadily through the desert. After fifteen minutes the flashlights the
men carried began to pick up spots of blood, still clear on the
hard-packed earth of the desert floor.

At last they came to the top of the canyon, where the trail came
to an abrupt end at the very edge of the precipice.

"Jesus," Billy Clark said softly, staring down into the dark chasm.
"What the hell happened up here?"

He and his men studied the terrain carefully, searching for any
sign of struggle, any sign at all that Heather had not been alone. But
there was none.

Only a set of bloody footprints, a dark outline on the windswept
sandstone of the precipice. Heather seemed to have been walking
normally; there was no sign that she was dragging her feet as if
someone were forcing her toward the edge, nor was there any hint
that she might have been running and seen where she was going too
late to stop herself.

At the very edge of the cliff there were two prints, side by side,
as if she'd stood there, staring into the abyss.

Stood there for a few seconds, then jumped.

"Jesus," Clark said once again, shaking his head slowly. "What
the hell would make a kid do something like that? Doesn't make
sense."

One of the other men shrugged. "Who knows?" he asked. "Maybe she was drugged up. Kids these days do all kinds of crazy things."

They stood silently at the edge for a few moments, looking down, then finally turned away and started back toward the town. They moved slowly, unconsciously putting off the moment that they would have to tell Reenie Fredericks that her daughter, an ordinary kid with no seemingly extraordinary problems, had committed suicide.

Frank Arnold said nothing as he drove his son home from the police station for the second time in the space of a week. He sat stolidly behind the wheel of the truck, his jaw set, his eyes fixed unwaveringly on the road ahead. But the tension in the heavy frame of his body was an almost palpable force within the confines of the truck's cab. Jed, his face drawn, sat silently in the passenger seat next to his father, staring out into the night, oblivious to his father's silent anger, still seeing Heather's dead eyes staring at him. When Frank finally turned into the driveway of their small house on Sixth East and switched the engine off, Jed made no move to get out.

"We're here," Frank said, opening the door on his side and jumping out of the cab. For a moment he wasn't sure his son had even heard him, but just as he was about to speak again, the other door of the truck opened and Jed slid out.

They walked down the driveway, entering the house through the back door, and Frank flipped on the kitchen light. Going to the refrigerator, he pulled out a beer. He thought a moment, then pulled out a second one and held it up toward Jed. "Want one? Or would you rather have a shot of brandy?"

Jed looked at his father uncertainly, and Frank managed a wry grin. "I'm still pretty damned mad at you, but I'm not so mad I don't have any idea what you're feeling right now. If you're old enough to pull a corpse out of a river, I guess you're old enough to have a shot of brandy to take the edge off it."

Jed hesitated, but shook his head. "I think maybe I'll just have a Coke," he said.

Frank waited until Jed had opened the soft drink and sat down at the table across from him before he spoke. After his son had taken his first long drink of the soda, Frank pulled at his beer, then set the bottle on the table. "You okay?" he asked.

Jed started to nod, but then shook his head. "I don't know. I just keep seeing her, looking at me. I—" His voice trembled, and he fell silent as his eyes welled with tears.

"What the hell were you doing out there, Jed?" Frank said quietly, staring at the bottle in front of him. "Didn't you think I meant it when I grounded you?"

"I didn't go out there to get in any trouble—" Jed began, but his father cut him off.

"Bullshit! Kids like Randy Sparks and Jeff Hankins don't go out and get drunk in the middle of the night without intending to get into trouble."

"They weren't drunk," Jed protested. "They'd had maybe one beer apiece when they came over here, and—"

"And nothin'!" Frank exploded, his fist slamming down on the table with enough force to knock the beer bottle over. He snatched it up just as the beer itself began to foam onto the table, but ignored the puddle as he glared at his son. "What the hell's going on with you, Jed? You're twice as smart as those jerks, but you keep on letting them get you into trouble. Why the hell don't you start listening to yourself for a change, instead of those two assholes?"

"They're not assholes," Jed flared, his own anger rising in the face of his father's wrath. "There's nothing wrong with them, and they don't make me do anything I don't want to do. I didn't have to go with them tonight! I could have sat home by myself, just like I did last night, and the night before, and the night before that. But why the hell should I? You're either sleeping or at work or at some goddammed meeting or something. What am I supposed to do, sit around talking to the walls all the time? And when I do see you, all you ever do is yell at me!"

Frank's eyes narrowed angrily and a vein in his forehead stood out. But then, taking control of his anger, he bit back the furious words on his lips and found himself slowly counting to ten, just as Alice had always insisted he do when his temper—almost as quick as his son's—threatened to get the best of him.

When he reached ten, he started over again.

By the third time through, his rage was back under control, and he finally began to think about what Jed had just said. For the last four years, ever since Alice had died, he'd tended more and more to let Jed raise himself. Part of the problem was the simple fact of his shift work, that his schedule matched Jed's only once every three weeks. During one of the other weeks he was just going to work as Jed was getting home, and the third week, he was just getting up, still groggy from the restless sleep that was all he was ever able to get when he came home from the graveyard shift. And Jed had a point about the meetings too. But what could he do? He was the president of the union local, and no matter how hard he tried to organize his schedule so he could spend as much time as possible with his son, there always seemed to be something in the way.

Recently, for the last six months, there had been a series of rumors that Max Moreland was finally going to have to sell the refinery. Max insisted there was nothing to the talk, but it had long been Frank's experience that when gossip was as plentiful as it was now, there was something to it. And so, ever since last winter, he'd involved himself in union business more than ever before, working with a group of lawyers and accountants in Santa Fe to see if an employee buyout of Borrego Oil might be possible.

Which meant that Jed was alone even more than usual, for too often Frank found himself spending most of his waking hours driving back and forth over the 150 miles between Borrego and Santa Fe. And, if he was honest with himself, he knew that Jed's problems— the problems Frank had been doing his best to ignore, or attribute to nothing more serious than typical adolescent angst—had increased in these last six months.

During the spring semester of school Jed's grades, which had never before been a problem, suddenly took a nosedive. Before Frank had even become aware of the situation, it was too late. It had been a failing grade in geometry that had sent Jed to summer school.

He and his son had a terrible row about that. Only Frank's threat to take Jed's car away from him had finally convinced the boy that he had no choice.

In the end, Reba Tucker had suffered a stroke, putting a quick end to the summer school session, and now Jed was without his car anyway.

"Look," he said at last, slumping in his chair and wondering why conversations like this always had to take place in the small hours of the morning rather than at a more reasonable time, "I know things have been tough for you lately. But they haven't been easy for me either. Sometimes I feel like I'm trying to do everything, and I guess I tend to let you take care of yourself too much. But up until recently, there's never been a problem."

Jed's eyes clouded. "There's always been a problem," he said, his voice taking on a defiant note. "If there hadn't been a problem, Mom would still be alive, wouldn't she?"

Jed's words hit Frank like a blow. He stared at Jed mutely, trying to decide whether what his son had said was only caused by his momentary anger or if this was something that had been eating at him for months, even years. And yet, as he studied the pain in his son's eyes, he knew the words had been prompted by something the boy had been harboring for a very long time. "Is that what all this is really about?" Frank asked quietly. "Your mother?"

Jed's expression hardened. "Well, it's true, isn't it?" he asked, his voice taking on an almost childish petulance. "Isn't that why she's gone? Because you treated her the same way you treat me?"

Fury welled up in Frank and he rose to his feet, towering over his son. "No, God damn it!" he roared. "What happened to your mother had nothing to do with me at all. I loved her, as much as I've ever loved anybody in my life, and she loved me too." And yet even as he spoke the words, Frank knew deep within himself that it was that very love between them that had, in the end, been at least partially responsible for her death. For Alice, despite the love they had shared, had never been able to make a place for herself in Borrego. Part of her always longed to be back in Kokatí with the people she'd grown up with. She hadn't talked about it often, but there had been times, particularly during the last months, when she'd curled in his arms late at night. "Nobody here likes me," she'd whispered, her arms tightening around him. "I can tell by the way they look at me. They think I'm stupid, and they don't think I hear the things they say about the Indians."

"But they don't mean to hurt you," Frank had told her. "It's because they don't even think of you as being an Indian anymore that you even hear those things."

But Alice hadn't been convinced. In the last weeks she'd spent more and more time by herself, walking in the desert.

That last day, she'd been gone before dawn, and Frank had nearly taken the day off to go look for her. But in the end he'd decided to leave her alone.

And at half-past three that afternoon Jed had called him, sobbing and hysterical. The boy had come home from school as usual, and opened the garage door to put his bicycle away.

And found his mother's body, hanging from the rafters, a thick rope tightly knotted around her neck.

Until this moment, though, he'd never known that Jed blamed him for what had happened to Alice. Now, keeping his voice as steady as he could, he tried to explain to his son what had really happened. Jed listened in silence, not interrupting until he was finished. Then, after several more minutes had passed, he nodded his head slowly.

"So Mom felt just like I do," he said. "Like she didn't fit in anywhere, like nobody really liked her."

"But it wasn't true," Frank insisted. "Everyone in town loved your mother."

Jed stared at him bleakly. "Did they?" he said. "I wonder. After all, she was an Indian, wasn't she? And don't give me any bullshit that everyone in town loves the Indians."

"But your mother was different—" Frank began, then realized the words had been a mistake.

"Was she?" Jed demanded. "She was never part of anything, not really. She wasn't part of this place, and up in Kokatí no one ever trusted her after she married you."

"That's not true," Frank replied. "She never said anything—"

"She didn't say anything to *you*," Jed broke in, his voice filled with anguish. "But she told me."

Frank wished he could shut out what he was certain was coming, but knew he had to hear it. "All right," he said, his voice choking. "What did she tell you?"

Jed's jaw tightened and his eyes reflected the pain deep within his soul. "That sometimes she wished she'd never had me," he whispered. "She said that sometimes she thought it would be easier for me not to exist at all than to spend my whole life never fitting in anywhere, never feeling like I'm really part of anything."

"But you are part of something," Frank protested. "You're my son."

"I'm your *half-breed* son," Jed said bitterly. "And that's all I'll ever be."

"Now that is bullshit," Frank replied. "If that's the way your mother really felt, I'm sorry. Because she was wrong. You're still you, and you can be anything you want to be. If you don't like it here, you can leave. And after you graduate from high school, you will leave. At college you'll find out that no one cares where you came from or what your background is. The only things that will count are your brains, and your talent. And you've got a lot of both."

"Yeah," Jed growled. "Except that I'm not going to college."

Frank stared at his son. "What the hell are you talking about? Of course you're going to college. Your mother and I—"

"The hell with Mom," Jed shouted, rising to his feet. "Can't you understand that she's dead? She killed herself, Dad. She didn't love you, and she didn't love me. So who the hell cares what she wanted? She didn't even care enough to stick around and help me! So all I want is to get a job and earn some money so I can get the hell out of here. Okay?"

Before Frank could say anything, Jed wheeled and stormed out of the kitchen. Frank sat staring at the beer bottle for a few moments, then silently drained it, tossed it into the trash, turned out the lights and headed for his bedroom. He paused outside Jed's door, his hand on the knob, then changed his mind.

Right now, in the hours before dawn, he suddenly felt as if he hadn't the slightest idea who his son was, nor did he have any idea what to say to him.

As he lay in bed a few minutes later, trying to go to sleep, he felt more lonely than he had in all the years since Alice had died. Until tonight, he'd always felt that he at least had Jed.

Now he was no longer certain he even had a son.

Greg Moreland walked into the hospital at eight o'clock the next morning and smiled a greeting to the duty nurse, Gloria Hernandez. "What's going on?" he asked. "Another quiet night?" His smile faded quickly as Gloria looked up at him, her expression haggard.

"I wish it had been," she said. "But we got a body in about one o'clock this morning. Dr. Banning's downstairs with it now."

The last vestige of Moreland's grin faded away. "A body? What happened?"

"It looks like a suicide," Gloria told him. "It's Heather Fredericks."

Greg nodded perfunctorily, then went into his office, slipped into a white smock, and went downstairs to the morgue beneath the hospital. He found Bob Banning in the single small autopsy room, nodded a greeting, then made himself look at Heather Fredericks.

Her body lay on the metal autopsy table, her abdomen slit open from the groin all the way up to her chest. Her organs, carefully removed from the thoracic cavity, lay where Banning had placed them, small samples of each cut away for testing by a lab in Santa Fe.

Greg turned away quickly, instinctively avoiding looking at Heather's face. It was the one thing about being a doctor he hated—he'd never gotten used to seeing corpses, never developed that clinical detachment most doctors managed in the face of death.

For him, a corpse was still a person, and though he knew it was irrational, he sometimes felt that even after death, a person might still be able to experience pain.

He picked up the clipboard that held Bob Banning's notes, and scanned them quickly. From the first gross examination, death appeared to have been instantaneous, and caused by severe trauma.

Nearly every bone in Heather's body seemed to have been broken in the fall: both arms and legs, her hips, her back and neck, as well as her collarbone. Her cranium was fractured as well, and there were severe lacerations on her back.

After he'd finished reading the notes, numbed by the shock of what had happened to his patient, he finally managed to speak to Banning. "Jesus Christ—how did all this happen?"

Banning shrugged, his eyes never leaving his work. "She fell over a thousand feet, and hit a rock in the river. She's broken up like a bunch of matchsticks."

"And it was definitely a suicide?"

Banning nodded. "As far as I can tell. I'll have to wait for the lab analyses before I can make a final report, but apparently she just walked from her house up to the rim of the canyon— barefoot, and wearing nothing but a pair of pajamas—and jumped off. No sign of a struggle—her mother didn't hear anything. She just went to bed, then got up a couple of hours later and went out and killed herself. Unless she was doing drugs—"

Greg Moreland's brows knit into a deep frown, and he shook his head. "Not Heather," he said. "I'd been treating her for that accident a week ago, and if she was on drugs, believe me, I'd have spotted it. I saw her yesterday, and she was just fine. Her wounds were healing, and the biggest problem she had was that her mother had grounded her. But you'd hardly think something like that would be enough to make a kid kill herself."

Banning stretched his aching muscles, and yawned against the fatigue that clouded his mind. "I don't know," he said. "I guess we've been pretty lucky around here. This kind of thing seems to happen every day now. Kids who seem fine just suddenly give up. It's as though the world has become too complicated for them, and anything seems better than having to cope with one more day." He moved to a sink, and began washing up. "By tomorrow we should know for sure. But if her blood comes up clean, I'm going to call it a suicide."

Later, back in his office, Greg found himself still thinking about Banning's words.

And he also thought about Heather Fredericks. He'd liked Heather, even though she had often been a bit manipulative, trying to get her own way about everything. But no one, he was sure, thought she was the kind who would commit suicide.

Perhaps, after all, they would find something indicating that it hadn't been suicide at all.

Sighing heavily, he picked up the phone and rang the front desk.

"Gloria? When the lab reports on Heather Fredericks come in, make sure I get a copy, will you?"

"Of course, Doctor," Gloria replied. "I'd have done it anyway. She was your patient, wasn't she?"

"Yes, she was," Greg agreed, then hung up.

But all that day, and into the next, he kept thinking about Heather, and wondering what, if anything, the lab would find.

Five

The funeral for Heather Fredericks took place three days later, on the kind of perfect summer day when the New Mexican skies are deep blue and cloudless, and even the heat of the desert is made bearable by the dryness of the air. But as Judith Sheffield stood with Max and Rita Moreland in the cemetery next door to the old Methodist church she herself had attended as a child, it seemed to her the atmosphere was wrong. Though cloudy skies would have been a cliché, she still thought they would have been more appropriate.

Ted and Reenie Fredericks stood gazing blankly at the coffin that contained the remains of their only child, as if they hadn't yet quite grasped what had happened. But as the minister uttered the final words of the service, and the coffin was slowly lowered into the ground, an anguished wail of grief suddenly welled up out of Reenie's throat, and she hurled herself into her husband's arms, burying her face in his chest. Judith, embarrassed to witness Reenie's unbearable pain, averted her eyes, letting them run over the crowd.

She was surprised by how many of the mourners she recognized, many of them people she'd grown up with. Now, as she identified them ten years later, she found herself unaccountably bewildered that they were no longer the teenagers she remembered. Most of them had children, ranging in age from ten downward, and as she watched them she couldn't help wondering what they were thinking. Were they, like her, wondering which of the other teenagers in the crowd might be considering following the course Heather had taken? Were they wondering if, in a few more years, or tomorrow, it might be their own child in that casket? Every face she studied wore an expression of shock—shock mixed with apprehension.

Heather's friends seemed to have clustered together of their own accord, taking up a position close to the casket but separated from Heather's parents by the casket itself.

Amazingly, Judith found she even recognized some of the dead girl's classmates, though they had been only five or six years old the last time she'd seen them.

Randy Sparks and Jeff Hankins were there—apparently still the inseparable friends they had been since they were little boys. But something about both of them had changed. Judith watched their faces—Randy's narrow and vaguely hollowed, in contrast to Jeff's tendency to chubbiness, which gave him a slightly baby-faced look— and realized, sadly, that their eyes, indeed their whole appearance, had lost any semblance of innocence. They stood together, their posture slouched as if to send a signal to whomever might be watching that even here, at the funeral of one of their friends, they were still cool, still somehow detached from it all. With them were two girls, one of whom Judith was certain was Gina Alvarez. Still as pretty as she had been as a child, Gina's dark eyes seemed to sparkle with life, and her chestnut-colored hair framed a face that already had matured beyond the prettiness of a little girl and into the beauty of a young woman.

Next to Gina stood a boy Judith recognized at once. Indeed, she would have recognized Jed Arnold by his eyes alone—those incredibly bright, almost turquoise-blue eyes, made even more remarkable by the crisp planes of his face and the bronze skin he had inherited from his mother.

Those eyes were his father's. Judith scanned the crowd, searching for Frank Arnold himself. A moment later she saw him, standing alone, staring at the coffin almost as if he weren't entirely certain he should have been at the funeral at all. Was he remembering another funeral, when it had been his wife whose remains were being consigned to the ground?

She was about to look away when Frank abruptly glanced up, as if he'd felt her eyes on him. His expression seemed puzzled for a moment, but then his eyes met hers and he shifted his weight slightly, straightening up to his full height. He offered her a small nod of recognition, and Judith felt herself flush, all her childhood memories of him flooding back to her.

She turned away, falling in with Rita and Max Moreland as they made their way toward the Frederickses. As they came to the head of the receiving line, Judith extended her hand to Reenie Fredericks.

"I'm so sorry," she said. "You might not remember me, but—"

"Of course I remember you," Reenie said, taking her hand firmly. "You used to be Judy Sheffield!"

"I still am," Judith replied. "Except it's Judith now. I never did really like 'Judy.' "

"I know," Reenie said, her faint smile fading as her eyes wandered to her daughter's grave. "Heather hated nicknames too. She even wanted me to start making everyone call me René." For a moment she seemed about to dissolve into tears once more, but then took her emotions under control. "Well, I'll remember to call you Judith. I can certainly do that for Heather, can't I?" Her voice trembled, but then the person behind Judith spoke, and Reenie turned away, once more forcing herself to smile, determined not to break down again.

Judith let herself drift away, moving through the crowd, stopping to talk briefly to some people, nodding to others. In a way, it was almost as if she'd never left Borrego at all. The same people were still there, doing the same things they'd been doing a decade ago.

No surprises.

An incredible feeling of familiarity.

And then she came face to face with Frank Arnold.

He was still standing by himself, but she hadn't seen him approach until he put out a hand and turned her around. "I suppose everyone's telling you you haven't changed a bit, but I'm not going to," he said.

Judith felt her heartbeat speed up slightly, and prayed it didn't show. "You mean you didn't recognize me?" she asked, then wished she hadn't. She'd never thought of herself as a flirt, and didn't intend to turn into one now. "That was a stupid thing to say," she went on without pausing, "since you nodded to me earlier."

"Oh, I recognized you all right," Frank replied. "But you've grown up. What are you now? Twenty-five?"

"Twenty-six," Judith told him.

Frank's brows rose slightly in a dismissive gesture.

"Same difference," he said. "It's not like when we were kids, and a couple of years' difference in age put us into different worlds." His eyes darkened slightly. "Have you seen Jed?"

Judith nodded, but there was something in his tone that told her the question was more than just casual conversation. "I haven't talked to him, but he's certainly just as handsome as ever. With your eyes and Alice's features and skin, he ought to be in the movies."

Frank smiled, but it seemed forced, and when he spoke, there was an edge to his voice. "Maybe you ought to suggest that to him."

Judith stepped back, abashed. "I'm sorry. I didn't mean—"

"Hey," Frank said quickly, "don't you be sorry. It's just that I'm having a rough time with Jed right now." He managed a crooked grin. "They don't give you a book of instructions when they give you the kid, and right now I guess I'm feeling a little inadequate. But I shouldn't take it out on you. I apologize."

Judith let herself relax a little, but when Frank reached out to squeeze her arm reassuringly, she felt something very like an electrical shock run through her. "It's all right," she assured him. Then she thought she understood what Frank had been talking about. "It was Jed who found Heather, wasn't it?"

Frank nodded. "It was pretty bad for him, but that's not really the problem." He seemed about to say more, then apparently changed his mind. "And I sure don't have any call to bother you with my troubles, do I? I hardly know you."

A twinge of unexplainable panic ran through Judith as Frank started to turn away. This time it was she who grabbed his arm. "Not so fast, Frank," she said, doing her best to keep her tone bantering. "You've known me all my life, and Jed was my favorite kid when I was a baby-sitter. Also, I happen to be a high school teacher, which is supposed to make me some kind of an expert on teenagers. Tell me what the problem is."

Frank eyed her appraisingly for a moment, then finally came to a decision. "All right," he said, matching her bantering tone on the surface, but making no attempt to cover the deep worry beneath. "He says he's going to quit school and get a job so he can get out of here. He thinks no one here likes him because he's half Indian, and he thinks his mother killed herself because she was an Indian and didn't think anyone here liked her either."

Almost to her own surprise, Judith's eyes met Frank's squarely, and she asked the first question that came into her mind. "Is he right?"

Words of denial immediately sprang to Frank's lips, but when he spoke, the words that came out were not the ones he had intended. "I don't know," he said softly, his pain clear not only in his voice, but in his eyes as well. "Maybe he is."

Judith said nothing for a moment, having to fight an urge to put her arms around Frank's broad-shouldered body and comfort him. "I-If there's anything I can do . . ." she began, then let the sentence hang, feeling suddenly awkward.

Now it was Frank who was silent for a moment. Then he grinned at her almost shyly. "Maybe you could come over for dinner some night," he suggested. He hesitated, and reddened slightly. "Jed always liked you."

Again their eyes met, and this time the look held for several seconds.

"Tonight?" Judith heard herself ask.

Plainly flustered, Frank managed a nod.

Max Moreland peered up at Judith over the rims of his half glasses, an almost comical expression of surprise giving him the look of an old Norman Rockwell *Saturday Evening Post* cover. "Frank Arnold invited you to dinner?"

Judith eyed him quizzically. "Is that so strange? We've known each other for years—I used to baby-sit for Jed, remember?"

Max ignored the second question, choosing to focus on the first instead. "Well, I don't know what you call strange, but Frank hasn't invited any woman anywhere since Alice died."

Judith felt a warm glow in her face, and hoped it didn't show. "It's hardly like a date," she said, but could see that Max didn't believe her. "It's just for dinner."

The old man's eyes gleamed with wicked humor, and Judith turned to Rita Moreland for support. "Aunt Rita, will you tell Max there's nothing to this, please?"

"There's nothing to this, Max," Rita parroted, not even looking up from the pillow she was working in an incredibly complex needlepoint design. "Do you believe me?"

"No," Max replied comfortably. "How about you?"

"I don't believe me either," Rita replied, then glanced fondly up at Judith. "Will you be home tonight?"

Now Judith's blush turned scarlet. "You're both terrible!" she exclaimed, but bent down to kiss each of them before she left. And yet, as she drove into Borrego the thought she had been suppressing all afternoon rose once more into her consciousness. What if her spending the night was exactly what Frank Arnold had in mind?

How did she feel about it?

The truth was, she didn't know, or at least wasn't yet willing to deal with what she did know, which was that she was definitely attracted to Frank, and was almost certain he was equally attracted to her. Part of her still thought of herself as that sixteen-year-old baby-sitter she'd been ten years ago, and of Frank as a mature man far older than she.

Now, though, nine years didn't seem like so much.

The Arnold house wore a coat of fresh white paint, and Judith smiled as she remembered: Frank and Alice had painted their house every year, refusing to abandon it to the weather the way most people in Borrego did. And apparently even without Alice, Frank was still determined to keep the house as fresh-looking as it had been the day he bought it.

She parked the Honda, hurried up the path that cut through the well-tended lawn in front of the little house, and knocked on the door. After a moment it opened and Jed Arnold stood facing her, his expression all but unreadable, as if he'd made a conscious decision not to let anyone know what was going on in his mind.

"Jed!" Judith exclaimed. "I'm sorry I didn't get to talk to you at Heather's funeral, but—"

"It's okay," Jed replied, stepping back from Judith's outstretched hand, but holding the door open so she could come into the house. "There were a lot of people there." He closed the door behind her, then stood where he was, as if uncertain of what to do next. "Dad's in the kitchen," he finally said, a small grin beginning to play around the corners of his mouth. "He's trying to cook a roast, but it doesn't look like he knows what he's doing." Jed's grin broadened. "Maybe you'd better go in and see if you can pry him loose from the roast before he wrecks it." Then, as Judith started through the living room toward the kitchen, he spoke again. "What am I supposed to call you?"

Judith turned and stared at him, then remembered her own embarrassment when she'd reached the age at which she felt foolish calling her parents' friends Mr. or Mrs. So-and-so, but hadn't quite dared to call them by their first names. There had been a couple of years when she simply hadn't called them anything at all. Now she shrugged. "I don't know," she said. "As long as it isn't Judy, which I hate, or Miss Sheffield, which makes me feel like an old-maid schoolteacher."

Jed's expression turned impish. "But that's what you are, isn't it?"

Judith eyed him for a moment, her lips pursed. "And I suspect I hate that term almost as much as you hate 'half-breed.' Right?"

Jed's mouth dropped open in shock, and for a split second his eyes glittered with anger. But a moment later he recognized her point, and his grin—the same one that had never failed to enchant Judith when she'd been a teenager—crept once more across his face. "You can play rough, can't you?" he observed. "Jude. That's what I'll call you. Like in that old song Dad's always playing—you know, the Beatles?"

"The patron saint of lost causes." Judith sighed. "Well, I suppose it's better than 'old-maid school-teacher.' And is 'Jed' all right with you?"

"It's better than 'half-breed,' " Jed offered, and finally put out his hand. Judith took it, then impulsively pulled him closer and hugged him.

"I really am glad to see you again," she said.

Jed hesitated, then returned the hug. "I'm kind of glad you came back too," he said. "I remember when I was a little kid, I always had more fun with you than with practically anybody."

Frank appeared in the kitchen door. "What's going on out here?" he asked, glancing almost anxiously at Jed.

"Nothing at all. We're just talking about the old days. Jed tells me your cooking hasn't improved over the years."

For a moment Frank looked stung, but then burst out laughing. "Well, if that's the way you two feel, why don't you cook dinner, and I'll watch the end of the football game." He peeled off the apron he was wearing, and tossed it to Jed.

A look passed between the father and son, a look Judith couldn't quite read. In the tense silence that followed, she was afraid Jed might hurl the apron to the floor and walk out. He had stiffened for a moment, the apron held uncertainly in his hand. Then, as if making a conscious decision, he gripped the cloth tightly and returned his father's grin. "You're on," he said. "Maybe for once we can have a decent meal around here."

It was nearly midnight when Judith finally started back to the Morelands' house, and before she left, she'd agreed to come back two nights later. The evening, after a strained beginning, had turned out all right, except for the uneasy feeling she'd had that somehow Alice Arnold was still in the house, watching them. The three of them had sat at the table talking long after the meal had been finished, at first hesitantly, then with increasing ease. Judith had formed the distinct impression that Frank and Jed spent little time talking to each other. Indeed, the two of them were almost like strangers living under the same roof, two people living such completely separate lives that they barely knew one another.

A tense moment had come when Judith suggested to Jed that the two of them go horseback riding the next day. Jed's eyes had lit up, but then his excitement had faded.

"I don't think I can," he'd said. "I'm grounded for a couple of weeks."

But Frank, after eyeing his son speculatively for a moment, had shaken his head. "It seems to me when I handed that grounding down, I meant to keep you away from some of your friends for a while. But I don't see how it applies to Judith. If you want to go, I don't see why you shouldn't."

Only after Jed had finally gone to bed and she was alone with Frank had Judith brought the subject up again. "I didn't mean to interfere between you and Jed," she said. "If you want to keep him home tomorrow, it's all right with me."

Frank shook his head. "No, it's okay. In fact, I'm not sure the punishment was the right thing to do in the first place. I have a feeling he'd take off as soon as I went to work anyway. You just can't control kids the way you used to. Something's changed. I worry about him, Judith. I worry about all the kids around here. It's not just Jed—it's all of them. There's something about them—they just don't seem very happy."

Judith thought back to the kids she'd been teaching—or at least trying to teach—for the last couple of years. Troubled, suspicious young people. Certainly they had not seemed happy. "The world's a much more complicated place now, Frank," she said softly. "When you were a kid, you pretty much knew what was going to happen when you grew up. You'd get married, have kids, get a job, and life would go on just as it always had. But what do these kids have to look forward to? Jobs are getting scarcer and scarcer, even for the ones who graduate from college. And they might get married, but where are they going to live? How much does a house right here in Borrego cost now?"

Frank shrugged. "I don't know—forty, maybe fifty thousand."

"And what did you pay for this one?"

"Seventeen five," Frank admitted. "And I had to borrow the down payment."

"And the kids know all that," she told him. "They know what things cost, and they know they're probably never going to be able to afford the things their parents have. So life doesn't seem fair to them. And you know what? They're right!"

"So what do you propose to do about it?" Frank had asked. They were outside by then, and she was already sitting behind the wheel of her car.

"I don't know," she'd replied.

Now, as she left the town behind and drove out into the desert, then turned left on the narrow track that led to the Morelands' house at the foot of the mesa, she reflected on her own words.

Every year, it seemed, the problems of the teenagers seemed to grow steadily worse.

And every year, no one seemed to come up with a solution.

Except that, unknown to Judith, there was one person in Borrego who *had* come up with a solution.

Indeed, that person had already applied that solution to Heather Fredericks.

And her death had finally proven that the solution worked.

Six

Judith and Jed rode in silence for a while the next morning, Judith relaxing in the saddle as all the old pleasures of riding through the desert came back to her. The morning was still cool, and the air, redolent with sage and juniper, filled her nostrils, reminding her once more of the difference between the air here and the smog-choked atmosphere she had left behind in Los Angeles. She was still lost in her reverie when Ginger, the mare she was riding, suddenly shied, uttered a frightened whinny, then rose up on her hind legs. Leaning forward and clutching at the horse, Judith held her seat, then spotted the rattlesnake, coiled tightly in the partial shelter of a rock a few feet ahead, its tail held erect and buzzing menacingly while its wedge-shaped head weaved dangerously back and forth.

Its tongue, flicking in and out of its mouth, looked almost like a living antenna, searching for its prey.

"Easy, Ginger," Judith murmured, her head close to the horse's ear. "Just take it easy."

The horse twisted, then came down on all fours once again. Judith allowed it to skitter off to the right, away from the snake, then brought it to a halt. When she looked again, the snake was gone.

"You okay?" she heard Jed ask.

"I'm fine. I guess I wasn't looking where I was going." She scrutinized Jed carefully. "Didn't you see it? The snake?"

Jed looked puzzled, and shook his head. "Why? Should I have?"

Judith opened her mouth to speak again, then changed her mind. Taking Ginger's reins firmly in hand, she brought the horse around, then urged it into a reluctant trot until they reached the foot of the steep trail that led up the mesa. When Jed caught up, she held her own horse aside until Blackie had passed, then let Ginger fall in behind the gelding.

Moving slowly, picking their way carefully over the rocky path that in some places had all but eroded away from the face of the mesa, the two horses moved steadily upward. Only when they reached the top did Judith allow herself the pleasure of turning to look out over the vista below.

The buildings of the town looked tiny from the mesa; indeed the town itself seemed almost lost in the vast grandeur of the desert that spread below, its expanse seeming to go on forever, broken only by the mesas dotted across its broad reach and the gullies of the washes that snaked aimlessly across it. Far in the distance an enormous rock rose up out of the desert like a watchtower, impossibly slender, standing alone in regal isolation.

"Did you ever climb it?" Judith asked.

Jed cocked his head, then grinned crookedly. "You remember everything, don't you?" he asked. But before Judith could reply, he shook his head. "I guess I sort of forgot about it. Anyway, I don't think I want to try it anymore. I'm not really crazy about heights."

"You?" Judith asked. "You used to run up and down the edge of the canyon as if it were only an irrigation ditch. It scared me half to death. I was always afraid you'd fall, and I'd be the one who'd have to tell your folks what happened."

Once again that odd cloud passed behind Jed's eyes, and now she made up her mind. "Come on," she said, pulling Ginger's head around and guiding the horse along a trail that cut straight down the middle of the long mesa, "I've decided where I want to go."

Half an hour later they came within view of the ancient village of Kokatí, and Judith reined Ginger to a halt. "Thank God," she breathed softly as Jed drew up abreast of her. "I was afraid they'd done to Kokatí what they've done to the Hopi towns."

Jed glanced at her questioningly, and she told him about the collections of squalid tin-roofed tarpaper shacks that had sprung up behind the villages that had stood for centuries on the rims of the three Hopi mesas. "I was afraid it might have happened here too," she finished. "But it hasn't. It looks just as I remember it."

With obvious distaste, Jed regarded the village in which his mother had grown up. "This is where you wanted to come?" he asked, his tone revealing his disbelief.

Judith nodded. "I love it," she said. "I always have. Even when I was a little girl I used to love to come up here. I always used to think there must be magic in the pueblo."

"The only magic would be if everybody smartened up and moved out," Jed groused. "I don't see how they can live up here at all— they have to haul water up from the lake, and they don't even have electricity."

"But that's their choice," Judith replied. "If they wanted to, they could bring power up from the dam. Max says the offer's been good since the day his father built the dam, but they've always turned it down."

"Stupid . . ." Jed mumbled.

"Maybe. But maybe not. Did you ever stop to think about what this place would look like if they took Max up on the power?"

"Sure," Jed replied. "They could have a decent life—real kitchens and bathrooms, and television, and everything else people have now."

"But what would it look like?" Judith pressed. She turned to gaze at the ancient structure once more. It spread along the rim of the mesa, a series of two- and three-storied stone, timber, and adobe structures, each of them built around a small central courtyard. The walls were thick—nearly four feet on parts of the lowest floor, and the roofs were flat. The only concession to the modern world the old pueblo seemed to have made was the installation of windows in some of the rooms; worn wooden casements with small panes, which even despite their own age, looked oddly out of place in the primitive adobe construction.

"Well, I guess it would have to look kind of different," Jed finally admitted. "I mean, you'd have to do some remodeling to get plumbing and wiring in—"

"You'd have to start over again," Judith told him. "You don't just start remodeling something like that. The pueblo's more than six hundred years old; at least parts of it are. You really think they should start tearing it apart just for some plumbing and electricity?"

"But what about the weather?" Jed asked, instantly wishing he hadn't, since he knew just as well as Judith that there was practically no better insulation available than those thick walls.

Judith didn't bother to respond. "Shall we see if your grandfather's home?" she asked instead.

Now Jed looked distinctly uncomfortable, and refused to meet her eyes.

"How long has it been since you've seen him, Jed?"

Jed shifted his weight in the saddle, but finally looked up, chewing uneasily at his lower lip. "I don't know," he mumbled almost inaudibly. "A while, I guess."

"Five years?" Judith asked, making a guess she was almost positive could not be far from the mark. Jed shrugged, but didn't deny it. Judith sat silently for a few moments, taking in the graceful beauty of the Kokatí pueblo and the lake that flooded the canyon on whose lip the pueblo sat. Finally she gazed out into the distance. Though the town of Borrego was invisible from here, the signs that it existed were scattered everywhere over the desert. "Look around, Jed," she said softly. "Look around the way you used to do, when you were a little boy, and tell me what you see. Tell me what looks right and what doesn't."

Jed cocked his head slightly, his eyes taking on a puzzled look, but Judith kept her face impassive, determined not to give him any clue as to what was in her mind. At last Jed's eyes shifted away from her, and as she watched, he began scanning the landscape around him. "I guess maybe the pueblo looks okay," he finally, reluctantly, admitted. "Except you have to wonder why anybody would want to live in it. But it sort of looks like it's part of the mesa."

"What else?" Judith pressed.

Jed grinned sourly at her. "What is this? A test?"

"Maybe. But there aren't any grades. Just look around some more."

Jed began to scan the landscape once more, finally focusing on the lake. "I don't like the lake," he said at last. "I like the part of the canyon below the dam, where the cottonwoods grow along the stream and there are all kinds of birds and animals." A memory stirred inside him, something he hadn't thought of for a long time. "Grandpa always said the lake looks too much like the sky, and the sky doesn't belong in the canyon. I never really thought much about it, but maybe he's right. Look . . ." He pointed down into the narrow chasm that held the lake. "See how the water's eating away at the sandstone? And there're stains running up it from the surface, where more water's soaking in. The whole damned thing's going to crumble some day. But of course it won't matter, because the whole canyon will be filled up with silt from upstream long before the walls start caving in. It's kind of stupid, when you think about it—I mean, to wreck the whole canyon just so you can get electricity for maybe a hundred years."

"What else?" Judith asked.

Jed's eyes moved on, roaming over the broad expanses of the desert. Once, three years ago, he'd ridden up here late in the afternoon and come to the top of the mesa just in time to see the sun setting in the west as the full moon rose in the east. Around the horizon, five separate thunderstorms were raging, so far away that even as the lightning bolts shot out of the sky, the thunder itself was a barely audible rumble. He'd sat down on a rock and just watched the sky for nearly an hour, until the sun had finally disappeared and the storms moved on, fading away past the horizon until only the glowing light of the moon illuminated the desert, casting long black shadows from the mesas in the distance. The night noises had begun, and he'd listened to them for a while, leaving only when the lights in the oil field and the refinery came on, wrecking the whole thing.

"The refinery," he said now. "And the oil wells and tanks. Sometimes I wish I could see the desert the way it used to be, before there were roads and power lines."

"But that's what you like, isn't it?" Judith asked. "I mean, without the oil, you wouldn't even be here, would you? There wouldn't be any reason for Borrego to exist at all. Not," she added, "that that would make much difference to you. I understand you're not too crazy about Borrego."

Jed's eyes glowed sullenly. "Why should I like it?" he demanded. "It's ugly, and there's nothing to do. It just sits there, and nobody cares about it. I mean, have you ever really looked at it? Jesus, everytime someone needs a new place to live, they just build another one of those crappy cinder-block houses, or drag in a trailer." His voice took on a scornful edge. "The trailers are the worst. They only last a few years, and then people just move out of them and leave them sitting there to rust. And there's junk all over the place—

Randy Sparks's dad must have ten wrecked cars sitting around their yard. But he doesn't ever do anything with them. He's always claiming he's going to fix them up, but everyone knows he's not!" His gaze shifted from Judith back to the pueblo. "Then you look at the Indians. At least they don't have a bunch of crap around they're never going to use." He snickered as another thought came to him. "Shit, they hardly have *any*thing!"

Judith spoke quietly. "Is that why you don't come up here anymore?" she asked. "Because you don't think there's anything here?"

Jed shrugged. "Maybe," he mumbled. "But it isn't just that. You know how the Kokatí are—if you're not one of them, they don't want to have much to do with you."

"But you are one of them," Judith reminded him. "At least your mother was, and your grandfather still is."

Jed shook his head. "You think that matters?" he demanded, making no attempt now to keep the anger out of his voice. "Mom's grandmother never even spoke to her again after she married Dad."

"Her grandmother was a different generation," Judith reminded him. "I used to come up here when I was a little girl." She fell silent for a few moments, remembering.

She'd been about eight the first time she'd come to the pueblo alone, riding the horse her father had given her for her birthday. Some Indian kids had been playing a game of baseball— work-ups— and she'd just watched for a while. Then one of them had asked her if she wanted to play, so she'd tied up her horse and joined the game. She'd started in right field, and slowly worked her way up to the point when she would be next at bat when someone had called the children home for lunch. It hadn't really occurred to her not to go with them, and a little while later she was in one of the courtyards, eating the grayish pita bread the Kokatí women still made the old way, grinding the corn with their mortars and pestles, then mixing the coarse flour with water and frying it on a hot stone. No one had suggested she shouldn't be there, and after lunch she'd gone back to the game with the rest of the kids, not getting home until late afternoon. When her mother had asked her where she'd been, she just told her she'd been up on the mesa, playing with some of the Indian kids. Her mother hadn't told her not to do it again, so a week later she'd gone back. From then on she'd always gone up to the pueblo at least once a week, and soon she knew practically everyone there.

"So they let you come and play with their kids," Jed told her. "What's the big deal?"

Judith shrugged. "Maybe *that's* the big deal," she replied. "As far as they were concerned, I was just another kid. And I came to play with the other kids, not to stare at them. How would you like it if people were always coming up and staring at you, and asking to take your picture, as if you were some kind of exhibit?''

Jed's expression took on a cynicism that was beyond his years. "Okay," he agreed, obviously reluctant to give her even that much. "But did any of them ever come down to Borrego and visit you?"

Judith nodded. "Sure. Why wouldn't they?"

Now Jed stared at her in utter disbelief. "Oh, come on—you know what most of the people in town think about the Indians."

"They think a lot of stupid things," Judith replied. "And most of them just don't apply to the Kokatí. Sure, there's a lot of Indians who spend too much time getting drunk, but there's plenty of white people in Borrego who do the same thing. Nothing to do is nothing to do, whether you're Indian or white. And I think maybe that's why the Kokatí have always stuck so close to the old ways. They have a lot to do in the pueblo. They're still farming their fields the old way, still hauling their water up from the canyon, still doing everything else just the way they've always done it. They don't have time to go out and get drunk, and they won't even accept any money from the Bureau. Of course," she admitted, "they're a lot luckier than most of the tribes. They still have almost all their old land, and they were never displaced."

Jed's expression reflected his scorn. "If everything in the pueblo is so great, then how come my mother didn't stay there?" he asked.

Judith held Jed's eyes with her own. "It seems to me," she said, "that maybe that's a question you ought to ask your grandfather."

Jed was silent for a moment, and when he spoke, his voice was hard. "All right," he said. "Let's do it."

Digging his heels into the flanks of the black gelding, he clucked to it, slapping the reins gently against the horse's neck. Immediately the big animal broke into a fast trot, and Jed guided it directly toward the pueblo.

They slowed the horses to a walk as they approached the pueblo, finally dismounting when they were still fifty yards away, tying the reins to a rail where five mules stood, their ribs showing clearly through their skin. They were work animals, nearly worn out from years of climbing up and down the steep trails that led from the mesa to the desert floor, their backs deeply swayed from the heavy weight of the ollas they carried as they hauled water up to the pueblo. They whinnied softly as Jed and Judith tied the two horses up, and shied away from the bigger animals, as if resenting their presence. For their part, Blackie and Ginger ignored the mules, choosing instead to begin munching on the straw that was strewn around the hitching rail.

Jed and Judith skirted the edge of the pueblo's ancient cemetery, then made their way down a narrow alley between two of the main structures of the pueblo. The alley opened into a plaza after fifty feet, and they paused to look around.

In the decade since Judith had last been here, nothing seemed to have changed at all. A few women were working in the courtyard, constructing pots out of coiled ropes of clay. A little girl, no more than two, was playing with a wad of the soft clay, already trying to imitate the actions of her mother, rolling the clay between her tiny hands, looking almost surprised when bits of it dropped away into the dust in which she sat.

For a few moments the women didn't seem to notice them at all, but finally one of them looked up and smiled. "Jed! You finally decided to come up and see us again?" Then her eyes shifted to Judith and suddenly lit up. "Judy Sheffield!" She began speaking fast in Kokatí, and a moment later Judith was surrounded by five women, all of them asking questions at once.

Jed watched the warm welcome Judith was receiving, and wished he hadn't agreed to come here at all. Once again he felt like an outsider, while Jude, who wasn't one of them at all, was being treated like a long lost relative. One of the women turned to him. "Are you looking for your grandfather?"

Jed felt himself flush slightly, but nodded his head.

The woman tilted her own toward another of the narrow alleys. "He's in the kiva." Then she turned her attention back to Judith, and a moment later Jed, feeling as if he was being watched from every dark door and window in the pueblo, crossed the plaza and stepped into the shadows of the narrow passageway.

He followed the alley, emerging onto the wide apron that lay between the pueblo and the rim of the canyon. Midway between the pueblo's wall and the lip of the precipice, a low dome rose up a few feet. From its center a ladder emerged from a hole in the dome, along with a steady wisp of smoke from the small fire that almost always burned within the kiva. Jed paused, uncertain what to do, gazing at the mouth of the kiva. Since he'd been a little boy, it had always seemed a dark and forbidding place. It was in the kiva that the Kokatí men gathered to carry out their spiritual rites. It was the place from which they emerged on festival days, wearing their elaborate costumes to dance in the courtyards.

But it was also the place they went to be alone, to chat quietly among themselves without the distractions of their wives and children, or to just sit and think, or commune with the spirits who resided beneath the kiva's floor.

Could he really do it? Simply walk up to the hatch in the roof and climb down inside? But he was only a boy, not even a member of the tribe.

And then he remembered.

He was sixteen, and among the Kokatí that made him a man. Taking a deep breath, he started toward the kiva.

He hesitated as he came to the hatchway, then took one more breath and descended the ladder into the chamber below. It was circular, some fifty-odd feet in diameter, and had been hacked out of the sandstone of the mesa centuries earlier. Around its perimeter there was a stone bench, and a circle of heavy posts formed a smaller ring midway between the walls of the kiva and the firepit in the center. As Jed stepped off the ladder onto the floor of the kiva, his eyes began to burn from the smoke of the fire. For a few moments he could see nothing in the gloom beneath the low ceiling. But after a while his eyes began to adjust to the darkness, and finally he spotted his grandfather.

Brown Eagle was sitting alone on the bench, facing eastward, his eyes closed, his body held perfectly still. Jed approached him almost warily, half expecting the old man's eyes to open and fix accusingly on him. But Brown Eagle seemed not to be aware of his presence at all. When Jed sat down on the bench next to him, the old man never so much as moved a muscle.

Jed sat nervously at first, feeling the hardness of the stone beneath his buttocks, gazing around curiously. He studied the construction of the dome carefully, examining the peeled tree trunks that extended from the walls of the kiva inward to the heavy beams that had long ago been laid on the tops of the posts, and the smaller logs that lay crosswise above the main stringers. There was a geometric orderliness to the dome, and a sense of timelessness that came from the blackened patina of the old wood. Except for the patch of sunlight that shone through the hatch, moving slowly across the floor as the sun moved across the sky above, there was little clue to what was happening beyond the confines of the kiva, and as he sat next to his grandfather, Jed found his own mind begin to drift in strange directions.

His eyes fixed on the fire and he began to imagine he saw shapes dancing in the flames.

A drowsiness came over him, and he began to feel his eyelids grow heavy. When at last he opened his eyes again, the patch of sunlight had moved far across the floor.

"How do you like it?" he heard his grandfather ask.

"I—I don't know," Jed murmured. "I guess I must have fallen asleep."

Brown Eagle regarded Jed with deep and impenetrable eyes. "You didn't go to sleep. It's something else that happens here. Something you won't understand for years. Some people never understand it." He stood up, stretched, then glanced down at Jed. "What do you say we go outside? Whatever happened to you is over now."

A moment later, as they emerged into brilliant daylight, Jed blinked, then glanced at the sun. "Jesus," he said. "I must have been in there almost three hours."

Brown Eagle shrugged. "It happens." Then he eyed Jed appraisingly. "You've grown. Not as big as your dad, but a lot bigger than any of the kids around here. Still, I see your mother in you."

Jed's voice took on a note of belligerence. "How come people can't just look like themselves?"

Brown Eagle's brows rose slightly. "What's wrong with looking like your mother?" he asked mildly. "She was a beautiful woman, my little girl." Then a flicker in Jed's eyes made the Indian frown. "Is that why you came up here? To ask me about your mother?"

Jed felt nonplussed, as if his grandfather had looked right inside him. "I—I don't know, really. You remember Judy Sheffield?" Brown Eagle nodded. "I rode up with her this morning. We got to talking about the pueblo, and the tribe, and . . ." His voice trailed off as he began to flounder over his own words.

Brown Eagle ignored Jed's discomfort. "I remember her. I remember the first day she came up here. She started playing with some of the kids, and before you knew it, she was acting as if she'd been born here. She's the kind who will always fit herself in anywhere she happens to be." His voice changed slightly, taking on a wistful tone. "There's other kinds of people too," he said. "Just the opposite of Judy Sheffield."

"She likes to be called Judith now," Jed broke in.

Brown Eagle's head tipped slightly in acknowledgment of the boy's words, but his penetrating eyes fixed on Jed's own. "It's your mother you want to talk about, isn't it? Not Judith Sheffield."

Jed's breath caught—how had his grandfather known what was on his mind? But then his grandfather had always seemed to know things without being told. He nodded.

"Your mother was one of those other people—people who can never be happy," Brown Eagle said. "No matter where they go, or who they're with. She always had the feeling that everyone else was part of something, but that she was an outsider." He stopped, placing a hand on Jed's shoulder. "I think that's why she did what she did, Jed. I think she finally figured out she wasn't ever going to be happy—whatever that means—and just gave up."

Jed glared angrily at the old man, shaking off his gnarled hand. "I don't believe you," he said. "It was a lot more than that. It was because of Dad, and everyone else down there."

Brown Eagle shook his head, but refused to respond to Jed's anger. "I'm not saying it was her fault. It was just the way things were. She was never happy here, and she was never happy in Borrego. And there was nothing anyone could do about it. Not me, and not your father. It was her nature. She wasn't of the world, so she left it."

Jed kicked at the dust beneath his feet, suddenly feeling frightened. His thoughts tumbled over one another as he recognized himself in his grandfather's words about his mother. Was the same thing going to happen to him too? Was he going to wake up some morning and just decide, to hell with it?

And then the specter of Heather Fredericks rose up in his mind once more, and with it a thought—one he voiced without even meaning to. "Maybe that's what happened to Heather too."

Brown Eagle's eyes narrowed. "The girl who died in the canyon a few days ago?"

Jed nodded. "She killed herself."

"Is that what they're saying down in Borrego?" Brown Eagle asked. He shook his head. "It isn't true. She didn't jump because she wanted to."

Jed eyed his grandfather suspiciously.

"No," Brown Eagle went on, speaking almost to himself now. "She didn't want to jump at all. Someone made her do it."

Jed's brows drew together angrily. "That's not what the cops said," he challenged.

Brown Eagle shrugged. "It doesn't matter what they said. I was in the kiva when it happened. I saw it."

Now Jed stared at his grandfather with open incredulity. "Come on," he said. "If you were in the kiva, you couldn't have seen it."

Brown Eagle gazed at his grandson impassively. "Is that what you think?" he asked. "Well, perhaps if you came up here more often, and found out just who you are, you might think otherwise."

Half an hour later, as they made their way back down the mesa, Judith finally decided the silence had lasted long enough.

"Well? What did you find out?"

Jed glanced at her. "From my *grandfather?*" he asked, his voice harsh, almost mocking. "Oh, I found out a lot. But not about my mom—about him! You know what? He's nuts. Stark, raving nuts."

Judith stared at him. Something, obviously, had happened. But what? Before she could ask him, Jed told her.

"You know what he said? He said Heather didn't kill herself at all. He said someone killed her, and that he saw it. He was in the kiva, and he saw it. Don't you just love it? Shit, the old man's a complete whacko!"

Spurring his horse, he shot ahead, leaving Judith staring after him.

Seven

J ed glared angrily at his father. It was the morning after he'd been up to Kokatí with Jude. By the time he'd returned the day before, his father had already gone to work, and when Frank finally got home a little before midnight, Jed had already gone to bed. So it hadn't been until a few minutes ago that he finally told his father what had happened in the pueblo. And now his father was angry at him again, as he had been nearly every other day lately. "I don't see what the big deal is," Jed muttered, staring into his coffee. "All I said was that Grandpa's nuts. So what?"

Frank's jaw tightened. "You don't know your grandfather, and you don't know a damned thing about the Kokatí."

Jed looked up now, his scornful eyes meeting his father's. "Jeez, Dad, it doesn't take any brains to figure it out. How the hell could Grandpa have seen what happened to Heather if he was in the kiva? What have they got? Some kind of TV monitor down there?"

Frank shook his head. He remembered the day Alice had died, and something that had happened, something he'd never told his son before. "You remember when your mom died?" he asked. The look in Jed's eyes, a sudden opaqueness that came into them, spoke more than any words Jed could have said. "Brown Eagle came down here that day," Frank went on. "He told me what had happened. He said he'd felt funny when he woke up that morning and had gone into the kiva." Hi voice dropped, turning husky. "And while he was down there, he saw Alice kill herself." He fell silent for a moment, then went on, his voice trembling now "That's why he came down here that day, Jed. He was hoping he was wrong. But he wasn't."

Now it was Jed who was silent, his eyes narrowed to no more

than angry slits as he stared at his father "That's not true," he whispered. "If he really thought something was wrong, he'd have come down earlier. He'd have stopped her. But he didn't, did he? So then he claims he saw what happened—"

The phone rang, a harsh jangling that cut through Jed's words. He fell silent as Frank reached over and picked up the receiver. "Arnold," he said. He listened for a few moments, grunting responses every now and then. "Okay. I'll be there right away." Putting the receiver back on the hook, he stood up. "I've got to get out to the plant," he told Jed. "They've got a problem and they're shorthanded."

Jed opened his mouth to protest, then shut it again. What the hell good would it do? His father wasn't going to listen to him anyway. "Great," he muttered to himself as Frank disappeared out the kitchen door a few minutes later, dressed in the gray overalls that were his work uniform. "Start talking about Mom, then just walk away." He slammed his fist down on the tabletop, the coffee in his cup slopping over into the saucer. "Well, who cares?" he shouted into the now empty house. "Who the hell cares?"

Frank arrived at the refinery five miles out of town and swung into his accustomed parking spot outside the gate. But instead of going directly into the plant, he crossed the street and stepped into the superintendent's office. As soon as he saw the frown on Bobbie Packard's normally sunny face, he knew something else had gone wrong. He glanced past the secretary into Otto Kruger's office, half expecting to see Kruger's face glowering with unconcealed rage, but the plant superintendent was nowhere to be seen. "Where's Otto?" he asked. "Out in the plant, making more trouble than they already have?"

The secretary shrugged. "They called him into town for a meeting in Mr. Moreland's office," she said. "It sounds like Max might finally be getting ready to sell out."

Frank felt a surge of anger rise up from his gut, but quickly put it down. It couldn't be true—it had to be just talk. The rumors had been flying for months, ever since the first feelers from UniChem had begun. But so far Max had insisted that he had no intention of selling the place out, and that if he ever did, it wouldn't be to some huge, impersonal conglomerate. It would be to the employees of Borrego Oil. So Frank put his brief spate of anger aside and shook his head. No use having Bobbie spreading the rumors all over town. "Take my word for it, Bobbie," he said. "If Max wants to sell, he'll come to us first."

"I don't know," Bobbie sighed. "From the way Otto was talking, it sounds like Max is almost broke." She winked conspiratorially at Frank. "And if you ask me, Otto will do his best to get Max to sell out to UniChem rather than us. He thinks you'd fire him if you ever got the chance."

Frank's lips twisted into a wry grin. "And just how would I get the chance?" he asked.

Bobbie giggled. "Come on, Frank. You think if the employees bought this place you wouldn't wind up on the board of directors?"

Frank shrugged noncommittally. "Even if I made the board, I'd only have one vote," he pointed out.

Now Bobbie was carefully repairing an already perfect fingernail. "And everybody else would vote right along with you, as Otto well knows."

Frank's grin broadened across his face. "Does Otto know how much you hate him?"

"Of course," Bobbie said blithely. "But it doesn't matter, because anybody else who was his secretary would hate him too."

Frank nodded absently, but his mind was no longer registering Bobbie's words. He was already wondering if he should call a union meeting for that evening. If there was, indeed, any truth to the rumor that Max was on the verge of selling out, then there was a lot of work to be done.

Months ago he'd found a lawyer and an accountant in Santa Fe and quietly hired them to begin studying the feasibility of an employee buyout of the company. It hadn't been a difficult job—Borrego Oil was a small company, and the same kind of transfer of ownership had been happening all over the country. He'd been pleased to note that in most cases, the turnaround of those companies into profitable organizations had been nearly immediate; when people were working for themselves, they tended to be a lot more efficient.

More efficient, and more careful, he reflected as he left the office and crossed the street once more, this time to deal with the problem that had brought him out here this morning in the first place. He walked into the loader's shack to check last night's output, nodding a greeting to Fred Cummings, and picked up the sheet that showed every gallon of gasoline pumped from the tank farm into the trucks.

He shook his head dolefully as he tried to decipher Fred's chicken scratchings, and wondered, yet again, why the whole system had yet to be computerized. But he knew the answer—the same lack of money that seemed to be strangling Borrego Oil at every turn. Still, oil prices were slowly rising again, and he'd thought the end of the steady losses was in sight. But then as his eye came to the bottom of the shipment list, he frowned.

Fred had stopped loading at four that morning.

"That's when the pump went out," Fred explained. "We tried to fix it, but someone screwed up 'on parts, and we didn't have any."

Frank scowled. He'd personally reviewed the inventory a month ago and given a list to Kruger. Apparently, the parts had never been ordered. "Okay," he said. "Give me the list of what you need, and I'll call down to Albuquerque. We should be able to get back in operation by this afternoon."

But Fred Cummings shook his head. "Won't work," he said. "I already talked to the supplier, and they say our credit's run out. We want parts for the pump, we pay cash."

Frank's scowl deepened. "Okay, then let's fix the parts we have. Can we do that?" he asked, knowing the answer even before he had uttered the words.

"I 'spose we could fix it," Cummings finally said, avoiding Frank's gaze. "But it'd take an overtime crew, and Kruger ain't authorizing overtime." Still avoiding Frank's eyes, he picked up his lunch bucket and headed toward the door, but Frank stopped him.

"You could hang around a couple of hours on your own," he pointed out.

Cummings spat into the dirt outside the door. "'Spose I could," he agreed amiably. "But it's not my outfit, and I don't notice Kruger, or Moreland, or anybody else comin' over to mow my lawn on their own time."

As Cummings left, Frank swore softly to himself. And yet the man was right—why should he work overtime, knowing full well he wouldn't get paid for his time? But in the long run, Borrego's inability to deliver gasoline, even for a day, would only add to the losses, and bring on more cost-cutting. Soon the layoffs would increase, and in the end the layoffs would only drop production even further.

Cursing again, Frank studied the work schedule, looking for a way to pull enough men off their regular jobs to put together a crew to repair the broken pump.

And when Kruger got back, he'd have a little talk with the man. If they weren't even paying their suppliers anymore, the situation must be a lot worse than anyone had told him.

What the hell was going on?

He picked up the phone to call Jed and explain what was happening. "I'm probably going to be tied up all day," he said. Jed listened to him silently, but as Frank talked he could picture clearly the dark look that would be coming into the boy's eyes, the look of resentment that always came over Jed when he had to change his schedule yet again. But there was nothing he could do about it.

*   *   *

By mid-afternoon Frank's temper was beginning to fray. The broken pump, totally disassembled, lay scattered in the dusty road. Two of his makeshift crew had disappeared after lunch, sent back to their regular jobs by Otto Kruger, who had insisted that the pump would be of little use if the refinery itself had to be shut down because nobody was looking after it. Frank had argued that there had been a general shutdown only two weeks ago and that every pipe and valve in the place had been thoroughly cleaned and inspected. Right now the plant was quite capable of running itself for a few hours. But Kruger had insisted, and in the end Frank decided the issue wasn't worth fighting about, since his two other men were going to be occupied for the next couple of hours with repairing the broken shaft of the pump's motor.

If they could repair it at all. Carlos Alvarez and Jerry Polanski had insisted they could make the weld easily enough, but Frank wasn't so sure. The shaft looked to him as if it had bent pretty badly when the break had occurred, and he suspected that even if they managed the weld, the pump might tear itself apart again as soon as they reassembled it and started it up.

But now the repair had been made, and Alvarez and Polanski were beginning the process of reassembling the pump. Denied the help of half his crew, Frank pitched in himself, holding the shaft steady while Carlos carefully adjusted the collar that would clamp it to the pump.

"What the hell's going on?" Otto Kruger's harsh voice demanded from behind. Frank waited until Carlos had tightened the last bolt before straightening up. Using the bandanna he habitually wore, which was now hanging out of his rear pocket, he mopped the sweat from his brow.

"Just about got her fixed—" he began, but Kruger didn't let him finish.

"By breaking every union rule in the book?" the superintendent growled. Frank tensed, tightening his grip on his temper. "Alvarez and Polanski aren't part of the yard crew," Kruger went on. "It's not their job to be working on that pump. And you're a shift foreman, right? That means you make sure your men are doing their jobs. It doesn't mean you do the work for them."

Frank felt his anger boiling up from the pit of his belly, but he was damned if he was going to get into a fight with Kruger. Not right here, anyway. "Maybe we'd better go into your office to talk about this, Otto." His voice was even but his eyes glittered with fury. What the hell was the man trying to do? Weren't things bad enough without Kruger making it impossible for him to do his job?

"If that's what you want," Kruger rumbled. He spat into the dirt, then turned his attention to Alvarez and Polanski. "Leave the pump and get back to your regular jobs."

Frank saw Carlos's hand tighten on the wrench he was holding, but he shook his head just enough to tell the man to leave it alone. Without a word, Carlos put the wrench down and turned away from the loading shed. A moment later Jerry Polanski followed him. Only when they'd both disappeared into the plant itself did Kruger turn away and stride across the street to his office. Frank followed him, managing only the tightest of nods for Bobbie Packard as he passed her desk.

Unseen by Kruger, she made a face at the superintendent's back, then gave Frank a thumbs-up sign.

"Shut the door," Kruger growled as he slouched low in his chair and propped his feet up on his desk. "No sense airing our problems in front of the hired help, is there?"

Frank closed the door gently, deliberately depriving Kruger of the pleasure of seeing his anger. "Seems to me we're both part of the hired help around here," he observed evenly, retaining his position by the door, but folding his arms across his chest as he leaned back against the wall. "Now why don't you just tell me what's going on? Our credit with the suppliers is shot, and the last of the yard crew got laid off a week ago. How the hell am I supposed to fix that pump if I don't use men from the plant? And don't give me any shit about it not being my job to work on it, 'cause you and I both know my job's to keep the shift running, even if I have to do it myself."

Kruger averted his eyes. "Those layoffs were temporary. We lost a bundle during the shutdown. The men will be hired back as soon as we can afford it."

"But if we can't move the gas out of the tanks—" Frank began. Once again Kruger didn't let him finish.

"As it happens, we should be getting a new loading pump up here within a week or two," he said. "And since we've got no problem with storage, it looks like all your work was sort of a waste of time, wasn't it?"

It wasn't only Kruger's refusal to meet his eyes that roused Frank's suspicions—it was the smugness in his voice. "What's going on?" he demanded. "Is Max getting a new line of credit?"

Now Kruger smiled, but it was a cruel twisting of his lips. "I 'spose you could call it that," he said, drawling elaborately. "Anyway, by the time we get the new pump, we should be ready to start hiring the men back."

Frank Arnold's eyes bored into Kruger's. "It's a sellout, isn't it?" he asked, but the words came out more as a statement than a question. A cold knot of anger formed in his belly. "Are you telling me Max is selling out?"

Kruger's hands spread noncommittally. "He hasn't yet," he said. His feet left the desk and went to the floor as his chair suddenly straightened and he leaned forward. "But the party's about over," he declared, his eyes meeting Frank's for the first time, "and if I were you I'd start thinking about how I could benefit if someone *does* buy this place."

"Are you telling me that's what's happened?" Frank asked. "Is that what the big meeting this morning was about?"

Kruger shrugged. "Someone wants to do a leveraged buyout, the way I heard it."

"But Max won't do that," Frank protested. "Everybody knows if he sells out, he'll offer the company to the employees first."

Kruger chuckled hollowly. "If you've got that in writing, I'd suggest you call a lawyer pretty damned quick. Because if you don't have it in writing, I think it's a pretty sure thing that by next month you and I will be working for someone else. Which," he added, finally allowing himself a genuine smile, "is just fine by me. How's it suit you?"

Every fiber in Frank wanted to strike out at Kruger, wanted to punch that smile right down the son of a bitch's throat. But that, he knew, was probably just what Kruger was hoping for. There weren't many things Kruger could use as grounds to fire him, but physical violence was certainly one of them. So Frank restrained himself, shoving his hands deep in his pockets, as if it was the only way to hold them in check. But when he spoke, he made no attempt to conceal his rage. "It doesn't suit me at all," he replied. "And there are a few things I can do about it." His mind was already working. He'd have to organize a union meeting and put a proposal to buy the company before the membership. That meant weeks of spending practically every waking hour when he wasn't at work dealing with the lawyer and accountant from Santa Fe.

But there had to be a way to counter any offer Max Moreland might already have on his desk.

He turned away from Kruger, jerking the door to the superintendent's office open with so much force it almost came off its hinges. Bobbie Packard, startled by his sudden presence, looked up at him. "What is it?" she asked.

Frank's eyes glared malevolently. "You mean he didn't tell you? Someone's trying to buy Max out. And you can bet they're not going to be interested in the refinery—without a lot of improvements, it won't even break even. And the new takeover people aren't interested in investment—they're interested in fast bucks, which means they'll keep the wells and close down the plant. Pretty neat, huh?" He jerked his head toward Kruger's office. "And I'll bet that son of a bitch has already cut himself a deal to keep an eye on the wells while the rest of us go looking for work that doesn't happen to exist around here."

Bobbie shook her head dazedly. "Mr. Moreland said—"

Frank leaned down so he could look into the secretary's eyes. "Don't you get it, Bobbie?" he asked. "Max is at the end of his rope. He's sunk every nickel he has into this place, but it's not enough. It's old and obsolete, and you can bet no outsider is planning to spend a lot of money out here. All they'll want is the wells."

Without waiting for her to reply, he pushed his way but of the office and crossed back into the plant.

From his office window Otto Kruger watched Frank Arnold disappear into the refinery, and knew exactly what he was up to. He sat quietly for a while, savoring the anger he'd seen in Frank Arnold, enjoying the rage he'd induced in the man. It wasn't often that he got the best of Frank Arnold, and whenever he did, it gave him an intense pleasure.

He'd hated Frank for years, and knew exactly why: Frank knew the refinery better than he did, and had the trust of the men.

Even Max Moreland had more respect for Frank than he had for him, Kruger thought. A year ago, when he'd demanded to know why, if Frank Arnold was so smart, he hadn't been promoted past shift supervisor, Kruger remembered Max smiling at him almost pityingly.

"I need him where he is, Otto," he'd explained. "You can't run an oil refinery without a man like Frank Arnold. Oh, you do fine, overseeing the whole operation. But without Frank in the plant, there wouldn't be an operation for you to oversee."

He, of course, had said nothing in response, but ever since that day he'd hated Frank.

Hated him almost as much as he hated Max Moreland himself.

Finally he turned back to his desk and picked up the phone. He dialed a number quickly, then spoke as soon as the phone was answered at the other end, not waiting for a greeting.

"I just talked to Arnold," he said. "I told him just enough to gauge his reaction, and it's just like I told you. He's going to make trouble."

Then, knowing he'd said enough, and knowing there would be no reply, he hung up, his face wearing a satisfied smile.

Soon, very soon, Frank Arnold would be out of his hair.

It was a thought that gave him a great deal of pleasure.

Eight

F rank Arnold glanced up from his newspaper as his son came into the kitchen, dressed—as usual—in a manner carefully calculated to tell the world he didn't give a damn what it thought. Frank bit back the words of criticism that immediately came to his lips. During the last two weeks, while it seemed he'd spent every waking moment with the lawyers and accountants, the situation with Jed had only worsened. Indeed, over the Labor Day weekend that had just ended, the two of them had barely spoken, except for Friday night, when Judith Sheffield had come for dinner.

That night there had been no question of who would do the cooking. When Frank had come home from work, the house was already redolent with the aroma of a roast in the oven. That night, as on the other nights Judith had spent the evening with them in the little house on Sixth East, Jed had seemed perfectly happy, as though his resentments had magically vanished. But the next morning, with Judith gone, he had retreated again behind his sullen mask, and they had barely spoken over breakfast. Maybe if Judith had spent the night.

He quickly abandoned the thought, although there were several nights during the last few weeks when he'd been almost certain she would have stayed if he'd asked her. Every time, he'd lost his nerve, terrified of looking like a fool for even thinking she might find him as attractive as he found her. Yet had Judith only been here this morning, he was absolutely sure things would be better between him and Jed. Everything seemed to be better when Judith was around. She seemed to understand his moods, even to understand the importance of what he was trying to do.

But then, despite the holiday weekend, Frank had had to leave for Santa Fe, for yet another series of meetings which would culminate tonight at the union lodge when he would finally present to the employees a plan for them to buy the company.

Assuming, of course, that by tonight the company had not yet been sold to UniChem.

And if his plan succeeded, would Jed finally forgive all the time he had spent? Frank wondered. Would pride in his father's accomplishment bridge the chasm between them? Leaning back, Frank folded his arms across his chest, and his eyes settled again on Jed's self consciously "cool" clothes. Idly, he wondered if Jed was aware that his scrupulous attention to his dress only gave the lie to the message he was trying to project: if he truly didn't care how he looked, why were his jeans always so meticulously torn, why was his black leather jacket inspected for missing studs every day, and why was Jed's hair always greased into total submission to the whim of the moment? Why, if his son truly didn't care what anyone thought, did he constantly do his best to look like a thug and hide the quickness of his mind?

Frank knew the answer, or at least most of it. But aside from the loss of his mother, Jed had weathered more than his fair share of fights over the years—practically all of them having to do with his Kokatí heritage—and had finally built a shell around himself that told people not to mess with him, that warned them he would strike back if pushed too far. Frank supposed the shell Jed had built served a purpose, protecting the boy from things he didn't want to deal with. But now he was almost grown, and in danger of wrecking his life. Frank had seen too many kids like Jed—bright but angry—just give up and drift into a job on the oil field or at the refinery, spending their evenings drinking too much in the bar at the café. And that wasn't what he wanted for Jed. Jed was going to go to college, and get out of Borrego, and do more with his life than he had done with his own. Unless Jed gave in to his image, and decided going to school was no longer cool.

"Hope they're not planning to take the class pictures today," Frank said mildly, pushing the newspaper aside.

Instantly, Jed's eyes began to smolder, as he understood what his father was really saying. "You don't like the way I look?" he demanded.

"I didn't say that," Frank countered. "It's just that on the first day of school—"

Jed cut him off. "What's the big deal about the first day of school?" he pressed. "It's just another day of sitting around listening to a bunch of dull teachers say dull things—"

"That's enough!" The sharpness in Frank's voice made Jed fall silent, and the boy slouched low in his chair. "I know what you think about school, and I'm tired of hearing it."

"I do okay," Jed muttered. "And I don't notice how not finishing school hurt you."

Frank's eyes fixed on Jed. "You think being a shift foreman at the refinery is a big deal? If I'd paid attention when I was your age, I could be managing the whole thing."

"Sure," Jed shot back, his voice dark. "And Mr. Moreland would still own the whole thing. Come on, Dad! I don't care if you'd gotten every goddamn degree they can give you—you'd still be working for Max Moreland. Nothing ever changes—if you don't start out rich, you don't get rich. So why the hell should I keep going to school? What's the big deal if I graduate or not? I'm going to wind up working in the refinery, just like you! In fact," he added, shoving his chair back and standing up, "maybe I'll do it today. Maybe instead of going to school, I'll go down to the company office and get a job!"

So that's what it's all about, Frank thought. That's what he hasn't been talking about. He looked at Jed and knew the boy was waiting for him to explode, waiting for him to start yelling. Controlling himself, he leaned back and shrugged. "Well, if that's what you want to do, there isn't much I can do to stop you. You're sixteen—there's no law that says you have to go to school." Jed's eyes flickered with uncertainty. "I can save you a little time, though—there aren't any jobs at the company. The only reason I'm still working is seniority. So you'd better start checking with some of the stores—maybe they can use some help." He glanced up at the calendar on the wall. "Let's see . . . I guess I can give you a week or ten days, so what do you say we start the rent on the fifteenth? That should give you time to find a job."

Jed blinked. "Rent?" he asked, his voice suddenly hollow. "What are you talking about?"

Frank shrugged again, his arms spreading in a helpless gesture. "What do you expect? If you're going to school, I pay the bills. If you're not, you pay your share." He watched Jed carefully and could almost see the thoughts going through his son's mind, see him calculating how much money he might earn bagging groceries at the market or clerking in the lumberyard. At last Jed finished his coffee, then stood up, his face a mask of belligerence.

"Maybe I'll do it," he said. "Maybe I'll start looking around, and see what kind of job I can find."

Frank nodded affably. "Sounds good to me." He picked up the paper again and pretended to read, but he kept one eye on Jed, not missing the fact that when Jed went out the back door a few minutes later, he was carrying his book bag.

Stuart Beckwith, the high school principal, smiled thinly as Judith Sheffield came into his office. He remembered her well—the blond, blue-eyed girl who always sat in the front row of his social studies class and asked too many questions. And now here she was, back in Borrego, once more looking at him with those bright blue eyes, obviously just as inquisitive as ever. He pushed a stack of folders across the desk, then nervously ran his right hand over his nearly bald pate as if pushing back a lock of hair that had long since disappeared. "So," he said as she took the chair opposite him and began quickly thumbing through the folders, "how does it feel to be back home?"

Judith shrugged, the nervousness she had been feeling earlier that morning dissolving. Ten years ago, when she'd been a teenager, she'd always thought of Beckwith as mean, but now she could see that what had once seemed like petty spitefulness was actually nothing more than weakness. She knew the type perfectly from Los Angeles—the sort of administrator whose prime rule was "don't rock the boat."

She, of course, had always been a boat-rocker, and had no intention of changing. Still, she didn't want to alienate Beckwith on her very first day on the job. "It's interesting," she said carefully. "Actually, the town hasn't changed much. In fact," she added without thinking, "it doesn't even look like it's been painted since I left." She immediately regretted her words, as a defensive tightening pinched Beckwith's sallow face. "I didn't mean—" she began apologetically, but to her surprise, he cut her off.

"Of course you meant it," he said. Judith felt herself reddening slightly, and an uncomfortable silence filled the room until, as if he'd come to a decision, Beckwith leaned forward and rested his forearms on the top of the desk. "I'm afraid I seem to be getting off on the wrong foot, don't I? But I have to confess that I'm still at a bit of a loss. Losing Reba Tucker was very upsetting, and . . ." He paused then, his lips pursing into what struck Judith as a phony smile. "And I have to confess," he went on, "that having one of my own students return as one of my teachers is making me feel just a little old."

Judith didn't know whether she was expected to laugh, but decided not to. "I was very sorry to hear about Mrs. Tucker," she said, choosing to ignore Beckwith's feeble joke. "She always seemed so—well, strong, I guess."

Beckwith's head bobbed and his expression took on a too mournful cast. "We all thought she was," he said. "And it seemed to come on her quite suddenly. She was teaching summer school, and everything seemed to be fine at first. And then she began to have strange moods, and finally, well . . ." His voice trailed off and he made a helpless gesture, as if there were really nothing else to say.

Judith tensed. Rita Moreland had distinctly said that Mrs. Tucker had suffered a stroke, and Greg, Reba's doctor, had concurred. But Beckwith's implication was something else entirely. "You mean she had some sort of breakdown?"

Beckwith hesitated, then sighed. "I suppose that's what one

would have to call it, yes," he said. "Of course, young Greg More-land says it was a stroke, but it seems to me it was a lot more than that. In the weeks before the . . . episode, she seemed to get list-less." He clucked almost like a ruffled hen. "Not like Reba. Not like herself at all." Pointedly, he glanced at his watch, then pushed another folder toward Judith. "At any rate, these are her lesson plans. She used the same ones every year, and I'm sure she'd have no problem with your using them too."

Judith made no move to pick up the folder. "That's very kind of you," she said, "but as it happens, I've got my own lesson plans. As I'm sure you know, I've been teaching in L.A. for the last couple of years, and I think it might be easier for me to do what I know how to do than try to turn myself into Mrs. Tucker."

Beckwith leaned back, his hands folded over his stomach. His lips tightened in a show of disapproval that made Judith suddenly feel as if she had been undergoing some kind of oral exam she'd just flunked. Gathering the folders that contained the records of her homeroom students into a neat stack, she stood up. "If I'm going to go through these before classes begin, I'd better be going," she said.

Beckwith seemed about to let her go without comment, but as if changing his mind, he stood as she turned toward the door and smiled at her, then came around his desk to shake her hand. "Let me welcome you back to Borrego," he said. "I have to confess, I had terrible misgivings about your coming here. I was afraid you might want to come in and start changing everything, modernizing every-thing, that sort of thing. But we don't have the money to do much, and you know we're just a little backwater high school in the middle of nowhere. If you can deal with that, then I'm sure we'll get along just fine."

Judith hesitated only a moment before taking Beckwith's ex-tended hand. Yet as she left his office she wondered if she had, after all, made the right decision in returning to Borrego and taking this job. The interview had been odd, and Beckwith, once her least favorite teacher, had not become any more appealing now that he was principal of Borrego High. But what troubled her most, what would not leave her mind as she hurried through the building to find her classroom, was his strange description of what had happened to Reba Tucker.

What had he meant? Had what happened to Mrs. Tucker been something other than a stroke?

The house sat at the top of a small rise on the floor of Mordida Canyon, nestled almost invisibly into a grove of cottonwoods. Even during the hottest part of the day, it was always cool here, and as the woman emerged from the building, she felt a slight chill. The sun had moved far enough across the sky so that even without the trees, the house would still be lying in shadows, and it occurred to her— not for the first time—that it was an odd place for a rehabilitation center. How was anyone supposed to get well when they never got any sunlight? Still, the spot was beautiful, and the pay was good, and God knew, the work was simple enough.

She balanced the tray on one raised knee and quickly pushed the door to the little cabin open. There were no lights on, and she groped for the switch, wondering, not for the first time, how people could stand to sit all day in the dark.

Not that this newest patient could do much about it, she reminded herself.

The lights came on, and the woman looked over at the bed.

There she was, sitting by the window, staring out at the canyon just as Reba Tucker had been doing an hour ago, the last time she'd looked in on her.

"Here's lunch," the attendant said, summoning up a cheeriness she knew sounded false, but not really worrying about it, since she wasn't at all certain the woman even heard her.

Stroke victim, was what Dr. Moreland called her.

Just plain old senile, the woman thought.

Still, she had a job to do. She set the tray on the rolling table, then pushed the table around so it swung over the chair in which the woman sat. Finally she eased the patient around so she was no longer staring blankly out the window, and shoved an extra pillow behind her back.

Lifting the cover off the single dish on the luncheon tray, the attendant plunged a spoon into the soft grayish mush, then brought it close to the patient's lips.

"Come on, Mrs. Tucker," she crooned. "We have to eat, don't we? We don't want to starve to death."

The spoon touched Reba Tucker's lips, and, as always, they parted just enough for the attendant to slide the pablum into her mouth.

The woman waited a moment, until she felt Mrs. Tucker's tongue wrap itself around the spoon, removing the food from it so that it could slip down her throat. Then she scooped up a second serving.

Slowly, concentrating the small part of her mind that still functioned on the task at hand, Reba Tucker managed to swallow the gruel.

Sometimes, as she did now, she wished she could bring herself to speak. Indeed, when she was alone, she sometimes practiced it, moving her tongue slowly, struggling to form the sounds that had once been so natural to her.

She knew the attendant didn't think she could talk, didn't even think she could hear.

And that was fine with Reba.

Let them all think she couldn't hear, and couldn't talk.

She still didn't know who they were, or even where she was.

All she remembered was waking up and finding herself here.

Except she didn't know where "here" was or what had happened to her.

Panic had set in, and she'd screamed and screamed, but mercifully, she didn't know how long the screaming had lasted, for she no longer had any more sense of time than of place.

There was darkness, and there was light.

And there were the nightmares.

Perhaps, she thought in that tiny corner of her mind that still seemed to work now and then, she should stop eating and let herself starve to death.

She wasn't sure, because sometimes, in those fleeting moments when she could think at all, she thought she must already have died and gone to Hell.

But there wasn't any point to dying again, and besides, if she wasn't dead already, she knew they wouldn't let her die.

If they let her die, they couldn't give her the nightmares anymore.

For Reba Tucker, that was what life had become.

Waiting for the nightmares.

Nine

"Will you please hurry?" Gina Alvarez pleaded, though she knew her words would fall on deaf ears. As far as Jed Arnold was concerned, it was definitely not cool to hurry on the way to a class. The whole idea, in fact, was to look as though you didn't care whether you got there or not. Now she looked up at Jed's face to see his incredible blue eyes twinkling happily at her. She knew he was testing her, knew he was waiting to see if she'd wait for him or hurry off by herself so she wouldn't be late to class. She wrestled with herself, part of her wanting to leave him standing there lounging against his locker, idly passing time with his friends. She didn't even like his friends—they seemed to her like a bunch of jerks who didn't know what they wanted to do with their lives.

Gina knew perfectly well what she was going to do with her own. She was going to graduate with honors from Borrego High, then win a full scholarship to Vassar. Her mother had told her she was wasting her time, that girls from Borrego didn't go to Vassar—they didn't go to college at all, especially when their father was a drunk who had abandoned them, and their mother had raised them by working as a waitress in a rundown café. But Gina didn't care what other girls did. She just didn't want to wind up like her mother, getting married right away, having a couple of kids, and wondering what happened when her husband suddenly took off and she was left to raise her children on whatever she could earn waiting tables.

So Gina went her own way, ignoring the flickering television while she studied every night, and still finding time to be a cheer-leader for the football team, serve on the student council, look after her little sister, and maintain her relationship with Jed Arnold.

But sometimes, like now, she wondered why she bothered with Jed. Partly, of course, it was his dark good looks—there wasn't any question that Jed was the handsomest boy in town. But it was some-thing else too. She'd always had a feeling that there was more to Jed than what he showed to the world, that his tough-guy image was only that—an image. In fact, sometimes when they were alone to-gether, hiking out by the canyon, he changed. He'd sprawl on his back, looking up at the clouds, and show her things he saw in them—fantastic cities in the air, whole circuses of animals and ac-robats. Once he'd even told her stories he'd heard from his Indian grandfather, about the gods who lived on the mesas and in the canyon itself, looking after the Kokatí. "It means 'the People,' " he'd explained. But his voice had taken on an almost scornful edge as he continued. "That's what they call themselves, as if nobody else in the world is real. Grandpa says the gods are all waiting right now, but someday soon something is going to happen, and all the land is going to be given back to the Kokatí." She'd tried to get him to explain what he meant, but he'd only shrugged. "How should I know? You know how the Kokatí are—they never tell everything, and they don't trust white people."

"But you're one of them," Gina had protested, and immediately a dark curtain had dropped behind Jed's eyes.

"No, I'm not," he'd protested. "I'm not anything, remember? I'm not white, and I'm not Kokatí."

Ever since that day she'd realized there was a part of Jed Arnold that she barely knew. And so, in spite of his sometimes infuriating manner, she still went out with him, and tried to find a way to uncover what was really going on inside him.

As the final bell for the first class rang, breaking her reverie, she made up her mind. "Maybe you don't care if you're late, but I do," she said. She turned away from Jed and started down the hall.

"You're already late," she heard him say as he caught up to her. "But so what? The teacher's Jude Sheffield, and you know how crazy she is about me. I could walk in thirty minutes late and she wouldn't say a word." Sweeping Gina an exaggerated bow, he held the door to the classroom open and gestured her inside. The rest of the class, already in their seats, giggled appreciatively.

Judith, standing at the blackboard outlining the study program for the semester, turned to see what had caused the ripple of laughter in the room. Gina Alvarez, her face red with embarrassment, avoided Judith's eyes as she slid quickly into an empty seat in the back row. But Jed Arnold, his startlingly blue eyes fixed on her with the same cocksure expression she had seen all too often in East Los Angeles, was strolling nonchalantly toward a desk at the front.

"I'm terribly sorry, Jed," Judith said evenly. "I'm afraid I don't accept tardiness. If I can be here on time, so can you."

Jed stopped in his tracks, then grinned crookedly at the teacher. "Hey, what's the big deal? A couple of lousy minutes?"

Judith nodded. "They're *my* lousy minutes, Jed, and I don't like to waste them. If you'll come back during the next break, I'll give you the homework assignment."

Jed's mouth dropped open. Recovering himself he asked: "What do you mean, come back? I'm not going anywhere." He made another move toward the empty desk.

Judith's expression hardened. "If you mean you're not going to that desk, you're right," she agreed. "I don't really care where you go or what you do, but please don't expect to come wandering in here any time the mood strikes you."

A tense silence fell over the room, but Judith kept her eyes firmly fixed on Jed. He still stood in the aisle next to the wall, but she already knew she'd won. If he intended to defy her, he'd have taken the seat and challenged her to remove him. But he didn't. Instead, his brows furrowed into an uncertain frown, which he quickly deepened into a deliberate scowl.

But the scowl didn't come quickly enough to hide from Judith the hurt that had come into his eyes. Ducking his head, he turned and strode out of the room.

For a split second Judith felt an urge to go after him, to bring him back into the room, but she put the urge aside, determined that her friendship with Jed was not going to interfere with the discipline of her classroom. As if nothing at all had happened, she turned back to the blackboard. But the silence she'd commanded lingered on, and as the chalk continued to scratch across the board, she heard none of the whispering that had preceded her confrontation with Jed.

She smiled to herself. Now that she had their attention, she could begin the process of teaching them. She reminded herself to find a way of thanking Jed for the opportunity he'd offered her. Unless she'd hurt him too badly. Unless he now felt that she too had betrayed him.

As the bell signaling lunch period rang and Judith watched her last morning class stream out of the room, she smiled to herself—obviously the word was getting around already that Miss Sheffield was not to be messed with. She'd sensed it at the start of the third period, when she'd spotted two potential troublemakers ambling in at precisely the moment the bell rang. They were Randy Sparks and Jeff Hankins—friends of Jed's. So as they grinned insolently at her, she called them by name and told them to sit by the door. "That way there'll be less disruption when I throw you out," she'd explained with deliberate blandness. The rest of the class had snickered appreciatively, and both Randy and Jeff had reddened. But for the rest of the hour they'd sat quietly watching her, as if trying to figure her out. Since then there'd been no trouble at all.

Her door opened and a face appeared. "You have a date for lunch, or may I escort you to the lounge myself?" Judith's brow rose questioningly, and the man stepped inside. About the same age as Judith, he could have been handsome with his sandy hair and soft gray eyes, except for a tired cast to his face that Judith had seen before. Here, she thought immediately, is a man who shouldn't be teaching. Already, before he was thirty, he seemed to be worn out. "I'm Elliott Halvorson," he said, thrusting a hand toward her. "I thought you might like to meet some of your colleagues."

Judith took the proffered hand, then withdrew it when Halvorson seemed to hold it a little too long. You mean you thought you might make a pass at the new teacher, she thought to herself, more amused than offended. "Fine," she said, slinging her purse over her shoulder. She followed Halvorson out of the room, then turned right, toward the cafeteria. Halvorson reached out and took her arm. "Not that way," he said. "That direction leads only to the zoo."

"The zoo?" Judith repeated.

"That's what we call the cafeteria," Halvorson replied, grinning sourly. "All of us steer pretty clear of it. If you want to enjoy your lunch, the teachers' lounge is the only place."

Judith shook her head. "You go ahead," she said. "I think for at least today I'd like to see what's going on in the cafeteria."

Halvorson stared at her for a moment as if he thought she'd lost her marbles, but then he shrugged. "This," he said, "is going to be worth seeing." He fell in beside her, then paused when they were outside the cafeteria itself. "Tell you what," he offered. "If you last out the hour, I'll pay for your lunch."

Judith smiled. "You're on," she said. "And you might as well pay for it while we go through the line. It'll make the bookkeeping easier." She pulled open the door and was immediately assaulted by the blare of rock music, which almost drowned out the babble of voices as some of the kids tried to talk over the roar of heavy metal.

She glanced around and immediately saw the source of the din. At a table in the far corner, Jed Arnold sat with Randy Sparks, Jeff Hankins, Gina Alvarez, and a couple of other kids whom Judith didn't recognize. As the ghetto-blaster on their table continued to fill the room with the roar of heavy metal, Jed leaned back in his chair and, using a knife as a catapult, flicked a pat of butter up to the ceiling, where it stuck, one more yellow blob in the midst of an already thick layer of previous shots. She watched in silence as Randy Sparks repeatedly tried to match Jed's achievement, raining butter down onto the surrounding tables. She began threading her way through the tables until she stood over Randy.

Reaching down, she pressed a button on the ghetto-blaster, cutting off the tape. In the sudden silence Randy looked up at her angrily.

"Hey, what do you think you're doing?" he demanded.

"Turning off the music," Judith replied. "In case you hadn't noticed, some of the people in here are trying to talk to each other."

Randy pushed his chair back and rose to his feet, spinning around to tower over Judith. But even as he turned, she expertly grasped his wrist, then twisted his arm back and up into a tight hammerlock. Randy winced with pain.

"Don't ever try to hit me," she told him so quietly only he could hear her words. "I threw Jed out of my class this morning, and I can throw you out of the cafeteria right now. So just sit down and be quiet, and let everyone enjoy his lunch. All right?"

Randy, his arm hurting too much for him to speak, managed to nod, and Judith released him, easing him back down into his chair as her eyes shifted to Jed. "Good trick with the butter," she observed, then gazed up at the ceiling. "If we say two and a half cents a pat, how much do you think all that's worth up there? And don't forget the cost of paint, at six dollars a gallon." All the kids at the table were silent now, glancing nervously at each other.

Judith, knowing she had their full attention, went on talking, keeping her tone almost conversational. "Of course, to get a good match, we'll have to paint the whole ceiling, and I think you can figure about two hundred square feet per gallon. Figure the price of the painter at $12.75 an hour, for, let's say, three and a quarter hours." She smiled at the six kids at the table who were in one or another of her classes. "Any of you who come within ten dollars of the total value of the damage and the repairs gets an automatic A on tomorrow morning's quiz, and I'll be back in five minutes to answer questions." Then, leaving all of the kids at the table except Jed staring at her in dumbfounded silence, she headed toward the cafeteria line, where Elliott Halvorson was waiting for her.

Jed, she noticed, was looking almost smug, as if she'd just done exactly what he'd expected her to do.

Elliott Halvorson, on the other hand, was anything but smug. "Are you out of your mind?" he asked as they started through the line. "Randy Sparks could sue the school for what you just did."

Judith nodded in agreement. "But he won't," she said. "In order for him to do that, he's going to have to own up to exactly what happened. And what's going to happen to his image when he has to admit to everyone in town that a teacher—a woman teacher, no less—took him?"

"But everybody already saw it," Halvorson pointed out.

"Ah, but that's different. If he tells them all he let me twist his arm on purpose because he didn't want to hurt me, he saves face." She loaded up her tray, then, after Halvorson had paid for both of them, started back toward the table.

Randy Sparks refused to meet her eyes, and Jed was no longer at the table at all. For a moment Judith wondered if perhaps she'd been wrong and he'd simply taken off, but then she spotted him.

He was walking along the far wall, carefully pacing off the dimensions of the cafeteria. Saying nothing, Judith sat down at the table and began eating, at the same time beginning her count of the butter pats that were stuck to the ceiling above her. Finally, as she began to work out the formula that would solve the problem she'd set for the kids, she reached over and turned the tape player back on, but with the volume turned so low that only the students at that table could hear it.

Five minutes before the end of the hour, she began collecting the napkins on which the kids had scribbled their solutions to the problem.

At last she looked up, not surprised to find all six of the kids at the table watching her warily. "Okay," she said. "It's not bad at all. It's good enough so everyone except Jed gets an A tomorrow." Her eyes met Jed's. "You want to tell me why your price is so high?"

Jed shrugged. "You forgot something," he said. "You didn't figure in how much it was going to cost for someone to clean up the mess before the painting could start. Paint won't stick to grease."

Judith was silent for a moment, then slowly nodded. "Touché," she said, as she marked Jed's napkin with an A+, then handed it back to him.

As she left the cafeteria a few minutes later with a very quiet Elliott Halvorson at her side, she could feel not only Jed's eyes, but the eyes of all the students, staring speculatively at her.

Greg Moreland glanced up at the clock, surprised to see that the day was half over. Already this morning he'd been out to The Cottonwoods, where he'd examined Reba Tucker once more. Her condition had deteriorated—she'd been through yet another series of tiny strokes the night before—but still she hung on. Her vital signs were almost as strong as ever, and so far her heart and lungs seemed totally unaffected by what was happening to her brain.

Her brain, Greg knew, was being slowly destroyed, and he couldn't help but wonder how much longer Reba would be able to hang on.

One more massive stroke—the kind she'd had the day she collapsed in her classroom—would do it. Indeed, Greg wasn't sure that such a thing wouldn't be a blessing for the woman now.

Her eyes, as she'd stared up at him that morning, had been terrified, and her mouth had worked almost as if she was trying to speak. But speech had long since become impossible for her; all she was capable of now was a stream of incoherent screams that occasionally erupted from her, screams generated by pain or by terror.

He wasn't sure which, for he knew full well that it could be either one. The strokes Reba had suffered could as easily induce phantom pain as phantom terror. The anguish for Reba would be as great whichever emotion she experienced, assuming she was aware of her condition at all. Greg hoped that Reba's mind was now so far gone that she had no knowledge of her own situation.

In a week—two at the most—she would be dead, and it would, indeed, be a blessing.

He put Reba out of his mind, and picked up the reports on his desk, studying them carefully.

Five minutes later Greg left his office, heading downtown toward the Borrego Building and the last appointment of his day.

It was an appointment he wasn't looking forward to.

Ten

Otto Kruger glanced out the window of the small office in the control building of the dam, far up Mordida Canyon. He didn't need to look at the clock to see that it was almost quitting time—the dark shadow of the descending sun creeping up the canyon's wall told him the time to within a few minutes. Then, uneasily, his eyes went to the rim of the canyon itself, and the lone figure who stood watching there.

It was Brown Eagle. He stood at the canyon's edge, unmoving, his figure imbued with the same unsettling concentration Otto had only seen before in the birds for which the Indian was named. At first, when Brown Eagle had taken up his sentry's stance early in the afternoon, Otto had only glanced at him casually, then forgotten about him. Bill Watkins, the dam supervisor, had told him people from Kokatí often appeared above the dam, looking down at it for a few moments, their faces set in silent reproof at the dam's very existence, then quietly moving off to go about their business.

But Brown Eagle had remained all afternoon, his stance never changing, not a muscle in his lean body so much as twitching. It had finally begun to make Otto nervous, and he'd considered sending someone up to send the man on his way, but Brown Eagle was doing no harm. If the Indian wanted to stand around like a fool, what concern was it of his?

Still, the presence of the Indian watcher was making him increasingly uneasy, as if something in the Kokatí's gaze compelled his attention; as if it wasn't actually the dam the old man was concentrating on, but he himself.

It was almost, indeed, as if the Indian somehow knew why he was up at the dam that afternoon, and was waiting for the same thing he was waiting for.

The hell with him, Otto finally told himself. So they all hate us, and hate the dam. So what? Irritated, he finished reading Watkins's reports of the day's activities and shoved them in the envelope he would drop off at Max Moreland's office on his way home.

Like a damned messenger boy, he thought, resenting once more the extra workload that had been put on his shoulders as the company was forced to lay off more and more people.

But not for long, he reminded himself. The company was losing too much money for Max to hang on much longer. Soon—perhaps even today—Moreland would face up to reality.

His thoughts were interrupted as a red light began to flash on the control panel in front of him. At the same time a bell sounded sharply in the building, while a siren began to wail outside, echoing eerily off the canyon walls.

His pulse quickening, Kruger dropped the reports back onto the desk. A moment later Bill Watkins burst in the door, shoving Otto aside as he began scanning the dials and indicators on the control board.

"What the hell's happening?" Kruger demanded. Watkins didn't answer. The tendons of his neck standing out starkly, he began twisting knobs and throwing switches. He snatched up a telephone and began barking orders into it.

"Get the main diversion valve open now, then close the number-one intake. And get that shaft clear! Shut down the turbine and get it drained."

Otto's eyes widened slightly as the implications of Watkins's words penetrated his mind, and his eyes instinctively left the control panel to gaze out the window at the dam itself. Though nothing appeared to have changed, men were suddenly spilling out of the doorway that led to the interior of the dam. Some of them were sprinting toward the control shack; others were leaning out over the dam, staring down at its concrete face.

Abruptly, as quickly as it had begun, the siren and bell fell silent.

Otto looked back to Watkins, who was now perched on a chair while he studied the array of meters spread out on the control panel before him.

"What was it?" Otto asked again, and this time Watkins replied.

"Something's gone haywire in the main power shaft. Looks like it may have developed a crack."

"Jesus," Otto breathed, turning back to gaze at the dam. "It isn't going to—"

Watkins gave Otto's back a sour look. "It's not gonna come down, no. Far from it. When Sam Moreland built that dam, he did it right." He leaned back in the chair, unconsciously rubbing at the tension in his neck. "What we've got here is what you might call a minor inconvenience," he said in a laconic drawl. "I'd reckon we're gonna have to cut the power to the refinery in about half, maybe more. 'Course, we're gonna have to shut the wells off completely in order to keep the refinery going at all."

Otto swallowed, trying to keep his expression impassive. But it was plain that this was the final blow. Max would have to sell out now. Watkins gazed at him steadily, almost as if he could read Otto's mind.

"Wouldn't have happened if you'd shown some balls about the maintenance program last month," he pointed out.

Otto's eyes narrowed. "We needed to save money," he said, his voice tight. "I was told we could save twenty-five thousand by skipping it, and not sacrifice safety at all. Max approved it." It wasn't quite the truth, for the maintenance reports Max had signed were slightly different from the ones Kruger had placed in the files. For the most part they were accurate; only one page had been changed.

One page, detailing the maintenance work that Kruger had ordered not to be done. But the signature at the bottom of the work order was still Max Moreland's.

"Is that so?" Watkins drawled, his tongue exploring the hollow where he'd lost a wisdom tooth a year ago. "Well, now, it looks like whoever told you that was a little off target, weren't they?" He hauled himself to his feet, then, without saying another word to Otto, left the control shack to go inspect the power shaft personally.

Alone, Otto savored the moment, then finally picked up the phone. He wished he could see the look on Max's face when Moreland understood that it was all over, that he was finally going to have to sell Borrego Oil.

This time, Kruger knew, there were no funds left to repair the damage.

As he waited for someone to pick up the call at the other end, Otto's eyes went once more to the rim of the canyon.

Brown Eagle was gone.

Otto frowned deeply. It was almost as if the Indian had known what was going to happen to the dam, and had been waiting to see it.

But that was impossible—he couldn't have known.

Could he?

A cold chill passed through Otto Kruger's body.

Max Moreland sat behind the huge mahogany desk his father had shipped out to the wilds of New Mexico almost seventy years earlier. His eyes were fixed on the papers laid out neatly in front of him, but his mind kept drifting back over all those years, the years when he'd been a little boy, accompanying his father as the old man wildcatted the area, spending most of his time capping the artesian wells he'd hit while drilling for oil, then moving on to the next likely spot. Finally Sam Moreland had found what he was looking for. First one well, then another and another. He'd borrowed against the wells to build the first small refinery, and gone on reinvesting his profits to drill more wells and expand the refinery, building Borrego Oil into an enterprise large enough to support a town of nearly ten thousand people. Now it looked as if his father's work and his own were all going to crumble away.

Slowly, he looked up from the papers he had been studying. He loved this office, with its softly glowing mahogany paneling, and the perfectly woven Two Grey Hills rug that had covered the floor since the day the Borrego Building had been completed at the corner of First and E Streets, establishing a new center for the dusty village. His eyes swept over the collection of Kachina dolls his father had begun and he had kept expanding. They covered a whole wall now. For some reason he found himself idly wondering if he should leave them where they were or take them with him if he had to vacate this office.

It was becoming increasingly clear that vacating the office was something he was going to have to do. Though part of Borrego's problems lay with the crash in oil prices a few years ago, he also knew that part of the problem lay within himself.

He simply hadn't kept up with the times.

Much of the refinery was obsolete, and there were all kinds of new drilling methods that could conceivably double or even triple crude oil output. He had fallen behind.

But to make Borrego Oil prosper again would take money, and there was no more. He'd spent it all to keep his obsolete refinery operating, then borrowed more.

Yet something in him refused to accept the inevitable. He stared again at the papers in front of him—the papers that would sell the whole outfit, lock, stock, and barrel, to UniChem for what he knew was more than a fair price. He was still having trouble bringing himself to sign them.

All day he'd been looking for a way to keep his promise to Frank Arnold—and a lot of other people—that the employees would have first crack at buying the company if it ever became necessary for him to sell it.

But what would he be giving them?

A pile of debts on an obsolete plant.

And they'd have to take on more debt if they were ever to have a hope of making the company pay off.

If, of course, they could find a lender, which was highly unlikely, given the climate of the oil industry and the net worth of Borrego's assets.

And yet he still kept working, searching for something he might have forgotten, hunting for something that might postpone the inevitable.

But he hadn't been able to refuse to see Paul Kendall, the representative from UniChem who had first approached him with a buy-out offer months earlier. He'd instinctively liked Kendall, a large, ruddy-faced man in his mid-forties who vaguely reminded Max of himself at the same age. And Kendall knew how he felt, even taking the time to show Max some of the places where things had gone wrong over the suddenly all-too-quick passing of the last quarter of a century.

"Nobody could ever accuse you of mismanagement, Mr. Moreland," Kendall had assured him. "Lord knows, you did your best, and for a long time it was about as good as it gets. But you were all by yourself out here, and the industry just sort of passed you by. And who could predict what was going to happen to oil prices? It's been years, and they're just starting to recover."

As the weeks went by, he and Kendall had continued bargaining. Max had to admit that Kendall had been more than fair. He and Rita would come out of it with more money than they'd ever need, and UniChem had committed to an immense infusion of new capital into the operation.

Max had been suspicious at first, certain, just as Frank Arnold was, that UniChem would shut down the refinery and simply begin piping the crude to their own facilities farther west. Kendall had insisted that that wasn't the intention at all. He and the rest of UniChem's management projected a strong market ahead, and foresaw a need for more refineries, not fewer. Max had finally called his bluff.

With a stare so intense it chilled Kendall's soul, he asked: "Then you're willing to sign a guarantee that the refinery remains in operation for twenty-five years?"

Kendall laughed out loud. "Of course not," he said. "But I think you'd settle for ten, wouldn't you?"

At that moment Max knew he could not resist much longer.

Now, he focused his attention once more on the papers in front of him, and took up his pen. He was just signing the last page of the agreement when his intercom chimed softly and his secretary informed him that Otto Kruger was on the line.

Tiredly, he picked up the receiver. "Yes, Otto? What is it?"

Across the room, Paul Kendall looked up when the phone rang. He had been sitting at a conference table with Greg Moreland, quietly explaining to the younger man the complex series of documents that comprised the offer for the company, while he let the older man adjust to the inevitable in any way he could. He gestured to the extension on the conference table, and when Max nodded, pressed a button that amplified Kruger's voice so both he and Greg could hear it clearly.

"... it's going to mean a shutdown of the dam, Max," they heard Kruger saying. "And the wells, and maybe the refinery too." Kendall saw the blood drain from Max Moreland's face.

When the call was over, Paul Kendall faced Max. "If it'll make you feel any better, Mr. Moreland, none of this will affect our offer. The offer stands as it is, and we'll deal with the problem at the dam."

Max said nothing for a moment. His expression grim, he punched at a button on his intercom. "I want the maintenance files on the dam," he said. The color had come back into his face, and his voice seemed suddenly to have strengthened.

Kendall glanced questioningly at Greg, who shrugged but said nothing, as Max's secretary entered the office, carrying three thick file folders. She laid them on Max's desk, then turned to go.

"Take him with you, please," Max snapped, nodding toward Kendall and already beginning to flip through the files. Kendall started to object, but Max silenced him with a glance. "I'm sorry, Mr. Kendall," he said. "I want to know what happened out there at that dam, and until I know, I'm afraid I can't let you sign these papers. For the moment this deal is on hold." He slid Kendall's documents into the center drawer of his desk, then locked it.

Kendall frowned. "But I already told you—"

"I heard what you said," Max interrupted. "And it may not make any difference to you and your company, but it makes a hell of a difference to me. I don't sell shit for the price of fertilizer."

Kendall's brows rose slightly, but he followed the secretary out of the office without another word. When the door had closed behind him, Max looked up again, this time fixing his gaze on Greg. "Something's going on," he said, his voice dropping. "Take a look at this."

Greg crossed to his uncle's desk and leaned over to look at the page that lay exposed in the file folder. The notations on the page were as indecipherable to him as his prescriptions were to his patients. "What is it?"

"The results of the last inspection of the dam, and the orders for repairs that needed to be made. Except that what's here and what I signed are not the same."

Greg frowned. "I'm not sure I understand . . ."

Max's fist clenched angrily. "It means that what I authorized— hell, what I *ordered*—wasn't done. I may be getting old, but I remember what I read, and what I sign. And what I signed was an order that all the cracks in the main drive flume were to be repaired. But those orders aren't here. Christ, anyone who looks at this would have to assume I'd lost my grip completely!" His voice was rising now and a vein was beginning to stand out on his forehead. "God damn it—look at this! Here's Watkins's report on the damage they found at the last inspection." He picked up the page and began reading it out loud. " 'Transverse cracking at the intake—erosion of the primary casing in the area of the turbine.' Hell, there's ten or fifteen items here, and every single one should have been taken care of. But according to this, I didn't authorize any repairs. Which is a damned lie!" His fist slammed down on the desk and he fairly trembled with rage.

"Now take it easy," Greg said, alarmed by his uncle's fury. "You might be wrong. You might have thought you authorized those repairs but forgot—"

"No!" Max roared. "I don't forget things like that. Not something as important as that dam." He fell silent for a moment, sitting still, his mind working quickly as he tried to figure out what might have happened.

"All right," he said, his breathing slowly coming back to normal as his rage subsided and reason took over. "Here's what we're going to do. You tell Kendall he's going to have to wait until at least tomorrow. And in the meantime I'm going to have a little talk with Otto Kruger. This whole thing smells, and the only thing that could have happened is that Kruger changed the orders after I signed them. And that," he added, "seems to me like a pretty good indication that someone's been paying him off." A cold grin spread across his face and his eyes shifted to the door through which Paul Kendall had passed only a few moments ago. "Now, who do you suppose would have been interested in paying Otto off to sabotage the dam?" he asked. His voice hardened. "If I can pin this on that son of a bitch, we won't need to sell this company at all."

"Even if you can prove it, what difference will it make?" Greg asked. "It would mean a lawsuit, and that would drag on for years. We don't have the time for something like that, let alone the money—"

"We'll find it," Max declared, his voice suddenly stronger than Greg had heard it in years. "I'm damned if I'm going to let them just squeeze me out like this." He picked up the phone and began dialing, then gestured toward the door. "Go on—get rid of Kendall, and don't say a word about these orders. If I'm right, I want to take him by surprise."

Greg, knowing there was no point in arguing with his uncle, stood up and left the office. Paul Kendall was waiting in the anteroom beyond the secretary's office. As he came in, Kendall rose to his feet.

"What's going on?"

Greg shrugged. "Nothing much. He just wants to find out what happened to the dam. I don't think anything else is going to happen until tomorrow."

Kendall eyed Greg shrewdly. "He's not thinking of backing out of this deal, is he? He'll never get a better offer."

Greg shook his head. "That's not it at all," he said. "You just don't know Uncle Max. If the dam's in really bad shape, he'll insist on lowering the price of the company."

"Come off it, Greg," Kendall replied. "If we're still willing to pay the price, why should he accept less?"

Greg's lips curved in a thin smile. "Because that's the way he is. Maybe he's the last honest businessman."

Again Kendall regarded Greg narrowly. "But he'll go through with the deal?" he pressed.

Greg hesitated, then nodded. "Yes," he said. "He'll go through with the deal. He's already signed the papers, and no matter what he thinks, he doesn't really have much choice, does he?" He offered Kendall his hand. "Now, if you'll excuse me, I've got some things I have to attend to at my office."

Kendall grasped Greg's proffered hand, shaking it firmly. "Then I'll see you here tomorrow."

Once again Greg nodded. "Tomorrow."

Max drove slowly, his mind only half concentrating on the road ahead of him. The sun was dropping low, and the sky to the west was beginning to glow a brilliant red, shot through with orange, purple, and magenta. But Max saw none of it. Instead, his mind was whirling. Was it really possible, after all these years, that Otto Kruger had betrayed him?

Of course it was. Kruger was as aware as anyone of the financial condition of the company, and Max had known almost since the day he'd hired Kruger that the man's number-one interest was himself. If someone had come along and offered him a deal, Kruger wasn't the sort who would refuse, particularly when the alternative would almost certainly be to end up working for Frank Arnold.

Frank Arnold.

How the hell was he going to explain to Frank what had happened? How many times had he told Frank that when the time came to sell, the employees would have the first opportunity?

But he'd waited too long, and now selling to the employees, no matter the condition of the dam, would be the wrong thing to do. Despite the bravado of his words, he knew that Greg was right.

He had neither the time nor the money for a long legal battle which, in the end, he'd probably lose anyway.

He was on the mesa now, driving along the dirt road that led up to the dam, and as he finally looked out over the canyon, the last of his cold fury drained away from him. It wasn't just the time and money he was lacking for a fight with UniChem, he realized.

He lacked the stomach for it too.

Better to give it up gracefully, he decided, admit when he'd been beaten. Losing, after all, was losing, whether Kruger had sold out or not. In the end it really didn't matter, for in the end the condition of the dam was his responsibility, not Kruger's. He knew what repairs he'd ordered, and he should have been up at the dam to make sure they were done.

If he wasn't going to do his job, it was time to step down. With a UniChem buyout, at least he could secure the future of all the people who worked for him for another ten years, and none of them would have to live with the constant specter of debt that had hung over him for more than a decade.

It would be all right, once they got over the shock of it.

And he'd be all right too.

No!

He'd be damned if he would be betrayed like this, and just fade quietly away into oblivion.

Never!

He frowned suddenly as a sharp stab of pain lashed through his head.

His fingers tightened on the wheel and he reflexively closed his eyes for a moment, as if to shut out the searing pain in his skull. A noxious odor, rotten and pervasive, invaded his nostrils. When he opened his eyes, his vision was blurred behind a thick red haze.

The pain slashed at his brain again, even more powerfully this time, and his whole body went into a convulsive spasm.

A second later the spasm passed, and Max's own weight pulled the steering wheel around as he slumped over into the passenger seat.

The car veered off the road, lurched toward the edge of the canyon, then struck a boulder.

It jerked to a halt, its front end collapsing under the sudden impact. The engine died almost immediately.

The windshield didn't shatter, and the driver's door swung open, one of its hinges broken from the stress of the impact.

It would have been easy for anyone to have crawled out of the wreckage, unharmed.

Anyone, that is, except Max Moreland.

For Max, at the age of seventy-five, had already died even before the car left the road and slammed into the boulder.

Perhaps he'd died even before that.

Perhaps he'd died in his office when he'd finally affixed his signature to the UniChem documents, giving up the company that had been his whole life.

It no longer made any difference *when* Max had died.

The only thing that would make a difference was *how* he had died.

Eleven

The chill of the desert night had already settled in. Frank Arnold lingered in the cab of his pickup truck, gazing at the squat building that had once been the social center of Borrego. Only a few years ago, when the company had been making plenty of money, the union hall had been well-kept, its exterior freshly painted every year, its lawns regularly watered and mowed at least once a week during the summer. Now, even in the shadowed light from a rising moon, the deterioration of the building was visible. The union hall, like the rest of Borrego, was showing the effects of the ill-fortune that had befallen the company. Its paint was beginning to peel away, and the lawns had been allowed to die, slowly becoming overgrown with sagebrush and tumbleweed.

Part of the neglect, Frank knew, was a simple lack of money. As raises had become scarcer—and smaller—but prices had continued to rise, the union's support from its members had begun to dwindle. The negative attitude had grown slowly, but pervasively: What good was the union, if it couldn't win a better standard of living for its members? And so the weekend get-togethers at the hall, the Friday-night dances and the Saturday softball games on the field behind the hall, had slowly dwindled away too, until there were no longer either the funds or the interest to keep them up.

The glare of headlights swept through the cab of the truck as another car pulled into the parking lot and came to a stop a few feet away. Frank stirred, then got out and greeted Tom Kennedy, the attorney who had driven up from Santa Fe to help Frank answer the mass of questions tonight's meeting would surely generate.

Together the two men went inside the hall, and while Frank

turned on the lights and heat, Kennedy began setting up a table on the small platform at the far end of the main meeting room.

"How many do you think will turn up?" Kennedy asked as Frank straightened the rows of folding chairs facing the platform.

"Couple hundred, maybe. I should think a lot of the wives would show up too."

But half an hour later, when Frank finally banged his gavel on the table and stood to call the meeting to order, he had counted fewer than a hundred people. It was not surprising, really. A rumor that the company had already been sold had spread like wildfire, and even most of the men who had come to the meeting looked as though they didn't think anything could be done. He knew he had already lost. But still, he had to try. He glanced down at the notes he had put together over dinner that evening, but just as he was about to begin, the door opened and Jerry Polanski stepped into the room, his face pale. He signaled to Frank, but then, instead of waiting for Frank to come to him, he hurried down the center aisle and leaped up onto the platform.

"Max is dead, Frank," he said, bending over the table and keeping his voice so low that no one except Frank and Tom Kennedy could hear him.

Frank stared numbly at Polanski.

"They found him half an hour ago," Polanski went on. "He was on his way to the dam, and his car went off the road."

Frank's hands clenched into tight fists, his knuckles turning white. "Jesus," he breathed, sinking back into his chair.

He struggled against his own emotions for a moment, his eyes moistening as a choking sob rose in his throat. He'd known Max Moreland all his life. He'd both liked and respected the man, and known his feelings had been reciprocated. And even though in recent years they'd often been forced to meet as adversaries, their personal relationship had never changed.

Now Max was gone.

Finally conquering the emotions that threatened to overwhelm him, Frank gazed uncertainly out at the crowd. They were all looking at him with guarded expressions, as if they knew that some new disaster was about to be revealed. His voice shaking slightly, Frank began to speak.

"You all know why I called this meeting," he began. "It was my hope that we could find a way to buy Borrego Oil from Max Moreland, even though he apparently agreed to sell it to UniChem today." He hesitated, then forged on. "Tom Kennedy, here, thought there might have been a way, but . . ." His voice trailed off again, but once more he gripped his emotions in the vise of his will. "But I'm afraid all that is past us now. I've just been told that Max is dead."

There was a moment of shocked silence in the hall, and then a babble of voices rose. Frank banged the gavel hard on the table. Slowly the rumbling began to subside. "I'm afraid we don't know exactly what happened," he went on. "But given the circumstances, I don't see any reason for this meeting to go on. So, if there is no objection, it's adjourned."

He banged the gavel once more, then dropped back into his chair.

Immediately the room came to life. A crowd gathered around the table, and voices shouted questions at Jerry Polanski, who could only repeat what he'd already told Frank. After several minutes Frank leaned over to Tom Kennedy.

"Let's get out of here. I need a drink."

As Kennedy began shoving papers in his briefcase, Frank pushed his chair back and began making his way through the crowd, ignoring the hands that plucked at his sleeve and the voices that shouted questions in his ear. Outside the hall, he paused for a moment, taking a deep breath of the cold night air in a vain effort to wash his mind clear of the ugly suspicions that were already beginning to take form in his head.

An hour later, he sat by himself at a table in the bar at the back of the café. Tom Kennedy, Jerry Polanski, Carlos Alvarez, and a few other men sat at other tables, the faces changing as they drifted from spot to spot. Frank stared at the shot glass in front of him, which contained the first half of his fourth boilermaker. He was looking for numbness in the liquor, a cessation of thought. So far, though, his mind was still clear.

Clear, and functioning all too well.

He knocked back the whiskey, then took three fast swallows of beer, finally banging the stein down on the table with a force that silenced the conversation.

"They killed him," he said, giving voice for the first time to the suspicions that had been roiling in his mind since the moment he'd left the union hall.

One of the recent arrivals—Jesus Hernandez, an electrician from the dam—heard his remark and stared at him, his mouth twisting into a half-drunken grin. "Killed him? C'mon, Frank," he mumbled. "Why the hell would anyone wanta kill ol' Max? He was a good ol' boy." He raised an arm and waved to the waitress. "Hey, Katie. Bring us another round, and come listen to what ol' Frank says."

Katie Alvarez came over with a tray of drinks. After she'd placed glasses on several tables and another boilermaker in front of Frank, she shifted her attention to Jesus Hernandez. "So what's Frank say that I've got to hear?'' she asked, feigning more interest than she actually felt. She'd learned long ago that customers left better tips if you listened to their hard-luck stories.

"He thinks the guys from UniChem killed Max Moreland,'' Hernandez replied, downing half his fresh drink. "Can you believe that?''

For the first time in weeks something a customer said finally seized Katie's attention. "Killed him?'' she repeated, echoing Hernandez's words. "Why would they want to do that?''

Frank tossed back his fifth shot of whiskey, chased it with a gulp of beer, then wiped his mouth with his shirtsleeve.

"Keep him from making trouble,'' he said, his words slurring now as the alcohol in his blood began to penetrate his brain. "I coulda talked him out of it, and everybody knew it,'' he went on. "I told Kruger that just the other day. Told him I could figure out a way. So they fixed it so I couldn't even talk to 'im.'' His eyes wandered over the messy tabletop. "Bastards,'' he mumbled, only half aloud. "The bastards jus' went ahead an' killed ol' Max.''

Katie glanced around the bar nervously. If what he'd said got back to UniChem, Frank would be fired for sure, but no one at any of the other tables seemed to have heard. If she could get him to go home and sleep it off ... "Come on, Frank,'' she said. "You've had too much to drink, and you're just upset. That's crazy talk, and you don't believe it any more than anyone else does.'' She had a hand on his arm now and was easing him gently to his feet. "Now, why don't you just go on home and get some sleep. Okay?''

Frank shook her hand off, then wheeled around to glare drunkenly at her. He staggered, then braced himself against the table to keep from falling. "I'm telling you,'' he said. "Somethin's goin' on around here.'' His eyes narrowed and he searched Katie's face. "What are you, part of the whole thing?'' he asked. "You got something goin' with that guy from UniChem—what's his name? Kendall?''

Katie felt her temper rise. She knew what a lot of people in town thought of her; it was no different from what people thought of cocktail waitresses everywhere. But she'd thought Frank Arnold was different. Then she remembered that he was drunk. "Right,'' she said, forcing herself to grin at him. "I've never even met the man, but I'm screwing his brains out every night. Okay? Now come on.'' She took his arm again, steering him gently toward the door, and by the time she got him outside, he seemed to have steadied slightly. "You think you can drive?'' she asked. "I can get someone to take you.''

But Frank shook his head. "I'm okay,'' he said, taking a deep breath of air, then shaking his whole body almost like a dog ridding itself of water. He pulled open the door of the truck and swung up into the cab. Then he rolled down the window and spoke to Katie once more. "Sorry about what I said in there. I guess maybe I've had too much to drink."

Katie chuckled. "I guess maybe you have," she agreed, then patted his arm reassuringly. "Look, Frank, take it easy, okay? Drive carefully, and don't go shooting your mouth off about Max. If what you said in there gets back to UniChem or Otto Kruger, they might can you."

"Kruger'll try to do that anyhow," Frank replied. "But he can't, 'cause I won't give him any reason to. That's what the union's for, right?"

Katie shook her head in mock despair, but decided to have one last try at reasoning with him. "Frank, you don't know what happened to Max. But if you start telling everyone he was killed, that's libel, or slander, or something, and I bet they can fire you for it."

"They can't if it's true," Frank growled. He slammed the truck into gear, his rear wheels spinning in the loose gravel as he took off. The free-spinning tires screeched in protest when they finally hit the pavement, then they caught and the truck jackrabbited across the road. For a split second Katie thought Frank had lost control completely, but then the vehicle swerved around, straightened out, and took off down the street. She watched him go until he turned the corner two blocks away, then shook her head tiredly and went back into the café. She had a feeling Frank Arnold wasn't the only drunk she was going to have to deal with that night. The bar seemed to be full of them.

Frank rolled both windows down, and the cold air washed over his face, sobering him slightly. He was driving well, keeping his speed ten miles below the limit, and the steering steady. But one more drink and he wouldn't have been able to drive at all.

It was another five minutes before he realized where he was going, although as he turned onto the long gravel drive that led up a rise to the foot of the mesa where Max Moreland's parents had built their great Victorian pile of a house so many years ago, he knew he'd decided to come out here as soon as he'd left the café.

He wanted to talk to Judith Sheffield, wanted her to listen to him, to believe him.

And besides, he rationalized, the least he could do right now was pay his respects to Rita Moreland.

Kill two birds with one stone. The trite words seemed to slur even in his mind.

He pulled unsteadily up in front of the house, slewing his truck in next to Greg Moreland's worn Jeep Wagoneer. He climbed the steep flight of steps to the wide veranda that fronted the house, then leaned heavily against the doorframe for a moment as a wave of dizziness swept over him. Maybe, after all, he shouldn't have come out here. But then the door opened and Judith Sheffield, her face ashen and streaked with tears, looked out at him.

They stared at each other wordlessly for a moment, then Judith took a step forward. Frank's arms slid around her, and her face pressed against his chest. A single sob shook her, and then she felt Frank gently stroking her hair. Regaining her composure, she stepped back. "I—I'm so glad you're here. It's terrible."

Frank, feeling suddenly sober, nodded. "How's Rita taking it?"

Judith managed a weak smile. "On the surface, better than I am, I guess. But you know Rita—no matter what happens, she never loses her composure. She's in the living room." Taking Frank's hand, she led him into the house.

Rita Moreland, her lean body held erect and every strand of her white hair in place, stood up as they entered. "Frank," she said, taking his hand and clasping it tightly. "I'm so glad you've come. I was going to call you, but . . ." Her voice trailed off.

"I should have called you, Rita," Frank replied. "In fact, I should have come out as soon as I heard."

Rita shook her head. "Don't even think it. Greg is here, and there have been people in and out all evening."

Frank felt a wave of nausea as the alcohol in his blood regained its grip on him, and he swayed slightly. "I—I don't know what to say," he mumbled. "I just can't believe he's dead. Not Max. He was so—" He faltered, unable to find the words he was looking for.

"I know," Rita told him, gently steering him toward a sofa and signaling Greg to pour a cup of coffee from the immense silver urn that stood on a sideboard. "We're all going to miss him terribly, but we're going to go on, just as he would have wanted us to." She perched stiffly on the edge of a wing-backed chair opposite the sofa.

Greg came over and set a cup of coffee on the table in front of Frank. "Looks like you've had a couple of drinks—" he began, but before he could finish the sentence, Rita Moreland's melodic voice smoothly cut in.

"I think I could use one myself, Greg. I think perhaps a shot of your uncle's bourbon might be in order." Though she spoke to Greg her eyes never left Frank Arnold. "Frank?"

Frank hesitated, then shook his head. "I think I've had enough, Rita. In fact, I probably shouldn't have come out here tonight—"

"Nonsense," Rita replied, letting just enough sharpness come into her voice to let Frank know she meant what she was saying and was not simply being polite. "Outside the family, no one in town was closer to Max than you were."

Frank nodded, then licked nervously at his lips. He knew he shouldn't say what he was about to say; but he also knew he wasn't going to be able to stop himself. And there was something in the way Rita was looking at him that told him she already knew what he was about to say. "I think they killed him," he blurted.

Rita Moreland, hand extended to accept the drink Greg was holding out to her, didn't so much as flinch. Her eyes remained on Frank. "Go on," she said softly.

Frank met her steady gaze. "I don't know what happened to Max, but I can't believe it was just an accident. I think they must have run him off the road or something." He began speaking faster, his words tumbling over one another as they rushed from his mind to his mouth. "Max was a good driver. He would never have just run off the road like that. And think about it—UniChem wanted the company, and Max didn't want them to have it—he wanted to sell it to us, he told me so—"

"Now just a minute," Greg Moreland interrupted. He set the drink on the coffee table in front of his aunt, as Rita's eyes remained fixed on Frank, her face an expressionless mask. Greg glared at Frank. "You've had way too much to drink, Frank, and I don't know what you're thinking, coming in here tonight—of all nights—and throwing around charges like that. You don't know what you're talking about."

"I know what I think—" Frank began, but once again an indignant Greg Moreland cut him off.

"You know what you imagine," he shot back. "If you want to know what happened, I—or even Aunt Rita—will be glad to tell you! It was a one-car accident, Frank. And it wasn't even Uncle Max's fault. He was already dead when the car went off the road."

Frank frowned, as if he couldn't quite put the words together. "I don't—"

"You don't get it?" Greg finished for him, his voice crackling with anger. "Well, maybe if you hadn't gone out and gotten drunk tonight, you *would* get it. He died at the wheel, Frank. He'd just sold the company, which except for Aunt Rita was the only thing that meant anything to him. He was under a lot of strain, and he had a stroke while at the wheel. That's what killed him, Frank. Not the accident. A stroke. He was already dead when the accident happened."

Frank, dazed, sank back into his chair. His eyes fixed on Greg Moreland, but he could see by the anger in Greg's eyes that Max's nephew was telling him the truth. Finally he managed to shift his gaze to Rita Moreland, a wave of shame sweeping over him as he saw the pain in her eyes.

The pain he'd caused her, with his drunken accusations.

"I—I'm sorry, Rita," he said, pulling himself to his feet and managing a single step toward her before collapsing back onto the chair.

His words seemed to trigger something in Rita Moreland, and suddenly she came alive again. "It's all right," she said, the forgiving words coming to her almost automatically. "We've all had a terrible shock today."

"It's not all right," Greg Moreland broke in, his voice cold. "He had no right to come out here and upset you that way, Aunt Rita. I ought to call the police."

But Rita held up a protesting hand. "There's no need for that, Greg. I've known Frank for a good many more years than I've known even you. If you'll just call Jed, perhaps—"

"It seems to me he got out here under his own steam—" Greg began, but Rita shook her head.

"We don't need any more cars going off the road today, Greg. Please, just call Jed."

"You don't need to call him," Judith put in quickly, anxious to calm the situation before Frank's temper might erupt. "I'll take him home, and Jed can drive me back."

Greg seemed about to argue, but a look from his aunt changed his mind. As he stalked out of the room a moment later, he glared at Judith, and for an instant she had the strangest feeling that he was jealous. But why would he be? Since she'd been back in Borrego, he hadn't shown the slightest interest in her. "I—I'll just go up and get my coat," she stammered, feeling as if she had somehow inadvertently made a bad situation even worse.

When Judith too was out of the room, Rita Moreland finally picked up the untouched drink from the coffee table, stared at it for a moment, then drained it. She paused as if waiting for the alcohol to fortify her, then once more met Frank's eyes. "I want you to know I understand how you feel," she said gently, her voice now free of the carefully controlled graciousness she had mastered so many years ago that it had become second nature to her. "In fact, the same thought you just expressed crossed my mind too. Max called me just before he died. Something had happened, and even though he'd already signed the papers, he said he had time to back out. And he intended to do it." She shrugged helplessly. "I'm not sure what the problem was—he didn't tell me. But I have to tell you the first thing I thought when Greg told me what had happened was that somehow—for some reason—they'd killed him. But I was wrong, Frank. Greg assures me it was a stroke, Frank, pure and simple. Max was at an age when those things can happen, and Greg had warned him about the possibility for months. It was just one of those things that nobody can predict."

Frank's sense of shame deepened.

He'd come out here to offer his condolences and express his sorrow.

Instead, Rita Moreland was comforting him.

Jed came awake slowly. Darkness surrounded him, yet his room was filled with a strange silvery glow, as if a full moon was somehow shining through the ceiling itself. But when he looked at the window, the night outside was a velvety black.

The glow was somehow coming from within the room itself.

He sat up, then gasped.

Perched on the top rail of his cast-iron bedstead was an enormous bird. It looked like an eagle, but Jed was certain he'd never seen one this large. Indeed, as he watched, it suddenly spread its wings and its feathers filled the room, spreading from one wall to the other. Jed felt his heart begin to pound, and he involuntarily shrank back. But a second later the bird settled down again and its head turned sideways so that one of its eyes fixed on Jed.

It was from the giant bird's eye that the silvery light emanated, a cold radiance that hung in the room, yet did not wash away the darkness. When Jed held up his hand to shield his eyes against it, he found that his hand was invisible. Though he could feel his fingers touching his face, the bird's image remained before him, as clear as ever.

The bird's beak opened, and a single word issued forth from its throat.

"Come."

Jed froze as he recognized the voice that had risen from the maw of the great bird.

It was his grandfather's voice, as clear as if it had been the old man himself standing at the foot of the bed.

The enormous bird spoke the word once more.

"Come."

And then it spread its wings and the room filled with a great roaring noise as the bird rose straight upward. It seemed to pass right through the ceiling, and as it rose higher into the pitch-blackness of the night, Jed could still see the silvery light radiating from its eyes. It hovered in the air for a moment, then wheeled around, and with a great rushing sound as its wings found the breeze, it soared toward the mesa.

As it disappeared, Jed came awake for the second time.

This time he was lying on the sofa, the television droning in the background. In his mind the dream he'd just awakened from was still fresh and vivid.

So vivid, it hadn't been like a dream at all. Even now that he was fully awake, he still felt as if he had actually experienced the presence of the enormous bird.

He had a strange urge to go to the mesa, to Kokatí, right now, and find his grandfather.

His reverie was broken by the sound of his father's truck pulling into the driveway, and a moment later Frank, leaning heavily on Judith Sheffield, lurched through the back door and into the kitchen. Jed stared stupidly at his father for a second, then his eyes shifted to Judith.

"He's drunk," she said. "Help me get him into his room, and then I'll tell you what happened."

Jed took his father's other arm, and between the two of them they managed to get Frank through the living room and down the hall into the master bedroom. He collapsed onto the bed, rolled over on his back and held out his arms toward Judith. "Stay with me?" he asked.

Judith felt herself reddening, and glanced toward Jed. To her surprise, the boy was grinning broadly. "It's not funny," she snapped. "Of all the things for him to say—"

Jed tried to control his grin and failed. "Why shouldn't he say it? He's been wanting to all week. Haven't you seen the way he looks at you?"

Judith's blush deepened. "Jed!"

"Well, it's true, even if he's too drunk to know what he said," Jed insisted. His eyes fixed on her, twinkling impudently. "You want to get him undressed, or shall I?"

"You do it," Judith mumbled, her cheeks still burning. "I'll go make some coffee."

Five minutes later Jed joined her in the kitchen, still snickering. "What happened?" he asked. "I don't think I've ever seen him drunk before. Not like this, anyway. He's really blitzed."

"Max Moreland died this afternoon," Judith told him.

Jed's laughter faded away. "Mr. Moreland?" he echoed. "Wh-What happened?"

Judith explained, then added: "Your father got the idea in his head that someone from UniChem killed Max."

"Oh, Christ," Jed groaned. "What's going to happen now?"

Frank Arnold's voice filled the kitchen. "Now," he said, "I'm going to find out what *did* happen."

Jed and Judith spun around to stare at him. He was standing in the kitchen door, a bathrobe wrapped around his large frame, his face still wet from the cold shower he'd just taken.

"I thought you were asleep," Judith said.

Frank shook his head. "I wasn't asleep, and I wasn't so drunk I didn't know what I was saying." His eyes met hers squarely, and his voice dropped. "And Jed was right—I *have* been wanting to ask you to stay all week."

Once again Judith felt herself beginning to flush, and once again she found herself glancing involuntarily toward Jed.

Jed, realizing that whether or not Judith spent the night with his father was up to him, hesitated only a second. "I think maybe I'll take off for a while," he said, his eyes shifting to his father. "Okay if I take the truck?"

"The keys are in it," Frank replied, his eyes never leaving Judith.

Jed started toward the back door, then turned and winked at Judith. "See you in the morning. And pancakes would be great for breakfast. We haven't had a decent pancake around here for years."

It wasn't until he was a block away from the house that he realized where he was going. When he'd left, he thought he'd drive around for a while, or maybe go see if Gina Alvarez was still up.

But now that he was in the truck, he knew.

He was going to Kokatí, to see his grandfather.

Brown Eagle emerged from the kiva. He'd been sitting on the stone bench facing the firepit for hours, his body motionless, his mind turned outward from his own spirit to accept whatever might emerge from the sipapu in the center of the floor.

He had maintained a silence during his long vigil, listening only to the voices from the underworld. When at last he came back to himself, he discovered he was alone in the kiva. There had been ten others in the holy place when he'd come in so many hours ago, and he had no recollection of them leaving. But that was all right; it often happened to him when he was in communion with the spirits, and when the communion was over he had no memory of where he'd been or what he'd done, much less of what anyone around him might have done.

Indeed, for all he remembered, he might never have been in the kiva at all.

Tonight, as he climbed out of the hatch in the chamber's roof, he had the distinct feeling that this wasn't the first time he'd left the kiva since the vigil began.

Tonight he'd been possessed by Rakantoh, the greatest of all the Kokatí spirits, who had dwelt in the canyon until the dam had forced him to fly away from his home.

Yes, tonight the great spirit eagle Rakantoh had come to him, and they had flown together. Flown, and seen many things; things that he needed, for reasons the spirit had not yet revealed to him, to tell his grandson.

So he strode away from the kiva and went to look out over the canyon and the lake that flooded Rakantoh's ancient home.

He stood at the edge of the canyon, waiting in the darkness, and when, half an hour later, he saw headlights bobbing across the mesa far in the distance, he knew at once that it was Jed.

Rakantoh had summoned him, and he had answered.

Tonight Brown Eagle would introduce his grandson to the mysteries of the kiva.

Twelve

It was close to midnight, and Rita Moreland knew she should feel exhausted. Until an hour ago the phone hadn't stopped ringing, and though Greg had argued with her, she'd insisted on taking every call, exchanging a few words with all the people who had offered her their sympathy. After a while the words had come almost automatically, but still she'd listened, and spoken, and been amazed at how much her husband had been loved. For the last hour, though, the phone had been mercifully silent, and she and Greg had sat alone in front of a small fire that had now burned down to no more than a few glowing embers.

"You should go to bed, Aunt Rita," Greg said, rising from the sofa to sweep a few coals off the hearth and place the screen in front of the huge brass andirons that had been in the fireplace as long as the house had stood.

Rita's hand fluttered dismissively. "I wouldn't sleep. I'd just lie there, waiting for Max to come home." Her eyes, their normal curtain of reserve lifted, were bleak and lonely as she gazed at her nephew. "But he's not coming home, is he?" she asked.

Greg made no answer, knowing none was expected.

Rita leaned forward and picked up her glass. A half inch of Max's favorite bourbon still remained, and Rita held it up to the light of the fire, the glowing coals flickering eerily in the amber liquid. "We have to decide what to do, Greg," she said.

Greg nodded briefly and sank back onto the sofa. "The funeral will be on Friday morning," he told her. "I've already made most of the arrangements. It'll be at the old church."

"I wasn't thinking of that," Rita replied, her voice oddly detached, as if she hadn't yet brought herself to deal with Max's funeral. "I was thinking of the company."

Greg's brows rose slightly. "I'm not sure there's anything that needs to be done. Uncle Max signed the sale today—the papers are in his desk."

Rita's lips tightened. "But there was something wrong—he was going up to the dam to talk to Otto Kruger."

Greg nodded. "It was something about the maintenance reports," he said. "There was a problem up there today. Some damage to the main power flume. Uncle Max thought there was some kind of irregularity—"

"Irregularity?" Rita repeated. "What do you mean?"

Greg's eyes shifted to the floor, and when he spoke again he sounded almost embarrassed by what he had to say. "I'm afraid Uncle Max didn't read the last reports very well," he said. "He seemed to think he'd ordered some repairs that weren't made. But he'd signed the report, and the repair orders."

Rita frowned. "I find it hard to believe Max would have let the dam go," she said.

Greg met her eyes. "Aunt Rita, he was getting old. He was already suffering from high blood pressure, and his arteries weren't in the best condition. He should have retired five years ago."

Rita turned the matter over in her mind, hearing again the last conversation she'd had with Max. He'd sounded upset—indeed, he'd sounded furious—but he hadn't told her exactly what the problem was.

At whom had he been angry? Himself, after discovering his own mistake?

Or someone else?

She'd never know.

She took a deep breath. "All right," she said. "I suppose there's no point in trying to figure out exactly what happened. But what do we do about the sale? Max seemed to think it shouldn't go through."

"Not exactly," Greg replied. "He wanted to find out what had happened up at the dam—how bad the damage was. I suppose it would have affected the value of the company."

"You mean UniChem might not want it anymore," Rita translated. To her surprise, Greg shook his head.

"Not at all. In fact, Paul Kendall heard everything Otto Kruger had to say about the dam, and it didn't seem to bother him at all. He's quite willing to let the deal go through with no changes."

Rita stared at him. "But that doesn't make sense. If the dam's damaged badly, the company's not worth as much."

Greg shrugged. "I suppose when you have as much money as UniChem does, whatever it will take to fix the damage doesn't mean much to them. They just seem to want the company, and they don't seem to care what it costs."

"But why?" Rita insisted. "Max always said that if a deal looked too good to be true, it was too good to be true. If they're willing to pay the same price, disregarding the condition of the dam—"

Before she could complete her thought, a loud crash echoed through the house, followed by the tinkling of glass. Rita and Greg stared at each other for a moment, then Greg was on his feet, charging out to the foyer.

On the hardwood floor, amid the shattered remains of the broken judas window in the large oaken door, was a rock the size of a fist. Ignoring the rock, Greg jerked the door open and stepped out onto the broad veranda that fronted the house. But he already knew it was too late. The moon was low in the sky, and the darkness of the desert night surrounded him.

Whoever had thrown the rock had already disappeared into the vast emptiness around the house. Still, Greg left the porch and quickly searched the grounds before going back in and gingerly picking the rock from among the shards of glass.

It was a river cobble, round, flat, and worn smooth from eons of tumbling. But on one of its surfaces a word had been scrawled with a laundry marker.

Bitch

Greg stared at it in puzzlement, then finally looked up at his aunt, who was standing in the wide arched opening of the living room.

"What does it say?" Rita demanded, her voice clear and calm.

Greg handed the rock to his aunt, who turned it over and read the single word. "Why the hell would anyone want to do something like this?" he asked. "And tonight, of all nights?"

Rita shook her head. "I don't know," she said, her voice sorrowful. "Apparently I don't have the sympathy of everyone in town after all."

Greg's eyes hardened. "I'm calling the police," he said. "There's no reason why we should have to put up with vandalism."

Rita took a deep breath, then shook her head. "No," she said, the exhaustion of the long evening finally closing in on her. "Not tonight. I don't want to talk to anyone else right now, Greg. I just want to go to bed and think for a while."

But a few minutes later, when she was at last alone in the large bed she'd shared with Max for almost half a century, she found she didn't think at all.

She fell asleep, and dreamed of Max.

Jed had no idea what time it was, except that the sun had risen and a bright patch of light lay trapped on the western edge of the kiva floor. The fire still smoldered, tendrils of smoke drifting up to dance for a moment in the rays of the sun, only to climb onward, escaping out of the hatch and riding away on the breeze.

He was still uncertain exactly what had happened last night. When he'd arrived at Kokatí and found his grandfather waiting for him, he had been unsurprised, as if there were nothing abnormal about Brown Eagle having known he was coming. He'd told his grandfather about the dream, and a bemused smile had come over Brown Eagle's face as he listened. "Maybe," the old man had mused when Jed was finished, "your grandpa isn't so crazy after all, eh?"

"But what happened?" Jed had asked. "What did I see?"

Brown Eagle shrugged. "You can see anything in dreams. Some of it is real—some of it might not be. Some of it means something, some of it doesn't." At the look of puzzlement on Jed's face, he continued, "The trouble with your father's people is that they won't open their minds. When they dream, they say everything they see comes from inside their minds. When their eyes are closed, they don't think there's any other way to see. But to the People, sleep is a different world. When we sleep, we see different things."

"I don't get it."

Brown Eagle put an arm around Jed's shoulders. "Why do you have to? If you don't understand why the sky is blue, does it make it another color? Just because you don't know where something comes from doesn't make it less real. Come on." He guided Jed toward the kiva, but as they approached the ladder, Jed hesitated, remembering the strange loss of time he'd experienced when he'd gone into the kiva on his last visit to Kokatí.

"Wh-What's going to happen?"

"Who knows?" Brown Eagle countered. "Maybe nothing. Maybe we'll just sit for a while and I'll tell you stories, like I did when you were still five years old." He nudged Jed forward, and Jed climbed down into the gloom of the subterranean chamber. As always, a fire crackled in the pit, but the suffocating heat that built up in the day had long since dispersed through the hatchway. Tonight, the room held only an intimate warmth, with none of the stultifying closeness that bore in on it when the sun was at its zenith.

"You can learn practically anything down here," Brown Eagle told him as they seated themselves on the bench. "To me, this place is a doorway. I can sit here for hours, looking out at things I can't see anywhere else. If I want, sometimes I can even pass through the door and go to other places." He grinned at Jed. "Tonight, for example. I went with Rakantoh tonight, and spoke to you."

Jed smiled nervously. "Come on, you don't think I'm gonna believe that, do you?" But even as he spoke, he remembered the word that had risen from the bird's throat, a word he had heard in his grandfather's voice.

"Look at the fire," Brown Eagle told him. "Watch the flames. Let yourself drift. Let the fire guide you, and don't be afraid."

Jed leaned back against the stone wall. For a few minutes he looked around the dimly lit chamber, peering into the shadows around its circumference, examining the stones that paved the floor. But soon the fire itself seemed to beckon to his eyes and he stared into the flames themselves.

For a while he saw nothing, but slowly the flames began to take on shapes, and he began to imagine that they had come alive. Amorphous forms began to appear—a brilliantly hued snake slithered among the coals, only to disappear a second later, transformed into a bird which rose up from the ashes, then disappeared as quickly as it had come.

The fire came alive, and a whole new world appeared within the stone ring that surrounded it. Life came and went, strange creatures lived for a moment, then died, or were transformed into something else. Jed felt his mind begin to expand and reach out toward the world within the fire, wanting to explore every corner of it.

The fire grew then, surrounding him, and suddenly he himself was walking among the coals. Yet he felt no fear, no burning of his flesh; and his nostrils, instead of filling with the acrid aroma of smoke, thrilled instead to the myriad perfumes of the desert night— sage and juniper, and the scents of earth.

A bird appeared before him, the same bird he'd seen in his dream, and when the bird spread its wings to soar into the sky, Jed let himself go with it.

He rose out of the fire, drifted like the smoke up through the hatchway and into the coolness of the night sky. The huge eagle rose beside him, and Jed felt as if he could reach out and touch the creature's feathers. He reached out. Suddenly the bird turned on the breeze and soared higher.

As they rose upward, Jed gazed down on the pueblo spread along the edge of the mesa. From the sky it seemed a perfect reflection of the landscape around it. The plazas appeared to wander through the buildings just as the floor of the desert meandered among the mesas that lay scattered across it, and the whispers of smoke that rose from the firepits of the village gathered over it like so many clouds. Seen from the night sky, Kokatí seemed perfect.

Jed wheeled with the great bird and sailed out over the canyon. There was a coldness to the air above the lake, and for a moment Jed felt as if he was going to fall out of the sky and plunge into the waters below. He could stand to look into their black depths for only a moment, for a feeling of desolate loneliness and longing came over him, wrenching at his spirit. Then he was above the ugly concrete scar of the dam, and the canyon spread out before him. Even from the great height at which he soared, he could hear the soft babbling of the stream as it made its way through the rocks, and hear the muted rustlings of small animals scavenging in the night.

The mouth of the canyon opened before him, and the vastness of the desert spread away from the banks of the wash. He breathed deeply, sucking the clean air into his lungs, feeling the rush of the wind against his face.

But a moment later his nostrils recoiled as they were choked with a noxious odor, and Jed realized he was above the refinery now. Like a hideous pit of vipers, the tangle of blackened pipes writhed among themselves, twisting around the furnaces that glowed with the light of Hell and belched fumes into the sky. Sickened, he turned away, only to be faced with the oil fields themselves, the drilling rigs poised like giant insects sucking the blood from the planet's body. Once again that bleakness of spirit overcame him; once more he turned away.

He was above the village now, and in the distance he could see the angry glare of artificial light, far too bright against the darkness of the night, and he flew toward it.

Below him now was the ungainly Victorian shape of the Morelands' house, all its windows glowing brightly, as if its occupants were trying to fend off the night itself.

There was a movement then, and Jed's eyes shifted. A figure was moving through the night, darting across the desert, crouched low to the ground. Jed let himself drop downward, following closely as the shadow dodged among the boulders and trees. Then at last he lost interest, drifting once more on the wind, feeling at one with the sky.

He let his eyes close, let his mind soar free . . .

And now it was morning, and the kiva was already beginning to take on the heat of the sun as well as the fire. Jed blinked and stretched, prepared for the pain he expected to wash over him as he flexed his muscles after the many hours of sitting on the hard stone bench.

But his body felt relaxed, as if he'd been sleeping all night.

Yet in his mind all the images he'd seen as he stared at the fire, and then imagined himself soaring free with the great bird, were still clear.

Nor were they the vague, fleeting fragments of dreams that sometimes caught in his memory for a few seconds upon awakening, only to disappear forever a moment later. No, these were clear memories, as bright and vivid as his memories of riding up to the mesa with Jude; as vivid, indeed, as his ride up the mesa last night in his father's truck.

The memories were not the memories of dreams at all. They were memories of something that truly happened. As the realization hit him, he felt a hollowness in his belly and his heart began to pound. When he turned to his grandfather, his face frightened, Brown Eagle only chuckled softly.

"What happened?" the old man asked. "What did you see?"

Jed did his best to explain the strange thing that had happened to him during the night, but even as he listened to his own words he realized they sounded crazy.

It was impossible, all of it.

But when he was finished, Brown Eagle nodded. "The bird is Rakantoh," he said, his eyes fixing once more on the fire. "He is the totem of our clan. What you felt when you were over the lake was what he feels. His home is there somewhere, under the water, and he tried to go back. But he can't." He laid a gentle hand on Jed's knee. "Maybe he feels the way you do," he went on. "Maybe he feels he has no home and doesn't belong anywhere. But it's not true, of course." Brown Eagle sighed heavily. "His home is still there. Someday he will reclaim it."

Jed made a hollow snorting sound. "Yeah?" he asked. "How?"

Brown Eagle shook his head. "Some things none of us can know." He stood up and moved toward the ladder. "Time for you to go," he said. "Up here time might not mean much, but down in Borrego your father will be worried about you."

Jed steered the truck down the winding road that led off the mesa, then stopped at one of the turns to look out over the desert. In the distance he could see the refinery and the oil fields, something he'd seen all his life. But this morning, after what happened to him during the night, they looked different.

They looked wrong.

Wrong, and somehow evil. He drove more slowly now, looking at all the things the people of Borrego had brought to the area.

The refinery and the dam, and paved roads and electric cables.

Great pipes, shooting straight across the desert like scars made by a surgeon's scalpel.

All the things that were supposed to make life better for the people who had built them. But as he thought about it now, he realized that wasn't quite what had happened.

For the people of Borrego, unlike the Kokatí, had become slaves to what they had built, spending most of their time tending to the machinery that was supposed to take care of them.

The only good thing, he supposed, was that at least most of them didn't know they were slaves.

Idly, he wondered what would happen if they ever found out . . .

"Well," Judith Sheffield said, glancing at the clock and dropping her chalk on the ledge below the blackboard, "shall we all line up and play kindergarten?"

The sound of laughter rippled through the class, and Gina Alvarez grinned. "Maybe we should all pin our permission slips to our shirts," she suggested.

Judith smiled at her. When she'd briefed the class earlier about what was to occur at exactly 8:45 that morning, she'd made no attempt to disguise her disdain of Stuart Beckwith's precise logistical plans. Indeed, she'd hardly listened at the staff meeting yesterday afternoon, when he'd made his laborious explanation of how the distribution of flu shots was to be carried out. It had sounded to her more like a military campaign than a simple inoculation, and as soon as he'd begun repeating himself—which had happened in about the second minute of his presentation—Judith found herself thinking not about the logistics of administering the shots, but of the shots themselves.

After all, it was only last spring that she'd heard that flu shots were no longer going to be administered on a mass basis. If people wanted them, they were going to have to get them privately. Nor, for that matter, had she heard anything about an epidemic sweeping the country, which was the kind of thing that invariably got some mention on the evening news. Finally, out of pique at what she considered Beckwith's wasting of the staff's time, she'd decided to call her doctor in Los Angeles, who was also a close friend. "Actually," Sally Rosen had told her, "there is an epidemic going on, a small one, though, and pretty well localized in New England. But there's no inoculation against it. It's some new strain." Judith hadn't made a big deal about it; indeed she'd soon been more interested in hearing about Sally's latest boyfriend. Then, when Greg had arrived at the Morelands' the night before, with the news of Max's death, it had vanished from her mind completely.

This morning, as Frank scribbled his name on the inoculation permission slip Jed had left for him on the refrigerator door— and which was now in Judith's purse—she'd remembered her conversation with Sally, and gone to talk to Beckwith as soon as she'd arrived at the school.

He'd pasted a smile on as she stepped into his office, but it had immediately disappeared when she'd told him she had some questions about the shots the students were to receive that day.

"Really," he'd said, his eyes fixing on her as if he'd just detected a cockroach creeping across the floor of his office. "I hadn't been aware of your medical background, Judy."

"It's not my background," Judith replied. "It's a friend of mine. I happened to be talking to her yesterday. She told me there's no epidemic around here, and even if there were, there's no immunization shot available."

Beckwith's scowl deepened. "I'm afraid you're talking to the wrong person," he said. "It was Greg Moreland who arranged for these shots to be given. If you have a problem, you should take it up with him."

Judith felt her face burning. "It just seems to me that if there's any question—" she began, but this time Beckwith didn't let her finish.

"What you're saying is that you expect me to jeopardize the students' health simply because some friend of yours hasn't kept up with this epidemic."

"If that's the way you want to put it, fine!" Judith replied, then wished she'd been able to keep the anger out of her voice. But it was too late.

"That is the way I want to put it, Judy," Beckwith had told her. "And until you're the principal here, I think you'd be well advised to leave administrative decisions up to me. Now, if you'll excuse me, I have a great deal of work this morning." He'd nodded toward the door in a gesture of dismissal that Judith had found infuriating. Still, he was right in one way—the shots were his business, and Greg Moreland's business, not hers.

"Okay," she said now, "let's go." She watched in amusement as the class trooped out of the room, their permission slips neatly pinned to their chests just as Gina had suggested.

Lining themselves up in alphabetical order, they all joined hands like a kindergarten class trooping through a museum. "Do we get cookies and milk if we're good?" someone asked.

Despite herself, Judith laughed out loud. "I'm just hoping none of you embarrasses me by passing out," she replied. Then, deciding that if the class were going to make a joke out of it, she might as well too, she stepped to the head of the line.

Stuart Beckwith was waiting outside the nurse's office, a clipboard in his hand, and Judith had to suppress an urge to snap him a sharp salute. His eyes swept her class, and a flicker of anger crossed his face as he saw the slips pinned to their chests. "Well, at least you're prompt," he observed tightly. "Line them up against the wall. Laura will be ready for them in a moment."

Judith glanced at the class, who, not being deaf, had managed to translate the principal's words for themselves, then moved closer to Gina Alvarez. "You didn't see Jed this morning, did you?" she asked, hoping her words sounded as casual as she intended them.

Gina shook her head. "Maybe he's already got the flu," she suggested.

Or maybe he's upset about me sleeping with his father, Judith said to herself. And yet, when he'd left last night, he'd actually seemed pleased. In fact, she reflected, he'd seemed downright smug about it.

Her thoughts were interrupted as the last of the preceding class emerged from the nurse's office. Beckwith, still posted against the far wall, nodded tersely at Judith. She stepped into the nurse's office, and Laura Sanders smiled at her. "All set?" she asked.

"All lined up, just as Beckwith wanted," Judith replied as she handed that morning's attendance report—the space next to Jed's name still blank—to Laura. Then her eyes fell on the boxes containing the disposable syringes, and she frowned as she recognized the bright red UniChem logo emblazoned on each of them.

"Okay," Laura said. "Bring them in."

Judith stepped out into the hall and waved the class inside. The first in line was Gina Alvarez.

Gina unpinned her permission slip, handed it to the nurse, then rolled up her sleeve. Then, as Laura Sanders slipped a needle beneath Gina's skin, Jed Arnold appeared. He waved and started toward Judith, grinning broadly.

Judith glanced back into Laura's office. The shot administered, the nurse pulled the needle out of Gina's arm, but instead of throwing it away immediately, she carefully copied a number from the syringe onto the attendance sheet on the clipboard. Judith frowned. She'd seen inoculations before—dozens of them, in her years of teaching—but she'd never seen anything like this. Suddenly, as all the elements came together, a warning bell sounded in her head.

No epidemic, at least not around here.

No vaccination, even if there was an epidemic.

Needles, supplied by UniChem, on the day UniChem was taking over the town's single major employer.

Judith glanced around. Beckwith was nowhere to be seen. Jed was next to her now, still smiling. "I know I'm late," he began, "but I couldn't help it. I—"

Judith didn't let him finish. "Go back out," she said, her voice an urgent whisper. "Go back outside, and don't come in until the second period bell."

Jed stared at her, mystified. "What?" he began. "What's going on? I got here as—"

"Never mind!" Judith exclaimed. "Will you just do it? I'll tell you later on, at lunchtime."

Jed still hesitated. What was wrong? Was she mad at him or something? Then he saw the look in her eyes and realized that it wasn't anger.

It was fear.

He backed away, then turned and disappeared down the hall.

Only when he was gone did Judith turn back to her class, watching in uneasy silence as the rest of her students received their shots.

She had no idea what the purpose of these inoculations was. But she was suddenly very certain they had nothing whatever to do with the flu.

Thirteen

With tired eyes Paul Kendall surveyed the three people gathered in the darkly paneled room. He'd been up most of the night; he'd spent most of those long hours here in this very office, the office that only yesterday had been Max Moreland's—and now was his. In a gesture that was not lost on the group gathered opposite him, he moved behind the immense desk and lowered himself into the large leather swivel chair.

Kendall's eyes moved from one face to another as he tried to read the minds of these men to whom he had been a total stranger only yesterday, but for whom, just half an hour ago, he had become of paramount importance. Now that he had countersigned the papers

Max had left in the top drawer of his desk, the deal was done. UniChem was in control of Borrego Oil.

The men in the room were gazing at him guardedly now, their expressions half expectant, half apprehensive. Except for Greg Moreland, of course, who had been for the sale right from the start. Indeed, had it not been for the rumors that had begun last night, and continued to fly around the town this morning—rumors that wouldn't exist at all if Frank Arnold hadn't lost control of himself— Kendall's job right now would be much simpler.

He brushed the thought aside, concentrating not on what had already happened, but on what needed to happen now.

Otto Kruger, of course, he already knew. Kruger was mean, and essentially weak, but would do whatever was needed without wasting anyone's time with unnecessary questions.

Ted Whittiker, though, was another story. The mayor of Borrego was a politician, which meant that above and beyond anything else, in the end he would be worried only about his own skin. The impact of UniChem's acquisition of Borrego Oil would matter to him only in terms of votes.

Finally there was Greg Moreland. Though Kendall knew he could deal with the change in management without Greg Moreland's presence, he also knew the transition would be accepted in a far more positive way with Max's sole male heir offering his full support. And that, at least, Kendall knew he could count on. Greg had assured him the papers would be signed today, and indeed they had been. Already, Greg's cooperation had made the takeover much easier.

"Okay," he said, passing each man a folder that contained both a copy of the executed agreement between Max and UniChem, and a copy of the hastily constructed outline of his proposed plan of action. "We all know what's happened, and if the rest of you have heard the same rumors I've heard today, then you all know we've got a problem."

"The only problem we have is Frank Arnold," Otto Kruger interrupted. "It seems to me the first thing you ought to do is fire him."

Kendall's eyes fixed coolly on Kruger. "I'm not firing him or anybody else, Otto," he said. "Frankly, though I wish it hadn't happened, I can understand what must have been in Arnold's mind last night." He could almost hear Ted Whittiker's silent sigh of relief. Nothing would lose a mayor votes faster than a mass firing, even if he couldn't be held directly responsible. "The point of this meeting," he went on, "is for me to find out if I have your support. I intend to put my cards on the table, and I'd appreciate it if you'd put yours the same place. I don't know if there are rumors I haven't heard, but if there are, this is the time and place for me to hear them.

I want to answer every question you have, and then, if you're satisfied with my answers"—he grinned encouragingly—"we can get down to the business of getting this company going again." He sat back in the chair, predicting that it would be the mayor who spoke first. He wasn't wrong.

Whittiker shifted in his chair and cleared his throat nervously. "I suppose what concerns us all most is the future of the refinery," he said.

"We intend to keep it going," Kendall promptly assured him. "As you know, it's going to be shut down today, until the problem at the dam is fixed. But—"

His words died on his lips as the door to the office flew open and Frank Arnold stormed in. Otto Kruger rose to his feet immediately, but Kendall, sizing up the situation instantly, motioned him to sit down again.

"What the hell's going on?" Frank demanded. His eyes, blazing with indignation, fixed on Kendall. "Judging by the fact that Whittiker's here," he growled, "I'm assuming this is something more than a management meeting. And if it is, it seems to me that I should have been invited, since I'm still president of the union local."

Before he spoke, Kendall shot Kruger one more warning glance. "If you'd gone to the plant this morning," he said, judging the redness in Arnold's eyes and taking a gamble, "Otto here would have brought you along with him. Have a seat, Frank."

Taken aback by Kendall's unexpected welcome, Frank stared uncertainly at the other man, then sank into a chair. Kendall turned his attention back to the group, but as he went on he made certain to address himself directly to Frank Arnold as often as he did to any of the others.

He talked steadily for nearly thirty minutes, outlining UniChem's plans to keep the refinery going and to expand it. There would be a huge investment of capital into Borrego Oil; within four years, employment would at least double.

"It all sounds good," Frank Arnold said after Kendall had finished sketching UniChem's plans. "But it seems to me there's a catch. The hydroelectric plant at the dam is already working to capacity. When," he added, "it's working at all. How are you planning to power this new refinery?"

"Power is hardly a problem," Kendall replied. He tossed a document to Frank. "That's a commitment from the state to run a major line up here."

Frank studied the paper for a moment, then eyed Kendall warily. "How'd you get this? Max Moreland tried for years, and couldn't get to first base."

Kendall smiled. "Shall we just say UniChem is a lot bigger than Borrego Oil?" he said. Not to his surprise, Ted Whittiker chuckled appreciatively. "I also want you all to know," he went on, this time addressing himself almost exclusively to Frank Arnold, "that we intend to fulfill the union contract, and bring the pay in the refinery up to industry standards."

Frank's face turned ruddy. "Are you saying I haven't been doing a good job for my men?"

Kendall held up his hands in a mollifying gesture. "All I'm saying is there's now enough money to pay everyone what he's worth," he said. "Everyone in this room, including me, knows you did the best you could for the workers, given the situation. My company did a lot of research on this outfit before we made our offer. There isn't much we don't know about it, and we believe it's worth every cent we spent and every other cent we plan to invest." He paused then went on, choosing his words carefully. "Now, there's one more thing I want to show you, he said, passing each of the men another sheet of paper. "This is the autopsy report on Max Moreland. Greg, here, brought it along this morning." His eyes came to rest on Frank. "I've already told everyone else in this room that I understand what happened last night, and I'm not holding it against you. But this town is going to be going through a lot of changes in a short time, and the fewer rumors we have flying around, the better. So I want all of you to know exactly what happened to Max Moreland. If nothing else, at least we can get that settled here and now.

Frank Arnold took the sheet of paper Kendall offered him and studied it carefully. It had been prepared by the county coroner, a man Frank had known most of his life. And the words were clear. Cause of death: massive cerebral hemorrhage in the region of the hypothalamus.

He absorbed the words slowly, then handed the page back to Kendall as his gaze shifted to Greg Moreland. "I'm sorry," he said, his voice turning gruff. "I was drunk last night, and out of order. I'll call Rita this afternoon and apologize to her too."

Greg Moreland nodded once as an acceptance of the apology, but said nothing.

Paul Kendall stood up and came around the desk as the rest of the men in the room rose to their feet too. "Well, how about it?" he asked. "Do I have your support?"

One by one the men shook his hand and assured him they were behind him.

Finally he came to Frank Arnold. "How about it?" Kendall asked. "Truce?"

Frank hesitated, his lips curving into a thin smile. "We'll see," he said. Then he turned and walked out the door.

Jed stood in the hall outside Judith Sheffield's room, waiting for the corridor to empty out before he went inside. He still wasn't certain how much he was going to tell her of what had happened last night. All morning, since he'd come back down onto the desert floor and the reality of Borrego, he'd been wondering himself exactly what had happened to him in the kiva.

Vivid as they were, his memories were impossible. He couldn't fly—no one could. And he had seen nothing on his journey with Rakantoh that he hadn't seen before—the view from the top of the mesa, of the refinery and the town, was a panorama he had viewed many times. No, he'd simply let the fire hypnotize him, and let his mind drift. His own imagination had conjured up all the rest.

The corridors finally emptied as the students hurried toward the cafeteria, and Jed at last stepped into the room. But when he looked at Judith, he hesitated. Instead of the smile he'd been expecting, she looked angry.

"Where were you last night?" she demanded. "If you think you can just go out and vandalize houses all night, I think you're going to find out you're wrong. When I tell Frank—"

Jed gaped at her. "What are you talking about?" he broke in.

Judith's eyes narrowed. "I talked to Rita Moreland during the morning break," she said, her voice cold. "She told me about the rock." When Jed didn't flinch at the word, but only looked puzzled, she felt the first pang of uncertainty. She had assumed that when Jed had left the house last night, knowing she was about to sleep with his father, he'd felt jealous. And he'd vented that jealousy by throwing a rock through a window of the house where she lived. And yet now, as she faced him, she was suddenly not so sure her assumption was correct. Could he really mask his guilt this well? She chewed nervously at her lower lip, then started over again. "Someone threw a rock through the Morelands' front door last night," she said. "There was a word on it. 'Bitch.' " She watched Jed carefully, but his expression still betrayed nothing more than bewilderment. "I— Well, I guess I simply assumed you did it," she finished.

Jed shook his head slowly, a memory already stirring in his mind. Then it came back to him. It was fuzzy at first, but as he focused in on it, the scene etched itself sharply in his mind.

There had been lights on in the Morelands' house, and he'd sailed closer.

A form, darting away from the house.

Dropping lower, following the running figure.

Suddenly, starkly, like a black-and-white landscape emerging in a photographer's darkroom, the scene came clear in his mind. From the shadows, the face of the figure came into focus.

"Randy Sparks," he said out loud.

Judith stared at him. "Randy Sparks?" she echoed.

Jed nodded. "I—I saw him," he said. Then, slowly, trying not to make the tale sound too unbelievable, he told her what had happened to him the previous night. When he was done, though, he could see that she didn't believe him.

"I see." Her voice was cold. "In that case, I think maybe both of us should go talk to Randy and see what he has to say."

To her own surprise, Randy Sparks looked almost guilty when he saw her, and only reluctantly responded to Jed's beckoning wave. They stood just outside the cafeteria, Randy slouching nonchalantly against the wall.

"What's up?" he asked.

"What's up is that you threw a rock through a window in the Morelands' front door last night," Jed said, fixing as closely on Randy's face as Judith.

Randy shook his head, his eyes averted. "I don't know what you're talkin' about—" he began, but Jed cut him off.

"I saw it, Randy," he said. "I saw you running away from the house."

"Bullshit!" Randy exploded. "There wasn't anybody out there! I made sure—" Too late, he realized his mistake. He swallowed hard, then managed to glare truculently at Judith. "What the hell did you expect?" he muttered. "After what you did to me yesterday..."

But Judith wasn't listening. Her mouth slightly agape, she was staring at Jed, her eyes searching his. Finally, impatiently, she turned back to Randy. "You'll pay for the window," she said, "and apologize to Mrs. Moreland. You scared her half to death."

Randy stared at the floor, but nodded miserably. "And you might also be interested to know," Judith added, "I wasn't even there. I was out for the night. So the next time you have a problem with me, make sure you know where I am before you come to—" She hesitated, searching for the right word, then went on, her voice sarcastic: "Shall we say before you come to 'talk' to me about it?"

Randy's head came up. "You mean you're not going to tell Beckwith?" he asked, his voice trembling like a guilty eight-year-old's. "Or the cops?"

Judith shook her head. "Let's just call a truce, okay?"

Randy swallowed once more and nodded. Then his eyes shifted to Jed. "Where the hell were you?" he demanded. "If you were close enough to see me, how come I didn't see you?"

Jed said nothing. A slow, sardonic grin spread over his face. "I'm a half-breed, remember?" he drawled. "Us Indians can sneak around where you guys can never spot us." Leaving Randy staring at his back, he turned and followed Judith back to her classroom.

"So do you believe me now?" Jed asked when the door closed behind him.

Judith dropped into the chair behind her desk, regarding him thoughtfully. "You know," she said, her voice vague, as if she were thinking out loud, "this kind of thing isn't exactly unheard-of." Jed frowned uncertainly. "There's a phenomenon called an out-of-body experience. There are a lot of reports of them from people who have come close to dying. They say they actually leave their bodies and can watch what's going on around them. There are reports of people who almost died in surgery—some of them did die, but were brought back to life—who can recount what happened when they died. What was done, what was said—everything. Yet they were completely unconscious at the time."

Jed looked doubtful as Judith fell silent, lost in thought. Then, softly, he asked, "You believe me, don't you?"

Judith sighed, nodding reluctantly. She glanced up at the clock on the wall. "Do you want to get some lunch? We still have twenty minutes."

Jed was about to agree, then remembered the note his third-period teacher had handed him. "I can't," he said. "I have to go to the nurse's office and get my shot." His eyes narrowed quizzically. "What was going on this morning?" he asked. "Why did you shove me out of there?"

Judith's expression hardened. She glanced toward the door as if she expected to see someone standing outside, listening. "I got you out of there," she told him, her voice dropping, "because I don't understand what those shots are all about, and I don't know why the kids are being given them."

"They're just flu shots—" Jed began, but Judith didn't let him finish.

"Maybe. But something is wrong." She told him about the conversation she'd had with Sally Rosen the day before. "The thing that really got to me," she finished, "was the UniChem label on the boxes."

Jed's eyes narrowed. "UniChem?"

Judith nodded. "It just seems strange to me that on the day UniChem is taking over Borrego Oil, they're also giving shots to every kid in town. Especially when someone I trust tells me there is no effective inoculation against the latest strain of flu."

"Jesus," Jed whispered, his tongue running over his lower lip. "What are you going to do?"

Judith shrugged. "I don't know," she said. "In fact, I don't even know what I ought to do. But I know I'd just as soon you skipped that shot."

Jed smiled crookedly. "That's okay by me," he said. "The last time I had a shot I passed out."

Together they headed back to the cafeteria, but as Judith toyed with the limp sandwich that was all that remained by the time they passed through the line, she kept thinking about those shots.

By the time her afternoon classes began, she had come up with an idea.

Judith stepped out into the hall, closing the door of the lounge behind her. It was almost four, and the school was nearly deserted, only a few teachers left in the lounge, lingering over gossip rather than work.

Across the hall, the door to Laura Sanders's office stood slightly ajar. Inside, Judith could see the boxes of syringes sitting on the table where Laura had apparently left them. Laura herself had come into the teachers' lounge a few minutes ago, looking harried and announcing that she intended to take a good long break. "I missed lunch waiting for Jed Arnold," she grumbled, rolling her eyes balefully at Judith, "and he didn't even show up. Can you beat that?"

Judith had shrugged sympathetically, then waited until Laura had settled into conversation with Elliott Halvorson. Certain that she had at least ten minutes to herself, she had finally slipped out of the lounge.

Now she hesitated, glancing in both directions.

The hall was empty.

Quickly, furtively, Judith crossed the hall, slipped into Laura's office and quietly shut the door behind her.

On the table, neatly stacked, were all the class lists of the day, duplicates of her own. Beside each name there was either a five-digit number or a notation that the student had been absent that day. Clipped to each class list were the permission slips that had been collected from the students.

On the floor by the table next to the window, boxes with the UniChem logo were carefully stacked. All but one of them were empty, but on the table itself were two more boxes. The seal on one of them was broken. Judith opened it. The box was nearly full. Good! No one would notice if one of the syringes disappeared. Making up her mind, she took one of the needles out of the box and started to slip it into her purse.

And then she saw the serial number neatly printed on the tube of the syringe.

She frowned, then picked up the class lists once more. Scanning through them, she counted the number of students from throughout the school listed as absent that day.

Twenty-two.

On the table was one box of twelve syringes, its seal unbroken.

The open box had contained ten more, but one of them was now in her hand.

Apparently UniChem had supplied exactly enough syringes to inoculate the entire student body, and had insisted on an accounting.

Judith's sense of unease over the whole inoculation program congealed into fear. Why would UniChem be so concerned about accounting for all the needles?

Still, because of what she'd seen that morning, she was prepared for this accounting system, and now flipped through the lists once more, until she found the one for her own first-period class.

The second name from the top was Jed Arnold's, and the space next to his name was still blank. She breathed a sigh of relief as she realized that, expecting him later in the day, Laura Sanders had not yet marked Jed as absent.

Judith fished in her purse and found the permission slip she'd taken from Frank's refrigerator that morning. Her eyes flitting guiltily toward the door, she added the slip to the stack attached to the top of the class list. Next she picked up a pen, tested it to make certain its ink matched that of the pen Laura had used to fill in the class lists, then carefully copied the number from the syringe she'd taken from the box into the space next to Jed's name.

The handwriting match wasn't perfect, but it was so close that she didn't think anyone would notice.

Leaving everything as she had found it, Judith slipped the syringe into her purse, and moved quietly to the door.

She listened for a moment, but heard nothing from the corridor outside.

Finally she opened the door a crack and peered out into the hall.

It was empty.

Unconsciously drawing her breath in, Judith pulled the door open and slipped through. Leaving it a few inches ajar, just as she had found it five minutes before, she walked quickly away, her mind already fully occupied with figuring out the fastest way to get the syringe to Sally Rosen in Los Angeles. And then she remembered Peter Langston.

She'd dated Peter in Los Angeles for a few months, until he'd moved to Los Alamos to take a position with a think tank. The work was highly technical, he'd explained, and secret. It was, he'd added, the opportunity of a lifetime.

And here was her opportunity: Peter was a chemist—he'd be able to tell her exactly what was in the syringe.

If Judith had looked back at that moment, she would have seen Stuart Beckwith emerge from his office and frown as he saw her disappear around the corner toward the cafeteria, then turn his attention to the open door to Laura Sanders's office.

He stood where he was for a moment, apparently lost in thought, then went to the nurse's office himself.

He scanned the lists carefully, then took his own count of the syringes.

He repeated the process, assuring himself that the number of needles matched the number of students who'd been absent that day.

Perhaps, he finally decided, he'd been wrong.

Perhaps Judy Sheffield hadn't been in Laura's office at all.

Still, as he left the nurse's office a moment later, he made certain the door was firmly closed, and locked it as well.

He made a mental note to reprimand Laura Sanders. Greg Moreland, after all, had made it absolutely clear that the syringes were to be kept under lock and key at all times.

Well, nothing had gone awry, so there was really no point in even mentioning the incident to Greg.

Laura Sanders, on the other hand, was another matter.

He went into the teachers' lounge, already silently relishing the tongue-lashing he was about to give her.

Fourteen

Frank drove quickly down the narrow dirt road that edged the canyon. Only a fraction of his attention was focused on driving, for the ruts in the road were so deep that the pickup essentially drove itself. His mind kept turning over what he'd seen at the dam.

He still wasn't certain why he'd decided to start poking around after the meeting in Max Moreland's office; he only knew that, despite Kendall's assurances to the contrary, he had not been expected to attend. He'd seen it in Otto Kruger's eyes.

He also knew, regardless of Kendall's claims, that UniChem's plans were not going to be nearly as beneficial to Borrego as Kendall maintained. Over the past two days, despite the hectic schedule of the plant shutdown, he'd still managed to do his homework, and now, on Thursday morning, he knew more about UniChem than Kendall—or anyone else, for that matter—suspected. This morning, with the shifts already juggled so he could attend Max's funeral, he'd decided to drive up to the dam and have a look around.

He hadn't liked what he'd seen.

Everywhere he'd looked, there had been signs of sloppy maintenance.

Greasy rags, which should have been stowed away in a fireproof bin until they were ready to be washed, were scattered haphazardly through the passages.

Valves had been allowed to rust and corrode, some of them so badly they should have been replaced weeks, if not months, earlier.

When he'd finally taken a look at the main flume, the shaft that carried water from the lake down through the dam to power the huge main turbine itself, he'd been downright scared. Cracks had developed in the flume's lining—cracks too big to have developed overnight, or even over a period of days. In fact, they'd been damned lucky they hadn't lost the entire turbine. If a sizable chunk of concrete had come loose, they would have had a major disaster on their hands.

When he'd asked Bill Watkins why the dam had been let go so badly, the operator had shrugged helplessly. "Otto just kept telling us to make do," he explained. "He kept telling us Max didn't have the money."

Though he'd said nothing, Frank knew that whatever Watkins believed, Otto Kruger had been lying to him. Max Moreland would have closed the dam down before he'd have let it run in the condition he had just observed.

As Frank's anger built, his foot pressed down on the accelerator and the truck shot forward. He knew Kruger would be at the plant, and no doubt Kendall was with him. Whatever they were up to Frank was not going to let them get away with it.

As he suspected, the two were in Kruger's office when Frank stormed in. Paul Kendall looked up, a smug smile playing at the corners of his lips as Frank spoke.

"I've just been up at the dam, Otto," Frank said, steel in his voice.

"And I want to know what the hell is going on. The shaft's ready to blow, and that didn't happen overnight."

"Now just a minute," Kruger broke in, his face livid. "Max Moreland ordered those maintenance cuts, not me—"

He'd given Frank the opening he was waiting for. Staring straight into the other man's eyes, he finished the sentence for him. "And Max, conveniently enough, isn't here to defend himself, right, Otto?"

Though he'd been careful to make no direct accusation, the implication was clear. Without another word, he turned and left the office.

Paul Kendall stared at the door Frank had just slammed, then turned to Kruger. "What's going on with him?" he asked. "I thought you had him under control."

Kruger's eyes fixed malevolently on Kendall. "He's shooting blind," he said. "He doesn't know what he's talking about."

Kendall regarded his plant supervisor darkly. "Well, if that's the way he wants to fight, there's a few things I can do too."

"Listen to Frank," Max said.

Rita Moreland froze. She felt suddenly cold, although above her the sun was blazing down, and she could feel the midday heat radiating from the sandstone boulder on which she sat; her legs, clad in a pair of worn jodhpurs, curled beneath her, her back as ramrod straight as ever.

She wasn't certain how long she'd been sitting there, high up on the mesa above her house, gazing out over the town.

It lay spread out before her, the sun glinting off the tin roofs of its small rectangular houses. Beyond the town she could see the refinery, and even a few of the oil wells. And then, in the distance, the mouth of Mordida Canyon, its sandstone walls sloping gently down to the desert floor, a winding double row of cottonwoods lining the banks of the Mordida wash as it emerged from the confines of the canyon itself.

She knew why she'd come to the mesa; it had always been one of Max's favorite places, indeed the only place where he could stand and gaze out over everything he and his father before him had built.

Gone now, all gone.

Her jaw clenched as she turned to look at Max.

He was standing a few yards from her, his hands on his hips, his eyes fixed on the distance. When he looked up, Rita's eyes instinctively followed her husband's.

High up, almost invisible against the brilliant blue glare of the sky, an eagle soared, its wings outstretched as it effortlessly rode the invisible currents of a thermal over the mesa.

As she watched, the bird drifted lower, and she imagined that it was coming down to look at her.

"He knows," Max said. "He knows everything."

Rita's eyes left the soaring eagle and returned to Max. Now he was smiling at her and his hand was outstretched, as if to take her own.

She stood up and took a step toward him, then another.

But he was no closer, and she suddenly felt a stab of fear.

She took another step, and then another. Then she was running, stumbling toward Max along the rough path hewn out of the mesa's crumbling sandstone. But no matter how fast she ran, Max seemed only to slip farther and farther away from her.

And yet he still smiled, and his hand was still outstretched. Then, so abruptly she didn't realize it had happened, her foot slipped and she lost her balance. She stumbled, fell, slipped over the edge of the path.

"Max!"

And then she was falling, tumbling through the air, and the eagle was swooping down toward her, its talons extended.

"Max!" she cried out again.

This time, as she cried out her husband's name, she woke from the dream.

She blinked in the late-morning sunlight, her whole body still trembling from the memory of the dream. Slowly she regained control of herself. She was all right, she repeated to herself. She was at home, in her bed, and nothing had happened to her at all.

Automatically she reached out to touch Max, reached out to feel his solid strength next to her in the bed.

He wasn't there; would never be there again.

Her hand, feeling suddenly heavy, dropped to the sheet, and for just a moment she wondered if she would be able to get through this day.

In only another hour she was going to bury Max, lay him to rest in the small graveyard on the edge of town, next to his father and mother.

Summoning her will, she threw off the covers and left the bed, moving to the window to close it against the growing heat of the day, but pausing to glance up toward the mesa. Even from here she could see the spot from which she'd fallen in the dream. High up, it was a dangerous place in the path, a place that Max had always warned her about. Even now, fully awake, she half expected to see him there. Almost against her will, her hand came up to wave to him.

But the path was empty, the mesa standing in its placid majesty like some great sentry looking out over the desert. And then, soaring high, she saw the eagle.

Now, in the morning sunlight, it looked exactly as it had in the dream, its wings fixed, circling slowly on whatever faint traces of breeze there might be, its eyes hunting the ground below for prey.

Except that, as in the dream, Rita had the strange sensation that the eagle was watching her.

Shivering despite the warmth of the morning, she closed the window and began dressing. But even as she slipped into the simple black silk dress she would wear to her husband's funeral, she heard once more the words he'd spoken to her in the dream.

"Listen to Frank."

She seated herself at the small vanity in her dressing room, then willed her hands to stop trembling as she began carefully applying the mask of makeup that would hide her emotions. One hour from now she would sit in the church, trying to look at Max's coffin without really seeing it, for she knew that if she let herself truly accept that it was Max inside that dark mahogany box, she might well lose the bulwark of self-control she had so carefully built since the moment she'd been told he was dead.

Finally satisfied with the image she saw in the mirror, she went downstairs, where Greg was already waiting for her in the breakfast room at the back of the house.

He stood as his aunt came into the room, and his eyes seemed to search her, as if looking for a chink in her serene armor. "Are you all right, Aunt Rita?"

Rita managed a slight smile. "I dreamed I was falling this morning," she said, apparently out of nowhere. Greg gazed blankly at her. "And it's odd, but Max was there, trying to help me," Rita went on. "But of course he couldn't, and it seemed I couldn't help myself either." She took a sip of coffee. "Have you ever dreamed you were falling, Greg?"

Greg frowned, trying to puzzle out what his aunt was saying. If there was some hidden message in her words, he couldn't fathom what it might be. "Everybody dreams of falling," he said at last.

Rita's eyes clouded for a moment as she remembered once more the words Max had spoken to her in the dream. "I haven't," she replied, setting the cup back on its saucer. "And I don't think I ever shall again."

An hour later Rita, with Greg at her side, watched the pallbearers slowly lower her husband's coffin into the hard ground of the cemetery. A dense crowd surrounded her, for nearly the whole town had turned out for Max Moreland's funeral, but still she felt alone, even with Greg on one side of her and Judith Sheffield on the other.

At last, as the pallbearers stepped back, she moved forward, stooped down, and picked up a clod of earth. She held it for a moment, and then, feeling eyes on her, she looked up.

A few feet away, on the other side of Max's grave, Frank Arnold stood watching her, his eyes glistening with the tears he refused to give in to.

Rita hesitated a moment, and yet again Max's words in the dream sounded softly in her head. Her eyes met Frank's and she smiled at him.

Her fingers closed on the lump of earth in her hand and the clod broke up, sifting down onto the coffin in the grave.

Rita looked up into the sky. There, as if at her command, the form of an eagle appeared, hovering for a moment, then wheeling around, its wings beating strongly. A moment later it disappeared over the rim of the mesa and was gone.

Rita stepped back from the grave, and as if accepting her silent signal, the townspeople began filing past, some of them adding their own small lump of earth to Max's grave, others pausing only to murmur soft condolences to his widow.

Finally Paul Kendall appeared, his face grave, his eyes dark with concern. "Rita," he said quietly. "I'm so sorry."

It was as if she didn't hear him, didn't even see him. Her eyes swept past him as if he didn't exist, and came to rest on another person, a person who seemed to have been waiting silently for the right moment to approach her.

"Frank," Rita said, her voice carrying clearly through the morning as she beckoned him to her side. "Come and stand with me, will you? Help me say goodbye to Max."

Paul Kendall's jaw tightened and his right hand clenched into an angry fist, then relaxed. He moved on, stepping aside so that Frank Arnold could take his place.

A few minutes later Kendall found Otto Kruger in the crowd.

"I've had it," he said, drawing Kruger aside. "I've had it with both of them. Clear?"

Kruger nodded, his lips twisting into a cruel smile. "Clear," he agreed.

At four o'clock that afternoon Frank Arnold wheeled his pickup truck into the dusty lot in front of the refinery gate and shut off the engine. There weren't many cars there—all but a handful of men had been laid off yesterday, and today more would go. It was only temporary, according to Kruger, but Frank didn't believe him any more than he believed Kendall. Why should they start up the refinery again when they could make more money by simply selling off the crude as it was pumped out of the ground?

An eerie feeling came over him as he moved through the refinery. The usual cacophony of hissing steam and clanging pipes was silent now, and there wasn't even the usual racket caused by the rattling out of the pipes during a regular shutdown.

Today the refinery had an atmosphere of death about it, and Frank kept glancing back over his shoulder, as if half expecting to see some strange specter closing in on him. But there was nothing there.

He came finally to the catalytic cracking plant at the far end of the refinery. When it was built thirty-odd years ago, the plant had been Max Moreland's pride and joy. It was a semiexperimental installation back then, and Max had been one of the few men in the country who was willing to take a gamble on the new refining process.

Now, though, it was as obsolete as the rest of the refinery. In the control room, as Frank began scanning the gauges, he wondered if maybe Max hadn't been right in selling out to UniChem. Now, with the deal done, and his own dream of taking the place over gone forever, he began to realize just what an expense it would take to bring the plant up to date. He sighed, but as the crew began drifting in for the afternoon shift, the sigh gave way to a frown.

"Where's Polanski?" he asked Carlos Alvarez.

Carlos shrugged. "Same place as Phil Garcia. Laid off this morning." He forced a humorless grin. "Good thing they're shutting us down, eh, amigo? There's nobody left to run it anyway."

"I've got to tell you," Frank said to Alvarez and the others who had gathered, his voice somber, "I wouldn't be surprised if the rest of the layoffs come today. We should be done by ten or eleven, and if I know Kruger, he'll be out here with the checks and the pink slips, even if it's the middle of the night."

Alvarez spread his hands philosophically. "So what can we do? It's not your fault." Then he brightened. "Anyway, I hear they're gonna move a lot of people up to the dam. Get it fixed right away, huh? Then we'll all be back in business."

Frank nodded, wishing he could believe it.

But that night, exactly as he'd predicted, Otto Kruger was waiting for them as he and the rest of the men came out the front gate.

"Damn it!" he heard Carlos mutter. "Here it comes."

Kruger, an appropriately serious expression on his face, handed out the envelopes, then turned to face Frank, his eyes glowing with malice. "I need to talk to you in my office," he growled.

Frank's eyes narrowed angrily as Kruger turned and fairly swaggered away, then he heard Carlos Alvarez's cautioning voice.

"Take it easy, Frank. Don't let him get your goat. Come down to the café afterward, and I'll buy you a beer."

As Alvarez and the rest of the crew climbed into their cars, Frank headed toward the supervisor's building. Inside, Kruger was lounging in his chair, hands behind his head, legs sprawled across his desk. "Don't bother to sit down, Arnold," he said, a satisfied smirk spreading across his face.

Frank remained where he was, standing next to the door. "You can't lay me off too, Otto," he said. "You're still going to need a mothball crew around here, and I'll be part of it."

Kruger shook his head. "It seems Kendall has something else in mind for you," he said. "He thinks—and don't ask me why—that your talents would be wasted around here."

Frank shifted his weight uneasily. From Kruger's smug look a few minutes ago, he'd been certain that he too was going to be laid off, despite the union rule dictating that his seniority would make him the last man to go. But apparently that wasn't going to happen. "Okay," he said, when it was obvious that Kruger would wait for him to ask about his new assignment. "What is it?"

"The dam," Kruger replied. "It seems Kendall's been studying the union rules, and given an emergency situation, he can assign you to pretty much anything he wants. At least," he added, his smirk broadening into a malicious grin, "for as long as the emergency lasts."

Frank tipped his head in silent concession. It was true, though it hadn't occurred to him that Kendall might use the emergency provision like this.

Kruger's grin spread even wider. "You don't know enough about the dam to be a foreman," he went on, "so you're going to be on one of the labor crews. Chopping concrete, Frank. Working down there in the shaft, where it's cold and dirty and cramped. Breaking up old concrete, and building forms to pour new. How do you like that?"

Frank knew what they wanted him to do. They wanted him to refuse the job and quit entirely.

And it wasn't Paul Kendall's idea at all. It was Otto Kruger's.

Once before, Frank had worked in the pipes. He could still remember the day ten years ago—long before he'd become a foreman—when he'd crept into one of the immense pipes during a shutdown, dragging the rattler behind him, intent on knocking the deposits of coke and sludge from the interior of the pipe.

But he'd panicked, and the pipe had seemed to close in on him, threatening to crush him, strangling his breath until he could barely even scream.

In the end they'd had to pull him out, so paralyzed with unreasoning terror that he couldn't move at all.

Max Moreland had told him to forget about it—that it could happen to anyone.

Otto Kruger, obviously, had not forgotten about it.

So now Frank was faced with a choice.

Accept the new assignment, in compliance with the rules that he himself had helped to formulate, or quit.

Quit, with no prospect of any other job.

He forced himself to keep his face impassive, and met Kruger's eyes. "All right," he said. "When do I start?"

Kruger frowned, and Frank knew his answer had thrown the man off balance. Then Kruger appeared to recover.

"Tomorrow," he said. "And you know what? I think I might just come out and take a look. Should be fun, watching you crawl into those shafts."

As Kruger began to laugh, Frank walked out.

Fifteen

"Maybe you should quit," Judith suggested early the next morning. She'd spent the night with Frank again. He had called shortly before midnight, and though he hadn't managed to ask her directly to come over, his voice told her how upset he was. Finally, it had been Rita Moreland who convinced her to drive over in the middle of the night.

"Go," the older woman had said. "I don't expect to sleep much myself tonight, and I have to get used to being alone in this house."

So Judith had driven to the house on Sixth East and they had sat up until almost two, she listening and Frank talking. Eventually they'd gone to bed and made love, but when it was over, Frank had lain beside her, his body still tense. "I don't know whether I can do it," he'd said, his voice hollow in the darkness. "Just thinking about those shafts gives me the willies."

"You'll be all right," she'd reassured him once more, but even as she spoke the words, she knew they were meaningless. The rest of the night had been spent restlessly as Frank tossed and turned.

Now he said tersely, "I can't afford to quit."

"I know," Judith sighed. "But if you're—"

Her words were cut off by the shrill jangling of the telephone. Frank picked it up. "Hello?" He listened for a moment, then his brows arched and he held the phone toward her. "For you," he said, puzzled. "A man."

"Judith?" It was Peter Langston. "What's going on? First Mrs. Moreland tells me you're not home, and then a man answers at the number she gives me. May I assume you've thrown me over completely and are now having an affair?"

"Peter!" Judith exclaimed, ignoring the question. "I was going to call you in a couple of hours. Have you found anything?"

The timbre of Peter's voice changed instantly. "I have, and I haven't," he said carefully. "I can't tell you what was in that syringe you sent me, but I can tell you that whatever it is, it's not a flu vaccine."

Judith felt a chill, and the look on Frank's face told her the blood had drained from her own. "Then what is it?" she asked.

"I don't know," Peter went on. "I gave a sample of it to our lab guys, and they were able to determine that it's not a vaccine for flu, or anything else. In fact, it seems to be a simple saline solution, but with some impurities in it."

"Impurities?" Judith repeated, her brows knitting into a deep frown. "What kind?"

"I wish I could tell you," Peter replied. "I'm working on it, but it's going to take a couple of days. Okay?" Judith managed a wry smile. "Do I have a choice?" she asked.

"I'm sorry," Peter told her. "This place is all tied up with government work, and I just have to work this thing in when I can." He paused, but when Judith said nothing he continued, "Look—I'll do my best, and get back to you as soon as I know something."

Judith nodded automatically. "Thanks," she said. Then: "Peter? Why would anyone want to inject a saline solution into a bunch of kids?"

There was a silence, then Peter spoke once more.

"That's the thing that's got me curious," he said. "I can't think of any reason at all. So whatever the reason, it must have something to do with the impurities in the stuff. Is anything happening to the kids up there? Anything at all?"

"Not that I can see. And believe me, I've been watching. But nothing's happening to the kids at all. In fact, I was starting to think I was wrong about the shots."

"Okay," Peter sighed, his own bafflement clear in his voice. "And who knows? Maybe there *isn't* anything to it."

―――――

But as Judith hung up the phone she knew that Peter hadn't believed his own last words any more than she did. You didn't give a whole school full of kids a mass inoculation for no reason at all.

As she was telling Frank what Peter had told her, Jed came in and slid into his chair at the kitchen table, instantly plunging into the business of eating the plate of pancakes Judith put in front of him. As she finished her recounting of the call, her eyes moved to Jed. "What about it?" she asked. "Have you noticed anything about any of the kids? Anything I might have missed?"

Jed shrugged. "They're not dropping dead, or anything like that." He finished off the last morsel of pancakes, then picked up his book bag and headed for the back door. Abruptly he turned back, his eyes fixing on his father. "Dad?"

Frank looked up inquiringly. There was an odd look on Jed's face, and when he spoke again, his voice quavered.

"Be careful today, Dad. Okay?"

Frank felt a sudden tightening in his throat. It was the first time in years—perhaps even the first time since Alice had died—that Jed had exposed his feelings so openly. "I—I will, son," he said, surprised at the gruffness in his own voice. "And you too, right?"

But Jed shook his head. "I'm okay," he said. "It's you I'm worried about. Just be careful."

Before either Judith or Frank could say anything else, he turned and disappeared out the back door. At last Frank turned to Judith. "Do you have any idea what might have brought that on?"

Judith chewed thoughtfully at her lower lip for a moment, her eyes fixed on the back door. "He must have heard us talking last night," she said. And yet just before Jed had left, she'd seen an odd look in his eyes.

The same kind of odd look he'd had as he'd told her about his experience up at Kokatí three nights ago, when he'd seen things he couldn't possibly have seen.

Had he seen something else last night?

Frank Arnold shivered as he stared into the pipe. He hated the dam, hated the total lack of natural light in the narrow winding passages that honeycombed the massive concrete structure; hated the chill of the place, whose temperature never varied from 54° Fahrenheit; hated, most of all, his unreasoning fear of being trapped within the dam's confining spaces.

He'd stood above the dam that morning, looking down at it from the canyon's rim, telling himself it was perfectly safe, that there was no reason to fear it.

But even then his emotions had threatened to betray him, as he began to think about going down into it—not for a brief tour of inspection like last week's, but to spend the next eight hours crawling through its maze of passages.

Brown Eagle had suddenly appeared beside him that morning, seeming to come out of nowhere.

"It is a bad place," he'd said, as if reading Frank's mind. Frank had looked up, startled. He nodded grimly, then managed a grin. "Oh, I don't know. Not really much different from a kiva, I suppose. Dark, and closed in. Seems to me you'd like it."

Brown Eagle eyed Frank solemnly. "The kiva honors nature," he said. "The dam destroys it."

Frank had heard it all before, heard Brown Eagle ramble on for hours sometimes, talking about the patience of the Kokatí, and his faith that in the end the land would be restored to them. Then everything would be as it had been before the white men ever came. But the white men had been around for centuries now, and the dam for more than half of one, and Frank sometimes wondered if the Kokatí ever noticed that their spirits never seemed to do much about the situation. His eyes had drifted back to the dam for a moment. When he'd turned to speak to Brown Eagle again, the Indian was gone, having disappeared back into the desert as silently as he'd come.

Now, as he prepared himself to creep through the access hatch into the pipe that would take him to the main power shaft, opening into it just above the turbine itself, he heard Brown Eagle's words once more and decided he agreed with him. The dam was, indeed, a thoroughly bad place, and right now—if he weren't inside it—he might almost wish that the spirits, whatever they were, would destroy it.

He took a deep breath, hunched his shoulders, and snapped on the miner's light attached to his hard hat. Then he pushed his way through the hatch into the pipe itself.

Instantly, the space seemed to shrink around him, and he felt an almost irresistible urge to draw his knees up, push his back against the tight curve of concrete above him, and try to rise to his feet.

But he couldn't stand up, couldn't even get to his knees. The pipe, barely two feet in diameter, forced him to creep along, using only his fingers and toes to find slippery holds in the algae-covered concrete.

He felt bands of panic tighten around his chest, and stopped moving, concentrating his entire being on fighting the overwhelming urge to thrash himself free from the constrictions of the pipe.

He heard a sound, a crunching noise, and wanted to scream out as he imagined himself trapped inside the pipe as parts of the dam gave way.

No, he told himself. *It's not breaking up, and the pipe's not getting smaller and I'm not trapped.*

He began talking to himself, whispering silently, giving himself a steady stream of encouragement.

It helped to keep the panic slightly at bay, and after a moment he began creeping forward again, down the pipe's slope.

He had moved no more than a few yards when the light on his helmet went out and he was plunged into total darkness. Instinctively he clamped his eyes shut, as if by doing that he could convince himself the suffocating blackness wasn't real.

Clumsily he pulled the hat off his head and fumbled with the switch on the miner's lamp. The light came on for a second, then went out again.

Panic was creeping up on him inexorably now. Before, he'd at least been able to see the pipe stretching away in front of him.

Now there was nothing but blackness around him, and everywhere he moved, the unforgiving hardness of cold concrete.

Terror loomed up inside him, and he tried to rear up to face it head-on.

The pipe let him move only an inch, then stopped him.

The terror grew, and he felt his mind beginning to give way.

He was going to die here. He knew it. The pipe was going to crush him, close around him, snuff out his life the way it had snuffed out the dim light of the lantern.

He felt as though he were going to explode. Finally he gave way to the panic, thrashing himself against the walls of the pipe, as if to break loose from the clutches of the concrete.

He knew now what it would feel like to be buried alive, knew the hopelessness of it.

He clawed at the concrete, his fingernails tearing and breaking as he scratched away the algae and gouged at the stone and cement beneath.

Vaguely, he was aware of another sound, a keening wail that echoed though the pipe like the cry of a tortured animal.

But it wasn't an animal.

It was himself.

And as he understood that the scream was his own, a tiny fragment of his mind escaped the terror and took hold of him.

He began moving again, but no longer with the mindless churning the panic had dictated.

Now he was seized with a single overwhelming imperative.

He would keep his mind intact, and escape from the pipe.

He slithered faster, pushing himself along, his eyes still shut against the terrifying blackness.

He could hear something ahead of him now. He must be near the end of the pipe, but he dared not stop, dared not even open his eyes to search for a faint glimmer of light.

He had to get out. Had to escape. Had to keep going.

And then, suddenly, the pipe fell away beneath him.

His eyes flew open and he reached out wildly, searching for a handhold to stop his fall.

It was too late.

His own momentum carried his body out of the pipe, and then he was in the main shaft itself. There was light around him, shining down from above, and he could hear voices calling out to him.

Instinctively he twisted himself around as he fell, so that when he hit the turbine, it was his feet that made contact first.

He thought he heard a distinct snapping sound from somewhere, and then a blinding pain gripped his right leg.

He came to a stop.

"Don't move, Frank," he heard a voice saying.

He couldn't identify where the voice was coming from, couldn't see its source.

But it didn't matter, really. He knew he couldn't move, even if he tried. Blackness closed in around him again, but this time it didn't bring the stark terror of panic with it. This time, it brought only relief from the pain in his leg.

He had no idea how long he'd been unconscious, but when he opened his eyes, he was stretched out on the floor of one of the passages. He tried to sit up, but the pain in his leg stopped him even more effectively than Bill Watkins's restraining hands.

"Take it easy, Frank," Watkins told him. "You're okay, and we've got an ambulance on its way. Shouldn't be more than a few more minutes."

Frank winced against the pain, then forced himself to relax. "What happened?" he breathed.

"You panicked. Came shooting out of the feeder pipe like all the demons of Hell were chasing you. Except when you came out, there wasn't anything to grab onto."

Frank groaned softly. "How far'd I fall?"

Watkins smiled. "Not that far. Fifteen feet maybe." Then his expression sobered. "You were lucky. If you'd hit headfirst, you'd have broken your neck instead of your leg."

There were sounds of footsteps echoing hollowly in the passage, and two men in white uniforms appeared, followed by Greg Moreland. While the medics began unfolding a portable stretcher, Greg himself knelt beside Frank and took a syringe out of a small medical kit.

"What's that?" Frank asked, eyeing the needle suspiciously.

"Morphine," Greg told him.

Frank shook his head. "Forget it," he said. "It doesn't hurt that much."

"Don't be a hero," Greg replied, slipping the needle into a vein in Frank's forearm and pressing the plunger. "It might not hurt now, but when we start carrying you up topside, it's going to hurt like hell."

Frank started to protest once more, but as the drug quickly began to take hold, a feeling of euphoria came over him.

What the hell, he thought. Might as well enjoy it.

As the medics eased him onto the stretcher, he felt his mind begin to drift. Then they picked the stretcher up, and Frank closed his eyes until, a few minutes later, he felt the warmth of the sun on his face.

He blinked in the sunshine.

Overhead, the sky was clear, and an even deeper blue than he remembered having ever seen before. And then, soaring above the canyon, he saw an eagle.

His vision seemed to telescope, and suddenly he thought the eagle's head had changed, and it wasn't a bird at all that was staring down at him from the sky.

For a moment he thought it was his father-in-law, Brown Eagle.

Bullshit, he told himself. It's just the morphine. I'm stoned out of my mind, that's all.

He blinked, and looked up into the sky again.

The bird was gone.

Otto Kruger looked up at the sound of the ambulance siren and smiled with satisfaction. He'd already heard what had happened to Frank. It had worked. Frank was going to be out of his hair for a while. His musings were interrupted by a muffled roar, and he turned to gaze southward. Flying low, just clearing the top of the mesa, a huge helicopter was approaching. Hanging below it, suspended by steel cables, was a large object shaped like an enormous dish.

"Here she comes!" Otto yelled to the crew he'd been overseeing for the last two days.

The five men looked up, shielding their eyes from the sun, then scuttled off the concrete pad whose wooden forms they'd only torn away an hour ago. The chopper came closer, then hovered overhead, the huge antenna, complete with its rotating base, suspended only three feet above its pad. As Otto shouted orders, three of the men moved forward to guide the antenna onto the centering pins that rose up from the freshly hardened concrete. Two minutes later the antenna settled down and the men quickly freed the steel cables. Otto waved to the pilot, and the 'copter rose once more into the air, swung around, and headed back south.

"Okay," Otto called to the crew as the pounding of the chopper's huge blades began to dwindle, "let's get her bolted down, and then start hooking her up. Kendall wants it in full operation by five o'clock this afternoon."

One of the men threw Kruger a dark look. "Who the hell do you think we are?" he muttered, already beginning the job of sorting out the leads that emerged from a piece of PVC pipe that had been laid into the concrete. A shadow passed over him, and he looked up to see Otto Kruger scowling at him.

"You being paid to talk or work?" Kruger demanded.

The man rose to his feet, towering three full inches above Kruger. When he spoke, his voice held a dangerous edge. "Look, smart boy," he said. "It takes exactly two and a half days to put one of these things in, start to finish. Five guys, two and a half days. This is the sixth one this crew has put in. Everything's on schedule. The pad, the chopper, the pipe down into the canyon. Only thing that's going to hold us up now is you. So why don't you just shut up and let us do our job, huh? Then we'll be out of this dump and you can go back to being King Shit. Okay?"

Kruger glared angrily at the man, but then subsided. Kendall had told him this crew knew what they were doing; in fact, Kendall had told him merely to give them whatever they needed. "Just make sure you get it done," Kruger growled. "If it isn't, it's your asses, not mine."

"Sure," the big man replied, deliberately spitting into the dirt at Kruger's feet. "I'll remember that." Turning his back on Kruger, he went to work. By five-thirty Borrego Oil Company, the newest acquisition of UniChem, would be fully integrated into the company's worldwide communications network.

As if, the man reflected, anybody really cared.

Borrego Oil Company, like its town, was a failing backwater.

In fact, he couldn't imagine why UniChem even wanted it.

What the hell could they possibly do with it?

Judith Sheffield was just about to leave her classroom to go have a cup of coffee in the teachers' lounge when her door slammed open and Jed, his face pale, rushed in.

Rising to her feet, her heart pounding with a premonition of what was coming, she took a step toward him. "What is it, Jed?" she asked. "What's happened?"

Jed leaned against the wall for a moment, catching his breath from the dash up the stairs to Judith's room on the second floor. "It's Dad," he gasped. "They just called Beckwith from the hospital. He's had an accident."

Judith's eyes widened in shock. "Frank?" she asked. "But what—" She cut off her own words. Obviously, whatever had happened, Jed didn't yet know the details himself. "Come on," she said, grasping his arm and steering him toward the side door and the parking lot. "I'll drive you to the hospital myself."

Sixteen

J udith pulled the Honda into the parking lot next to the small hospital. A low, single-story building constructed of the ubiquitous cinder blocks, it had an emergency room at the front, with two small wings extending back to partially enclose a tiny courtyard. It appeared that the hospital had been painted green at some time in the past, but most of the paint had weathered away, and now the clinic had a strange speckled look to it, almost as if the building itself had contracted some rare disease. By the time she'd brought the car to a stop in a slot between two battered pickup trucks, Jed already had the passenger door open.

They found the waiting room deserted, but a moment later Gloria Hernandez, looking harried, emerged from the double doors that led to the emergency room. When she recognized Jed, she hurried toward him. At the look on the nurse's face, Jed froze.

"What is it?" he asked, his voice shaking. "What's wrong? Dad isn't . . ." His voice trailed off as he found himself unable even to finish his question.

Gloria shook her head quickly. "He's in the back," she said. "Dr. Moreland doesn't think it's too bad." Then, turning to Judith, she forced herself to smile. "I'm sorry," she said. "When I called the school, I didn't mean for them to make you drive Jed over here."

"It's all right, Gloria," Judith replied. "I—Well, I've been seeing Frank a bit lately. What happened?"

Gloria shook her head helplessly. "I'm not sure. They said he fell—"

She was interrupted by Greg Moreland, who strode into the room, wiping his hands on a white towel which he handed to Gloria. His brows arched slightly as he recognized Judith, and he offered her a quick nod before turning his attention to Jed, who was watching him anxiously.

"Your father's a very lucky man," he said. "It's a clean fracture of the right tibia and fibula, and he may have a slight concussion from hitting his head against the turbine, but given the circumstances, it could have been a lot worse."

Judith's eyes closed for a moment as she heard the words, and she felt some of the tension drain out of her body. "Thank God," she breathed. She stepped forward then, and unconsciously laid a hand on Jed's shoulder. "May we see him?"

Greg spread his hands expansively. "No reason for you not to," he said. "He's a bit groggy, and might not make much sense, but I'll bet he'll be glad to see you. They've just put him in a room . . . one-oh-six, I think."

As Jed moved toward the doors that led to the wing containing the rooms, Judith hung back. "What happened?" she asked when she and Greg were alone.

Greg shrugged. "A freak accident, from what I understand," he told her. "He was working at the dam, and apparently he panicked."

Judith nodded. "He was in the pipes, wasn't he?" she asked, her voice trembling from anger now, rather than from shock.

Greg cocked his head. "I'm not sure what you're getting at."

"He's claustrophobic," Judith told him. "He was afraid of going to work this morning. He was sure they were going to send him into the intake pipes, and he was sure that if they did, he was going to panic. Dear God," she went on, "this isn't the dark ages. There are all kinds of jobs up there. They didn't have to put Frank into a position like that!"

"Stop it!" Greg snapped, his voice commanding her to silence. "You're out of control, Judith," he said, then softened. "I didn't do anything. If you want to get mad at someone, get mad at Kendall or Kruger. They're the ones who sent him up there."

He was right. Judith took a deep breath as she struggled to regain control of herself. "I'm sorry," she finally said "You're right, of course. I just—" She stopped. She'd been about to tell him that what had just happened to Frank wasn't the only thing on her mind, but then she'd remembered that it was Greg himself who had ordered the shots the other day. "I—Well, I guess I'd better go in and see him," she finished, glancing at her watch. "Damn . . . do me a favor, will you? Have someone call the school so they can cover my next class?''

Without waiting for a reply, Judith hurried toward the doors of the emergency room, unaware of Greg's eyes, still fixed on her, watching her speculatively as she left.

She'd been about to say something else—he'd seen it in her eyes. And then she had changed her mind.

Why?

What was it she had suddenly decided not to tell him?

Judith reached out and gently stroked Frank's brow with the damp washcloth Jed had brought from the tiny bathroom that connected Frank's room to the one next door. For a moment he made no sign that he even felt the wet coolness on his face, but then he stirred in the bed and his eyes opened. He gazed at her blankly, and then his vision cleared. His eyes darted around the room as if searching for something, and finally came back to her. He reached up and gently squeezed her hand.

"Judith?" he breathed, his voice raspy, his throat feeling unnaturally dry.

She picked up the glass of water on the stand next to his bed and held it to his lips, gently raising his head to make it easier for him. "Drink a little water," she urged.

He drank thirstily, then let his head fall back to the pillow.

"Hi, Dad," Jed said, stepping forward and reaching out to lay his hand tentatively on his father's shoulder. Frank looked up at his son, smiled and covered Jed's hand with his own. Then, as if embarrassed by the affectionate gesture, he dropped his hand to his side.

"What time is it?" he asked.

"Almost eleven," Judith replied.

"Jesus," Frank groaned. "It just seemed like a couple of minutes." Then, as his mind cleared further, he shuddered at the memory of what had happened to him.

Once again he glanced suspiciously around the room. "Who's here?" he asked, his voice dropping so it was barely above a whisper.

Judith frowned uncertainly. "Just Jed and me," she said.

"Nobody from work?" Frank asked.

Above him, he saw Judith and Jed exchanging a worried glance. He struggled to sit up straighter, wincing against the stab of pain that shot through his right leg.

"Don't," Judith protested, but Frank ignored her.

Gritting his teeth against the pain, he shoved himself up and back until he rested propped up against the pillows. Then he took Judith's hand again. "What did they say?" he asked. "Did they tell you what happened?"

Judith bit her lip as she nodded. "Greg said you were in a pipe, and panicked," she said. "It was an accident."

Frank was silent for a few seconds, but then his jaw set and his eyes met Judith's. "It was no accident," he said, his voice taking on a belligerent tone, as if he expected to be contradicted. Before either Jed or Judith could speak, he turned to his son and said, "Do you hear me, Jed? They tried to kill me today."

"Aw, come on, Dad," Jed began again, but Frank turned away and fixed his gaze on Judith.

"It was no accident," he repeated. "There was something they didn't tell me. That pipe doesn't go straight across to the shaft. It slopes a little, and then at the end it starts slanting real bad. But there's nothing to hold onto. Even if I hadn't panicked, I'd have fallen. And that's just what they were counting on."

Judith stared at him. "Frank, I can't believe that. It's well, it's just crazy—"

Frank shook his head. "It's not crazy," he said, his voice taking on a note of obstinacy that told both Judith and Jed it would be useless to argue with him. "They're pissed at all the yelling I've been doing, and they want to get rid of me. And they almost got away with it." He was silent for a moment, then his eyes clouded before he spoke once more. "And they won't stop," he said. "They'll do something else. They're going to kill me, just like they did Max Moreland."

Gina Alvarez glanced over at Jed and wondered once more if her idea of going for a horseback ride that afternoon was a good one. It had seemed like a terrific idea at the time, when she'd found Jed waiting for her after school, his face pale, and his eyes worried. But he'd barely even spoken to her, apparently off somewhere in a world of his own.

"What do you think?" she'd asked as they came to a fork in the trail, the one to the left leading up to the rim of the canyon, the other following the river into the canyon itself. When Jed made no response, she'd made the decision herself, opting to wind along through the cottonwoods, enjoying their shelter from the afternoon heat.

Finally, when the horses stopped to take a drink from the stream, she decided she'd had enough.

"Look," she said. "Either tell me what's bugging you or tell me you're mad at me or tell me to go home. If you aren't having a good time, I'm sorry. Maybe this was just a dumb idea in the first place. Okay?"

At last Jed seemed to come out of his reverie. "I'm not mad at you, Gina," he said. Then, after a short silence, he added in a whisper, "If I tell you something, will you promise not to tell anyone else?"

Gina's brows creased into a rare frown, and she nodded.

Jed still hesitated, then made up his mind. "Dad thinks the company tried to kill him today," he said.

Gina stared at him, trying to decide if he was pulling her leg, but the look in his eyes told her he wasn't. "Come on," she said. "Why would they want to do that?"

Jed repeated what his father had told him earlier, and Gina listened to it all in silence. When he was done, she shook her head.

"That's nuts," she said. Jed's eyes instantly clouded, and Gina quickly apologized. "I'm sorry. I didn't mean your father's nuts. But it just seems like kind of a crazy idea, that's all. I mean, your dad was probably still in shock, or something, and besides, why would the company want to hurt him?"

"Because he's been making a lot of trouble for them," Jed replied.

"But that's nothing new," Gina protested. "He's always made trouble for the company. That's his job, isn't it? I mean, if the head of the union isn't supposed to make trouble, what is he supposed to do? Uncle Carlos says that's what makes him so good at it—he's never been afraid to say what he thinks."

"Yeah," Jed agreed, his voice bitter now. "And with Mr. Moreland, it didn't matter, 'cause they were friends. But it's all different now."

The horses, their thirst slaked, began moving along the trail again, and Gina was silent for a few minutes, her eyes fixed on the clear water of the stream. "Okay, so let's say the company did try to kill your dad," she said. "Can he prove it?"

Jed shook his head. "I don't see how. I mean, even he admitted it was partly his fault. If he hadn't panicked, he would have felt the bend in the pipe and stopped. But he says they were counting on him to panic. He says . . ." His voice faded away, and when Gina turned to look at him, he was looking the other way, across to the other side of the canyon.

Her own eyes followed his gaze. At first she didn't see anything unusual. They were about halfway up to the dam now, near the weathered frame building nestled against the canyon wall, that had served as the construction headquarters back when the dam was being built. And then she realized what Jed was staring at.

The building, unused for years, had been repainted.

In front of it, several cars were parked, and when she looked up, there seemed to be some kind of plastic pipe—like a water pipe—

rising up from the side of the building and snaking up the side of the canyon.

Gina looked at Jed, her expression puzzled. "I don't get it," she said. "I thought that building was abandoned."

Jed nodded. "It was," he said. "Or anyway, it used to be. But it doesn't look like it is now, does it? Come on."

He clucked to his horse and laid the reins over to the left. Obediently, the horse turned off the path, hesitated only a second, then began splashing across the river. Gina, kicking gently at her own mount, followed after him.

The bank was higher on the other side of the river, and Jed's horse stumbled as it searched for footing, then steadied itself, climbed the bank and came to a halt, as if waiting for Jed to indicate where it should go next. Jed waited until Gina caught up with him, then slapped the reins against the horse's neck. It began moving slowly forward until Jed drew it to a halt at the dirt road that ran past the front of the building.

The road, for years nothing more than a pair of nearly overgrown ruts, now showed clear signs of use. And there was a sign on the building:

BORREGO OIL COMMUNICATIONS CENTER
AUTHORIZED PERSONNEL ONLY

"Communications Center?" Jed read. "What does that mean?"

Gina's eyes followed the plastic pipe up to the canyon's rim. "Why don't we go up to the top and see what's there?" she asked.

Jed nodded, and they turned their horses back toward the mouth of the canyon, this time following the track of the old road. "Whatever it is, why would they put it up here?" Jed wondered out loud as they rode. "Nobody's used that building since the dam was built. It's not even safe anymore."

"It looked like they rebuilt it," Gina replied.

"But it's dumb," Jed objected. "I mean, it's stuck way up here in the middle of nowhere."

But when they finally came to the rim of the canyon above the old construction headquarters, Jed thought he understood.

The crew was just finishing up the installation. A six-foot Cyclone fence surrounded the antenna pad now, and the two teenagers stared at it curiously. Otto Kruger, his face florid from the long days in the sun on top of the mesa, jogged over to them. "What are you kids doing up here?" he demanded.

Jed gazed down at him. "We're riding horses, obviously," he said, making no attempt to keep his voice calm. "What's this supposed to be?"

"An antenna," Kruger told him. "UniChem flew the whole thing in this morning. Something, isn't it?"

Jed gazed at the huge machine for a moment. As he watched, it suddenly came to life.

There was a low humming noise, the base of the antenna began to rotate, and the dish itself tipped southward.

The humming noise stopped, and Jed found himself straining to hear the transmissions he was certain were now emanating from the huge dish. Indeed, he imagined he could actually feel them, vibrating through his body. But that was stupid—whatever frequencies they were using would be far out of the range of hearing.

"It's really something, isn't it?" Kruger repeated, his voice filled with as much pride as if he'd designed and built the thing himself.

Jed glared down at him. "Yes," he said finally. "It's something— something really ugly. As ugly as the wells, and the refinery, and everything else that's wrecking this place." Jerking on the reins, he turned his horse away and started back down the trail toward the town. A few moments later Gina caught up with him.

"What was that all about?" she asked. "I know you're worried about your dad, but—"

"But maybe I've just decided I don't like it, okay?" Jed asked. "Maybe I just don't like any of it."

They rode in silence for a while, until the town came into view. As Jed looked at it, after seeing the strange antenna that had suddenly appeared on the mesa and feeling the odd vibrations coming from it, he thought even Borrego itself looked different now.

The space age, apparently, had finally come to Borrego.

Maybe that's all it's really all about, Jed found himself thinking as he let the horse find its own way home, and his mind drifted back to his father.

Maybe it's not that I've changed. Maybe I'm just like dad. Maybe I'm just pissed off because things aren't like they used to be.

Rita Moreland sighed as she stepped out of the heat of the afternoon into the coolness of the house. She stopped in the entry hall, took off her hat and carefully placed it on the shelf in the coat closet. Then, as her eyes fell on Max's three coats, which still hung in their assigned places as if waiting for their owner to come and claim them, she bit her lip.

"I think perhaps it's time I started getting rid of some of Max's things," she said to Greg, but didn't turn to face him, unwilling to let him see the tears she could feel in her eyes.

"There isn't any rush," Greg replied. "You have plenty of time."

Rita's back straightened as she regained her composure, and when she finally looked at him, the tears that had threatened her only a moment ago were gone. "Perhaps I do," she observed. "But one never knows, does one?" She moved across the entry hall and into the library, her thoughts shifting to the hospital she had left only a few minutes before. "Look at poor Frank Arnold," she said. "He could have died today—he was lucky he didn't. And of course Max—" She broke off her own words as once more her emotions welled up within her, and quickly searched for something to take her mind off her husband. On the desk the red light of the answering machine was blinking, and though she often ignored it, she now punched at it hopefully.

But instead of a message of condolence, she heard an unfamiliar voice: "Mrs. Moreland, this is Forrest Frazier, with Southwest Properties in Las Cruces. I have a client who is very interested in buying your house. If you could give me a call, I'd like to discuss the details with you." A phone number followed, then the slightly metallic sound of the machine's synthesized voice as it announced the exact time the call had come in. Rita frowned, and looked at Greg.

"Now what on earth was that all about?" she asked. "What could he have meant?"

Greg shrugged. "Apparently someone wants to buy the place," he said.

"*This* place?" Rita asked. "But it isn't for sale."

"Maybe you ought to at least consider it," Greg said slowly, glancing around the large library. "I mean, given the circumstances."

Rita eyed her nephew acerbically. "You mean because Max died?" she said, willing her voice not to catch as she uttered the words. "Surely you aren't going to suggest that I'm going to . . ." She searched quickly for the right phrase, then: "Rattle around in this big old place," she finished. "Isn't that what they always say when half of a couple is gone?"

Greg swallowed uncomfortably. "I didn't mean that exactly, Aunt Rita," he said. "But in a way, it's true, isn't it? I mean, it *is* a big house, and—"

"It wasn't too big for Max and me," Rita retorted. Regretting the sharpness of her words, she cocked her head, and forced a smile. "Or are you just trying to get your old auntie out of town?"

And then, quite suddenly, Rita thought she understood. "That's it, isn't it?" she said, more to herself than Greg.

"Oh, come on, Aunt Rita," Greg began, but Rita waved his words aside.

"Not you, darling," she said. "I was just making a joke. But let's face it—there *are* people who would just as soon see me leave Borrego, aren't there? You don't suppose it's UniChem that's making the offer, do you?"

Greg shrugged. "Well, it would certainly be easy to find out. Call up what's-his-name—was it Frazier?—and ask him."

Rita shook her head. "If it were UniChem, they wouldn't be foolish enough to do it directly," she said.

"Oh, Jesus," Greg groaned. "Now you're starting to sound like Frank Arnold!"

Rita's eyes flashed with anger. "Am I?" she asked. "Well, let me tell you something, young man. Your uncle was listening to Frank Arnold long before you arrived on the scene, and he trusted Frank. And I also know what Max would want me to do now, and it certainly wouldn't include selling my house and going elsewhere."

Greg took a deep breath. "Aunt Rita," he said. "I don't know why we're arguing. Nobody's told you to sell your house, and nobody's told you to leave town. All I'm saying is that it's something you should think about. The house *is* big, and it *is* full of memories, and you know as well as I do that Uncle Max often talked about getting rid of it when he retired. You two were going to travel, and he'd even talked about maybe moving to Hawaii." He shrugged as he saw his aunt's eyes narrow. "Anyway, I'm not trying to tell you what to do. If it hadn't been for that phone call, we wouldn't even be talking about it right now. But the call *was* on the machine, and all I'm saying is that maybe you should think about it."

Rita reached out and took Greg's hand, squeezing it fondly. "I'm sorry," she told him. "You'll have to forgive me. None of this has been easy for me, but I shouldn't take it out on you." She moved to the window and stood looking out over the desert. And then, almost unbidden, her eyes drifted up to the mesa, to the spot where she'd been in the dream the morning of Max's funeral.

Once more, she heard Max's words. *Listen to Frank.*

Then, in her mind, she heard Frank's own words, uttered only half an hour before, when she'd sat alone with him in the hospital room.

They tried to kill me, Rita. Just like they killed Max.

She stood still for a few seconds, the two voices echoing in her head. Finally she turned to face her nephew.

"All right," she said quietly. "I've thought it over, and I've made up my mind. I'm not selling my house, Greg. I'm going to stay right here, and I'm going to find out exactly who wants to buy my house, and why, and I'm also going to find out exactly what happened to Frank, and to Max too. Something is happening here, Greg, and I intend to find out what it is. I intend to find out, and put a stop to it."

She showed Greg out of the house, then went to Max's desk. Taking out a piece of his heavy stationery, and picking up his favorite pen, she began jotting notes; notes of what had been happening in Borrego over the past few weeks. She scratched down random thoughts, even impressions. And through it all she kept hearing Max's words from the dream once again: *Listen to Frank.*

She kept writing, kept searching for a pattern in the events she'd noted on the paper.

But there was no pattern, at least not yet.

Still, she was certain that sooner or later a pattern would emerge.

A pattern of death.

Seventeen

Darkness had fallen and the first chill of the night had set in. Above Judith and Jed the sky was clear, the great swath of the Milky Way glimmering gently against a velvety backdrop. They stood silently for a few moments, gazing upward.

"Are you going to be okay?" Judith finally asked.

Jed nodded absently. "I guess," he said. Then, after a moment or two, his eyes shifted. "What about Dad?" he asked, his voice trembling. "Is he going to be all right?"

"Of course he is," Judith replied. "Why wouldn't he? A broken leg isn't exactly the end of the earth. He'll be in the hospital a few more days, and then he'll come home." She forced a smile. "Our biggest problem will be getting him to take it easy for a while."

Jed nodded, but Judith could sense that something was bothering him. "What is it?" she asked. "What's wrong?"

Jed took a deep breath, then let it out in a long sigh. "I don't know. I guess it's just that this morning, when I woke up, I had this weird feeling something was going to happen to him today. And it did." He shivered, though the night wasn't that cold. "I keep thinking it was my fault, that I should have told him not to go to work today."

Judith shook her head. "It wouldn't have done any good. In fact," she went on, smiling wryly, "I tried it myself. I even suggested he quit. But you know your father . . ." Her voice trailed off. "Look," she said. "Do you want me to come home with you? I could spend the night, if you don't want to be alone in the house."

Jed considered it for a moment, but shook his head. "I'll be okay—Christ knows, there've been enough nights when Dad was working graveyards."

But later, as he pulled his father's truck into the driveway, he realized that tonight would be different. He let himself in the front door, and immediately felt the emptiness of the place. Always before, even when he'd been alone, he'd felt his father's presence. But tonight, knowing his father wouldn't be home in a few hours, a desolate loneliness seemed to emanate from the house.

He tried to ignore it, switching on the television and stretching out on the couch. But he couldn't concentrate on the TV. Instead of hearing the soundtrack of the movie, his ears kept picking up the sounds of the night outside.

He felt fidgety, nervous.

At last he got up from the sofa, picked up the remote control, and switched the television off again.

Silence closed in on him.

He wandered around the house for a few minutes, his nervousness growing by the second. Finally, making up his mind, he grabbed his leather jacket and went back out to the truck.

The A&W stand.

His friends would be there—it was Friday night. Maybe someone would even have gotten hold of a keg of beer. At least tonight there wasn't any chance of his father finding out what he'd been doing.

There were five of them up on the mesa an hour later. Randy Sparks and Jeff Hankins had already been at the A&W, and a few minutes later Gina Alvarez and JoAnna Garcia arrived on their way home from the movies. When Gina had seen the keg of beer in the trunk of Jeff's Plymouth, her eyes had narrowed ominously, but it had been JoAnna who had finally convinced her to come along. "We can tell my folks we watched the movie twice, and your mom won't even be home till after midnight."

Gina's eyes had shifted over to Jed. "No drag racing?" she asked. "If you wreck your dad's truck—"

"I promise," Jed had replied, putting on his best solemn face and crossing his heart. And he'd stuck to the promise, despite the way

Jeff had tauntingly revved the Plymouth's engine as they'd left the A&W and started up toward the mesa.

Now the keg was half gone, and Jed was stretched out on his back, staring up into the sky. Gina was beside him, her head resting on his shoulder, her body snuggled close to his. He'd found an old blanket behind the seat of the pickup, and he was about to pull it over them when he felt something prod roughly at his side. He looked up to see Randy Sparks glaring down at him.

Randy was weaving slightly, and in his hand was a paper cup full of beer. "I wanta talk to you, half-breed," he said, his words slurred.

Jed felt his stomach tighten. When he'd arrived at the A&W, Randy had nodded to him but not said much. Since they'd come up to the mesa and started drinking, he'd noticed Randy eyeing him speculatively, as if he was trying to decide whether or not he could take Jed in a fight. For a while Jed had been on his guard, but when Randy had simply kept drinking, Jed had concluded that nothing was going to happen.

Now Randy's foot jammed into his side once more. "I said I wanta talk to you!"

Gina was sitting up now, one of her hands pressed against Jed's chest. "Come on, Randy," she said. "What's the big deal? You're the one who threw the rock through the Morelands' window, not Jed."

Randy glowered drunkenly down at her. "Yeah, but your Indian boyfriend's the one who told."

Jed thought quickly. The last thing any of them needed right now was a fight. And if they got caught out here with a keg of beer . . . "Look," he said, scrambling to his feet and picking up the blanket. "Let's just forget about it, okay? Maybe I didn't see you at all. Maybe it was just a lucky guess." Taking Gina's hand, he started toward the truck, with Randy staggering after him.

"Whatsa matter?" he shouted. "You scared to fight me? Huh? You a chicken-shit Indian?"

Jed froze, his anger finally beginning to rise, but Gina kept pulling him to the truck. "Don't listen to him," she said. "He's drunk, and he just wants to make trouble. Let's just split, okay?"

They were at the truck now, and Gina pulled the passenger door open, half shoving Jed inside. "Let's go," she pleaded. "Please?"

Randy was still shouting, but now Jeff Hankins was next to him, trying to calm him down. Jed started the engine of the pickup and backed away, then shifted gears. But as he pulled out onto the road, Randy bent down and picked up a rock, hurling it toward the oncoming truck.

Instinctively both Jed and Gina ducked as the rock came at them, and neither of them saw it strike the windshield. But a moment later they both saw the cracks, a spiderweb spreading out from the pit the rock had left in the glass.

"Shit!" Jed yelled, slamming on the brakes and starting to jump out of the cab. But even before the door was fully open, Gina grabbed at his arm, pulling him back.

"Don't, Jed!" she said. "Don't make it any worse! We'll figure out something to tell your father—maybe we can even get a new windshield before he gets out of the hospital."

Jed hesitated, torn. He wanted to jump out of the truck, grab Randy, and throw him down in the dirt. He wanted to make Randy eat his words, and a lot more. And he knew he could do it. He was bigger and stronger than Randy—always had been. And Randy was so drunk he'd barely be able to even throw a punch.

Maybe.

And what would happen tomorrow, when he had to explain to his father where he'd gotten a black eye, or a split lip, or any of the other injuries he'd brought home from fights over the last few years?

Taking a deep breath, he slammed the door once again, venting his anger by jamming the accelerator to the floor. All four wheels spun gratifyingly for a moment before the truck shot forward into the night.

"Slow down, will you?" Gina begged a couple of minutes later as they approached the hairpin turns of the switchbacks that led down to the desert floor.

Still breathing hard, Jed eased up on the gas pedal, then pressed the brakes as he steered into the first of the curves. As he approached the second curve, he slammed on the brakes, at the same time reaching down to switch off the headlights.

"What's wrong?" Gina asked. "Why are we stopping?"

Jed pointed out into the desert. "Look."

Far in the distance a pair of dim lights glowed. It was a car, moving slowly, its headlights extinguished and only its parking lights on. It was heading along the same road Jed and the rest of the kids had traveled two hours earlier.

"You think it's the cops?" Gina asked.

Jed shrugged. "I don't know. But why would anyone else be coming up here at this time of night? And with their headlights off?"

Gina's lips tightened. "I told you we shouldn't have come. If we get caught, Mom's gonna—"

"Just take it easy," Jed told her. Leaving the headlights off, he began carefully steering the truck down the twisting road. A few moments later they were close to the bottom, and Jed brought the pickup to a stop behind a large boulder. "Come here," he said, holding out his arms. "If it's the cops, it'll look like we just came out here to neck. They probably won't even stop."

Gina hesitated, then decided the ruse was at least worth a try. She slid across the seat and snuggled herself into Jed's arms.

The faint beams of the oncoming car's parking lights were brightening now, casting a dim glow onto the mesa's wall. Jed held his breath, knowing the car was approaching the fork in the road. If the twin shafts of light didn't swing away in a moment, it would mean the car was coming up the mesa road.

And then the beams suddenly moved toward them, only to disappear as the car took the turnoff just past the boulder that concealed the truck. Instantly, Jed opened the door and scrambled out of the truck, scuttling around the boulder until he could see the car as it started up the canyon. A moment later he was back, his brows furrowed.

"It's Dr. Moreland's car," he said. "What's he doing going up in the canyon in the middle of the night?"

Gina shrugged. "Maybe something happened up at The Cottonwoods," she suggested.

Jed shook his head. "If it's some kind of an emergency, how come he didn't have his headlights on? The way he was driving, it's like he didn't want anyone to see him."

Gina giggled softly. "Maybe he didn't," she said. "Maybe he's got a girlfriend up there and doesn't want anyone to know about her."

But Jed was barely listening, for he was once more feeling the strange vibrations he'd felt earlier that afternoon, when he and Gina had come across the new antenna UniChem had installed.

Frank Arnold lay in his bed, sleeping peacefully. Then, as midnight came, his eyes opened and he sat up.

Something was wrong.

There was a strange smell in the room, almost as if something was burning. And then the scent grew stronger, and changed slightly.

Garbage.

The air seemed redolent now with the putrid stink of a dump on a hot summer afternoon.

He could even taste the stuff. It was as if his mouth was filled with rotting eggs, and he felt himself begin to gag, then tried to reach for the glass of water on his nightstand.

He missed it, his hand brushing against it, knocking it to the floor.

Suddenly, streaks of light slashed through the darkness of the room, and he saw flickering images of strange creatures lurking in the corners. But when he tried to look straight at them, they seemed to disappear, only to reappear a moment later, coming at him from another direction.

A guttural sound rose from his throat as a wave of pure terror washed over him.

Something was coming at him out of the darkness, and he tried to strike out at it. His arms flailed wildly, and then, as a flash of pain lashed through his head, he tumbled from the bed.

He began screaming then, bellowing out in fear and rage, and a moment later the room filled with blinding light. On the floor, his body writhing, Frank tried to scrabble away from this newest assailant. He cowered against the wall, his arms wrapped around his body.

His mouth filled with the sickening flavor of bile, and then he was retching, vomit spewing from his lips in glutinous streams.

From the doorway Susan Paynter, the night nurse, stared in frozen horror at the spectacle on the floor.

Then her years of training took over and she came to life. Pressing the buzzer that would summon an orderly to the room, she dropped onto the floor next to Frank and reached out to touch him. "It's all right, Mr. Arnold," she said soothingly, though she wasn't sure if he could hear her or not. "Just take it easy. I'm here to help you."

As her fingers touched his left arm, Frank screamed out again. His arm jerked convulsively, as if she'd burned him, and he tried to roll away from her.

His head struck the wall, hard. A second later he smashed it against the wall again, and yet again.

Susan heard a sound at the door and looked up. "Get Dr. Banning," she said. "Then call Dr. Moreland and tell him to get over here."

The orderly disappeared, and a moment later she heard his voice on the paging speaker, summoning Bob Banning to the room. Though the sound was barely audible in the room, it seemed to stimulate something in Frank Arnold, and now his whole body went into convulsions.

His broken leg swung around and the cast smashed painfully against Susan Paynter's knee. And then, as if someone had turned a switch inside him, he went limp.

For a split second Susan thought he had died. She seized his wrist, pressed her fingers into his flesh and counted quickly as she found his pulse.

At the same time, her eyes watched his chest begin to move in the slow and steady rhythm of strong breathing.

At last she heard Bob Banning's voice behind her.

"Jesus, Susan. What's happening in here?"

Susan glanced up. "I don't know. I found him like this." She slipped an arm under Frank's shoulders, and the doctor immediately squatted down to help her. The orderly appeared, and together they managed to get Frank back into bed.

Banning quickly began examining Frank, double checking his pulse and breathing, wrapping the rubber sleeve of a sphygmomanometer around his arm. But as he began inflating the sleeve, Frank's eyes opened and he stirred in the bed.

He looked up at the three faces above him, and his mouth opened. "Wh-What's happening? Is something wrong?"

Susan Paynter stared at him. "Wrong?" she repeated. "Don't you remember what just happened, Mr. Arnold?"

Frank's eyes clouded slightly. "Nightmare," he said at last. "I think I had a nightmare."

Susan glanced quickly at Dr. Banning, who nodded.

"It was a lot more than a nightmare, Mr. Arnold," she told him. "You started screaming, and when I came in, you were on the floor. You smashed your head against the wall, and then you started throwing up."

Frank's eyes widened and his gaze shifted to the doctor.

"You don't remember any of this, Frank?"

Frank shook his head and made a slight movement toward the glass of water that was no longer there. Susan brought him another from the bathroom, then held it while he drank.

"I—I thought it was a dream," he said. "I woke up, and everything smelled funny. Then I got this horrible taste in my mouth, and I started seeing things . . ." His voice trailed off and he dropped back against the pillows.

"Okay," Bob Banning said, squeezing Frank's shoulder reassuringly. "Let's just check a few things and see where we are. And how does that leg feel?"

Frank's lips tightened. "Hurts like hell," he admitted. "Feels like I kicked something."

"You did," Susan Paynter told him. "Me." Then she smiled. "Don't worry about it. I have a feeling that in this case, it really *did* hurt you a lot more than it hurt me."

"Great," Banning commented dryly. "Well, when we're done here, we'll take him in and X-ray the leg again." He peeled Frank's left eyelid back, examined the pupil carefully, then repeated the procedure on his right eye. A few moments later he was at the foot of the bed, running the tip of a pencil up the bare soles of Frank's feet.

Instantly Frank jerked his feet away, then groaned as the flash of pain shot through his broken leg.

"Serves you right." Banning commented wryly. "Kicking nurses, indeed! Well, your reflexes seem to be in good shape. Other than your leg, how do you feel?"

Frank shrugged uncertainly, then leaned forward so Susan could strip off his filthy hospital gown. "Given what Susan says happened, not too bad, I suppose. But what *did* happen?"

Banning shook his head. "I wish I could tell you," he said, starting to make notations on Frank's medical chart. He glanced at his watch, frowned slightly, and turned to Susan Paynter. "How long ago did the seizure begin?"

Susan's eyes darted toward Frank, then returned to the doctor. "It was strange," she said, her voice muted. "I have my watch set to beep on the hour. And it had just beeped when I heard Frank scream. It was midnight. Exactly midnight."

Eighteen

I t had been more than a year since Brown Eagle had last been in Borrego, and as he left the pueblo at the first light of dawn the next morning, he felt as if he were embarking on a journey into an alien territory. He fell into the steady pace that could carry him across the desert all day if need be, but instead of turning his mind inward to close out the tedium of a long walk, he watched and listened eagerly as the landscape around him changed.

The last rustlings of the night creatures fell silent as they crept back into their burrows, shielding themselves from the heat of the day and the predators that stalked them from the sky as well as on the desert's floor. As the sun rose, Brown Eagle turned to face it, silently welcoming it back to the mesas. His eyes swept the sky, searching for the familiar shape of the bird whose name he bore, but this morning the sky was empty.

Brown Eagle took it as an omen. Today his personal totem had abandoned him. As he continued on his way toward the town, he felt lonely and unprotected.

He paused on the fringes of Borrego, feeling the familiar hostility that seemed to emanate from the town like an invisible sandstorm. During the months he'd stayed in Kokatí, avoiding the town completely, he'd almost forgotten the hostility toward his people that hung over it. But he'd never learned to ignore the way people looked at him, or, more exactly, failed to look at him, acting for the most part as if he didn't exist at all. He'd never grown used to their silent contempt for the Kokatí, and over the years, as his senses had sharpened with age instead of growing dull, he felt the malice clearly whenever he was forced to come down off the mesa. It seemed to reach out to him, as if it were trying to crush him.

He moved on, his head down, the pavement under his feet feeling too hard, the acrid smell of the refinery and the ugly cinder-block houses offending his senses. Finally he came to the house where his daughter had once lived. He walked around to the back door and let himself into the kitchen, sensing immediately that his grandson had not wakened yet.

He sat down at the kitchen table and waited.

Almost an hour later Jed, a bathrobe hanging loosely from his shoulders, came into the kitchen to start a pot of coffee. He stopped short, shocked by the sight of someone sitting at the table, then realized who it was.

"Grandpa? What are you doing here? How long have you been here?"

Brown Eagle grinned at Jed's surprise. "About an hour. I came to find out about your father. Is he going to be all right?"

Jed nodded, but then he eyed his grandfather suspiciously. "How did you know?" he asked.

"I saw them bring him down from the dam yesterday. In fact, I told him not to go into it at all."

Jed scowled darkly. "Great," he said. "I told him to be careful, Jude told him to quit his job, and you warned him not to go in the dam. He really listens to all of us, doesn't he?"

Brown Eagle eyed his grandson dispassionately. When Jed came up to the pueblo to visit him, there was so much of the Kokatí about him that he sometimes forgot the other half of the boy's heritage. But here, in his home in Borrego, Brown Eagle could see the other side of Jed, the side that would forever be alien to the Kokatí, the side he'd inherited from his father.

"Maybe he's as stubborn as you," he said. "It wasn't so very long ago you thought I was a crazy old Indian. Frank probably still thinks so."

There was a knock at the back door, and a moment later Jed let Judith Sheffield in. She put a box of fresh doughnuts on the counter, then noticed Brown Eagle. "I—I'm sorry," she stammered. "I thought Jed was by himself. If I'm interrupting something—"

"It's okay," Brown Eagle told her. "Jed didn't know I was here either." He eyed the box on the counter, and Judith handed it to him. He bit into one of the doughnuts, then, spoke again. "Tell me about Frank. Is he really going to be all right?"

Judith's eyes darted toward Jed. "I—I'm not sure," she said. "I called the hospital this morning, and they wouldn't tell me much, but I got the feeling something happened during the night. I came over to get Jed so we could both go see him."

Brown Eagle stood up. "We'll all go," he said. "He's still my grandson's father. He might not listen to me, but I care what happens to him."

As they drove to the hospital, Judith glanced at Brown Eagle in the rearview mirror. His face looked odd: his eyes, open and unmoving, seemed fixed on some object a few feet in front of him.

She turned her concentration to the road ahead, but a minute or so later, when she glanced in the mirror again, nothing had changed.

Brown Eagle seemed unaware of his very surroundings as if he'd disappeared somewhere within himself, some place neither she nor anyone else could follow. Finally she turned to Jed. "Is he all right?" she whispered, nodding toward the backseat of the Honda where Brown Eagle sat, staring sightlessly out the window.

Jed glanced back, then nodded. "He's fine," he said. "He doesn't like the town, you know. So in his mind, he's gone somewhere else. The mesa, probably."

Jed's words echoed in Judith's mind as she continued driving. He'd said them so matter-of-factly, as if there were nothing strange about them at all.

She wondered if he even realized that until a few days ago, when he'd gone up there himself and spent the night in the kiva, he'd never have said such a thing, much less understood it.

Margie Sparks, her ample figure clad in a fading pink housedress, tapped at Randy's door, then let herself in. Randy was sprawled on his back, his eyes closed, and for a moment Margie thought he was still asleep. But when she spoke softly to her son, Randy's eyes opened and he sat up.

Margie eyed him carefully. His eyes were rimmed with red, and his complexion had the same sallow look her husband's always had the night after he'd been out on a toot. "You've got a hangover, haven't you?" Margie challenged, going to the window and pulling the drapes back, deliberately letting the morning sun glare into Randy's eyes. When the groan of protest she'd expected didn't come, she glanced back at Randy, then opened the window itself to air out the stuffy room. When she turned to face Randy again, fully expecting him to have buried his head under the pillow, she was surprised to find him still sitting up in bed, the sun in his eyes, exactly as she'd left him a moment before.

"What's wrong with you?" she demanded. "Don't feel so good?"

Randy shook his head. "I feel fine," he replied.

Margie frowned. Well, at least that was normal: no matter how bad he looked on a Saturday morning, he always insisted he felt fine. And he always lied about drinking, just as if she was blind and couldn't see how he looked. "What were you doin' last night?" she demanded.

"Me and some of the kids went up on the mesa," Randy mumbled.

Margie rolled her eyes knowingly. "And I 'spose you're going to tell me you was just lookin' at the stars, and nobody brought no keg of beer, right?"

Randy said nothing.

"Well?" Margie pressed, her voice taking on a shrill note.

Randy's eyes met hers. "We were just lookin' at the stars," he said. "Nobody brought no keg of beer." Margie glared angrily at him. "You sassin' me? 'Cause if you are, I'm gonna have to have a talk with your pa. Now you tell me what you was doin'!"

Randy's face remained impassive. "We got a keg of beer, and we got drunk."

"Who?" Margie asked, suddenly suspicious. What was Randy up to this time? she wondered. "Who was with you?"

Obediently, Randy recited the list of names. When he was finished, Margie nodded knowingly. "Well, I might have known that half-breed Arnold kid would be there. He bring the beer?"

Randy shook his head. "I did," he said, his voice almost toneless.

Margie's mouth dropped open in surprise. What was going on? She'd have sworn that no matter how much she browbeat him, he'd never have admitted to having gotten the beer himself. Then she thought she understood.

"You're lyin' again, aren't you?" she prodded.

Randy shook his head, and once more Margie looked at him, trying to puzzle out what might have happened to him. Then she remembered the flu shots they'd given at school the other day. Vaguely, she remembered reading somewhere that sometimes the shots caused the disease instead of preventing it. She laid her wrist against Randy's forehead.

It seemed a little hot to her, but that could just have been the hangover.

"You sure you're not sick?"

"I'm okay, I guess," Randy said, his voice still listless. Then he fell silent, staring off into space.

Margie cocked her head. "Randy? Is something wrong?"

Randy slowly turned to gaze blankly at his mother. "No," he said in the same dull monotone as before. "I'm fine."

Margie frowned thoughtfully. How many times had Randy claimed he felt lousy just so she'd let him stay in bed? And now, even looking like death warmed over, and owning up that he'd been out drinking till God knows when, he claimed he was fine. "Maybe you better go wash your face," she said. "It might make you feel better."

Immediately Randy got out of the bed and padded out of his room. A moment later Margie heard the sound of water running in the bathroom down the hall. She plumped up Randy's pillow then headed toward the kitchen. "You come into the kitchen as soon as you're through in there, hear?" she called as she passed the bathroom door, expecting no reply and already sure that as soon as he finished in the bathroom, Randy would go back to bed.

"Okay," Randy replied.

Margie stopped in her tracks and gazed perplexedly at the closed door to the bathroom.

A few minutes later Randy appeared in the kitchen. He slid onto his chair, then sat still, as if waiting for his mother to serve him. "What's the matter?" Margie carped at him. "Can't you get your own orange juice?" She started toward the refrigerator, knowing Randy would never bestir himself—something he'd learned from his father. By the time she got there, Randy already had the door open and the pitcher of orange juice in his hand.

Margie regarded the boy in puzzlement, then slid a bowl of cereal in front of him as he sat back down at the table. To her surprise, Randy made no move to drink the juice or start eating the cereal. "Well?" she asked. "Aren't you going to drink it?"

Randy stared at the glass for a moment, then picked it up and began to drink. Only when the glass was empty did he put it back on the table.

Margie frowned. "Do you want another?" she asked.

Randy shrugged. "It's all right," he said. "I'm fine."

"Well, you don't seem fine to me," Margie groused, her lips pursing.

Her frown deepened as she studied Randy's eyes. There seemed to be something odd about them—they had a dazed look, as if there were something Randy didn't quite understand. "I think maybe you'd better go back to bed," Margie said at last.

Silently, Randy rose to his feet and disappeared back down the hall toward his room.

For a moment Margie considered calling Dr. Banning, but then changed her mind. Hangovers could do funny things to people. Probably all Randy needed was another few hours in bed.

After all, there wasn't really anything wrong with him, except for that funny look in his eyes. He just seemed totally listless; not at all like his regular self.

Well, for today, at least, she wouldn't worry about it. She'd just keep an eye on Randy, she decided, and if he wasn't better by tomorrow, she'd take him to see the doctor.

Frank Arnold was sitting up in bed, glowering angrily when Judith and Jed, followed by Brown Eagle, spotted him through the open door to his room. Judith was about to ask him what was wrong, when they entered the room and she saw Otto Kruger standing at the foot of Frank's bed.

"Will you tell him to get out of here?" Frank growled, jerking his thumb at Kruger.

"Now, come on, Frank," Otto said. "I didn't come here to get you upset. I just wanted to find out how you are."

"And I told you," Frank grated, his jaw clenching so that his words shot through his teeth like tiny darts. "I'm going to hire a lawyer, and I *am* going to sue. What happened yesterday was no accident. Bill Watkins knew that pipe turned into a chute, and you knew it too. I know what happened, Kruger. They want me to shut up, and they're willing to kill me to do it. So I'm going to sue them. The whole bunch—UniChem, Borrego Oil, Kendall, Watkins, and you. Then we can all find out what's going on. Who knows?" he added. "Maybe we'll even find out what happened to Max!"

Kruger's face flushed angrily. "God damn it, Frank! Will you shut up and listen to reason for once in your life? You think I want to be here? I'm here because Kendall sent me. He says you should have had some kind of safety line if you were going to be in that pipe. UniChem's already agreed to take responsibility for the accident! You're getting all your expenses taken care of, and you'll get a big settlement as well." His eyes hardened and his voice took on a note of scorn. "If it was up to me, you wouldn't get a thing. But it's gonna be our word against yours, Frank. It was just an accident, pure and simple. So why the hell do you have to keep raving about some plot? You're starting to sound paranoid, for Chrissake!"

"Paranoid?" Frank repeated, heaving himself up into an upright position. "You listen to me, Kruger—" he began, but Judith cut him off.

"Stop it, both of you," she demanded. Her eyes fixed on Frank warningly, and she held his gaze for a moment. At last, reluctantly, he let his body relax.

Judith turned to Otto Kruger. "I think you'd better leave," she said coldly. "I don't know what this is all about, but I won't let you upset Frank."

"I'm only trying to reason with him—" Kruger began, but Judith shook her head.

"By telling him he's crazy?" she asked. "Please, just leave. All right?"

Kruger seemed about to argue, then turned and strode toward the door. Frank's voice stopped him just as he was stepping into the hallway.

"You can tell Kendall to get ready," he said. "I'm not kidding about this, Kruger. I am going to sue."

Kruger nodded. "I'll tell him," he said, his voice etched with sarcasm. "It's not going to make him feel particularly generous toward you, which I'd think you'd be worrying about right now, but I'll tell him." Then he was gone.

Deprived of his adversary, Frank was silent for a moment, then smiled weakly. "I guess I lost my temper, huh?" he said. "Seems like that's happening a lot lately."

Judith leaned over and kissed him. "Well, the way Kruger was talking, he had it coming. Frankly, I doubt the man even knows what a paranoid is!"

Frank slid his arms around her and gave her a squeeze, then nodded to Brown Eagle. "I guess you were right yesterday," he observed ruefully. "Thank you for coming." His eyes fixed on Jed. "You behaving yourself?"

Instantly, Jed thought of the shattered windshield on his father's truck, but then nodded. "Everything's fine," he said. "Nothing's going on that I can't handle."

Frank frowned slightly. There was something in Jed's eyes that told him the boy wasn't quite telling the truth. He was tempted to press the issue, but then changed his mind. If Jed thought he could deal with whatever was going on, he supposed the boy was old enough to try. He sighed heavily, then let himself sink back onto the pillow. "It seems I might have more of a problem than we thought yesterday," he said, choosing his words carefully. "I guess maybe you'd all better sit down." He glanced up at the clock on the wall. "Dr. Banning said he'd be here at eight-thirty."

Judith felt her knees weaken. "Did something happen last night?" she asked, sinking into the chair next to the bed. "If something happened, how come nobody called me? Or Jed?"

"Now, just take it easy," Frank said. "I had some kind of little seizure last night, that's all. It's probably nothing, but they've been giving me a lot of tests, and—"

"If it's nothing, why were they giving you tests?" Jed broke in. "If something happened, they should have called me. I would have come."

Frank eyed his son sardonically. "Were you home?" he asked.

Jed looked guilty. "I was out for a while," he admitted. "But I was back by eleven."

"And just where were you till eleven?" Frank demanded, unable to set aside his disciplinarian's role, even though confined to the hospital. Jed was spared having to face his father's probing stare by the appearance of Bob Banning. In his hand was a thick sheaf of papers, the results of the tests he'd administered to Frank during the long night. Frank fell silent as Banning began telling them what he thought had occurred.

Paul Kendall's eyes turned cold as he listened to Otto Kruger's report of his conversation with Frank Arnold. When Kruger was done, Kendall thanked him tersely, then sat for a moment, his fingers drumming on the top of his desk. He weighed his options carefully, but even as he conducted the mental exercise, he knew he was only wasting time: he'd made up his mind what he was going to do even as Kruger had been making his report.

Finally he picked up the phone.

As far as he was concerned, the problem of Frank Arnold was now solved.

"Unfortunately," Bob Banning finished, "we don't have a CAT scanner up here, and until we can get Frank down to Santa Fe or Las Cruces, we won't know for sure. But he definitely underwent a brain seizure of some kind last night, at about midnight. It might have been a minor cerebral hemorrhage, but if it was, I think we'd have seen something on the X rays. And given the state of his reflexes, I'm more inclined to think it was something involving his nervous system. We discovered a slight fracture in his skull, just a hairline, really, but any blow to the head can cause all kinds of reactions, some of them immediate, some of them delayed."

Judith, her face ashen, stared at Banning. She'd tried to follow him as he reviewed the test results, but she'd been only half listening, her mind occupied instead with an image of Frank writhing in agony on the floor, bashing his head against the wall. "I—I'm sorry," she said finally, her voice barely audible. "I'm afraid I don't understand. Are you saying he had a *stroke?*"

Banning hesitated, then nodded. "I'm saying it's certainly a possibility."

Judith felt her blood run cold. First Reba Tucker, then Max Moreland, now Frank. "I see," she breathed. Then: "Is it going to happen again?"

Banning spread his hands helplessly. "It's hard to say," he said. "Until we know more, I wouldn't want to try to predict anything. But it seems to me . . ." His voice trailed off as Frank's body appeared to stiffen. "Frank?" he said. "You okay?"

"I—I smell something," Frank whispered. Then, as a sour taste began to fill his mouth, he felt a twinge of panic. "It's happening again, Dr. Ban—"

His voice faltered, and suddenly his eyes opened wide as his whole body went rigid.

"Frank!" Judith cried out. She rose to her feet, staring in horror at the figure on the bed. "My God! What's happening to him?"

She instinctively reached out to touch Frank, but as another convulsion seized him, he bellowed in agony and his right arm swung up, his hand smashing against Judith's cheek, sending her reeling against the wall.

As Brown Eagle moved quickly to Judith, and Jed stared at his father in shock, Banning jammed his finger against the signal button, but the instruments wired to Frank's body had already sounded an alarm at the nurses' station, and the door flew open. Two orderlies and a nurse came into the room, surrounding the bed. Frank was thrashing wildly now, his face scarlet. His spine arched grotesquely and his left leg began twitching spasmodically.

"Get restraints," Banning barked. Instantly, one of the orderlies darted from the room. Frank's voice, his words unintelligible now, rose to an anguished scream, then was suddenly cut off as his body went limp.

"Hold him!" Banning snapped. The nurse and one of the orderlies grasped Frank by the upper arms, and then the second orderly reappeared. Working quickly, he strapped Frank's big body to the bed, attaching the last of the wide nylon straps just as another seizure gripped Frank.

His eyes popped open and his tongue protruded from his mouth. His throat began strangling, cutting off his anguished screams, and he struggled wildly against the bonds that held him to the bed.

"Can't you do something for him?" Judith moaned, her face smeared with tears as she stared helplessly at Frank. "My God, he's going to die!"

Banning spoke quickly to the nurse, and she disappeared from the room. A moment later she returned and handed the doctor a hypodermic.

But instead of plunging it into Frank's arm, he waited, watching.

"My God," Judith screamed. "Can't you see what's happening to him? For God's sake, do something!"

Then, as suddenly as it had begun, the seizure was over. Banning hesitated a moment, then handed the needle, unused, back to the nurse.

Ignoring Judith's sobs, he bent over Frank, checking his pulse and respiration, peering into his eyes.

"He's unconscious," he said. He looked at Brown Eagle, who was standing between Jed and Judith, his arms encircling them both. "You'd better take them out to the waiting room," he said, his voice gentle. "We have a lot of work to do."

Brown Eagle and Judith moved toward the door, but Jed remained where he was. His eyes met the doctor's. "Is he dying?" he asked, his voice eerily calm.

Banning hesitated. "I don't know," he said at last. "But I'm afraid I can't tell you right now that he's not." He saw Jed struggling with his emotions. "I'm sorry," he said. "We'll do the best we can."

Tears welled in Jed's eyes, then spilled over. But he said nothing, silently leaving the room to join Judith and his grandfather in the waiting room.

Nineteen

The three of them sat quietly in the waiting room, each occupied with their own thoughts.

For Judith, the vision of Frank, his strong body contorted by the horrible spasms, was etched sharply in her mind. But slowly the image changed, and she saw him lying back against the pillows, drained, his eyes closed, all his vitality suddenly gone.

It wasn't fair, losing Frank now, just when she'd found him. She shivered as she remembered the feel of his arms around her body, the touch of his lips on hers. Now she might never experience that again.

No!

She shoved the thought out of her mind. People recovered from strokes—it happened every day. And Frank was strong and healthy. He'd be all right.

For a moment, just a moment, she almost believed her own thoughts. But then she remembered Reba Tucker, and Max Moreland.

And the shots.

Her mind went back to the previous day. They'd given Frank a shot.

No. Not "they."

Greg Moreland had given Frank a shot, just as he'd arranged to give every teenager at the high school shots.

She gasped, then covered her mouth as both Jed and Brown Eagle turned to look at her.

Greg? she repeated to herself.

Was it possible?

Of course not—she'd known Greg Moreland for years.

Except, of course, she hadn't. She'd known him once, ten years ago, when he'd been a medical student. But it had been a full decade since she'd seen him. And yet her mind still rejected her own thoughts. Greg was a doctor—a doctor who truly cared about his patients. He'd even spent a lot of his own money to build a private rehabilitation center. . . .

A rehabilitation center where Reba Tucker still lay, helpless after her own stroke.

But Max?

Surely Greg wouldn't have done something to his own uncle. No. It was simply not possible.

And yet the thought wouldn't let go of her.

She picked up a magazine and began to leaf through it, determined to put the terrible thoughts out of her mind. But her imaginings kept reaching out to her, twisting themselves around her mind like the tendrils of a plant, squeezing at her until she thought she'd scream. And then, when she thought she could stand it no longer, the doors from the back wing opened and Bob Banning stepped through.

For a moment, until she saw the look on his face, Judith felt a surge of hope.

Banning motioned them to stay where they were, coming to perch uneasily on the edge of a chair, his hands clasped together, his eyes grave.

"What's happening?" she heard Jed ask. "What's going on with dad?"

Banning shook his head, and Judith instinctively reached out to take Jed's hand. But Jed, his wary eyes never leaving the doctor's face, barely seemed to notice her gesture.

"I'm afraid the news isn't very good," Banning said.

"He's awake again, but he's very groggy, and he's having a hard time speaking. I've checked his reflexes, and they don't look good. He's lost most of his control over his left arm, and he can't move his left leg at all. This time I'm sure of what happened. He definitely had a stroke, and it looks like a bad one."

A tiny wail of anguish tore itself from Judith's lips, but she quickly bit it back, determined not to let herself come apart. Jed, feeling dazed by what he'd just heard, stared anxiously at the doctor.

"But . . . he'll be okay, won't he?" Jed asked, his voice taking on a desperate tone. "I mean, people can get better after strokes, can't they?"

Banning chewed at his lower lip, choosing his words carefully before he spoke. "Yes, they can," he said at last. "And Frank's got a lot going for him. He's comparatively young, and he's strong as an ox." Then, as both Judith and Jed appeared ready to grasp at the straws he'd offered them, he added: "The problem is that we don't yet know how serious his head injuries are. They looked pretty minor until last night, but now I have to tell you that he's in grave danger. Apparently he has some blood clots in his brain. We're analyzing the possibilities of trying to relieve the pressure in his head surgically—"

"You can do that?" Brown Eagle asked. "You can operate on him?"

Banning spread his hands helplessly. "We don't know yet. We're trying to lower his blood pressure, and then we'll do another evaluation. But if he should have another hemorrhage while he's on the operating table, it could be pretty serious."

Judith's eyes closed for a moment, as if to shut out the implications of the doctor's words, and suddenly her mind filled with another image of Frank, this time sitting bolt upright in his bed, his face scarlet as he raged at Otto Kruger.

"Kruger," she breathed. "If he hadn't been here—"

Banning held up a restraining hand. "I thought about that," he said. "And of course if I'd known what was going to happen, I wouldn't have let him see Frank. But it isn't necessarily related."

Jed's eyes darkened. "I don't believe that," he said, his voice trembling with anger. "If you ask me, he came just because he knew it would piss dad off—" He cut off his own words, and his shoulders slumped. "What the hell difference does it make?" he asked hollowly. Then his eyes went back to Banning. "Can I see him?"

Banning hesitated, then nodded. "But don't be surprised if he doesn't recognize you," he said. "And don't stay long."

Jed nodded, then stood up. For just a moment his legs threatened to buckle under him, but he steadied himself and pushed through the doors into the east wing. He paused outside his father's room, took a deep breath and let himself in.

His father, lying flat on his back now, with a Levine tube in his nose and an array of wires connecting his body to a bank of monitors on a portable rack next to the bed, seemed to have shrunk since Jed had last seen him. His face was a pasty white, and his arms, lying limply by his sides, looked like the flaccid limbs of a man nearly twice his age. As Jed came in, Gloria Hernandez glanced up at him and gave him an encouraging smile.

"You've got a visitor, Frank," she said, motioning Jed over to the bed.

Jed stared down at his father's sallow face, and his eyes flooded with tears once again. He tried to speak, but his voice failed him. Then he saw that his father was trying to smile, and heard a garbled sound bubble up from his lips.

Jed leaned closer, and Frank's lips worked spasmodically. When he finally managed to speak again, the words came out slowly, one at a time.

"I ... said ... I ... really ... blew ... a ... fuse ... this ... morning."

The words seemed to break the tension in Jed. He reached out and touched his father's hand. "Gee," he said, forcing his voice not to tremble, "out there, they told me you were really sick. I guess they don't know what they're talking about, do they?"

Frank's head moved in a tiny nod and he managed to wink approvingly at Jed. "Good boy," he whispered, his words barely intelligible. "Never let 'em see you sweat ..."

He gasped for breath, the effort of enunciating the words seeming to have drained him. Jed felt a knot of fear grip his stomach, and he squeezed his father's hand. "It's okay, Dad," he said. "Don't try to talk."

But Frank's head moved again, and as his lips began to work, Jed leaned close. "Take ... care ... of ... Judith. ..." He winced slightly, then strained to speak once more. "They're ... killing ... me. ..." He whispered, his voice all but inaudible. "They're—"

Frank's voice strangled and his fingers tightened on Jed's hand like a vise. Jed's head jerked up and he instinctively looked at Gloria Hernandez just as the nurse roughly pushed him aside.

"He's having another stroke," she said.

But this time it was over almost as soon as it began.

Frank's body went rigid for a moment, and his face twisted into a brief grimace of pain. Then, quite suddenly, he relaxed. His body went limp and his head rolled to one side. Jed, terrified, stared at his father. "Dad?" he said. *"Dad!"*

The door flew open and Bob Banning, followed by an orderly, rushed into the room. "What's happened?" Banning asked, his eyes scanning the machines.

"Another stroke," Gloria told him. "It didn't last long, but it looked real bad."

"Damn." Banning cursed quietly, his eyes fixed on the monitor that displayed Frank Arnold's brain waves.

The lines running steadily across the screen were jagged and uneven, accurately reflecting the chaos that was occurring in Frank Arnold's brain.

Given what was happening to him, Banning could only believe that it was a blessing that Frank had sunk deep into a coma.

Judith sat in her car, trying to gather her wits together. She still wasn't certain what it was she hoped to accomplish by coming to The Cottonwoods. But as she'd sat waiting for Jed, then heard about Frank's third stroke, she'd known she had to come out here and at least try to find out exactly what had happened to Reba Tucker. Not, really, that she expected much, but at least she felt like she was *doing* something.

She stared at the place, slowly realizing that she'd subconsciously expected to see something quite different; perhaps even something sinister. But there was nothing about it that was out of the ordinary at all. It seemed to be nothing more than an old frame ranch house, together with what had apparently been a stable, a small barn, and a few smaller buildings that might have been guest quarters or bunkhouses, all of them scattered through a large grove of cottonwoods that was nestled against the canyon's northern wall. It was quiet here—birds chirped softly as they hopped among the branches of the trees, and the stream, flowing lazily in its bed along the south wall, was nearly silent; only a faint babbling sound revealed its presence at all.

She got out of her car and walked toward the main building, enjoying the coolness of the canyon. A few moments later she stepped through the front door, and almost immediately a woman she didn't recognize appeared from an office in the rear. The woman greeted Judith warmly enough, but when Judith told her she was there to see Reba Tucker, the welcoming smile was replaced with a small frown.

"Are you a relative?" she asked, eyeing Judith doubtfully.

"No, I'm not," Judith told her. "My name's Judith Sheffield. I—I used to be a student of Mrs. Tucker's." She wasn't sure quite why she hadn't told the woman she had also taken over Mrs. Tucker's job at the school, but something in the back of her mind told her to reveal as little as possible.

"Well, I don't know," the woman mused doubtfully. "Mrs. Tucker doesn't have many visitors . . ."

Judith's nerves, already frayed from the hours at the hospital, snapped. "Is there any reason why I can't see her?" she demanded.

The woman appeared flustered. "Well, no," she began, but Judith, sensing that she was about to qualify her words, let her go no further.

"In that case, why don't you just tell me where she is?"

The woman, looking trapped, glanced around as if hoping someone might appear to relieve her of the decision as to whether or not to allow Judith access to the patient. When no one appeared, she sighed heavily. "She's in Cabin Three," she said. "Just follow the path around the back, then keep to the right."

Moments later, as Judith gazed curiously at the small cabin that was set in a grove of cotton woods, she realized that from the woman's attitude, she'd half expected to see heavy wire-mesh panels covering the windows of the building, or perhaps even bars. But there seemed nothing odd about the cabin at all. It was simply a square frame building, maybe twenty feet on a side, painted a neutral shade of beige with dark brown shutters flanking the windows on either side of the door. Unconsciously drawing herself up straighter, Judith walked up to the cabin's door and rapped sharply. The door opened and a heavyset woman whose features had all but disappeared into the puffy flesh of her face looked at her suspiciously. The woman wore a rumpled white nurse's uniform, and a badge on her ample bosom identified her as Elsie Crampton.

"I—I came to see Mrs. Tucker," Judith stammered uncertainly as the nurse said nothing to her at all. "Is this the right cabin?"

Elsie Crampton shrugged. "This is it," she said. She held the door open, and Judith stepped into the cabin. Its walls were paneled with knotty pine, and a worn carpet covered most of the wooden floor. A hospital bed sat next to the window on the far wall, and by another window there was a worn chair.

In the chair, staring out at the canyon, sat the huddled form of Reba Tucker. In the ten years since Judith had seen her, the woman had aged terribly, though Judith had no doubt that most of the aging had taken place in the last few weeks.

"Mrs. Tucker?" Judith breathed.

There was no response from the figure in the chair. Judith glanced at the nurse. "Can she hear me?" she asked.

"Hard to say," Elsie replied. "The doctor says she can, but you couldn't make me swear to it. They say she's had some kind of stroke, but if you ask me, she's just gone senile."

Judith felt a flash of anger toward the nurse, but did her best to conceal it.

"Well, I got some things to take care of." Elsie Crampton went on. "If you need me, there's a bell there by the bed." she added, her tone clearly implying that she hoped Judith wouldn't use the bell. Turning her back on Judith, she walked out of the cabin, pulling the door shut behind her.

Judith stood still for a moment, then moved over to the chair by the window. Kneeling down, she gently touched Reba Tucker's arm. "Mrs. Tucker?" she asked again. "It's me. Judith Sheffield. Can you hear me?" As if from a great distance, Reba Tucker heard the voice speaking to her, and a memory stirred within the fragments of her mind.

This was a voice from the past, not one of the voices she knew from the endless expanses of time since she had awakened and found herself in this frightening place. Concentrating hard, she turned her head slightly, and her eyes examined the face that seemed suspended in front of her.

She recognized the face too. It was from somewhere long ago, before she'd died and gone to Hell. "Judy . . ." she breathed, her own voice sounding strange and unfamiliar to her.

A surge of excitement welled up in Judith. Mrs. Tucker *could* hear her; had even recognized her. "I came to find out what happened to you, Mrs. Tucker," she said, enunciating each syllable slowly and distinctly.

Reba felt her mind drifting, saw the image of the face fading slowly away. She concentrated harder, struggling to keep the image intact and to make sense out of the words Judy had spoken.

"Dead," she whispered at last. "Hell."

Judith's heart sank. Had Mrs. Tucker completely lost her mind after all? "No," she said. "You aren't dead, Mrs. Tucker."

Reba's mind grappled with the words. "Live?" she gasped. Then, her eyes flooding with tears, she shook her head.

"You *are* alive, Mrs. Tucker," Judith insisted. "You're alive, and you got sick, and they brought you here. They're trying to make you well again."

Reba's shattered brain picked at the words, then, once more, she shook her head slowly. "Hurt . . ." she breathed.

Judith frowned. "Hurt?" she repeated. "They hurt you?"

Reba Tucker's eyes clouded and her head moved slightly as she nodded. Then her voice crept forth from her lips again, and her hand reached out to seize Judith's own. "Smells," she managed to say. "Bad. See things . . . Bad . . ." She paused for a moment, then gasped one more word. "Hurts."

Judith felt tears in her eyes as she saw the pain and suffering that was etched in Reba Tucker's face. The woman's fingers, swollen with arthritis, clutched at Judith again, and she watched helplessly as Reba struggled to speak once more.

"Night," she managed to whisper. "Night . . . hurts."

Judith looked at her helplessly, but there was something flickering in the depths of the woman's eyes that told her that whatever had happened to Reba Tucker, she was certainly not senile. She seemed to be trying to reach out, trying to tell Judith what had happened, but finding the task nearly impossible. Desperately searching for something that might help her understand, Judith's eyes scanned the room.

And there, hanging at the foot of Reba Tucker's bed, was a metal clipboard.

Gently extracting her hand from Reba's grip, Judith hurried to the bed and took the clipboard off its hook. Her eyes ran down it quickly, trying to comprehend all the abstruse words and phrases that were jotted there in a nearly incomprehensible medical shorthand. She flipped through the pages, and then her eyes stopped at the last entry. In a sloppy handwriting—a scrawl that Judith automatically matched to Elsie Crampton—was a single word. "Seizure." Next to the word was the time: 12:15 A.M.

Judith's lips tightened and she put the clipboard back on its hook, then went back to kneel by Reba Tucker once again. "You had a seizure last night, Mrs. Tucker," she said. "Can you tell me anything about it? Anything at all?"

But Reba Tucker's eyes had glazed over, and she was once more staring out the window. Judith spoke to her again, then gently stroked her hand.

There was no response from the old woman.

Judith stood next to the chair for a few minutes, trying to think of something—anything—she might be able to do for Reba Tucker. But she knew there was nothing. Indeed, if it hadn't been for that strange, desperate light that had come into Reba's eyes, and the fact that she had spoken the name that Judith hadn't used for nearly a decade, she would have tended to agree with Elsie Crampton's judgment that Reba Tucker had turned senile. But that flicker of intelligence she'd seen had told her that Reba had been struggling to tell her as much as she could, or at least as much as she understood, of what had happened to her. And what had happened to her, as far as Judith was able to see, was that her mind had been destroyed.

Turning away, she moved to the cabin door and stepped outside. She spotted Elsie Crampton standing under a cottonwood tree a few yards away, smoking a cigarette. Making up her mind, Judith walked over to her.

"I saw her chart," she said. "I—I hope it's all right."

Elsie shrugged. "It's all right with me," she said. "I don't guess it's any big secret, if they leave it hanging there."

Judith nodded. "I was wondering what happened last night," she said. "I saw that she had some kind of seizure or something."

Elsie took another drag on her cigarette, then dropped it to the ground, grinding it into the dirt with her toe. "She started scream-ing," she said, her face setting in disapproval. "She went to sleep right after dinner—not that she ate much—and then in the middle of the night she just started yelling her head off. Don't know exactly what happened. By the time I got there, it was all over with."

Judith stared at the woman in disbelief. "You mean she's in there all by herself at night?" she asked. "How can they do that? She's helpless!"

Elsie shrugged. "Don't ask me," she said. "I don't make up the policies around here. I just do what they tell me." But her eyes darted toward the main building and her voice dropped a notch. "If you ask me," she said, "it doesn't seem like anyone around here really cares if the patients live or die. 'Course," she added, "that's the way most of these places are, isn't it? The checks come in, and nobody pays much attention to what happens." She shook her head. "Seems like a crappy way to spend your last years, though, doesn't it?" She looked at Judith. "She say anything? Mrs. Tucker, I mean?"

Judith hesitated, then shook her head. "No," she said. "I'm not even sure she knew I was there."

Elsie Crampton nodded. "Yeah, that's the way she is, all right. Just nothing left of her at all."

Judith nodded absently, already thinking of something else. "The seizure," she said. "On the chart, it said it happened at a quarter after twelve."

Elsie shrugged. "Well, that's what time I got there, I guess," she said. "Actually, I think it hit her just about midnight."

Judith felt a chill run through her.

It was at midnight last night that Frank had suffered his first stroke.

Gina Alvarez stood outside the Sparkses' house, hoping she wouldn't lose her nerve. But why should I? she asked herself. After all, Randy was the one who broke the windshield. Why should Jed have to pay for it? Especially after what had happened this morning.

She'd called Jed earlier, and when he hadn't answered the phone, she'd called the hospital. But when Gloria Hernandez let her know what had happened to Jed's father, Gina told the nurse not to call him to the phone. "I'll come over after a while," she'd said. "There's something I have to do first."

Finally, summoning up her courage, she went up to the front door and pressed the bell. A few seconds later Mrs. Sparks opened the door a crack, looked suspiciously out, then opened the door wider.

"Well, for heaven's sakes," she said. "Look who's here! Come on in."

But her welcoming smile faltered when Gina asked if Randy was home. "Oh, yeah," she said, jerking her head toward the hall. "He's still in bed, sleeping it off." Her eyes narrowed slightly. "You weren't up on the mesa with him last night, were you?"

Gina hesitated, then nodded.

"Hmph," Margie snorted. "Thought you were better than that."

"I—I really need to talk to Randy," Gina said.

Margie Sparks shrugged carelessly. "Suit yourself," she said. "But I warn you—he's acting kind of weird this morning. Not that he's getting any sympathy from me—the idea, a sixteen-year-old kid waking up with a hangover. Well, like father, like son, I always say."

As Margie moved off toward the kitchen, Gina made her way down the hall until she came to a closed door that she assumed was Randy's. She knocked, and when there was no response, tried the door. It was unlocked, and when she opened it a crack and looked inside, she saw Randy lying in bed, his eyes open, staring at the ceiling. "Randy?" she asked.

His head rolled over and he gazed at her blankly.

"It's me," Gina said. She stepped into the room, and Randy finally sat up. "Your mom says you're sick."

Randy shrugged. "I'm fine," he said.

Gina cocked her head. There *was* something weird about Randy today. His eyes looked strange—empty and his mouth seemed to have lost the sneer he usually affected.

"Well, you shouldn't be fine," Gina said. "Not after what you did last night."

Randy made no reply. Instead he simply sat up in bed, staring at her.

"You broke the windshield on Mr. Arnold's truck, you know," Gina said. "Or don't you remember?"

Randy nodded. "I remember."

It was the tonelessness of his voice that finally made Gina mad. It was as if he didn't even care. "Well, what are you going to do about it?" she demanded.

Randy only seemed puzzled. "What am I supposed to do about it?"

Gina glared at him. What was wrong with him? "Well, the least you can do is pay for it!" she exclaimed. "Why should Jed have to pay for it? He didn't do anything to you."

"All right," Randy said.

Gina stared at him, shocked. She couldn't imagine he wasn't even going to argue with her. Now she eyed him suspiciously. "It costs two hundred and fifty dollars," she said. "I called the Ford dealer in Las Cruces this morning."

She'd expected Randy to start laughing at her now, but instead he got out of bed, stark naked, and went to the chest of drawers that stood against the wall under the window. Too shocked even to speak, Gina simply stared at him. Randy pulled the bottom drawer completely out of the dresser, then reached in and fished out an envelope that had been taped to the inside of the dresser's frame. Opening it, he counted out $250, then replaced the envelope and the drawer. Handing Gina the money, he climbed back into bed.

Stunned, Gina gaped at the money in her hand, then turned to gaze at Randy, again. "Wh-Where did you get this?" she asked.

Randy shrugged. "I stole some of it. I made the rest selling drugs at school."

Gina felt her knees start to shake. It was crazy—all of it. She'd expected him to laugh at her—in fact, she'd expected him to flat-out refuse to pay for the windshield. She thought she'd at least have to plead with him, maybe even threaten to tell his mother what had happened.

But she'd never expected what had just happened.

And now Randy was just lying there in bed, as though he hadn't done anything strange at all. "L-Look," she stammered. "I've got to go, okay?"

Randy said nothing. She wasn't even certain he'd heard her. He was just looking off into space again, with the weird, empty look in his eyes. Stuffing the money into her pocket, she hurried out of the Sparkses' house, not even stopping to say good-bye to Randy's mother.

Twenty minutes later she was outside the hospital, wishing there were some way she could avoid going in. She hated hospitals, hated the smell of them, and the whole atmosphere of sick people. She could remember vividly the time when she was only five and her mother had brought her here to visit her grandmother. She had barely recognized the old woman lying in the bed, her eyes—eyes that had always before twinkled so merrily at Gina—now dull and lifeless. Her grandmother had held out a hand to Gina, and though she hadn't wanted to take it in her own, her mother had made her, and finally she'd touched the old lady's damp and clammy flesh, then let go immediately, hiding her hands behind her back. Ever since that day, whenever she had to come to the hospital she remembered her dying grandmother, and felt again her strange, cold touch. Still, she had to see Jed. Taking a deep breath against her apprehension, she pushed open the door and went into the waiting room.

Jed was slumped on the sofa, staring into space, and it wasn't until she sat down beside him and took his hand in her own that he finally noticed her.

"What's happened?" Gina breathed, though she was certain she already knew. "Your dad didn't . . ." Her voice trailed off as she found herself unable to utter the word.

Jed bit his lip, then shook his head. "He's not dead," he said, his voice rough with emotion. Then his eyes met hers. "But he might as well be. He—He's in a coma." Jed's eyes flooded with tears. "He's just lying there, Gina. He doesn't move, and when you touch him, he doesn't react, or anything."

Gina squeezed his hand, uncertain what to say. They sat silently for a few minutes, then Jed turned to look at her. "Oh, Jeez," he said. "I was going to come over this morning, wasn't I?"

"It's all right," Gina told him. And then she began telling Jed what had happened at Randy's house. "It was weird," she finished, almost fifteen minutes later. "He just did what I told him to do. And when he got out of bed, it was like he didn't even know he was naked."

Jed gazed at her. "You sure he wasn't stoned?"

Gina shook her head. "Uh-uh," she said. "It was like he was dead. It was like something had gotten into his brain and killed it."

Twenty

Rita Moreland was upstairs in the room she'd shared with Max, slowly going through the painful process of sorting through his things. The windows were opened wide to catch the afternoon breezes, and when she heard the crunching of tires on the gravel drive, she felt relieved to have an excuse to take a break from her work.

She arrived at the foot of the stairs just as the front door opened and Judith Sheffield stepped in.

"You're home," Rita said, starting down the stairs. But then, as she saw Judith's ashen face, she paused. "It's Frank, isn't it?" she breathed. "Has he died?"

Judith closed the door behind her, leaning against it for a few seconds, trying to gather her thoughts before she spoke. How could she tell Rita what she was thinking? Finally she shook her head. "No," she said. "He's not dead. But he's had a series of—" Her eyes met Rita's then. "He's had a series of strokes, Rita."

Rita froze on the stairs and her face paled, but then she recovered herself. She came to the bottom of the stairs and took Judith by the arm. "You look like you need a drink," she said. She guided Judith into the living room, steered her into a chair, then went to the bar and took out the decanter that contained the last of Max's favorite bourbon. Pouring an inch and a half into each of two tumblers, she handed one of them to Judith. "Drink this," she said. "Then tell me what's happening." Her eyes, clear and unfrightened, fixed on Judith.

"There is something happening, isn't there?" she asked.

Judith nodded, feeling the tension in her own body easing in the face of the older woman's cool control. She raised the tumbler to her lips. The whiskey burned her throat as it went down, but as it hit her stomach, a reassuring warmth spread through her body, and the chill that had seized her as she'd driven down from The Cottonwoods began to loosen its grip. Slowly, she began to tell Rita everything that had happened, everything she was thinking. The only thing she left out was the single common denominator.

Greg Moreland and his shots.

"I know it sounds crazy," she said when she was finished. "I know I must sound just as paranoid as everyone claims Frank is."

For a long time Rita said nothing. She leaned back in her chair, her eyes leaving Judith to study the glass in her hands, which she began slowly rolling one way and then another. At last, as if she'd come to some kind of internal decision, she faced Judith once again.

"We don't all think Frank is paranoid," she said. "Certainly I don't. But there's something you've left out, Judith."

Judith gazed warily at the elderly woman.

"You haven't mentioned my nephew."

Judith's breath drew in sharply. "I didn't—"

"You wanted to spare my feelings," Rita said, her words clipped. She rose to her feet and began pacing the room. "I keep finding myself wondering at what age it is that people decide they must begin sparing your feelings." She sniffed dismissively, and the fingers of her left hand flicked at the air as if brushing an insect away. "Well, of course it doesn't matter, does it. The point is, you do think Greg has something to do with this, don't you? After all, he was Reba's doctor and Max's doctor. He was also on duty when Frank had his accident yesterday, and I'm certainly well aware that it is Greg who coordinates all inoculations for the school." Judith remained silent, certain that no response was necessary. Rita turned away, and moved to a window, where she stood looking out, her back to Judith. But finally she turned around again. "Did you know I've always found my nephew to be something of an anomaly?"

Judith frowned.

"It's true," Rita went on. "When he was young, he was quite an insufferable snob. Oh, he was smart, and handsome, and had plenty to be proud of, but with him it was more than that. There was an arrogance about him, as if other people only existed to serve him." She smiled ironically. "He thought Max and I were fools when he was young, you know. Every year, after Max's brother died, and Greg started coming out to spend a month or two with us each summer, he used to try to convince us to move away from here. Thought we ought to live in New York, where his mother was, and have a mansion with a staff. 'Clodhoppers' is what he used to call the people around here."

Judith's frown deepened. "But you've seemed so proud of him."

Rita took a deep breath. "Oh, I have been. Ever since he came back that last summer, after poor Mildred died, too. That was the year he stayed. And he'd changed so much. To begin with, I was suspicious of it—I thought he must have some dark ulterior motive. Frankly, I always half suspected that he was trying to make sure Max and I didn't forget him in our wills. But over the last five years, I decided I was wrong." Now her eyes met Judith's. "But perhaps I wasn't," she said, her voice trembling for the first time since she'd begun to speak. "Perhaps nothing about Greg ever changed at all." She fell silent wishing she didn't have to go on, but knowing she did. "There's something about Greg that I've never told anyone before," she continued, her voice barely audible. "When he was a little boy, he—well, he suffocated a puppy once, just to see how long it would take to die, and to find out if he could revive it again."

"Dear God," Judith breathed. For several minutes the two women simply sat staring silently at each other, and then there was the sound of a car pulling into the driveway. A moment later the front door opened.

"Aunt Rita?" Greg Moreland called out.

Rita shot Judith a look of warning. "In here, dear," she called back. "Judith and I are just having a drink."

Greg Moreland appeared in the doorway, his face grave as he faced Judith. "I talked to Bob Banning this afternoon," he said. "I can't tell you how sorry I am about Frank."

Judith gazed at him, trying to read something—anything—into his expression that would give the lie to the sincerity of his words. But there was nothing. His eyes were large and sympathetic, and his smile gentle.

She was wrong—she had to be.

And then she remembered Rita's words of only a few seconds ago.

He suffocated a puppy once, just to see how long it would take to die.

She rose shakily to her feet and managed to force a smile. "Thank you," she said, then set her glass on the coffee table. "If you'll excuse me, I have a few phone calls to make."

Without waiting for a reply from either Rita or Greg, she hurried out of the room.

She imagined she could feel Greg's eyes on her back, watching her speculatively as she left.

Or was it her imagination?

At ten o'clock, as had been her habit for more than twenty years, Rita Moreland began preparing to go to bed. She moved through the house slowly, locking the doors and windows, following the same routine Max himself had always carried out until the day he'd died. Rita found the ritual comforting, in an odd way. It was almost as if, as she moved through the rooms on the lower floor, Max was beside her, giving her quiet instructions.

"Check the French doors twice," she imagined she heard him say as she went into the dining room. "That lock never worked quite right."

She twisted the lock, then rattled the doors in silent compliance with Max's equally silent instructions. Satisfied, she moved on to the library.

Max's presence was stronger here. His desk was covered with papers—even yesterday, when she'd worked at the desk herself, she hadn't disturbed Max's things. A book still lay open, facedown, on the table next to his favorite chair. Rita paused for a moment, fingering the volume, then abruptly picked it up, closed it, and returned it to its place on the walnut shelves that lined the room.

She crossed to the windows, checked their latches, then pulled closed the heavy damask curtains. When she returned to the door, she paused a moment, looking back into the room before she switched out the light.

A vague feeling of apprehension swept over her, and for a moment she thought she might cry. Resolutely, she flicked the switch, plunging the room into darkness, then pulled the door shut.

At last she went upstairs, but she went through the house on the second floor, opening the windows to let the cool night air drift through the rooms.

Finally, in the master bedroom, she began folding the clothes— Max's clothes—that were spread out on the bed, and packing them away in the boxes Greg had brought her yesterday.

Greg.

She felt an icy chill as she remembered the conversation she'd had with him after Judith had left the living room. She'd done her best to mask her emotions, but she was almost certain he'd known something was wrong.

Still, nothing had actually been said. They'd simply made small talk for a while, and she'd assured him she was doing just fine. No, she wasn't lonely.

No, she hadn't thought any more about selling the house.

Yes, she'd heard about Frank Arnold—Judith had told her.

She'd searched his face as they'd talked about Frank, looking for any sign that would tell her his concern was anything less than genuine. But even as he'd finally said good-bye, he'd spoken once more of Frank. "It's a shame," he'd said, his voice filled with what sounded to Rita like genuine sympathy. "He could be a pain in the neck sometimes, but no one deserves what's been happening to him today."

Rita had searched his eyes as he spoke, but they had revealed nothing. When he left, she went upstairs to talk to Judith again.

"I don't know," she'd sighed, perching on the edge of Judith's bed. "Perhaps we're wrong—"

"We're not," Judith had insisted. "I called my friend in Los Alamos. He doesn't have any answers yet, but he promised to keep trying." She glanced at her watch, then her eyes shifted back to Rita. "Look, I promised Jed I'd meet him at the hospital, then take him out for dinner. Why don't you come with me? I don't think you should be alone here."

Rita had brushed her words aside. "Don't be silly," she'd said. "I didn't say a word to Greg. And I need some time to think about all this. It's just . . . well, it just seems so unbelievable. You go ahead, dear. I'll be fine."

She'd fixed herself a small dinner, but had been unable to eat it.

She'd tried to work on some needlepoint, but her hobby hadn't soothed her either.

In the end she'd spent most of the evening simply sitting in front of an unlit fire, thinking about Greg and the experiment he'd carried out on his puppy.

And suddenly she was certain she knew the truth of what Greg was doing now.

Once again he was carrying on some kind of experiment. Only this time it wasn't a puppy that was dying.

This time it was people.

Tomorrow, she would find a way to stop him.

Tiredly, she put the last of the things on the bed into the boxes, then undressed and put on a robe. She sat at her vanity, pulled the pins out of her hair, then began giving it the hundred brushstrokes it had received every night since she was ten years old.

Usually, the ritual brushing of her hair relaxed her, made her put the worries of the day aside, but tonight it didn't seem to work, and when she was finished with the task, she still felt nervous.

She wandered restlessly to the window and looked out into the night.

The moon was high, and a silvery light danced on the face of the mesa. She could see bats darting through the night, and heard the soft hoot of an owl as it coasted on the breeze, searching the ground for mice.

She was about to turn away when she thought she saw a movement in the shadows outside the house, but when she looked again, there was nothing there. At last she turned away and slid into bed.

She read for a while, but the conversation with Greg kept replaying in her mind, and she had to go back over the pages again and again, the words holding no meaning for her.

At last she drifted into sleep.

She had no idea what time it was when she woke up, but she sensed immediately that something was wrong. The air in her room was heavy, and acrid with smoke.

She came fully awake, and then she could hear it.

A crackling sound, as if someone were crumpling paper.

She ran to the window and looked out, half expecting to see a brush fire burning in the desert.

But the bright yellow glow that filled the yard was not coming from the desert beyond her property. It was coming from the house itself.

Rita gasped, instinctively slammed the window shut, then

snatched her robe from the foot of the bed, shoving her arms into its sleeves as she hurried to the bedroom door.

The hall was choked with smoke. As she pulled the door open, it rolled into the room, filling her nostrils and making her gasp for air. She slammed the door closed again, then ran once more to the window.

No way down.

If she jumped, she would surely break her legs, if not her back.

She thought quickly. If she took a deep breath, she could make it down the stairs and out the front door before she had to take another.

What if she tripped and fell on the stairs?

She put the thought out of her mind.

She returned to the door once more, then steeled herself as she took three deep breaths, holding the last one.

Throwing the door open, she hurled herself toward the top of the stairs twenty-odd feet away.

She could hear the fire roaring now, and almost turned back, but then she was at the top of the staircase. The walls of the foyer were blazing, their ancient handcarved wood panels crackling and curling as the fire consumed them.

Now it was too late to turn back. She drew the robe tighter around her as she hurried down the marble stairs. Then she was in the foyer itself. The front door was only a few yards away.

She ran to it, twisting at the knob, her aching lungs releasing her breath as they anticipated the fresh air on the other side of the door.

The door refused to open. Rita's fingers fumbled with the lock mechanism, struggling to turn it.

Her lungs expanded and she choked as smoke was sucked into her throat.

Coughing, she twisted at the lock again, then jerked hard on the door.

It gave way slightly, then stuck again.

The chain!

Panic was overwhelming her now, and as she tried to breathe again, smoke gorged her lungs and she felt her legs weaken beneath her. She hurled herself against the door, then tried to reach the chain, but it was too late.

Her legs betrayed her, and she slid to the floor, overwhelmed by the smoke that was trapped in the room.

The fire seemed to close in on her, reaching out to take her in its arms, its flames whispering to her, calling to her.

As her lungs filled once more with the bitter, stinging miasma, she gave in to the beckoning arms, gave herself up to the fire.

And as she passed into the blackness that now surrounded her, she thought she saw Max, coming toward her, his hand held out to her.

That was how they found her when the fire finally died: her hand stretched out as if reaching for help. They thought she was reaching for the door, trying to make good her escape from the flames.

In truth, though no one would ever know it, she had not been reaching for the door at all in those last fleeting seconds of her life.

She had been reaching for Max, and she had found him.

Night fell in Borrego. High above the town, at the rim of the canyon, there was a low hum of well-oiled machinery. The huge antenna came slowly to life.

Midnight.

Gina Alvarez was lying in her bed, her eyes closed, a book propped on her knees. She'd fallen asleep earlier that evening, but then awakened when the fire trucks screamed by the little house she shared with her mother and younger sister. She'd gotten up and looked out the window. At first she'd seen nothing, but then, off in the distance somewhere near the mesa, an orange glare had flared up. She'd thought about going outside and trying to get a better look, but then decided against it and gone back to bed. But by then she was wide awake again, so she'd decided to do some reading for her American literature class. The book was *The Deerslayer*, and though she found the story interesting enough, the style seemed kind of old-fashioned to her, and she'd found her eyes growing heavy.

Now she wasn't quite asleep, but neither was she quite awake. She was in that half state somewhere in between, where she was vaguely aware of what was going on around her, but the images of dreams to come were already beginning to sneak up from her subconscious like night creatures emerging from their holes.

A haze of color played around her vision, and she idly wondered if it could be morning already. But she knew it was impossible—her reading light was still on, and she could feel the weight of her book resting on her legs. She toyed abstractly with the idea of moving the book to her night table and switching off the light, but knew the movement itself would banish the sleep that had almost overcome her. Then she would be lying in the darkness, fully awake again, and her mind would start working overtime, going over her schedule for tomorrow, worrying about a quiz in history, trying to think of things she might be able to do to help Jed.

Suddenly, despite herself, she was wide awake again.

Sighing, she picked up her book, stared at its open pages for a moment, then closed it and set it aside.

She snapped off the light, rolled over, and tried to will herself to fall instantly asleep.

Seconds ticked by.

She smelled something.

She frowned slightly and sniffed at the air, then sat up. Something smelled terrible. Like burning rubber. Or garbage rotting.

Gina's frown deepened, but when she drew another breath in through her nose, the strange odor seemed to be gone. She hesitated a moment, then lay down again. She concentrated on making each of the muscles in her body relax, starting with her toes, then working her way up her legs, through her torso, then down her arms to her fingertips. Usually, by the time she was finished, she was almost asleep.

A few minutes later she was almost done. She felt totally relaxed, almost as if she were floating in space. Soft tendrils of sleep stroked at the edges of her mind, and she began reaching out toward them, welcoming them.

Dreams began to form, shapeless images of swirling colors, spinning out of the blackness, dancing in front of her eyes. Then, as she watched, they began to take shape, but just as she was about to recognize what they might be, they would disappear.

And then, quite suddenly, her whole body went into a spasm, every muscle in her jerking in unison.

And she was awake again.

She was sure she knew what had happened. The spasms came over her every now and then, just when she was on the verge of falling asleep. They always seemed to come jumping out at her, taking her by surprise, just when she was most comfortable, just when she had curled in the most perfect position, feeling neither too hot nor too cold. Then she would lie awake for another half hour, having to start all over again with her complicated program of relaxing.

Except that tonight was different.

Tonight, after the spasm hit her, she felt really relaxed. She stretched languidly in the bed for a moment, then yawned.

She had no urge to turn the light back on and read some more, nor did she even feel her usual impatience at the prospect of losing another half hour or so to nothing more productive than trying to go to sleep.

Within the space of a minute she drifted off into a deep, dreamless sleep.

Jeff Hankins rolled over in bed, kicking out at the covers, then jerking awake.

The dream had been vivid.

He'd been on the football field, and he'd just caught the kickoff in the second half. The ball had come into his arms solidly, and he was already on the run.

In the stands he could hear all his friends cheering wildly as he sprinted down the field.

Then, out of the corner of his eye, he spotted one of the opposing players, bearing down on him from the left. He'd feinted, then darted right across the other player's path, feeling the boy's fingers try to grasp his ankle as he went by.

The field seemed to be clear then, and he could see the end zone, only twenty more yards away.

The crowd was going crazy, and the band was already playing a series of fanfares, urging him on as he charged down the field.

Ten yards to go, then five.

And then, out of nowhere, they appeared.

Three of them. Big boys, each of them towering over him, barreling down on him. He tried to turn away, but suddenly there were two more of them, even bigger than the first three, blocking his way.

And then they hit him.

He felt the shock of their weight as they slammed down on him, felt his lungs collapse as the wind was knocked out of him.

He woke up with a start, sitting bolt upright in bed. He gasped for breath, struggling to recapture his wind. Then he realized where he was, and that it had been nothing more than a dream.

Christ, he wasn't even on the football team. In fact, his interest in football went no further than in taking a six-pack to the games and getting drunk under the grandstand with a couple of his friends. Then, after the game, they'd go out and raise a little hell around town until they got bored or the cops sent them home.

And yet, from the way he felt, it sure seemed like he'd been playing just now. The whole thing was clear in his mind, and his head even hurt, just as though someone had kicked him.

He lay back down and his breathing slowly returned to normal. He thought about the dream, even imagined he heard the crowd cheering him on again.

Fat chance of that ever happening. He'd never been any good at team sports—he'd always thought they were stupid. If you couldn't do something your own way, he'd decided long ago, it probably wasn't worth doing.

But now, as he remembered the dream once more and imagined what it would feel like to actually hear a crowd of people rooting for you, he wondered if maybe he'd been wrong.

He snickered softly as he thought about what his friends would say if tomorrow, instead of going down to the A&W to hang out after school, he tried out for the football team.

Maybe, he decided, he'd just do it.

A few minutes later, half hoping the dream would come back so he could try the play again, Jeff drifted back to sleep.

Susan Paynter stood up and stretched. It had been a quiet night. The hospital was almost empty, and most of the patients were sleeping, except for old Mrs. Bosworth, who was lying in her bed staring up at the television on the wall of her room. Mrs. Bosworth barely slept at all, but it didn't seem to bother her, and as long as Susan left the TV on, she didn't complain about anything.

She wandered down the hall, glancing into each of the rooms as she went, then turned into the staff lounge at the end of the hall. The night orderly was sitting at the table leafing through a magazine. He glanced up, then went back to the magazine as Susan poured herself a cup of coffee. Wincing as she sipped at the stale and bitter brew, she reached for the sugar. But before she could pick it up, a scream shattered the quiet of the little hospital. Instantly, the orderly was on his feet.

"It's Frank," Susan said as they ran out of the lounge and headed down the hall. "Find Dr. Banning."

But from the other end of the hall, Bob Banning was already racing toward them.

Susan reached the room first, flinging the door open and snapping on the lights. When she'd stopped in no more than five minutes before, Frank had been lying peacefully in the bed, his breathing slow and regular, all his vital signs strong. Indeed, except for the abnormal patterns of his brain waves, he would have appeared merely to be asleep.

But now his eyes were wide open and he was once more struggling violently against the straps that held him to the bed. The veins on his neck and arms were standing out starkly against his flesh, and strangled sounds were bubbling from his throat.

"Jesus," the orderly whispered, his eyes widening as he stared at Frank. "Is he awake again?"

Bob Banning quickly surveyed the monitors on the wall. Frank's brain waves were going crazy now, forming a jagged line that bore no pattern at all. It was as if a storm were raging in his brain, sending stimuli to every muscle in his body at the same time.

Other monitors showed that his breathing and heartbeat had gone wild as well.

And then, as they watched, it stopped.

Frank went limp, his arms and legs dropping onto the bed, his head lolling on the pillow.

His eyes, staring up at the ceiling, remained open, but held a glassy, sightless look.

Susan Paynter gasped, her own heart pounding. She'd never seen anybody actually die before. Her eyes went to the monitors that tracked Frank's vital signs, and she saw that although the man's heartbeat had evened out, his breathing had all but stopped.

Though Frank Arnold wasn't dead yet, in a few more minutes he would be.

Without waiting to be told, Susan raced to get a respirator. In less than a minute she was back, wheeling the machine through the door and into the space that had been cleared for it next to the bed.

Almost silently, each of them knowing his job so well that few words were necessary, the three of them set to work.

Fifteen minutes later, Frank's condition had stabilized, and Bob Banning sighed heavily. "Get him into X ray," he told Susan. "Whatever happened in there must have been massive, and I want to see how bad it is."

Susan nodded. "Shall I call Jed?" she asked.

Banning hesitated. By rights, he supposed, Frank's son should be notified immediately of what had happened. But what good would it do, really? At the moment he could tell Jed nothing more than that his father had apparently suffered yet another stroke.

And what could he tell the boy when he asked about his father's condition?

Only that although his body was still alive, his brain was now, to all intents and purposes, dead.

"Let him sleep," he said. "There's nothing he can do for Frank, and tomorrow he's going to have to make the hardest decision of his life." His eyes drifted to the inert form in the bed. "He's going to have to decide whether to keep his father this way, or let his body die too."

A few minutes later, as he prepared to take Frank, still in his bed, down to the X ray room, he wondered if it wouldn't have been kinder for him to have ignored the respirator when Susan had brought it in, and simply let Frank go.

But that wasn't his decision.

That was a decision only Jed Arnold could make.

Then again, Jed might not have to make it at all. For it was quite possible that Frank Arnold would have yet another stroke before the morning came, and his suffering would be over.

But it was not to be: midnight had come, and now was gone.

Twenty-two

J ed stirred restlessly in his bed, then came abruptly awake. It wasn't a lingering waking, the kind of quiet emergence from sleep he usually enjoyed, reluctant to leave the comfort of his bed. Instead it was a sudden sharpening of all his senses, a tensing of his body, as if some unseen danger lurked nearby. He sat up, pushing aside the single blanket he had slept under, then rubbed at the ache in his right shoulder where his muscles had knotted from lying too long in one position.

He hadn't slept well. He'd gone to bed early, his mind confused with everything that had happened the day before. But as he'd lain awake, he'd remembered the strange sense of peace that had come over him the night he'd sat in the kiva with his grandfather. He'd begun to picture himself there, visualizing the glowing fire and the low roof, summoning from the depths of his memory every sensation he'd seen and heard and felt.

Slowly, as he lay in his bed, that strange trancelike state had come over him once more.

He still wasn't certain if he'd actually slept at all, for last night, in the end, had been another night spent with the spirits, and the memories of the things they had shown him were still fresh in his mind.

He had flown with Rakantoh again, soaring over the desert, seeing the world once more through the eyes of the spirit.

Everywhere, there had been evil. The earth below was scarred with the ravages of the white men, and from the sky he had been able to see them creeping through the darkness, feel the malevolence radiating from them.

For a time his vision had been filled with the brilliant yellow of flames, but after flaring up into a blinding radiance, they had quickly died away.

A little later—he had no idea how long, for time itself seemed to warp as he flew with the spirit—he had felt a strange vibration in the air and become disoriented. He'd felt himself tumbling through the sky, falling toward the earth, certain he was about to die. He had called out to Rakantoh, but the spirit was rolling and yawing in the air too, his enormous wings flapping uselessly. And then the curious vibrations suddenly stopped and he regained his bearings.

But from the earth below he felt a new sensation, a perception of pain such as he had never felt before. Rakantoh, screaming with rage, had wheeled on the wind, and they had soared away above the canyon, as the spirit searched in vain for his lost refuge beneath the lake.

Now, in the growing light of dawn, Jed lay motionless, his mind examining what he had seen in the visions of the night, trying to fathom the meaning of his strange fantasies.

It was nearly six-thirty when Judith emerged from Frank's bedroom. Though Jed had insisted he didn't need her to spend the night in the house with him, she'd stayed anyway, knowing that if she'd be able to sleep at all that night, it would be easier in Frank's bed, where at least she would feel his presence. It had worked, for she had slept soundly, and when she awoke, felt herself oddly comforted by the faint smell of him that still clung to the sheet in which she was wrapped. Now she paused outside Jed's room, his door ajar. She tapped lightly, then pushed it farther open. He was lying on the bed, and though he seemed to be looking right at her, he didn't acknowledge her presence at all.

"Jed?" she said. "Jed, are you all right?"

He stirred slightly, and then his eyes cleared. "I think we should call the hospital," he said quietly. "I think something else happened to dad during the night."

Judith felt a pang of fear pricking at her, but forced herself to reject it. What could Jed possibly know? If there had been a problem with Frank during the night, surely they would have called here. She said nothing, as she turned and walked through the small living room and into the kitchen, where she started a pot of coffee. But she kept eyeing the phone, the fear Jed had aroused in her growing by the minute. She remembered the other day, when he'd known it had been Randy Spark's who threw the rock through Rita's window.

At last, as Jed came in and sat down silently at the table, she picked up the phone and punched in the hospital's number.

As she listened to Dr. Banning's brief description of what had happened during the night, her legs weakened beneath her. Then she hung up and faced Jed.

"You were right," she said, her voice quavering.

Twenty minutes later, with Jed at her side, Judith entered the hospital. As soon as she saw the look on Bob Banning's face, she knew it was even worse than she'd thought.

Banning led them into Frank's room, standing quietly as Judith took Frank's hand in her own, her eyes flooding with tears. She gazed down at him, trying to see the vital man she'd come to love so much. But the man in the bed seemed a stranger.

His face was expressionless, his jaw sagging. Though his eyes were closed, he didn't look as if he were sleeping.

Despite the motion of his chest as the respirator forced him to breathe, he looked dead.

Though she was absolutely certain he was totally unaware of his surroundings now, Judith leaned over and kissed his cheek. Still holding his hand in her own, she whispered aloud the thought that was in her mind. "Oh, Frank, what do you want us to do?"

They stayed with him a few minutes, then finally left his room, following Bob Banning into his office.

"He—He could still come out of it, couldn't he?" Jed asked, his voice taking on a desperate tone. "I mean, people wake up from comas, don't they?"

Banning was silent for a moment. It would have been easier, he knew, if Frank had died during the night. Indeed, without the respirator he would have. But the respirator had been there, and it had been Banning's duty to use it. So now he had to explain the reality of Frank Arnold's condition to the two people who loved him most.

"I'm afraid he won't," he said, forcing himself to meet Jed's eyes as he spoke the words. The boy flinched as if he'd been struck, and his jaw tightened; but he said nothing, and managed to control the tears that glistened in his eyes. "Without the respirator," Banning, went on, "I don't think he'd survive more than a few minutes."

He stood up and went to a light panel on the wall where the latest X rays of Frank's brain were displayed As his fingers pointed out large dark masses within Frank's skull, he resumed speaking. "The damage is very extensive. There are parts of his brain that are still functioning, but his mind is essentially dead. In fact, I don't think it's fair to say he's either asleep or awake. He isn't even in what I personally would call a coma. To me a condition of coma implies that there is still a functioning mind within the brain, a mind that has a possibility, no matter how slim, of recovering." He took a deep breath, then went on. "But unfortunately, for Frank that just isn't true anymore. What he's in is more like a state of suspended animation. Though his body is still alive, he has no control over it, let alone awareness of it. He's conscious of nothing, and never will be." He paused for a second, then forced himself to utter the words he knew he had to speak. "I'm very sorry, Jed, but I'm afraid your father is dead."

Judith gasped, and reached out to clutch Jed's hand, "But there must be something you can do," she pleaded. "His heart is still beating, and he's breathing—"

Banning spread his hands helplessly. "Only because of the respirator," he replied. "Without it . . ." He left the sentence hanging, and Judith nodded numbly, forcing herself to accept the unacceptable. At last, taking a deep breath and unconsciously straightening herself on the sofa, she faced the doctor again.

"What can we do?" she asked, her voice almost eerily calm.

Banning chose his words carefully. "I'm afraid there isn't much we can do. Here—at the hospital—it's our policy to keep a . . . shall we say 'keep a body viable' as long as we can."

Jed gazed uncertainly at the doctor, and Judith felt her eyes moisten. Steeling herself, she forced the translation of Banning's words from her lips. "You mean you won't let Frank die, even though he can no longer live on his own," she said.

Banning nodded gratefully. It wasn't a policy he totally agreed with, but he wasn't at liberty to suggest that perhaps the best thing for Frank, and Jed too, was simply to turn off the respirator. But if one of them brought it up, he was more than willing to discuss it with them. Now, to his relief, Judith did just that.

"If we decided to move Frank," she said. "Is there a place where they would allow us to turn off the respirator?"

An anguished wail erupted from Jed's throat. "Jude, I could never do that—" he began, but Judith pressed his hand, silencing him.

"I didn't say that, Jed. I said *if*. We have to understand all the possibilities. And we have to do what's right for Frank, even if it's hard for us." Her eyes shifted to Dr. Banning in a silent plea for help.

"She's right, Jed," Banning said. "I know how hard this is for you. Deciding what to do is going to be the hardest choice you've ever had to make. It's possible that with the respirator and intravenous feeding your father could live for years. Or he could die at any time. But as long as he's here, we'll do whatever has to be done to keep him alive. On the other hand," he went on, barely pausing, "if he were in a sanitarium, or nursing home, you would have the right to ask them do nothing for Frank except make him comfortable. And if you should change your mind about the respirator, there are places that would be willing to accommodate you.''

Jed chewed at his lip for a moment, then faced the doctor, his eyes stormy. "If he were your father," asked finally, his voice holding a note of challenge, "What would you do?"

Banning gazed steadily at the boy. "I'd let him go," he said, and saw Jed flinch away from the words. "I don't believe in keeping someone alive simply because I *can*. Here, I have to do it. It's the rule of the hospital. But if it were up to me . . ." He shook his head "There is a time to live, and a time to die," he quoted softly.

The words seemed to hang in the air, and then Jed spoke again. There was a new strength in his voice. "Can I do that?" he asked. "I'm only sixteen, but Dad doesn't have any other family. Can I make the decisions?"

Banning shifted uneasily. "I don't know," he finally admitted. "But it seems to me we'll have to find someone to act as your guardian, or trustee."

"Jude," Jed said instantly. His eyes shifted to meet hers. "Will you do it?" he asked, his eyes pleading. "You know it's what Dad would want."

Judith's eyes brimmed over and tears began to run down her cheeks. Jed reached out and gently brushed them away. "Hey," he said, his voice ineffably gentle. "It's gonna be all right. We'll make all the decisions together. Okay?"

Judith's whole body trembled for a moment, and then she regained her composure. "Is there a place we could move Frank to?" she asked.

Banning turned to Jed. Something in the boy had changed just now. His face was still pale and drawn, but in the depths of his eyes, Banning saw a new maturity. Quite suddenly, Jed had been forced to grow up. "There's a place up in the canyon," he began. "I don't know much about it, really—"

"The Cottonwoods?" Jed asked, his voice suddenly hard. Banning nodded.

"No," Jed said immediately.

Confused, Banning turned to Judith, but her expression had taken on the same look of determination as Jed's. "It's the only place I can think of right now—" Banning began, but Judith cut him off.

"Then we won't do anything for now," she said. "Frank can stay here, can't he?"

"Of course," Banning replied. Abruptly, the mood in the room had changed. Judith and Jed were looking at each other, and though neither said a word, Banning sensed that a communication was taking place between them.

Jed stood up. "I think we need to talk about this for a while," he said. "And then we'll decide what we have to do. Is that all right?"

Banning nodded, and a moment later watched helplessly as they left his office. Something, obviously, had happened, but he had no idea what it might have been

Judith was sitting in the waiting room with Jed. They hadn't spoken for several minutes, each of them trying to absorb what the doctor had told them. They felt numb, their minds spinning helplessly as each tried to accept that Frank was now irretrievably gone.

A shadow passed over Judith, and she glanced up. A figure was silhouetted in the main doors, framed against the brilliant morning sky, but the glare from beyond the doors prevented her from seeing who it was. Then the doors opened and the person stepped into the lobby.

It was Greg Moreland.

He stopped, staring at Judith almost as if he'd seen a ghost. And then, seeming to recover himself, he came toward her. "Judith? Are you all right? Where have you been?"

There was an urgency in his voice that made Judith rise to her feet. "It's Frank—" she said, then broke off. Her eyes hardened, fixing on Greg. "But you already know what's happened, don't you?" she asked.

Greg hesitated, appearing confused. Then his expression dissolved into one of sympathy. "Oh, God," he said quietly. "You don't know, do you?"

Now it was Judith who looked confused. "F-Frank," she repeated, stammering. "He's had another stroke."

"Oh, Christ," Greg groaned. "No, it's Aunt Rita." He lowered himself into a chair and reached out to take Judith's hand. "I'm sorry." He felt Judith stiffen, then she jerked her hand away. "There was a fire last night," Greg went on, "out at her house. She—Well, I'm afraid she didn't get out."

Judith stared at him, stunned. "I don't believe it," she said, her voice hollow. But the words, she knew, were as hollow as her voice, for she could read the truth in Greg's eyes. "What happened?" she demanded, too shocked, too exhausted, too emotionally drained to hold back the cold fury that washed over her now. "What did you make it look like? A short in the wiring? A coal popping out of the fireplace?"

Greg paled and his jaw tightened. "My God," he breathed. "How can you even suggest such a thing? She was my aunt, Judith. She was almost as close to me as my own mother.''

''Yes,'' Judith said, the word escaping her lips in a furious hiss. ''And Max could have been your father. And what about Reba Tucker? Were you close to her too? What are you doing, Greg? Why?''

She buried her face in her hands, sobbing, and Greg gestured to Gloria Hernandez, who was just coming in for her shift. Gloria hurried over, and Greg spoke to her softly.

''She's hysterical, Gloria,'' he said. ''There's a sedative in the cabinet in my office. If you'll just bring it.''

At his words, Judith's wits returned to her. ''No!'' she exclaimed loudly. ''It's all right, Gloria. I'm upset, that's all. But I'll be all right.'' She turned to Jed, grasping his hand tightly in her own. ''Maybe you'd better take me home, Jed,'' she said. ''I—I think I need to lie down for a while.''

Instantly Jed rose to his feet, and with Judith leaning heavily on him, he led her out to her car. She fumbled in her purse, pulled out her keys and handed them to him. Then she collapsed into the front seat, once more burying her face in her hands. Only when she was certain that they were at least a block from the hospital did she straighten up in the seat again.

''Stupid!'' she said out loud. ''Stupid, stupid, stupid!''

Jed looked over at her, his eyes wide. ''What the hell—'' he began, but Judith shook her head impatiently.

''Not you, Me. How could I be so stupid as to sit there and accuse him like that?''

Jed glanced at her out of the corner of his eye. ''You really think he killed Mrs. Moreland?'' he asked.

Judith sank back in the seat. ''Oh, God,'' she groaned. ''I don't know. Maybe I'm crazy.'' They were in front of Jed's house now, but neither of them made a move to get out of the car. ''What do you think, Jed? Am I crazy?''

Jed turned and looked at her. ''I don't think so,'' he said. ''But what can we do? We can't go to the cops—all they'd say is that we're both nuts. And everybody around here is crazy about Greg anyway. Shit, they think he's the next thing to God.''

Judith's lips tightened into a hard line. ''Wouldn't you think they'd notice that most of his patients are either dead or dying?''

Jed shrugged. ''Even Heather Fredericks,'' he said. ''Except I don't see how you can blame . . .'' The words died on his lips as he remembered something. Starting the car again, he shoved it into reverse and shot back into the street. ''We're going up to the mesa to

see my grandfather," he said. "Remember the first time we went up
there, when I said he was crazy?"

Judith nodded numbly.

"Well, I was wrong. He said someone made Heather jump into
the canyon, remember? He said he'd seen it from the kiva, just like
I saw Randy Sparks from the kiva. And if he saw what happened,
maybe he knows *how* they did it too."

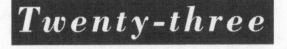

Twenty-three

J udith Sheffield stood at the doorway of her classroom on Monday morning, her eyes searching the hall for any sign of Jed. The
first bell had already rung, but this morning the kids were slow
in heading toward their classes, and Judith knew why. They, like the
teachers in the lounge a few minutes ago, were talking among themselves about the fire in which Rita Moreland had died. Indeed, little
else had been talked about in Borrego since the morning after the
fire, when nearly everyone in town had gone out to the charred
ruins of the house. There, they had gathered in small groups, murmuring quietly, speculating on what might have happened.

Judith herself had said little about it, either yesterday or this morning. Not that she hadn't wanted to tell them what she thought—that
the fire had been deliberately set, and that perhaps she, as well as
Rita Moreland, was supposed to have died. But as she listened to the
talk, she realized that so far there wasn't even a rumor that the fire
might have been arson. Indeed, according to Elliott Halvorson—
who, as always, had stopped at the café that morning to pick up the
latest gossip—the fire had apparently started in the basement, where
the remains of a pile of oily rags had been found. She had imagined
the looks on the teachers' faces if she'd told them what she suspected—that Greg Moreland himself had set the fire.

Frustration was building inside her. So far all she had were suspicions. But even those suspicions had grown stronger yesterday,
when she'd listened to Brown Eagle describe what he'd "seen" the
night Heather Fredericks died.

"There was someone with her," Brown Eagle had said. "He was
talking to her, telling her what to do. And she did everything he

wanted her to. When he told her to jump, she jumped.'' But when Judith had suggested that Brown Eagle tell the police about the vision he'd had, he'd shaken his head. "I was in the kiva, remember? I couldn't possibly have seen anything. I'm a Kokatí—an Indian." His voice had taken on a rare bitterness. "We all lie about everything, you know."

And so, in the end, she and Jed had found themselves with nothing to do but wait.

Wait until Peter Langston called, and told them what was in the syringe Judith had sent him; in the end, it was the only solid evidence they had. If, indeed, it turned out to be evidence at all. There was still a chance that she was wrong, she reminded herself.

Now, as the corridor began to clear and the bell rang signaling the beginning of the first period, she stepped inside, closing the door behind her. But Jed's absence preyed on her. He'd insisted he'd only stop at the hospital for a few minutes and would be at school in plenty of time. She decided if he didn't show up by the end of the hour, she would call the hospital.

She moved quickly up and down the aisles, collecting homework assignments, then went to the blackboard and raised the map to expose the morning quiz, a daily ritual always accompanied by groans of anguish from the class.

Today, however, there were no groans. Frowning, Judith ran her eyes over the class, doing a quick head count. Three people were absent, which was a little better than on Friday. So the lack of groaning wasn't simply a matter of fewer people. She tried to tell herself that they were just getting used to her ways.

The trouble was, she was used to their ways too, and she found she missed the loud complaint. It was almost as if they suddenly didn't care enough to protest. Still, they were all hunched over their papers, working diligently at the equation she'd put on the board. She began checking off names in her attendance book, then turned her attention to the stack of homework on her desk. She was about to begin correcting the first paper when the door at the back of the room opened and Jed stepped inside. Their eyes met, and she knew immediately that something had gone wrong. Signaling him back out into the hall, she walked quickly down the aisle to join him.

"They moved him out of the hospital," he said, his voice taut. "Gloria Hernandez told me."

Judith stared at him. It wasn't possible. "How?" she breathed. "Who authorized it?"

"Dr. Moreland," Jed replied, his voice cold, his eyes glittering with anger. "Gloria says he's always been Dad's primary physician—whatever the hell that's supposed to mean—and that when he came in this morning, he had Dad moved out to The Cottonwoods. He claimed it would be a lot cheaper, and that there wasn't any reason why Dad had to stay in the hospital.''

Judith closed her eyes for a moment, cursing under her breath. Her mind raced, but she didn't have the slightest idea what she could do. "We have to get a lawyer," she finally said. "Look, why don't you skip school today. You've got to—"

But to her surprise, Jed shook his head. "I already thought about that," he said. "There isn't really anything I can do for Dad, is there? I mean, you heard what Dr. Banning said. And we both saw those monitors they had hooked up to him."

Judith bit her lip. "But to have him out there . . ." she said, remembering the terror she'd seen in Reba Tucker's eyes.

Once again Jed shook his head. "If we make a stink, it's only going to make Moreland more suspicious. And they can't hurt Dad, Jude," he added, his voice trembling now. "Remember? Dr. Banning says he can't feel anything at all. He—He's already dead."

"Then what are you going to do?"

Jed struggled with his emotions for a moment, then managed a trace of an almost wry smile. "I guess right now I'm gonna do what dad would want me to do. And that's stay in school. At least for today."

Judith took a deep breath, then let it out in a sigh of frustration. But Jed was right. For the moment there was absolutely nothing they could do that wouldn't make Greg more suspicious than he already was. "All right," she agreed. "But this afternoon we're going out there."

They went back into the classroom. When Judith returned to her desk, she found two of the quizzes waiting for her, already completed. She glanced at the names at the tops of the papers, then looked at them again.

Both of them belonged to students who only last week had hung onto their papers until the last possible moment, not out of any inability to do the work, but simply because they both preferred to daydream their time away. It wasn't, Judith knew, that they were stupid; they simply had no ability to concentrate on a task.

But today, both of them had finished, and their solutions were perfect. Surprised, Judith looked up and scanned the class until she found the two students. The two were sitting at their desks, their expressions serene, their eyes facing forward.

But they didn't seem to be looking at anything.

The bell rang at the end of the fourth period, and Jed picked up his books, wondering if he'd been right when he'd decided to stay at school that day. He couldn't concentrate on anything at all, and so far he hadn't taken a single note during any of his classes. His mind had been occupied with his father.

He kept seeing his father lying inert in the hospital bed, oblivious to everything around him. For some reason he didn't quite understand yet, he'd at last been able to accept the fact that his father was never going to wake up again. Perhaps it had happened last night, when he and Judith had stopped into the hospital one last time, late in the evening, and he'd hoped that something—anything—had changed. But as he'd stared at the flat lines running across the monitors displaying his father's brain activity, and looked once more into his father's expressionless face, he hadn't felt that he was seeing his father at all.

What he had seen was only a shell that his father had once lived in.

All morning he'd half expected to be called out of class to be told his father's body had finally died too.

But the call hadn't come, and by the fourth period he'd begun thinking about what he would do if his father *didn't* die. He had no idea how much it would cost to keep his father in a nursing home, but he suspected it didn't really matter. Whatever it was, he knew he couldn't afford it.

Nor, without his father working, would he be able to pay the mortgage on the house, or make the payments on the truck, or anything else.

He found himself wondering if his father had any insurance, and if so, what it might cover. Maybe, instead of going to the cafeteria for lunch, he should find a telephone and start hunting for answers to all his questions.

He stepped out of the room into the corridor and looked around for Gina, who almost always met him here on her way to the cafeteria. But she was nowhere to be seen.

In fact, now that he thought about it, she'd barely spoken to him during first period either. His brows furrowing into a puzzled frown, he started toward the cafeteria, stopping at his locker to drop off his books.

When he got to the lunchroom, he felt an immediate sense of relief when he spotted Gina sitting at their usual table with JoAnna Garcia, Randy Sparks, and Jeff Hankins.

He waved to them, then joined the line of kids waiting for food. But as he made his way through the line, instead of following his usual habit of taking double portions of everything, he caught himself looking at the prices of each item. Almost to his own surprise, he settled for a cheese sandwich and a glass of milk. It didn't look very good, but it cost a couple of dollars less than he usually spent. Taking his almost empty tray to the table, he set it down, then slid into the chair next to Gina's.

"Hi," he said. "I looked for you outside Mr. Moreno's room, but you weren't there."

Gina looked vaguely puzzled. "Was I supposed to be?" she asked.

Jed frowned slightly. "I—Well, I don't know," he said. "You just usually are, that's all." He turned to look at her, but she seemed to be concentrating on the food on her plate. Suddenly he thought he understood. "Hey, I'm sorry I didn't meet you on the way to school this morning."

She looked over at him, a half smile on her lips.

"That's okay," she said, her voice carrying an odd, languid note. "I can walk by myself."

"I—I had to go to the hospital this morning," Jed said. "They moved my dad."

Gina's eyes gazed at him vacantly. "Is he going to be all right?" she asked.

Jed stared at her. She'd been at the hospital Saturday—she knew how bad he had been then. "No," he said, his voice shaking slightly. "He's not going to be all right. He—He's going to die, Gina."

Gina's eyes widened slightly and she looked vaguely confused. "Oh, Jed," she said. "I—I'm sorry. I didn't mean—it's just—" She faltered, then fell silent.

Jed was sure he understood. She just didn't know what to say, didn't have any idea how to handle the situation. "Hey, Gina, it's all right," he said. He took her hand and squeezed it. "And maybe something will happen," he went on. "Maybe he'll get better after all." Then, when Gina made no response, he looked at her again. "Gina? Are you sure you're okay? Is something wrong?"

Gina smiled at him and her eyes cleared. "I'm fine," she said. "I'm just eating my lunch. Isn't that what I'm supposed to be doing?"

Jed's eyes moved away from Gina then, flitting from one face to another.

Suddenly it occurred to him that Gina wasn't the only one at the table who looked strange.

JoAnna Garcia looked the way she always did, slouching comfortably in her chair, her feet sprawled out beneath the table so there wasn't much room for anyone else's, but uncharacteristically, she hadn't said a word since Jed had joined them.

Jeff Hankins was simply sitting there, his eyes focused only on the tray in front of him, slowly consuming the food on his plate.

And next to Jeff, Randy Sparks had the same faraway look, as if he was only barely aware of where he was or what he was doing.

Now Jed remembered bits and pieces of what Gina had told him about Randy on Saturday. *It was weird . . . he just did what I told him to.* He eyed Randy for a moment, then said, "Hey, Randy. Bet you can't hit the clock with a butter patty."

Ordinarily it was a challenge Randy would have risen to instantly. Today, he only looked at Jed curiously. "Why would I want to do that?" he asked.

Jed felt flustered. "J-Just to see if you *can*," he stammered. "Why do we ever do it?"

Randy's eyes fixed blankly on him for a moment, then he turned his attention back to his food.

Jed waited a few seconds, then spoke again. This time, though, the words were uttered as an order instead of a question. "Randy, hit the ceiling with a pat of butter."

Instantly, Randy placed a butter patty on the end of his knife and flicked it upward, where it stuck to the ceiling. But as he went back to his lunch, he seemed totally unaware of what he'd done.

Jed shifted his gaze to JoAnna Garcia. "What the hell's going on?" he asked.

JoAnna shrugged. "What's going on?" she repeated mildly. "Is something wrong?"

"What's the matter with you guys?" Jed was nearly shouting in his frustration now. "If you're all sick or something, why don't you go home?"

Randy, Jeff, JoAnna, and Gina all gazed blankly at him.

"But I'm not sick," Gina said. "I feel fine. There's nothing wrong at all."

"Well, you don't look fine," Jed told Gina. "You look weird. Maybe you'd better go see the nurse."

Without a word, Gina stood and started toward the cafeteria door. Jed hesitated a moment, then got up and quickly threaded his way through the tables. He caught up to her just as she reached the door.

"Hey," he said. "Are you mad at me?"

Gina gazed at him, her eyes expressionless. "No," she said. "I'm just going to the nurse's office. That's what you told me to do."

Without a flicker of emotion, she turned and walked out the door.

"I don't think you can wait for your friend to call you," Jed said as he got into Judith's car after school that day.

Judith, about to start the engine, paused, looking over at Jed. "Why?" she asked. "Has something else happened?"

Jed nodded, his eyes grim. "Didn't you notice it today? It's the kids—they're starting to act real weird." He began telling her what had happened in the cafeteria at lunchtime that day, and what had happened afterward.

When Gina left the cafeteria, Jed had gone along with her, trying to talk to her, but it had been difficult. Not that she'd acted as though she was mad at him—she just didn't seem to care at all. She'd answered all his questions, but her voice, usually filled with excitement about whatever she might be talking about, had sounded flat, taking on a listless quality Jed had never heard before.

She'd sat patiently in Ms. Sanders's office, answering the nurse's questions but volunteering nothing, only insisting in that strange lifeless voice that she felt just fine.

"Well," Laura Sanders had finally said after taking Gina's temperature, examining her throat, and checking her for swollen glands, "you certainly *seem* all right." But Jed had been able to tell from the nurse's expression that she too had noticed Gina's peculiar apathy. "Would you like to go home?" she asked.

"If you want me to," Gina replied.

The nurse frowned. "It's not what *I* want, Gina. It's what would be best for you."

Gina had said nothing. In the end she had walked back to the cafeteria with Jed and quietly finished her lunch. For the rest of the day, whenever Jed had seen her, she'd been the same: calm and placid, moving steadily from class to class, but never stopping to chat with her friends, speaking to them only if they spoke to her first.

"Jeff Hankins is acting the same way, and so is Randy Sparks," Jed finished. "Didn't you notice it? They're all wandering around like sleepwalkers."

She realized he was right—indeed, if she hadn't been so consumed with worry about Frank. . . . She abandoned the thought, concentrating instead on remembering her classes that day. Yes, there definitely *had* been a difference in some of her students. The two in her first period, for instance, who had suddenly managed to complete a quiz in the allotted ten minutes. And all her classes, she realized now, had been more subdued that day, almost as if the students had been given a tranquilizer.

The shots.

Could that have been what they were? But it seemed crazy. Why would they give a whole school sedatives?

And if the shots *were* some kind of sedative, why were many of the kids behaving perfectly normally?

Silently, she cursed Peter Langston—she'd tried to get through to him twice already, but had been told both times that he was in meetings. And no, he couldn't be disturbed, except for an emergency. She would have dreamed one up, but both calls had been made from the lounge, and she'd been certain that Elliott Halvorson, at least, was listening to her curiously. She ignored him, determined not to let him see how worried she was. Besides, she'd told herself, if Peter had anything to tell her, he knew how to reach her.

But Peter still didn't know how important the shot might be. Suddenly she knew what she would do. "I'm going down there," she said. Only as she spoke the words did she realize that Jed had been talking. She hadn't heard a word he'd said

"I said I've decided to quit school," he repeated.

Judith stared at him. "You're what?" she repeated.

"I said I know Dad wouldn't want me to quit school, but I don't see how I can pay Dad's bills if I don't get a job."

Judith shook her head, confused. "But this morning you said—"

"I *know* what I said," Jed interrupted doggedly. "But I've been thinking about it all day, and there just doesn't seem to be any way out of it. Besides," he added, his voice hardening, and his eyes meeting hers for the first time since he'd suggested quitting school, "if I can get a job with the company—and I bet I can, even if they are laying people off," he added darkly, "—maybe I can find out what they did to Dad. They're doing something, Jude. It's not just Dad and the Morelands and Mrs. Tucker. They're doing something to all of us."

Part of Judith wanted to argue with him, but another part of her knew he was right. "All right," she said tiredly. "Look. You go out and see your father. Don't act upset that he's there—don't do anything at all. Can you do that?"

Jed hesitated, then nodded. "Yeah," he said. "I can do it."

"Good. I'm going to drive down to Los Alamos right now, and light a fire under Peter Langston. Tonight, when I get back, we'll decide what to do. All right?"

For a moment Judith thought Jed was going to argue with her, but then he nodded. "Okay," he said. He opened the door of her car and slid out, then leaned down to stick his head in the window. "Be careful, huh?"

Judith managed a smile she hoped was reassuring, but Jed had already turned away, loping across the parking lot to his father's truck.

A moment later she pulled out of the parking lot, too preoccupied to notice the dark blue car that fell in behind her, following her closely as she drove through Borrego, but discreetly dropping back nearly half a mile as she headed south and east toward Los Alamos.

Twenty-four

The heat of the afternoon rippled over the desert. Ahead Judith could see a familiar mirage of water apparently lying across the road. But the shimmering image, as always, stayed far in the distance, hovering just below the horizon so the water seemed endless, merging finally with the sky itself.

She was forty minutes, and fifty miles, away from Borrego, driving fast, the speedometer hovering between seventy and eighty. The road was straight here, and though Judith ordinarily felt relaxed behind the wheel, today she was tense, the muscles of her back and shoulders already beginning to knot under the strain that seemed to make every nerve in her body tingle.

Now she frowned as she glanced in the rearview mirror. Behind her, maybe a quarter of a mile, was the dark blue car she'd first noticed ten minutes before. She told herself she was being paranoid, that there was no reason to think it might be following her. She hadn't, after all, noticed it as she'd left Borrego. And yet it seemed to her that if it had been coming down from farther north, and had only just now caught up with her, it ought to be passing her.

Instead, it seemed to linger behind her, almost as if it were deliberately keeping pace with her.

Frowning, she eased up on the accelerator, and the Honda began to slow. When she glanced into the mirror again, the blue car was closer.

Perhaps she ought to stop entirely. Would he simply pass, ignoring her completely? Or would he stop, asking her if she needed help?

And why do I keep thinking of the driver as *he?* Judith suddenly thought. It could just as easily be a woman.

Making up her mind, Judith braked the car, pulling off the road. A cloud of dust rose behind her as the tires struck the hard adobe shoulder, and then the Honda came to a stop.

The blue car zipped past her, and Judith frowned. She was positive that the man in the car—at least she was now certain it *was* a man—had seen her. But what had she learned by the fact that he hadn't stopped?

Either he thought she had a problem and didn't care, or he didn't want her to get a good look at him.

Feeling foolish, she put the car in gear again and moved back onto the road. Ahead, barely visible, she could just make out the blue car; every few seconds it seemed to disappear into the mirage, only to reappear a moment later.

She drove another thirty minutes and then, ahead, saw a gas station by the side of the road—one of those strange lonely-looking places stuck out in the middle of nowhere.

As she approached it, she saw the blue car pull off the road, and when she passed it a few seconds later, she could see the person in the car talking to a weathered old man who apparently owned the place. But this time the man in the blue car waved to her as she passed. Suddenly she felt better. At least he'd acknowledged her presence. Surely he wouldn't have done that if he'd been following her?

An hour later she was on the outskirts of Los Alamos. She hadn't seen the blue car again, and the simple fact of its absence had made her begin to relax.

As the traffic thickened and she began threading her way toward the Brandt Institute, where Peter worked, she didn't notice the beige sedan that had picked her up as she'd reached the edges of the town.

Judith pulled to a stop in front of a heavy chain-link gate. Beyond the gate there was a wide lawn, in the center of which stood a large two-story building. It was fairly new, constructed in a Spanish-Moorish style, its white plaster facade plain and unadorned, broken only by small windows covered with heavy wrought-iron gratings. It was capped by a gently sloping red tile roof, and the driveway, which cut straight across the lawn from the gates, ended abruptly at a pair of immense oaken doors, suspended from ornate iron hinges fastened to the wooden planks with large bolts. Except for that huge pair of doors, Judith couldn't see another entrance to the building. Nor was there much around it. She'd had to drive all the way through Los Alamos to find it; it wasn't even in the town itself. Around the high fence that surrounded the Brandt Institute, there was little to be seen except the desert itself, and Judith found the broad expanse of lawn to be faintly unsettling. It was as if whoever had designed the building and its landscaping had wished to separate it from its environment, but had instead succeeded only in making the building appear totally out of place.

The whole estate—for that was what it would have looked like, had it not been for the fence, the gate, and the guardhouse that sat in the center of the drive—was situated a quarter of a mile back from the road, and only a small sign at the main road identified it at all.

A guard stepped out of the shack, and Judith gave her name, asking for Peter Langston. The guard returned to his kiosk and picked up a telephone. A few seconds later he came back to the car and handed Judith a plastic badge. It had Judith's name embossed across the top. "I don't believe it," she murmured, staring at the badge.

The guard grinned. "Computer. Once you're okayed, I just type in your name and she spits the badge right out." When Judith remained puzzled, he added: "Yellow just means you're a visitor. Don't forget to turn it in before you leave. There's a magnetic strip on the back that can be detected from anywhere inside the fence. If you take the badge outside the fence, the computer knows it's missing and alarms go off."

Judith stared at the badge, then turned it over. It looked for all the world like a credit card, right down to the brown stripe across the back. "Am I supposed to sign it?" she asked, only half in jest.

The guard grinned again. "Only if you're permanent," he said. "Then you have to sign for it every day."

The guard watched as she clipped the badge to her blouse, then he stepped back into the kiosk. The gate rolled back, and Judith put the car into gear and drove onto the grounds of the institute.

The heavy chain-link gate swung closed behind her, and a moment later, as the car approached the wooden doors of the building itself, the huge portals began to swing outward, allowing the car to pass between them, through a short tunnel that ran below the second floor and into an enormous courtyard.

Judith's eyes opened in shock.

There was a parking lot at the near end of the courtyard, but beyond that a park had been constructed. Tropical foliage burgeoned everywhere, and there was an artificial brook meandering through the gardens, spanned here and there by low wooden bridges.

Peter Langston, a tall, angular man with hair that was grayer than Judith remembered it, was waiting for her, apparently bemused by her shock at the jungle contained within the building. "I don't believe this," Judith said as she got out of the car. "How on earth does it survive in the winter?"

Peter pointed upward. "There's a roof—see? It retracts when the weather's right."

"Incredible," Judith said.

"Isn't it just?" Peter replied dryly. He gave her an affectionate hug before holding her away from him, his eyes growing serious. "What's going on?" he asked. "I was going to call you tonight."

Judith shook her head. "I couldn't wait. There's too much going on, and I'm scared, Peter."

The last traces of his smile vanished. "Come on," he said. "Let's go up to my office." He led her up a flight of stairs to a broad loggia that ran around the entire second floor of the building's inner wall.

"I suppose there's no point in asking you what's going on out here, is there?" Judith asked. "From what happened out in front, I gather it's all pretty secret."

Langston shrugged. "Some of it is, I suppose. But a lot of it's only a secret if you have a financial interest in it, which Willard Brandt certainly does. We're doing a lot of work with superconductors here, and there's one group over in the east wing that's supposed to be working on a new computer that's going to make the best Cray look like a Model-T Ford." He turned into an office, then gestured to a comfortable-looking chair before folding himself up into a wooden rocker that looked oddly out of place to Judith. "Back problems," he said. "Now, what's this all about? And why the sudden rush?"

Judith explained what had happened in Borrego over the weekend and the odd behavior of some of her students that day. "I'm absolutely certain it has something to do with those shots," she concluded. "But until you tell me what they are, I can't prove anything."

"Well, as a matter of fact," Peter said, "I just managed to get some time on the electron microscope this afternoon. Let's go take a look."

He led Judith back out to the loggia, but this time they used an elevator instead of the stairs, descending to what was apparently the second of three underground levels. When the doors slid open, they emerged into a corridor tiled with glistening white porcelain and shadowlessly illuminated from fluorescent panels in the ceiling. All along the length of the corridor closed doors hid whatever activity was taking place down here from Judith's view. "Real space-age, huh?" Langston asked.

Judith made no reply, and at last Peter turned into one of the rooms and spoke to a technician who was studying a display on a computer monitor. "Is that my stuff?" he asked.

The technician nodded. "But I can't quite figure out what it is."

Judith stared at the image on the monitor. It looked like nothing she'd ever seen before, but at the same time it struck her as being vaguely familiar.

It was roughly rectangular, with two nibs, almost like the tips of ballpoint pens, protruding from one end. The body of the thing seemed to be wrapped in wire, and at what Judith assumed was the base of the object, there was another pair of points, these two mounted to the body in such a way that they appeared to be able to swing toward each other.

The technician, his expression as puzzled as Judith's own, finally spoke. "I give up," he said. "I can't tell you what it is, but I can tell you what it isn't. It isn't cellular, and it isn't organic. And it doesn't look like any molecule I've ever seen either."

Peter Langston nodded in agreement, his bushy brows knitting as he concentrated on the strange object the screen displayed. "It's definitely not a molecule," he said. "It's way too big. But it's too small to be anything organic. That thing could fit right into any cell in the human body, with plenty of room to spare."

Judith glanced at Peter. "Okay," she said, certain he already knew the answer. "What is it?"

"Off the top of my head," Peter replied, "I'd say it's some kind of a micromachine."

Judith's eyes left the display and fixed on Peter. "A what?" she asked.

Peter smiled at her. "A micromachine. If I'm right and I'd give at least a hundred-to-one odds I am—it's a tiny mechanism, probably etched out of silicon."

Judith stared at him. "You mean it actually does something?" she asked.

Peter's finger moved to the screen and he traced along the twin protuberances at the object's base. "I'd be willing to swear that those two things swing on those pivots," he said, his finger stopping on what looked like the head of a tiny pin penetrating through the protuberance and fixed to the body of the object. "In fact," he said, "that looks like some kind of a switch. See?" he went on. "Look how the ends of those are beveled. If you brought them together, the two beveled faces would match perfectly, making a contact point."

Judith stared at him. "But how big is it? If it can actually work . . . ." Her voice trailed off as Peter glanced inquiringly at the technician.

"A couple of microns," he said, "one point eighty-seven, to be exact."

Peter whistled. "Small, indeed," he said.

"But what does it do?" Judith asked.

Langston sighed heavily. "I'm going to have to get a lot of images of this thing, then have the computer put it together in three dimensions. At that point I should be able to get a pretty good sense of what it is."

Judith pulled her eyes away from the strange image on the screen to look worriedly at Peter. "How long will it take?" she asked.

Peter shook his head. "I wish I could tell you. A few hours, probably. But once I know what it is, I'll need more time to figure out how it works and exactly what it does."

"But I don't *have* time," Judith replied, fear sharpening her voice. "Peter, two people are already dead up in Borrego, and two more might as well be. And now something's happening to the children—"

Peter held up a restraining hand. "I understand," he said. "Look, I'll find someone to help me, and if I have to, I'll work all night, and all day tomorrow. Now, the best thing you can do is go find a hotel room and wait for me to call. All right?"

Judith shook her head. "I have to go home. Frank needs me, and Jed—"

Peter eyed her worriedly. "Look. Whatever's going on, it's got to be dangerous. And if anyone finds out you stole that syringe, it's going to be especially dangerous for you."

Judith took a deep breath and slowly let it out. It did nothing to relieve her fear. But she still knew she had to go back to Borrego today. "I can't stay," she said. "I just can't."

Peter started to argue with her, but knew by the look in her eye that it would do no good. "All right," he said, reluctantly giving in. "But be careful, okay?"

Judith nodded tightly. "I will," she replied. "But promise me, Peter. As soon as you know what that thing is, call me. No matter what time it is."

Ten minutes later, after Judith had left, Peter Langston set to work. Within an hour, as the truth of what the micromachines were began to dawn on him, a cold knot of fear began to form in his stomach.

The children of Borrego were in a lot more trouble than even Judith suspected.

Jed stared at the dark brick mass of the four-story building that stood at the corner of First and E streets and felt a twinge of doubt. The Borrego Building, still the largest in town, seemed to have taken on an ominous look this afternoon, but Jed knew that its foreboding air was only a figment of his own imagination. The building itself, with its vaguely Gothic facade, looked as it always had—faintly dingy, like the rest of the town, but with a feeling of solidity to it.

Still, as he pulled the pickup truck into an empty slot in front of the building, he hesitated. But he'd made his decision, and there didn't seem to be any point in waiting until tomorrow. Once he was working for the company, he might be able to find out the truth about what they had done to his father.

Jed swung out of the cab of the truck and walked through the door next to the bank that occupied the ground floor of the building, hurrying up the stairs to the second floor. At the top of the stairs there was a glass-fronted directory. Jed scanned it quickly, then studied the numbers on the doors on either side of him. Finally he turned left and made his way down the narrow corridor until he came to Room 201, its number emblazoned on the opaque glass panel in flaking gold leaf. Taking a deep breath, he turned the knob and stepped inside.

There were two desks in the room, but only one of them was occupied. Charlie Hodges, a gray-haired man of about fifty-five, whom Jed had known all his life, glanced idly up from his work, then smiled broadly as he rose to his feet and strode toward him, his hand out.

"Jed!" Charlie said. "This is a coincidence." His smile faded and his eyes grew somber. "I was just working on some of the forms regarding your father. Getting his insurance straightened out, and starting a disability claim." He shook his head sadly. "This is one of the worst things I've ever had to do. Every time I think of Frank . . ." His voice trailed off, then he seemed to recover himself. "How is he? Is there any change?"

Jed shook his head. "I went out to see him this afternoon. He's just the same. I—" His voice faltered, but then he managed to steady it. "I don't know what I'm going to do yet," he said, leaving it to Hodges to figure out what he meant. Though he'd already thought about it, and was going to talk to Jude about it tonight, he still couldn't accept the idea of deliberately letting his father die.

Hodges, though, understood immediately, and grasped his shoulder reassuringly. "It's hard," he said. "How's that girlfriend of his doing? The teacher."

"Okay," Jed replied. Then he gazed directly at Hodges. "I didn't really come down here about Dad," he said. "What I need to do is get a job."

Hodges looked at him in surprise, then repressed his automatic urge to ask Jed if he'd talked to his father about going to work. He nodded firmly. "Well, as you know, we've been laying men off all week, but I think maybe we can make an exception in your case. I mean, given the circumstances," he added, sounding flustered.

Waving to Jed to follow him, he returned to his desk, pulled a form from the bottom drawer and handed it to the boy. "You might start filling this out," he said. "Let me just call upstairs." He punched three digits into the phone on his desk, then waited.

"Mr. Kendall?" he said a moment later. "Charlie Hodges, downstairs. I have someone here looking for work." He was silent for a moment, nodding a couple of times as the other man spoke. "I know that," he said after Kendall had finished speaking. "But I think this may be a special case. It's Frank Arnold's boy—Jed." He listened again, then winked at Jed, and after a moment hung up. "Just as I thought," he said. "One thing around here hasn't changed this week. The company is still doing its best to look after its people."

Jed looked up from the application form he was filling out, his lips twisted in a wry grin. "How about the guys who are getting laid off?" he asked.

Hodges shrugged. "It's only temporary," he said. But as he read the doubt in Jed's eyes, he added, "Look, I know what your father thought about what's happened, but he's wrong. UniChem has big plans for this company. Within two years the refinery is going to be twice the size it is now, and there are plans to build a factory, as well."

"A factory?" Jed echoed. "Come on, Mr. Hodges. What kind of factory would they build out here?"

Hodges shrugged. "All I know is it's some kind of real high-tech deal. They're talking about new kinds of fusion, and that kind of thing. Three years from now there are going to be more jobs out here than we can fill."

The application form completed, Jed pushed it across the desk. Could what Hodges had just said really be true? Had his father been wrong? But then an image of his father flashed into his mind, followed by another, this time of Gina Alvarez.

His father, he decided, had not been wrong, but nothing in Jed's expression revealed his doubts as he faced the personnel director. "Sounds great," he said. "Maybe I'm getting in on the ground floor of something terrific."

Hodges's head bobbed enthusiastically, and he handed Jed a card. "Take this over to the hospital. Then report to Bill Watkins tomorrow morning, up at the dam."

Half an hour later, at the small hospital on the edge of Borrego, Jed sat uneasily facing Dr. Banning for the second time that day. This time, instead of studying Frank Arnold's tests, the doctor was looking at Jed's own. Jed had already produced a urine sample, and the nurse had taken a blood sample as well. Jed had felt uneasy as the needle had slipped into his vein, and had had to fight down an urge to jerk away from the instrument in the nurse's hand.

"Well, I guess that's it," Banning told him at last. "We've got all the specimens we need, and you don't seem to have any problems at all. And according to your records at school, you got your flu shot last week, so I guess we're covered."

Almost automatically, Jed opened his mouth to correct the error in his school records, but then quickly shut it again. If they thought he'd already had his shot, he certainly wasn't about to tell them otherwise. "Then that's it?" he asked, standing up.

Banning smiled. "That's it. Not too bad, was it?"

Jed shrugged, said good-bye, and hurried out of the hospital into the warmth of the late afternoon. As he started home, he felt a twinge of uneasy excitement.

The answers to all his questions were somewhere within the company he now worked for.

And somehow he would find out what those answers were.

Twenty-five

T he man in the dark blue Chevy parked across the street from Frank Arnold's house slouched low in the passenger seat as the glare of headlights swept his windshield. He hated having to sit by himself in a car in the middle of a residential neighborhood; he always had the feeling that eyes were watching him from every home. But his instructions had been explicit—as long as there was a light on in the Arnold house, he was to remain posted where he was, and he wasn't to leave for at least an hour after the last light in the house went off. Well, maybe the teacher and the kid were the kind who went to bed early.

The source of the headlights turned out to be the same pickup truck with the broken windshield that had left half an hour earlier, and the man in the car relaxed as he saw Jed Arnold, now accompanied by a girl he was sure must be Gina Alvarez, get out of the truck and disappear through the front door. When they were safely inside, he left his car and strolled up the street, glancing into the window of the house as he passed it. The two kids were talking to the Sheffield woman, but it didn't look like any big deal—they just seemed to be chatting. He wandered on up the street, crossed, then walked back along the other side until he was even with his car. Glancing around, still with the uneasy sense that he was being watched from every window on the block, he got back in his car and decided it was time to ignore his orders.

He turned on the engine and drove away. From now on, he would keep an eye on the house from a distance, driving by every half hour or so. But in a dumpy little town like Borrego, he didn't really think there was much likelihood that the Sheffield woman would be going anywhere that night.

The three of them were sitting in the small living room, Jed and Gina side by side on the sofa, Judith in Frank's big easy chair. Almost half an hour had gone by since Jed had brought Gina into the house, and as the minutes had ticked away, Judith had become more and more frightened.

Everything about Gina seemed to have changed. Gone were her expressive voice and animated gestures.

Her eyes, always sparkling with interest in everything around her, had lost their luster, as well as their movement. Her gaze seemed to fasten on objects from time to time, but Judith had a strange feeling that Gina wasn't truly seeing whatever she was looking at. It was as if her whole mind had simply gone into neutral. For the most part she sat silently next to Jed, answering questions only when they were directed specifically to her, seeming lost in some private world of her own.

Except Judith had the eerie feeling that there was nothing whatsoever in that world. The girl seemed to be existing in a void.

"Gina," Judith said, leaning forward in her chair, her voice rising, as if she were speaking to a deaf person. "I want you to tell me if anything happened Saturday night. Anything strange, or out of the ordinary."

Gina shook her head.

But what if she doesn't think whatever happened was strange? Judith suddenly thought.

"All right, let's try it another way. What time did you go to bed?"

Gina frowned. "About ten o'clock, I guess."

Judith nodded encouragingly. "All right. Now, did you go right to sleep or did you read for a while? Maybe listen to the radio?"

"I read," Gina said. "I was trying to read *The Deerslayer*, but I couldn't concentrate on it. And I fell asleep."

"Okay," Judith said. "And did you sleep all night?"

"No. I woke up when the fire truck went by, and I went to look out the window. Then I tried to read some more."

She fell silent again, and Judith began to feel like an inquisitor, painfully dragging information out of a subject, bit by bit. "How much longer did you read?"

Gina shrugged. "Not much. I kept sort of drifting off."

"But you didn't actually go back to sleep?"

There was a silence while Gina seemed to think. "No," she said finally. "That's when I started to smell something."

Judith cocked her head. "Smell something? Like what?"

"I—I'm not sure," Gina stammered. Then: "It smelled bad. Like garbage."

"And it woke you up?"

Gina nodded. Her nose screwed up as she remembered the odor. "It was really bad."

In her mind Judith heard an echo of Reba Tucker's voice, barely audible, croaking out words one by one: "Smells . . . bad. See things . . . bad."

"Gina," Judith said, her voice quavering, "I want you to think very carefully. When the smell came, did you see anything? Anything at all?"

Gina's eyes narrowed and her brows furrowed as she concentrated. Finally she nodded. "There were colors," she said. "And something else. There were things around me. I couldn't quite see them, but they were there."

Judith felt her heart beating faster. "All right. Anything else? Did you *feel* anything?"

Gina thought again, then slowly nodded. "Something funny. It was one of those spasms, you know? Like when you're just about to go to sleep, and your whole body jerks?"

Judith nodded. "That happened Saturday night too?"

"Just as I was going back to sleep. But it was funny. Usually when that happens to me, I'm wide awake again. But Saturday, after it happened, I just felt real relaxed and went right to sleep."

"Okay," Judith told her. "That's very good, Gina. And yesterday and this morning, you woke up feeling fine. Is that right?"

Gina nodded.

"Now, I want you to think once more, Gina. I want you to try to remember what time all this happened. We know it was after you heard the fire truck, which was around eleven-thirty."

"Well, it had to have happened before twelve-thirty because that's what time Mom gets home. And it seemed like I tried to read for about half an hour after I heard the sirens."

Judith's whole body tensed.

Midnight.

Whatever had happened to Gina Saturday night had happened at the same time that Frank had had his stroke the night before.

And Reba Tucker had had her seizure.

An hour later, when Jed came back to the house after driving Gina home, he found Judith sitting pensively at the kitchen table, staring at a piece of paper. Jed slid into the chair opposite her, then turned the sheet around to look at it.

It was a list of names, starting with his father's and Reba Tucker's. Below that were more names.

Max Moreland
Gina Alvarez
Randy Sparks
JoAnna Garcia
Jeff Hankins
Heather Fredericks

There were three more names, but Jed skipped over them, for at the bottom of the list a single name jumped out at him.

His own.

And next to his name, Judith had placed a large question mark, underlined twice. After a few seconds his eyes left the sheet of paper and he looked questioningly at her.

"I'm trying to find a common denominator," Judith said. "There has to be a pattern."

Jed's eyes scanned the list again, and suddenly he thought he saw it. "It's the company," he said. "All these kids? Every one of them has a parent who works for Borrego Oil."

Judith frowned. "Gina? Her father's gone, and her mother works at the café."

"Her uncle," Jed replied. "Carlos."

"But what about Reba Tucker?"

Jed studied the list again, and then realized that there was something else the names on the list had in common. "Troublemakers," he breathed. "That's what it is!"

Judith stared at him quizzically. "Troublemakers?" she echoed.

Jed nodded. "That's got to be it—look. The kids? Christ, every one of them has been in trouble except Gina, and she hangs out with the rest of us. And you know what Greg Moreland and Otto Kruger think of Dad. Hell, he made life miserable for Kruger, and didn't want Max to sell the company."

"But what about Reba?" Judith said again. "I still don't know how she fits in."

"Oh, yeah?" Jed replied. "Well, I do. She was making all kinds of trouble at the school. She was always after them to fix the place up and get better equipment. She screamed about the books, the pay, everything. And last spring she got so mad she decided to try to get the teachers to form a union. Christ, she was over here all the time, talking to dad about it."

Judith stared at him. Could it possibly be true? It seemed so crazy, and yet . . .

And then she remembered something Frank had told her. *UniChem's put two of its companies into bankruptcy, just to bust the unions. They want everyone to shut up and do their jobs and not make trouble. But it won't work—they won't shut me up.*

But they had.

And then another thought struck her.

Jed.

As far as anyone except the two of them knew, Jed had had one of the shots too. If he was on their list . . .

And then she knew what had to be done. "You have to do something tomorrow, Jed," she said. She talked for almost five minutes, telling him what she had in mind. "Can you do it?" she asked at last.

Jed said nothing for a moment, then nodded slowly. "I guess I'll have to," he said. "If I don't, they might just kill me, like they did Dad."

J ed negotiated the dirt track along the canyon's edge the next morning almost automatically, most of his mind occupied with what Judith Sheffield had told him the night before. After they'd gone to bed, he'd lain in the darkness, wide awake, wondering if he could actually pull it off. Despite what he'd told Judith, he wasn't sure he could. For a while he'd even considered not showing up for work at all.

Quitting the company now, on his very first day, would be like a red flag to Kendall—for Jed was certain that Paul Kendall was behind whatever was being done as much as Greg Moreland. But he managed to keep himself under control yesterday, about Greg Moreland sending his father to The Cottonwoods, and he'd do it again today, with Kendall watching him.

And so, all night, he'd thought about what he had to do. He remembered Gina, and Randy Sparks, and a few of the other kids he'd seen at school. And he kept in mind that he too was supposed to have gotten one of the murderous shots.

Now, as he parked the truck in the lot above the dam, he looked at himself in the rearview mirror. He let the muscles of his face go slack, making his features expressionless. Then he let his eyes lose their focus slightly, so they took on the strange, blank look he'd seen in Gina Alvarez's eyes last night and the night before.

Finally he got out of the truck, picked up his father's lunch bucket, and slammed the door. As he started down the trail to the dam, he kept his head down, staring only at the path in front of his feet. As he came to the operations office at the end of the dam itself, he paused, steeling himself to show no emotion, no reaction except cooperation, no matter what was said to him.

He stepped into the office. Bill Watkins, busy with some paper-work, glanced up at him. In the inner office, clearly visible through an open door, Otto Kruger was talking to someone on the phone.

"I'll send them down in groups of four," he heard Kruger saying. "It looks like everyone's here today, so there shouldn't be any prob-lem." He was silent for a moment, then swung around as if he were about to speak to Bill Watkins, but stopped short when he saw Jed. His eyes narrowed, and Jed had to concentrate hard to keep himself from reacting to the man's stare. Then Kruger said, "Arnold just came in," his voice dropping, but still clearly audible. "He looks fine. He's just standing in Watkins's office, waiting for his orders."

He dropped the phone back on its hook, then stood up and came to lounge in the door to his office, his lips twisted in a quizzical half smile. "Hey, Jed," he said. "How you doing this morning?"

Jed let his head come up, but slowly. "Okay. I feel fine."

Kruger's brows rose a fraction of an inch. "Sleep okay last night? No problems?"

Jed shrugged. "I'm okay," he said again.

Kruger's eyes seemed to bore into him, but then he nodded. "Great," he said. "Well, don't just stand around here like an idiot—there's a lot to be done down below, and we're going to be short-handed all day."

A twinge of anger plucked at Jed as the word "idiot" struck him, but he managed to shunt it aside. Nodding, he turned and walked out of the office, never even looking at Bill Watkins. But when he was gone, Watkins scratched his head pensively. "What's with Jed?" he asked.

Otto Kruger's lips twisted into an unpleasant grin. "Maybe he finally decided his old man had the wrong attitude," he said. "Looks to me like he figured out you're better off if you just shut up and do what you're told."

Watkins grunted. "Well, I wish all the men were like that," he said. "It'd sure make my job a lot easier."

Kruger said nothing, but as he went back into the inner office, he smiled to himself. Bill Watkins was going to get his wish a lot sooner than he ever could have imagined.

Jed moved steadily down the spiral staircase that led into the depths of the dam, his steps echoing in a regular rhythm on the metal risers, sending an eerie resonance through the shaft. Finally he reached the bottom and moved slowly along the tight confines of the corridor—lit only by bare bulbs in metal cages hung every twenty-five feet or so—toward the damaged power shaft. As he approached, the crew foreman's eyes fixed on him.

"You'll be working in the pipes today, Arnold," he said. "There's a miner's light and probe waiting for you. All you got to do is look for cracks. When you find 'em, use the probe to open 'em up and clean 'em out as best you can."

Jed said nothing. He set his lunch bucket on a shelf, took one of the miner's hard hats off the rack, put it on, then found the probe. It was a piece of thick, hardened metal, its tip bent slightly, attached to a wooden handle. Finally he moved into the base of the power shaft itself.

A conveyor had been rigged up, a tall cranelike object that rose from the base of the shaft all the way to the top. A moving belt was already operating, carrying an endless circle of scoops upward, where their contents would be dumped onto another conveyor that would carry them out and drop them into a chute leading down to a dump truck waiting at the base of the dam itself.

On scaffolding high above, men were already working, chipping away at the damaged concrete of the shaft, dropping pieces of debris into a temporary chute that was designed to let men work at the bottom of the shaft in relative safety. Still, there was a steady rain of tiny fragments of concrete pattering down from above, and the air was thick with dust.

"Up here!" one of the men on the scaffolding called. Jed peered up, seeing the narrow opening of one of the intake pipes.

It might have been the same pipe from which his father had fallen on Friday morning. Taking a deep breath, he began climbing the scaffolding until he came to the platform where the man stood.

He stared into the black hole, no more than two feet in diameter.

A knot of fear formed in his stomach, but he forced it down, telling himself there was nothing to be afraid of.

"Headfirst," the man told him. "Turn on the light, and keep your head up. The beam'll give you enough light to work by." The man glanced down then, and when he spoke, his voice had dropped. "If you start to panic," he said, "just relax and give me a holler. I'm gonna tie a line around your ankle, and I'll be able to pull you right out.''

Jed kept his eyes fixed on the hole in the side of the shaft. "I'll be okay," he said, doing his best to keep his voice clear of the fear he hadn't quite been able to rid himself of. "I'll be fine."

He reached up and switched on the tiny light fixed to his helmet, then, gripping the probe tightly in his right hand, ducked down and thrust his torso into the hole.

The first thing he noticed was the suffocating heaviness of the air in the pipe. Stale and musty, it threatened to choke him.

The fear in his belly blossomed, and he felt the first fingers of panic reaching out toward him. He closed his eyes for a moment, willing the panic to subside, making himself breathe in the dank air.

"You okay?" he heard a voice asking him.

Gritting his teeth, he forced himself to open his eyes again. The dim beam of light glowed softly ahead of him, disappearing quickly into the blackness of the pipe. But the panic had eased slightly. "I'm okay," he managed to say. "I'm fine."

He crept ahead, using his fingers to explore the concrete tube. A moment later he felt a rough spot and twisted his head slightly so that the light on the helmet shone on the wall. Using the probe, he dug at the crack, scraping mud and algae away from it. A piece of concrete broke loose, then another. He kept at it, chipping away, until finally the probe could pry no more fragments out of the break.

He moved on.

He came to another crack, this one in the top of the shaft.

He tipped his head up, but there wasn't enough room for the lantern to find the break.

He would have to roll over and lie on his back.

He began twisting his body, working it around in the narrow confines of the pipe.

A moment later he was looking at the top of the tube, only a few inches above his face.

Above it, he realized, were the thousands of tons of concrete of which the dam was made. And now, lying on his back, his belly exposed, he felt the full weight of the dam pressing down on him.

Once again panic closed in on him, and this time he couldn't put it aside.

Instinctively, he tried to sit up, and instantly hit the close confines of the pipe.

He felt it tightening around him, and suddenly he couldn't breathe. He wanted to scream, wanted to scramble to his feet and begin running.

His muscles contracted as he tried to draw his legs up, and then he felt them jam against the wall of the shaft.

He couldn't move, but he had to. He struggled for a moment, and the panic threatened to overwhelm him entirely.

A scream of unreasoning terror built in his throat.

And then, just as it was about to burst from his lips, he clamped his mouth closed.

He wouldn't do it—he wouldn't give in to the urge to scream, wouldn't give in to the panic that had seized him. He struggled again, but this time the battle took place within his own mind. He closed his eyes, then forced himself to imagine that he wasn't in the dam at all.

He was on the mesa, high up above the desert, with nothing around him except clean, dry air.

He imagined the air filling his lungs, washing away the dankness of the pipe.

Slowly the tension in his body eased, and at last he moved again, easing his torso forward to release his legs from the pressure of the pipe. He closed his eyes then and concentrated, as he had in the kiva with his grandfather; as he had alone in his room on Saturday night.

It worked.

Part of him stayed in the pipe, directing his body as it carried out the work he had been told to do.

But most of his mind moved elsewhere, traveling beyond the dam, breathing freely.

The panic—the terror of the pipe, which had overwhelmed his father—could no longer reach him.

After two hours he felt a tug on his ankle. "Take a break, kid," he heard a voice calling. "Nobody can keep that up all day."

Jed stopped working, and a moment later felt himself being pulled out of the pipe. The part of his mind that had been occupied with evading the terrible panic rejoined his body, and for a moment he felt another twinge of the paralyzing fear. Then he was free of the tunnel, back in the main shaft. He scrambled down the scaffolding, then stepped out of the shaft into the turbine room. There was a sudden silence as the conveyor belt stopped moving, and then the rest of the men who had been working on the scaffolding above began to appear.

Thermoses were opened and someone handed Jed a cup of steaming coffee. Around him he could hear the voices of the men, swapping jokes and casual insults, but Jed took no part in it. He sat still, staring at nothing, sipping with careful disinterest at his coffee.

When the allotted fifteen minutes was nearly up, the foreman spoke.

"Hey, Gomez. Take Harris, Sparks, and Hankins and head down to the hospital, okay? Company's springing for flu shots."

Jed froze, but managed to say nothing, managed even to keep himself from looking up as Randy's and Jeff's fathers got up and, demanding to know if they were getting paid for their time away from the job, followed the other two men toward the stairs that would take them to the top of the dam. "Yes, you're getting paid," the foreman called after them. "If the company wants you to do something, the company pays you to do it."

A rowdy cheer erupted from the four men as they disappeared into the narrow corridor.

Jed wanted to yell after them, to warn them not to take the shots, but he knew he couldn't.

If he did, he would only give himself away.

Judith watched in silent dismay as her third-period class filed into the room and quietly took their seats. Randy Sparks, along with two others, was absent, but of the twenty-two students who were there, five had that strange glassy-eyed look that Gina, Randy, and the others had exhibited yesterday. The room was almost unnaturally silent, for in this class, as in her two previous classes of the day, it was the liveliest of the students who seemed to have been affected by whatever was being done to them.

Judith, like Jed, had done her best to betray nothing of what she suspected. During the just completed mid-morning break, she'd even managed to force a small laugh when Elliott Halvorson had joked that he wished that whatever kind of flu was going around this year would stay on. His classes seemed to have calmed down, and for the first time in years the students were actually paying attention to what he was saying.

Judith had felt like screaming at him that what was happening to the students had nothing at all to do with the flu, but she'd suppressed her words and coerced a smile from her lips instead.

It had been that way all morning.

She'd tried to tell herself that she was getting paranoid, just as she had yesterday when she'd thought that blue car was following her. Even on her way to work this morning she'd found herself glancing around, searching in every direction for something that might tell her she was indeed being watched.

There had been nothing.

No cars parked where they shouldn't have been; certainly no one who appeared to be following her. And yet, why should there have been? If anyone wanted to know where she was, it wouldn't be hard to locate her in Borrego. All anyone would have to do, really, was keep an eye on the main road leading north and south. Unless you had a four-wheel drive and were just a little bit crazy, there was no other way out of town. And as long as she was in town, anyone could find her in ten minutes.

She'd avoided the teachers' lounge entirely before classes that morning, certain she wouldn't be able to fake even an appearance of being relaxed, but by the time the break came, her paranoia had overcome her once more, and she'd decided that not to show up for a quick cup of coffee would look suspicious. Besides, if the rest of the classes were like hers, by then it must have been obvious that something was haywire.

Yet during the break none of the teachers seemed the least bit concerned. Most of them—like Elliott Halvorson—actually appeared to welcome the change. Their disciplinary problems had evaporated, and their classes actually seemed attentive.

But Judith wasn't certain exactly how attentive they really were. Now, as she looked at the class, an idea came to her.

She turned to the board and began quickly writing out a series of problems. Deliberately, she put some of the harder ones first, then scattered out the simpler ones toward the end.

Finally she turned to face the class. "You have five minutes to copy these," she said. "Copy them in order please."

A few groans drifted up—groans Judith welcomed as at least a small sign that some of her students were still perfectly normal.

Judith watched carefully as they set to work. Most of the class kept glancing up at the blackboard, then turning their attention to the paper in front of them while they wrote in short bursts, only to look up at the blackboard once more a few seconds later.

The affected students—the sleepwalkers, as Judith had begun to think of them—seemed to look at the board less often, and their writing, though Judith couldn't actually see it, appeared to proceed at a much steadier pace.

At the end of the five minutes Judith reached up and pulled the map down to cover the board. "All right," she said. "Begin working on the problems. You have thirty minutes."

She sat down at her desk, apparently grading a stack of homework assignments, but glancing up every few seconds to study one student after another.

The seventeen unaffected students seemed to be working normally. Some of their faces screwed up in expressions that looked almost painful as they concentrated, and several of them tapped their pencils nervously on their desktops as they pondered their solutions. Others turned now and then to gaze out the window for a moment, or stared at the ceiling.

Three of them were surreptitiously trying to see what their class-mates had already written.

The five sleepwalkers, however, all sat at their desks, their faces expressionless, their eyes fixed on the papers in front of them.

Their pencils moved steadily, except for two of them, who seemed to have frozen in place.

The minutes ticked by.

After twenty minutes three of the unaffected students had come up and placed their quiz sheets on her desk.

Two of the sleepwalkers had laid their pencils down and were now sitting quietly, their eyes staring straight ahead.

One of them was still working, while the last two were still staring at their papers, their pencils, unmoving, still in their hands.

At the end of the allotted thirty minutes, Judith stood up. "Time's up," she said.

Immediately, the fourteen unaffected students began passing their papers forward.

The five others didn't move.

"Please pass your papers forward," Judith said quietly.

The five students passed their papers forward.

Judith collected the papers, then glanced at the clock. There were still five minutes before the bell would ring. "All right," she said. "That's it for today. And there'll be no homework tonight. See you all tomorrow."

As the room began to empty, Judith began scanning the quizzes.

Seventeen of them seemed perfectly normal—most of the students had finished the quiz, or at least come close. All of them had finished the easiest of the problems, and there was a normal spread of right and wrong answers. Some of the harder problems, as Judith had expected, had simply been skipped entirely.

Then she turned to the quizzes turned in by the five strangely subdued students.

Two of them had finished the quiz, and both of them, not surprisingly, since they were her brightest students, had done the work perfectly. Their solutions were laid out neatly, with nothing either crossed out or erased.

The other three quizzes were strange. The work, as on the first two, was neatly written, with no changes having been made. And what was done had been done correctly.

But one of the students hadn't even finished the first problem; the second had gotten no more than halfway through the quiz; and the third had apparently given up on the next to the last problem.

The very last problem, which read simply $2 + 2 = x$, hadn't been touched by any of the three students.

Judith's throat tightened and a knot formed in her stomach as she realized what had happened.

The five students had, like Gina Alvarez night before last, done exactly as they had been told.

They had been told to "begin working on the problems," and they had. They had worked steadily and methodically, and they had not given up.

But when they had gotten stuck, they simply stopped.

And of course Judith knew why.

She hadn't told them to go through the quiz and solve the simplest equations first, then go back and work on the harder ones, solving them in the order of difficulty, which would have been the most efficient way to complete the test.

Instead she had simply told them to begin working on the problems, and they had followed her instructions to the letter.

What work they had done was perfect, until they got stuck. But when they got stuck, they were like robots that had walked into a wall.

They did nothing.

They just sat quietly, their gears spinning, and waited.

Twenty-seven

Judith's nerves jangled as she approached the counseling office of Borrego High School. Despite herself, she kept glancing back over her shoulder to see if anyone was watching. But it was ridiculous—she was a teacher, and she had a perfect right to look at the records of any of her students at any time she chose. Still, she'd spent several minutes alone in her classroom after the fourth-period bell had sounded, devising a cover story should anyone ask her what she was doing. A review of her classes was what she'd finally settled on. She was thinking of advancing her lesson plans a bit, and wanted to see just how much preparation her students had had in the event she decided to introduce them to some of the intricacies of trigonometry.

She paused outside the office door, glancing up and down the corridor one more time, but there was no one there. Finally she pushed the door open and stepped inside. Carla Bergstrom, who served as the school's sole full-time student counselor, was just taking her purse out of the bottom drawer of her desk. "Judith," she said.

"You just barely caught me."

Judith forced what she hoped was a disarming smile. "Actually, it isn't you I need at all," she said. "I just wanted to go over some of my kids' records."

Carla shrugged dismissively. "Be my guest," she said. "Do you know how to use the computer?"

Now Judith uttered a genuine laugh. "Is there anyone in the modern world who doesn't?" she asked. "But you could save me a little time by bringing up the right program."

Carla nodded, sat down at her desk and hit a few keys. "There it is," she said. "Just enter the names of the students you want, and your password and go to it." She stood up, picked up her purse, and started toward the door. "If you get stuck, I'll be hiding out in the staff lounge with everyone else."

A moment later Judith was sitting at the desk, typing in the names of her students. The work went slowly at first, and after ten minutes she realized she was going at it the wrong way—at this rate, she wouldn't even finish getting the names in by the time the lunch hour was over.

Clearing the screen, she brought up a directory of the computer's hard drive, and almost immediately spotted what she was looking for.

A data management program, the same one the school in East Los Angeles had used. Breathing a sigh of relief, she brought up the program's main menu, then began making her selections, typing in specific words and phrases.

The computer itself would sort through the records, compiling a list of students whose records contained the key words. All she would have to do was look over the list it produced. If she and Jed had been right last night, she knew which names should be on the list. She thought carefully, finally constructing a program designed to dig from the records the names of every student who had a relative working for Borrego Oil and a history of disciplinary problems.

At last she pressed the Enter key, then stared at the screen as images flashed by. A few seconds later a report form generated itself on the screen and names began to appear.

The pattern was there.

The names of every one of her affected students, along with many others—some she recognized, and others she did not— appeared on the list.

She narrowed the focus of the search, linking several of the variables together.

A much shorter list appeared, but still, all the names of those strange, emotionless kids who had sat so quietly through her morning classes were still there.

Her mind in turmoil, Judith printed out a copy of the list of names, folded it carefully, and stuck it into her purse. Turning off the computer, she stepped out into the hall. She still had fifteen minutes left of her lunch hour, time at least to grab a snack from one of the machines outside the cafeteria door. But as she started down the hall, the sound of voices caught her attention. She glanced across the corridor to the open door to Laura Sanders's office. A man was standing in front of the nurse's desk. Even from the back, Judith recognized him.

Greg Moreland.

As Laura's voice, sounding furious now, erupted once more, Judith slipped silently across the corridor.

Laura Sanders knew she was losing her temper, but she wasn't sure she cared anymore. Though Greg Moreland had been perfectly polite when he'd appeared in her office ten minutes ago, his implication was clear, he was accusing her of incompetence. And if there was one thing that annoyed Laura more than anything else, it was to have the thoroughness with which she did her job questioned.

"I don't really care what you think, Greg," she said now, her voice rising as she fixed her eyes on him. "I administered every one of the inoculations myself. I kept the records precisely as Mr. Beckwith instructed me, and I cross-checked my work after every class was inoculated."

Greg's expression hardened. He'd been working all morning, ever since Kendall had called him at seven, demanding to know if one of the syringes could possibly have gotten away from them. Since the call, he'd reviewed the records again and again, but been unable to find a mistake.

Every one of the needles was accounted for in the records, either as having been administered to someone or as being in the safe in his office.

Indeed, more than an hour had been wasted in examining the contents of the safe itself, physically matching the syringes against the inventory lists.

Every needle appeared to have been accounted for.

"I'm not accusing you of anything, Laura," Greg said, deliberately keeping his own anger out of his voice. "I just want you to check these lists one more time. There seems to be a mistake somewhere, and all I want you to do is help me find it."

Laura's lips set angrily, but she picked up the lists and began scanning them one more time. Everything, just as she expected—in fact just as it had been the last time she'd looked at it, not two minutes ago—was in order. And then she glanced once more at the second name on the list of Judith Sheffield's first-period class.

Jed Arnold.

Her eyes focused on the number next to his name.

It was out of sequence; indeed, it wasn't even close to the numbers of the rest of his class, nor the class preceding.

And then she remembered.

"Well, there is one thing," she said, looking up. She paused as she saw Judith Sheffield herself, standing outside the office, apparently listening. She was about to nod a greeting to Judith, but when the other woman shook her head and held a finger to her lips, she changed her mind. "It's Jed Arnold," she said. "Actually, he missed his shot that morning. He was late that morning."

Laura saw Judith shaking her head violently. For a split second she didn't understand. And then she realized what must have happened. Her mind raced, and then, as she saw the anger in Greg Moreland's eyes, she decided what to do.

"That's why his number is out of sequence," she went on smoothly. "He came in after school and I gave him his shot then." She let her voice harden slightly. "In fact, if you remember, I was cross-checking the lists when you came to pick everything up."

Greg stared at Laura, trying to decide if she was telling the truth. But of course there was a way to find out—a call to the dam would tell him if Jed had become as compliant as the rest of them. But wherever the mistake had occurred—if, indeed, there had been one at all—it no longer mattered. If Jed was behaving as the rest of the teenagers were, all the syringes were accounted for.

He thanked Laura for her cooperation and turned to leave the office.

Judith Sheffield had disappeared around the corner toward the cafeteria only seconds before.

Peter Langston stared at the telephone.

Twenty-four hours.

That was all it had taken, but it seemed much longer. He and the technician had been in the second subterranean level of the Brandt Institute almost all night, and both of them had been back early this morning just a little after dawn. It hadn't taken too long to figure out what the micromachines were. That had been the simplest part.

They were nothing more than minute transformers. When the switch at the bottom was thrown, whatever electrical source was entering them from their base would be stepped up, and the protuberances at the top, made of a high-resistance ceramic, would heat up. Nor had the source of electricity been difficult to decipher.

He'd calculated the amount of electricity the machines would need to operate. Not surprisingly, it had matched the tiny amount of electricity the human body itself generated.

But there had been some anomalies too, and finally, this morning, he had called in Tom Patchell, a neurosurgeon who had often served as a consultant to the institute.

"There's some kind of coating on the things," Langston had told Patchell. "It's a protein of some kind, but I can't figure out why it's there or what it's for."

It had been Patchell's idea to inject a sample of the fluid in the syringe into a lab animal and see what happened. They'd selected a chimpanzee, and an hour after giving it the injection, had anesthetized it and strapped it to the bed on the institute's nuclear magnetic resonator.

A moment later images began to form on the screen as the machine bombarded the chimpanzee's body with incredibly brief bursts of powerful electromagnetic energy, then measured the reaction of the atomic nuclei within the animal, reconstructing in visual form the structures of the tissues themselves.

After some fine-tuning by the technician, the tiny micromachines began to show up as dark flecks in the bloodstream.

"I don't get it," Langston murmured almost under his breath. "They just seem to be floating around."

Tom Patchell frowned but said nothing, his mind already struggling to remember something he'd read several months earlier. Then it came back to him. "Let's wait a few minutes," he said, "then focus on the chimp's brain."

Fifteen minutes went by, and then, as Patchell issued instructions to the technician, images of the ape's brain began to take form, greatly magnified, only a few millimeters showing at any single moment.

The clock on the wall kept moving, and the minutes crawled by as they kept searching through the depths of the chimpanzee's brain, looking for anything out of the ordinary.

Finally, Tom Patchell thought he saw something.

"There!" he said.

He leaned forward to study the screen. Although most of the dark specks representing the micromachines were still surging through the capillary system like leaves floating in a swift-moving stream, a few of them seemed to have adhered to the walls of cells, almost as if some of the leaves had been caught in the exposed roots of trees along the stream's banks. "I don't get it," Langston said. But Tom Patchell wasn't listening to him.

"Blow that one up," he instructed the technician, using the tip of a pencil to touch one of the specks on the screen.

The technician's fingers flew over the control panel of the resonator, and a few seconds later a new image appeared. This time the image on the screen was of only a few molecules, enlarged millions of times, to the point where the molecular structure itself was visible.

The technician touched a button and the image froze on the screen. Patchell studied the images produced by the resonator for a few moments, then whistled softly. "For Chrissake," he muttered. "Someone's done it."

Langston was bouncing impatiently on the balls of his feet now. "Done what?" he demanded.

"Look at that," Patchell told him. "See those molecules there? The ones that are slightly intertwined?" Langston looked closely at the screen and nodded. "Well, what they've done is something that's supposed to be only in the early experimental stages," Patchell explained. "What you're seeing there are two different molecules, one of which is a part of a nerve cell, the other of which is part of the coating on one of those micromachines."

"So?" Langston asked.

"Every type of cell in the human body has a distinctive protein coating to it. Whoever made those micromachines has coated them with specific kinds of substances that will allow them to adhere only to specific kinds of cells. In other words, what the micromachines do is keep traveling through the bloodstream at random, until they come into contact with the type of cell they were designed to adhere to. When they do, they lock onto that cell. It's almost as if each of the machines has a unique set of fingers, and it's searching for a perfectly fitting glove."

Langston's eyes widened. "So what you're telling me is that there could be any number of different coatings on those things, and it doesn't matter how or where they're injected into the blood system. Once released, they'll sort themselves out all by themselves."

Patchell's expression set grimly. "You've got it," he said. "I think we ought to wait a couple of hours, then take another look and see what we've got. And in the meantime, let's see what we can do about figuring out the triggering method."

Leaving the still-unconscious chimpanzee under the watchful eye of the technician, Peter Langston and Tom Patchell had returned to the physics lab, where they'd been working most of the time since then. The answer had come to Peter quickly enough. "It has to be radio waves," he'd said. "From what Judith said, they have to be triggering these things by remote control." He'd tapped a tiny area near the base of the object displayed on the screen of the electron microscope. "That area right there looks as if it could be some kind of a simple receiver."

By early afternoon they'd been ready. Several slides bad been prepared, each slide containing a drop of the saline solution from the hypodermic syringe. The syringe itself was sealed in a lead-lined container; the container was in a safe in Langston's office. Now they were in the microscopy lab, where Langston had jury-rigged a small transmitter capable of broadcasting a weak signal in a broad range of frequencies, and there were electrodes attached to the microscope slide itself.

The technician adjusted the electron microscope, and on the monitor images of half a dozen of the tiny devices appeared. Patchell touched a switch, and a tiny electrical charge, measurable only in millivolts, began coursing through the solution in which the micro-machines floated. Finally Langston turned on the transmitter, chose a range of frequencies near the high end, then began turning a dial. For a few seconds nothing happened at all.

And then, so suddenly neither of them actually saw it happen, the image of one of the micromechanisms disappeared from the display screen.

"What the hell?" Tom Patchell muttered.

Patchell frowned, made a note of the exact frequency at which the transmitter had been broadcasting when the object suddenly disappeared, then readjusted it.

A moment later another of the objects disappeared. "I want to get this on tape," Langston said, and the technician nodded.

"It's already done. If you want, I can play that last one back."

"Do it," Langston replied.

The monitor went blank, and then the images reappeared. At the top of the screen a chronometer displayed the lapse of time in microseconds, and another scale monitored the changing frequency of the radio waves to which the sample was being exposed.

As they watched, the switch at the base of one of the devices began to close, and a few microseconds later the contacts touched. Then the protuberances at the opposite end of the device began to change, and finally the whole device started to disintegrate.

"I was right," Langston breathed to himself. "A soon as the contact closes, the transformer begins drawing current out of the solution, and the whole thing heats up to the point where it burns."

Now it was Patchell who frowned. "But why didn't they all go?"

"They've tuned the switches to different frequencies," Langston explained. "It wouldn't surprise me if we find out that there's a correlation between the frequencies that activate the switches and the kinds of cells they attach themselves to."

A few minutes later they were back on the second level beneath the surface. The chimpanzee, still unconscious, lay inert on the bed of the resonator. The technician glanced up from the magazine he was reading. "Ready to take another look?"

Patchell nodded, and the technician set the magazine aside and began manipulating the controls of the machine in the next room. The scan began, and a greatly enhanced image of the chimpanzee's brain appeared on the screen.

Tom Patchell studied the screen carefully. Satisfied, he nodded. "They've clustered all right," he said. "See? There's a mass of them here in the hypothalamus region, and more here and here, in the area of the cortex."

They removed the chimpanzee from the resonator, transferred it to a gurney, and wheeled it back to its cage. By the time the two men had brought their small transmitter downstairs and set it up, the sedative had begun to wear off. The chimpanzee was beginning to stir.

Half an hour later the transmitter had been set up near the chimp's cage, and two syringes filled with a powerful tranquilizer were on a counter next to the lab sink. The chimpanzee, awake now but still lying on the gurney, watched them languidly.

At last Peter Langston turned on the transmitter and began broadcasting a sequence of frequencies, each of which had activated some of the micromechanisms in the lab.

As they watched, the chimpanzee's eyes suddenly widened and it sat up on the gurney, its head turning as if it was trying to focus on something invisible to either Langston or Patchell.

"Change the frequency," Patchell said.

Langston made a small adjustment on the transmitter. The chimp began to spit, wiping its mouth with its hands as if trying to rid itself of something bitterly distasteful. Then, as Langston once more readjusted the transmitter, the chimp began screaming with either rage or pain, and flung itself off the gurney, leaping up to grasp the bars of the cage.

"Shut it off!" Patchell yelled, but the order was unnecessary. Peter Langston had already cut the power to the transmitter.

Both men stared at the animal, which was now lying inert on the floor. Its face bore an oddly human expression, part frightened, part almost puzzled by what had just happened to it. Patchell hesitated a moment, then carefully opened the door to the cage, keeping a wary eye on the animal within.

The chimp watched him but made no move either to attack or to try to escape as the neurosurgeon slowly stepped inside the cage.

"Hand me one of the needles," Patchell said quietly his body tense, his eyes never leaving the chimp.

Langston passed him one of the syringes, and Patchell approached the chimp slowly, making no sudden moves, talking quietly to it.

He tentatively touched the chimp's right arm, expecting the ape to jerk its limb away, but instead the chimp simply stared at him, its head cocked slightly, flinched as the needle pierced its skin and slid into a vein, but made no move to try to pull away.

After a few minutes, it was asleep once more. Patchell lifted it back onto the gurney, and five minutes later they were back in the resonator lab.

"Jesus," Peter Langston breathed, whistling softly as the images of the chimpanzee's brain once more began to appear on the resonator screen. "Look at that."

Tom Patchell nodded, his lips compressing into a tight line.

Though many of the micromechanisms were still visible, others had disappeared entirely, to be replaced with the vivid lesions that were the physical evidence of a series of strokes the chimp had apparently suffered.

"It's horrible," Patchell said at last, shaking his head in awe. "If we'd set them all off, there'd be practically nothing left of the chimp's brain. And all you'd be able to find would be those lesions, without so much as a trace of what caused them."

Both men fell silent as they realized they were looking at the perfect tool for nuclear-age torture.

Or murder.

Peter Langston glanced at the clock on the wall. It was almost four o'clock. He started back to his office to call Judith Sheffield.

Twenty-eight

J udith Sheffield felt as though the walls were closing in around her. All afternoon she had been telling herself she was being paranoid, that no one was following her, or watching her. Still, she kept finding herself drawn to the window. What did she expect to see out there? A man in a trench coat, a battered fedora pulled low on his forehead, his hands stuffed deep in his pockets as he lounged against a lamp post?

Well, there wasn't any lamp post, let alone a man in a trench coat and a fedora. And if she was being watched, she suspected that the methods would be far more sophisticated than those she was imagining.

Her eyes drifted up to the mesa, where there could be someone with high-powered binoculars—even a telescope—hiding in any one of a hundred crevices in the worn sandstone. There could even be high-tech listening devices directed at the house or tapping into the telephone.

Stop it! she commanded herself, then nearly jumped out of her skin as the phone in the kitchen suddenly rang, its bell jangling her nerves, making her almost run to snatch it up.

"Peter?" she asked, her voice quavering despite her determination not to let him know how nervous she was.

"Judith?" Peter replied, and almost immediately she felt some of the tension drain out of her body. "Are you okay?" Then: "Stupid question. Anyway, I've got it figured out. The micromachines are transformers with electrodes, and when we triggered some of them in a chimpanzee, they induced a series of what looks—after it's all over—exactly like strokes. But I've talked to a neurosurgeon, and he thinks the devices could induce hallucinations—both visual and olfactory. I won't go into all the details right now—hell, Tom and I don't even *have* most of the details yet—but it looks like they've got this thing down to the point where they can do damned near anything they want to anybody who's got these things in their bodies. Different ones seem to adhere to different parts of the brain, but in the end, if there are enough of them tuned to enough different frequencies, you could play a person like an organ. You could drive them insane, take away their will power—hell, if you set off enough of them, you could kill a person almost instantly.''

Judith felt weak as she thought of Reba Tucker and Frank Arnold. Neither was dead, but they had been punishing Frank Arnold, and experimenting with Reba Tucker.

And they'd killed Max Moreland outright.

"My God," she whispered, the words issuing from her throat in a strangled moan. "Wh-What can we do?"

"Right now, not much except find out how they're setting the things off, and stop them. Then we'll start working on a way to flush the mechanisms out of the brain. If we can find a way to dissolve the protein coating—"

The sound of the doorbell shattered what little concentration Judith had been able to devote to Peter. Her mind numb, she tried to gather her wits together "J-Just a minute, Peter," she said. "There's someone at the door."

She laid the phone on the counter. Still preoccupied with what Peter had told her, and the possible implications of it, she hurried to the front door and opened it.

The moment it was open, she realized her mistake.

All the paranoid feelings that had been growing in her yesterday and today, all the suspicions and intuitions that she was being watched or followed, had been right. For now, standing on her porch, were two men she'd never seen before. They were dressed in a perfectly ordinary manner—both of them in faded blue jeans and plaid western-cut shirts with mother-of-pearl snaps. They wore scuffed cowboy boots, and one of them had a light denim jacket draped over his right arm, covering his hand.

Instinctively, Judith knew the jacket was concealing a gun.

She gasped slightly, stepping backward as she tried to swing the door closed again, but it was too late. One of the men simply stepped forward, his left hand coming up to push against the door, and then he was inside.

His companion followed a split second later, gently closing the door behind him.

Judith's mind lurched. It was all impossible. Two men—two strangers—couldn't simply come barging in on her like this! And from outside, she already knew, it would look exactly as if she had invited them in.

She opened her mouth to scream, but the first man, nearly six and a half feet tall, with jet-black hair and broad shoulders that appeared even wider because of the narrow cut of his shirt, reached out with an immense hand as if to grasp her neck.

Her training in karate and judo—the training that had allowed her to overpower Randy Sparks so easily that day in the lunchroom—came to the fore, and she quickly stepped aside, ready to twist the man's arm around behind him. But even as she made her move, he anticipated it, countering it with an instantaneous shift of his own that put him behind her. As his right arm snaked around her neck, choking off her scream so quickly it was no more than a tiny yelp, Judith understood with terrible clarity that his own first move had been nothing more than a feint, a trap she had instantly fallen into.

"Not a word," he said, his voice quiet but hard as steel. "If you try to scream, I'll kill you right here, right now." As if to prove his point his arm tightened around her neck while the fingers of his left hand found a nerve and applied just enough pressure to send a blinding pain screaming through her body. Her lungs automatically contracted as she tried to scream again, then she began choking as her windpipe closed tight.

The man holding her nodded to his companion, a sandy-haired man with cold blue eyes, who immediately went into the kitchen. Judith could hear the sound of the telephone being put gently back onto its hook.

"I'm going to let you breathe now," the black-haired man said in a tone so casually conversational that it sent chills through Judith's body. "But if you try to scream, or speak, or do anything else I don't tell you to do, it will be the last thing you do."

As he stopped speaking his right arm relaxed enough so that she could suck air into her aching lungs. A part of her mind focused on the fact that before allowing her to breathe, he hadn't bothered to wait for any sign that she'd even heard his instructions, let alone agreed to them. That added to the terror that now threatened to overwhelm her, for she was certain he would do exactly as he had said, and didn't really care whether she agreed to his conditions or not.

The sandy-haired man was back in the living room now, and he casually lifted his jacket so she could see the gun in his hand. She hadn't the slightest idea what kind of gun it was, but it was small and compact, with a snub nose that made it look mean and ugly.

"It's a thirty-eight," Sandy-hair told her, his lips curling slightly. "And this," he went on, pulling a metal tube from a pocket of the jacket, "is a silencer. Actually, it doesn't really do the aim of this thing much good, and if you were to get away from us, I'd probably miss you from anything beyond ten or fifteen yards. But at close range, like if it's jammed into your back, aim doesn't count for much, does it?" He smiled coldly, and neither he nor Black-hair even seemed to notice the phone when it rang.

"What the neighbors are going to see," Sandy-hair continued, "if they're looking at all, is us helping you out to the car. You're not feeling so good, see? So that way, if I have to shoot you, you'll just look like you're feeling even worse."

"Wh-Why?" Judith managed to ask. Her throat hurt where Black-hair had crushed her larynx, and the word was no more than a croak.

Sandy-hair shrugged. "A man wants to talk to you," he said. "He sent us to pick you up."

"I'll need your car keys," Black-hair said, his voice still carrying that eerily conversational quality that made his request sound so ominous.

"M-My purse," Judith managed, nodding toward a small table next to the sofa.

Black-hair moved to the table, picked up Judith's purse, then groped in it until his hands closed on her keys. Then he handed her the purse and opened the front door. "If you'll just take my arm," he said.

Numbly, Judith slipped her hand through his arm, and he led her outside onto the porch. Sandy-hair pulled the door closed, almost shutting out the sound of the still-ringing telephone, then fell in beside her, gripping her other arm and letting her feel the pressure of the pistol against her rib cage. Sitting outside, behind her own car, was the blue Chevy she'd seen the day before.

Black-hair opened the passenger door for her, and as she climbed into the front seat, Sandy-hair slid behind the wheel. "My friend here still has his gun," Black-hair told her. "He'll be driving with one hand, and he'll be holding the gun with the other. If you make any attempt to get out of the car, or scream, or do anything else except sit there quietly, he'll kill you."

A moment later, after Sandy-hair had disappeared around the corner, Black-hair ambled up the driveway, got into Judith's car, backed into the street, and shifted the transmission into Drive.

Across the street and two houses up, a woman stood watering her front lawn. As he passed her, Black-hair smiled and waved.

The woman seemed puzzled, but then she grinned uncertainly and returned his wave before going back to her watering.

Peter Langston stared at the receiver in his hand and rattled the button on the phone. "Judith?" he said. He held the button down a moment, then quickly redialed the number. He let the phone ring fifteen times, then finally hung up. "Something's happened up there," he told Tom Patchell, who was looking at him, his head cocked worriedly to one side. "Someone came to the door, and then they hung up her phone."

Patchell's eyes narrowed. "Better call the police up there." But his words were unnecessary, for Peter was already dialing again. A few minutes later he began talking urgently to the Borrego police department.

"I'm telling you, something's gone wrong!" He repeated what had happened, then spoke again. "I don't know the address. She's living at her boyfriend's house." He searched his memory, but couldn't remember the name of Judith's new boyfriend. Possibly she had never told him the name. Then he had an idea. "Look, the guy's in the hospital. He had a stroke." A moment later he slammed the receiver down. "I'm driving up there," he told Patchell. "They knew who the guy was, but they said he's some kind of kook. I don't think they're even going to check his place out."

"You want me to go with you?" Patchell asked, but Peter shook his head.

"Stay here and see what else you can find out about those damned machines. Like maybe a way to disable them."

Patchell looked at Peter, his eyes bleak. "I've already been thinking about that," he said. "I'm not sure there is a way to disable them, short of destroying them. And the only way I can think of to do that is to set them off."

Peter Langston's eyes turned to flint. "There has to be a way," he said. "If there isn't . . ."

But he left the sentence unfinished, unwilling to accept that for all the teenagers of Borrego, there might already be no means of escape from the bombs that had been planted inside their heads.

By the end of his shift Jed Arnold didn't have to pretend to move like a somnambulist. As he climbed the long circular staircase that led up to the top of the dam, his whole body felt numb. He'd spent the afternoon in the main shaft, shoveling debris into the conveyor belt, and his arms felt as if he could barely lift them. He took the stairs one by one, moving his legs stolidly, willing them to carry his weight upward. At last he reached the surface and emerged, blinking into the bright afternoon sunlight. He paused, sucking fresh air into his lungs, hacking and coughing in an attempt to dislodge the dust and grime of the power shaft from his throat. A moment later, realizing he was in full view of the operator's shack at the end of the dam, he let his head hang once more and started along the dam, as though unconscious of his surroundings.

"Arnold!" Otto Kruger's voice barked as he passed the open door to the control room.

He stopped, and slowly raised his head, keeping his expression carefully impassive. Kruger was holding a brown manila envelope out to him.

"Take this down to the communications center on your way home. Give it to the first person you see." It wasn't a request; it was an order. From the way Kruger had spoken, it was clear to Jed that he anticipated no argument, no questions.

He expected that Jed would silently comply with his command.

Wordlessly, Jed held out his hand and took the thin package, then proceeded on his way to the truck, being careful not even to so much as look at the envelope.

Ignoring the rest of the crew, who had gathered around the bed of Carlos Alvarez's old pickup to enjoy an after-work beer, he climbed up into the cab of the truck, started the engine, and pulled out onto the road along the canyon's edge. Only when certain he was no longer within view of anyone at the dam did he pick up the envelope and look for any markings that might identify what was inside. There was nothing on it. No name, no address, not even a logo for either Borrego Oil or UniChem. It was simply a plain brown envelope.

Jed dropped the envelope on the seat beside him, then sped up, enjoying the wind in his face as it blew through the open window. He slowed the truck only when he came to the part of the road that switchbacked down the shoulder of the mesa, then sped up again as he started back up into the canyon itself.

Four hundred yards into the canyon, in the shelter of a thick stand of cottonwoods, he pulled the truck to a stop. He got out and stripped off his shirt, then splashed water from the stream over his face and torso. Finally he went back to the truck, pulled a ragged towel out from behind the passenger seat and wiped himself dry, removing the worst of the sweat and grime from his aching body. Only when he'd put his sticky work shirt back on did he finally pick up the brown envelope again, this time testing the flap to see if it was sealed. To his surprise, it wasn't.

And yet, he reflected, why should it be? It was obvious they were certain he would simply do as he was told, and show no curiosity at all about what might be in the envelope.

Well, they were wrong.

Quickly he opened the envelope and slid the single sheet of paper out far enough so he could see what it was.

It was a list of the men he'd been working with all day, the men who had disappeared in groups of four at various times through the morning and afternoon, sent down to the hospital to receive their "flu" shots.

Beside each name there was a five-digit number.

Except for the list of names and numbers, the envelope was empty. Jed stared at the sheet for a few seconds, then rummaged in the glove compartment of the truck until he found a stub of a pencil and a crumpled paper bag.

He copied the names and their corresponding numbers, then shoved the bag and pencil back where he'd found them. He slid the sheet back into its envelope and carefully flattened the metal fastener.

Ten minutes later he pulled up in front of the communications center and climbed out of the truck.

He hesitated.

He wanted to see more of the building than simply whatever lay just inside the door. As he looked at the cars in the parking lot, an idea came to him. He hurried from car to car, until he found what he was looking for. Lying on the dashboard of a blue Buick was an envelope, addressed to someone named Stan Utley. He checked the other cars, but they were all locked, and he found nothing useful. He would have to gamble on the Utley envelope.

Making his face expressionless once more, he walked through the gate and into the building itself.

A girl he didn't recognize looked up at him. "Give me the envelope," she said, exactly as if she were talking to a robot rather than a human being.

Jed shook his head. "They said to give it to Utley," he said. "Stan Utley."

The girl stared at him for a moment, then nodded her head. "In the back," she said. "Go through the door into the transmitter room. He's in there."

Jed stifled a sigh of relief as he followed the girl's instructions. He stepped through the door, and almost immediately the temperature dropped as he came into the cavern that formed the back chamber of the building.

It looked to Jed like a control room. There seemed to be computer monitors everywhere, and at several of the monitors, blank-eyed, expressionless people sat tapping data into keyboards.

Jed stopped, his head down but his eyes darting everywhere, taking in everything he could. On a desk a few feet from him, propped up by one of the monitors, was a list of names and numbers. On the screen of the monitor, more numbers were flashing.

Suddenly a man in a technician's coat appeared in front of Jed. "I'm Stan Utley," he said. Nothing more.

Jed handed him the envelope.

"That's all," Utley said. "You can go home now."

Silently Jed turned and started out of the room, but as he reached the door, he heard Utley's voice speaking to someone else. "Get these entered, and have them matched to the Parameter B frequencies."

As he left the communications center a few seconds later and started driving back down the canyon, Jed was certain he'd found the source of what was being done to the people of Borrego.

The communications center wasn't broadcasting to other UniChem offices at all.

It was broadcasting to the town.

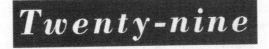

P eter Langston hurried up the walk in front of the nondescript cinder-block house and rapped sharply on the door. Darkness had already fallen, the first star beginning to glimmer in the sky, and Peter shivered, though he wasn't sure if it was the chill of the evening that had brought on the sudden tremor. He was about to knock again when the door opened and a teenage boy, dark-complected, with fine planes in his face and startlingly blue eyes, looked out at him. Despite his dusky complexion, the boy's face looked pale and seemed almost expressionless, and as Peter remembered Judith's description of her "affected" students, he felt a pang of apprehension. But if this was Jed Arnold, he couldn't possibly be feeling the effects of a shot he hadn't had.

"Jed?" he asked. "Jed Arnold?" A hint of a frown creased the boys brow and he nodded warily. "I'm Peter Langston, Judith Shef- field's—"

Jed's face came to life, and he quickly pulled Langston into the house, closing the door behind him. "Where's Jude?" he demanded. "Isn't she with you? She wasn't here when I got home and—" His words faded away as he saw the look on Langston's face. "Oh, Jesus," he breathed. "Something's happened to her, hasn't it?"

Peter nodded. "I think she's been kidnapped. I know it sounds crazy, but—"

Jed shook his head. "Nothing sounds crazy around here anymore. What happened?"

For a moment Peter hesitated. What, after all, could a teenage kid do? He should go to the police, put the whole thing in the hands of people who would know what to do. But as Jed's eyes fixed on him, Peter changed his mind. There was a strength in Jed he'd never seen before in someone as young. Quickly he told Jed what had happened.

"The antenna," Jed said as soon as Peter was finished. "That's where they're sending the transmissions from." His eyes darkened. "And I know where they've got Jude too."

"Then let's call the police," Peter said.

Jed seemed to think about it for a moment, then shook his head. "No," he said. "It'll take too much time. Even if they believe us, it'll be too late. We'll do it ourselves."

Without waiting for Peter to argue further, Jed grabbed his jacket and headed out the back door. A second later Peter followed him.

Judith strained against the heavy straps that held her to the bed, her wrists and ankles already abraded from her struggles against the thick leather bonds. From the chair a few feet away, Black-hair watched her indolently. "It won't do much good, you know," he said in that infuriatingly conversational tone. "You might just as well lie there and enjoy yourself until Mr. Kendall gets here."

Judith wanted to scream, but wasn't about to give Black-hair the satisfaction.

She didn't know how long it had been since the two men had appeared at her house and calmly taken her away, a gun in her back, with no one apparently either knowing or caring. She'd known where they were taking her as soon as they started up the road into the canyon. They'd brought her into one of the cabins at The Cottonwoods, tied her up and gagged her. A little while later an orderly had appeared, and, as Judith's heart pounded with terror, administered a shot to her. She'd expected to fall asleep then, but when nothing happened, her terror only grew as she realized that the shot could have been only one thing—a dose of the micromechanisms that had already been administered to nearly all the teenagers in town.

But finally, as the hours went on, her terror had given way to cold fury, and when Black-hair had at last removed the gag, she'd screamed out at him in rage, not fear.

He'd only chuckled quietly, settling himself back into a chair. "Scream all you want," he'd told her. "Around here, I guess that's what people are supposed to do, isn't it?"

Since then she'd remained silent, but still struggled against the bonds, knowing even as she did that she wasn't strong enough to break them.

Even if she were, Black-hair was still there, and she had no doubt that if it became necessary, he would kill her. Indeed, she was certain that he would even take pleasure in the act.

After a while the door opened and Greg Moreland entered the room. Nodding to Black-hair, he came over to the bed and looked down at Judith, his eyes glittering with cold anger.

Judith stopped struggling and glared up at him.

"Why?" she demanded. "Why are you doing this?"

Greg ignored the question. "I want to know where you got that sample of my flu inoculation."

Judith said nothing.

"Look, Judith," Greg told her, speaking exactly as if they were conversing at a cocktail party, rather than in a room where she was being held prisoner, "I don't know how much you've discovered about what I'm doing, but I can assure you that at this point, it won't make any difference. What I want to know from you is how you got your hands on one of our syringes. And you *did* get hold of one of them. There isn't any other reason why you'd have gone down to the Brandt Institute yesterday."

Judith's mind raced. He didn't *know*. So far, he was still just guessing. If she simply refused to speak—

It was as if Greg had read her mind. "You'll tell me, you know. The question is whether you tell me now or tomorrow morning."

Judith's eyes betrayed the sudden surge of panic that gripped her.

Moreland smiled. "I gather you figured out what was in that shot the orderly gave you a while ago. Actually, I considered having them put some sodium pentothal in it too, but the trouble with that is that you might have slept through the night. And I wouldn't want to deprive you of the experience of being realigned."

Judith stared balefully up at Moreland. "Is that what you call murdering people?" she asked, her voice trembling with both fear and anger. "Realigning them?"

Moreland's voice hardened. "Judith, you haven't the slightest idea of what it is we're doing here, but I can assure you that it has nothing whatever to do with killing people."

Anger overrode fear in Judith now. "Then what happened to Frank Arnold, and Max Moreland, and Reba Tucker?" she demanded.

Greg shrugged as if what Judith was saying had no importance. "You could call them victims of research, I suppose," he replied.

"Dear God," Judith breathed. "You're playing with people, just like you played with your puppy . . ."

Greg's face paled. "So Aunt Rita told you about that, did she? She always hated me after that. She always looked at me as if I was some kind of freak. And she wasn't the only one. She told everyone what I did, you know. That's why everyone's always hated me.''

His voice went on and on, but Judith had heard enough to understand the truth.

He was paranoid, certain that everyone in Borrego hated him. And it would have been the same anywhere he'd gone. Everywhere, he would have felt people watching him, listening to him, plotting against him.

But here in Borrego he'd found a way to vent his insane rage, to get even for the imagined hatred he'd felt.

Only when the stream of Greg's words died away did Judith speak again. "You don't even know what you're doing, do you?" she asked.

Greg's expression hardened, and Judith realized she'd struck a nerve. "You don't, do you?" she pressed. "You're just striking out blindly, seeing what will happen."

"Don't pretend to be stupid," Greg snapped. "You've already seen the beginnings of what we're doing. And if you think about it, you'll realize that it isn't so bad. Haven't you noticed that your classes have been better behaved the last couple of days? And don't some of your students concentrate on their work more than they used to?"

"They're like sleepwalkers!" Judith flared. "Whatever you're doing, it's destroying their minds."

"No," Greg replied. "That's where you're wrong. What we're doing is freeing their minds. By the time we get finished, we're going to be able to create a population such as the world has never seen before!"

Judith gasped, and suddenly thought she understood the whole thing. "Slaves," she breathed. "You're turning people into slaves, aren't you?"

Greg's features hardened. "That's an ugly word, Judith," he said. He began pacing the floor, then stopped and looked at her again. "You're a teacher, Judith. It seems to me you, of all people, would be able to see what's going on in this country. What we're faced with is economic ruin. It hasn't happened yet, but it's on the horizon. America simply can't compete. Our people aren't well enough educated, and they have no self-discipline. They spend half their time wanting things they can never have, and the other half being miserable about it. Christ, look at this town. Is anyone here really happy? No. They hate the town, they hate their jobs, they hate their whole lives. Well, I've figured out a way to change all that. It's simply a matter of making some adjustments to the brain itself. And what we're going to wind up with is a whole population that is going to have powers of concentration such as no one has ever seen before. They're going to be able to take orders from their managers, and then carry out their jobs with so few mistakes that even the Japanese will sit up and take notice."

Judith stared up at Greg, almost unable to believe what she was hearing. "But they're not people," she said. "For God's sake, haven't you even *seen* what you've done to them? Gina Alvarez was a bright, vivacious child three days ago. Now she doesn't speak unless she's asked a direct question. She doesn't seem to be interested in doing anything. She just sits and stares!"

Greg Moreland looked at her almost pityingly. "But if you asked her, she'd tell you she was feeling just fine, wouldn't she?" he demanded. "And that's the whole point—for the rest of her life, Gina—and all the others—will be happy."

"Happy?" Judith echoed. "My God, Greg, she won't be happy—she doesn't feel anything anymore. You've killed her, just like you killed Frank and Max and—" Her voice broke and her body was wracked with a sob she couldn't control.

Greg Moreland's lips twisted into a sardonic smile. "Well, that's a matter of opinion, isn't it?" he asked. "At any rate, it won't be much longer until you can experience a realignment for yourself." Judith shrank back on the bed, and Greg's smile broadened. "Don't worry about it," he said. "For most people, it doesn't seem to be too unpleasant. Nothing more than a bad dream. Except that I expect you'll be wide awake when it happens. And tomorrow, when I ask you where you got that syringe, you'll tell me. You'll want to tell me."

Nodding once more to Black-hair, he walked out into the night.

"That's it," Jed said quietly. He brought the truck to a stop a few yards from the antenna on the rim of the canyon. Jed's first impulse had been to go directly to The Cottonwoods, but Peter had talked him out of it. "If they've got Judith, they've probably already given her a shot. By now those things will have lodged in her brain, and they can activate them any time. Is there a way we can disable the antenna? If we can get it shut down for a while, at least it'll buy us some time."

Now Peter stared through the windshield at the chain-link fence surrounding the antenna. It had an ugly look to it in the silvery light of the moon, though for the moment it seemed totally inactive. Finally Jed opened the door of the truck and got out, Peter following him.

There was a large toolbox in the bed of the truck, and Jed immediately went to it, taking out a hacksaw and a large plastic-handled screwdriver. He and Peter approached the fence.

"Don't touch it," Peter warned, remembering the fence that surrounded the Brandt Institute. "It might be electrified."

Jed stepped forward, and making sure he was touching nothing of the screwdriver except its plastic handle, laid the tool against the fence.

Nothing happened.

Jed shook his head. "I don't get it," he said. "There's got to be an alarm system."

Peter frowned. "Maybe they figured an alarm would make it look too important," he suggested.

Jed shrugged. "Well, there's only one way to find out." Putting the screwdriver in his hip pocket and slipping his right arm through the frame of the hacksaw, he quickly climbed to the top of the fence, swung over the top, then dropped to the other side.

Instantly, a siren began to wail and four bright floodlights came on, wiping away the darkness with a brilliant artificial glare.

"Holy Christ," Peter swore. "Get out of there, Jed. They'll have guards up here in a minute!"

But Jed made no move to reclimb the fence. Instead, he moved to the antenna itself, where the PVC pipe that snaked up the canyon wall emerged from the concrete floor of the antenna pad. "We have some time," he yelled over the din of the sirens. "It'll take at least twenty minutes for anyone to get up here." Kneeling down, he began sawing at the PVC.

Peter, feeling almost naked in the glare of the floodlights, looked around for a way to turn them off, but it was impossible. They hung from the tops of metal posts, and the lamps were covered with thick Plexiglas, itself protected by heavy metal mesh.

For a moment he felt a twinge of panic, but inside the fence Jed, apparently unaffected by the lights and sirens, pumped steadily at the saw. The blade penetrated the top of the PVC pipe, then moved quickly as it cut downward. But then the blade struck the cables within the pipe and Jed paused.

One of the cables inside, he was sure, would be a power line. He pulled the saw from the kerf in the pipe, examining its handle carefully.

It was all metal. If he'd kept sawing and hit that power line, he would have electrocuted himself. "Peter!" he called out. "Look in the box. I need electrical tape."

Peter dashed to the truck and quickly rummaged through the tool chest. Finally, near the bottom, half buried under a confusion of wrenches, he felt a roll of plastic tape. He jerked it free of the tools, then tossed it over the fence.

Jed snagged the roll of tape in midair and quickly began binding the handle of the saw. After he'd covered it with five layers of tape, he began working again.

The blade bit into the cables once more, and now the work slowed down. But suddenly there was a shower of sparks, and then the lights went out and the wailing of the siren abruptly died away. Jed cursed softly as his eyes—their pupils constricted against the brilliance of the floodlights—failed him completely for a moment, but despite his blindness, he kept sawing.

A few moments later, as his eyes once more adjusted to the dim moonlight, the saw bit into the last centimeters of PVC, and then the pipe parted.

Jed jerked at the saw, trying to get it to come back up through the kerf it had left between the two ends of the pipe, but the cables within had shifted slightly, and the blade jammed firmly. Finally he gave it up, abandoning the saw as he quickly scaled the fence once more and dropped to the other side.

"I don't know how much time we have," he said. "But it's going to take them a while to get that back together again."

They rushed back to the truck, but Peter stopped short to stare at Jed.

"Where do we go?" he asked. "If we go back the way we came, we're going to run right into them."

"We go the other way," Jed said.

Peter shook his head. "But the mouth of the canyon's behind us. If we're going to go after Judith—" Jed was already in the truck. "Just do what I say, okay? Or do you want to wait around here and see what happens?"

Jed started the engine of the truck, and then, as they saw the first glow of headlights moving toward them along the canyon's rim, headed farther up the rutted road.

The track narrowed as it wound eastward, finally disappearing altogether. Peter glanced nervously over at Jed.

Jed kept going. What he was looking for was no more than a quarter of a mile up the canyon's rim.

Thirty

Greg Moreland was halfway between The Cottonwoods and the communications center when the quiet of the night was shattered by the high-pitched wailing of the siren. He leaned forward over the wheel and gazed upward at the brilliant white glow of the floodlights surrounding the antenna installation, then slammed his right foot down hard on the gas pedal. The car's rear wheels skidded on the loose dirt of the road, and the rear end fishtailed violently; a second later the tires caught and the car shot forward. Within less than a minute he braked to a sharp stop in front of the communications building and dashed inside. The front office was deserted, but in the cavern hollowed out of the cliff's wall he found Paul Kendall and Stan Utley huddled around a computer terminal.

"What the hell is going on?" Greg demanded.

Utley didn't even look up from the screen he was studying. "Not sure yet," he said. "Something tripped the alarm topside, but so far everything's working fine." He studied the display for a few more seconds, then glanced up at Paul Kendall. "Could have been a bird," he said. "If a mouse was poking around up there and an owl went for it, it could break the trip beam."

Moreland shook his head. Whatever had happened at the antenna had nothing to do with an owl, or any other kind of wild animal. If Judith Sheffield had discovered what was going on, then other people had too. "I want a crew up there," he ordered. "Right now!"

Utley shot him an irritated glance, but knew better than to argue. He picked up a phone and entered a number on the keypad, drumming his fingers impatiently on his desk until he recognized Otto Kruger's voice at the other end. Less than a minute later he hung up. "Kruger's going up there himself with a couple of the men from the dam," he said. "But if there's a real problem—"

Abruptly, the sirens stopped wailing. Utley started to smile, but as his eyes moved to the computer screen, the smile faded. "Shit," he muttered.

Paul Kendall, his fury mounting, shoved Utley aside and studied the display on the screen. It indicated clearly that not only was the signal cable to the antenna cut, but the power cable was broken as well. "I want that fixed," he said, his voice taking on a dangerous edge. "We've got a lot to do tonight, and none of it can wait."

Utley's tongue ran nervously across his lower lip. Until Kruger got to the antenna and assessed the damage, there was no way of telling how long it would take before the antenna would be functional again. But he'd worked for Kendall long enough to know better than to suggest the possibility that one of his orders might not be met. "I'll let you know when I've heard from Kruger," he said.

Kendall nodded curtly, his mind already on other things. He'd made his decision about what was to be done tonight much earlier, and there were preparations to be made. But instead of sitting down at one of the computers with Greg Moreland to begin designing the new program that would be broadcast out over Borrego as soon as the antenna was repaired, he found himself drawn out of the little building into the serene quiet of the canyon.

He glanced upward, but the lights around the antenna were out now, and all he could see were the black shadows of the canyon's northern wall. On the southern wall the pale light of the moon shone softly on the sandstone, its glorious daylight hues muted now to myriad shades of gray. Directly above, the sky glittered with stars, more stars than Paul Kendall ever remembered having seen before.

He moved away from the building, and a small breeze, redolent with sage, tweaked at him. Then, to the right, there was a flickering movement, nothing more than a shadow within a shadow, as a bat fluttered by.

The stream, running in its bed a few yards away, babbled softly in the darkness, and Kendall could hear the chirruping of frogs as they called out in an endless search for mates.

Kendall liked the canyon—even was beginning to appreciate the desert itself.

He hadn't wanted to come to Borrego at all. Indeed, his first choice for the experiment that was taking place here had been Alaska. Up there were towns with no roads leading in or out, towns that were all but cut off from the rest of the world during the long northern winter. But in the end he'd realized that the very isolation of those places could become a liability rather than an asset. While it was true that no one could get to those towns, neither could anyone leave them.

And Greg Moreland had assured him that Borrego would be perfect. "No one cares what happens there," he'd insisted five years ago when he'd brought his first sketchy ideas to Kendall. "No one will even notice what we're doing." But now, after all the years of research and planning, after all the experiments that had, in the end, proved the project to be completely feasible; now, when he was on the very verge of success, he was going to have to fold his tents, move on, and start over again.

Well, perhaps not completely over again. The mechanisms were perfected now, he was certain of that. If they'd had another month—maybe even as little as two weeks—they'd have been ready to unveil Greg's technique to the consortium of corporations that had funded the massive project he'd headed for the last five years.

And abandoning Borrego had its advantages. Before the successes of the past few days, there had been some failures.

Reba Tucker.

No one had meant for Reba to die, not really. But they'd had to have a subject for that first human experiment, and there had been compelling reasons for selecting Reba. The teacher, from the moment Greg had suggested her, had struck Kendall as one of those women who was devoted to her students, even sometimes capable of inspiring them. But she was also the kind who was overprotective of them, just as Frank Arnold had been overprotective of his men. And it wasn't protection anyone in the country needed. Americans, as far as Paul Kendall was concerned, had had entirely too much protection. And now, in the last decade of the century, they were paying for it.

The whole nation had become lazy, assuming that its forty years of economic supremacy was a permanent fixture on the planet's landscape. Too many people, inspired by other people like Reba Tucker, were taking the attitude that their own personal fulfillment was more important than carrying their economic weight. And the country was paying for it.

And then Greg Moreland had come to him with his plan to realign the minds of the nation's youth.

The most elegant aspect of the scheme—the aspect that had truly seized Kendall's imagination—was that by its very nature the realignment would allow subjects to be customized perfectly to suit whatever tasks society—or Paul Kendall—required of them.

People with unique talents could be provided with the personalities best suited to utilize those talents. Other people—the masses of individuals who would never stand out from the crowd—would simply have their minds adjusted so that, no matter what their station in life, they would feel a contentment that nature would never have allowed them.

That, of course, was still in the future. But in Borrego the final experimentation would have taken place over the next few weeks, possibly even months. Despite Greg Moreland's own eagerness to move forward as quickly as possible, Kendall had planned to move slowly, sending out only narrow ranges of frequencies at any given time, then monitoring the people who were affected. Already it was obvious that there were still areas in which the process needed refinement. Right now it appeared there were too many hypothalamus probes, and some of the subjects had already become almost too lethargic ever to be useful.

On the other hand, those extra probes could prove useful. Indeed, with Frank Arnold, they already had. Frank had gotten out of line, and he'd been punished.

Given time, it all could have been worked out. He and Greg Moreland would have been able to record the changes in each subject, and eventually devise perfect combinations of probes to affect any given subject's mind in almost any way imaginable.

That was why he'd insisted on keeping such meticulous records of who had received which shot. The probes were tuned to hundreds of frequencies. Until now they'd been very careful in their selection of subjects for realignment.

They'd started with the troublemakers, the kids who made life difficult not only for their teachers, but for everyone else as well. But now there had been a leak in the security of the project, long before they were willing to make it public. Until people could see the benefits of what they were doing, they could hardly expect them to approve. Right now, given the condition of the Alvarez girl, and the Sparks kid, they would surely be accused of "crimes against humanity."

Kendall had decided that he simply wouldn't let that happen.

Tonight he was going to eliminate the evidence.

Tonight, as soon as the antenna was repaired, he would send out powerful transmissions of the entire frequency spectrum to which the probes were tuned.

In the space of a few seconds every probe in the Borrego area would fire, burning itself away and leaving no trace whatever of its existence.

A lot of people would die.

Some of them might survive physically, of course, but Kendall knew there would be little left of their minds.

And then there would be the inevitable investigation, but in the end, with no evidence to show what had happened, none of the micromachines left in anyone's brain, there would be nothing left but questions.

Paul Kendall and Greg Moreland wouldn't be around to answer any of those questions. They would already be somewhere else, in some other small town in the middle of nowhere, preparing to repeat their experiments.

But next time there would be no leaks.

As he started back to the communications center to begin putting together the program that would wreak havoc in the brains of nearly thirty percent of Borrego's population, Paul Kendall wondered how the town would react to what they would find in the morning.

It was a shame, really, that he wouldn't be able to stay here and study it. Aside from the sociological implications of the whole thing, he had come to like Borrego.

But not enough that he was unwilling to destroy it.

"We're here," Jed said quietly, braking the truck to a stop.

Peter Langston looked around. They were a few yards back from the edge of the canyon. The road had deteriorated into no more than a nearly invisible track winding through the scrub juniper on the top of the mesa, and Peter saw nothing unusual about the area. But Jed was already out of the truck. Peter followed him.

Jed was once more rummaging through the toolbox, finally sliding a rusty carpet knife under his belt and handing Peter a long screwdriver. "That's not much, but if you have to, at least you can shove it in someone's eye," he said.

Langston winced at the boy's words, telling himself they were nothing but adolescent bravado, but reluctantly took the screwdriver and secured it under his own belt. "Where are we?" he asked as Jed started toward the rim of the canyon.

"There's a trail," Jed replied.

A few minutes later the two of them stood on the edge of the precipice. The edge of the cliff dropped straight into the canyon. Peter, after glancing down, took a step backward, his groin tightening as the chasm seemed to draw him toward it, seemed to urge him to throw himself into its gaping maw. He looked away, following as Jed turned northward and trotted quickly along the brink of the cliff, apparently unaffected by the height. Twenty yards away there was a small cleft in the canyon's wall.

Peter peered doubtfully down into the rift. It notched no more than fifteen feet into the canyon's wall, and as it went down it seemed to get smaller, until it finally disappeared entirely. "Jesus, kid, that's not a trail."

Jed grinned in the moonlight. "Sure it is," he said. "My grandfather's been using it for years. He showed it to me when I was about ten." He didn't tell Peter that he'd never before attempted to use the trail, even in broad daylight.

He dropped down onto the edge of the cleft, rolled over onto his stomach, then lowered himself down until he was hanging only by his fingers. Closing his eyes and uttering a silent prayer, he let go, and dropped straight downward.

Peter froze. He couldn't believe what he'd just seen. The kid must be crazy. Then, from the darkness, he heard Jed's voice.

"Come on." The words drifted eerily up from the darkness of the cleft.

Peter approached the edge and reluctantly looked down. Jed was standing on a narrow ledge, his head five feet below Peter's feet.

Peter realized it was his turn.

He sat down gingerly, then let his legs drop over the edge. His groin tightened again, and for a moment he felt an almost uncontrollable urge to throw himself into the abyss. But the urge passed. Finally he rolled over and inched his way out until only his torso and arms were still on the mesa's surface.

"Good," he heard Jed encouraging him. "Now just a little more."

He inched outward, and then his whole body was hanging over the edge, his fingers clawing at the ground as if trying to dig into the rock itself.

He felt his fingers slip.

A scream rose up in his throat, but he choked it back. The instant during which he fell seemed to expand into an eternity, but then he felt hands grasping him, and suddenly his feet struck the ledge below. As the hands steadied him he pressed against the sandstone, his heart pounding, his breath coming in short gasps. "I knew there was a reason why I never wanted to climb mountains." he said, his voice trembling.

"It's not so bad," Jed said. "Just don't look down unless you have to." He was already sidling along the ledge, and a moment later he crouched down once more. This time, instead of lowering himself to another ledge directly below, he leaped across the gap itself, his feet coming to rest on another outcropping that was four feet farther down and as many across.

Peter stared down at the depths of the abyss, realizing that if he missed his footing, he would plunge down the wall into the canyon itself. Instantly, what was left of his nerve deserted him. "I—I'm not sure I can do it," he said, and his words seemed to bounce off the rock walls, echoing back to taunt him.

"You don't have a choice," Jed told him. "My grandfather told me this is a one-way trail. Without ropes, I can't get back to your ledge, and you can't get back up to the top without me."

Panic seized Peter. He pressed once more against the suddenly comforting stone behind him. But when he looked up, he realized that Jed was right. The only way out was down.

Steeling himself, he took the jump before he had enough time really to think about it.

"Yeah!" Jed exclaimed as he once more steadied Peter's landing. "It's not so bad, huh?"

They dropped farther into the cleft, moving as fast as they could. The lower they went, the darker it became, until Peter could barely see at all. But Jed moved quickly and steadily, using his inner senses to guide him along the invisible path.

The cleft finally dwindled away entirely, and they had to creep several yards along a narrow ledge that was more than three hundred feet above the canyon floor, until they came to another break in the wall. Peter negotiated it only by keeping his back flat against the cliff's facade, his eyes averted, and his feet moving only a few inches at a time.

Then they were into the second fissure. This one, only three feet wide, dropped away as vertically as a chimney, but all along it there were small fractures in the stone. Many of them appeared to have been deliberately hollowed out to provide hand and footholds, and when they finally came to the bottom of the crevice, Peter asked Jed about them.

"I think my grandfather did it," Jed replied. "But he only cut them where nobody could see them from above or below. He said sometimes it's good to have a path no one knows about."

Twenty minutes later they finally dropped from the lowest ledge down to the canyon floor. There was a turn in the canyon here, and the stream flowed next to the wall, so when they released their grips on the stone lip, they dropped into two feet of cold water.

Peter flinched in shock, then reached down and splashed water over his face, only now realizing that his whole body was drenched in sweat despite the chill of the night. He took a drink, then waded ashore, where Jed was waiting for him. Two hundred yards down the canyon there was a soft glow of lights from the buildings of The Cottonwoods. For the moment, though, the two of them, lost in the black shadows of the canyon, were totally invisible.

They moved quickly and quietly along the bank of the stream, then Jed seemed to melt away into the grove of cottonwoods.

Peter, suddenly finding himself alone in the darkness, froze. He strained his ears, trying to hear even the faintest sound that would tell him where Jed had gone, but there was nothing.

Jed glided through the cottonwood grove, his sense absorbing every vibration of the night. It was as if he could actually see the tiny creatures that scurried in the darkness, and smell the faint odors of animals that had long ago passed over the ground on which he trod.

He stopped. Though he couldn't see it yet, he knew there was a cabin close by.

The cabin his father was in.

He hesitated, knowing he should move on, find the right cabin, the one in which Judith Sheffield was being held. Yet even as he hesitated he knew why that strange spirit that seemed to have been guiding him from within had brought him here.

There was something he had to do.

He slipped silently through the darkness until he reached the deep shadow of the cabin. Only a faint light showed in the cabin's window—the glow of the screen on the monitors attached to his father.

His father was alone.

Jed moved around the cabin, coming to the front door like a shadow.

The door was unlocked.

He slipped inside.

He knew what it was that had to be done; indeed, he suspected he'd known it since yesterday, when he'd first seen his father here. He hadn't done it then; hadn't been able to summon up the courage. But now there was no other choice to be made. He gazed at his father in the dim light of the cathode tubes, trying once more to see some remnant of the man he'd known all his life. There was none. All that lay in the bed were the ruined remains of what his father had once been.

His face, coldly pale even under the soft light, held no expression whatsoever.

Surrounding him were the machines that were keeping him alive, but now, as Jed watched his lifeless body being manipulated by the machinery, he finally grasped that his father wasn't truly alive at all.

He reached down for a moment, as if to touch his father's cheek, but then his hand trembled and he withdrew it. At last he drew a deep breath and straightened up. It was time for him to release his father's spirit from the body that had already died.

Steeling himself, Jed reached out and switched off the respirator that kept his father alive.

He stood perfectly still, watching in silence as his father's chest stopped moving.

Seconds ticked by.

Jed was about to turn away when he thought he saw something in the darkness.

A pale wraith of silvery light was drifting up from the bed where his father lay. It hovered in the air for a moment, and Jed felt a strange serenity come over him, as if the aura he beheld had reached out and touched him.

Then it was gone.

Jed glanced at the monitors: all the lines were flat now.

His father's body was truly dead, and his spirit was gone.

Turning away, Jed slipped out of the cabin as silently as he'd come, moving once more through the night until he was certain that what he'd come looking for was here.

At last he returned to the spot where Peter Langston waited.

"She's here," Jed said. "I can feel it."

Three pickup trucks, each of them carrying two men, pulled up to the antenna installation. They formed a crescent around the site, so their headlights flooded the area within the fence with a bright halogen glow. Otto Kruger jumped out of the first truck and hurried to the gate, a ring of keys jangling in his right hand. He flipped through the keys quickly, found the right one, and unlocked the gate. Once inside, it took him no time at all to discover the cut in the PVC pipe. "Hernandez," he called out. "Bring the toolbox in here and get to work. Briggs, you and Alvarez take your truck and keep on going."

"Shit, man," Joe Briggs complained. He had been almost ready to go home for the night when Kruger had commandeered him for this job. "They could be anywhere. If they had a four-wheel, they could've taken off cross-country."

"Maybe so," Kruger agreed. "But I'm sure not going to tell Kendall we didn't even look, and since we didn't see anyone coming down the road, maybe they went up. So quit bitching and move your ass."

Briggs, with Carlos Alvarez slouched in the seat beside him, backed the truck away from the chain-link enclosure, spun the wheel and jammed the transmission into low gear. Popping the clutch, he let the wheels spin in a gratifying release of his own anger. The truck skidded out of control and spun around, but Briggs steered into the curve, caught his traction, and sped off into the night.

Otto Kruger, watching him, shook his head dolefully. "Son of a bitch is going to kill himself at that rate."

Jesus Hernandez, carrying a large toolbox, came into the enclosure, frowned at the cut in the PVC, then pulled a hacksaw out and set to work. Within less than a minute a section of PVC a foot long came loose from the pipe. Jesus tossed it aside, then knelt down and, using a flashlight, peered into the tube itself. "God damn," he swore softly.

"What's wrong?" Kruger demanded.

Hernandez shrugged. "Lot of cable in there. Its own weight pulled it down. I can see the ends, but they're about five feet back from the opening."

"So? Fish 'em out."

Hernandez stared at his boss contemptuously. "Yeah?" he asked. "How you going to do that, huh? First off, unless you brought some tool I don't know about, I don't see how we're going to get hold of the ends of those cables. And even if we do, it don't matter. I don't know about you, but I can't lift a thousand feet of that stuff. It's too heavy."

The muscles in Kruger's neck knotted with anger.

"Then what do we do?" he asked.

Hernandez shrugged. "Got to bust up the concrete," he said. "Only way to fix that tonight is break up the pad, get the pipe out of the way, and put in some jumpers."

Kruger nodded, his mind already made up. From Utley's tone earlier, he had been certain that Paul Kendall was standing at the man's elbow, listening to every word. And that meant it was Kendall who wanted the antenna repaired tonight.

Therefore, it would be done.

Kruger yelled at the two men who were leaning against the front fender of the third truck, smoking cigarettes. "There's a couple of sledgehammers and a wedge in the back of my truck. Bring 'em over here. We've got a lot of work to do."

The two men groaned, but tossed their cigarette butts away.

Twenty minutes later, as Kruger was pacing impatiently just outside the fence, Joe Briggs and Carlos Alvarez came back. Briggs swung out of the truck. "You were right," he said to Kruger. "We found a truck about a mile or so up."

"Did you recognize it?"

Briggs hesitated a split second, but nodded. "Oh, yeah. It's Frank Arnold's."

Kruger felt his temple throb with sudden fury. The man was as good as dead, for Chrissake—he was lying in a cabin up the canyon that very moment. Then he understood.

The kid.

"All right," he growled. "Where'd he go?"

Briggs shrugged. "How should I know? He wasn't around the truck, and there's no way he could have gotten down into the canyon from there, so he must be hiding up here somewhere. Hell, he could've hiked halfway back to town by now."

Kruger shook his head. "If he was going back to town, he'd have driven at least part of the way. But he wouldn't have gone in the exact opposite direction. So he's up here somewhere." He pulled a walkie-talkie out of its belt holster and snapped it on. Stan Utley's voice came through, scratchy but clear.

"Well, we know who did it," Kruger said, punching the button on the side of the unit in his hand. "A couple of my guys just found Frank Arnold's truck. I figure it had to be his kid, pissed off about what happened to his old man."

In the communications center below, Stan Utley glanced up at Paul Kendall. Kendall's face had gone scarlet with fury as he glared at Greg Moreland.

"That's where they got it," Kendall said, his voice shaking with rage. "That kid was supposed to have gotten his shot, and Watkins said he was doing just fine. Taking his orders, and keeping his mouth shut. But it was an act! The whole goddamned thing was an act!" His eyes went to the clock, then fixed on Stan Utley once more. "How much time have we got before that antenna's up again?" he asked.

"Half an hour, at least. Maybe an hour."

Kendall nodded tersely and began snapping orders to the technician.

Greg Moreland, filled with the same fury that had gripped Paul Kendall, turned and strode out of the room. He had half an hour, and there was something he wanted to do.

He wanted to watch Judith Sheffield suffer. Indeed, he wanted to torture her himself.

Thirty-one

J ed froze, his whole body tensing as he heard the soft cracking of a twig. Someone was coming. He was alone again, having left Peter concealed in the deep shadows of the cottonwood grove while he himself moved out of the trees' shelter to get a closer look at the little cabin. He'd moved swiftly and silently, dodging between the boulders that lay scattered near the canyon's wall, finally waiting for several long minutes, crouched in the shadows, sensing danger even though nothing was visible.

Now, as a second twig cracked, he spotted the presence he had only felt before.

At first he could see nothing but the faint glow of a cigarette tip, brightening briefly as its bearer drew in on it, then fading away, almost disappearing into the inky blackness of the canyon's depths. But Jed's night vision still saw it clearly, bobbing slowly toward him.

Then the figure emerged from the shadows for a moment, and Jed saw that it was a woman—heavyset and walking slowly, as if she were tired. She paused, and Jed could hear her muttering to herself, but then she ground the cigarette under her foot and began walking again, more quickly this time.

She approached the cottage, rapped on the door a couple of times, and tried the knob. When it didn't open, she knocked again, more loudly. A moment later the door opened a couple of inches and a large figure loomed in the gap. Again there was the faint sound of voices, and then the door opened wider and the woman stepped inside.

The door closed.

Jed waited.

Time stood still.

After what seemed an eternity, but had actually been no more than a couple of minutes, the door opened again and the woman emerged. She was carrying a tray with what looked like a few dirty dishes on it. As soon as she was out the door, the man inside closed it again.

Jed heard the click of the lock being thrown. He stayed where he was, as still as one of the boulders he crouched among. When the woman started in his direction, he held his breath.

But the woman passed by him, no more than six feet away, never so much as sensing his presence. Jed began breathing again, but waited to make a move until the woman had disappeared completely into the darkness and his inner senses told him the danger was over.

At last, darting silently away from the protection of the boulders, he approached the bungalow itself. There were several windows, and he thought for a moment before deciding which one to risk peering into. Finally he chose the one in which the small table lamp was framed. Its light would turn the inner surface of the glass into a mirror. Still, he approached it warily, every nerve in his body tingling, ready to dodge away into the dark shadows at the first hint of danger.

He came to the window and peered inside.

Immediately he let his body relax, for the man inside was sitting in a chair next to the lamp, his back to the window,

Jed stole closer, then finally stood up to his full height. In the bed, strapped down, he saw Judith Sheffield. Her eyes were closed, but Jed was certain she wasn't asleep. Now she stirred and struggled to sit up, her eyes moving toward the window as if she sensed his presence there.

In response to her movement, the man in the chair stood up. He was a big man, much larger than Jed himself. Still, there would be two of them . . .

Satisfied, Jed faded back into the darkness. Within seconds he was back in the black shadows of the cottonwoods, whispering softly to Peter. A few moments later both of them moved out of the grove, this time making no effort to conceal their presence.

They approached the cabin quickly, Jed pressing his back to the wall next to the door. Peter stepped up to the door, knocked sharply, then rapped again, as if impatient at being kept waiting.

Peter heard movement inside the cabin. A moment later the door opened a couple of inches. A large man with black hair eyed Peter suspiciously, squinting at him.

"I'm Dr. Langston," Peter said, loudly enough so he hoped Judith would be able to hear him, but not so loudly as to alert the man whose body blocked the door. He prayed his voice would not betray his nervousness. "Dr. Moreland wanted me to take a look at—" He hesitated, as if searching his memory. "Miss Sheffield, is it?" The black-haired man's eyes narrowed still more. "He didn't call me," he said doubtfully.

Peter thought quickly, then decided a good offense was his best defense. "Well, that's not my problem, is it? And I didn't drive all the way up here from Santa Fe just to turn around and start back." He reached in his hip pocket, pulled out his wallet, then flipped it open to reveal an ID card from the institute. "Maybe you'd better give Moreland a call, if it'll make you feel any better," he suggested.

The big man's eyes flicked to Peter's ID, and his expression cleared as he remembered the scene earlier when Moreland had been there. He'd been furious, and it was possible he'd simply forgotten to mention the doctor. Still . . .

And then he saw the name on the card. The Brandt Institute.

This guy hadn't been sent by Moreland at all! He was a friend of Sheffield's!

Peter saw the change in the big man's eyes. Instantly, as the door started to close, he launched himself against it, and the man, startled by the sudden move, reflexively took a step backward to catch his balance as the door smashed into him.

Peter shoved again and the door flew open, but the man was already recovering, crouching as he prepared to hurl a fist. Peter spun aside, and at the same moment Jed burst into the room. The rusted carpet knife already in his hand, Jed slammed the door closed behind him, then hurled himself at the man.

Judith, her eyes wide open now, choked back a scream as Black-hair's fist smashed into Jed. Jed fell back against the wall, but then Peter brandished the long screwdriver that had been concealed in his belt, now held tightly in his right hand. With no hesitation he hurled his whole weight at Black-hair, plunging the screwdriver into the man's stomach. Black-hair, eyes bulging with the shock of the sudden attack, grasped at the handle of the screwdriver, but before he could begin to pull it free from his guts, Jed was behind him.

As Judith watched, horrified, Jed's arm snaked around Black-hair's neck and he sank the curved blade of the carpet knife deep into the flesh and sinews of his throat just below his left ear. With a fast jerk he ripped the man's throat open, and blood began to spurt from his lacerated veins. His face twisting into a mask of fear and shock, Black-hair sank to his knees, his hands now grasping spasmodically at his neck. Then he toppled over and lay still.

Ignoring the dead man, Peter rushed to the bed and unfastened the straps that bound Judith to it. "Can you walk?" Peter asked.

Judith nodded, rubbing hard at the soreness in her ankles. She got off the bed and stood up, her head suddenly swimming. She lost her balance, falling heavily against Peter, who started to pick her up. She shook her head. "I can make it," she said. "I was just dizzy for a second."

Holding onto Peter's arm, she started toward the door, ducking her head away so she wouldn't have to look directly at the blood-sodden corpse of Black-hair sprawled out next to the door. Jed, who had already jerked the screwdriver out of the dead man's belly, held the door open, and Judith, with Peter right behind her, lurched out into the night. She paused for a moment filling her lungs with fresh air, then looked around in vain for the car or truck she had expected to be waiting for them.

"Jed—" she began, but her words were stifled as Jed's hand clamped over her mouth.

"Be quiet," he whispered. "Just keep quiet, and follow me."

He released her and darted toward the cottonwoods, Peter and Judith hurrying after him.

Just as they reached the shelter of the trees, headlights swept across the cabin, and then a car pulled up in front of it. But by the time Greg Moreland got out of his car and approached the bungalow's door, the three people in the cottonwood grove had already begun moving up the canyon.

Greg Moreland rapped sharply on the door of the cabin, then tried the knob.

It was locked.

He knocked again, louder this time. "Walters!"

There was no answer. Suddenly he had a presentiment that something had gone terribly wrong. He strode over to one of the windows and peered inside. The bed was empty, and on the floor, so close to the window he could only see part of it, was Lamar Walters's body. But the part Greg could see—the wide open, dead eyes, and the torn neck—told him as much as he needed to know. Cursing under his breath, he dashed to the main house, and burst in the front door. Elsie Crampton, slouched on a chair with a romance novel open on the desk in front of her, looked up in surprise. As she recognized Greg, she got quickly to her feet. "Dr. Moreland," she stammered. "What are—"

"Where is she?" he demanded, glaring furiously a her. "What the hell is going on around here?"

Elsie looked at him blankly. "Where's who?"

"Sheffield, you idiot," Moreland snarled. He wanted to smash his fist into the woman's stupid, cowlike eyes. "She's gone, and Walters is dead!"

Elsie gasped, her face paling. "But I was just out there," she said. "I picked up the dinner trays, and everything was fine. It wasn't more than five minute ago, ten at the most."

Moreland's fury got the better of him then. His hand came up, slapping Elsie's cheek so hard she reeled, then crumpled to the floor, sobbing. Moreland ignored her snatching up the phone on the desk and dialing quickly. A moment later Paul Kendall's voice came on the line.

"The Arnold kid's in the canyon," Moreland said not bothering to identify himself. "Somehow he managed to kill Lamar Walters, and Judith Sheffield is gone."

Kendall's voice crackled over the line. "I'll get some of Kruger's men down there right away," he said.

"Get the mouth of the canyon blocked," Moreland told him. "But don't take so many men that Kruger can't get that antenna fixed. I'll be there in a few minutes." He slammed the phone back on the hook, then completely ignoring Elsie Crampton, left the house and sprinted back to his car.

Elsie, rubbing at her burning cheek, pulled herself to her feet and hobbled to the door. Her hip was hurting where it had slammed against the floor, and it was painful to walk. She leaned her weight against the doorjamb, her eyes narrowing angrily as Moreland's car shot past a few seconds later.

This, she decided, was it.

She didn't like this place—didn't like it at all. In fact, she'd been thinking about getting out of here all evening, ever since they'd brought that nice woman in—the one who'd come to visit Mrs. Tucker. Elsie had seen her twice now—once when she'd taken the two dinner trays out to the cabin, and again when she'd picked them up a few minutes ago—and to her, Judith Sheffield hadn't looked sick at all. She'd looked scared, and the man in the cabin had looked very much like the kind of tough that Elsie had once found attractive, until she learned, painfully, that men like that tended to talk with their fists instead of their mouths.

As Moreland's taillights disappeared, she started toward her room at the back of the house. She'd just throw her things in her suitcase, and in ten minutes she'd be gone. To hell with the last couple of weeks' pay—it just wasn't worth it.

But then her mind shifted gears and she remembered what Moreland had said about that man in Cabin Five being dead. Her mind still working, she left the house and trudged slowly across the lawn, rubbing her sore hip as she went. Finally she came to Cabin Five, knocked at the door, then used her key to unlock it.

She stared at the body for a moment, frowning, her mind working. If she left now—just took off—they might try to blame the murder on her.

She puzzled at the problem for a moment, then smiled as she figured out what to do. She'd get herself off the hook, and get even with Moreland at the same time.

Leaving the cabin door standing open, Elsie hurried back to the main building and rummaged in the drawers of the desk until she found the thin Borrego telephone directory.

The number she was looking for was printed in large red type on the inside of the front cover. She dialed it, settling herself into the chair behind the desk.

"Borrego police department," a bored-sounding voice said after the phone had rung several times.

Elsie smiled to herself. "My name is Elsie Crampton," she said. "I work at The Cottonwoods. You know, up in Mordida Canyon?"

"Uh-huh," the policeman said.

"Well, we've had some trouble," Elsie went on. "One of our patients is missing, and the man who was attending her is dead."

"Beg pardon, ma'am?" the man said, all traces of boredom suddenly gone. "What did you say your name is?"

Elsie patiently repeated her name, "The patient's name is Sheffield," she went on. "Judith Sheffield."

In the Borrego police department Billy Clark stiffened. What the hell was one of the high school teachers doing up there? "You say she's a *patient* there?" he asked, his voice reflecting his doubt.

Elsie briefly explained what had happened, then hung up the phone and went to her room to start packing.

She'd wait for the police, tell them everything she knew, and answer all their questions. By the time she left, Dr. Moreland would be in big trouble.

She wasn't absolutely certain, but she had a vague idea that not reporting a crime to the police was some kind of crime itself.

And if the crime you didn't report was murder . . .

She let the thought drift along, smiling happily. She'd teach Greg Moreland not to slap *her* around.

Judith slipped on a rock in the stream bed and stumbled, her ankle twisting painfully. Instantly, Jed's hand grasped her arm, steadying her. She tested her weight on her ankle and winced, suppressing the yelp that rose in her throat.

"Are you all right?" Jed asked her.

Judith shook her head. "I—I'm sorry, but I have to sit down for a minute."

Jed's eyes bored into the darkness ahead. "A little farther," he said. "There's a big rock in the middle of the stream. You can sit down there."

Judith considered arguing, but quickly thought better of it. When Greg's men—and they were all certain that by now a search party had been formed—discovered they hadn't gone toward the mouth of the canyon at all, they would bring dogs up to find their trail, which meant the stream was their only safety.

"Can you make it?" Jed asked, his voice low.

Judith nodded, leaning heavily on him as she hobbled through the water.

Twenty yards farther on they came to the rock and Judith gratefully lowered herself onto its flat surface. She lifted her foot out of the water and started to massage it.

Peter looked at her anxiously. "Is it broken?"

"I don't think so," Judith said, then prodded at it again. "In fact, I don't think I even sprained it. It's just a twist. I'll be all right in a couple of minutes." She fell silent for a few seconds, catching her breath. Since they'd left the cottonwood grove, no one had said much, each of them concentrating on putting as much distance between themselves and the sanitarium as they could. But now, as the pain in her ankle began to ease and she was certain they were not yet being followed, the other fear—which had been growing within her since her arrival at the sanitarium—came to the fore.

"They gave me a shot, Jed," she said.

Jed nodded. "We figured on that." He gazed back down the canyon and up. High up on the canyon's rim he could see headlights. A crew was already working on the antennae putting it back into operating condition. And when they did . . .

He slid off the rock, back into the stream. "We don't have much time."

Peter shook his head. "But it doesn't matter, does it? Where can we go? Even if we can get out of the canyon, what good will it do? Once they get that antenna fixed—"

Judith stared at him through the darkness. "The antenna?" she asked, confused. "What does that have to do with it?"

His voice dulled by both his exhaustion and the certain knowledge that in the end, when the antenna was fixed, they would have failed, Peter explained to Judith how the tiny mechanisms were being triggered. "Jed cut the cables," he finished. "But they're up there now, fixing them."

Judith's eyes shifted upward, to the spot far down the canyon where a glow of lights created a bright splash in the darkness. "But there has to be something we can do," she said. "Can't we get up there?"

There was silence for a moment, then Jed spoke. "We don't have to get up there," he said. "There might be something else we can do." His eyes met Judith's. "Can you walk?"

Judith nodded, and as if to prove it to herself, she put her foot back in the water and stood up. A sharp spasm of pain shot up her leg, but it faded away a second or two later, and when she took a step, her limp was less pronounced than it had been just minutes ago.

They moved as quickly as they could, finally leaving the river when the bottom became too rocky for any of them to find a secure footing, and found a path that led along the riverbank, threading through the trees.

Ten minutes later they came to a dead stop. Twenty yards ahead of them the blank face of the dam rose up into the night, blocking their way.

Judith stared at the massive concrete structure, its surface looking almost glassily smooth in the moonlight. Then she heard Jed's voice.

"This way," he called out softly. He was moving quickly, heading off toward the north wall.

And then, finally, she realized where he was taking them.

Mounted in the concrete, starting about ten feet off the ground, were a series of metal bars—spaced about two feet apart—climbing up the face of the dam like a ladder. They ended at a small metal platform resembling a fire escape, a quarter of the way up.

"It's an emergency ladder," Jed explained. "We can climb up it, force that door, and get into the dam."

Peter gazed up doubtfully. "If we can get to that first bar."

"Take off your belt," Jed told him, removing his own even as he spoke. Peter hesitated, then did as he was told. Jed buckled the two belts together so they formed a loop more than two feet long. "Let's get me up there first, then Peter," he said.

Peter stood close to the dam and laced his fingers tightly together. A moment later Jed placed his foot in Peter's hands, and while Peter stood rigid, his back against the dam itself, Jed straightened himself up, keeping his balance by resting part of his weight against the concrete.

"A little higher," Jed said, and Peter strained to raise the boy's weight upward. "Got it," Peter heard Jed say, and a moment later Jed's weight lifted off him. Rubbing his hands, Peter stepped back and looked up.

Jed was hanging from the lowest rung. As Peter and Judith watched, he pulled himself up until his chin was level with the bar. Then, taking a deep breath, he let go of the bar with his right hand, which shot upward to grasp the second rung.

He repeated the action, and then managed to get his feet onto the bottom bar. "Easy—" he said. "Now toss me up the belts."

Peter cupped his hands for Judith while Jed waited, clinging to the second rung, the looped belt hanging down almost within reach. But Judith shook her head.

"You next," she said. "Someone's going to have to lift the last one, and I'm the lightest."

Peter felt an urge to argue with her, but then realized argument would only waste time. Besides, she was right.

Judith cupped her hands, and Peter bounced tentatively for a moment, then launched himself upward.

He missed the rung by nearly a foot, but Jed had anticipated him, and Peter's hand closed on the looped belts. He swung helplessly for a moment, but then, as Judith lifted and Jed pulled, he rose up until he could grasp the lowest rung. He hung there, then pulled himself up.

Jed's hand closed on the collar of his jacket, and a moment later Peter too was clinging to the ladder. Jed gestured upward. "Go ahead," he said. "I can handle Judith." Peter hesitated, then followed Jed's orders.

Jed crouched low on the bottom rung once again, his right hand gripping the one above. Stretching downward, he lowered the looped belts until they hovered just out of Judith's reach.

"Jump," he said, making the single word an urgent command.

Judith took a deep breath, then hurled herself upward, her hands closing on the leather band. Jed grunted slightly as he absorbed her weight. His body tensed and he began slowly straightening up. He paused for a moment, then swiftly released the second rung to grasp the third. Judith was able to transfer one of her hands to the lower rung. Jed kept lifting, and finally Judith's other hand came to the second rung. Releasing the belt entirely, she hauled herself up.

Less than a minute later they were on the balcony outside the door in the dam's face. Peter, with only the bloody screwdriver as a tool, was working at the doorjamb, prying at the wood, slowly splintering it away. At last he got a purchase on the lock itself, and as he leaned his weight against the hardened steel of the tool, the lock broke free from the wood and fell away.

They were inside the dam.

"That way," Jed said. There was a spiral staircase leading straight up, but Jed was pointing down a long, narrow corridor that curved away to the right, following the contour of the dam itself.

Jed began running along the corridor, and Peter and Judith followed him, Judith's ankle jarring painfully every time she put her weight on it. Finally they came to a branch in the corridor and Jed stopped. When the other two had caught up with him, he pointed down the corridor.

"Keep going," he said. "At the end, there's another staircase. It'll take you up to the top, near the south wall of the canyon. Then try to get to the pueblo."

Peter's eyes narrowed. "What about you?" he asked.

Jed took a deep breath. "I have an idea," he said. "It might not work, but I'm going to try it."

Now Peter did argue, but this time Judith intervened. "He knows what he's doing," she said. "He's gotten us this far, hasn't he?" She gazed at Jed for a moment, then turned away.

A moment later Jed was alone in the bowels of the dam.

Otto Kruger glared at Jesus Hernandez. A five-foot section of the PVC pipe had been cut away, and finally the ends of the cut cables were exposed. "How much longer?" Kruger demanded.

Hernandez shrugged. "Ten minutes. Maybe a little less."

Kruger's jaw tightened but he said nothing. As he turned away, something in the distance caught his attention.

Far away, off to the left beyond the mouth of the canyon, he saw a flashing red light moving across the desert.

A moment later he heard a faint siren.

Kendall, he decided, had finally called the police.

It wouldn't be long now before it was all over, and Jed Arnold got what was coming to him.

Thirty-two

J ed waited until Judith and Peter were out of sight, then moved quickly toward the main flume. He stopped dead as he came into the control area, for a man was sitting on a bench, chewing on a sandwich. The man looked at him, then frowned, as if searching his mind for some bit of information. Finally he got up and moved toward the intercom phone on the main control panel.

Jed's heart pounded. The man was much bigger than he was, and built like an ox. But as Jed watched the way the man moved, he thought he understood.

"Stop!" he said, his voice firm.

The watchman froze in his tracks as if some internal switch had been thrown.

"They sent me to relieve you," Jed said. "They want you to go home. Now."

Unhesitatingly, the man returned to the bench, closed his lunch bucket, and walked silently past Jed, leaving Jed alone in the control room.

He stared at the large board covered with gauges and switches, and for a moment nearly gave it up. But then he remembered Gina Alvarez and the strange, empty look in her eyes. If he failed, all his friends—almost everyone he knew—would soon look like that.

Eventually he too would be given one of the shots.

He shuddered, then put everything out of his mind except the problem at hand.

He moved to the main shaft and pulled the entry hatch closed, spinning the wheel in its center until it was dogged tight. Then he returned to the control panel.

To the left, mounted on the concrete wall, was another large wheel, nearly five feet in diameter, connected by a universal joint to a shaft that went straight up, disappearing into a pipe in the low ceiling. A thick chain had been run between two spokes of the wheel and attached to a heavy hasp mounted on the floor.

A padlock secured the two ends of the chain.

Jed tried the screwdriver first, sliding its blade through the hasp

806

of the lock, then twisting. But he could get no leverage, and the lock simply twisted out of his grip.

He glanced around, then saw a toolbox sitting by the wall next to the flume's hatch. He darted over to it, opened it, and pulled out the top tray. Beneath the tray he found a hacksaw.

He went back to the lock, tested the saw's blade against the metal of its hasp, then set to work. After what seemed an eternity, the lock finally gave way, and he ripped the chain free from the wheel. Grasping the wheel with both hands, he applied his weight to it.

Nothing happened.

He climbed up onto the wheel itself, but even his entire weight resting on one of its spokes didn't budge it. Tears of anger and frustration welling in his eyes, he scanned the room for another tool.

He remembered.

He darted back to the flume's hatch, spun its wheel and pushed it open. Inside, the flume was pitch-black but Jed ignored the darkness, stepping into it and groping along the wall until he found what he was looking for.

It was the same shovel he'd been using most of that day, still where he'd left it, leaning against the wall of the shaft. Grabbing it, he hurried back out of the hatch, dogging it closed once more.

Back at the immense wheel, he stuck the blade of the shovel between two of the spokes, then jammed it beneath the wheel's axle. Now, with three more feet added to the radius of the wheel, his weight was enough to break it loose. It moved a few inches, and Jed readjusted the shovel, then applied his weight again.

A few more inches, but he was almost certain the wheel was moving more easily.

He abandoned the shovel, grasping one of the spokes of the wheel, and pulled down hard. The wheel began to turn, and far above, he heard a faint grinding sound. A few seconds later, as the floodgate forty feet below the lake's surface began to lift, opening the inlets to the power flume, Jed could hear the first trickling of water running into the huge chute.

He kept turning the wheel, and the trickling of water grew into a rumbling, then a steady roar. Finally the wheel came to a stop. The floodgates at the top would be wide open now.

The noise was deafening, battering at his ears, and Jed was about to start his own dash for the surface when he thought of one more thing he could do. Scanning the control board quickly, he finally found what he was looking for. There was a large lever, and when he pulled it, there was a screech of protest before the enormous turbine at the base of the flume began to turn.

It emitted only a low growl at first, but as it began to pick up speed, its pitch quickly rose until it became a shrill scream floating above the roar of the moving water.

Suddenly there was a terrifying crash from somewhere within the flume. The sound galvanized Jed. Turning away from the control board, he raced out of the room and bolted down the corridor, turning left as he came to the main transverse that ran through the lower level of the dam.

His feet pounded on the concrete, but he could hear nothing except the roar of water, the scream of the turbine, and, increasingly, the terrible crashing sounds as chunks of concrete, torn loose from the damaged sides of the flume, struck the whirling blades of the turbine.

Jed knew what was happening—the turbine was flinging the concrete back, breaking some of it up, hurling fragments of stone and cement against the walls of the flume, damaging them even further.

Soon the turbine itself would begin to break up, and as its blades tore loose, the spinning monster would fall out of balance and begin tearing itself apart. And if it should come loose from its moorings before he'd reached the surface . . .

He blocked the thought out of his mind as he reached the base of the spiral staircase. His lungs already gasping for breath, his muscles worn first from the long day's labor in the dam, then abused further by the climb down the canyon wall, he started upward, his hands grasping the railing to pull himself up as his legs threatened to collapse beneath him.

Halfway up he tripped, pitching forward as his left foot missed one of the narrow steps, his head smashing against the sharp metal of one of the risers. Stunned, a wave of nausea swept over him and his vision blurred. He sank down on the steps, tears streaming from his eyes and mixing with the blood that was already running from a gash on his forehead.

Around him the cacophony built, battering at him.

He could feel the dam beginning to break up.

Judith stared in shock at the figure standing on top of the dam. She and Peter had emerged from the top of the spiral stairs only a few seconds earlier, and now she stood frozen, hardly able to believe her eyes.

"Brown Eagle," she whispered.

Jed's grandfather stepped forward. "I was in the kiva," he said. "I saw . . ." His words died on his lips as he saw Peter Langston, but then his gaze came back to Judith. "I know what Jed is doing," he said. Then he smiled. "I want to see it."

A puzzled frown formed on Peter Langston's face. He was about to ask the mysterious Indian who had appeared out of nowhere what he was talking about, when he heard a faint grinding sound.

It grew louder, and then Judith noticed it too. Instinctively she grasped Brown Eagle's arm. "What is it? What's happening?"

Brown Eagle's smile broadened. "I think Jed opened the main shaft," he said.

"The shaft?" Peter echoed. "Why?"

But Judith understood instantly. "They're repairing it, aren't they? If it's not ready—"

"If it's not ready, then it might tear the dam apart," Brown Eagle said, his voice placid. "I suspect that's what Jed is counting on."

Peter's eyes widened.

The roar of water into the flume was beginning to build, and as he looked over the edge of the dam, he could see water spurting out of the drainage spillway far below.

Suddenly lights came on, bathing the face of the dam, and at the other end, two hundred yards away, a man appeared, darting out of the control shack.

"Come," Brown Eagle said. "We'd better get away from here."

He started to move away, his hand on Judith's arm, but she planted herself firmly. "We have to wait for Jed."

Brown Eagle shook his head. "He didn't want you to wait," he said. "That's why he sent you ahead." But despite his words, he made no move to leave the dam. Instead, he looked over the railing, staring downward. Water was roaring from the lower spillway. Then a piece of concrete broke loose, propelled nearly a hundred feet out by the force of the water before it plunged into the stream below.

The stream itself was already beginning to grow into a river.

Now they heard what sounded like a series of explosions coming from within the dam.

But still none of them made a move to leave the dam, their eyes fixed on the hatchway where Jed would appear.

If he appeared at all.

Jed's vision cleared slightly and he wiped the tears and blood from his eyes. His head was throbbing, and the roar from within the dam was hammering him with a force that was almost physical. But he struggled to his feet and once more began climbing upward.

The steps were trembling beneath his feet now, and he thought he could hear the rending sounds of metal being torn from metal. He pushed himself harder, scrabbling up the steps, his legs threatening to betray him at any moment.

And then, above him, he saw the hatch.

A surge of adrenaline coursed through his system and he sprang up the last few steps, throwing himself out of the hatchway and scrambling back to his feet even as he sprawled out on top of the dam.

He was almost blinded by the glare of the flood lights, but then, ahead of him, he saw three people. His grandfather was already starting toward him, followed by Peter Langston.

"No," he yelled. Then, when he realized they couldn't possibly hear him, he waved his arms frantically, gesturing to them to get off the dam.

Brown Eagle hesitated, and Jed began running. "It's breaking up," Jed yelled. "Let's go!"

At last the others turned toward the south wall and began to run, Jed pounding after them, his legs burning in protest. Now they came to the end of the dam, where a narrow trail led upward, switch-backing across the face of the canyon all the way to the top, two hundred feet above.

They started up, but paused to look back.

Below them a fissure in the dam was climbing steadily upward as the pressure in the damaged flume continued to tear away at the walls of the chute. Suddenly there was a crashing sound, then a hole appeared in the dam as the turbine tore loose from its huge anchoring bolts and exploded through the concrete facing. Then the dam seemed to split, the center section breaking away.

Judith instinctively shrank back against the stone wall of the canyon, her eyes fixed on the spectacle below as if she were hypnotized.

The lights on the dam went out as the force of the lake exploded the structure, and a deafening roar issued forth as a wall of water, nearly two hundred feet high, began to move down the canyon.

"Climb!" Brown Eagle shouted into her ear. "That water will tear this whole wall apart. The path's going to collapse under our feet."

Judith still stood frozen until Brown Eagle slapped her across the face—not hard enough to hurt her, but with just enough force to snap her out of her trance.

Nodding dumbly, she started scrambling up the steep path, Brown Eagle behind her, followed by Peter and Jed.

Elsie Crampton was standing near the window in Cabin Five. On the floor the body of Lamar Walters still lay exactly as they had found it a few minutes ago when she'd led the two officers, Billy Clark and Dan Rogers, along the path from the main building of the sanitarium. Rogers, the blond one who didn't look old enough to be a cop, had immediately checked the corpse for a pulse, and though she hadn't said anything, Elsie thought it was a waste of time. The man's head was half cut off from his neck, and there was blood all over the place. Couldn't have been more than a pint or two left in his body, from the look of things.

Billy Clark opened his notebook and began scribbling in it, asking Elsie questions every now and then. Elsie didn't mind the questions, since it was already obvious they didn't think she was involved in whatever had happened to Walters. Even sprawled out on the floor, his empty eyes staring up at the ceiling, he looked dangerous, and anyone could have seen right away that there was no way Elsie could have done this to him.

"What about Dr. Moreland?" Clark asked.

Elsie shrugged, ground out her cigarette on a plate on the lamp table, then immediately lit another. "I don't think so," she said finally. He'd be in enough trouble, and right now Elsie figured she'd better stick to the truth. "He wasn't hardly here long enough, and he sure didn't act like he'd done it. I mean, he wasn't even paying any attention to me, and he sounded real upset when he told the other guy Walters was dead. Besides, Walters was a lot bigger than Moreland, and he sure wouldn't have just stood there and let someone cut his throat. You ask me, it must have been at least two people, and they must have been waiting outside when I came out for the dinner tray." She shuddered slightly. "Guess I'm lucky to be alive, huh?"

"Guess so," Clark commented.

Then, in the distance, they both heard a sound. It was a low rumbling, almost like thunder. Elsie cocked her head, then looked out the window.

Her eyes widened as she gazed up the canyon, where a wall of water, towering up the chasm's walls and glinting strangely in the moonlight, was bearing down on them.

She uttered a choked scream and stepped backward. Now it was Clark who looked out the window, freezing as he instantly realized what had happened.

The wall of water was only a hundred yards away now, and even though a part of Billy Clark's mind knew it was already too late, he still bellowed a warning to his partner. "The dam!"

Dan Rogers, startled, looked up just as the raging flood hit the cabin. The walls burst instantly, the roof collapsed, and all three occupants of the cabin were crushed beneath a maelstrom of rubble, part broken concrete from the dam itself, part trees that had been jerked up by their very roots as the deluge roared down the canyon. In a split second the cabin and its occupants had vanished into the flood.

*   *   *

In her own cabin, Reba Tucker had been sitting in her chair by the window all evening, staring out into the night, waiting for the next attack of the demons that always seemed to come in the darkness.

When the first faint rumblings of the raging torrent drifted down the canyon ahead of the flood itself, Reba wasn't even aware of them. But as the noise built, it finally penetrated her failing consciousness, and in her lap one of her hands twitched.

The rumbling rose to a thundering roar, and then Reba's dull eyes perceived the furious wave bearing down on her, its spume glittering silver in the moonlight.

For Reba those last instants of her life passed slowly, almost as if she were looking at old pictures, studying them one by one, savoring them.

She never understood precisely what had happened or knew how she was going to die.

But images burned into the remnants of her mind.

A tree, floating strangely, its roots up, its branches pointing toward the ground, flashed into her sight, then disappeared, lost forever in the roiling foam.

A block of concrete as big as the cabin suddenly rose up in front of her, and Reba gazed at it mutely.

It came closer, and then her window was filled by it, the foam suddenly gone.

She heard noises, worse noises than she'd ever heard during the times she'd been tortured here, and she felt the very floor shake beneath her feet.

Then the window exploded into her face, and her eyes, punctured by fragments of flying glass, failed her but it didn't really matter.

The huge mass of concrete, propelled by the force of millions of tons of water, crushed her beneath its weight then moved on, reducing the cabin to little more than fragments of flotsam churning in the melee.

It was all over in a matter of seconds.

Where before there had been a frame house and several small cabins scattered through a peaceful grove of cottonwood trees, there now was nothing.

Not a scrap of vegetation survived the scouring of the flood's furious bore; not even a fragment of the building's foundations remained.

All that was left was the naked rock bottom of the canyon, scraped clean of everything, its sandstone gouged deep with the scars of an assault that nature itself had never designed.

The water rushed on.

Thirty-three

J esus Hernandez began the last check of his work. The power was back on, and once more the concrete pad that supported the huge dish antenna was bathed in the white radiance of halogen floodlights. He examined the connections carefully, then finally nodded to Kruger. "Got it."

Kruger, who had been pacing nervously, urging Hernandez to work faster, punched a button on the walkie-talkie and spoke to Kendall. "Tell them to start testing."

Almost immediately the antenna came to life. The dish began to rotate, then tipped on its axis. "Okay," Kruger said. "Looks like it's good. It's just a jury rig, but it should hold up till morning."

In the control center Kendall felt a little of the tension drain out of his body. His eyes fixed on the screen of one of the computers as he quickly double-checked the codes once more, then he nodded to Stan Utley. "Send it," he said.

Utley glanced at the display, then whistled softly.

"Jesus Christ—you'll blow every one of them." His gaze shifted uncertainly to Greg Moreland.

Moreland nodded curtly.

Utley hesitated, then shrugged his acceptance of the order. He made some adjustments to the controls of the transmitter, then prepared the machine to accept the codes from the computer. His finger hovered over the Enter key on his own computer and he looked questioningly at Kendall and Moreland one last time.

Both men nodded, and Utley pressed the button.

On the display screen numbers began flashing as the antenna above came to life and the first of the high-frequency waves radiated out over Borrego.

And then, abruptly, the lights went out. The cavern was plunged into total darkness.

Paul Kendall froze for a split second, then rage welled up in him. He groped in the darkness, then found the walkie-talkie. "What the hell's going on?" he shouted. "We've lost power down here!"

On the rim of the canyon Otto Kruger felt the same anger as Paul Kendall when the power went out again. He was about to yell an

order at Jesus Hernandez when he heard a low rumble, almost like
an explosion, drifting down from the eastern end of the canyon. He
frowned, puzzled, but as the walkie-talkie in his hand came alive and
he heard Kendall's voice—its fury evident despite the crackling of
the transmission—he understood.

"The dam," he breathed, almost to himself. His whole body
tensed, then he pressed the transmitting button on his own instrument. "The dam!" he shouted. "I think it's gone!"

The distant roar was getting louder now, and a moment later, as
the wall of water hit a bend in the narrow chasm and shot a plume
high above the canyon's rim, Kruger and his men saw it.

Churning out of the darkness, it roared down the canyon like a
freight train gone out of control. The first enormous bore seemed
almost like the head of some kind of reptilian monster, weaving back
and forth across the canyon, smashing first against one wall and then
the other. Behind it the body of the monster spread out to fill the
canyon a hundred feet deep.

Trees, boulders, massive chunks of concrete churned on its surface, gouged up from the bottom by the force of the flood, only to
sink once more, then reappear.

Kruger stared at the spectacle, every muscle in his body frozen by
the sheer magnitude of it.

There was a bend in the canyon just above the antenna installation, and Jesus Hernandez, instinctively understanding what was
about to happen, began to run, charging away from the edge of the
chasm, stumbling through the sagebrush and juniper that spread
across the plateau's surface. By the time the bore struck, he was a
hundred yards away, but the force of the cascade of water that
welled up from the canyon, overflowing its walls, flattened him to
the ground. Then, as it began its backwash, the flood tried to drag
him with it.

His hands grappled along the ground, then closed on the lower
branches of a thick juniper.

The water, its force spent, released him. He scrambled to his feet
and looked back toward the antenna.

It had been reduced to a mass of twisted wreckage. The chain-link
fence had been flattened, and the one truck that had been left after
the other four men had gone down to cordon off the canyon's
mouth half an hour earlier now lay on its side, twenty yards in from
the canyon's rim.

Of Otto Kruger there was no sign at all.

As Hernandez watched, the ground beneath his feet trembled,
and suddenly fifty feet of the canyon's rim disappeared, dropping

away, crumbling into the roiling water below. The antenna, the pad upon which it sat, and the truck were all gone forever.

Jesus Hernandez, stunned, crossed himself, then fell to his knees and for the first time in years began to pray.

Already the roar of the flood's charge down the canyon was beginning to fade into the distance.

In the cave behind the old construction shack, Paul Kendall heard Otto Kruger's last words, though for a moment the full meaning of them didn't sink in. But a moment later, when he too heard the first ominous rumblings of the cataclysm that was hurtling toward him, he dropped the walkie-talkie and threw himself toward the door.

Kendall stumbled over a chair, lost his balance, and dropped to the floor. He scrambled to his feet, but felt disoriented in the pitch-blackness.

The roar was growing steadily, and panic began to overwhelm him. He groped in the darkness, his hands touching something hard.

A desk.

Which desk?

He didn't know.

"Utley!" he yelled. "Greg! Where are you?"

There was no answer, but he could hear the other men stumbling in the darkness, and tried to move toward the sounds.

Kendall's knee struck something hard and he recoiled, then tried another direction.

Greg Moreland, groping his way through the dark, fumbled with something that felt like a door. Then fingers reached out of the darkness and touched him. A second later he felt hands close around his neck, and then he was hurled to the floor as someone else—Kendall? Stan Utley?—tried to jerk the door open.

As the rumble of the flood grew, so also did Greg Moreland's own panic. Reason deserted him. He began thrashing in the darkness, stumbling first one way then another. But wherever he turned, something seemed to be in his way.

The roar was deafening now, and there was a crashing noise as the flimsy frame structure fronting the cavern was swept away. Then, as the inrushing water compressed the air in the cavern, he was struck by a blinding pain.

His eardrums, stressed beyond their capabilities, burst. Abruptly, Greg Moreland found himself in utter silence.

But even the silence lasted only a second before the water overcame him, knocking him to the floor, then picking him up again to hurl him against the rock wall of the cavern.

A fragment of concrete, carried from the dam on the pure force of the current, slammed into his head, crushing it like an egg against the rough sandstone wall.

The water swept on, scouring the cavern clean, gouging the bodies of Greg Moreland, Paul Kendall, and Stan Utley loose from the shelter of the cave, sweeping the transmitter and computers away, adding them to the great collection of debris the flood had gathered.

When the water finally ebbed a few minutes later, the cavern in the wall, like the rest of the canyon, had been swept clean of every trace that human beings had ever been there.

A moment later the wall of the canyon, undercut by the fury of the flood, collapsed, marking the spot with a pile of rubble that, if left undisturbed, would last for a millennium, slowly to be reshaped by rain and wind.

The four of them approached the rim of the canyon slowly. An eerie silence seemed to have fallen over the night. The roar of the flood had faded away completely, but the normal night sounds, the rustling of small animals, the flutter of the wings of bats as they hunted for prey, the chirping of insects calling for mates—all were gone.

It was as if every living thing on the plateau had been shocked into utter silence by the forces that had been unleashed when the dam crumbled.

Judith instinctively slipped her hand into Jed's as they crept toward the edge of the precipice.

The path they had come up a few minutes earlier was gone, and the verge of the canyon was twenty feet farther back than it had been before. The new face of the canyon, freshly exposed sandstone, was rough and uneven, like a gem waiting to be cut.

Far below them fragments of the great slab that had broken away from the heights lay shattered on what had once been the bed of the river but was now nothing more than the hard and wetly glittering surface of the bedrock beneath.

To their right was what had once been the bottom of the lake, a great layer of silt that had been carried downstream by the river over the course of half a century slowly sinking to the bottom of the lake, building up. Eventually, even if the dam had survived, the lake would have disappeared, the canyon filled by the silt. Now it lay gleaming in the moonlight, a huge mud slick thirty feet thick, its surface carved in strange patterns by the water that had left it behind.

Awestruck, they stood still, gazing out on the ruins of the reservoir and the canyon, each of them lost in his own private thoughts.

Jed stared down into the utter desolation below, the sheer magnitude of the fury he had unleashed threatening to overwhelm him.

Finally he looked away, gazing up into the sky. The moon and stars overhead were comforting, for unlike the landscape below, they were unchanged, oblivious to the cataclysm that had swept through the canyon. As he watched, a shadow swept past the moon. Jed felt his grandfather's hand on his shoulder, squeezing gently.

"What is it?" Jed asked, murmuring the words softly, as if even his voice would defile the strangely reverent silence of the night.

The pressure on his shoulder increased. "Don't speak," Brown Eagle whispered. "Just watch."

Now Judith and Peter too were staring up into the sky. As if seeking the light of the moon, the shadow appeared again, silhouetted against the silver disk, and then began lazily spiraling downward.

It was a bird, its great wings set as it coasted on the air currents. As it came lower and lower, growing larger, the four people watching it gasped at its sheer size. It circled over them, then soared eastward, its huge wings pounding as it gained altitude and once more began riding the breezes, sweeping back and forth over the canyon. It disappeared into the distance, then, a moment later, reappeared, beating its way back to swoop low over the small cluster of people on the canyon's rim.

It screamed, a shrill sound that echoed off the canyon's walls, then began climbing, higher with every wing beat, silhouetted once more against the brilliance of the moon. Finally, when it was almost out of sight, it dove, sweeping its wings back, stretching its neck so that its enormous curved beak sliced through the air.

It was over the canyon now; and then, as it dropped below the rim, it screamed once more.

Its wings spread wide as it neared the canyon wall only a few feet above the great mud slick that covered the chasm's floor, and then it screamed a third time.

Its talons reached out, clutching at the naked rock, and in an instant it disappeared.

The four of them watched in silence, unsure whether they'd seen and heard the strange phantom bird at all. In the silence, Brown Eagle spoke.

"Rakantoh," he said softly. "He's come home."

They had been walking for nearly an hour, pausing now and then to look down into the canyon.

They'd stared in silence at the spot where the sanitarium had been.

Now, as on the rest of the canyon floor, there was nothing left:

only a few boulders that the passing flood had almost whimsically dropped here and there.

Farther on they had paused again, and stared at the great slab of rubble where the ledge upon which the antenna had stood now lay shattered at the bottom, blocking the cavern that had been dug into the wall beneath.

At last they started down the gentle slope that led to the desert floor. In the distance they could see the town, a few of its windows glowing with candlelight.

Spread out across the desert, already disappearing quickly into the sands and gullies, draining down the myriad washes that cut through the flatlands, there was a sheen of water.

By morning it would be gone.

They'd paused, almost by common consent, and Judith turned to Jed Arnold.

"What do you want us to tell them?" she asked. Immediately, they all understood what she meant.

Jed was silent for a moment, but when he finally spoke, his voice was clear.

"We'll tell them the truth," he said. "They tried to kill us all. So I killed them first."

They started once more toward the town, with only the moon lighting their way.

But above them, high in the sky, the great bird soared.

Jed looked up at it, and smiled.

ABOUT THE AUTHOR

Author of 15 bestselling novels, John Saul is renowned for his tales of psychological terror. In 1977 he won instant success with his first novel, *Suffer the Children*, which topped national bestseller lists and sold more than one million copies. In addition to the three novels in this collection, his recent works include *Second Child, Darkness, Creature,* and *Shadows.* John Saul resides in Seattle, Washington, where he continues writing fascinating stories of supernatural and psychological suspense.